Praise for Michael Connelly

'Connelly is one of the great crime writers, a novelist who creates a fictional world so succinctly, and inhabits it so purposefully, that you are convinced it must be real. His mastery of place and character, his ease with dialogue, his control of plot gives his books a subtlety that is irresistible'
Daily Mail

'A clever plot, full of twists, to make a first-rate legal thriller'
Sunday Telegraph

'Connelly's fifth novel to feature roguish defence lawyer Mickey Haller is even better than last year's *The Black Box*'
Mail on Sunday

'Expect surprises and plenty of dark moments in this punchy legal drama from an ever-reliable writer' *Financial Times*

'Connelly is superb at building suspense' *Wall Street Journal*

'In the crime fiction stakes Connelly is comfortably in the upper bracket' *Daily Express*

'A clever thriller with a brilliant double twist but also a heart-felt examination of the difference between natural justice and the law' *Evening Standard*

'Connelly masterfully manages to marry an absorbing court-room drama with a tense and exciting thriller of detection'
The Times

'While the themes of Connelly's LA crime novels are familiar (power, envy, corruption), his plotting is anything but' *Esquire*

'A story that's as old as the genre itself but Connelly's skill is such that it all feel[...] heartbreakingly poignant t[...]

By Michael Connelly

Fiction

The Black Echo
The Black Ice
The Concrete Blonde
The Last Coyote
The Poet
Trunk Music
Blood Work
Angels Flight
Void Moon
A Darkness More Than Night
City of Bones
Chasing the Dime
Lost Light
The Narrows
The Closers
The Lincoln Lawyer
Echo Park
The Overlook
The Brass Verdict
The Scarecrow

Nine Dragons
The Reversal
The Fifth Witness
The Drop
The Black Box
The Gods of Guilt
The Burning Room
The Crossing
The Wrong Side of Goodbye
The Late Show
Two Kinds of Truth
Dark Sacred Night

Non-fiction

Crime Beat

Ebooks

Suicide Run
Angle of Investigation
Mulholland Dive
The Safe Man
Switchblade

A former police reporter for the *Los Angeles Times*, Michael Connelly is the internationally bestselling author of the Harry Bosch series, and several other bestsellers including the highly acclaimed legal thriller, *The Lincoln Lawyer*. The TV series – *Bosch* – is one of the most watched original series on Amazon Prime and is now in its fourth season. Connelly has been President of the Mystery Writers of America, and his books have been translated into thirty-nine languages. His writing has won awards all over the world, including the Edgar and Anthony Awards, and, most recently, the CWA Diamond Dagger, the highest honour in British crime writing. He spends his time in California and Florida.

To find out more, visit Michael's website or follow him on Twitter or Facebook.

www.michaelconnelly.com

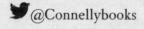 @Connellybooks

/MichaelConnellyBooks

MICHAEL CONNELLY

THE LINCOLN LAWYER

ORION

An Orion paperback

First published in Great Britain in 2005
by Orion Books
This paperback edition published in 2006
by Orion Books
an imprint of The Orion Publishing Group Ltd,
Carmelite House, 50 Victoria Embankment
London EC4Y ODZ
Hachette Ireland
8 Castlecourt Centre, Castleknock, Dublin 15

An Hachette UK company

Published by arrangement with
Little, Brown and Company Inc., New York, USA

18

Reissued 2014

A CIP catalogue record for this book
is available from the British Library.

ISBN 978-1-4091-5605-5

Printed and bound in Great Britain by
Clays Ltd, Elcograf S.p.A.

The Orion Publishing Group's policy is to use papers that
are natural, renewable and recyclable products and
made from wood grown in sustainable forests. The logging
and manufacturing processes are expected to conform to
the environmental regulations of the country of origin.

www.orionbooks.co.uk

This is for Daniel F. Daly
and Roger O. Mills

There is no client as scary as an innocent man.

— J. MICHAEL HALLER, CRIMINAL DEFENSE ATTORNEY,
LOS ANGELES, 1962

PART ONE
— PRETRIAL
INTERVENTION

ONE

The morning air off the Mojave in late winter is as clean and crisp as you'll ever breathe in Los Angeles County. It carries the taste of promise on it. When it starts blowing in like that I like to keep a window open in my office. There are a few people who know this routine of mine, people like Fernando Valenzuela. The bondsman, not the baseball pitcher. He called me as I was coming into Lancaster for a nine o'clock calendar call. He must have heard the wind whistling in my cell phone.

"Mick," he said, "you up north this morning?"

"At the moment," I said as I put the window up to hear him better. "You got something?"

"Yeah, I got something. I think I got a franchise player here. But his first appearance is at eleven. Can you make it back down in time?"

Valenzuela has a storefront office on Van Nuys Boulevard a block from the civic center, which includes two courthouses and the Van Nuys jail. He calls his business Liberty Bail Bonds. His phone number, in red neon on the roof of his establishment, can be seen from the high-power wing on the third floor of the jail. His number is scratched into the paint on the wall next to every pay phone on every other ward in the jail.

You could say his name is also permanently scratched onto my Christmas list. At the end of the year I give a can of salted nuts to everybody on it. Planters holiday mix. Each can has a ribbon and bow on it. But no nuts inside.

Just cash. I have a lot of bail bondsmen on my Christmas list. I eat holiday mix out of Tupperware well into spring. Since my last divorce, it is sometimes all I get for dinner.

Before answering Valenzuela's question I thought about the calendar call I was headed to. My client was named Harold Casey. If the docket was handled alphabetically I could make an eleven o'clock hearing down in Van Nuys, no problem. But Judge Orton Powell was in his last term on the bench. He was retiring. That meant he no longer faced reelection pressures, like those from the private bar. To demonstrate his freedom — and possibly as a form of payback to those he had been politically beholden to for twelve years — he liked to mix things up in his courtroom. Sometimes the calendar went alphabetical, sometimes reverse alphabetical, sometimes by filing date. You never knew how the call would go until you got there. Often lawyers cooled their heels for better than an hour in Powell's courtroom. The judge liked that.

"I think I can make eleven," I said, without knowing for sure. "What's the case?"

"Guy's gotta be big money. Beverly Hills address, family lawyer waltzing in here first thing. This is the real thing, Mick. They booked him on a half mil and his mother's lawyer came in here today ready to sign over property in Malibu to secure it. Didn't even ask about getting it lowered first. I guess they aren't too worried about him running."

"Booked for what?" I asked.

I kept my voice even. The scent of money in the water often leads to a feeding frenzy but I had taken care of Valenzuela on enough Christmases to know I had him on the hook exclusively. I could play it cool.

"The cops booked him for ag-assault, GBI and attempted rape for starters," the bondsman answered. "The DA hasn't filed yet as far as I know."

4

The police usually overbooked the charges. What mattered was what the prosecutors finally filed and took to court. I always say cases go in like a lion and come out like a lamb. A case going in as attempted rape and aggravated assault with great bodily injury could easily come out as simple battery. It wouldn't surprise me and it wouldn't make for much of a franchise case. Still, if I could get to the client and make a fee agreement based on the announced charges, I could look good when the DA later knocked them down.

"You got any of the details?" I asked.

"He was booked last night. It sounds like a bar pickup gone bad. The family lawyer said the woman's in it for the money. You know, the civil suit to follow the criminal case. But I'm not so sure. She got beat up pretty good from what I heard."

"What's the family lawyer's name?"

"Hold on a sec. I've got his card here somewhere."

I looked out the window while waiting for Valenzuela to find the business card. I was two minutes from the Lancaster courthouse and twelve minutes from calendar call. I needed at least three of those minutes in between to confer with my client and give him the bad news.

"Okay, here it is," Valenzuela said. "Guy's name is Cecil C. Dobbs, Esquire. Out of Century City. See, I told you. Money."

Valenzuela was right. But it wasn't the lawyer's Century City address that said money. It was the name. I knew of C. C. Dobbs by reputation and guessed that there wouldn't be more than one or two names on his entire client list that didn't have a Bel-Air or Holmby Hills address. His kind of client went home to the places where the stars seemed to reach down at night to touch the anointed.

"Give me the client's name," I said.

"That would be Louis Ross Roulet."

He spelled it and I wrote it down on a legal pad.

"Almost like the spinning wheel but you pronounce it Roo-*lay*," he said. "You going to be here, Mick?"

Before responding I wrote the name C. C. Dobbs on the pad. I then answered Valenzuela with a question.

"Why me?" I asked. "Was I asked for? Or did you suggest me?"

I had to be careful with this. I had to assume Dobbs was the kind of lawyer who would go to the California bar in a heartbeat if he came across a criminal defense attorney paying off bondsmen for client referrals. In fact, I started wondering if the whole thing might be a bar sting operation that Valenzuela hadn't picked up on. I wasn't one of the bar's favorite sons. They had come at me before. More than once.

"I asked Roulet if he had a lawyer, you know? A criminal defense lawyer, and he said no. I told him about you. I didn't push it. I just said you were good. Soft sell, you know?"

"Was this before or after Dobbs came into it?"

"No, before. Roulet called me this morning from the jail. They got him up on high power and he saw the sign, I guess. Dobbs showed up after that. I told him you were in, gave him your pedigree, and he was cool with it. He'll be there at eleven. You'll see how he is."

I didn't speak for a long moment. I wondered how truthful Valenzuela was being with me. A guy like Dobbs would have had his own man. If it wasn't his own forte, then he'd have had a criminal specialist in the firm or, at least, on standby. But Valenzuela's story seemed to contradict this. Roulet came to him empty-handed. It told me that there was more to this case I didn't know than what I did.

"Hey, Mick, you there?" Valenzuela prompted.

I made a decision. It was a decision that would

eventually lead me back to Jesus Menendez and that I would in many ways come to regret. But at the moment it was made, it was just another choice made of necessity and routine.

"I'll be there," I said into the phone. "I'll see you at eleven."

I was about to close the phone when I heard Valenzuela's voice come back at me.

"And you'll take care of me for this, right, Mick? I mean, you know, if this is the franchise."

It was the first time Valenzuela had ever sought assurance of a payback from me. It played further into my paranoia and I carefully constructed an answer that would satisfy him and the bar — if it was listening.

"Don't worry, Val. You're on my Christmas list."

I closed the phone before he could say anything else and told my driver to drop me off at the employee entrance to the courthouse. The line at the metal detector would be shorter and quicker there and the security men usually didn't mind the lawyers — the regulars — sneaking through so they could make court on time.

As I thought about Louis Ross Roulet and the case and the possible riches and dangers that waited for me, I put the window back down so I could enjoy the morning's last minute of clean, fresh air. It still carried the taste of promise.

TWO

The courtroom in Department 2A was crowded with lawyers negotiating and socializing on both sides of the bar when I got there. I could tell the session was going to start on time because I saw the bailiff seated at his desk. This meant the judge was close to taking the bench.

In Los Angeles County the bailiffs are actually sworn deputy sheriffs who are assigned to the jail division. I approached the bailiff, whose desk was right next to the bar railing so citizens could come up to ask questions without having to violate the space assigned to the lawyers, defendants and courtroom personnel. I saw the calendar on the clipboard in front of him. I checked the nameplate on his uniform — R. Rodriguez — before speaking.

"Roberto, you got my guy on there? Harold Casey?"

The bailiff used his finger to start down the list on the call sheet but stopped quickly. This meant I was in luck.

"Yeah, Casey. He's second up."

"Alphabetical today, good. Do I have time to go back and see him?"

"No, they're bringing the first group in now. I just called. The judge is coming out. You'll probably have a couple minutes to see your guy in the pen."

"Thank you."

I started to walk toward the gate when he called after me.

"And it's Reynaldo, not Roberto."

"Right, right. I'm sorry about that, Reynaldo."

"Us bailiffs, we all look alike, right?"

I didn't know if that was an attempt at humor or just a dig at me. I didn't answer. I just smiled and went through the gate. I nodded at a couple lawyers I didn't know and a couple that I did. One stopped me to ask how long I was going to be up in front of the judge because he wanted to gauge when to come back for his own client's appearance. I told him I was going to be quick.

During a calendar call incarcerated defendants are brought to the courtroom in groups of four and held in a wood-and-glass enclosure known as the pen. This allows the defendants to confer with their attorneys in the moments before their case is called for whatever matter is before the court.

I got to the side of the pen just as the door from the interior holding cell was opened by a deputy, and the first four defendants on the docket were marched out. The last of the four to step into the pen was Harold Casey, my client. I took a position near the side wall so that we would have privacy on at least one side and signaled him over.

Casey was big and tall, as they tend to recruit them in the Road Saints motorcycle gang — or club, as the membership prefers to be known. While being held in the Lancaster jail he had cut his hair and shaved, as I had requested, and he looked reasonably presentable, except for the tattoos that wrapped both arms and poked up above his collar. But there is only so much you can do. I don't know much about the effect of tattoos on a jury but I suspect it's not overly positive, especially when grinning skulls are involved. I *do* know that jurors in general don't care for ponytails — on either the defendants or the lawyers who represent them.

Casey, or Hard Case, as he was known in the club, was

charged with cultivation, possession and sale of marijuana as well as other drug and weapons charges. In a predawn raid on the ranch where he lived and worked, sheriff's deputies found a barn and Quonset hut complex that had been turned into an indoor growing facility. More than two thousand fully mature plants were seized along with sixty-three pounds of harvested marijuana packaged in various weights in plastic bags. Additionally, twelve ounces of crystal meth which the packagers sprinkled on the harvested crop to give it an extra kick were seized, along with a small arsenal of weapons, many of them later determined to be stolen.

It would appear that Hard Case was fucked. The state had him cold. He was actually found asleep on a couch in the barn, five feet from the packaging table. Added to this, he had twice previously been convicted of drug offenses and was currently still on parole for the most recent. In the state of California the third time is the charm. Realistically, Casey was facing at least a decade in prison, even with good time.

But what was unusual about Casey was that he was a defendant who was looking forward to trial and even to the likelihood of conviction. He had refused to waive his right to a speedy trial and now, less than three months after his arrest, eagerly wanted to bring it on. He was eager because it was likely that his only hope lay in an appeal of that likely conviction. Thanks to his attorney, Casey saw a glimmer of hope — that small, twinkling light that only a good attorney can bring to the darkness of a case like this. From this glimmer a case strategy was born that might ultimately work to free Casey. It was daring and would cost Casey time as he waited out the appeal, but he knew as well as I did that it was the only real shot he had.

The crack in the state's case was not in its assumption that Casey was a marijuana grower, packager and seller.

The state was absolutely correct in these assumptions and the evidence more than proved it. It was in how the state came to that evidence that the case tottered on an unsteady foundation. It was my job to probe that crack in trial, exploit it, put it on record and then convince an appellate court of what I had not been able to convince Judge Orton Powell of during a pretrial motion to suppress the evidence in the case.

The seed of the prosecution of Harold Casey was planted on a Tuesday in mid-December when Casey walked into a Home Depot in Lancaster and made a number of mundane purchases that included three lightbulbs of the variety used in hydroponic farming. The man behind him in the checkout line happened to be an off-duty sheriff's deputy about to purchase outdoor Christmas lights. The deputy recognized some of the artwork on Casey's arms — most notably the skull with halo tattoo that is the emblematic signature of the Road Saints — and put two and two together. The off-duty man then dutifully followed Casey's Harley as he rode to the ranch in nearby Pearblossom. This information was passed to the sheriff's drug squad, which arranged for an unmarked helicopter to fly over the ranch with a thermal imaging camera. The subsequent photographs, detailing rich red heat blooms from the barn and Quonset hut, along with the statement of the deputy who saw Casey purchase hydroponic lights, were submitted in an affidavit to a judge. The next morning Casey was rousted from sleep on the couch by deputies with a signed search warrant.

In an earlier hearing I argued that all evidence against Casey should be excluded because the probable cause for the search constituted an invasion of Casey's right to privacy. Using an individual's commonplace purchases at a hardware store as a springboard to conduct a further invasion of privacy through surveillance on the ground and in the air and by thermal imaging would surely be viewed as excessive by the framers of the Constitution.

Judge Powell rejected my argument and the case moved toward trial or disposition by plea agreement. In the meantime new information came to light that would bolster Casey's appeal of a conviction. Analysis of the photographs taken during the flyover of Casey's house and the focal specifications of the thermal camera used by the deputies indicated the helicopter was flying no more than two hundred feet off the ground when the photographs were taken. The U.S. Supreme Court has held that a law enforcement observation flight over a suspect's property does not violate an individual's right to privacy so long as the aircraft is in public airspace. I had Raul Levin, my investigator, check with the Federal Aviation Administration. Casey's ranch was located beneath no airport flight pattern. The floor for public airspace above the ranch was a thousand feet. The deputies had clearly invaded Casey's privacy while gathering the probable cause to raid the ranch.

My job now was to take the case to trial and elicit testimony from the deputies and pilot as to the altitude they were flying when they went over the ranch. If they told the truth, I had them. If they lied, I had them. I don't relish the idea of embarrassing law enforcement officers in open court, but my hope was that they would lie. If a jury sees a cop lie on the witness stand, then the case might as well end right there. You don't have to appeal a not-guilty verdict. The state has no comebacks from a not-guilty verdict.

Either way, I was confident I had a winner. We just had to get to trial and there was only one thing holding us back. That was what I needed to talk to Casey about before the judge took the bench and called the case.

My client sauntered over to the corner of the pen and

didn't offer a hello. I didn't, either. He knew what I wanted. We'd had this conversation before.

"Harold, this is calendar call," I said. "This is when I tell the judge if we're ready to go to trial. I already know the state's ready. So today's about us."

"So?"

"So, there's a problem. Last time we were here you told me I'd be getting some money. But here we are, Harold, and no money."

"Don't worry. I have your money."

"That's why I am worried. *You* have my money. I don't have my money."

"It's coming. I talked to my boys yesterday. It's coming."

"You said that last time, too. I don't work for free, Harold. The expert I had go over the photos doesn't work for free, either. Your retainer is long gone. I want some more money or you're going to have to get yourself a new lawyer. A public defender."

"No PD, man. I want you."

"Well, I got expenses and I gotta eat. You know what my nut is each week just to pay for the yellow pages? Take a guess."

Casey said nothing.

"A grand. Averages out a grand a week just to keep my ad in there and that's before I eat or pay the mortgage or the child support or put gas in the Lincoln. I'm not doing this on a promise, Harold. I work on green inspiration."

Casey seemed unimpressed.

"I checked around," he said. "You can't just quit on me. Not now. The judge won't let you."

A hush fell over the courtroom as the judge stepped out of the door to his chambers and took the two steps up to the bench. The bailiff called the courtroom to order. It was showtime. I just looked at Casey for a long moment and stepped away. He had an amateur, jailhouse knowledge of the law and how it worked. He knew more than most. But he was still in for a surprise.

I took a seat against the rail behind the defendant's table. The first case called was a bail reconsideration that was handled quickly. Then the clerk called the case of *California v. Casey* and I stepped up to the table.

"Michael Haller for the defense," I said.

The prosecutor announced his presence as well. He was a young guy named Victor DeVries. He had no idea what was going to hit him when we got to trial. Judge Orton Powell made the usual inquiries about whether a last-minute disposition in the case was possible. Every judge had an overflowing calendar and an overriding mandate to clear cases through disposition. The last thing any judge wanted to hear was that there was no hope of agreement and that a trial was inevitable.

But Powell took the bad news from DeVries and me in stride and asked if we were ready to schedule the trial for later in the week. DeVries said yes. I said no.

"Your Honor," I said, "I would like to carry this over until next week, if possible."

"What is the cause of your delay, Mr. Haller?" the judge asked impatiently. "The prosecution is ready and I want to dispose of this case."

"I want to dispose of it as well, Your Honor. But the defense is having trouble locating a witness who will be necessary to our case. An indispensable witness, Your Honor. I think a one-week carryover should be sufficient. By next week we should be ready to go forward."

As expected, DeVries objected to the delay.

"Your Honor, this is the first the state has heard about a missing witness. Mr. Haller has had almost three months to locate his witnesses. He's the one who wanted the speedy trial and now he wants to wait. I think this is just a delay tactic because he's facing a case that —"

"You can hold on to the rest of that for the jury, Mr. DeVries," the judge said. "Mr. Haller, you think one week will solve your problem?"

"Yes, Your Honor."

"Okay, we'll see you and Mr. Casey next Monday and you will be ready to go. Is that understood?"

"Yes, Your Honor. Thank you."

The clerk called the next case and I stepped away from the defense table. I watched a deputy lead my client out of the pen. Casey glanced back at me, a look on his face that seemed to be equal parts anger and confusion. I went over to Reynaldo Rodriguez and asked if I could be allowed back into the holding area to further confer with my client. It was a professional courtesy allowed to most of the regulars. Rodriguez got up, unlocked a door behind his desk and ushered me through. I made sure to thank him by his correct name.

Casey was in a holding cell with one other defendant, the man whose case had been called ahead of his in the courtroom. The cell was large and had benches running along three sides. The bad thing about getting your case called early in the courtroom is that after the hearing you have to sit in this cage until it fills with enough people to run a full bus back to the county jail. Casey came right up to the bars to speak to me.

"What witness were you talking about in there?" he demanded.

"Mr. Green," I said. "Mr. Green is all we need for this case to go forward."

Casey's face contorted in anger. I tried to cut him off at the pass.

"Look, Harold, I know you want to move this along and get to the trial and then the appeal. But you've got to pay the freight along the way. I know from long, hard experience that it does me no good to chase people for money after the horse is out of the barn. You want to play now, then you pay now."

I nodded and was about to turn back to the door that led to freedom. But then I spoke to him again.

"And don't think the judge in there didn't know what was going on," I said. "You got a young prosecutor who's wet behind the ears and doesn't have to worry about where his next paycheck's coming from. But Orton Powell spent a lot of years in the defense bar before he got to the bench. He knows about chasing indispensable witnesses like Mr. Green and he probably won't look too kindly upon a defendant who doesn't pay his lawyer. I gave him the wink, Harold. If I want off the case, I'll get off. But what I'd rather do is come in here next Monday and stand up out there and tell him we found our witness and we are ready to go. You understand?"

Casey didn't say anything at first. He walked to the far side of the cell and sat down on the bench. He didn't look at me when he finally spoke.

"As soon as I get to a phone," he said.

"Sounds good, Harold. I'll tell one of the deputies you have to make a call. Make the call, then sit tight and I'll see you next week. We'll get this thing going."

I headed back to the door, my steps quick. I hate being inside a jail. I'm not sure why. I guess it's because sometimes the line seems so thin. The line between being a criminal attorney and a *criminal* attorney. Sometimes I'm not sure which side of the bars I am on. To me it's always a dead-bang miracle that I get to walk out the way I walked in.

THREE

In the hallway outside the courtroom I turned my cell phone back on and called my driver to tell him I was coming out. I then checked voicemail and found messages from Lorna Taylor and Fernando Valenzuela. I decided to wait until I was in the car to make the callbacks.

Earl Briggs, my driver, had the Lincoln right out front. Earl didn't get out and open the door or anything. His deal was just to drive me while he worked off the fee he owed me for getting him probation on a cocaine sales conviction. I paid him twenty bucks an hour to drive me but then held half of it back to go against the fee. It wasn't quite what he was making dealing crack in the projects but it was safer, legal and something that could go on a résumé. Earl said he wanted to go straight in life and I believed him.

I could hear the sound of hip-hop pulsing behind the closed windows of the Town Car as I approached. But Earl killed the music as soon as I reached for the door handle. I slid into the back and told him to head toward Van Nuys.

"Who was that you were listening to?" I asked him.

"Um, that was Three Six Mafia."

"Dirty south?"

"That's right."

Over the years, I had become knowledgeable in the subtle distinctions, regional and otherwise, in rap and hip-hop. Across the board, most of my clients listened to it, many of them developing their life strategies from it.

I reached over and picked up the shoebox full of cassette tapes from the Boyleston case and chose one at random. I noted the tape number and the time in the little logbook I kept in the shoebox. I handed the tape over the seat to Earl and he slid it into the dashboard stereo. I didn't have to tell him to play it at a volume so low that it would amount to little more than background noise. Earl had been with me for three months. He knew what to do.

Roger Boyleston was one of my few court-appointed clients. He was facing a variety of federal drug-trafficking charges. DEA wiretaps on Boyleston's phones had led to his arrest and the seizure of six kilos of cocaine that he had planned to distribute through a network of dealers. There were numerous tapes — more than fifty hours of recorded phone conversations. Boyleston talked to many people about what was coming and when to expect it. The case was a slam dunk for the government. Boyleston was going to go away for a long time and there was almost nothing I could do but negotiate a deal, trading Boyleston's cooperation for a lower sentence. That didn't matter, though. What mattered to me were the tapes. I took the case because of the tapes. The federal government would pay me to listen to the tapes in preparation for defending my client. That meant I would get a minimum of fifty billable hours out of Boyleston and the government before it was all settled. So I made sure the tapes were in heavy rotation whenever I was riding in the Lincoln. I wanted to make sure that if I ever had to put my hand on the book and swear to tell the truth, I could say in good conscience that I played every one of those tapes I billed Uncle Sugar for.

I called Lorna Taylor back first. Lorna is my case manager. The phone number that runs on my half-page ad in the yellow pages and on thirty-six bus benches scattered through high-crime areas in the south and east county goes directly to the office/second bedroom of her Kings

Road condo in West Hollywood. The address the California bar and all the clerks of the courts have for me is the condo as well.

Lorna is the first buffer. To get to me you start with her. My cell number is given out to only a few and Lorna is the gatekeeper. She is tough, smart, professional and beautiful. Lately, though, I only get to verify this last attribute once a month or so when I take her to lunch and sign checks — she's my bookkeeper, too.

"Law office," she said when I called in.

"Sorry, I was still in court," I said, explaining why I didn't get her call. "What's up?"

"You talked to Val, right?"

"Yeah. I'm heading down to Van Nuys now. I got that at eleven."

"He called here to make sure. He sounds nervous."

"He thinks this guy is the golden goose, wants to make sure he's along for the ride. I'll call him back to reassure him."

"I did some preliminary checking on the name Louis Ross Roulet. Credit check is excellent. The name in the *Times* archive comes up with a few hits. All real estate transactions. Looks like he works for a real estate firm in Beverly Hills. It's called Windsor Residential Estates. Looks like they handle all exclusive pocket listings — not the sort of properties where they put a sign out front."

"That's good. Anything else?"

"Not on that. And just the usual so far on the phone."

Which meant that she had fielded the usual number of calls drawn by the bus benches and the yellow pages, all from people who wanted a lawyer. Before the callers hit my radar they had to convince Lorna that they could pay for what they wanted. She was sort of like the nurse behind the desk in the emergency room. You have to convince her you have valid insurance before she sends you back to see the doc. Next to Lorna's phone she keeps a rate schedule that starts with a $5,000 flat fee to handle a DUI and ranges to the hourly fees I charge for felony trials. She makes sure every potential client is a paying client and knows the costs of the crime they have been charged with. There's that saying, Don't do the crime if you can't do the time. Lorna likes to say that with me, it's Don't do the crime if you can't pay for my time. She accepts MasterCard and Visa and will get purchase approval before a client ever gets to me.

"Nobody we know?" I asked.

"Gloria Dayton called from Twin Towers."

I groaned. The Twin Towers was the county's main lockup in downtown. It housed women in one tower and men in the other. Gloria Dayton was a high-priced prostitute who needed my legal services from time to time. The first time I represented her was at least ten years earlier, when she was young and drug-free and still had life in her eyes. Now she was a pro bono client. I never charged her. I just tried to convince her to quit the life.

"When did she get popped?"

"Last night. Or rather, this morning. Her first appearance is after lunch."

"I don't know if I can make that with this Van Nuys thing."

"There's also a complication. Cocaine possession as well as the usual."

I knew that Gloria worked exclusively through contacts made on the Internet, where she billed herself on a variety of websites as Glory Days. She was no streetwalker or barroom troller. When she got popped, it was usually after an undercover vice officer was able to penetrate her check system and set up a date. The fact that she had cocaine on her person when they met sounded like an unusual lapse on her part or a plant from the cop.

"All right, if she calls back tell her I will try to be there and if I'm not there I will have somebody take it. Will you call the court and firm up the hearing?"

"I'm on it. But, Mickey, when are you going to tell her this is the last time?"

"I don't know. Maybe today. What else?"

"Isn't that enough for one day?"

"It'll do, I guess."

We talked a little more about my schedule for the rest of the week and I opened my laptop on the fold-down table so I could check my calendar against hers. I had a couple hearings set for each morning and a one-day trial on Thursday. It was all South side drug stuff. My meat and potatoes. At the end of the conversation I told her that I would call her after the Van Nuys hearing to let her know if and how the Roulet case would impact things.

"One last thing," I said. "You said the place Roulet works handles pretty exclusive real estate deals, right?"

"Yeah. Every deal his name was attached to in the archives was in seven figures. A couple got up into the eights. Holmby Hills, Bel-Air, places like that."

I nodded, thinking that Roulet's status might make him a person of interest to the media.

"Then why don't you tip Sticks to it," I said.

"You sure?"

"Yeah, we might be able to work something there."

"Will do."

"Talk to you later."

By the time I closed the phone, Earl had us back on the Antelope Valley Freeway heading south. We were making good time and getting to Van Nuys for Roulet's first appearance wasn't going to be a problem. I called Fernando Valenzuela to tell him.

"That's real good," the bondsman said. "I'll be waiting."

As he spoke I watched two motorcycles glide by my window. Each rider wore a black leather vest with the skull and halo patch sewn on the back.

"Anything else?" I asked.

"Yeah, one other thing I should probably tell you," Valenzuela said. "I was double-checking with the court on when his first appearance was going to be and I found out the case was assigned to Maggie McFierce. I don't know if that's going to be a problem for you or not."

Maggie McFierce as in Margaret McPherson, who happened to be one of the toughest and, yes, fiercest deputy district attorneys assigned to the Van Nuys courthouse. She also happened to be my first ex-wife.

"It won't be a problem for me," I said without hesitation. "She's the one who'll have the problem."

The defendant has the right to his choice of counsel. If there is a conflict of interest between the defense lawyer and the prosecutor, then it is the prosecutor who must bow out. I knew Maggie would hold me personally responsible for her losing the reins on what might be a big case but I couldn't help that. It had happened before. In my laptop I still had a motion to disqualify from the last case in which we had crossed paths. If necessary, I would just have to change the name of the defendant and print it out. I'd be good to go and she'd be as good as gone.

The two motorcycles had now moved in front of us. I turned and looked out the back window. There were three more Harleys behind us.

"You know what that means, though," I said.

"No, what?"

"She'll go for no bail. She always does with crimes against women."

"Shit, can she get it? I'm looking at a nice chunk of change on this, man."

"I don't know. You said the guy's got family and C. C.

Dobbs. I can make something out of that. We'll see."

"Shit."

Valenzuela was seeing his major payday disappear.

"I'll see you there, Val."

I closed the phone and looked over the seat at Earl.

"How long have we had the escort?" I asked.

"Just came up on us," Earl said. "You want me to do something?"

"Let's see what they —"

I didn't have to wait until the end of my sentence. One of the riders from the rear came up alongside the Lincoln and signaled us toward the upcoming exit for the Vasquez Rocks County Park. I recognized him as Teddy Vogel, a former client and the highest-ranked Road Saint not incarcerated. He might have been the largest Saint as well. He went at least 350 pounds and he gave the impression of a fat kid riding his little brother's bike.

"Pull off, Earl," I said. "Let's see what he's got."

We pulled into the parking lot next to the jagged rock formation named after an outlaw who had hid in them a century before. I saw two people sitting and having a picnic on the edge of one of the highest ledges. I didn't think I would feel comfortable eating a sandwich in such a dangerous spot and position.

I lowered my window as Teddy Vogel approached on foot. The other four Saints had killed their engines but remained on their bikes. Vogel leaned down to the window and put one of his giant forearms on the sill. I could feel the car tilt down a few inches.

"Counselor, how's it hanging?" he said.

"Just fine, Ted," I said, not wanting to call him by his obvious gang sobriquet of Teddy Bear. "What's up with you?"

"What happened to the ponytail?"

"Some people objected to it, so I cut it off."

"A jury, huh? Must've been a collection of stiffs from up this way."

"What's up, Ted?"

"I got a call from Hard Case over there in the Lancaster pen. He said I might catch you heading south. Said you were stalling his case till you got some green. That right, Counselor?"

It was said as routine conversation. No threat in his voice or words. And I didn't feel threatened. Two years ago I got an abduction and aggravated assault case against Vogel knocked down to a disturbing the peace. He ran a Saints-owned strip club on Sepulveda in Van Nuys. His arrest came after he learned that one of his most productive dancers had quit and crossed the street to work at a competing club. Vogel had crossed the street after her, grabbed her off the stage and carried her back to his club. She was naked. A passing motorist called the police. Knocking the case down was one of my better plays and Vogel knew this. He had a soft spot for me.

"He's pretty much got it right," I said. "I work for a living. If he wants me to work for him he's gotta pay me."

"We gave you five grand in December," Vogel said.

"That's long gone, Ted. More than half went to the expert who is going to blow the case up. The rest went to me and I already worked off those hours. If I'm going to take it to trial, then I need to refill the tank."

"You want another five?"

"No, I need ten and I told Hard Case that last week. It's a three-day trial and I'll need to bring my expert in from Kodak in New York. I've got his fee to cover and he wants first class in the air and the Chateau Marmont on the ground. Thinks he's going to be drinking at the bar with movie stars or something. That place is four hundred a night just for the cheap rooms."

"You're killing me, Counselor. Whatever happened to that slogan you had in the yellow pages? 'Reasonable doubt for a reasonable fee.' You call ten grand reasonable?"

"I liked that slogan. It brought in a lot of clients. But the California bar wasn't so pleased with it, made me get rid of it. Ten is the price and it is reasonable, Ted. If you can't or don't want to pay it, I'll file the paperwork today. I'll drop out and he can go with a PD. I'll turn everything I have over. But the PD probably won't have the budget to fly in the photo expert."

Vogel shifted his position on the window sill and the car shuddered under the weight.

"No, no, we want you. Hard Case is important to us, you know what I mean? I want him out and back to work."

I watched him reach inside his vest with a hand that was so fleshy that the knuckles were indented. It came out with a thick envelope that he passed into the car to me.

"Is this cash?" I asked.

"That's right. What's wrong with cash?"

"Nothing. But I have to give you a receipt. It's an IRS reporting requirement. This is the whole ten?"

"It's all there."

I took the top off of a cardboard file box I keep on the seat next to me. My receipt book was behind the current case files. I started writing out the receipt. Most lawyers who get disbarred go down because of financial violations. The mishandling or misappropriation of client fees. I kept meticulous records and receipts. I would never let the bar get to me that way.

"So you had it all along," I said as I wrote. "What if I had backed down to five? What would you have done then?"

Vogel smiled. He was missing one of his front teeth on the bottom. Had to have been a fight at the club. He patted the other side of his vest.

"I got another envelope with five in it right here, Counselor," he said. "I was ready for you."

"Damn, now I feel bad, leaving you with money in your pocket."

I tore out his copy of the receipt and handed it out the window.

"I receipted it to Casey. He's the client."

"Fine with me."

He took the receipt and dropped his arm off the window sill as he stood up straight. The car returned to a normal level. I wanted to ask him where the money came from, which of the Saints' criminal enterprises had earned it, whether a hundred girls had danced a hundred hours for him to pay me, but that was a question I was better off not knowing the answer to. I watched Vogel saunter back to his Harley and struggle to swing a trash-can-thick leg over the seat. For the first time I noticed the double shocks on the back wheel. I told Earl to get back on the freeway and get going to Van Nuys, where I now needed to make a stop at the bank before hitting the courthouse to meet my new client.

As we drove I opened the envelope and counted out the money, twenties, fifties and hundred-dollar bills. It was all there. The tank was refilled and I was good to go with Harold Casey. I would go to trial and teach his young prosecutor a lesson. I would win, if not in trial, then certainly on appeal. Casey would return to the family and work of the Road Saints. His guilt in the crime he was charged with was not something I even considered as I filled out a deposit slip for my client fees account.

"Mr. Haller?" Earl said after a while.

"What, Earl?"

"That man you told him was coming in from New York to be the expert? Will I be picking him up at the airport?"

26

I shook my head.

"There is no expert coming in from New York, Earl. The best camera and photo experts in the world are right here in Hollywood."

Now Earl nodded and his eyes held mine for a moment in the rearview mirror. Then he looked back at the road ahead.

"I see," he said, nodding again.

And I nodded to myself. No hesitation in what I had done or said. That was my job. That was how it worked. After fifteen years of practicing law I had come to think of it in very simple terms. The law was a large, rusting machine that sucked up people and lives and money. I was just a mechanic. I had become expert at going into the machine and fixing things and extracting what I needed from it in return.

There was nothing about the law that I cherished anymore. The law school notions about the virtue of the adversarial system, of the system's checks and balances, of the search for truth, had long since eroded like the faces of statues from other civilizations. The law was not about truth. It was about negotiation, amelioration, manipulation. I didn't deal in guilt and innocence, because everybody was guilty. Of something. But it didn't matter, because every case I took on was a house built on a foundation poured by overworked and underpaid laborers. They cut corners. They made mistakes. And then they painted over the mistakes with lies. My job was to peel away the paint and find the cracks. To work my fingers and tools into those cracks and widen them. To make them so big that either the house fell down or, failing that, my client slipped through.

Much of society thought of me as the devil but they were wrong. I was a greasy angel. I was the true road saint. I was needed and wanted. By both sides. I was the oil in the machine. I allowed the gears to crank and turn. I helped keep the engine of the system running.

But all of that would change with the Roulet case. For me. For him. And certainly for Jesus Menendez.

FOUR

Louis Ross Roulet was in a holding tank with seven other men who had made the half-block bus ride from the Van Nuys jail to the Van Nuys courthouse. There were only two white men in the cell and they sat next to each other on a bench while the six black men took the other side of the cell. It was a form of Darwinian segregation. They were all strangers but there was strength in numbers.

Since Roulet supposedly came from Beverly Hills money, I looked at the two white men and it was easy to choose between them. One was rail thin with the desperate wet eyes of a hype who was long past fix time. The other looked like the proverbial deer in the headlights. I chose him.

"Mr. Roulet?" I said, pronouncing the name the way Valenzuela had told me to.

The deer nodded. I signaled him over to the bars so I could talk quietly.

"My name is Michael Haller. People call me Mickey. I will be representing you during your first appearance today."

We were in the holding area behind the arraignment court, where attorneys are routinely allowed access to confer with clients before court begins. There is a blue line painted on the floor outside the cells. The three-foot line. I had to keep that distance from my client.

Roulet grasped the bars in front of me. Like the others in the cage, he had on ankle, wrist and belly chains. They wouldn't come off until he was taken into the courtroom. He was in his early thirties and, though at least six feet tall and 180 pounds, he seemed slight. Jail will do that to you. His eyes were pale blue and it was rare for me to see the kind of panic that was so clearly set in them. Most of the time my clients have been in lockup before and they have the stone-cold look of the predator. It's how they get by in jail.

But Roulet was different. He looked like prey. He was scared and he didn't care who saw it and knew it.

"This is a setup," he said urgently and loudly. "You have to get me out of here. I made a mistake with that woman, that's all. She's trying to set me up and —"

I put my hands up to stop him.

"Be careful what you say in here," I said in a low voice. "In fact, be careful what you say until we get you out of here and can talk in private."

He looked around, seemingly not understanding.

"You never know who is listening," I said. "And you never know who will say he heard you say something, even if you didn't say anything. Best thing is to not talk about the case at all. You understand? Best thing is not to talk to anyone about anything, period."

He nodded and I signaled him down to the bench next to the bars. There was a bench against the opposite wall and I sat down.

"I am really here just to meet you and tell you who I am," I said. "We'll talk about the case after we get you out. I already spoke to your family lawyer, Mr. Dobbs, out there and we will tell the judge that we are prepared to post bail. Do I have all of that right?"

I opened a leather Mont Blanc folder and prepared to take notes on a legal pad. Roulet nodded. He was learning.

"Good," I said. "Tell me about yourself. How old you are, whether you're married, what ties you have to the community."

"Um, I'm thirty-two. I've lived here my whole life — even went to school here. UCLA. Not married. No kids. I work —"

"Divorced?"

"No, never married. I work for my family's business. Windsor Residential Estates. It's named after my mother's second husband. It's real estate. We sell real estate."

I was writing notes. Without looking up at him, I quietly asked, "How much money did you make last year?"

When Roulet didn't answer I looked up at him.

"Why do you need to know that?" he asked.

"Because I am going to get you out of here before the sun goes down today. To do that, I need to know everything about your standing in the community. That includes your financial standing."

"I don't know exactly what I made. A lot of it was shares in the company."

"You didn't file taxes?"

Roulet looked over his shoulder at the others in the cell and then whispered his answer.

"Yes, I did. On that my income was a quarter million."

"But what you're saying is that with the shares you earned in the company you really made more."

"Right."

One of Roulet's cellmates came up to the bars next to him. The other white man. He had an agitated manner, his hands in constant motion, moving from hips to pockets to each other in desperate grasps.

"Hey, man, I need a lawyer, too. You got a card?"

"Not for you, pal. They'll have a lawyer out there for you."

I looked back at Roulet and waited a moment for the hype to move away. He didn't. I looked back at him.

"Look, this is private. Could you leave us alone?"

The hype made some kind of motion with his hands

and shuffled back to the corner he had come from. I looked back at Roulet.

"What about charitable organizations?" I asked.

"What do you mean?" Roulet responded.

"Are you involved in any charities? Do you give to any charities?"

"Yeah, the company does. We give to Make a Wish and a runaway shelter in Hollywood. I think it's called My Friend's Place or something like that."

"Okay, good."

"Are you going to get me out?"

"I'm going to try. You've got some heavy charges on you — I checked before coming back here — and I have a feeling the DA is going to request no bail, but this is good stuff. I can work with it."

I indicated my notes.

"No bail?" he said in a loud, panicked voice.

The others in the cell looked in his direction because what he had said was their collective nightmare. No bail.

"Calm down," I said. "I said that is what she is going to go for. I didn't say she would get it. When was the last time you were arrested?"

I always threw that in out of the blue so I could watch their eyes and see if there was going to be a surprise thrown at me in court.

"Never. I've never been arrested. This whole thing is —"

"I know, I know, but we don't want to talk about that here, remember?"

He nodded. I looked at my watch. Court was about to start and I still needed to talk to Maggie McFierce.

"I'm going to go now," I said. "I'll see you out there in a few minutes and we'll see about getting you out of here. When we are out there, don't say anything until you check with me. If the judge asks you how you are doing, you check with me. Okay?"

"Well, don't I say 'not guilty' to the charges?"

"No, they're not going to even ask you that. Today all they do is read you the charges, talk about bail and set a date for an arraignment. That's when we say 'not guilty.' So today you say nothing. No outbursts, nothing. Got that?"

He nodded and frowned.

"Are you going to be all right, Louis?"

He nodded glumly.

"Just so you know," I said. "I charge twenty-five hundred dollars for a first appearance and bail hearing like this. Is that going to be a problem?"

He shook his head no. I liked that he wasn't talking. Most of my clients talk way too much. Usually they talk themselves right into prison.

"Good. We can talk about the rest of it after you are out of here and we can get together in private."

I closed my leather folder, hoping he had noticed it and was impressed, then stood up.

"One last thing," I said. "Why'd you pick me? There's a lot of lawyers out there, why me?"

It was a question that didn't matter to our relationship but I wanted to test Valenzuela's veracity.

Roulet shrugged.

"I don't know," he said. "I remembered your name from something I read in the paper."

"What did you read about me?"

"It was a story about a case where the evidence got thrown out against some guy. I think it was drugs or something. You won the case because they had no evidence after that."

"The Hendricks case?"

It was the only one I could think of that had made the papers in recent months. Hendricks was another Road Saint client and the sheriff's department had put a GPS bug on his Harley to track his deliveries. Doing that on public roads was fine. But when he parked his bike in the kitchen of his home at night, that bug constituted unlawful entry by the cops. The case was tossed by a judge during the preliminary hearing. It made a decent splash in the *Times*.

"I can't remember the name of the client," Roulet said. "I just remembered your name. Your last name, actually. When I called the bail bondsman today I gave him the name Haller and asked him to get you and to call my own attorney. Why?"

"No reason. Just curious. I appreciate the call. I'll see you in the courtroom."

I put the differences between what Roulet had said about my hiring and what Valenzuela had told me into the bank for later consideration and made my way back into the arraignment court. I saw Maggie McFierce sitting at one end of the prosecution table. She was there along with five other prosecutors. The table was large and L-shaped so it could accommodate an endlessly revolving number of lawyers who could sit and still face the bench. A prosecutor assigned to the courtroom handled most of the routine appearances and arraignments that were paraded through each day. But special cases brought the big guns out of the district attorney's office on the second floor of the courthouse next door. TV cameras did that, too.

As I stepped through the bar I saw a man setting up a video camera on a tripod next to the bailiff's desk. There was no network symbol on the camera or the man's clothes. The man was a freelancer who had gotten wind of the case and would shoot the hearing and then try to sell it to one of the local stations whose news director needed a thirty-second story. When I had checked with the bailiff earlier about Roulet's place on the calendar, he told me the judge had already authorized the filming.

I walked up to my ex-wife from behind and bent down to whisper into her ear. She was looking at photographs in a file. She was wearing a navy suit with a thin gray stripe. Her raven-colored hair was tied back with a matching gray ribbon. I loved her hair when it was back like that.

"Are you the one who used to have the Roulet case?"

She looked up, not recognizing the whisper. Her face was involuntarily forming a smile but then it turned into a frown when she saw it was me. She knew exactly what I had meant by using the past tense and she slapped the file closed.

"Don't tell me," she said.

"Sorry. He liked what I did on Hendricks and gave me a call."

"Son of a bitch. I wanted this case, Haller. This is the second time you've done this to me."

"I guess this town ain't big enough for the both of us," I said in a poor Cagney imitation.

She groaned.

"All right," she said in quick surrender. "I'll go peacefully after this hearing. Unless you object to even that."

"I might. You going for a no-bail hold?"

"That's right. But that won't change with the prosecutor. That was a directive from the second floor."

I nodded. That meant a case supervisor must have called for the no-bail hold.

"He's connected in the community. And has never been arrested."

I studied her reaction, not having had the time to make sure Roulet's denial of ever being previously arrested was the truth. It's always amazing how many clients lie about previous engagements with the machine, when it is a lie that has no hope of going the distance.

But Maggie gave no indication that she knew otherwise. Maybe it was true. Maybe I had an honest-to-goodness first-time offender for a client.

"It doesn't matter whether he's done anything before," Maggie said. "What matters is what he did last night."

She opened the file and quickly checked through the photos until she saw the one she liked and snatched it out.

"Here's what your pillar of the community did last night. So I don't really care what he did before. I'm just going to make sure he doesn't get out to do this again."

The photo was an 8 × 10 close-up of a woman's face. The swelling around the right eye was so extensive that the eye was completely and tightly closed. The nose was broken and pushed off center. Blood-soaked gauze protruded from each nostril. There was a deep gash over the right eyebrow that had been closed with nine butterfly stitches. The lower lip was cut and had a marble-size swelling as well. The worst thing about the photo was the eye that was undamaged. The woman looked at the camera with fear, pain and humiliation undeniably expressed in that one tearful eye.

"If he did it," I said, because that is what I would be expected to say.

"Right," Maggie said. "Sure, if he did it. He was only arrested in her home with her blood on him, but you're right, that's a valid question."

"I like it when you're sarcastic. Do you have the arrest report there? I'd like to get a copy of it."

"You can get it from whoever takes the case over from me. No favors, Haller. Not this time."

I waited, expecting more banter, more indignation, maybe another shot across the bow, but that was all she said. I decided that getting more out of her on the case was a lost cause. I changed the subject.

"So," I said. "How is she?"

"She's scared shitless and hurting like hell. How else would she be?"

She looked up at me and I saw the immediate recognition and then judgment in her eyes.

"You weren't even asking about the victim, were you?"

I didn't answer. I didn't want to lie to her.

"Your daughter is doing fine," she said perfunctorily. "She likes the things you send her but she would rather *you* show up a little more often."

That wasn't a shot across the bow. That was a direct hit and it was deserved. It seemed as though I was always chasing cases, even on weekends. Deep down inside I knew I needed to start chasing my daughter around the backyard more often. The time to do it was going by.

"I will," I said. "Starting right now. What about this weekend?"

"Fine. You want me to tell her tonight?"

"Uh, maybe wait until tomorrow so I know for sure."

She gave me one of those knowing nods. We had been through this before.

"Great. Let me know tomorrow."

This time I didn't enjoy the sarcasm.

"What does she need?" I asked, trying to stumble back to just being even.

"I just told you what she needs. More of you in her life."

"Okay, I promise. I will do that."

She didn't respond.

"I really mean that, Maggie. I'll call you tomorrow."

She looked up at me and was ready to hit me with both barrels. She had done it before, saying I was all talk and no action when it came to fatherhood. But I was saved by the start of the court session. The judge came out of chambers and bounded up the steps to the bench. The bailiff called the courtroom to order. Without another word to Maggie I left the prosecution table and went back to one of the seats along the bar.

The judge asked his clerk if there was any business to be discussed before the custodies were brought out. There was none, so the judge ordered the first group out. As with the courtroom in Lancaster, there was a large holding area for in-custody defendants. I got up and moved to the opening in the glass. When I saw Roulet come through the door I signaled him over.

"You're going first," I told him. "I asked the judge to take you out of order as a favor. I want to try to get you out of here."

This was not the truth. I hadn't asked the judge anything, and even if I had, the judge would do no such thing for me as a favor. Roulet was going first because of the media presence in the courtroom. It was a general practice to deal with the media cases first. This was a courtesy to the cameramen who supposedly had other assignments to get to. But it also made for less tension in the courtroom when lawyers, defendants and even the judge could operate without a television camera on them.

"Why's that camera here?" Roulet asked in a panicked whisper. "Is that for me?"

"Yes, it's for you. Somebody tipped him to the case. If you don't want to be filmed, try to use me as a shield."

Roulet shifted his position so I was blocking the view of him from the camera across the courtroom. This lowered the chances that the cameraman would be able to sell the story and film to a local news program. That was good. It also meant that if he was able to sell the story, I would be the focal point of the images that went with it. This was also good.

The Roulet case was called, his name mispronounced by the clerk, and Maggie announced her presence for the prosecution and then I announced mine. Maggie had upped the charges, as was her usual MO as Maggie McFierce. Roulet now faced attempted murder along with the attempted rape count. It would make it easier for her to argue for a no-bail hold.

The judge informed Roulet of his constitutional rights and set an arraignment date for March 21. Speaking for Roulet, I asked to address the no-bail hold. This set off a spirited back-and-forth between Maggie and me, all of which was refereed by the judge, who knew we were formerly married because he had attended our wedding. While Maggie listed the atrocities committed upon the victim, I in turn listed Roulet's ties to the community and charitable efforts and pointed to C. C. Dobbs in the gallery and offered to put him on the stand to further discuss Roulet's good standing. Dobbs was my ace in the hole. His stature in the legal community would supersede Roulet's standing and certainly be influential with the judge, who held his position on the bench at the behest of the voters — and campaign contributors.

"The bottom line, Judge, is that the state cannot make a case for this man being a flight risk or a danger to the community," I said in closing. "Mr. Roulet is anchored in this community and intends to do nothing other than vigorously attack the false charges that have been leveled against him."

I used the word *attack* purposely in case the statement got on the air and happened to be watched by the woman who had leveled the charges.

"Your Honor," Maggie responded, "all grandstanding aside, what should not be forgotten is that the victim in this case was brutally —"

"Ms. McPherson," the judge interrupted. "I think we have gone back and forth on this enough. I am aware of the victim's injuries as well as Mr. Roulet's standing. I also have a busy calendar today. I am going to set bail at one million dollars. I am also going to require Mr. Roulet to be supervised by the court with weekly check-ins. If he misses one, he forfeits his freedom."

I quickly glanced out into the gallery, where Dobbs was sitting next to Fernando Valenzuela. Dobbs was a thin man who shaved his head to hide male-pattern balding. His thinness was exaggerated by Valenzuela's girth. I waited for a signal as to whether I should take the judge's bail order or try to argue for a lower amount. Sometimes, when a judge thinks he is giving you a gift, it can backfire to press for more — or in this case less.

Dobbs was sitting in the first seat in the first row. He simply got up and started to walk out of the courtroom, leaving Valenzuela behind. I took that to mean that I should leave well enough alone, that the Roulet family could handle the million. I turned back to the bench.

"Thank you, Your Honor," I said.

The clerk immediately called the next case. I glanced at Maggie as she was closing the file on the case she would no longer prosecute. She then stood up and walked out through the bar and down the center aisle of the courtroom. She spoke to no one and she did not look back at me.

"Mr. Haller?"

I turned to my client. Behind him I saw a deputy coming to take him back into holding. He'd be bused the half block back to jail and then, depending on how fast Dobbs and Valenzuela worked, released later in the day.

"I'll work with Mr. Dobbs and get you out," I said. "Then we'll sit down and talk about the case."

"Thank you," Roulet said as he was led away. "Thank you for being here."

"Remember what I said. Don't talk to strangers. Don't talk to anybody."

"Yes, sir."

After he was gone I walked to the bar. Valenzuela was waiting at the gate for me with a big smile on his face. Roulet's bail was likely the highest he had ever secured. That meant his cut would be the highest he'd ever received. He clapped me on the arm as I came through the gate.

"What'd I tell you?" he said. "We got ourselves a franchise here, boss."

"We'll see, Val," I said. "We'll see."

FIVE

Every attorney who works the machine has two fee schedules. There is schedule A, which lists the fees the attorney would like to get for certain services rendered. And there is schedule B, the fees he is willing to take because that is all the client can afford. A franchise client is a defendant who wants to go to trial and has the money to pay his lawyer's schedule A rates. From first appearance to arraignment to preliminary hearing and on to trial and then appeal, the franchise client demands hundreds if not thousands of billable hours. He can keep gas in the tank for two to three years. From where I hunt, they are the rarest and most highly sought beast in the jungle.

And it was beginning to look like Valenzuela had been on the money. Louis Roulet was looking more and more like a franchise client. It had been a dry spell for me. It had been almost two years since I'd had anything even approaching a franchise case or client. I'm talking about a case earning six figures. There were many that started out looking like they might reach that rare plateau but they never went the distance.

C. C. Dobbs was waiting in the hallway outside the arraignment court when I got out. He was standing next to the wall of glass windows that looked down upon the civic center plaza below. I walked up to him quickly. I had a few seconds' lead on Valenzuela coming out of the court and I wanted some private time with Dobbs.

"Sorry," Dobbs said before I could speak. "I didn't want

to stay in there another minute. It was so depressing to see the boy caught up in that cattle call."

"The boy?"

"Louis. I've represented the family for twenty-five years. I guess I still think of him as a boy."

"Are you going to be able to get him out?"

"It won't be a problem. I have a call in to Louis's mother to see how she wants to handle it, whether to put up property or go with a bond."

To put up property to cover a million-dollar bail would mean that at least a million dollars in the property's value could not be encumbered by a mortgage. Additionally, the court might require a current appraisal of the property, which could take days and keep Roulet waiting in jail. Conversely, a bond could be purchased through Valenzuela for a ten percent premium. The difference was that the ten percent was never returned. That stayed with Valenzuela for his risks and trouble and was the reason for his broad smile in the courtroom. After paying his insurance premium on the million-dollar bail, he'd end up clearing close to ninety grand. And he was worried about me taking care of *him*.

"Can I make a suggestion?" I asked.

"Please do."

"Louis looked a little frail when I saw him back in the lockup. If I were you I would get him out of there as soon as possible. To do that you should have Valenzuela write a bond. It will cost you a hundred grand but the boy will be out and safe, you know what I mean?"

Dobbs turned to the window and leaned on the railing that ran along the glass. I looked down and saw that the plaza was filling up with people from the government buildings on lunch break. I could see many people with the red-and-white name tags I knew were given to jurors.

"I know what you mean."

43

"The other thing is that cases like this tend to bring the rats out of the walls."

"What do you mean?"

"I mean other inmates who will say they heard somebody say something. Especially a case that gets on the news or into the newspapers. They'll take that info off the tube and make it sound like our guy was talking."

"That's criminal," Dobbs said indignantly. "That shouldn't be allowed."

"Yeah, I know, but it happens. And the longer he stays in there, the wider the window of opportunity is for one of these guys."

Valenzuela joined us at the railing. He didn't say anything.

"I will suggest we go with the bond," Dobbs said. "I already called and she was in a meeting. As soon as she calls me back we will move on this."

His words prompted something that had bothered me during the hearing.

"She couldn't come out of a meeting to talk about her son in jail? I was wondering why she wasn't in court today if this boy, as you call him, is so clean and upstanding."

Dobbs looked at me like I hadn't used mouthwash in a month.

"Mrs. Windsor is a very busy and powerful woman. I am sure that if I had stated it was an emergency concerning her son, she would have been on the phone immediately."

"Mrs. Windsor?"

"She remarried after she and Louis's father divorced. That was a long time ago."

I nodded, then realized that there was more to talk about with Dobbs but nothing I wanted to discuss in front of Valenzuela.

"Val, why don't you go check on when Louis will be back at Van Nuys jail so you can get him out."

"That's easy," Valenzuela said. "He'll go on the first bus back after lunch."

"Yeah, well, go double-check that while I finish with Mr. Dobbs."

Valenzuela was about to protest that he didn't need to double-check it when he realized what I was telling him.

"Okay," he said. "I'll go do it."

After he was gone I studied Dobbs for a moment before speaking. Dobbs looked to be in his late fifties. He had a deferential presence that probably came from thirty years of taking care of rich people. My guess was that he had become rich in the process himself but it hadn't changed his public demeanor.

"If we're going to be working together, I guess I should ask what you want to be called. Cecil? C.C.? Mr. Dobbs?"

"Cecil will be fine."

"Well, my first question, Cecil, is whether we are going to be working together. Do I have the job?"

"Mr. Roulet made it clear to me he wanted you on the case. To be honest, you would not have been my first choice. You may not have been any choice, because frankly I had never heard of you. But you are Mr. Roulet's first choice, and that is acceptable to me. In fact, I thought you acquitted yourself quite well in the courtroom, especially considering how hostile that prosecutor was toward Mr. Roulet."

I noticed that the boy had become "Mr. Roulet" now. I wondered what had happened to advance him in Dobbs's view.

"Yeah, well, they call her Maggie McFierce. She's pretty dedicated."

"I thought she was a bit overboard. Do you think there is any way to get her removed from the case, maybe get someone a little more . . . grounded?"

"I don't know. Trying to shop prosecutors can be

dangerous. But if you think she needs to go, I can get it done."

"That's good to hear. Maybe I should have known about you before today."

"Maybe. Do you want to talk about fees now and get it out of the way?"

"If you would like."

I looked around the hallway to make sure there were no other lawyers hanging around in earshot. I was going to go schedule A all the way on this.

"I get twenty-five hundred for today and Louis already approved that. If you want to go hourly from here, I get three hundred an hour and that gets bumped to five in trial because I can't do anything else. If you'd rather go with a flat rate, I'll want sixty thousand to take it from here through a preliminary hearing. If we end it with a plea, I'll take twelve more on top of that. If we go to trial instead, I need another sixty on the day we decide that and twenty-five more when we start picking a jury. This case doesn't look like more than a week, including jury selection, but if it goes past a week, I get twenty-five-a-week extra. We can talk about an appeal if and when it becomes necessary."

I hesitated a moment to see how Dobbs was reacting. He showed nothing so I pressed on.

"I'll need thirty thousand for a retainer and another ten for an investigator by the end of the day. I don't want to waste time on this. I want to get an investigator out and about on this thing before it hits the media and maybe before the cops talk to some of the people involved."

Dobbs slowly nodded.

"Are those your standard fees?"

"When I can get them. I'm worth it. What are you charging the family, Cecil?"

I was sure he wouldn't walk away from this little episode hungry.

46

"That's between me and my client. But don't worry. I will include your fees in my discussion with Mrs. Windsor."

"I appreciate it. And remember, I need that investigator to start today."

I gave him a business card I pulled from the right pocket of my suit coat. The cards in the right pocket had my cell number. The cards in my left pocket had the number that went to Lorna Taylor.

"I have another hearing downtown," I said. "When you get him out call me and we'll set up a meeting. Let's make it as soon as possible. I should be available later today and tonight."

"Perfect," Dobbs said, pocketing the card without looking at it. "Should we come to you?"

"No, I'll come to you. I'd like to see how the other half lives in those high-rises in Century City."

Dobbs smiled glibly.

"It is obvious by your suit that you know and practice the adage that a trial lawyer should never dress too well. You want the jury to like you, not to be jealous of you. Well, Michael, a Century City lawyer can't have an office that is nicer than the offices his clients come from. And so I can assure you that our offices are very modest."

I nodded in agreement. But I was insulted just the same. I was wearing my best suit. I always did on Mondays.

"That's good to know," I said.

The courtroom door opened and the videographer walked out, lugging his camera and folded tripod with him. Dobbs saw him and immediately tensed.

"The media," he said. "How can we control this? Mrs. Windsor won't —"

"Hold on a sec."

I called to the cameraman and he walked over. I immediately put my hand out. He had to put his tripod down to take it.

"I'm Michael Haller. I saw you in there filming my client's appearance."

Using my formal name was a code.

"Robert Gillen," the cameraman said. "People call me Sticks."

He gestured to his tripod in explanation. His use of his formal name was a return code. He was letting me know he understood that I had a play working here.

"Are you freelancing or on assignment?" I asked.

"Just freelancing today."

"How'd you hear about this thing?"

He shrugged as though he was reluctant to answer.

"A source. A cop."

I nodded. Gillen was locked in and playing along.

"What do you get for that if you sell it to a news station?"

"Depends. I take seven-fifty for an exclusive and five for a nonexclusive."

Nonexclusive meant that any news director who bought the tape from him knew that he might sell the footage to a competing news station. Gillen had doubled the fees he actually got. It was a good move. He must have been listening to what had been said in the courtroom while he shot it.

"Tell you what," I said. "How about we take it off your hands right now for an exclusive?"

Gillen was perfect. He hesitated like he was unsure of the ethics involved in the proposition.

"In fact, make it a grand," I said.

"Okay," he said. "You got a deal."

While Gillen put the camera on the floor and took the tape out of it, I pulled a wad of cash from my pocket. I had kept twelve hundred from the Saints cash Teddy Vogel had given me on the way down. I turned to Dobbs.

"I can expense this, right?"

"Absolutely," he said. He was beaming.

I exchanged the cash for the tape and thanked Gillen. He pocketed the money and moved toward the elevators a happy man.

"That was brilliant," Dobbs said. "We have to contain this. It could literally destroy the family's business if this — in fact, I think that is one reason Mrs. Windsor was not here today. She didn't want to be recognized."

"Well, we'll have to talk about that if this thing goes the distance. Meantime, I'll do my best to keep it off the radar."

"Thank you."

A cell phone began to play a classical number by Bach or Beethoven or some other dead guy with no copyright and Dobbs reached inside his jacket, retrieved the device and checked the small screen on it.

"This is she," he said.

"Then I'll leave you to it."

As I walked off I heard Dobbs saying, "Mary, everything is under control. We need now to concentrate on getting him out. We are going to need some money . . ."

While the elevator made its way up to me, I was thinking that I was pretty sure that I was dealing with a client and family for which "some money" meant more than I had ever seen. My mind moved back to the sartorial comment Dobbs had made about me. It still stung. The truth was, I didn't have a suit in my closet that cost less than six hundred dollars and I always felt good and confident in any one of them. I wondered if he had intended to insult me or he had intended something else, maybe trying at this early stage of the game to imprint his control over me and the case. I decided I would need to watch my back with Dobbs. I would keep him close but not that close.

SIX

Traffic heading downtown bottlenecked in the Cahuenga Pass. I spent the time in the car working the phone and trying not to think about the conversation I'd had with Maggie McPherson about my parenting skills. My ex-wife had been right about me, and that's what hurt. For a long time I had put my law practice ahead of my parenting practice. It was something I promised myself to change. I just needed the time and the money to slow down. I thought that maybe Louis Roulet would provide both.

In the back of the Lincoln I first called Raul Levin, my investigator, to put him on alert about the potential meeting with Roulet. I asked him to do a preliminary run on the case to see what he could find out. Levin had retired early from the LAPD and still had contacts and friends who did him favors from time to time. He probably had his own Christmas list. I told him not to spend a lot of time on it until I was sure I had Roulet locked down as a paying client. It didn't matter what C. C. Dobbs had said to me face-to-face in the courthouse hallway. I wouldn't believe I had the case until I got the first payment.

Next I checked on the status of a few cases and then called Lorna Taylor again. I knew the mail was delivered at her place most days right before noon. But she told me nothing of importance had come in. No checks and no correspondence I had to pay immediate attention to from the courts.

"Did you check on Gloria Dayton's arraignment?" I asked her.

"Yes. It looks like they might hold her over until tomorrow on a medical."

I groaned. The state has forty-eight hours to charge an individual after arrest and bring them before a judge. Holding Gloria Dayton's first appearance over until the next day because of medical reasons meant that she was probably drug sick. This would help explain why she had been holding cocaine when she was arrested. I had not seen or spoken to her in at least seven months. Her slide must have been quick and steep. The thin line between controlling the drugs and the drugs controlling her had been crossed.

"Did you find out who filed it?" I asked.

"Leslie Faire," she said.

I groaned again.

"That's just great. Okay, well, I'm going to go down and see what I can do. I've got nothing going until I hear about Roulet."

Leslie Faire was a misnamed prosecutor whose idea of giving a defendant a break or the benefit of the doubt was to offer extended parole supervision on top of prison time.

"Mick, when are you going to learn with this woman?" Lorna said about Gloria Dayton.

"Learn what?" I asked, although I knew exactly what Lorna would say.

"She drags you down every time you have to deal with her. She's never going to get out of the life, and now you can bet she's never going to be anything less than a twofer every time she calls. That would be fine, except you never charge her."

What she meant by *twofer* was that Gloria Dayton's cases would from now on be more complicated and time-consuming because it was likely that drug charges would always accompany solicitation or prostitution charges. What bothered Lorna was that this meant more work for me but no more income in the process.

"Well, the bar requires that all lawyers practice some pro bono work, Lorna. You know —"

"You don't listen to me, Mick," she said dismissively. "That's exactly why we couldn't stay married."

I closed my eyes. What a day. I had managed to get both my ex-wives angry with me.

"What does this woman have on you?" she asked. "Why don't you charge even a basic fee with her?"

"Look, she doesn't have anything on me, okay?" I said. "Can we sort of change the subject now?"

I didn't tell her that years earlier when I had looked through the dusty old account books from my father's law practice, I had found that he'd had a soft spot for the so-called women of the night. He defended many and charged few. Maybe I was just continuing a family tradition.

"Fine," Lorna said. "How did it go with Roulet?"

"You mean, did I get the job? I think so. Val's probably getting him out right now. We'll set up a meeting after that. I already asked Raul to sniff around on it."

"Did you get a check?"

"Not yet."

"Get the check, Mick."

"I'm working on it."

"How's the case look?"

"I've only seen the pictures but it looks bad. I'll know more after I see what Raul comes up with."

"And what about Roulet?"

I knew what she was asking. How was he as a client? Would a jury, if it came to a jury, like him or despise him? Cases could be won or lost based on jurors' impressions of the defendant.

"He looks like a babe in the woods."

"He's a virgin?"

"Never been inside the iron house."

"Well, did he do it?"

She always asked the irrelevant question. It didn't matter in terms of the strategy of the case whether the defendant "did it" or not. What mattered was the evidence against him — the proof — and if and how it could be neutralized. My job was to bury the proof, to color the proof a shade of gray. Gray was the color of reasonable doubt.

But the question of did he or didn't he always seemed to matter to her.

"Who knows, Lorna? That's not the question. The question is whether or not he's a paying customer. The answer is, I think so."

"Well, let me know if you need any — oh, there's one other thing."

"What?"

"Sticks called and said he owes you four hundred dollars next time he sees you."

"Yeah, he does."

"You're doing pretty good today."

"I'm not complaining."

We said our good-byes on a friendly note, the dispute over Gloria Dayton seemingly forgotten for the moment. Probably the security that comes with knowing money is coming in and a high-paying client is on the hook made Lorna feel a bit better about my working some cases for free. I wondered, though, if she'd have minded so much if I was defending a drug dealer for free instead of a prostitute. Lorna and I had shared a short and sweet marriage, with both of us quickly finding out that we had moved too quickly while rebounding from divorces. We ended it, remained friends, and she continued to work with me, not for me. The only time I felt uncomfortable about the arrangement was when she acted like a wife again and second-guessed my choice of client and who and what I charged or didn't charge.

Feeling confident in the way I had handled Lorna, I called the DA's office in Van Nuys next. I asked for Margaret McPherson and caught her eating at her desk.

"I just wanted to say I'm sorry about this morning. I know you wanted the case."

"Well, you probably need it more than me. He must be a paying customer if he's got C. C. Dobbs carrying the roll behind him."

By that she was referring to a roll of toilet paper. High-priced family lawyers were usually seen by prosecutors as nothing more than ass wipers for the rich and famous.

"Yeah, I could use one like him — the paying client, not the wiper. It's been a while since I had a franchise."

"Well, you didn't get as lucky a few minutes ago," she whispered into the phone. "The case was reassigned to Ted Minton."

"Never heard of him."

"He's one of Smithson's young guns. Just brought him in from downtown, where he was filing simple possession cases. He didn't see the inside of a courtroom until he came up here."

John Smithson was the ambitious head deputy in charge of the Van Nuys Division. He was a better politician than a prosecutor and had parlayed that skill into a quick climb over other more experienced deputies to the division chief's post. Maggie McPherson was among those he'd passed by. Once he was in the slot, he started building a staff of young prosecutors who did not feel slighted and were loyal to him for giving them a shot.

"This guy's never been in court?" I asked, not understanding how going up against a trial rookie could be unlucky, as Maggie had indicated.

"He's had a few trials up here but always with a babysitter. Roulet will be his first time flying solo. Smithson thinks he's giving him a slam dunk."

I imagined her sitting in her cubicle, probably not far from where my new opponent was sitting in his.

"I don't get it, Mags. If this guy's green, why wasn't I lucky?"

"Because these guys Smithson picks are all cracked out of the same mold. They're arrogant assholes. They think they can do no wrong and what's more . . ."

She lowered her voice even more.

"They don't play fair. And the word on Minton is that he's a cheater. Watch yourself, Haller. Better yet, watch him."

"Well, thanks for the heads-up."

But she wasn't finished.

"A lot of these new people just don't get it. They don't see it as a calling. To them it's not about justice. It's just a game — a batting average. They like to keep score and to see how far it will get them in the office. In fact, they're all just like junior Smithsons."

A calling. It was her sense of calling that ultimately cost us our marriage. On an intellectual level she could deal with being married to a man who worked the other side of the aisle. But when it came down to the reality of what we did, we were lucky to have lasted the eight years we had managed. *Honey, how was your day? Oh, I got a guy who murdered his roommate with an ice pick a seven-year deal. And you? Oh, I put a guy away for five years because he stole a car stereo to feed his habit* . . . It just didn't work. Four years in, a daughter arrived, but through no fault of her own, she only kept us going another four years.

Still, I didn't regret a thing about it. I cherished my daughter. She was the only thing that was really good about my life, that I could be proud of. I think deep down, the reason I didn't see her enough — that I was chasing cases instead of her — was because I felt unworthy of her. Her mother was a hero. She put bad people in jail. What could I tell her was good and holy about what I did, when I had long ago lost the thread of it myself?

"Hey, Haller, are you there?"

"Yeah, Mags, I'm here. What are you eating today?"

"Just the oriental salad from downstairs. Nothing special. Where are you?"

"Heading downtown. Listen, tell Hayley I'll see her this Saturday. I'll make a plan. We'll do something special."

"You really mean that? I don't want to get her hopes up."

I felt something lift inside me, the idea that my daughter would get her hopes up about seeing me. The one thing Maggie never did was run me down with Hayley. She wasn't the kind that would do that. I always admired that.

"Yes, I'm sure," I said.

"Great, I'll tell her. Let me know when you're coming or if I can drop her off."

"Okay."

I hesitated. I wanted to talk to her longer but there was nothing else to say. I finally said good-bye and closed the phone. In a few minutes we broke free of the bottleneck. I looked out the window and saw no accident. I saw nobody with a flat tire and no highway patrol cruiser parked on the shoulder. I saw nothing that explained what had caused the traffic tie-up. It was often like that. Freeway traffic in Los Angeles was as mysterious as marriage. It moved and flowed, then stalled and stopped for no easily explainable reason.

I am from a family of attorneys. My father, my half brother, a niece and a nephew. My father was a famous lawyer in a time when there was no cable television and no Court TV. He was the dean of criminal law in L.A. for almost three decades. From Mickey Cohen to the Manson girls, his clients always made the headlines. I was just an afterthought in his life, a surprise visitor to his second marriage to a B-level movie actress known for her exotic Latin looks but not her acting skills. The mix gave me my black Irish looks. My father was old when I came, so he was gone before I was old enough to really know him or talk to him about the calling of the law. He only left me his name. Mickey Haller, the legal legend. It still opened doors.

But my older brother — the half brother from the first marriage — told me that my father used to talk to him about the practice of law and criminal defense. He used to say he would defend the devil himself just as long as he could cover the fee. The only big-time case and client he ever turned down was Sirhan Sirhan. He told my brother that he had liked Bobby Kennedy too much to defend his killer, no matter how much he believed in the ideal that the accused deserved the best and most vigorous defense possible.

Growing up I read all the books about my father and his cases. I admired the skill and vigor and strategies he brought to the defense table. He was damn good and it made me proud to carry his name. But the law was different now. It was grayer. Ideals had long been downgraded to notions. Notions were optional.

My cell phone rang and I checked the screen before answering.

"What's up, Val?"

"We're getting him out. They already took him back to the jail and we're processing him out now."

"Dobbs went with the bond?"

"You got it."

I could hear the delight in his voice.

"Don't be so giddy. You sure he's not a runner?"

"I'm never sure. I'm going to make him wear a bracelet. I lose him, I lose my house."

I realized that what I had taken as delight at the windfall that a million-dollar bond would bring to Valenzuela was actually nervous energy. Valenzuela would be taut as a wire until this one was over, one way or the other. Even if the court had not ordered it, Valenzuela was going to put an electronic tracking bracelet on Roulet's ankle. He was taking no chances with this guy.

"Where's Dobbs?"

"Back at my office, waiting. I'll bring Roulet over as soon as he's out. Shouldn't be too much longer."

"Is Maisy over there?"

"Yeah, she's there."

"Okay, I'm going to call over."

I ended the call and hit the speed-dial combo for Liberty Bail Bonds. Valenzuela's receptionist and assistant answered.

"Maisy, it's Mick. Can you put Mr. Dobbs on the line?"

"Sure thing, Mick."

A few seconds later Dobbs got on the line. He seemed put out by something. Just in the way he said, "This is Cecil Dobbs."

"This is Mickey Haller. How is it going over there?"

"Well, if you consider I am letting my duties to other clients slide while I sit here and read year-old magazines, not good."

"You don't carry a cell phone to do business?"

"I do. But that's not the point. My clients aren't cell phone people. They're face-to-face people."

"I see. Well, the good news is, I hear our boy is about to be released."

"Our boy?"

"Mr. Roulet. Valenzuela should have him out inside the hour. I am about to go into a client conference, but as I said

58

before, I am free in the afternoon. Do you want to meet to go over the case with our mutual client or do you want me to take it from here?"

"No, Mrs. Windsor has insisted that I monitor this closely. In fact, she may choose to be there as well."

"I don't mind the meet-and-greet with Mrs. Windsor, but when it comes down to talking about the case, it's just going to be the defense team. That can include you but not the mother. Okay?"

"I understand. Let's say four o'clock at my office. I will have Louis there."

"I'll be there."

"My firm employs a crack investigator. I'll ask him to join us."

"That won't be necessary, Cecil. I have my own and he's already on the job. We'll see you at four."

I ended the call before Dobbs could start a debate about which investigator to use. I had to be careful that Dobbs didn't control the investigation, preparation and strategy of the case. Monitoring was one thing. But I was Louis Roulet's attorney now. Not him.

When I called Raul Levin next, he told me he was already on his way to the LAPD Van Nuys Division to pick up a copy of the arrest report.

"Just like that?" I asked.

"No, not just like that. In a way, you could say it took me twenty years to get this report."

I understood. Levin's connections, procured over time and experience, traded over trust and favors, had come through for him. No wonder he charged five hundred dollars a day when he could get it. I told him about the meeting at four and he said he would be there and would be ready to furnish us with the law enforcement view of the case.

The Lincoln pulled to a stop when I closed the phone. We were in front of the Twin Towers jail facility. It wasn't even ten years old but the smog was beginning to permanently stain its sand-colored walls a dreary gray. It was a sad and forbidding place that I spent too much time in. I opened the car door and got out to go inside once again.

SEVEN

There was an attorney's check-in window that allowed me to bypass the long line of visitors waiting to get in to see loved ones incarcerated in one of the towers. When I told the window deputy whom I wanted to see, he tapped the name into the computer and never said anything about Gloria Dayton being in medical and unavailable. He printed out a visitor's pass which he slid into the plastic frame of a clip-on badge and told me to put it on and wear it at all times in the jail. He then told me to step away from the window and wait for an attorney escort.

"It will be a few minutes," he said.

I knew from prior experience that my cell phone did not get a signal inside the jail and that if I stepped outside to use it, I might miss my escort and then have to go through the whole sign-in process again. So I stayed put and watched the faces of the people who came to visit those being held inside. Most were black and brown. Most had the look of routine on their faces. They all probably knew the ropes here much better than I.

After twenty minutes a large woman in a deputy's uniform came into the waiting area and collected me. I knew that she had not gotten into the sheriff's department with her current dimensions. She was at least a hundred pounds overweight and seemed to struggle just to carry it while walking. But I also knew that once somebody was in, it was hard to get them out. About the best this one could do if there was a jail break was lean up against a door to keep it closed.

"Sorry it took so long," she told me as we waited between the double steel doors of a mantrap in the women's tower. "I had to go find her, make sure we still had her."

She signaled that everything was all right to a camera above the next door and its lock clacked open. She pushed through.

"She was up in medical getting fixed up," she said.

"Fixed up?"

I wasn't aware of the jail having a drug-treatment program that included "fixing up" addicts.

"Yeah, she got hurt," the deputy said. "Got a little banged up in a scuffle. She can tell you."

I let the questions go at that. In a way, I was relieved that the medical delay was not due — not directly, at least — to drug ingestion or addiction.

The deputy led me to the attorney room, which I had been in many times before with many different clients. The vast majority of my clients were men and I didn't discriminate, but the truth was I hated representing women who were incarcerated. From prostitutes to murderers — and I had defended them all — there was something pitiful about a woman in jail. I had found that almost all of the time, their crimes could be traced back to men. Men who took advantage of them, abused them, deserted them, hurt them. This is not to say they were not responsible for their actions or that some of them did not deserve the punishments they received. There were predators among the female ranks that easily rivaled those among the males. But, even still, the women I saw in jail seemed so different from the men in the other tower. The men still lived by wiles and strength. The women had nothing left by the time they locked the door on them.

The visiting area was a row of booths in which an attorney could sit on one side and confer with a client who sat on the other side, separated by an eighteen-inch sheet of clear Plexiglas. A deputy sat in a glassed-in booth at the end of the room and observed but supposedly didn't listen. If paperwork needed to be passed to the client, it was held up for the booth deputy to see and approve.

I was led to a booth and my escort left me. I then waited another ten minutes before the same deputy appeared on the other side of the Plexiglas with Gloria Dayton. Immediately, I saw that my client had a swelling around her left eye and a single butterfly stitch over a small laceration just below her widow's peak. Gloria Dayton had jet-black hair and olive skin. She had once been beautiful. The first time I represented her, seven or eight years before, she was beautiful. The kind of beauty that leaves you stunned at the fact she was selling it, that she had decided that selling herself to strangers was her best or only option. Now she just looked hard to me. The lines of her face were taut. She had visited surgeons who were not the best, and anyway, there was nothing they could do about eyes that had seen too much.

"Mickey Mantle," she said. "You're going to bat for me again?"

She said it in her little girl's voice that I suppose her regular clients enjoyed and responded to. It just sounded strange to me, coming from that tightly drawn mouth and face with eyes that were as hard and had as much life in them as marbles.

She always called me Mickey Mantle, even though she was born after the great slugger had long retired and probably knew little about him or the game he played. It was just a name to her. I guess the alternative would have been to call me Mickey Mouse, and I probably wouldn't have liked it much.

"I'm going to try, Gloria," I told her. "What happened to your face? How'd you get hurt?"

She made a dismissive gesture with her hand.

"There was a little disagreement with some of the girls in my dorm."

"About what?"

"Just girl stuff."

"Are you getting high in there?"

She looked indignant and then she tried putting a pouting look on her face.

"No, I'm not."

I studied her. She seemed straight. Maybe she wasn't getting high and that was not what the fight had been about.

"I don't want to stay in here, Mickey," she said in her real voice.

"I don't blame you. I don't like being in here myself and I get to leave."

I immediately regretted saying the last part and reminding her of her situation. She didn't seem to notice.

"You think maybe you could get me into one of those pretrial whatchamacallits where I can get myself right?"

I thought it was interesting how addicts call both getting high and getting sober the same thing — *getting right.*

"The problem is, Gloria, we got into a pretrial intervention program last time, remember? And it obviously didn't work. So this time I don't know. They only have so many spaces in those things and the judges and prosecutors don't like sending people back when they didn't take advantage of it in the first place."

"What do you mean?" she protested. "I took advantage. I went the whole damn time."

"That's right. That was good. But then after it was over, you went right back to doing what you do and here we are again. They wouldn't call that a success, Gloria. I have to be honest with you. I don't think I can get you into a program this time. I think you have to be ready for them to be tougher this time."

Her eyes drooped.

"I can't do it," she said in a small voice.

"Look, they have programs in the jail. You'll get straight and come out with another chance to start again clean."

She shook her head; she looked lost.

"You've had a long run but it can't go on," I said. "If I were you I'd think about getting out of this place. L.A., I mean. Go somewhere and start again."

She looked up at me with anger in her eyes.

"Start over and do what? Look at me. What am I going to do? Get married, have kids and plant flowers?"

I didn't have an answer and neither did she.

"Let's talk about that when the time comes. For now, let's worry about your case. Tell me what happened."

"What always happens. I screened the guy and it all checked out. He looked legit. But he was a cop and that was that."

"You went to him?"

She nodded.

"The Mondrian. He had a suite — that's another thing. The cops usually don't have suites. They don't have the budget."

"Didn't I tell you how stupid it would be to take coke with you when you work? And if a guy even asks you to bring coke with you, then you know he's a cop."

"I know all of that and he didn't ask me to bring it. I forgot I had it, okay? I got it from a guy I went to see right before him. What was I supposed to do, leave it in the car for the Mondrian valets to take?"

"What guy did you get it from?"

"A guy at the Travelodge on Santa Monica. I did him earlier and he offered it to me, you know, instead of cash. Then after I left I checked my messages and I had the call from the guy at the Mondrian. So I called him back, set it up and went straight there. I forgot I had the stuff in my purse."

Nodding, I leaned forward. I was seeing a glimmer on this one, a possibility.

"This guy in the Travelodge, who was he?"

"I don't know, just some guy who saw my ad on the site."

She arranged her liaisons through a website which carried photos, phone numbers and e-mail addresses of escorts.

"Did he say where he was from?"

"No. He was Mexican or Cuban or something. He was sweaty from using."

"When he gave you the coke, did you see if he had any more?"

"Yeah, he had some. I was hoping for a call back . . . but I don't think I was what he was expecting."

Last time I had checked her ad on LA-Darlings.com to see if she was still in the life, the photos she'd put up were at least five years old and looked ten. I imagined that it could lead to some disappointment when her clients opened their hotel room doors.

"How much did he have?"

"I don't know. I just knew he had to have more because if it was all he had left, he wouldn't have given it to me."

It was a good point. The glimmer was getting brighter.

"Did you screen him?"

"'Course."

"What, his driver's license?"

"No, his passport. He said he didn't have a license."

"What was his name?"

"Hector something."

"Come on, Gloria, Hector what? Try to re—"

"Hector something Moya. It was three names. But I remember 'Moya' because I said 'Hector give me Moya' when he brought out the coke."

"Okay, that's good."

"You think it's something you can use to help me?"

"Maybe, depending on who this guy is. If he's a trade-up."

"I want to get out."

"Okay, listen, Gloria. I'm going to go see the prosecutor and see what she's thinking and see what I can do for you. They've got you in here on twenty-five thousand dollars' bail."

"What?"

"It's higher than usual because of the drugs. You don't have twenty-five hundred for the bond, do you?"

She shook her head. I could see the muscles in her face constricting. I knew what was coming.

"Could you front it to me, Mickey? I promise I'd —"

"I can't do that, Gloria. That's a rule and I could get in trouble if I broke it. You're going to have to be in here overnight and they'll take you over to arraignment in the morning."

"No," she said, more like a moan than a word.

"I know it's going to be tough but you have to nut it out. And you have to be straight in the morning when you come into court or I'll have no shot at lowering your bond and getting you out. So none of that shit they trade in here. You got that?"

She raised her arms over her head, almost as if she was protecting herself from falling debris. She squeezed her hands into tight fists of dread. It would be a long night ahead.

"You've got to get me out tomorrow."

"I'll do my best."

I waved to the deputy in the observation booth. I was ready to go.

"One last thing," I said. "Do you remember what room the guy at the Travelodge was in?"

She thought a moment before answering.

"Yeah, it's an easy one. Three thirty-three."

"Okay, thanks. I'm going to see what I can do."

She stayed sitting when I stood up. Soon the escort deputy came back and told me I would have to wait while she first took Gloria back to her dorm. I checked my watch. It was almost two. I hadn't eaten and was getting a headache. I also had only two hours to get to Leslie Faire in the DA's office to talk about Gloria and then out to Century City for the case meeting with Roulet and Dobbs.

"Isn't there somebody else who can take me out of here?" I said irritably. "I need to get to court."

"Sorry, sir, that's how it works."

"Well, please hurry."

"I always do."

Fifteen minutes later I realized that my complaining to the deputy had only succeeded in her making sure she left me waiting even longer than had I just kept my mouth shut. Like a restaurant customer who gets the cold soup he sent back to the kitchen returned hot with the piquant taste of saliva in it, I should have known better.

On the quick drive over to the Criminal Courts Building I called Raul Levin. He was back at his home office in Glendale, looking through the police reports on the Roulet investigation and arrest. I asked him to put it aside to make some calls. I wanted to see what he could find out about the man in room 333 at the Travelodge on Santa Monica. I told him I needed the information yesterday. I knew he had sources and ways of running the name Hector Moya. I just didn't want to know who or what they were. I was only interested in what he got.

As Earl pulled to a stop in front of the CCB, I told him that while I was inside he should take a run over to Philippe's to get us roast beef sandwiches. I'd eat mine on my way out to Century City. I passed a twenty-dollar bill over the seat to him and got out.

While waiting for an elevator in the always crowded

lobby of the CCB, I popped a Tylenol from my briefcase and hoped it would head off the migraine I felt coming on from lack of food. It took me ten minutes to get to the ninth floor and another fifteen waiting for Leslie Faire to grant me an audience. I didn't mind the wait, though, because Raul Levin called back just before I was allowed entrance. If Faire had seen me right away, I wouldn't have gone in with the added ammunition.

Levin had told me that the man in room 333 at the Travelodge had checked in under the name Gilberto Garcia. The motel did not require identification, since he paid cash in advance for a week and put a fifty-dollar deposit on phone charges. Levin had also run a trace on the name I had given him and came up with Hector Arrande Moya, a Colombian wanted on a fugitive warrant issued after he fled San Diego when a federal grand jury handed down an indictment for drug trafficking. It added up to real good stuff and I planned to put it to use with the prosecutor.

Faire was in an office shared with three other prosecutors. Each had a desk in a corner. Two were gone, probably in court, but a man I didn't know sat at the desk in the corner opposite Faire. I had to speak to her with him in earshot. I hated doing this because I found that the prosecutor I was dealing with in these situations would often play to the others in the room, trying to sound tough and shrewd, sometimes at the expense of my client.

I pulled a chair away from one of the empty desks and brought it over to sit down. I skipped the pleasantries because there weren't any and got right to the point because I was hungry and didn't have a lot of time.

"You filed on Gloria Dayton this morning," I said. "She's mine. I want to see what we can do about it."

"Well, we can plead her guilty and she can do one to three years at Frontera."

She said it matter-of-factly with a smile that was more of a smirk.

"I was thinking of PTI."

"I was thinking she already got a bite out of that apple and she spit it out. No way."

"Look, how much coke did she have on her, a couple grams?"

"It's still illegal, no matter how much she had. Gloria Dayton has had numerous opportunities to rehabilitate herself and avoid prison. But she's run out of chances."

She turned to her desk, opened a file and glanced at the top sheet.

"Nine arrests in just the last five years," she said. "This is her third drug charge and she's never spent more than three days in jail. Forget PTI. She's got to learn sometime and this is that time. I'm not open to discussion on this. If she pleads, I'll give her one to three. If she doesn't, I'll go get a verdict and she takes her chances with the judge at sentencing. I will ask for the max on it."

I nodded. It was going about the way I thought it would with Faire. A one-to-three-year sentence would likely result in a nine-month stay in the slam. I knew Gloria Dayton could do it and maybe should do it. But I still had a card to play.

"What if she had something to trade?"

Faire snorted like it was a joke.

"Like what?"

"A hotel room number where a major dealer is doing business."

"Sounds a little vague."

It was vague but I could tell by the change in her voice she was interested. Every prosecutor likes to trade up.

"Call your drug guys. Ask them to run the name Hector Arrande Moya on the box. He's a Colombian. I can wait."

She hesitated. She clearly didn't like being manipulated

by a defense attorney, especially when another prosecutor was in earshot. But the hook was already set.

She turned again to her desk and made a call. I listened to one side of the conversation, her telling someone to give her a background check on Moya. She waited awhile and then listened to the response. She thanked whoever it was she had called and hung up. She took her time turning back to me.

"Okay," she said. "What does she want?"

I had it ready.

"She wants a PTI slot. All charges dropped upon successful completion. She doesn't testify against the guy and her name is on no documents. She simply gives the hotel and room number where he's at and your people do the rest."

"They'll need to make a case. She's got to testify. I take it the two grams she had came from this guy. Then she has to tell us about it."

"No, she doesn't. Whoever you just talked to told you there's already a warrant. You can take him down for that."

She worked it over for a few moments, moving her jaw back and forth as if tasting the deal and deciding whether to eat more. I knew what the stumble was. The deal was a trade-up but it was a trade-up to a federal case. That meant that they would bust the guy and the feds would take over. No prosecutorial glory for Leslie Faire — unless she had designs on jumping over to the U.S. Attorney's Office one day.

"The feds will love you for this," I said, trying to wedge into her conscience. "He's a bad guy and he'll probably check out soon and the chance to get him will be lost."

She looked at me like I was a bug.

"Don't try that with me, Haller."

"Sorry."

She went back to her thinking. I tried again.

"Once you have his location, you could always try to set up a buy."

"Would you be quiet, please? I can't think."

I raised my hands in surrender and shut up.

"All right," she finally said. "Let me talk to my boss. Give me your number and I'll call you later. But I'll tell you right now, if we go for it, she'll have to go to a lockdown program. Something at County-USC. We're not going to waste a residency slot on her."

I thought about it and nodded. County-USC was a hospital with a jail wing where injured, sick, and addicted inmates were treated. What she was offering was a program where Gloria Dayton could be treated for her addiction and released upon completion. She would not face any charges or further time in jail or prison.

"Fine with me," I said.

I looked at my watch. I had to get going.

"Our offer is good until first appearance tomorrow," I said. "After that I'll call the DEA and see if they want to deal directly. Then it will be taken out of your hands."

She looked indignantly at me. She knew that if I got a deal with the feds, they would squash her. Head to head, the feds always trumped the state. I stood up to go and put a business card down on her desk.

"Don't try to back-door me, Haller," she said. "If it goes sideways on you, I'll take it out on your client."

I didn't respond. I pushed the chair I had borrowed back to its desk. She then dropped the threat with her next line.

"Anyway, I'm sure we can handle this on a level that makes everybody happy."

I looked back at her as I got to the office door.

"Everybody except for Hector Moya," I said.

EIGHT

The law offices of Dobbs and Delgado were on the twenty-ninth floor of one of the twin towers that created the signature skyline of Century City. I was right on time but everyone was already gathered in a conference room with a long polished wood table and a wall of glass that framed a western exposure stretching across Santa Monica to the Pacific and the charter islands beyond. It was a clear day and I could see Catalina and Anacapa out there at the very edge of the world. Because the sun was going down and seemed to be almost at eye level, a film had been rolled down over the window to cut the glare. It was like the room had sunglasses on.

And so did my client. Louis Roulet sat at the head of the table with a pair of black-framed Ray-Bans on. Out of his gray jail jumpsuit, he now wore a dark brown suit over a pale silk T-shirt. He looked like a confident and cool young real estate executive, not the scared boy I saw in the holding pen in the courthouse.

To Roulet's left sat Cecil Dobbs and next to him was a well-preserved, well-coiffed and bejeweled woman I assumed to be Roulet's mother. I also assumed that Dobbs hadn't told her that the meeting would not include her.

To Roulet's right the first seat was empty and waiting for me. In the seat next to it sat my investigator, Raul Levin, with a closed file in front of him on the table.

Dobbs introduced Mary Alice Windsor to me. She shook my hand with a strong grip. I sat down and Dobbs explained

73

that she would be paying for her son's defense and had agreed to the terms I had outlined earlier. He slid an envelope across the table to me. I looked inside and saw a check for sixty thousand dollars with my name on it. It was the retainer I had asked for, but I had expected only half of it in the initial payment. I had made more in total on cases before but it was still the largest single check I had ever received.

The check was drawn on the account of Mary Alice Windsor. The bank was solid gold — First National of Beverly Hills. I closed the envelope and slid it back across the table.

"I'm going to need that to come from Louis," I said, looking at Mrs. Windsor. "I don't care if you give him the money and then he gives it to me. But I want the check I get to come from Louis. I work for him and that's got to be clear from the start."

I knew this was different from even my practice of that morning — accepting payment from a third party. But it was a control issue. One look across the table at Mary Alice Windsor and C. C. Dobbs and I knew I had to make sure that they knew this was my case to manage, to win or to lose.

I wouldn't have thought it could happen but Mary Windsor's face hardened. For some reason she reminded me of an old grandfather clock, her face flat and square.

"Mother," Roulet said, heading something off before it started. "It's all right. I will write him a check. I should be able to cover it until you give me the money."

She looked from me to her son and then back to me.

"Very well," she said.

"Mrs. Windsor," I said. "Your support for your son is very important. And I don't mean just the financial end of things. If we are not successful in getting these charges dropped and we choose the alternative of trial, it will be very important for you to show your support in public ways."

"Don't be silly," she said. "I will back him come hell or high water. These ridiculous charges must be removed, and that woman . . . she isn't going to get a penny from us."

"Thank you, Mother," Roulet said.

"Yes, thank you," I said. "I will be sure to inform you, probably through Mr. Dobbs, where and when you are needed. It's good to know you will be there for your son."

I said nothing else and waited. It didn't take her long to realize she had been dismissed.

"But you don't want me here right now, is that it?"

"That's right. We need to discuss the case and it is best and most appropriate for Louis to do this only with his defense team. The attorney-client privilege does not cover anyone else. You could be compelled to testify against your son."

"But if I leave, how will Louis get home?"

"I have a driver. I will get him home."

She looked at Dobbs, hoping he might have higher standing and be able to overrule me. Dobbs smiled and stood up so he could pull her chair back. She finally let him and stood up to go.

"Very well," she said. "Louis, I will see you at dinner."

Dobbs walked her through the door of the conference room and I saw them exchange conversation in the hallway. I couldn't hear what was said. Then she left and Dobbs came back, closing the door.

I went through some preliminaries with Roulet, telling him he would have to be arraigned in two weeks and submit a plea. He would have the opportunity at that time to put the state on notice that he was not waiving his right to a speedy trial.

"That's the first choice we have to make," I said. "Whether you want this thing to drag out or you want to move quickly and put the pressure on the state."

"What are the options?" Dobbs asked.

I looked at him and then back at Roulet.

"I'll be very honest with you," I said. "When I have a client who is not incarcerated, my inclination is to drag it out. It's the client's freedom that is on the line — why not get the most of it before the hammer comes down."

"You're talking about a guilty client," Roulet said.

"On the other hand," I said, "if the state's case is weak, then delaying things only gives them time to strengthen their hand. You see, time is our only leverage at this point. If we refuse to waive our right to a speedy trial, it puts a lot of pressure on the prosecutor."

"I didn't do what they are saying I did," Roulet said. "I don't want to waste any time. I want this shit behind me."

"If we refuse to waive, then theoretically they must put you on trial within sixty days of arraignment. The reality is that it gets pushed back when they move to a preliminary hearing. In a prelim a judge hears the evidence and decides if there is enough there to warrant a trial. It's a rubber-stamp process. The judge will hold you over for trial, you will be arraigned again and the clock is reset to sixty days."

"I can't believe this," Roulet said. "This is going to last forever."

"We could always waive the prelim, too. It would really force their hand. The case has been reassigned to a young prosecutor. He's pretty new to felonies. It may be the way to go."

"Wait a minute," Dobbs said. "Isn't a preliminary hearing useful in terms of seeing what the state's evidence is?"

"Not really," I said. "Not anymore. The legislature tried to streamline things a while back and they turned the prelim into a rubber stamp because they relaxed hearsay rules. Now you usually just get the case cop on the stand and he tells the judge what everybody said. The defense usually doesn't get a look at any witnesses other than the cop. If you ask me, the best strategy is to force the prosecution to put up or shut up. Make them go sixty days from first arraignment."

"I like that idea," Roulet said. "I want this over with as soon as possible."

I nodded. He had said it as though a not-guilty verdict was a foregone conclusion.

"Well, maybe it doesn't even get to a trial," Dobbs said. "If these charges don't hold muster —"

"The DA is not going to drop this," I said, cutting him off. "Usually, the cops overcharge and then the DA cuts the charges back. That didn't happen here. Instead, the DA upped the charges. That tells me two things. One is that they believe the case is solid and, two, they upped the charges so that when we start to negotiate they will deal from a higher ground."

"You're talking about a plea bargain?" Roulet asked.

"Yeah, a disposition."

"Forget it, no plea bargain. I'm not going to jail for something I didn't do."

"It might not mean going to jail. You have a clean rec—"

"I don't care if it means I could walk. I'm not going to plead guilty to something I didn't do. If that is going to be a problem for you, then we need to part company right here."

I looked closely at him. Almost all of my clients make protestations of innocence at one point along the way. Especially if it is our first case together. But Roulet's words came with a fervor and directness I hadn't seen in a long time. Liars falter. They look away. Roulet's eyes were holding mine like magnets.

"There is also the civil liability to consider," Dobbs added. "A guilty plea will allow this woman to —"

"I understand all of that," I said, cutting him off again. "I think we're all getting ahead of ourselves here. I only wanted to give Louis a general idea of the way this was going to go. We don't have to make any moves or any hard-and-fast decisions for at least a couple of weeks. We just need to know at the arraignment how we are going to play it."

"Louis took a year of law at UCLA," Dobbs said. "I think he has baseline knowledge of the situation."

Roulet nodded.

"Okay, good," I said. "Then let's just get to it. Louis, let's start with you. Your mother said she expects to see you at dinner. Do you live at home? I mean at her home?"

"I live in the guesthouse. She lives in the main house."

"Anyone else live on the premises?"

"The maid. In the main house."

"No siblings, boyfriends, girlfriends?"

"That's it."

"And you work at your mother's firm?"

"More like I run it. She's not there too much anymore."

"Where were you Saturday night?"

"Satur— you mean last night, don't you?"

"No, I mean Saturday night. Start there."

"Saturday night I didn't do anything. I stayed home and watched television."

"By yourself?"

"That's right."

"What did you watch?"

"A DVD. An old movie called *The Conversation*. Coppola."

"So nobody was with you or saw you. You just watched the movie and then went to bed."

"Basically."

"Basically. Okay. That brings us to Sunday morning. What did you do yesterday during the day?"

"I played golf at Riviera, my usual foursome. Started at ten and finished at four. I came home, showered and changed, had dinner at my mother's house   you want to know what we had?"

"That won't be necessary. But later on I probably will need the names of the guys you played golf with. What happened after dinner?"

"I told my mother I was going to my place but instead I went out."

I noticed that Levin had started taking notes on a small notebook he had taken out of a pocket.

"What kind of car do you drive?"

"I have two, an oh-four Range Rover I use for taking clients around in and an oh-one Carrera I use for myself."

"You used the Porsche last night, then?"

"That's right."

"Where'd you go?"

"I went over the hill and down into the Valley."

He said it as though it was a risky move for a Beverly Hills boy to descend into the working-class neighborhoods of the San Fernando Valley.

"Where did you go?" I asked.

"Ventura Boulevard. I had a drink at Nat's North and then I went down the street a ways to Morgan's and I had a drink there, too."

"Those places are pickup bars, wouldn't you say?"

"Yes. That's why I went to them."

He was matter-of-fact about it and I appreciated his honesty.

"So you were looking for someone. A woman. Anyone in particular, someone you knew?"

"No one in particular. I was looking to get laid, pure and simple."

"What happened at Nat's North?"

"What happened was that it was a slow night, so I left. I didn't even finish my drink."

"You go there often? Do the bartenders know you?"

"Yeah, they know me. A girl named Paula was working last night."

"Okay, so it wasn't working for you there and you left. You drove down to Morgan's. Why Morgan's?"

"It's just another place I go."

"They know you there?"

"They should. I'm a good tipper. Last night Denise and Janice were behind the bar. They know me."

I turned to Levin.

"Raul, what is the victim's name?"

Levin opened his file to pull out a police report but answered before having to look it up.

"Regina Campo. Friends call her Reggie. Twenty-six years old. She told police she's an actress working as a telephone solicitor."

"And hoping to retire soon," Dobbs said.

I ignored him.

"Louis, did you know Reggie Campo before last night?" I asked.

Roulet shrugged.

"Sort of. I'd seen her around the bar scene. But I had never been with her before. I'd never even spoken to her."

"Had you ever tried?"

"No, I never could really get to her. She always seemed to be with someone or more than one person. I don't like to have to penetrate the crowd, you know? My style is to look for the singles."

"What was different last night?"

"Last night she came to me, that was what was different."

"Tell us about it."

"Nothing to tell. I was at the bar at Morgan's, minding

my own business, having a look at the possibilities, and she was at the other end and she was with some guy. So she wasn't even on my radar because she looked like she was already taken, you know?"

"Uh-huh, so what happened?"

"Well, after a while the guy she was with gets up to go take a leak or go outside for a smoke, and as soon as he's gone she gets up and slides on down the bar to me and asks if I'm interested. I said I was but what about the guy she's already with? She says don't worry about him, he'll be out the door by ten and then she's free the rest of the night. She wrote her address down for me and said to come by after ten. I told her I'd be there."

"What did she write the address down on?"

"A napkin, but the answer to your next question is no, I don't still have it. I memorized the address and threw out the napkin. I work in real estate. I can remember addresses."

"About what time was this?"

"I don't know."

"Well, she said come by at ten. Did you look at your watch at any point to see how long you would have to wait until then?"

"I think it was between eight and nine. As soon as the guy came back in they left."

"When did you leave the bar?"

"I stayed for a few minutes and then I left. I made one more stop before I went to her place."

"Where was that?"

"Well, she lived in an apartment in Tarzana so I went up to the Lamplighter. It was on the way."

"Why?"

"Well, you know, I wanted to see what the possibilities were. You know, see if there was something better out there, something I didn't have to wait around for or ..."

"Or what?"

He still didn't finish the thought.

"Take seconds on?"

He nodded.

"Okay, so who'd you talk to at the Lamplighter? Where is that, by the way?"

It was the only place so far I was unfamiliar with.

"It's on Ventura near White Oak. I didn't really talk to anybody. It was crowded but there really wasn't anybody I was interested in there."

"The bartenders know you there?"

"No, not really. I don't go there all that much."

"You usually get lucky before you hit the third option?"

"Nah, I usually just give up after two."

I nodded just to buy a little time to think about what else to ask before we got to what happened at the victim's house.

"How long were you at the Lamplighter?"

"About an hour, I'd say. Maybe a little less."

"At the bar? How many drinks?"

"Yeah, two drinks at the bar."

"How many drinks in all did you have last night before getting to Reggie Campo's apartment?"

"Um, four at the most. Over two, two and a half, hours. I left one drink untouched at Morgan's."

"What were you drinking?"

"Martinis. Gray Goose."

"Did you pay for any of these drinks in any of these places with a credit card?" Levin asked, offering his first question of the interview.

"No," Roulet said. "When I go out, I pay cash."

I looked at Levin and waited to see if he had anything else to ask. He knew more about the case than I did at this moment. I wanted to give him free rein to ask what he wanted. He looked at me and nodded. He was good to go.

"Okay," I said. "What time was it when you got to Reggie's place?"

"It was twelve minutes to ten. I looked at my watch. I wanted to make sure I didn't knock on her door early."

"So what did you do?"

"I waited in the parking lot. She said ten so I waited till ten."

"Did you see the guy she left Morgan's with come out?"

"Yeah, I saw him. He came out and left, then I went up."

"What kind of car was he driving?" Levin asked.

"A yellow Corvette," Roulet said. "It was a nineties version. I don't know the exact year."

Levin nodded. He was finished. I knew he was just trying to get a line on the man who had been in Campo's apartment before Roulet. I took the questioning back.

"So he leaves and you go in. What happens?"

"I go in the building and her place is on the second floor. I go up and knock and she answers and I walk in."

"Hold on a second. I don't want the shorthand. You went up? How? Stairs, elevator, what? Give us the details."

"Elevator."

"Anybody else on it? Anybody see you?"

Roulet shook his head. I signaled him to continue.

"She opened the door a crack, saw it was me and told me to come in. There was a hallway by the front door so it was kind of a tight space. I walked by her so she could close the door. That's how come she was behind me. And so I didn't see it coming. She had something. She hit me with something and I went down. It got black real fast."

I was silent while I thought about this, tried to picture it in my mind.

"So before a single thing happened, she just knocked you out? She didn't say anything, yell anything, just sort of came up behind and *bang*."

"That's right."

"Okay, then what? What do you remember next?"

"It's still pretty foggy. I remember waking up and these two guys are sitting on me. Holding me down. And then the police came. And the paramedics. I was sitting up against the wall and my hands were cuffed and the paramedic put that ammonia or something under my nose and that's when I really came out of it."

"You were still in the apartment?"

"Yeah."

"Where was Reggie Campo?"

"She was sitting on the couch and another paramedic was working on her face and she was crying and telling the other cop that I had attacked her. All these lies. That I had surprised her at the door and punched her, that I said I was going to rape her and then kill her, all these things I didn't do. And I moved my arms so I could look down at my hands behind my back. I saw they had my hand in like a plastic bag and I could see blood on my hand, and that's when I knew the whole thing was a setup."

"What do you mean by that?"

"She put blood on my hand to make it look like I did it. But it was my left hand. I'm not left-handed. If I was going to punch somebody, I'd use my right hand."

He made a punching gesture with his right hand to illustrate this for me in case I didn't get it. I got up from my spot and paced over to the window. It now seemed like I was higher than the sun. I was looking down at the sunset. I felt uneasy about Roulet's story. It seemed so far-fetched that it might actually be true. And that bothered me. I was always worried that I might not recognize innocence. The possibility of it in my job was so rare that I operated with the fear that I wouldn't be ready for it when it came. That I would miss it.

"Okay, let's talk about this for a second," I said, still facing the sun. "You're saying that she puts blood on your hand to set you up. And she puts it on your left. But if she was going to set you up, wouldn't she put the blood on your right, since the vast majority of people out there are right-handed? Wouldn't she go with the numbers?"

I turned back to the table and got blank stares from everyone.

"You said she opened the door a crack and then let you in," I said. "Could you see her face?"

"Not all of it."

"What could you see?"

"Her eye. Her left eye."

"So did you ever see the right side of her face? Like when you walked in."

"No, she was behind the door."

"That's it!" Levin said excitedly. "She already had the injuries when he got there. She hid it from him, then he steps in and she clocks him. All the injuries were to the right side of her face and that dictated that she put the blood on his left hand."

I nodded as I thought about the logic of this. It seemed to make sense.

"Okay," I said, turning back to the window and continuing to pace. "I think that'll work. Now, Louis, you've told us you had seen this woman around the bar scene before but had never been with her. So, she was a stranger. Why would she do this, Louis? Why would she set you up like you say she did?"

"Money."

But it wasn't Roulet who answered. It had been Dobbs. I turned from the window and looked at him. He knew he had spoken out of turn but didn't seem to care.

"It's obvious," Dobbs said. "She wants money from him, from the family. The civil suit is probably being filed as we speak. The criminal charges are just the prelude to the suit, the demand for money. That's what she's really after."

I sat back down and looked at Levin, exchanging eye contact.

"I saw a picture of this woman in court today," I said. "Half her face was pulped. You are saying that's our defense, that she did that to herself?"

Levin opened his file and took out a piece of paper. It was a black-and-white photocopy of the evidence photograph Maggie McPherson had showed me in court. Reggie Campo's swollen face. Levin's source was good but not good enough to get him actual photos. He slid the photocopy across the table to Dobbs and Roulet.

"We'll get the real photos in discovery," I said. "They look worse, a lot worse, and if we go with your story, then the jury — that is, if this gets to a jury — is going to have to buy that she did that to herself."

I watched Roulet study the photocopy. If it had been he who attacked Reggie Campo, he showed no tell while studying his handiwork. He showed nothing at all.

"You know what?" I said. "I like to think I'm a good lawyer and a good persuader when it comes to juries. But even I'm having trouble believing myself with that story."

NINE

It was now Raul Levin's turn in the conference room. We'd spoken while I had been riding into Century City and eating bites of roast beef sandwich. I had plugged my cell into the car's speaker phone and told my driver to put his earbuds in. I'd bought him an iPod his first week on the job. Levin had given me the basics of the case, just enough to get me through the initial questioning of my client. Now Levin would take command of the room and go through the case, using the police and evidence reports to tear Louis Roulet's version of events to shreds, to show us what the prosecution would have on its side. At least initially I wanted Levin to be the one to do this because if there was going to be a good guy/bad guy aspect to the defense, I wanted to be the one Roulet would like and trust. I wanted to be the good guy.

Levin had his own notes in addition to the copies of the police reports he had gotten through his source. It was all material the defense was certainly entitled to and would receive through the discovery process, but usually it took weeks to get it through court channels instead of the hours it had taken Levin. As he spoke he held his eyes down on these documents.

"At ten-eleven last night the LAPD communications center received a nine-one-one emergency call from Regina Campo of seventeen-sixty White Oak Boulevard, apartment two-eleven. She reported an intruder had entered her home and attacked her. Patrol officers

87

responded and arrived on the premises at ten-seventeen. Slow night, I guess, because that was pretty quick. Better than average response to a hot shot. Anyway, the patrol officers were met in the parking lot by Ms. Campo, who said she had fled the apartment after the attack. She informed the officers that two neighbors named Edward Turner and Ronald Atkins were in her apartment, holding the intruder. Officer Santos proceeded to the apartment, where he found the suspect intruder, later identified as Mr. Roulet, lying on the floor and in the command and control of Turner and Atkins."

"They were the two faggots who were sitting on me," Roulet said.

I looked at Roulet and saw the flash of anger quickly fade.

"The officers took custody of the suspect," Levin continued, as if he had not been interrupted. "Mr. Atkins —"

"Wait a minute," I said. "Where was he found on the floor? What room?"

"Doesn't say."

I looked at Roulet.

"It was the living room. It wasn't far from the front door. I never got that far in."

Levin wrote a note to himself before continuing.

"Mr. Atkins produced a folding knife with the blade open, which he said had been found on the floor next to the intruder. The officers handcuffed the suspect, and paramedics were called to treat both Campo and Roulet, who had a head laceration and slight concussion. Campo was transported to Holy Cross Medical Center for continued treatment and to be photographed by an evidence technician. Roulet was taken into custody and booked into Van Nuys jail. The premises of Ms. Campo's apartment were sealed for crime scene processing and the case was assigned to Detective Martin Booker of Valley Bureau detectives."

Levin spread more photocopies of the police photos of Regina Campo's injuries out on the table. There were front and profile shots of her face and two close-ups of bruising around her neck and a small puncture mark under her jaw. The copy quality was poor and I knew the photocopies weren't worthy of serious study. But I did notice that all the facial injuries were on the right side of Campo's face. Roulet had been correct about that. She had either been repeatedly punched by someone's left hand — or possibly her own right hand.

"These were taken at the hospital, where Ms. Campo also gave a statement to Detective Booker. In summary, she said she came home about eight-thirty Sunday night and was home alone when there was a knock at her door at about ten o'clock. Mr. Roulet represented himself as someone Ms. Campo knew and so she opened the door. Upon opening the door she was immediately struck by the intruder's fist and driven backwards into the apartment. The intruder entered and closed and locked the door. Ms. Campo attempted to defend herself but was struck at least twice more and driven to the floor."

"This is such bullshit!" Roulet yelled.

He slammed his fists down on the table and stood up, his seat rolling backwards and banging loudly into the glass window behind him.

"Hey, easy now!" Dobbs cautioned. "You break the window and it's like a plane. We all get sucked out of here and go down."

No one smiled at his attempt at levity.

"Louis, sit back down," I said calmly. "These are police reports, nothing more or less. They are not supposed to be the truth. They are one person's view of the truth. All we are doing here is getting a first look at the case, seeing what we are up against."

Roulet rolled his chair back to the table and sat down without further protest. I nodded to Levin and he continued. I noted that Roulet had long stopped acting like the meek prey I had seen earlier in the day in lockup.

"Ms. Campo reported that the man who attacked her had his fist wrapped in a white cloth when he punched her."

I looked across the table at Roulet's hands and saw no swelling or bruising on the knuckles or fingers. Wrapping his fist could have allowed him to avoid such telltale injuries.

"Was it taken into evidence?" I asked.

"Yes," Levin said. "In the evidence report it is described as a cloth dinner napkin with blood on it. The blood and the cloth are being analyzed."

I nodded and looked at Roulet.

"Did the police look at or photograph your hands?"

Roulet nodded.

"The detective looked at my hands but nobody took pictures."

I nodded and told Levin to continue.

"The intruder straddled Ms. Campo on the floor and grasped one hand around her neck," he said. "The intruder told Ms. Campo that he was going to rape her and that it didn't matter to him whether she was alive or dead when he did it. She could not respond because the suspect was choking her with his hand. When he released pressure she said she told him that she would cooperate."

Levin slid another photocopy onto the table. It was a photo of a black-handled folding knife that was sharpened to a deadly point. It explained the earlier photo of the wound under the victim's neck.

Roulet slid the photocopy over to look at it more closely. He slowly shook his head.

"This is not my knife," he said.

I didn't respond and Levin continued.

"The suspect and the victim stood up and he told her to lead the way to the bedroom. The suspect maintained a position behind the victim and pressed the point of the knife against the left side of her throat. As Ms. Campo entered a short hallway that led to the apartment's two bedrooms she turned in the confined space and pushed her attacker backwards into a large floor vase. As he stumbled backwards over the vase, she made a break for the front door. Realizing that her attacker would recover and catch her at the front door, she ducked into the kitchen and grabbed a bottle of vodka off the counter. When the intruder passed by the kitchen on his way to the front door to catch her, Ms. Campo stepped out of the blind and struck him on the back of the head, knocking him to the floor. Ms. Campo then stepped over the fallen man and unlocked the front door. She ran out the door and called the police from the first-floor apartment shared by Turner and Atkins. Turner and Atkins returned to the apartment, where they found the intruder unconscious on the floor. They maintained control of him as he started to regain consciousness and remained in the apartment until police arrived."

"This is incredible," Roulet said. "To have to sit here and listen to this. I can't believe what has happened to me. I DID NOT do this. This is like a dream. She is lying! She —"

"If it is all lies, then this will be the easiest case I ever had," I said. "I will tear her apart and throw her entrails into the sea. But we have to know what she has put on the record before we can construct traps and go after her. And if you think this is hard to sit through, wait until we get to trial and it's stretched out over days instead of minutes. You have to control yourself, Louis. You have to remember that you will get your turn. The defense always gets its turn."

Dobbs reached over and patted Roulet on the forearm, a nice fatherly gesture. Roulet pulled his arm away.

"Damn right you are going to go after her," Roulet said, pointing a finger across the table at my chest. "I want you to go after her with everything we've got."

"That's what I am here for, and you have my promise I will. Now, let me ask my associate a few questions before we finish up here."

I waited to see if Roulet had anything else to say. He didn't. He leaned back into his chair and clasped his hands together.

"You finished, Raul?" I asked.

"For now. I'm still working on all the reports. I should have a transcript of the nine-one-one call tomorrow morning and there will be more stuff coming in."

"Good. What about a rape kit?"

"There wasn't one. Booker's report said she declined, since it never got to that."

"What's a rape kit?" Roulet asked.

"It's a hospital procedure where bodily fluids, hair and fibers are collected from the body of a rape victim," Levin said.

"There was no rape!" Roulet exclaimed. "I never touched —"

"We know that," I said. "That's not why I asked. I am looking for cracks in the state's case. The victim said she was not raped but was reporting what was certainly a sex crime. Usually, the police insist on a rape kit, even when a victim claims there was no sexual assault. They do this just in case the victim actually has been raped and is just too humiliated to say so or might be trying to keep the full extent of the crime from a husband or family member. It's standard procedure, and the fact that she was able to talk her way out of it might be significant to us."

"She didn't want the first guy's DNA showing up in her," Dobbs said.

"Maybe," I said. "It might mean any number of things. But it might be a crack. Let's move on. Raul, is there any mention anywhere about this guy who Louis saw her with?"

"No, none. He's not in the file."

"And what did crime scene find?"

"I don't have the report but I am told that no evidence of any significant nature was located during the crime scene evaluation of the apartment."

"That's good. No surprises. What about the knife?"

"Blood and prints on the knife. But nothing back on that yet. Tracing ownership will be unlikely. You can buy those folding knives in any fishing or camping store around."

"I'm telling you, that is not my knife," Roulet interjected.

"We have to assume the fingerprints will be from the man who turned it in," I said.

"Atkins," Levin responded.

"Right, Atkins," I said, turning to Louis. "But it would not surprise me to find prints from you on it as well. There is no telling what occurred while you were unconscious. If she put blood on your hand, then she probably put your prints on the knife."

Roulet nodded his agreement and was about to say something, but I didn't wait for him.

"Is there any statement from her about being at Morgan's earlier in the evening?" I asked Levin.

He shook his head.

"No, the interview with the victim was in the ER and not formal. It was basic and they didn't go back with her to the early part of the evening. She didn't mention the guy and she didn't mention Morgan's. She just said she had been home since eight-thirty. They asked about what happened at ten. They didn't really get into what she had been doing before. I'm sure that will all be covered in the follow-up investigation."

"Okay, if and when they go back to her for a formal, I want that transcript."

"I'm on it. It will be a sit-down on video when they do it."

"And if crime scene does a video, I want that, too. I want to see her place."

Levin nodded. He knew I was putting on a show for the client and Dobbs, giving them a sense of my command of the case and all the irons that were going into the fire. The reality was I didn't need to tell Raul Levin any of this. He already knew what to do and what to get for me.

"Okay, what else?" I asked. "Do you have any questions, Cecil?"

Dobbs seemed surprised by the focus suddenly shifting to him. He quickly shook his head.

"No, no, I'm fine. This is all good. We're making good progress."

I had no idea what he meant by "progress," but I let it go by without question.

"So what do you think?" Roulet asked.

I looked at him and waited a long moment before answering.

"I think the state has got a strong case against you. They have you in her home, they have a knife and they have her injuries. They also have what I am assuming is her blood on your hands. Added to that, the photos are powerful. And, of course, they will have her testimony. Having never seen or spoken to the woman, I don't know how impressive she will be."

I stopped again and milked the silence even longer before continuing.

"But there is a lot they don't have — evidence of break-in, DNA from the suspect, a motive or even a suspect with a past record of this or any sort of crime. There are a lot of reasons — legitimate reasons — for you to have been in that apartment. Plus . . ."

I looked past Roulet and Dobbs and out the window. The sun was dropping behind Anacapa and turning the sky pink and purple. It beat anything I ever saw from the windows of my office.

"Plus what?" Roulet asked, too anxious to wait on me.

"Plus you have me. I got Maggie McFierce off the case. The new prosecutor is good but he's green and he'll have never come up against someone like me before."

"So what's our next step?" Roulet asked.

"The next step is for Raul to keep doing his thing, finding out what he can about this alleged victim and why she lied about being alone. We need to find out who she is and who her mystery man is and to see how that plays into our case."

"And what will you do?"

"I'll be dealing with the prosecutor. I'll set something up with him, try to see where he's going and we'll make our choice on which way to go. I have no doubt that I'll be able to go to the DA and knock all of this down to something you can plea to and get behind you. But it will require a concession. You —"

"I told you. I will not —"

"I know what you said but you have to hear me out. I may be able to get a no-contest plea so that you don't actually ever say the word 'guilty,' but I am not seeing the state completely dropping this. You will have to concede responsibility in some regard. It is possible to avoid jail time but you will likely have to perform community service of some sort. There, I've said it. That is the first recitation. There will be more. I am obligated as your attorney to tell you and make sure you understand your options. I know it's not what you want or are willing to do but it is my duty to educate you on the choices. Okay?"

"Fine. Okay."

"Of course, as you know, any concession on your part will pretty much make any civil action Ms. Campo takes against you a slam dunk. So, as you can guess, disposing of the criminal case quickly will probably end up costing you a lot more than my fee."

Roulet shook his head. The plea bargain was already not an option.

"I understand my choices," he said. "You have fulfilled your duty. But I'm not going to pay her a cent for something I didn't do. I'm not going to plead guilty or no contest to something I didn't do. If we go to trial, can you win?"

I held his gaze for a moment before answering.

"Well, you understand that I don't know what will come up between now and then and that I can't guarantee anything . . . but, yes, based on what I see now, I can win this case. I'm confident of that."

I nodded to Roulet and I think I saw a look of hope enter his eyes. He saw the glimmer.

"There is a third option," Dobbs said.

I looked from Roulet to Dobbs, wondering what wrench he was about to throw into the franchise machine.

"And what's that?" I asked.

"We investigate the hell out of her and this case. Maybe help Mr. Levin out with some of our people. We investigate six ways from Sunday and establish our own credible theory and evidence and present it to the DA. We head this off before it ever gets to trial. We show this greenhorn prosecutor where he will definitely lose the case and get him to drop all charges before he suffers that professional embarrassment. Added to this, I am sure this man works for a man who runs that office and is susceptible, shall we say, to political pressures. We apply it until things turn our way."

I felt like kicking Dobbs under the table. Not only did his plan involve cutting my biggest fee ever by more than half, not only did it see the lion's share of client money going to the investigators, including his own, but it could only have come from a lawyer who had never defended a criminal case in his entire career.

"That's an idea but it is very risky," I said calmly. "If you can blow their case out of the water and you go in before trial to show them how, you are also giving them a blueprint for what to do and what to avoid in trial. I don't like to do that."

Roulet nodded his agreement and Dobbs looked a bit taken aback. I decided to leave it at that and to address Dobbs further on it when I could do it without the client present.

"What about the media?" Levin asked, thankfully changing the subject.

"That's right," Dobbs said, anxious to change it himself now. "My secretary says I have messages from two newspapers and two television stations."

"I probably do as well," I said.

What I didn't mention was that the messages left with Dobbs were left by Lorna Taylor at my direction. The case had not attracted the media yet, other than the freelance videographer who showed up at the first appearance. But I wanted Dobbs and Roulet and his mother to believe they all could be splashed across the papers at any moment.

"We don't want publicity on this," Dobbs said. "This is the worst kind of publicity to get."

He seemed to be adept at stating the obvious.

"All media should be directed to me," I said. "I will handle the media and the best way to do that is to ignore it."

"But we have to say something to defend him," Dobbs said.

"No, we don't have to say anything. Talking about the case legitimizes it. If you get into a game of talking to the media, you keep the story alive. Information is oxygen. Without it they die. As far as I am concerned, let 'em die. Or at least wait until there is no avoiding them. If that happens, only one person speaks for Louis. That's me."

Dobbs reluctantly nodded his agreement. I pointed a finger at Roulet.

"Under no circumstances do you talk to a reporter, even to deny the charges. If they contact you, you send them to me. Got it?"

"I got it."

"Good."

I decided that we had said enough for a first meeting. I stood up.

"Louis, I'll take you home now."

But Dobbs wasn't going to release his grasp on his client so quickly.

"Actually, I've been invited to dinner by Louis's mother," he said. "I could take him, since I am going there."

I nodded my approval. The criminal defense attorney never seemed to get invited to dinner.

"Fine," I said. "But we'll meet you there. I want Raul to see his place and Louis needs to give me that check we spoke about earlier."

If they thought I had forgotten about the money, they had a lot to learn about me. Dobbs looked at Roulet and got an approving nod. Dobbs then nodded to me.

"Sounds like a plan," he said. "We'll meet again there."

Fifteen minutes later I was riding in the back of the Lincoln with Levin. We were following a silver Mercedes carrying Dobbs and Roulet. I was checking with Lorna on the phone. The only message of importance had come from Gloria Dayton's prosecutor, Leslie Faire. The message was we had a deal.

"So," Levin said when I closed the phone. "What do you really think?"

"I think there is a lot of money to be made on this case and we're about to go get the first installment. Sorry I'm dragging you over there. I didn't want it to seem like it was all about the check."

Levin nodded but didn't say anything. After a few moments I continued.

"I'm not sure what to think yet," I said. "Whatever happened in that apartment happened quick. That's a break for us. No actual rape, no DNA. That gives us a glimmer of hope."

"It sort of reminds me of Jesus Menendez, only without DNA. Remember him?"

"Yeah, but I don't want to."

I tried not to think about clients who were in prison without appellate hopes or anything else left but years of time in front of them to nut out. I do what I can with each case but sometimes there is nothing that can be done. Jesus Menendez's case was one of those.

"How's your time on this?" I asked, putting us back on course.

"I've got a few things but I can move them around."

"You are going to have to work nights on this. I need you to go into those bars. I want to know everything about him and everything about her. This case looks simple at this point. We knock her down and we knock the case down."

Levin nodded. He had his briefcase on his lap.

"You got your camera in there?"

"Always."

"When we get to the house take some pictures of Roulet. I don't want you showing his mug shot in the bars. It'll taint things. Can you get a picture of the woman without her face being all messed up?"

"I got her driver's license photo. It's recent."

"Good. Run them down. If we find a witness who saw her come over to him at the bar in Morgan's last night, then we're gold."

"That's where I was thinking I'd start. Give me a week or so. I'll come back to you before the arraignment."

I nodded. We drove in silence for a few minutes, thinking about the case. We were moving through the flats of Beverly Hills, heading up into the neighborhoods where the real money was hidden and waiting.

"And you know what else I think?" I said. "Money and everything aside, I think there's a chance he isn't lying. His story is just quirky enough to be true."

Levin whistled softly between his teeth.

"You think you might have found the innocent man?" he said.

"That would be a first," I said. "If I had only known it this morning, I would have charged him the innocent man premium. If you're innocent you pay more because you're a hell of a lot more trouble to defend."

"Ain't that the truth."

I thought about the idea of having an innocent client and the dangers involved.

"You know what my father said about innocent clients?"

"I thought your father died when you were like six years old."

"Five, actually. They didn't even take me to the funeral."

"And he was talking to you about innocent clients when you were five?"

"No, I read it in a book long after he was gone. He said the scariest client a lawyer will ever have is an innocent client. Because if you fuck up and he goes to prison, it'll scar you for life."

"He said it like that?"

"Words to that effect. He said there is no in-between with an innocent client. No negotiation, no plea bargaining, no middle ground. There's only one verdict. You have to put an NG up on the scoreboard. There's no other verdict but not guilty."

Levin nodded thoughtfully.

"The bottom line was my old man was a damn good lawyer and he didn't like having innocent clients," I said. "I'm not sure I do, either."

Thursday, March 17

TEN

The first ad I ever put in the yellow pages said "Any Case, Anytime, Anywhere" but I changed it after a few years. Not because the bar objected to it, but because *I* objected to it. I got more particular. Los Angeles County is a wrinkled blanket that covers four thousand square miles from the desert to the Pacific. There are more than ten million people fighting for space on the blanket and a considerable number of them engage in criminal activity as a lifestyle choice. The latest crime stats show almost a hundred thousand violent crimes are reported each year in the county. Last year there were 140,000 felony arrests and then another 50,000 high-end misdemeanor arrests for drug and sex offenses. Add in the DUIs and every year you could fill the Rose Bowl twice over with potential clients. The thing to remember is that you don't want clients from the cheap seats. You want the ones sitting on the fifty-yard line. The ones with money in their pockets.

When the criminals get caught they get funneled into a justice system that has more than forty courthouses spread across the county like Burger Kings ready to serve them — as in serve them up on a plate. These stone fortresses are the watering holes where the legal lions come to hunt and to feed. And the smart hunter learns quickly where the most bountiful locations are, where the paying clients graze. The hunt can be deceptive. The client base of each courthouse does not necessarily reflect the socioeconomic structure of the surrounding environs.

Courthouses in Compton, Downey and East Los Angeles have produced a steady line of paying clients for me. These clients are usually accused of being drug dealers but their money is just as green as a Beverly Hills stock swindler's.

On the morning of the seventeenth I was in the Compton courthouse representing Darius McGinley at his sentencing. Repeat offenders mean repeat customers and McGinley was both, as many of my clients tend to be. For the sixth time since I had known him, he had been arrested and charged with dealing crack cocaine. This time it was in Nickerson Gardens, a housing project known by most of its residents as Nixon Gardens. No one I ever asked knew whether this was an abbreviation of the true name of the place or a name bestowed in honor of the president who held office when the vast apartment complex and drug market was built. McGinley was arrested after making a direct hand-to-hand sale of a balloon containing a dozen rocks to an undercover narcotics officer. At the time, he had been out on bail after being arrested for the exact same offense two months earlier. He also had four prior convictions for drug sales on his record.

Things didn't look good for McGinley, who was only twenty-three years old. After he'd taken so many previous swings at the system, the system had now run out of patience with him. The hammer was coming down. Though McGinley had been coddled previously with sentences of probation and county jail time, the prosecutor set the bar at the prison level this time. Any negotiation of a plea agreement would begin and end with a prison sentence. Otherwise, no deal. The prosecutor was happy to take the two outstanding cases to trial and go for a conviction and a double-digit prison sentence.

The choice was hard but simple. The state held all of

the cards. They had him cold on two hand-to-hand sales with quantity. The reality was that a trial would be an exercise in futility. McGinley knew this. The reality was that his selling of three hundred dollars in rock cocaine to a cop was going to cost him at least three years of his life.

As with many of my young male clients from the south side of the city, prison was an anticipated part of life for McGinley. He grew up knowing he was going. The only questions were when and for how long and whether he would live long enough to make it there. In my many jailhouse meetings with him over the years, I had learned that McGinley carried a personal philosophy inspired by the life and death and rap music of Tupac Shakur, the thug poet whose rhymes carried the hope and hopelessness of the desolate streets McGinley called home. Tupac correctly prophesied his own violent death. South L.A. teemed with young men who carried the exact same vision.

McGinley was one of them. He would recite to me long riffs from Tupac's CDs. He would translate the meanings of the ghetto lyrics for me. It was an education I valued because McGinley was only one of many clients with a shared belief in a final destiny that was "Thug Mansion," the place between heaven and earth where all gangsters ended up. To McGinley, prison was only a rite of passage on the road to that place and he was ready to make the journey.

"I'll lay up, get stronger and smarter, then I'll be back," he said to me.

He told me to go ahead and make a deal. He had five thousand dollars delivered to me in a money order — I didn't ask where it came from — and I went back to the prosecutor, got both pending cases folded into one, and McGinley agreed to plead guilty. The only thing he ever asked me to try to get for him was an assignment to a prison close by so his mother and his three young children wouldn't have to be driven too far or too long to visit him.

When court was called into session, Judge Daniel Flynn came through the door of his chambers in an emerald green robe, which brought false smiles from many of the lawyers and court workers in the room. He was known to wear the green on two occasions each year — St. Patrick's Day and the Friday before the Notre Dame Fighting Irish took on the Southern Cal Trojans on the football field. He was also known among the lawyers who worked the Compton courthouse as "Danny Boy," as in, "Danny Boy sure is an insensitive Irish prick, isn't he?"

The clerk called the case and I stepped up and announced. McGinley was brought in through a side door and stood next to me in an orange jumpsuit with his wrists locked to a waist chain. He had no one out in the gallery to watch him go down. He was alone except for me.

"Top o' the morning to you, Mr. McGinley," Flynn said in an Irish brogue. "You know what today is?"

I lowered my eyes to the floor. McGinley mumbled his response.

"The day I get my sentence."

"That, too. But I am talking about St. Patrick's Day, Mr. McGinley. A day to revel in Irish heritage."

McGinley turned slightly and looked at me. He was street smart but not life smart. He didn't understand what was happening, whether this was part of the sentencing or just some form of white man disrespect. I wanted to tell him that the judge was being insensitive and probably racist. Instead I leaned over and whispered in his ear, "Just be cool. He's an asshole."

"Do you know the origin of your name, Mr. McGinley?" the judge asked.

"No, sir."

"Do you care?"

"Not really, sir. It's a name from a slaveholder, I 'spect. Why would I care who that motherfucka be?"

"Excuse me, Your Honor," I said quickly.

I leaned over to McGinley again.

"Darius, cool it," I whispered. "And watch your language."

"He's dissing me," he said back, a little louder than a whisper.

"And he hasn't sentenced you yet. You want to blow the deal?"

McGinley stepped back from me and looked up at the judge.

"Sorry about my language, Y'Honor. I come from the street."

"I can tell that," Flynn said. "Well, it is a shame you feel that way about your history. But if you don't care about your name, then I don't either. Let's get on with the sentencing and get you off to prison, shall we?"

He said the last part cheerfully, as if he were taking great delight in sending McGinley off to Disneyland, the happiest place on earth.

The sentencing went by quickly after that. There was nothing in the presentencing investigation report besides what everybody already knew. Darius McGinley had had only one profession since age eleven, drug dealer. He'd had only one true family, a gang. He'd never gotten a driver's license, though he drove a BMW. He'd never gotten married, though he'd fathered three babies. It was the same old story and same old cycle trotted out a dozen times a day in courtrooms across the county. McGinley lived in a society that intersected mainstream America only in the courtrooms. He was just fodder for the machine. The machine needed to eat and McGinley was on the plate. Flynn sentenced him to the agreed-upon three to five years in prison and read all of the standard legal language that came with a plea agreement. For laughs — though only his own courtroom staff complied — he read the boilerplate using his brogue again. And then it was over.

I know McGinley dealt death and destruction in the form of rock cocaine and probably committed untold violence and other offenses he was never charged with, but I still felt bad for him. I felt like he was another one who'd never had a shot at anything but thug life in the first place. He'd never known his father and had dropped out of school in the sixth grade to learn the rock trade. He could accurately count money in a rock house but he had never had a checking account. He had never been to a county beach, let alone outside of Los Angeles. And now his first trip out would be on a bus with bars over the windows.

Before he was led back into the holding cell for processing and transfer to prison I shook his hand, his movement restricted by the waist chain, and wished him good luck. It is something I rarely do with my clients.

"No sweat," he said to me. "I'll be back."

And I didn't doubt it. In a way, Darius McGinley was just as much a franchise client as Louis Roulet. Roulet was most likely a one-shot deal. But over the years, I had a feeling McGinley would be one of what I call my "annuity clients." He would be the gift that would keep on giving — as long as he defied the odds and kept on living.

I put the McGinley file in my briefcase and headed back through the gate while the next case was called. Outside the courtroom Raul Levin was waiting for me in the crowded hallway. We had a scheduled meeting to go over his findings in the Roulet case. He'd had to come to Compton because I had a busy schedule.

"Top o' the morning," Levin said in an exaggerated Irish accent.

"Yeah, you saw that?"

"I stuck my head in. The guy's a bit of a racist, isn't he?"

"And he can get away with it because ever since they unified the courts into one countywide district, his name goes on the ballot everywhere. Even if the people of Compton rose up like a wave to vote him off, the Westsiders could still cancel them out. It's fucked up."

"How'd he get on the bench in the first place?"

"Hey, you get a law degree and make the right contributions to the right people and you could be a judge, too. He was appointed by the governor. The hard part is winning that first retention election. He did. You've never heard the 'In like Flynn' story?"

"Nope."

"You'll love it. About six years ago Flynn gets his appointment from the governor. This is before unification. Back then judges were elected by the voters of the district where they presided. The supervising judge for L.A. County checks out his credentials and pretty quickly realizes that he's got a guy with lots of political connections but no talent or courthouse experience to go with it. Flynn was basically an office lawyer. Probably couldn't find a courthouse, let alone try a case, if you paid him. So the presiding judge dumps him down here in Compton criminal because the rule is you have to run for retention the year after being appointed to the bench. He figures Flynn will fuck up, anger the folks and get voted out. One year and out."

"Headache over."

"Exactly. Only it didn't work that way. In the first hour on the first day of filing for the ballot that year, Fredrica Brown walks into the clerk's office and puts in her papers to run against Flynn. You know Downtown Freddie Brown?"

"Not personally. I know of her."

"So does everybody else around here. Besides being a

pretty good defense lawyer, she's black, she's a woman and she's popular in the community. She would have crushed Flynn five to one or better."

"Then how the hell did Flynn keep the seat?"

"That's what I'm getting to. With Freddie on the ballot, nobody else filed to run. Why bother, she was a shoo-in — though it was kind of curious why she'd want to be a judge and take the pay cut. Back then she had to have been well into mid six figures with her practice."

"So what happened?"

"What happened was, a couple months later on the last hour before filing closed, Freddie walks back into the clerk's office and withdraws from the ballot."

Levin nodded.

"So Flynn ends up running unopposed and keeps the seat," he said.

"You got it. Then unification comes in and they'll never be able to get him out of there."

Levin looked outraged.

"That's bullshit. They had some kind of deal and that's gotta be a violation of election laws."

"Only if you could prove there was a deal. Freddie has always maintained that she wasn't paid off or part of some plan Flynn cooked up to stay on the bench. She says she just changed her mind and pulled out because she realized she couldn't sustain her lifestyle on a judge's pay. But I'll tell you one thing, Freddie sure seems to do well whenever she has a case in front of Flynn."

"And they call it a justice system."

"Yeah, they do."

"So what do you think about Blake?"

It had to be brought up. It was all anybody else was talking about. Robert Blake, the movie and television actor, had been acquitted of murdering his wife the day before in Van Nuys Superior Court. The DA and the LAPD had lost another big media case and you couldn't go anywhere without it being the number one topic of discussion. The media and most people who lived and worked outside the machine didn't get it. The question wasn't whether Blake did it, but whether there was enough evidence presented in trial to convict him of doing it. They were two distinctly separate things but the public discourse that had followed the verdict had entwined them.

"What do I think?" I said. "I think I admire the jury for staying focused on the evidence. If it wasn't there, it wasn't there. I hate it when the DA thinks they can ride in a verdict on common sense — 'If it wasn't him, who else could it have been?' Give me a break with that. You want to convict a man and put him in a cage for life, then put up the fucking evidence. Don't hope a jury is going to bail your ass out on it."

"Spoken like a true defense attorney."

"Hey, you make your living off defense attorneys, pal. You should memorize that rap. So forget Blake. I'm jealous and I'm already tired of hearing about it. You said on the phone that you had good news for me."

"I do. Where do you want to go to talk and look at what I've got?"

I looked at my watch. I had a calendar call on a case in the Criminal Courts Building downtown. I had until eleven to be there and I couldn't miss it because I had missed it the day before. After that I was supposed to go up to Van Nuys to meet for the first time with Ted Minton, the prosecutor who had taken the Roulet case over from Maggie McPherson.

"I don't have time to go anywhere," I said. "We can go sit in my car and grab a coffee. You got your stuff with you?"

In answer Levin raised his briefcase and rapped his knuckles on its side.

"But what about your driver?"

"Don't worry about him."

"Then let's do it."

ELEVEN

After we were in the Lincoln I told Earl to drive around and see if he could find a Starbucks. I needed coffee.

"Ain' no Starbuck 'round here," Earl responded.

I knew Earl was from the area but I didn't think it was possible to be more than a mile from a Starbucks at any given point in the county, maybe even the world. But I didn't argue the point. I just wanted coffee.

"Okay, well, drive around and find a place that has coffee. Just don't go too far from the courthouse. We need to get back to drop Raul off after."

"You got it."

"And Earl? Put on your earphones while we talk about a case back here for a while, okay?"

Earl fired up his iPod and plugged in the earbuds. He headed the Lincoln down Acacia in search of java. Soon we could hear the tinny sound of hip-hop coming from the front seat and Levin opened his briefcase on the fold-down table built into the back of the driver's seat.

"Okay, what do you have for me?" I said. "I'm going to see the prosecutor today and I want to have more aces in my hand than he does. We also have the arraignment Monday."

"I think I've got a few aces here," Levin replied.

He sorted through things in his briefcase and then started his presentation.

"Okay," he said, "let's begin with your client and then we'll check in on Reggie Campo. Your guy is pretty squeaky. Other than parking and speeding tickets — which he seems to have a problem avoiding and then a bigger problem paying — I couldn't find squat on him. He's pretty much your standard citizen."

"What's with the tickets?"

"Twice in the last four years he's let parking tickets — a lot of them — and a couple speeding tickets accumulate unpaid. Both times it went to warrant and your colleague C. C. Dobbs stepped in to pay them off and smooth things over."

"I'm glad C.C.'s good for something. By 'paying them off,' I assume you mean the tickets, not the judges."

"Let's hope so. Other than that, only one blip on the radar with Roulet."

"What?"

"At the first meeting when you were giving him the drill about what to expect and so on and so forth, it comes out that he'd had a year at UCLA law and knew the system. Well, I checked on that. See, half of what I do is try to find out who is lying or who is the biggest liar of the bunch. So I check damn near everything. And most of the time it's easy to do because everything's on computer."

"Right, I get it. So what about the law school, was that a lie?"

"Looks like it. I checked the registrar's office and he's never been enrolled in the law school at UCLA."

I thought about this. It was Dobbs who had brought up UCLA law and Roulet had just nodded. It was a strange lie for either one of them to have told because it didn't really get them anything. It made me think about the psychology behind it. Was it something to do with me? Did they want me to think of Roulet as being on the same level as me?

"So if he lied about something like that..." I said, thinking out loud.

"Right," Levin said. "I wanted you to know about it. But

I gotta say, that's it on the negative side for Mr. Roulet so far. He might've lied about law school but it looks like he didn't lie about his story — at least the parts I could check out."

"Tell me."

"Well, his track that night checks out. I got wits in here who put him at Nat's North, Morgan's and then the Lamplighter, bing, bing, bing. He did just what he told us he did. Right down to the number of martinis. Four total and at least one of them he left on the bar unfinished."

"They remember him that well? They remember that he didn't even finish his drink?"

I am always suspicious of perfect memory because there is no such thing. And it is my job and my skill to find the faults in the memory of witnesses. Whenever someone remembers too much, I get nervous — especially if the witness is for the defense.

"No, I'm not just relying on a bartender's memory. I've got something here that you are going to love, Mick. And you better love me for it because it cost me a grand."

From the bottom of his briefcase he pulled out a padded case that contained a small DVD player. I had seen people using them on planes before and had been thinking about getting one for the car. The driver could use it while waiting on me in court. And I could probably use it from time to time on cases like this one.

Levin started loading in a DVD. But before he could play it the car pulled to a stop and I looked up. We were in front of a place called The Central Bean.

"Let's get some coffee and then see what you've got there," I said.

I asked Earl if he wanted anything and he declined the offer. Levin and I got out and went in. There was a short line for coffee. Levin spent the waiting time telling me about the DVD we were about to watch in the car.

"I'm in Morgan's and want to talk to this bartender named Janice but she says I have to clear it first with the manager. So I go back to see him in the office and he's asking me what exactly I want to ask Janice about. There's something off about this guy. I'm wondering why he wants to know so much, you know? Then it comes clear when he makes an offer. He tells me that last year they had a problem behind the bar. Pilferage from the cash register. They have as many as a dozen bartenders working back there in a given week and he couldn't figure out who had sticky fingers."

"He put in a camera."

"You got it. A hidden camera. He caught the thief and fired his ass. But it worked so good he kept the camera in place. The system records on high-density tape from eight till two every night. It's on a timer. He gets four nights on a tape. If there is ever a problem or a shortage he can go back and check it. Because they do a weekly profit-and-loss check, he rotates two tapes so he always has a week's worth of film to look at."

"He had the night in question on tape?"

"Yes, he did."

"And he wanted a thousand dollars for it."

"Right again."

"The cops don't know about it?"

"They haven't even come to the bar yet. They're just going with Reggie's story so far."

I nodded. This wasn't all that unusual. There were too many cases for the cops to investigate thoroughly and completely. They were already loaded for bear, anyway. They had an eyewitness victim, a suspect caught in her apartment, they had the victim's blood on the suspect and even the weapon. To them, there was no reason to go further.

"But we're interested in the bar, not the cash register," I said.

"I know that. And the cash register is against the wall behind the bar. The camera is up above it in a smoke detector on the ceiling. And the back wall is a mirror. I looked at what he had and pretty quickly realized that you can see the whole bar in the mirror. It's just reversed. I had the tape transferred to a disc because we can manipulate the image better. Blow it up and zero in, that sort of thing."

It was our turn in line. I ordered a large coffee with cream and sugar and Levin ordered a bottle of water. We took our refreshments back to the car. I told Earl not to drive until after we'd viewed the DVD. I can read while riding in a car but I thought looking at the small screen of Levin's player while bumping along south county streets might give me a dose of motion sickness.

Levin started the DVD and gave a running commentary to go with the visuals.

On the small screen was a downward view of the rectangular-shaped bar at Morgan's. There were two bartenders on patrol, both women in black jeans and white shirts tied off to show flat stomachs, pierced navels and tattoos creeping up out of their rear belt lines. As Levin had explained, the camera was angled toward the back of the bar area and cash register but the mirror that covered the wall behind the register displayed the line of customers sitting at the bar. I saw Louis Roulet sit down by himself in the dead center of the frame. There was a frame counter in the bottom left corner and a time and date code in the right corner. It said that it was 8:11 P.M. on March 6.

"There's Louis showing up," Levin said. "And over here is Reggie Campo."

He manipulated buttons on the player and froze the image. He then shifted it, bringing the right margin into the center. On the short side of the bar to the right a woman and a man sat next to each other. Levin zoomed in on them.

"Are you sure?" I asked.

I had only seen pictures of the woman with her face badly bruised and swollen.

"Yeah, it's her. And that's our Mr. X."

"Okay."

"Now watch."

He started the film moving again and widened the picture back to full frame. He then started moving it in fast-forward mode.

"Louis drinks his martini, he talks with the bartenders and nothing much happens for almost an hour," Levin said.

He checked a notebook page that had notes attributed to specific frame numbers. He slowed the image to normal speed at the right moment and shifted the frame again so that Reggie Campo and Mr. X were in the center of the screen. I noticed that we had advanced to 8:43 on the time code.

On the screen Mr. X took a pack of cigarettes and a lighter off the bar and slid off his stool. He then walked out of camera range to the right.

"He's heading to the front door," Levin said. "They have a smoking porch in the front."

Reggie Campo appeared to watch Mr. X go and then she slid off her stool and started walking along the front of the bar, just behind the patrons on stools. As she passed by Roulet she appeared to drag the fingers of her left hand across his shoulders, almost in a tickling gesture. This made Roulet turn and watch her as she kept going.

"She just gave him a little flirt there," Levin said. "She's heading to the bathroom."

"That's not how Roulet said it went down," I said. "He claimed she came on to him, gave him her —"

"Just hold your horses," Levin said. "She's got to come back from the can, you know."

I waited and watched Roulet at the bar. I checked my watch. I was doing okay for the time being but I couldn't miss the calendar call at the CCB. I had already pushed the judge's patience to the max by not showing up the day before.

"Here she comes," Levin said.

Leaning closer to the screen I watched as Reggie Campo came back along the bar line. This time when she got to Roulet she squeezed up to the bar between him and a man on the next stool to the right. She had to move into the space sideways and her breasts were clearly pushed against Roulet's right arm. It was a come-on if I had ever seen one. She said something and Roulet bent over closer to her lips to hear. After a few moments he nodded and then I saw her put what looked like a crumpled cocktail napkin into his hand. They had one more verbal exchange and then Reggie Campo kissed Louis Roulet on the cheek and pulled backwards away from the bar. She headed back to her stool.

"You're beautiful, Mish," I said, using the name I gave him after he told me of his mishmash of Jewish and Mexican descent.

"And you say the cops don't have this?" I added.

"They didn't know about it last week when I got it and I still have the tape. So, no, they don't have it and probably don't know about it yet."

Under the rules of discovery, I would need to turn it over to the prosecution after Roulet was formally arraigned. But there was still some play in that. I didn't technically have to turn over anything until I was sure I planned to use it in trial. That gave me a lot of leeway and time.

I knew that what was on the DVD was important and no

doubt would be used in trial. All by itself it could be cause for reasonable doubt. It seemed to show a familiarity between victim and alleged attacker that was not included in the state's case. More important, it also caught the victim in a position in which her behavior could be interpreted as being at least partially responsible for drawing the action that followed. This was not to suggest that what followed was acceptable or not criminal, but juries are always interested in the causal relationships of crime and the individuals involved. What the video did was move a crime that might have been viewed through a black-and-white prism into the gray area. As a defense attorney I lived in the gray areas.

The flip side of that was that the DVD was so good it might be too good. It directly contradicted the victim's statement to police about not knowing the man who attacked her. It impeached her, showed her in a lie. It only took one lie to knock a case down. The tape was what I called "walking proof." It would end the case before it even got to trial. My client would simply walk away.

And with him would go the big franchise payday.

Levin was fast-forwarding the image again.

"Now watch this," he said. "She and Mr. X split at nine. But watch when he gets up."

Levin had shifted the frame to focus on Campo and the unknown man. When the time code hit 8:59 he put the playback in slow motion.

"Okay, they're getting ready to leave," he said. "Watch the guy's hands."

I watched. The man took a final draw on his drink, tilting his head far back and emptying the glass. He then slipped off his stool, helped Campo off hers and they walked out of the camera frame to the right.

"What?" I said. "What did I miss?"

Levin moved the image backwards until he got to the

moment the unknown man was finishing his drink. He then froze the image and pointed to the screen. The man had his left hand down flat on the bar for balance as he reared back to drink.

"He drinks with his right hand," he said. "And on his left you can see a watch on his wrist. So it looks like the guy is right-handed, right?"

"Yeah, so? What does that get us? The injuries to the victim came from blows from the left."

"Think about what I've told you."

I did. And after a few moments I got it.

"The mirror. Everything's backwards. He's left-handed."

Levin nodded and made a punching motion with his left fist.

"This could be the whole case right here," I said, not sure that was a good thing.

"Happy Saint Paddy's Day, lad," Levin said in his brogue again, not realizing I might be staring at the end of the gravy train.

I took a long drink of hot coffee and tried to think about a strategy for the video. I didn't see any way to hold it for trial. The cops would eventually get around to the follow-up investigations and they would find out about it. If I held on to it, it could blow up in my face.

"I don't know how I'm going to use it yet," I said. "But I think it's safe to say Mr. Roulet and his mother and Cecil Dobbs are going to be very happy with you."

"Tell them they can always express their thanks financially."

"All right, anything else on the tape?"

Levin started to fast-forward the playback.

"Not really. Roulet reads the napkin and memorizes the address. He then hangs around another twenty minutes and splits, leaving a fresh drink on the bar."

He slowed the image down at the point Roulet was

leaving. Roulet took one sip out of his fresh martini and put it down on the bar. He picked up the napkin Reggie Campo had given him, crumpled it in his hand and then dropped it to the floor as he got up. He left the bar, leaving the drink behind.

Levin ejected the DVD and returned it to its plastic sleeve. He then turned off the player and started to put it away.

"That's it on the visuals that I can show you here."

I reached forward and tapped Earl on the shoulder. He had his sound buds in. He pulled out one of the ear plugs and looked back at me.

"Let's head back to the courthouse," I said. "Keep your plugs in."

Earl did as instructed.

"What else?" I said to Levin.

"There's Reggie Campo," he said. "She's not Snow White."

"What did you find out?"

"It's not necessarily what I found out. It's what I think. You saw how she was on the tape. One guy leaves and she's dropping love notes on another guy alone at the bar. Plus, I did some checking. She's an actress but she's not currently working as an actress. Except for private auditions, you could say."

He handed me a professional photo collage that showed Reggie Campo in different poses and characters. It was the kind of photo sheet sent to casting directors all over the city. The largest photo on the sheet was a head shot. It was the first time I had seen her face up close without the ugly bruises and swelling. Reggie Campo was a very attractive woman and something about her face was familiar to me but I could not readily place it. I wondered if I had seen her in a television show or a commercial. I flipped the head shot over and read her credits. They were for shows I never watched and commercials I didn't remember.

"In the police reports she lists her current employer as Topsail Telemarketing. They're over in the Marina. They take the calls for a lot of the crap they sell on late-night TV. Workout machines and stuff like that. Anyway, it's day work. You work when you want. The only thing is, Reggie hasn't worked a day there for five months."

"So what are you telling me, she's been tricking?"

"I've been watching her the last three nights and —"

"You what?"

I turned and looked at him. If a private eye working for a criminal defendant was caught tailing the victim of a violent crime, there could be hell to pay and I would be the one to pay it. All the prosecution would have to do is go see a judge and claim harassment and intimidation and I'd be held in contempt faster than the Santa Ana wind through the Sepulveda Pass. As a crime victim Reggie Campo was sacrosanct until she was on the stand. Only then was she mine.

"Don't worry, don't worry," Levin said. "It was a very loose tail. Very loose. And I'm glad I did it. The bruises and the swelling and all of that have either gone away or she's using a lot of makeup, because this lady has been getting a lot of visitors. All men, all alone, all different times of the night. It looks like she tries to fit at least two into her dance card each night."

"Is she picking them up in the bars?"

"No, she's been staying in. These guys must be regulars or something because they know their way to her door. I got some plate numbers. If necessary I can visit them and try to get some answers. I also shot some infrared video but I haven't transferred it to disc yet."

"No, let's hold off on visiting any of these guys for now. Word could get back to her. We have to be very careful around her. I don't care if she's tricking or not."

I drank some more coffee and tried to decide how to move with this.

"You ran a check on her, right? No criminal record."

"Right, she's clean. My guess is that she's new to the game. You know, these women who want to be actresses, it's a tough gig. It wears you down. She probably started by taking a little help from these guys here and there, then it became a business. She went from amateur to pro."

"And none of this is in the reports you got before?"

"Nope. Like I told you, there hasn't been a lot of follow-up by the cops. At least so far."

"If she graduated from amateur to pro, she could've graduated to setting a guy like Roulet up. He drives a nice car, wears nice clothes . . . have you seen his watch?"

"Yeah, a Rolex. If it's real, then he's wearing ten grand right there on his wrist. She could have seen that from across the bar. Maybe that's why she picked him out of all the rest."

We were back by the courthouse. I had to start heading toward downtown. I asked Levin where he was parked and he directed Earl to the lot.

"This is all good," I said. "But it means Louis lied about more than UCLA."

"Yeah," Levin agreed. "He knew he was going into a pay-for-play deal with her. He should have told you about it."

"Yeah, and now I'm going to talk to *him* about it."

We pulled up next to the curb outside a pay lot on Acacia. Levin took a file out of his briefcase. It had a rubber band around it that held a piece of paper to the outside cover. He held it out to me and I saw the document was an invoice for almost six thousand dollars for eight days of investigative services and expenses. Based on what I had heard during the last half hour, the price was a bargain.

"That file has everything we just talked about, plus a copy of the video from Morgan's on disc," Levin said.

I hesitantly took the file. By taking it I was moving it into the realm of discovery. Not accepting it and keeping everything with Levin would have given me a buffer, wiggle room if I got into a discovery scrap with the prosecutor.

I tapped the invoice with my finger.

"I'll call this in to Lorna and we'll send out a check," I said.

"How is Lorna? I miss seeing her."

When we were married, Lorna used to ride with me a lot and go into court with me to watch. Sometimes when I was short a driver she would take the wheel. Levin saw her more often back then.

"She's doing great. She's still Lorna."

Levin cracked his door open but didn't get out.

"You want me to stay on Reggie?"

That was the question. If I approved I would lose all deniability if something went wrong. Because now I would know what he was doing. I hesitated but then I nodded.

"Very loose. And don't farm it out. I only trust you on it."

"Don't worry. I'll handle it myself. What else?"

"The left-handed man. We have to figure out who Mr. X is and whether he was part of this thing or just another customer."

Levin nodded and pumped his left-handed fist again.

"I'm on it."

He put on his sunglasses, opened the door and slid out. He reached back in for his briefcase and his unopened bottle of water, then said good-bye and closed the door. I watched him start walking through the lot in search of his car. I should have been ecstatic about all I had just learned.

It tilted everything steeply toward my client. But I still felt uneasy about something I couldn't quite put my finger on.

Earl had turned his music off and was awaiting direction.

"Take me downtown, Earl," I said.

"You got it," he replied. "The CCB?"

"Yeah and, hey, who was that you were listening to on the 'Pod? I could sort of hear it."

"That was Snoop. Gotta play him up loud."

I nodded. L.A.'s own. And a former defendant who faced down the machine on a murder charge and walked away. There was no better story of inspiration on the street.

"Earl?" I said. "Take the seven-ten. We're running late."

TWELVE

Sam Scales was a Hollywood con man. He specialized in Internet schemes designed to gather credit card numbers and verification data that he would then turn and sell in the financial underworld. The first time we had worked together he had been arrested for selling six hundred card numbers and their attendant verification information — expiration dates and the addresses, social security numbers and passwords of the rightful owners of the cards — to an undercover sheriff's deputy.

Scales had gotten the numbers and information by sending out an e-mail to five thousand people who were on the customer list of a Delaware-based company that sold a weight-loss product called TrimSlim6 over the Internet. The list had been stolen from the company's computer by a hacker who did freelance work for Scales. Using a rent-by-the-hour computer in a Kinko's and a temporary e-mail address, Scales then sent out a mass mailing to all those on the list. He identified himself as counsel for the federal Food and Drug Administration and told the recipients that their credit cards would be refunded the full amount of their purchases of TrimSlim6 following an FDA recall of the product. He said FDA testing of the product proved it to be ineffective in promoting weight loss. He said the makers of the product had agreed to refund all purchases in an effort to avoid fraud charges. He concluded the e-mail with instructions for confirming the refund. These included providing the credit card number, expiration date and all other pertinent verification data.

Of the five thousand recipients of the message, there were six hundred who bit. Scales then made an Internet contact in the underworld and set up a hand-to-hand sale, six hundred credit card numbers and vitals for ten thousand in cash. It meant that within days the numbers would be stamped on plastic blanks and then put to use. It was a fraud that would reach into the millions of dollars in losses.

But it was stunted in a West Hollywood coffee shop where Scales handed over a printout to his buyer and was given a thick envelope containing cash in return. When he walked out carrying the envelope and an iced decaf latte he was met by sheriff's deputies. He had sold his numbers to an undercover.

Scales hired me to get him a deal. He was thirty-three years old at the time and had a clean record, even though there were indications and evidence that he had never held a lawful job. By focusing the prosecutor assigned to the case on the theft of card numbers rather than the potential losses of the fraud, I was able to get Scales a disposition to his liking. He pleaded guilty to one felony count of identity theft and received a one-year suspended sentence, sixty days of CalTrans work and four years of probation.

That was the first time. That was three years ago. Sam Scales did not take the opportunity afforded him by the no-jail sentence. He was now back in custody and I was defending him in a fraud case so reprehensible that it was clear from the start that it was going to be beyond my ability to keep him out of prison.

On December 28 of the previous year Scales used a front company to register a domain name of SunamiHelp.com on the World Wide Web. On the home page of the website he put photographs of the destruction and death left two days earlier when a tsunami in the Indian Ocean devastated parts of Indonesia, Sri Lanka, India and Thailand. The site asked viewers to please help by making a donation to SunamiHelp which would then distribute it among the numerous agencies responding to the disaster. The site also carried the photograph of a handsome white man identified as Reverend Charles, who was engaged in the work of bringing Christianity to Indonesia. A personal note from Reverend Charles was posted on the site and it asked viewers to give from the heart.

Scales was smart but not that smart. He didn't want to steal the donations made to the site. He only wanted to steal the credit card information used to make the donations. The investigation that followed his arrest showed that all contributions made through the site actually were forwarded to the American Red Cross and did go to efforts to help victims of the devastating tsunami.

But the numbers and information from the credit cards used to make those donations were also forwarded to the financial underworld. Scales was arrested when a detective with the LAPD's fraud-by-trick unit named Roy Wunderlich found the website. Knowing that disasters always drew out the con artists in droves, Wunderlich had started typing in possible website names in which the word *tsunami* was misspelled. There were several legitimate tsunami donation sites on the web and he typed in variations of these, always misspelling the word. His thinking was that the con artists would misspell the word when they set up fraud sites in an effort to draw potential victims who were likely to be of a lower education level. SunamiHelp.com was among several questionable sites the detective found. Most of these he forwarded to an FBI task force looking at the problem on a nationwide scale. But when he checked the domain registration of SunamiHelp.com, he found a Los Angeles post office box. That gave Wunderlich jurisdiction. He was in business. He kept SunamiHelp.com for himself.

The PO box turned out to be a dead address but Wunderlich was undeterred. He floated a balloon, meaning he made a controlled purchase, or in this case a controlled donation.

The credit card number the detective provided while making a twenty-dollar donation would be monitored twenty-four hours a day by the Visa fraud unit and he would be informed instantly of any purchase made on the account. Within three days of the donation the credit card was used to purchase an eleven-dollar lunch at the Gumbo Pot restaurant in the Farmers Market at Fairfax and Third. Wunderlich knew that it had simply been a test purchase. Something small and easily coverable with cash if the user of the counterfeit credit card encountered a problem at the point of purchase.

The restaurant purchase was allowed to go through and Wunderlich and four other detectives from the trick unit were dispatched to the Farmers Market, a sprawling blend of old and new shops and restaurants that was always crowded and therefore a perfect place for credit card con artists to operate. The investigators would spread out in the complex and wait while Wunderlich continued to monitor the card's use by phone.

Two hours after the first purchase the control number was used again to purchase a six-hundred-dollar leather jacket at the Nordstrom in the market. The credit card approval was delayed but not stopped. The detectives moved in and arrested a young woman as she was completing the purchase of the jacket. The case then became what is known as a "snitch chain," the police following one suspect to the next as they snitched each other off and the arrests moved up the ladder.

Eventually they came to the man sitting at the top of that ladder, Sam Scales. When the story broke in the press Wunderlich referred to him as the Tsunami Svengali because so many victims of the scam turned out to be women who had wanted to help the handsome minister pictured on the website. The nickname angered Scales, and in my discussions with him he took to referring to the detective who had brought him down as Wunder Boy.

I got to Department 124 on the thirteenth floor of the Criminal Courts Building by 10:45 but the courtroom was empty except for Marianne, the judge's clerk. I went through the bar and approached her station.

"You guys still doing the calendar?" I asked.

"Just waiting on you. I'll call everybody and tell the judge."

"She mad at me?"

Marianne shrugged. She wouldn't answer for the judge. Especially to a defense attorney. But in a way, she was telling me that the judge wasn't happy.

"Is Scales still back there?"

"Should be. I don't know where Joe went."

I turned and went over to the defense table and sat down and waited. Eventually, the door to the lockup opened and Joe Frey, the bailiff assigned to 124, stepped out.

"You still got my guy back there?"

"Just barely. We thought you were a no-show again. You want to go back?"

He held the steel door open for me and I stepped into a small room with a stairwell going up to the courthouse jail on the fourteenth floor and two doors leading to the smaller holding rooms for 124. One of the doors had a glass panel. It was for attorney-client meetings and I could see Sam Scales sitting by himself at a table behind the glass. He was wearing an orange jumpsuit and had steel cuffs on his wrists. He was being held without bail because his latest arrest violated his probation on the TrimSlim6 conviction. The sweet deal I had gotten him on that was about to go down the tubes.

"Finally," Scales said as I walked in.

"Like you're going anywhere. You ready to do this?"

"If I have no choice."

I sat down across from him.

"Sam, you always have a choice. But let me explain it again. They've got you cold on this, okay? You were caught ripping off people who wanted to help the people caught in one of the worst natural disasters in recorded history. They've got three co-conspirators who took deals to testify against you. They have the list of card numbers found in your possession. What I am saying is that at the end of the day, you are going to get about as much sympathy from the judge and a jury — if it should come to that — as they would give a child raper. Maybe even less."

"I know all of that but I am a useful asset to society. I could educate people. Put me in the schools. Put me in the country clubs. Put me on probation and I'll tell people what to watch out for out there."

"*You* are who they have to watch out for. You blew your chance with the last one and the prosecution said this is the final offer on this one. You don't take it and they're going to go to the wall on this. The one thing I can guarantee you is that there will be no mercy."

So many of my clients are like Sam Scales. They hopelessly believe there is a light behind the door. And I'm the one who has to tell them the door is locked and that the bulb burned out long ago anyway.

"Then I guess I have to do it," Scales said, looking at me with eyes that blamed me for not finding a way out for him.

"It's your choice. You want a trial, we'll go to trial. Your exposure will be ten years plus the one you've got left on the probation. You make 'em real mad and they can also ship you over to the FBI so the feds can take a swing at you on interstate wire fraud if they want."

"Let me ask you something. If we go to trial, could we win?"

I almost laughed but I still had some sympathy left for him.

"No, Sam, we can't win. Haven't you been listening to what I've been telling you for two months? They got you. You can't win. But I'm here to do what you want. Like I said, if you want a trial we'll go to trial. But I gotta tell you that if we go, you'll have to get your mother to pay me again. I'm only good through today."

"How much did she pay you already?"

"Eight thousand."

"Eight grand! That's her fucking retirement account money!"

"I'm surprised she has anything left in the account with you for a son."

He looked at me sharply.

"I'm sorry, Sam. I shouldn't have said that. From what she told me, you're a good son."

"Jesus Christ, I should have gone to fucking law school. You're a con no different from me. You know that, Haller? Only that paper they give you makes you street legal, that's all."

They always blame the lawyer for making a living. As if it's a crime to want to be paid for doing a day's work. What Scales had just said to me would have brought a near violent reaction back when I was maybe a year or two out of law school. But I'd heard the same insult too many times by now to do anything but roll with it.

"What can I say, Sam? We've already had this conversation."

He nodded and didn't say anything. I took it to mean he would take the DA's offer. Four years in the state penal system and a ten-thousand-dollar fine, followed by five years' parole. He'd be out in two and a half but the parole would be a killer for a natural-born con man to make it through unscathed. After a few minutes I got up and left the room. I knocked on the outer door and Deputy Frey let me back into the courtroom.

"He's good to go," I said.

I took my seat at the defense table and soon Frey brought Scales out and sat him next to me. He still had the cuffs on. He said nothing to me. In another few minutes Glenn Bernasconi, the prosecutor who worked 124, came down from his office on the fifteenth floor and I told him we were ready to accept the case disposition.

At 11 A.M. Judge Judith Champagne came out of chambers and onto the bench and Frey called the courtroom to order. The judge was a diminutive, attractive blonde and ex-prosecutor who had been on the bench at least as long as I'd had my ticket. She was old school all the way, fair but tough, running her courtroom as a fiefdom. Sometimes she even brought her dog, a German shepherd named Justice, to work with her. If the judge had had any kind of discretion in the sentence when Sam Scales faced her, he would have gone down hard. That was what I did for Sam Scales, whether he knew it or not. With this deal I had saved him from that.

"Good morning," the judge said. "I am glad you could make it today, Mr. Haller."

"I apologize, Your Honor. I got held up in Judge Flynn's court in Compton."

That was all I had to say. The judge knew about Flynn. Everybody did.

"And on St. Patrick's Day, no less," she said.

"Yes, Your Honor."

"I understand we have a disposition in the Tsunami Svengali matter."

She immediately looked over at her court reporter.

"Michelle, strike that."

She looked back at the lawyers.

"I understand we have a disposition in the Scales case. Is that correct?"

"That is correct," I said. "We're ready to go on that."

"Good."

Bernasconi half read, half repeated from memory the legalese needed to take a plea from the defendant. Scales waived his rights and pleaded guilty to the charges. He said nothing other than the word. The judge accepted the disposition agreement and sentenced him accordingly.

"You're a lucky man, Mr. Scales," she said when it was over. "I believe Mr. Bernasconi was quite generous with you. I would not have been."

"I don't feel so lucky, Judge," Scales said.

Deputy Frey tapped him on the shoulder from behind. Scales stood up and turned to me.

"I guess this is it," he said.

"Good luck, Sam," I said.

He was led off through the steel door and I watched it close behind them. I had not shaken his hand.

THIRTEEN

The Van Nuys Civic Center is a long concrete plaza enclosed by government buildings. Anchoring one end is the Van Nuys Division of the LAPD. Along one side are two courthouses sitting opposite a public library and a city administration building. At the end of the concrete and glass channel is a federal administration building and post office. I waited for Louis Roulet in the plaza on one of the concrete benches near the library. The plaza was largely deserted despite the great weather. Not like the day before, when the place was overrun with cameras and the media and the gadflies, all crowding around Robert Blake and his lawyers as they tried to spin a not-guilty verdict into innocence.

It was a nice, quiet afternoon and I usually liked being outside. Most of my work is done in windowless courtrooms or the backseat of my Town Car, so I take it outside whenever I can. But I wasn't feeling the breeze or noticing the fresh air this time. I was annoyed because Louis Roulet was late and because what Sam Scales had said to me about being a street-legal con was festering like cancer in my mind. When finally I saw Roulet crossing the plaza toward me I got up to meet him.

"Where've you been?" I said abruptly.

"I told you I'd get here as soon as I could. I was in the middle of a showing when you called."

"Let's walk."

I headed toward the federal building because it would

give us the longest stretch before we would have to turn around to cross back. I had my meeting with Minton, the new prosecutor assigned to his case, in twenty-five minutes in the older of the two courthouses. I realized that we didn't look like a lawyer and his client discussing a case. Maybe a lawyer and his realtor discussing a land grab. I was in my Hugo Boss and Roulet was in a tan suit over a green turtleneck. He had on loafers with small silver buckles.

"There won't be any showings up in Pelican Bay," I said to him.

"What's that supposed to mean? Where's that?"

"It's a pretty name for a super max prison where they send violent sex offenders. You're going to fit in there pretty good in your turtleneck and loafers."

"Look, what's the matter? What's this about?"

"It's about a lawyer who can't have a client who lies to him. In twenty minutes I'm about to go up to see the guy who wants to send you to Pelican Bay. I need everything I can get my hands on to try to keep you out of there and it doesn't help when I find out you're lying to me."

Roulet stopped and turned to me. He raised his hands out, palms open.

"I haven't lied to you! I did not do this thing. I don't know what that woman wants but I —"

"Let me ask you something, Louis. You and Dobbs said you took a year of law at UCLA, right? Did they teach you anything at all about the lawyer-client bond of trust?"

"I don't know. I don't remember. I wasn't there long enough."

I took a step toward him, invading his space.

"You see? You are a fucking liar. You didn't go to UCLA law school for a year. You didn't even go for a goddamn day."

He brought his hands down and slapped them against his sides.

"Is that what this is all about, Mickey?"

"Yeah, that's right and from now on, don't call me Mickey. My friends call me that. Not my lying clients."

"What does whether or not I went to law school ten years ago have to do with this case? I don't —"

"Because if you lied to me about that, then you'd lie to me about anything, and I can't have that and be able to defend you."

I said it too loud. I saw a couple of women on a nearby bench watching us. They had juror badges on their blouses.

"Come on. This way."

I started walking back the other way, heading toward the police station.

"Look," Roulet said in a weak voice. "I lied because of my mother, okay?"

"No, not okay. Explain it to me."

"Look, my mother and Cecil think I went to law school for a year. I want them to continue to believe that. He brought it up with you and so I just sort of agreed. But it was ten years ago! What is the harm?"

"The harm is in lying to me," I said. "You can lie to your mother, to Dobbs, to your priest and to the police. But when I ask you something directly, do not lie to me. I need to operate from the standpoint of having facts from you. Incontrovertible facts. So when I ask you a question, tell me the truth. All the rest of the time you can say what you want and whatever makes you feel good."

"Okay, okay."

"If you weren't in law school, where were you?"

Roulet shook his head.

"Nowhere. I just didn't do anything for a year. Most of the time I stayed in my apartment near campus and read and thought about what I really wanted to do with my life. The only thing I knew for sure was that I didn't want to be a lawyer. No offense intended."

"None taken. So you sat there for a year and came up with selling real estate to rich people."

"No, that came later."

He laughed in a self-deprecating way.

"I actually decided to become a writer — I had majored in English lit — and I tried to write a novel. It didn't take me long to figure out that I couldn't do it. I eventually went to work for Mother. She wanted me to."

I calmed down. Most of my anger had been a show, anyway. I was trying to soften him up for the more important questioning. I thought he was now ready for it.

"Well, now that you are coming clean and confessing everything, Louis, tell me about Reggie Campo."

"What about her?"

"You were going to pay her for sex, weren't you?"

"What makes you say —"

I shut him up when I stopped again and grabbed him by one of his expensive lapels. He was taller than me and bigger, but I had the power in this conversation. I was pushing him.

"Answer the fucking question."

"All right, yes, I was going to pay. But how did you know that?"

"Because I'm a good goddamn lawyer. Why didn't you tell me this on that first day? Don't you see how that changes the case?"

"My mother. I didn't want my mother to know I . . . you know."

"Louis, let's sit down."

I walked him over to one of the long benches by the police station. There was a lot of space and no one could overhear us. I sat in the middle of the bench and he sat to my right.

"Your mother wasn't even in the room when we were talking about the case. I don't even think she was in there when we talked about law school."

"But Cecil was and he tells her everything."

I nodded and made a mental note to cut Cecil Dobbs completely out of the loop on case matters from now on.

"Okay, I think I understand. But how long were you going to let it go without telling me? Don't you see how this changes everything?"

"I'm not a lawyer."

"Louis, let me tell you a little bit about how this works. You know what I am? I'm a neutralizer. My job is to neutralize the state's case. Take each piece of evidence or proof and find a way to eliminate it from contention. Think of it like one of those street entertainers you see on the Venice boardwalk. You ever gone down there and seen the guy spinning all those plates on those little sticks?"

"I think so. I haven't been down there in a long time."

"Doesn't matter. The guy has these thin little sticks and he puts a plate on each one and starts spinning the plate so it will stay balanced and upright. He gets a lot of them going at once and he moves from plate to plate and stick to stick making sure everything is spinning and balanced and staying up. You with me?"

"Yes. I understand."

"Well, that's the state's case, Louis. A bunch of spinning plates. And every one of those plates is an individual piece of evidence against you. My job is to take each plate, stop it from spinning and knock it to the ground so hard that it shatters and can't be used anymore. If the blue plate contains the victim's blood on your hands, then I need to find a way to knock it down. If the yellow plate has a knife with your bloody fingerprints on it, then once again I need to knock that sucker down. Neutralize it. You follow?"

"Yes, I follow. I —"

"Now, in the middle of this field of plates is a big one. It's a fucking platter, Louis, and if that baby falls over it's going to take everything down with it. Every plate. The whole case goes down. Do you know what that platter is, Louis?"

He shook his head no.

"That big platter is the victim, the chief witness against you. If we can knock that platter over, then the whole act is over and the crowd moves on."

I waited a moment to see if he would react. He said nothing.

"Louis, for almost two weeks you have concealed from me the method by which I could knock the big platter down. It asks the question why. Why would a guy with money at his disposal, a Rolex watch on his wrist, a Porsche out in the parking lot and a Holmby Hills address need to use a knife to get sex from a woman who sells it anyway? When you boil it all down to that question, the case starts to collapse, Louis, because the answer is simple. He wouldn't. Common sense says he wouldn't. And when you come to that conclusion, all the plates stop spinning. You see the setup, you see the trap, and now it's the defendant who starts to look like the victim."

I looked at him. He nodded.

"I'm sorry," he said.

"You should be," I said. "The case would have started coming apart almost two weeks ago and we probably wouldn't be sitting here right now if you had been up-front with me from the start."

In that moment I realized where my anger was truly coming from and it wasn't because Roulet had been late or had lied or because of Sam Scales calling me a street-legal con. It was because I saw the franchise slipping away. There would be no trial in this case, no six-figure fee. I'd be lucky just to keep the retainer I'd gotten at the start. The case was going to end today when I walked into the DA's office and told Ted Minton what I knew and what I had.

"I'm sorry," Roulet said again in a whiny voice. "I didn't mean to mess things up."

I was looking down at the ground between my feet now. Without looking at him I reached over and put my hand on his shoulder.

"I'm sorry I yelled at you before, Louis."

"What do we do now?"

"I have a few more questions to ask you about that night, and then I'm going to go up into that building over there and meet the prosecutor and knock down all his plates. I think that by the time I come out of there this may all be over and you'll be free to go back to showing your mansions to rich people."

"Just like that?"

"Well, formally he may want to go into court and ask a judge to dismiss the case."

Roulet opened his mouth in shock.

"Mr. Haller, I can't begin to tell you how —"

"You can call me Mickey. Sorry about that before."

"No problem. Thank you. What questions do you want to ask?"

I thought for a moment. I really didn't need anything else to go into the meeting with Minton. I was locked and loaded. I had walking proof.

"What did the note say?" I asked.

"What note?"

"The one she gave you at the bar in Morgan's."

"Oh, it said her address and then underneath she wrote 'four hundred dollars' and then under that she wrote 'Come after ten.'"

"Too bad we don't have that. But I think we have enough."

I nodded and looked at my watch. I still had fifteen minutes until the meeting but I was finished with Roulet.

"You can go now, Louis. I'll call you when it's all over."

"You sure? I could wait out here if you want."

"I don't know how long it will take. I'm going to have to lay it all out for him. He'll probably have to take it to his boss. It could be a while."

"All right, well, I guess I'll go then. But you'll call me, right?"

"Yes, I will. We'll probably go in to see the judge Monday or Tuesday, then it will all be over."

He put his hand out and I shook it.

"Thanks, Mick. You're the best. I knew I had the best lawyer when I got you."

I watched him walk back across the plaza and go between the two courthouses toward the public parking garage.

"Yeah, I'm the best," I said to myself.

I felt the presence of someone and turned to see a man sit down on the bench next to me. He turned and looked at me and we recognized each other at the same time. It was Howard Kurlen, a homicide detective from the Van Nuys Division. We had bumped up against each other on a few cases over the years.

"Well, well, well," Kurlen said. "The pride of the California bar. You're not talking to yourself, are you?"

"Maybe."

"That could be bad for a lawyer if that got around."

"I'm not worried. How are you doing, Detective?"

Kurlen was unwrapping a sandwich he had taken out of a brown bag.

"Busy day. Late lunch."

He produced a peanut butter sandwich from the wrap. There was a layer of something else besides peanut butter in it but it wasn't jelly. I couldn't identify it. I looked at my watch. I still had a few minutes before I needed to get in line for the metal detectors at the courthouse entrance but I wasn't sure I wanted to spend them with Kurlen and his horrible-looking sandwich. I thought about bringing up the Blake verdict, sticking it to the LAPD a little bit, but Kurlen stuck one in me first.

"How's my man Jesus doin'?" the detective asked.

Kurlen had been lead detective on the Jesus Menendez case. He had wrapped him up so tightly that Menendez had no choice but to plead and hope for the best. He still got life.

"I don't know," I answered. "I don't talk to Jesus anymore."

"Yeah, I guess once they plead out and go upstate they're not much use to you. No appeal work, no nothing."

I nodded. Every cop had a jaundiced eye when it came to defense lawyers. It was as if they believed their own actions and investigations were beyond questioning or reproach. They didn't believe in a justice system based on checks and balances.

"Just like you, I guess," I said. "On to the next one. I hope your busy day means you're working on getting me a new client."

"I don't look at it that way. But I was wondering, do you sleep well at night?"

"You know what I was wondering? What the hell is in that sandwich?"

He held what was left of the sandwich up on display.

"Peanut butter and sardines. Lots of good protein to get me through another day of chasing scumbags. Talking to them, too. You didn't answer my question."

"I sleep fine, Detective. You know why? Because I play an important part in the system. A needed part — just like your part. When somebody is accused of a crime, they have the opportunity to test the system. If they want to do that, they come to me. That's all any of this is about. When you understand that, you have no trouble sleeping."

"Good story. When you close your eyes I hope you believe it."

"How about you, Detective? You ever put your head on the pillow and wonder whether you've put innocent people away?"

"Nope," he said quickly, his mouth full of sandwich. "Never happened, never will."

"Must be nice to be so sure."

"A guy told me once that when you get to the end of your road, you have to look at the community woodpile and decide if you added to it while you were here or whether you just took from it. Well, I add to the woodpile, Haller. I sleep good at night. But I wonder about you and your kind. You lawyers are all takers from the woodpile."

"Thanks for the sermon. I'll keep it in mind next time I'm chopping wood."

"You don't like that, then I've got a joke for you. What's the difference between a catfish and a defense attorney?"

"Hmmm, I don't know, Detective."

"One's a bottom-feeding scum sucker and one's a fish."

He laughed uproariously. I stood up. It was time to go.

"I hope you brush your teeth after you eat something like that," I said. "I'd hate to be your partner if you don't."

I walked away, thinking about what he had said about the woodpile and what Sam Scales had said about my being a street-legal con. I was getting it from all sides today.

"Thanks for the tip," Kurlen called after me.

FOURTEEN

Ted Minton had arranged for us to discuss the Roulet case in private by scheduling our conference at a time he knew the deputy district attorney he shared space with had a hearing in court. Minton met me in the waiting area and walked me back. He did not look to me to be older than thirty but he had a self-assured presence. I probably had ten years and a hundred trials on him, yet he showed no sign of deference or respect. He acted as though the meeting was a nuisance he had to put up with. That was fine. That was the usual. And it put more fuel in my tank.

When we got to his small, windowless office, he offered me his office partner's seat and closed the door. We sat down and looked at each other. I let him go first.

"Okay," he said. "First off, I wanted to meet you. I'm sort of new up here in the Valley and haven't met a lot of the members of the defense bar. I know you're one of those guys that covers the whole county but we haven't run across each other before."

"Maybe that's because you haven't worked many felony trials before."

He smiled and nodded like I had scored a point of some kind.

"That might be true," he said. "Anyway, I gotta tell you, when I was in law school at SC I read a book about your father and his cases. I think it was called *Haller for the Defense*. Something like that. Interesting guy and interesting times."

I nodded back.

"He was gone before I really knew him, but there were a few books about him and I read them all more than a few times. It's probably why I ended up doing this."

"That must have been hard, getting to know your father through books."

I shrugged. I didn't think that Minton and I needed to know each other that well, particularly in light of what I was about to do to him.

"I guess it happens," he said.

"Yeah."

He clapped his hands together once, a let's-get-down-to-business gesture.

"Okay, so we're here to talk about Louis Roulet, aren't we?"

"It's pronounced Roo-*lay*."

"Roooo-*lay*. Got it. So, let's see, I have some things for you here."

He swiveled his seat to turn back to his desk. He picked up a thin file and turned back to hand it to me.

"I want to play fair. That's the up-to-the-minute discovery for you. I know I don't have to give it to you until after the arraignment but, hell, let's be cordial."

My experience is that when prosecutors tell you they are playing fair or better than fair, then you better watch your back. I fanned through the discovery file but didn't really read anything. The file Levin had gathered for me was at least four times as thick. I wasn't thrilled because Minton had so little. I was suspicious that he was holding back on me. Most prosecutors made you work for the discovery by having to demand it repeatedly, to the point of going to court to complain to the judge about it. But Minton had just casually handed at least some of it over. Either he had more to learn than I imagined about felony prosecutions or there was some sort of play here.

"This is everything?" I asked.

"Everything I've gotten."

That was always the way. If the prosecutor didn't have it, then he could stall its release to the defense. I knew for a fact — as in having been married to a prosecutor — that it was not out of the ordinary for a prosecutor to tell the police investigators on a case to take their time getting all the paperwork in. They could then turn around and tell the defense lawyer they wanted to play fair and hand over practically nothing. The rules of discovery were often referred to by defense pros as the rules of dishonesty. This of course went both ways. Discovery was supposed to be a two-way street.

"And you're going to trial with this?"

I waved the file as if to say its thin contents were as thin as the case.

"I'm not worried about it. But if you want to talk about a disposition, I'll listen."

"No, no disposition on this. We're going balls out. We're going to waive the prelim and go right to trial. No delays."

"He won't waive speedy?"

"Nope. You've got sixty days from Monday to put up or shut up."

Minton pursed his lips as though what I had just told him were only a minor inconvenience and surprise. It was a good cover-up. I knew I had landed a solid punch.

"Well, then, I guess we ought to talk about unilateral discovery. What do you have for me?"

He had dropped the pleasant tone.

"I'm still putting it together," I said. "But I'll have it at the arraignment Monday. But most of what I've got is probably already in this file you gave me, don't you think?"

"Most likely."

"You have that the supposed victim is a prostitute who had solicited my client in here, right? And that she has continued that line of work since the alleged incident, right?"

Minton's mouth opened maybe a half inch and then closed, but it was a good tell. I had hit him with another solid shot. But then he recovered quickly.

"As a matter of fact," he said, "I am aware of her occupation. But what surprises me is that you know this already. I hope you aren't sniffing around my victim, Mr. Haller?"

"Call me Mickey. And what I am doing is the least of your problems. You better take a good look at this case, Ted. I know you're new to felony trials and you don't want to come out of the box with a loser like this. Especially after the Blake fiasco. But this one's a dog and it's going to bite you on the ass."

"Really? How so?"

I looked past his shoulder at the computer on his desk.

"Does that thing play DVDs?"

Minton looked back at the computer. It looked ancient.

"It should. What have you got?"

I realized that showing him the surveillance video from the bar at Morgan's would be giving an early reveal of the biggest ace that I held, but I was confident that once he saw it, there would be no arraignment Monday and no case. My job was to neutralize the case and get my client out from under the government's weight. This was the way to do it.

"I don't have all my discovery together but I do have this," I said.

I handed Minton the DVD I had gotten earlier from Levin. The prosecutor put it into his computer.

"This is from the bar at Morgan's," I told him as he tried to get it playing. "Your guys never went there but my guy did. This is the Sunday night of the supposed attack."

"And this could have been doctored."

"It could have been but it wasn't. You can have it checked. My investigator has the original and I will tell him to make it available after the arraignment."

After a short struggle Minton got the DVD to play. He watched silently as I pointed out the time code and all the same details Levin had pointed out to me, including Mr. X and his left-handedness. Minton fast-forwarded as I instructed and then slowed it to watch the moment when Reggie Campo approached my client at the bar. He had a frown of concentration on his face. When it was over he ejected the disc and held it up.

"Can I keep this until I get the original?"

"Be my guest."

Minton put the disc back in its case and placed it on top of a stack of files on his desk.

"Okay, what else?" he asked.

Now my mouth let some light in.

"What do you mean, what else? Isn't that enough?"

"Enough for what?"

"Look, Ted, why don't we cut the bullshit?"

"Please do."

"What are we talking about here? That disc blows this case out of the water. Let's forget about arraignment and trial and talk about going into court next week with a joint motion to dismiss. I want this shit-canned with prejudice, Ted. No coming back at my guy if somebody in here decides to change their mind."

Minton smiled and shook his head.

"Can't do that, Mickey. This woman was injured quite badly. She was victimized by an animal and I'm not going to dismiss anything against —"

"Quite badly? She's been turning tricks again all week. You —"

"How do you know that?"

I shook my head.

"Man, I am trying to help you here, save you some embarrassment, and all you're worried about is whether I've crossed some line with the victim. Well, I've got news for you. She ain't the victim. Don't you see what you have here? If this thing gets to a jury and they see that disc, all the plates fall, Ted. Your case is over and you have to come back in here and explain to your boss Smithson why you didn't see it coming. I don't know Smithson all that well, but I do know one thing about him. He doesn't like to lose. And after what happened yesterday, I would say that he feels a little more urgent about that."

"Prostitutes can be victims, too. Even amateurs."

I shook my head. I decided to show my whole hand.

"She set him up," I said. "She knew he had money and she laid a trap. She wants to sue him and cash in. She either hit herself or she had her boyfriend from the bar, the left-handed man, do it. No jury in the world is going to buy what you're selling. Blood on the hand or fingerprints on the knife — it was all staged after he was knocked out."

Minton nodded as if he followed the logic but then came out with something from left field.

"I'm concerned that you may be trying to intimidate my victim by following her and harassing her."

"What?"

"You know the rules of engagement. Leave the victim alone or we'll next talk about it with a judge."

I shook my head and spread my hands wide.

"Are you listening to anything I'm saying here?"

"Yes, I have listened to it all and it doesn't change the course I am taking. I do have an offer for you, though, and it will be good only until Monday's arraignment. After that, all bets are off. Your client takes his chances with a judge and jury. And I'm not intimidated by you or the sixty days. I will be ready and waiting."

I felt like I was underwater and everything that I said

was trapped in bubbles that were drifting up and away. No one could hear me correctly. Then I realized that there was something I was missing. Something important. It didn't matter how green Minton was, he wasn't stupid and I had just mistakenly thought he was acting stupid. The L.A. County DA's office got some of the best of the best out of law school. He had already mentioned Southern Cal and I knew that was a law school that turned out top-notch lawyers. It was only a matter of experience. Minton might be short on experience but it didn't mean he was short on legal intelligence. I realized that I should be looking at myself, not Minton, for understanding.

"What am I missing here?" I asked.

"I don't know," Minton said. "You're the one with the high-powered defense. What could you be missing?"

I stared at him for a moment and then knew. There was a glitch in the discovery. There was something in his thin file that was not in the thick one Levin had put together. Something that would get the prosecution past the fact that Reggie Campo was selling it. Minton had so much as told me already. *Prostitutes can be victims, too.*

I wanted to stop everything and look through the state's discovery file to compare it with everything about the case that I knew. But I could not do it now in front of him.

"Okay," I said. "What's your offer? He won't take it but I'll present it."

"Well, he's got to do prison time. That's a given. We're willing to drop it all down to an ADW and attempted sexual battery. We'll go to the middle of the guidelines, which would put him at about seven years."

I nodded. Assault with a deadly weapon and attempted sexual battery. A seven-year sentence would likely mean four years actual. It wasn't a bad offer but only from the standpoint of Roulet having committed the crime. If he was innocent, then no offer was acceptable.

I shrugged.

"I'll take it to him," I said.

"Remember, only until the arraignment. So if he wants it you better call me Monday morning first thing."

"Right."

I closed my briefcase and stood up to go. I was thinking about how Roulet was probably waiting for a phone call from me, telling him the nightmare was over. Instead, I would be calling about a seven-year deal.

Minton and I shook hands and I said I would call him, then I headed out. In the hallway leading to the reception area I ran into Maggie McPherson.

"Hayley had a great time Saturday," she said about our daughter. "She's still talking about it. She said you were going to see her this weekend, too."

"Yeah, if that's okay."

"Are you all right? You look like you're in a daze."

"It's turning into a long week. I'm glad I have an empty calendar tomorrow. Which works better for Hayley, Saturday or Sunday?"

"Either's fine. Were you just meeting Ted on the Roulet thing?"

"Yeah. I got his offer."

I raised my briefcase to show I was taking the prosecution's plea offer with me.

"Now I have to go try to sell it," I added. "That's going to be tough. Guy says he didn't do it."

"I thought they all said that."

"Not like this guy."

"Well, good luck."

"Thanks."

We headed opposite ways in the hallway and then I remembered something and called back to her.

"Hey, Happy St. Patrick's."

"Oh."

She turned and came back toward me.

"Stacey's staying a couple hours late with Hayley and a bunch of us are going over to Four Green Fields after work. You feel like a pint of green beer?"

Four Green Fields was an Irish pub not far from the civic center. It was frequented by lawyers from both sides of the bar. Animosities grew slack under the taste of room-temperature Guinness.

"I don't know," I said. "I think I have to head over the hill to see my client but you never know, I might come back."

"Well, I only have till eight and then I have to go relieve Stacey."

"Okay."

We parted again and I left the courthouse. The bench where I had sat with Roulet and then Kurlen was empty. I sat down, opened my case and pulled out the discovery file Minton had given me. I flipped through reports I already had gotten copies of through Levin. There seemed to be nothing new until I came to a comparative fingerprint analysis report that confirmed what we had thought all along; the bloody fingerprints on the knife belonged to my client, Louis Roulet.

It still wasn't enough to justify Minton's demeanor. I kept looking and then I found it in the weapon analysis report. The report I had gotten from Levin was completely different, as if from another case and another weapon. As I quickly read it I felt perspiration popping in my hair. I had been set up. I had been embarrassed in the meeting with Minton and worse yet had tipped him early to my hole card. He had the video from Morgan's and had all the time he would need to prepare for it in court.

Finally, I slapped the folder closed and pulled out my cell phone. Levin answered after two rings.

"How'd it go?" he asked. "Bonuses for everybody?"

153

"Not quite. Do you know where Roulet's office is?"

"Yeah, on Canon in Beverly Hills. I've got the exact address in the file."

"Meet me there."

"Now?"

"I'll be there in thirty minutes."

I punched the button, ending the call without further discussion, and then called Earl on speed dial. He must have had his iPod plugs in his ears because he didn't answer until the seventh ring.

"Come get me," I said. "We're going over the hill."

I closed the phone and got off the bench. Walking toward the opening between the two courthouses and the place where Earl would pick me up, I felt angry. At Roulet, at Levin, and most of all at myself. But I also was aware of the positive side of this. The one thing that was certain now was that the franchise — and the big payday that came with it — was back in play. The case was going to go the distance to trial unless Roulet took the state's offer. And I thought the chances of that were about the same as the chances for snow in L.A. It could happen but I wouldn't believe it until I saw it.

FIFTEEN

When the rich in Beverly Hills want to drop small fortunes on clothes and jewelry, they go to Rodeo Drive. When they want to drop larger fortunes on houses and condominiums, they walk a few blocks over to Canon Drive, where the high-line real estate companies roost, photographs of their multimillion-dollar offerings presented in showroom windows on ornate gold easels like Picassos and Van Goghs. This is where I found Windsor Residential Estates and Louis Roulet on Thursday afternoon.

By the time I got there, Raul Levin was already waiting — and I mean waiting. He had been kept in the showroom with a fresh bottle of water while Louis worked the phone in his private office. The receptionist, an overly tanned blonde with a haircut that hung down one side of her face like a scythe, told me it would be just a few minutes more and then we both could go in. I nodded and stepped away from her desk.

"You want to tell me what's going on?" Levin asked.

"Yeah, when we get in there with him."

The showroom was lined on both sides with steel wires that ran from ceiling to floor and on which were attached 8 × 10 frames containing the photos and pedigrees of the estates offered for sale. Acting like I was studying the rows of houses I couldn't hope to afford in a hundred years, I moved toward the back hallway that led to the offices. When I got there I noticed an open door and heard Louis Roulet's voice. It sounded like he was setting up a showing of a Mulholland Drive mansion for a client he told the realtor on the other end of the phone wanted his name kept confidential. I looked back at Levin, who was still near the front of the showroom.

"This is bullshit," I said and signaled him back.

I walked down the hallway and into Roulet's plush office. There was the requisite desk stacked with paperwork and thick multiple-listing catalogs. But Roulet wasn't there. He was in a sitting area to the right of the desk, slouched on a sofa with a cigarette in one hand and the phone in the other. He looked shocked to see me and I thought maybe the receptionist hadn't even told him he had visitors.

Levin came into the office behind me, followed by the receptionist, the hair scythe swinging back and forth as she hurried to catch up. I was worried that the blade might cut off her nose.

"Mr. Roulet, I'm sorry, these men just came back here."

"Lisa, I have to go," Roulet said into the phone. "I'll call you back."

He put the phone down in its cradle on the glass coffee table.

"It's okay, Robin," he said. "You can go now."

He made a dismissive gesture with the back of his hand. Robin looked at me like I was wheat she wanted to cut down with that blond blade and then left the room. I closed the door and looked back at Roulet.

"What happened?" he said. "Is it over?"

"Not by a long shot," I said.

I was carrying the state's discovery file. The weapon report was front and center. I stepped over and dropped it onto the coffee table.

"I only succeeded in embarrassing myself in the DA's office. The case against you still stands and we'll probably be going to trial."

Roulet's face dropped.

"I don't understand," he said. "You said you were going to tear that guy a new asshole."

"Turns out the only asshole in there was me. Because once again you didn't level with me."

Then, turning to look at Levin, I said, "And because you got us set up."

Roulet opened the file. On the top page was a color photograph of a knife with blood on its black handle and the tip of its blade. It was not the same knife that was photocopied in the records Levin got from his police sources and that he had showed us in the meeting in Dobbs's office the first day of the case.

"What the hell is that?" said Levin, looking down at the photo.

"That is a knife. The real one, the one Roulet had with him when he went to Reggie Campo's apartment. The one with her blood and his *initials* on it."

Levin sat down on the couch on the opposite side from Roulet. I stayed standing and they both looked up at me. I started with Levin.

"I went in to see the DA to kick his ass today and he ended up kicking mine with that. Who was your source, Raul? Because he gave you a marked deck."

"Wait a minute, wait a minute. That's not —"

"No, you wait a minute. The report you had on the knife being untraceable was bogus. It was put in there to fuck us up. To trick us and it worked perfectly, because I waltzed in there thinking I couldn't lose today and just gave him the Morgan's bar video. Just trotted it out like it was the hammer. Only it wasn't, goddamn it."

"It was the runner," Levin said.

"What?"

"The runner. The guy who runs the reports between the police station and the DA's office. I tell him which cases

I'm interested in and he makes extra copies for me."

"Well, they're onto his ass and they worked it perfectly. You better call him and tell him if he needs a good criminal defense attorney I'm not available."

I realized I was pacing in front of them on the couch but I didn't stop.

"And you," I said to Roulet. "I now get the real weapon report and find out not only is the knife a custom-made job but it is traceable right back to you because it has your fucking initials on it! You lied to me again!"

"I didn't lie," Roulet yelled back. "I tried to tell you. I said it wasn't my knife. I said it twice but nobody listened to me."

"Then you should have clarified what you meant. Just saying it wasn't your knife was like saying you didn't do it. You should have said, 'Hey, Mick, there might be a problem with the knife because I did have a knife but this picture isn't it.' What did you think, that it was just going to go away?"

"Please, can you keep it down," Roulet protested. "There might be customers out there."

"I don't care! Fuck your customers. You're not going to need customers anymore where you're going. Don't you see that this knife trumps everything we've got? You took a murder weapon to a meeting with a prostitute. The knife was no plant. It was yours. And that means we no longer have the setup. How can we claim she set you up when the prosecutor can prove you had that knife with you when you walked through the door?"

He didn't answer but I didn't give him a lot of time to.

"You fucking did this thing and they've got you," I said, pointing at him. "No wonder they didn't bother with any follow-up investigation at the bar. No follow-up needed when they've got *your* knife and *your* fingerprints in blood on it."

"I didn't do it! It's a setup. I'm TELLING YOU! It was —"

"Who's yelling now? Look, I don't care what you're telling me. I can't deal with a client who doesn't level, who doesn't see the percentage in telling his own attorney what is going on. So the DA has made an offer to you and I think you better take it."

Roulet sat up straight and grabbed the pack of cigarettes off the table. He took one out and lit it off the one he already had going.

"I'm not pleading guilty to something I didn't do," he said, his voice suddenly calm after a deep drag off the fresh smoke.

"Seven years. You'll be out in four. You have till court time Monday and then it disappears. Think about it, then tell me you want to take it."

"I won't take it. I didn't do this thing and if you won't take it to trial, then I will find somebody who will."

Levin was holding the discovery file. I reached down and rudely grabbed it out of his hands so I could read directly from the weapon report.

"You didn't do it?" I said to Roulet. "Okay, if you didn't do it, then would you mind telling me why you went to see this prostitute with a custom-made Black Ninja knife with a five-inch blade, complete with your initials engraved not once, but twice on both sides of the blade?"

Finished reading from the report, I threw it back to Levin. It went through his hands and slapped against his chest.

"Because I always carry it!"

The force of Roulet's response quieted the room. I paced back and forth once, staring at him.

"You always carry it," I said, not a question.

"That's right. I'm a realtor. I drive expensive cars. I wear expensive jewelry. And I often meet strangers alone in empty houses."

Again he gave me pause. As hyped up as I was, I still knew a glimmer when I saw one. Levin leaned forward and looked at Roulet and then at me. He saw it, too.

"What are you talking about?" I said. "You sell homes to rich people."

"How do you know they are rich when they call you up and say they want to see a place?"

I stretched my hands out in confusion.

"You must have some sort of system for checking them out, right?"

"Sure, we can run a credit report and we can ask for references. But it still comes down to what they give us and these kind of people don't like to wait. When they want to see a piece of property, they want to see it. There are a lot of realtors out there. If we don't act quickly, there will be somebody else who will."

I nodded. The glimmer was getting brighter. There might be something here I could work with.

"There have been murders, you know," Roulet said. "Over the years. Every realtor knows the danger exists when you go to some of these places alone. For a while there was somebody out there called the Real Estate Rapist. He attacked and robbed women in empty houses. My mother..."

He didn't finish. I waited. Nothing.

"What about your mother?"

Roulet hesitated before answering.

"She was showing a place in Bel-Air once. She was alone and she thought it was safe because it was Bel-Air. The man raped her. He left her tied up. When she didn't come back to the office, I went to the house. I found her."

Roulet's eyes were staring at the memory.

"How long ago was this?" I asked.

"About four years. She stopped selling after it happened. Just stayed in her office and never showed another property again. I did the selling. And that's when and why I got the knife. I've had it for four years and carry it everywhere but on planes. It was in my pocket when I went to that apartment. I didn't think anything about it."

I dropped into the chair across the table from the couch. My mind was working. I was seeing how it could work. It was still a defense that relied on coincidence. Roulet was set up by Campo and the setup was aided coincidentally when she found the knife on him after knocking him out. It could work.

"Did your mother file a police report?" Levin asked. "Was there an investigation?"

Roulet shook his head as he stubbed out his cigarette in the ashtray.

"No, she was too embarrassed. She was afraid it would get into the paper."

"Who else knows about it?" I asked.

"Uh, me . . . and Cecil I'm sure knows. Probably nobody else. You can't use this. She would —"

"I won't use it without her permission," I said. "But it could be important. I'll have to talk to her about it."

"No, I don't want you —"

"Your life and livelihood are on the line here, Louis. You get sent to prison and you're not going to make it. Don't worry about your mother. A mother will do what she has to do to protect her young."

Roulet looked down and shook his head.

"I don't know . . ." he said.

I exhaled, trying to lose all my tension with the breath. Disaster may have been averted.

"I know one thing," I said. "I'm going to go back to the DA and say pass on the deal. We'll go to trial and take our chances."

SIXTEEN

The hits kept coming. The other shoe didn't drop on the prosecution's case until after I'd dropped Earl off at the commuter lot where he parked his own car every morning and I drove the Lincoln back to Van Nuys and Four Green Fields. It was a shotgun pub on Victory Boulevard — maybe that was why lawyers liked the place — with the bar running down the left side and a row of scarred wooden booths down the right. It was crowded as only an Irish bar can be the night of St. Patrick's Day. My guess was that the crowd was swollen even bigger than in previous years because of the fact that the drinker's holiday fell on a Thursday and many revelers were kicking off a long weekend. I had made sure my own calendar was clear on Friday. I always clear the day after St. Pat's.

As I started to fight my way through the mass in search of Maggie McPherson, the required "Danny Boy" started blaring from a jukebox somewhere in the back. But it was a punk rock version from the early eighties and its driving beat obliterated any chance I had of hearing anything when I saw familiar faces and said hello or asked if they had seen my ex-wife. The small snippets of conversation I overheard as I pushed through seemed to all be about Robert Blake and the stunning verdict handed down the day before.

I ran into Robert Gillen in the crowd. The cameraman reached into his pocket and pulled out four crisp hundred-dollar bills and handed them to me. The bills were probably four of the original ten I had paid him two weeks earlier in the Van Nuys courthouse as I tried to impress Cecil Dobbs with my media manipulation skills. I had already expensed the thousand to Roulet. The four hundred was profit.

"I thought I'd run into you here," he yelled in my ear.

"Thanks, Sticks," I replied. "It'll go toward my bar tab."

He laughed. I looked past him into the crowd for my ex-wife.

"Anytime, my man," he said.

He slapped me on the shoulder as I squeezed by him and pushed on. I finally found Maggie in the last booth in the back. It was full of six women, all prosecutors or secretaries from the Van Nuys office. Most I knew at least in passing but the scene was awkward because I had to stand and yell over the music and the crowd. Plus the fact that they were prosecutors and viewed me as being in league with the devil. They had two pitchers of Guinness on the table and one was full. But my chances of getting through the crowd to the bar to get a glass were negligible. Maggie noticed my plight and offered to share her glass with me.

"It's all right," she yelled. "We've swapped spit before."

I smiled and knew the two pitchers on the table had not been the first two. I took a long drink and it tasted good. Guinness always gave me a solid center.

Maggie was in the middle on the left side of the booth and between two young prosecutors whom I knew she had taken under her wing. In the Van Nuys office, many of the younger females gravitated toward my ex-wife because the man in charge, Smithson, surrounded himself with attorneys like Minton.

Still standing at the side of the booth, I raised the glass in toast to her but she couldn't respond because I had her glass. She reached over and raised the pitcher.

"Cheers!"

She didn't go so far as to drink from the pitcher. She put it down and whispered to the woman on the outside of the booth. She got up to let Maggie out. My ex-wife stood up and kissed me on the cheek and said, "It's always easier for a lady to get a glass in these sorts of situations."

"Especially beautiful ladies," I said.

She gave me one of her looks and turned toward the crowd that was five deep between us and the bar. She whistled shrilly and it caught the attention of one of the pure-bred Irish guys who worked the tap handles and could etch a harp or an angel or a naked lady in the foam at the top of the glass.

"I need a pint glass," she yelled.

The bartender had to read her lips. And like a teenager being passed over the heads of the crowd at a Pearl Jam concert, a clean glass made its way back to us hand to hand. She filled it from the freshest pitcher on the booth's table and then we clicked glasses.

"So," she said. "Are you feeling a little better than when I saw you today?"

I nodded.

"A little."

"Did Minton sandbag you?"

I nodded again.

"Him *and* the cops did, yeah."

"With that guy Corliss? I told them he was full of shit. They all are."

I didn't respond and tried to act like what she had just said was not news to me and that Corliss was a name I already knew. I took a long and slow drink from my glass.

"I guess I shouldn't have said that," she said. "But my opinion doesn't matter. If Minton is dumb enough to use him, then you'll take the guy's head off, I'm sure."

I guessed that she was talking about a witness. But I had

seen nothing in my review of the discovery file that mentioned a witness named Corliss. The fact that it was a witness she didn't trust led me further to believe that Corliss was a snitch. Most likely a jailhouse snitch.

"How come you know about him?" I finally asked. "Minton talked to you about him?"

"No, I'm the one who sent him to Minton. Doesn't matter what I think of what he said, it was my duty to send him to the right prosecutor and it was up to Minton to evaluate him."

"I mean, why did he come to you?"

She frowned at me because the answer was so obvious.

"Because I handled the first appearance. He was there in the pen. He thought the case was still mine."

Now I understood. Corliss was a *C*. Roulet was taken out of alphabetical order and called first. Corliss must have been in the group of inmates taken into the courtroom with him. He had seen Maggie and me argue over Roulet's bail. He therefore thought Maggie still had the case. He must have made a snitch call to her.

"When did he call you?" I asked.

"I am telling you too much, Haller. I'm not —"

"Just tell me when he called you. That hearing was on a Monday, so was it later that day?"

The case did not make any notice in the newspapers or on TV. So I was curious as to where Corliss would have gotten the information he was trying to trade to prosecutors. I had to assume it didn't come from Roulet. I was pretty sure I had scared him silent. Without a media information point, Corliss would have been left with the information gleaned in court when the charges were read and Maggie and I argued bail.

It was enough, I realized. Maggie had been specific in detailing Regina Campo's injuries as she was trying to impress the judge to hold Roulet without bail. If Corliss had been in court, he'd have been privy to all the details he would need to make up a jailhouse confession from my client. Add that to his proximity to Roulet and a jailhouse snitch is born.

"Yes, he called me late Monday," Maggie finally answered.

"So why did you think he was full of shit? He's done it before, hasn't he? The guy's a professional snitch, right?"

I was fishing and she knew it. She shook her head.

"I am sure you will find out all you need to know during discovery. Can we just have a friendly pint of Guinness here? I have to leave in about an hour."

I nodded but wanted to know more.

"Tell you what," I said. "You've probably had enough Guinness for one St. Patrick's Day. How about we get out of here and get something to eat?"

"Why, so you can keep asking me about your case?"

"No, so we can talk about our daughter."

Her eyes narrowed.

"Is something wrong?" she asked.

"Not that I know of. But I want to talk to you about her."

"Where are you taking me to dinner?"

I mentioned an expensive Italian restaurant on Ventura in Sherman Oaks and her eyes got warm. It had been a place we had gone to celebrate anniversaries and getting pregnant. Our apartment, which she still had, was a few blocks away on Dickens.

"Think we can eat there in an hour?" she asked.

"If we leave right now and order without looking."

"You're on. Let me just say some quick good-byes."

"I'll drive."

And it was a good thing I drove because she was unsteady on her feet. We had to walk hip to hip to the Lincoln and then I helped her get in.

I took Van Nuys south to Ventura. After a few moments

Maggie reached beneath her legs and pulled out a CD case she had been uncomfortably sitting on. It was Earl's. One of the CDs he listened to on the car stereo when I was in court. It saved juice on his iPod. The CD was by a dirty south performer named Ludacris.

"No wonder I was so uncomfortable," she said. "Is this what you're listening to while driving between courthouses?"

"Actually, no. That's Earl's. He's been doing the driving lately. Ludacris isn't really to my liking. I'm more of an old school guy. Tupac and Dre and people like that."

She laughed because she thought I was kidding. A few minutes later we drove down the narrow alley that led to the door of the restaurant. A valet took the car and we went in. The hostess recognized us and acted like it had only been a couple weeks since the last time we had been in. The truth was, we had probably both been in there recently, but each with other partners.

I asked for a bottle of Singe Shiraz and we ordered pasta dishes without looking at a menu. We skipped salads and appetizers and told the waiter not to delay bringing the food out. After he left I checked my watch and saw we still had forty-five minutes. Plenty of time.

The Guinness was catching up with Maggie. She smiled in a fractured sort of way that told me she was drunk. Beautifully drunk. She never got mean under a buzz. She always got sweeter. It was probably how we'd ended up having a child together.

"You should probably lay off the wine," I told her. "Or you'll have a headache tomorrow."

"Don't worry about me. I'll lay what I want and lay off what I want."

She smiled at me and I smiled back.

"So how you been, Haller? I mean really."

"Fine. You? And I mean really."

"Never better. Are you past Lorna now?"

"Yeah, we're even friends."

"And what are we?"

"I don't know. Sometimes adversaries, I guess."

She shook her head.

"We can't be adversaries if we can't stay on the same case together. Besides, I'm always looking out for you. Like with that dirtbag, Corliss."

"Thanks for trying, but he still did the damage."

"I just have no respect for a prosecutor who would use a jailhouse snitch. Doesn't matter that your client is an even bigger dirtbag."

"He wouldn't tell me exactly what Corliss said my guy said."

"What are you talking about?"

"He just said he had a snitch. He wouldn't reveal what he said."

"That's not fair."

"That's what I said. It's a discovery issue but we don't get a judge assigned until after the arraignment Monday. So there's nobody I can really complain to yet. Minton knows that. It's like you warned me. He doesn't play fair."

Her cheeks flushed. I had pushed the right buttons and she was angry. For Maggie, winning fair was the only way to win. That was why she was a good prosecutor.

We were sitting at the end of the banquette that ran along the back wall of the restaurant. We were on both sides of a corner. Maggie leaned toward me but went too far and we banged heads. She laughed but then tried again. She spoke in a low voice.

"He said that he asked your guy what he was in for and your guy said, 'For giving a bitch exactly what she deserved.' He said your client told him he punched her out as soon as she opened her door."

She leaned back and I could tell she had moved too

quickly, bringing on a swoon of vertigo.

"You okay?"

"Yes, but can we change the subject? I don't want to talk about work anymore. There are too many assholes and it's too frustrating."

"Sure."

Just then the waiter brought our wine and our dinners at the same time. The wine was good and the food was like home comfort. We started out eating quietly. Then Maggie hit me with a pitch right out of the blue.

"You didn't know anything about Corliss, did you? Not till I opened my big mouth."

"I knew Minton was hiding something. I thought it was a jailhouse —"

"Bullshit. You got me drunk so you could find out what I knew."

"Uh, I think you were already drunk when I hooked up with you tonight."

She was poised with her fork up over her plate, a long string of linguine with pesto sauce hanging off it. She then pointed the fork at me.

"Good point. So what about our daughter?"

I wasn't expecting her to remember that. I shrugged.

"I think what you said last week is right. She needs her father more in her life."

"And?"

"And I want to play a bigger part. I like watching her. Like when I took her to that movie on Saturday. I was sort of sitting sideways so I could watch her watching the movie. Watch her eyes, you know?"

"Welcome to the club."

"So I don't know. I was thinking maybe we should set up a schedule, you know? Like make it a regular thing. She could even stay overnight sometimes — I mean, if she wanted."

"Are you sure about all of that? This is new from you."

"It's new because I didn't know about it before. When she was smaller and I couldn't really communicate with her, I didn't really know what to do with her. I felt awkward. Now I don't. I like talking to her. Being with her. I learn more from her than she does from me, that's for sure."

I suddenly felt her hand on my leg under the table.

"This is great," she said. "I am so happy to hear you say that. But let's move slow. You haven't been around her much for four years and I am not going to let her build up her hopes only to have you pull a disappearing act."

"I understand. We can take it any way you want. I'm just telling you I am going to be there. I promise."

She smiled, wanting to believe. And I made the same promise I just made to her to myself.

"Well, great," she said. "I'm really glad you want to do this. Let's get a calendar and work out some dates and see how it goes."

She took her hand away and we continued eating in silence until we both had almost finished. Then Maggie surprised me once again.

"I don't think I can drive my car tonight," she said.

I nodded.

"I was thinking the same thing."

"You seem all right. You only had half a pint at —"

"No, I mean I was thinking the same thing about you. But don't worry, I'll drive you home."

"Thank you."

Then she reached across the table and put her hand on my wrist.

"And will you take me back to get my car in the morning?"

She smiled sweetly at me. I looked at her, trying to read this woman who had told me to hit the road four years before. The woman I had never been able to get by or get over, whose rejection sent me reeling into a relationship I knew from the beginning couldn't go the distance.

"Sure," I said. "I'll take you."

SEVENTEEN

In the morning I awoke to find my eight-year-old daughter sleeping between me and my ex-wife. Light was leaking in from a cathedral window high up on the wall. When I had lived here that window had always bothered me because it let in too much light too early in the mornings. Looking up at the pattern it threw on the inclined ceiling, I reviewed what had happened the night before and remembered that I had ended up drinking all but one glass of the bottle of wine at the restaurant. I remembered taking Maggie home to the apartment and coming in to find our daughter had already fallen asleep for the night — in her own bed.

After the babysitter had been released, Maggie opened another bottle of wine. When we finished it she took me by the hand and led me to the bedroom we had shared for four years, but not in four years. What bothered me now was that my memory had absorbed all the wine and I could not remember whether it had been a triumphant return to the bedroom or a failure. I also could not remember what words had been spoken, what promises had possibly been made.

"This is not fair to her."

I turned my head on the pillow. Maggie was awake. She was looking at our sleeping daughter's angelic face.

"What isn't fair?"

"Her waking up and finding you here. She might get her hopes up or just get the wrong idea."

"How'd she get in here?"

"I carried her in. She had a nightmare."

"How often does she have nightmares?"

"Usually, when she sleeps alone. In her room."

"So she sleeps in here all the time?"

Something about my tone bothered her.

"Don't start. You have no idea what it's like to raise a child by yourself."

"I know. I'm not saying anything. So what do you want me to do, leave before she wakes up? I could get dressed and act like I just came by to get you and drive you back to your car."

"I don't know. Get dressed for now. Try not to wake her up."

I slipped out of the bed, grabbed my clothes and went down the hall to the guest bathroom. I was confused by how much Maggie's demeanor toward me had changed overnight. Alcohol, I decided. Or maybe something I did or said after we'd gotten back to the apartment. I quickly got dressed and went back up the hallway to the bedroom and peeked in.

Hayley was still asleep. With her arms spread across two pillows she looked like an angel with wings. Maggie was pulling a long-sleeve T-shirt over an old pair of sweats she'd had since back when we were married. I walked in and stepped over to her.

"I'm going to go and come back," I whispered.

"What?" she said with annoyance. "I thought we were going to get the car."

"But I thought you didn't want her to wake up and see me. So let me go and I'll have some coffee or something and be back in an hour. We can all go together and get your car and then I'll take Hayley to school. I'll even pick her up later if you want. My calendar's clear today."

"Just like that? You're going to start driving her to school?"

"She's my daughter. Don't you remember anything I told you last night?"

She shifted the line of her jaw and I knew from experience that this was when the heavy artillery came out. I was missing something. Maggie had shifted gears.

"Well, yes, but I thought you were just saying that," she said.

"What do you mean?"

"I just thought you were trying to get into my head on your case or just plain get me into bed. I don't know."

I laughed and shook my head. Any fantasies about us that I'd had the night before were vanishing quickly.

"I wasn't the one who led the other up the steps to the bedroom," I said.

"Oh, so it was really about the case. You wanted what I knew about your case."

I just stared at her for a long moment.

"I can't win with you, can I?"

"Not when you're underhanded, when you act like a criminal defense attorney."

She was always the better of the two of us when it came to verbal knife throwing. The truth was, I was thankful we had a built-in conflict of interest and I would never have to face her in trial. Over the years some people — mostly defense pros who suffered at her hands — had gone so far as to say that was the reason I had married her. To avoid her professionally.

"Tell you what," I said. "I'll be back in an hour. If you want a ride to the car that you were too drunk to drive last night, be ready and have her ready."

"It's okay. We'll take a cab."

"I will drive you."

"No, we'll take a cab. And keep your voice down."

I looked over at my daughter, still asleep despite her parents' verbal sparring.

"What about her? Do you want me to take her tomorrow or Sunday?"

"I don't know. Call me tomorrow."

"Fine. Good-bye."

I left her there in the bedroom. Outside the apartment building I walked a block and a half down Dickens before finding the Lincoln parked awkwardly against the curb. There was a ticket on the windshield citing me for parking next to a fire hydrant. I got in the car and threw it into the backseat. I'd deal with it the next time I was riding back there. I wouldn't be like Louis Roulet, letting my tickets go to warrant. There was a county full of cops out there who would love to book me on a warrant.

Fighting always made me hungry and I realized I was starved. I worked my way back to Ventura and headed toward Studio City. It was early, especially for the morning after St. Patrick's Day, and I got to the DuPar's by Laurel Canyon Boulevard before it was crowded. I got a booth in the back and ordered a short stack of pancakes and coffee. I tried to forget about Maggie McFierce by opening up my briefcase and pulling out a legal pad and the Roulet files.

Before diving into the files I made a call to Raul Levin, waking him up at his home in Glendale.

"I've got something for you to do," I said.

"Can't this wait till Monday? I just got home a couple hours ago. I was going to start the weekend today."

"No, it can't wait and you owe me one after yesterday. Besides, you're not even Irish. I need you to background somebody."

"All right, wait a minute."

I heard him put down the phone while he probably grabbed pen and paper to take notes.

"Okay, go ahead."

"There's a guy named Corliss who was arraigned right after Roulet back on the seventh. He was in the first group out and they were in the holding pen at the same time. He's now trying to snitch Roulet off and I want to know everything there is to know about the guy so I can put his dick in the dirt."

"Got a first name?"

"Nope."

"Do you know what he's in there for?"

"No, and I don't even know if he is still in there."

"Thanks for the help. What's he saying Roulet told him?"

"That he beat up some bitch who had it coming. Words to that effect."

"Okay, what else you got?"

"That's it other than I got a tip that he's a repeat snitch. Find out who he's crapped on in the past and there might be something there I can use. Go back as far as you can go with this guy. The DA's people usually don't. They're afraid of what they might find. They'd rather be ignorant."

"Okay, I'll get on it."

"Let me know when you know."

I closed the phone just as my pancakes arrived. I doused them liberally with maple syrup and started eating while looking through the file containing the state's discovery.

The weapon report remained the only surprise. Everything else in the file, except the color photos, I had already seen in Levin's file.

I moved on to that. As expected with a contract investigator, Levin had larded the file with everything found in the net he had cast. He even had copies of the parking tickets and speeding citations Roulet had accumulated and failed to pay in recent years. It annoyed me at first because there was so much to weed through to get to what was going to be germane to Roulet's defense.

I was nearly through it all when the waitress swung by my booth with a coffee pot, looking to refill my mug. She recoiled when she saw the battered face of Reggie Campo in one of the color photos I had put to the side of the files.

"Sorry about that," I said.

I covered the photo with one of the files and signaled her back. The waitress came back hesitantly and poured the coffee.

"It's work," I said in feeble explanation. "I didn't mean to do that to you."

"All I can say is I hope you get the bastard that did that to her."

I nodded. She thought I was a cop. Probably because I hadn't shaved in twenty-four hours.

"I'm working on it," I said.

She went away and I went back to the file. As I slid the photo of Reggie Campo out from underneath it I saw the undamaged side of her face first. The left side. Something struck me and I held the file in position so that I was only looking at the good half of her face. The wave of familiarity came over me again. But again I could not place its origin. I knew this woman looked like another woman I knew or was at least familiar with. But who?

I also knew it was going to bother me until I figured it out. I thought about it for a long time, sipping my coffee and drumming my fingers on the table, and then decided to try something. I took the face shot of Campo and folded it lengthwise down the middle so that one side of the crease showed the damaged right side of her face and the other showed the unblemished left side. I then slipped the folded photo into the inside pocket of my jacket and got up from the booth.

There was no one in the restroom. I quickly went to the sink and took out the folded photo. I leaned over the sink and held the crease of the photo against the mirror with the undamaged side of Reggie Campo's face on display. The mirror reflected the image, creating a full and undamaged face. I stared at it for a long time and then finally realized why the face was familiar.

"Martha Renteria," I said.

The door to the restroom suddenly burst open and two teenagers stormed in, their hands already tugging on their zippers. I quickly pulled the photo back from the mirror and shoved it inside my jacket. I turned and walked toward the door. I heard them burst into laughter as I left. I couldn't imagine what it was they thought I was doing.

Back at the booth I gathered my files and photos and put them all back into my briefcase. I left a more than adequate amount of cash on the table for tab and tip and left the restaurant in a hurry. I felt like I was having a strange food reaction. My face felt flushed and I was hot under the collar. I thought I could hear my heart pounding beneath my shirt.

Fifteen minutes later I was parked in front of my storage warehouse on Oxnard Avenue in North Hollywood. I have a fifteen-hundred-square-foot space behind a double-wide garage door. The place is owned by a man whose son I defended on a possession case, getting him out of jail and into pretrial intervention. In lieu of a fee, the father gave me the warehouse rent-free for a year. But his son the drug addict kept getting into trouble and I kept getting free years of warehouse rent.

I keep the boxes of files from dead cases in the warehouse as well as two other Lincoln Town Cars. Last year when I was flush I bought four Lincolns at once so I could get a fleet rate. The plan was to use each one until it hit sixty thousand on the odometer and then dump it on a limousine service to be used to ferry travelers to and from the airport. The plan was working out so far. I was on the second Lincoln and it would soon be time for the third.

Once I got one of the garage doors up I went to the archival area, where the file boxes were arranged by year on industrial shelving. I found the section of shelves for boxes from two years earlier and ran my finger down the list of client names written on the side of each box until I found the name Jesus Menendez.

I pulled the box off the shelf and squatted down and opened it on the floor. The Menendez case had been short-lived. He took a plea early, before the DA pulled it back off the table. So there were only four files and these mostly contained copies of the documents relating to the police investigation. I paged through the files looking for photographs and finally saw what I was looking for in the third file.

Martha Renteria was the woman Jesus Menendez had pleaded guilty to murdering. She was a twenty-four-year-old dancer who had a dark beauty and a smile of big white teeth. She had been found stabbed to death in her Panorama City apartment. She had been beaten before she was stabbed and her facial injuries were to the left side of her face, the opposite of Reggie Campo. I found the close-up shot of her face contained in the autopsy report. Once more I folded the photo lengthwise, one side of her face damaged, one side untouched.

On the floor I took the two folded photographs, one of Reggie and one of Martha, and fitted them together along the fold lines. Putting aside the fact that one woman was dead and one wasn't, the half faces damn near formed a perfect match. The two women looked so much alike they could have passed for sisters.

EIGHTEEN

Jesus Menendez was serving a life sentence in San Quentin because he had wiped his penis on a bathroom towel. No matter how you looked at it, that is what it really came down to. That towel had been his biggest mistake.

Sitting spread-legged on the concrete floor of my warehouse, the contents of Menendez files fanned out around me, I was reacquainting myself with the facts of the case I had worked two years before. Menendez was convicted of killing Martha Renteria after following her home to Panorama City from a strip club in East Hollywood called The Cobra Room. He raped her and then stabbed her more than fifty times, causing so much blood to leave her body that it seeped through the bed and formed a puddle on the wood floor below it. In another day it seeped through cracks in the floor and formed a drip from the ceiling in the apartment below. That is when the police were called.

The case against Menendez was formidable but circumstantial. He had also hurt himself by admitting to police — before I was on the case — that he had been in her apartment on the night of the murder. But it was the DNA on the fluffy pink towel in the victim's bathroom that ultimately did him in. It couldn't be neutralized. It was a spinning plate that couldn't be knocked down. Defense pros call a piece of evidence like this the iceberg because it is the evidence that sinks the ship.

I had taken on the Menendez murder case as what I

would call a "lost leader." Menendez had no money to pay for the kind of time and effort it would take to mount a thorough defense but the case had garnered substantial publicity and I was willing to trade my time and work for the free advertising. Menendez had come to me because just a few months before his arrest I had successfully defended his older brother Fernando in a heroin case. At least in my opinion I had been successful. I had gotten a possession and sales charge knocked down to a simple possession. He got probation instead of prison.

Those good efforts resulted in Fernando calling me on the night Jesus was arrested for the murder of Martha Renteria. Jesus had gone to the Van Nuys Division to voluntarily talk to detectives. A drawing of his face had been shown on every television channel in the city and was getting heavy rotation in particular on the Spanish channels. He had told his family that he would go to the detectives to straighten things out and be back. But he never came back, so his brother called me. I told the brother that the lesson to be learned was never to go to the detectives to straighten things out until after you've consulted an attorney.

I had already seen numerous television news reports on the murder of the exotic dancer, as Renteria had been labeled, when Menendez's brother called me. The reports had included the police artist's drawing of the Latin male believed to have followed her from the club. I knew that the pre-arrest media interest meant the case would likely be carried forward in the public consciousness by the television news and I might be able to get a good ride out of it. I agreed to take the case on the come line. For free. Pro bono. For the good of the system. Besides, murder cases are few and far between. I take them when I can get them. Menendez was the twelfth accused murderer I had defended. The first eleven were still in prison but none of them were on death row. I considered that a good record.

By the time I got to Menendez in a holding cell at Van Nuys Division, he had already given a statement that implicated him to the police. He had told detectives Howard Kurlen and Don Crafton that he had not followed Renteria home, as suggested by the news reports, but had been an invited guest to her apartment. He explained that earlier in the day he had won eleven hundred dollars on the California lotto and had been willing to trade some of it to Renteria for some of her attention. He said that at her apartment they had engaged in consensual sex — although he did not use those words — and that when he left she was alive and five hundred dollars in cash richer.

The holes Kurlen and Crafton punched in Menendez's story were many. First of all, there had been no state lotto on the day of or day before the murder and the neighborhood mini-market where he said he had cashed his winning ticket had no record of paying out an eleven-hundred-dollar win to Menendez or anyone else. Additionally, no more than eighty dollars in cash was found in the victim's apartment. And lastly, the autopsy report indicated that bruising and other damage to the interior of the victim's vagina precluded what could be considered consensual sexual relations. The medical examiner concluded that she had been brutally raped.

No fingerprints other than the victim's were found in the apartment. The place had been wiped clean. No semen was found in the victim's body, indicating her rapist had used a condom or had not ejaculated during the assault. But in the bathroom off the bedroom where the attack and murder had taken place, a crime scene investigator using a black light found a small amount of semen on a pink towel hanging on a rack near the toilet. The theory that came into play was that after the rape and murder the killer had stepped into the bathroom, removed the condom and flushed it down the toilet. He had then wiped his penis with the nearby towel and then hung the towel back on the rack. When cleaning up after the crime and wiping surfaces he might have touched, he forgot about that towel.

The investigators kept the discovery of the DNA deposit and their attendant theory secret. It never made it into the media. It would become Kurlen and Crafton's hole card.

Based on Menendez's lies and the admission that he had been in the victim's apartment, he was arrested on suspicion of murder and held without bail. Detectives got a search warrant, and oral swabs were collected from Menendez and sent to the lab for DNA typing and comparison to the DNA recovered from the bathroom towel.

That was about when I entered the case. As they say in my profession, by then the *Titanic* had already left the dock. The iceberg was out there waiting. Menendez had badly hurt himself by talking — and lying — to the detectives. Still, unaware of the DNA comparison that was under way, I saw a glimmer of light for Jesus Menendez. There was a case to be made for neutralizing his interview with detectives — which, by the way, became a full-blown confession by the time it got reported by the media. Menendez was Mexican born and had come to this country at age eight. His family spoke only Spanish at home and he had attended a school for Spanish speakers until dropping out at age fourteen. He spoke only rudimentary English, and his cognition level of the language seemed to me to be even lower than his speaking level. Kurlen and Crafton made no effort to bring in a translator and, according to the taped interview, not once asked if Menendez even wanted one.

This was the crack I would work my way into. The

interview was the foundation of the case against Menendez. It was the spinning platter. If I could knock it down most of the other plates would come down with it. My plan was to attack the interview as a violation of Menendez's rights because he could not have understood the Miranda warning he had been read by Kurlen or the document listing these rights in English that he had signed at the detective's request.

This is where the case stood until two weeks after Menendez's arrest when the lab results came back matching his DNA to that found on the towel in the victim's bathroom. After that the prosecution didn't need the interview or his admissions. The DNA put Menendez directly on the scene of a brutal rape and murder. I could try an O.J. defense — attack the credibility of the DNA match. But prosecutors and lab techs had learned so much from that debacle and in the years since that I knew I was unlikely of prevailing with a jury. The DNA was the iceberg and the momentum of the ship made it impossible to steer around it in time.

The district attorney himself revealed the DNA findings at a press conference and announced that his office would seek the death penalty for Menendez. He added that detectives had also located three eyewitnesses who had seen Menendez throw a knife into the Los Angeles River. The DA said the river was searched for the weapon but it was not recovered. Regardless, he characterized the witness accounts as solid — they were Menendez's three roommates.

Based on the prosecution's case coming together and the threat of the death penalty, I decided the O.J. defense would be too risky. Using Fernando Menendez as my translator, I went to the Van Nuys jail and told Jesus that his only hope was for a deal the DA had floated by me. If Menendez would plead guilty to murder I could get him a life sentence with the possibility of parole. I told him he'd be out in fifteen years. I told him it was the only way.

It was a tearful discussion. Both brothers cried and beseeched me to find another way. Jesus insisted that he did not kill Martha Renteria. He said he had lied to the detectives to protect Fernando, who had given him the money after a good month selling tar heroin. Jesus thought that revealing his brother's generosity would lead to another investigation of Fernando and his possible arrest.

The brothers urged me to investigate the case. Jesus told me Renteria had had other suitors that night in The Cobra Room. The reason he had paid her so much money was because she had played him off another bidder for her services.

Lastly, Jesus told me it was true that he had thrown a knife into the river but it was because he was afraid. It wasn't the murder weapon. It was just a knife he used on day jobs he picked up in Pacoima. It looked like the knife they were describing on the Spanish channel and he got rid of it before going to the police to straighten things out.

I listened and then told them that none of their explanations mattered. The only thing that mattered was the DNA. Jesus had a choice. He could take the fifteen years or go to trial and risk getting the death penalty or life *without* the possibility of parole. I reminded Jesus that he was a young man. He could be out by age forty. He could still have a life.

By the time I left the jailhouse meeting, I had Jesus Menendez's consent to make the deal. I only saw him one more time after that. At his plea-and-sentencing hearing when I stood next to him in front of the judge and coached him through the guilty plea. He was shipped off to Pelican Bay initially and then down to San Quentin after that. I had heard through the courthouse grapevine that his brother had gotten himself popped again — this time for using heroin. But he didn't call me. He went with a different lawyer and I didn't have to wonder why.

On the warehouse floor I opened the report on the autopsy of Martha Renteria. I was looking for two specific things that had probably not been looked at very closely by anyone else before. The case was closed. It was a dead file. Nobody cared anymore.

The first was the part of the report that dealt with the fifty-three stab wounds Renteria suffered during the attack on her bed. Under the heading "Wound Profile" the unknown weapon was described as a blade no longer than five inches and no wider than an inch. Its thickness was placed at one-eighth of an inch. Also noted in the report was the occurrence of jagged skin tears at the top of the victim's wounds, indicating that the top of the blade had an uneven line, to wit, it was designed as a weapon that would inflict damage going in as well as coming out. The shortness of the blade suggested that the weapon might be a folding knife.

There was a crude drawing in the report that depicted the outline of the blade without a handle. It looked familiar to me. I pulled my briefcase across the floor from where I had put it down and opened it up. From the state's discovery file I pulled the photo of the open folding knife with Louis Roulet's initials etched on the blade. I compared the blade to the outline drawn on the page in the autopsy report. It wasn't an exact match but it was damn close.

I then pulled out the recovered weapon analysis report and read the same paragraph I had read during the meeting in Roulet's office the day before. The knife was described as a custom-made Black Ninja folding knife with a blade measuring five inches long, one inch wide and one-eighth of an inch thick — the same measurements belonging to the unknown knife used to kill Martha

Renteria. The knife Jesus Menendez supposedly threw into the L.A. River.

I knew that a five-inch blade wasn't unique. Nothing was conclusive but my instincts told me I was moving toward something. I tried not to let the burn that was building in my chest and throat distract me. I tried to stay on point. I moved on. I needed to check for a specific wound but I didn't want to look at the photos contained in the back of the report, the photos that coldly documented the horribly violated body of Martha Renteria. Instead I went to the page that had two side-by-side generic body profiles, one for the front and one for the back. On these the medical examiner had marked the wounds and numbered them. Only the front profile had been used. Dots and numbers 1 through 53. It looked like a macabre connect-the-dots puzzle and I didn't doubt that Kurlen or some detective looking for anything in the days before Menendez walked in had connected them, hoping the killer had left his initials or some other bizarre clue behind.

I studied the front profile's neck and saw two dots on either side of the neck. They were numbered 1 and 2. I turned the page and looked at the list of individual wound descriptions.

The description for wound number 1 read: *Superficial puncture on the lower right neck with ante-mortem histamine levels, indicative of coercive wound.*

The description for wound number 2 read: *Superficial puncture on the lower left neck with ante-mortem histamine levels, indicative of coercive wound. This puncture measures 1 cm larger than wound No. 1.*

The descriptions meant the wounds had been inflicted while Martha Renteria was still alive. And that was likely why they had been the first wounds listed and described. The examiner had suggested it was likely that the wounds resulted from a knife being held to the victim's neck in a coercive manner. It was the killer's method of controlling her.

I turned back to the state's discovery file for the Campo case. I pulled the photographs of Reggie Campo and the report on her physical examination at Holy Cross Medical Center. Campo had a small puncture wound on the lower left side of her neck and no wounds on her right side. I next scanned through her statement to the police until I found the part in which she described how she got the wound. She said that her attacker pulled her up off the floor of the living room and told her to lead him toward the bedroom. He controlled her from behind by gripping the bra strap across her back with his right hand and holding the knife point against the left side of her neck with his left hand. When she felt him momentarily rest his wrist on her shoulder she made her move, suddenly pivoting and pushing backwards, knocking her attacker into a large floor vase, and then breaking away.

I thought I understood now why Reggie Campo had only one wound on her neck, compared with the two Martha Renteria ended up with. If Campo's attacker had gotten her to the bedroom and put her down on the bed, he would have been facing her when he climbed on top of her. If he kept his knife in the same hand — the left — the blade would shift to the other side of her neck. When they found her dead in the bed, she'd have coercive punctures on both sides of her neck.

I put the files aside and sat cross-legged on the floor without moving for a long time. My thoughts were whispers in the darkness inside. In my mind I held the image of Jesus Menendez's tear-streaked face when he had told me that he was innocent — when he'd begged me to believe him — and I had told him that he must plead guilty. It had been more than legal advice I was dispensing.

He had no money, no defense and no chance — in that order — and I told him he had no choice. And though ultimately it was his decision and from his mouth that the word *guilty* was uttered in front of the judge, it felt to me now as though it had been me, his own attorney, holding the knife of the system against his neck and forcing him to say it.

NINETEEN

I got out of the huge new rent-a-car facility at San Francisco International by one o'clock and headed north to the city. The Lincoln they gave me smelled like it had last been used by a smoker, maybe the renter or maybe just the guy who cleaned it up for me.

I don't know how to get anywhere in San Francisco. I just know how to drive through it. Three or four times a year I need to go to the prison by the bay, San Quentin, to talk to clients or witnesses. I could tell you how to get there, no sweat. But ask me how to get to Coit Tower or Fisherman's Wharf and we have a problem.

By the time I got through the city and over the Golden Gate it was almost two. I was in good shape. I knew from past experience that attorney visiting hours ended at four.

San Quentin is over a century old and looks as though the soul of every prisoner who lived or died there is etched on its dark walls. It was as foreboding a prison as I had ever visited, and at one time or another I had been to every one in California.

They searched my briefcase and made me go through a metal detector. After that they still passed a wand over me to make extra sure. Even then I wasn't allowed direct contact with Menendez because I had not formally scheduled the interview the required five days in advance. So I was put in a no-contact room — a Plexiglas wall between us with dime-size holes to speak through. I showed the guard the six-pack of photos I wanted to give

Menendez and he told me I would have to show him the pictures through the Plexiglas. I sat down, put the photos away and didn't have to wait long until they brought Menendez in on the other side of the glass.

Two years ago, when he was shipped off to prison, Jesus Menendez had been a young man. Now he looked like he was already the forty years old I told him he could beat if he pleaded guilty. He looked at me with eyes as dead as the gravel stones out in the parking lot. He saw me and sat down reluctantly. He didn't have much use for me anymore.

We didn't bother with hellos and I got right into it.

"Look, Jesus, I don't have to ask you how you've been. I know. But something's come up and it could affect your case. I need to ask you a few questions. You understand me?"

"Why questions now, man? You had no questions before."

I nodded.

"You're right. I should've asked you more questions back then and I didn't. I didn't know then what I know now. Or at least what I think I know now. I am trying to make things right."

"What do you want?"

"I want you to tell me about that night at The Cobra Room."

He shrugged.

"The girl was there and I talked. She tol' me to follow her home."

He shrugged again.

"I went to her place, man, but I didn't kill her like that."

"Go back to the club. You told me that you had to impress the girl, that you had to show her the money and you spent more than you wanted to. You remember?"

"Is right."

"You said there was another guy trying to get with her. You remember that?"

"Si, he was there talking. She went to him but she came back to me."

"You had to pay her more, right?"

"Like that."

"Okay, do you remember that guy? If you saw a picture of him, would you remember him?"

"The guy who talked big? I think I 'member."

"Okay."

I opened my briefcase and took out the spread of mug shots. There were six photos and they included the booking photo of Louis Ross Roulet and five other men whose mug shots I had culled out of my archive boxes. I stood up and one by one started holding them up on the glass. I thought that by spreading my fingers I would be able to hold all six against the glass. Menendez stood up to look closely at the photos.

Almost immediately a voice boomed from an overhead speaker.

"Step back from the glass. Both of you step back from the glass and remain seated or the interview will be terminated."

I shook my head and cursed. I gathered the photos together and sat down. Menendez sat back down as well.

"Guard!" I said loudly.

I looked at Menendez and waited. The guard didn't enter the room.

"Guard!" I called again, louder.

Finally, the door opened and the guard stepped into my side of the interview room.

"You done?"

"No. I need him to look at these photos."

I held up the stack.

"Show him through the glass. He's not allowed to receive anything from you."

"But I'm going to take them right back."

"Doesn't matter. You can't give him anything."

"But if you don't let him come to the glass, how is he going to see them?"

"It's not my problem."

I waved in surrender.

"All right, okay. Then can you stay here for a minute?"

"What for?"

"I want you to watch this. I'm going to show him the photos and if he makes an ID, I want you to witness it."

"Don't drag me into your bullshit."

He walked to the door and left.

"Goddamn it," I said.

I looked at Menendez.

"All right, Jesus, I'm going to show you, anyway. See if you recognize any of them from where you are sitting."

One by one I held the photos up about a foot from the glass. Menendez leaned forward. As I showed each of the first five he looked, thought about it and then shook his head no. But on the sixth photo I saw his eyes flare. It seemed as though there was some life in them after all.

"That one," he said. "Is him."

I turned the photo toward me to be sure. It was Roulet.

"I 'member," Menendez said. "He's the one."

"And you're sure?"

Menendez nodded.

"What makes you so sure?"

"Because I know. In here I think on that night all of my time."

I nodded.

"Who is the man?" he asked.

"I can't tell you right now. Just know that I am trying to get you out of here."

"What do I do?"

"What you have been doing. Sit tight, be careful and stay safe."

"Safe?"

"I know. But as soon as I have something, you will know about it. I'm trying to get you out of here, Jesus, but it might take a little while."

"You were the one who tol' me to come here."

"At the time I didn't think there was a choice."

"How come you never ask me, did you murder this girl? You my lawyer, man. You din't care. You din't listen."

I stood up and loudly called for the guard. Then I answered his question.

"To legally defend you I didn't need to know the answer to that question. If I asked my clients if they were guilty of the crimes they were charged with, very few would tell me the truth. And if they did, I might not be able to defend them to the best of my ability."

The guard opened the door and looked in at me.

"I'm ready to go," I said.

I checked my watch and figured that if I was lucky in traffic I might be able to catch the five o'clock shuttle back to Burbank. The six o'clock at the latest. I dropped the photos into my briefcase and closed it. I looked back at Menendez, who was still in his chair on the other side of the glass.

"Can I just put my hand on the glass?" I asked the guard.

"Hurry up."

I leaned across the counter and put my hand on the glass, fingers spread. I waited for Menendez to do the same, creating a jailhouse handshake.

Menendez stood, leaned forward and spit on the glass where my hand was.

"You never shake my hand," he said. "I don't shake yours."

I nodded. I thought I understood just where he was coming from.

The guard smirked and told me to step through the door. In ten minutes I was out of the prison and crunching across the gravel to my rental car.

I had come four hundred miles for five minutes but those minutes were devastating. I think the lowest point of my life and professional career came an hour later when I was on the rent-a-car train being delivered back to the United terminal. No longer concentrating on the driving and making it back in time, I had only the case to think about. Cases, actually.

I leaned down, elbows on my knees and my face in my hands. My greatest fear had been realized, realized for two years but I hadn't known it. Not until now. I had been presented with innocence but I had not seen it or grasped it. Instead, I had thrown it into the maw of the machine like everything else. Now it was a cold, gray innocence, as dead as gravel and hidden in a fortress of stone and steel. And I had to live with it.

There was no solace to be found in the alternative, the knowledge that had we rolled the dice and gone to trial, Jesus would likely be on death row right now. There could be no comfort in knowing that fate was avoided, because I knew as sure as I knew anything else in the world that Jesus Menendez had been innocent. Something as rare as a true miracle — an innocent man — had come to me and I hadn't recognized it. I had turned away.

"Bad day?"

I looked up. There was a man across from me and a little bit further down the train car. We were the only ones on this link. He looked to be a decade older and had receding hair that made him look wise. Maybe he was even a lawyer, but I wasn't interested.

"I'm fine," I said. "Just tired."

And I held up a hand, palm out, a signal that I did not want conversation. I usually travel with a set of earbuds like Earl uses. I put them in and run the wire into a jacket pocket. It connects with nothing but it keeps people from talking to me. I had been in too much of a hurry this morning to think about them. Too much of a hurry to reach this point of desolation.

The man across the train got the message and said nothing else. I went back to my dark thoughts about Jesus Menendez. The bottom line was that I believed that I had one client who was guilty of the murder another client was serving a life sentence for. I could not help one without hurting the other. I needed an answer. I needed a plan. I needed proof. But for the moment on the train, I could only think of Jesus Menendez's dead eyes, because I knew I was the one who had killed the light in them.

TWENTY

As soon as I got off the shuttle at Burbank I turned on my cell. I had not come up with a plan but I had come up with my next step and that started with a call to Raul Levin. The phone buzzed in my hand, which meant I had messages. I decided I would get them after I set Levin in motion.

He answered my call and the first thing he asked was whether I had gotten his message.

"I just got off a plane," I said. "I missed it."

"A plane? Where were you?"

"Up north. What was the message?"

"Just an update on Corliss. If you weren't calling about that, what were you calling about?"

"What are you doing tonight?"

"Just hanging out. I don't like going out on Fridays and Saturdays. It's amateur hour. Too many drunks on the road."

"Well, I want to meet. I've got to talk to somebody. Bad things are happening."

Levin apparently sensed something in my voice because he immediately changed his stay-at-home-on-Friday-night policy and we agreed to meet at the Smoke House over by the Warner Studios. It was not far from where I was and not far from his home.

At the airport valet window I gave my ticket to a man in a red jacket and checked messages while waiting for the Lincoln.

Three messages had come in, all during the hour flight down from San Francisco. The first was from Maggie McPherson.

"Michael, I just wanted to call and say I'm sorry about how I was this morning. To tell you the truth, I was mad at myself for some of the things I said last night and the choices I made. I took it out on you and I should not have done that. Um, if you want to take Hayley out tomorrow or Sunday she would love it and, who knows, maybe I could come, too. Either way, just let me know."

She didn't call me Michael too often, even when we were married. She was one of those women who could use your last name and turn it into an endearment. That is, if she wanted to. She had always called me Haller. From the day we met in line to go through a metal detector at the CCB. She was headed to orientation at the DA's office and I was headed to misdemeanor arraignment court to handle a DUI.

I saved the message to listen to again sometime and went on to the next. I was expecting it to be from Levin but the automated voice reported the call came from a number with a 310 area code. The next voice I heard was Louis Roulet's.

"It's me, Louis. I was just checking in. I was just wondering after yesterday where things stood. I also have something I want to tell you."

I hit the erase button and moved on to the third and last message. This was Levin's.

"Hey, Bossman, give me a call. I have some stuff on Corliss. Anyway, the name is Dwayne Jeffery Corliss. That's Dwayne with a *D-W.* He's a hype and he's done the snitch thing a couple other times here in L.A. What's new, right? Anyway, he was actually arrested for stealing a bike he probably planned to trade for a little Mexican tar. He has parlayed snitching off Roulet into a ninety-day lockdown program at County-USC. So we won't be able to get to him and talk to him unless you got a judge that will set it up. Pretty shrewd move by the prosecutor. Anyway, I'm still running him down. Something came up on the Internet in Phoenix that looks pretty good for us if it was the same guy. Something that blew up in his face. I should be able to confirm it by Monday. So that's it for now. Give me a call over the weekend. I'm just hanging out."

I erased the message and closed the phone.

"Say no more," I said to myself.

Once I heard that Corliss was a hype, I needed to know nothing else. I understood why Maggie had not trusted the guy. Hypes — needle addicts — were the most desperate and unreliable people you could come across in the machine. Given the opportunity, they would snitch off their own mothers to get the next injection, or into the next methadone program. Every one of them was a liar and every one of them could easily be shown as such in court.

I was, however, puzzled by what the prosecutor was up to. The name Dwayne Corliss was not in the discovery material Minton had given me. Yet the prosecutor was making the moves he would make with a witness. He had stuck Corliss into a ninety-day program for safekeeping. The Roulet trial would come and go in that time. Was he hiding Corliss? Or was he simply putting the snitch on a shelf in the closet so he would know exactly where he was and where he'd been in case the time came in trial that his testimony would be needed? He was obviously operating under the belief that I didn't know about Corliss. And if it hadn't been for a slip by Maggie McPherson, I wouldn't. It was still a dangerous move, nevertheless. Judges do not look kindly on prosecutors who so openly flout the rules of discovery.

It led me to thinking of a possible strategy for the

defense. If Minton was foolish enough to try to spring Corliss in trial, I might not even object under the rules of discovery. I might let him put the heroin addict on the stand so I would get the chance to shred him in front of the jury like a credit card receipt. It would all depend on what Levin could come up with. I planned to tell him to continue to dig into Dwayne Jeffery Corliss. To hold nothing back.

I also thought about Corliss being in a lockdown program at County-USC. Levin was wrong and so was Minton if he was thinking I couldn't reach his witness in lockdown. By coincidence, my client Gloria Dayton had been placed in a lockdown program at County-USC after she snitched off her drug-dealing client. While there were a number of such programs at County, it was likely that she shared group therapy sessions or even mealtime with Corliss. I might not be able to get directly to Corliss but as Dayton's attorney I could get to her, and she in turn could get a message to Corliss.

The Lincoln pulled up and I gave the man in the red jacket a couple dollars. I exited the airport and drove south on Hollywood Way toward the center of Burbank, where all the studios were. I got to the Smoke House ahead of Levin and ordered a martini at the bar. On the overhead TV was an update on the start of the college basketball tournament. Florida had defeated Ohio in the first round. The headline on the bottom of the screen said "March Madness" and I toasted my glass to it. I knew what real March Madness was beginning to feel like.

Levin came in and ordered a beer before we sat down to dinner. It was still green, left over from the night before. Must have been a slow night. Maybe everybody had gone to Four Green Fields.

"Nothing like hair of the dog that bit ya, as long as it's green hair," he said in that brogue that was getting old.

He sipped the level of the glass down so he could walk with it and we stepped out to the hostess station so we could go to a table. She led us to a red padded booth that was shaped like a U. We sat across from each other and I put my briefcase down next to me. When the waitress came for a cocktail order we ordered the whole shooting match: salads, steaks and potatoes. I also asked for an order of the restaurant's signature garlic cheese bread.

"Good thing you don't like going out on weekends," I said to Levin after she was gone. "You eat the cheese bread and your breath will probably kill anybody you come in contact with after this."

"I'll have to take my chances."

We were quiet for a long moment after that. I could feel the vodka working its way into my guilt. I would be sure to order another when the salads came.

"So?" Levin finally said. "You called the meeting."

I nodded.

"I want to tell you a story. Not all of the details are set or known. But I'll tell it to you in the way I think it goes and then you tell me what you think and what I should do. Okay?"

"I like stories. Go ahead."

"I don't think you'll like this one. It starts two years ago with —"

I stopped and waited while the waitress put down our salads and the cheese bread. I asked for another vodka martini even though I was only halfway through the one I had. I wanted to make sure there was no gap.

"So," I said after she was gone. "This whole thing starts two years ago with Jesus Menendez. You remember him, right?"

"Yeah, we mentioned him the other day. The DNA. He's the client you always say is in prison because he wiped his prick on a fluffy pink towel."

He smiled because it was true that I had often reduced Menendez's case to such an absurdly vulgar basis. I had often used it to get a laugh when trading war stories at Four Green Fields with other lawyers. That was before I knew what I now knew.

I did not return the smile.

"Yeah, well, it turns out Jesus didn't do it."

"What do you mean? Somebody else wiped his prick on the towel?"

This time Levin laughed out loud.

"No, you don't get it. I'm telling you Jesus Menendez was innocent."

Levin's face grew serious. He nodded, putting something together.

"He's in San Quentin. You were up at the Q today."

I nodded.

"Let me back up and tell the story," I said. "You didn't do much work for me on Menendez because there was nothing to be done. They had the DNA, his own incriminating statement and three witnesses who saw him throw a knife into the river. They never found the knife but they had the witnesses — his own roommates. It was a hopeless case. Truth is, I took it on the come line for publicity value. So basically all I did was walk him to a plea. He didn't like it, said he didn't do it, but there was no choice. The DA was going for the death penalty. He'd have gotten that or life without. I got him life with and I made the little fucker take it. I made him."

I looked down at my untouched salad. I realized I didn't feel like eating. I just felt like drinking and pickling the cork in my brain that contained all the guilt cells.

Levin waited me out. He wasn't eating, either.

"In case you don't remember, the case was about the murder of a woman named Martha Renteria. She was a dancer at The Cobra Room on East Sunset. You didn't end up going there on this, did you?"

Levin shook his head.

"They don't have a stage," I said. "They have like a pit in the center and for each number, these guys dressed like Aladdin come out carrying this big cobra basket between two bamboo poles. They put it down and the music starts. Then the top comes off the basket and the girl comes up dancing. Then her top comes off, too. Kind of a new take on the dancer coming out of the cake."

"It's Hollywood, baby," Levin said. "You gotta have a show."

"Well, Jesus Menendez liked the show. He had eleven hundred dollars his brother the drug dealer gave him and he took a fancy to Martha Renteria. Maybe because she was the only dancer who was shorter than him. Maybe because she spoke Spanish to him. After her set they sat and talked and then she circulated a little bit and came back and pretty soon he knew he was in competition with another guy in the club. He trumped the other guy by offering her five hundred if she'd take him home."

"But he didn't kill her when he got there?"

"Uh-uh. He followed her car in his. Got there, had sex, flushed the condom, wiped his prick on the towel and then he went home. The story starts after he left."

"The real killer."

"The real killer knocks on the door, maybe fakes like it's Jesus and that he's forgotten something. She opens the door. Or maybe it was an appointment. She was expecting the knock and she opens the door."

"The guy from the club? The one Menendez was bidding against?"

I nodded.

"Exactly. He comes in, punches her a few times to soften her up and then takes out his folding knife and holds it against her neck while he walks her to the bedroom.

Sound familiar? Only she isn't lucky like Reggie Campo would be in a couple years. He puts her on the bed, puts on a condom and climbs on top. Now the knife is on the other side of her neck and he keeps it there while he rapes her. And when he's done, he kills her. He stabs her with that knife again and again. It's a case of overkill if there ever was one. He's working out something in his sick fucking mind while he's doing it."

My second martini came and I took it right from the waitress's hand and gulped half of it down. She asked if we were finished with our salads and we both waved them away untouched.

"Your steaks will be right out," she said. "Or do you want me to just dump them in the garbage and save you the time?"

I looked up at her. She was smiling but I was so caught up in the story I was telling that I had missed what it was she had said.

"Never mind," she said. "They'll be right out."

I got right back to the story. Levin said nothing.

"After she's dead the killer cleans up. He takes his time, because what's the hurry, she's not going anywhere or calling anybody. He wipes the place down to take care of any fingerprints he might have left. And in the process he wipes away Menendez's prints. This will look bad for Menendez when he later goes to the police to explain that he is the guy in the sketches but he didn't kill Martha. They'll look at him and say, 'Then why'd you wear gloves when you were there?'"

Levin shook his head.

"Oh man, if this is true . . ."

"Don't worry, it's true. Menendez gets a lawyer who once did a good job for his brother but this lawyer wouldn't know an innocent man if he kicked him in the nuts. This lawyer is all about the deal. He never even asks the kid if he did it. He just assumes he did it because they got his fucking DNA on the towel and the witnesses who saw him toss the knife. The lawyer goes to work and gets the best possible deal he could get. He actually feels pretty good about it because he's going to keep Menendez off death row and get him a shot at parole someday. So he goes to Menendez and brings down the hammer. He makes him take the deal and stand up there in court and say 'Guilty.' Jesus then goes off to prison and everybody's happy. The state's happy because it saves money on a trial and Martha Renteria's family is happy because they don't have to face a trial with all those autopsy photos and stories about their daughter dancing naked and taking men home for money. And the lawyer's happy because he got on TV with the case at least six times, plus he kept another client off death row."

I gulped down the rest of the martini and looked around for our waitress. I wanted another.

"Jesus Menendez goes off to prison a young man. I just saw him and he's twenty-six going on forty. He's a small guy. You know what happens to the little ones up there."

I was looking straight down at the empty space on the table in front of me when an egg-shaped platter with a sizzling steak and steaming potato was put down. I looked up at the waitress and told her to bring me another martini. I didn't say please.

"You better take it easy," Levin said after she was gone. "There probably isn't a cop in this county who wouldn't love to pull you over on a deuce, take you back to lockup and put the flashlight up your ass."

"I know, I know. It will be my last. And if it's too much I won't drive. They always have a cab out front of this place."

Deciding that food might help I cut into my steak and ate a piece. I then took a piece of cheese bread out of the napkin it was folded into a basket with, but it was no longer warm. I dropped it on my plate and put my fork down.

"Look, I know you're beating yourself up over this but you are forgetting something," Levin said.

"Yeah? What's that?"

"His exposure. He was facing the needle, man, and the case was a dog. I didn't work it for you because there was nothing to work. They had him and you saved him from the needle. That's your job and you did it well. So now you think you know what really went down. You can't beat yourself up for what you didn't know then."

I held my hand up in a *stop there* gesture.

"The guy was innocent. I should've seen it. I should've done something about it. Instead, I just did my usual thing and went through the motions with my eyes closed."

"Bullshit."

"No, no bullshit."

"Okay, go back to the story. Who was the second guy who came to her door?"

I opened my briefcase next to me and reached into it.

"I went up to San Quentin today and showed Menendez a six-pack. All mug shots of my clients. Mostly former clients. Menendez picked one out in less than ten seconds."

I tossed the mug shot of Louis Roulet across the table. It landed facedown. Levin picked it up and looked at it for a few moments, then put it back facedown on the table.

"Let me show you something else," I said.

My hand went back into the briefcase and pulled out the two folded photographs of Martha Renteria and Reggie Campo. I looked around to make sure the waitress wasn't about to deliver my martini and then handed them across the table.

"It's like a puzzle," I said. "Put them together and see what you get."

Levin put the one face together from the two and nodded as he understood the significance. The killer — Roulet zeroed in on women that fit a model or profile he desired. I next showed him the weapon sketch drawn by the medical examiner on the Renteria autopsy and read him the description of the two coercive wounds found on her neck.

"You know that video you got from the bar?" I asked. "What it shows is a killer at work. Just like you, he saw that Mr. X was left-handed. When he attacked Reggie Campo he punched with his left and then held the knife with his left. This guy knows what he is doing. He saw an opportunity and took it. Reggie Campo is the luckiest woman alive."

"You think there are others? Other murders, I mean."

"Maybe. That's what I want you to look into. Check out all the knife murders of women in the last few years. Then get the victim's pictures and see if they match the physical profile. And don't look at unsolved cases only. Martha Renteria was supposedly among the closed cases."

Levin leaned forward.

"Look, man, I'm not going to throw a net over this like the police can. You have to bring the cops in on this. Or go to the FBI. They got their serial killer specialists."

I shook my head.

"Can't. He's my client."

"Menendez is your client, too, and you have to get him out."

"I'm working on that. And that's why I need you to do this for me, Mish."

We both knew that I called him Mish whenever I needed something that crossed the lines of our professional relationship into the friendship that was underneath it.

"What about a hitman?" Levin said. "That would solve our problems."

I nodded, knowing he was being facetious.

"Yeah, that would work," I said. "It would make the world a better place, too. But it probably wouldn't spring Menendez."

Levin leaned forward again. Now he was serious.

"I'll do what I can, Mick, but I don't think this is the right way to go. You can declare conflict of interest and dump Roulet. Then work on jumping Menendez out of the Q."

"Jump him out with what?"

"The ID he made on the six-pack. That was solid. He didn't know Roulet from a hole in the ground and he goes and picks him out of the pack."

"Who is going to believe that? I'm his lawyer! Nobody from the cops to the clemency board is going to believe I didn't set that up. This is all theory, Raul. You know it and I know it to be true but we can't prove a damn thing."

"What about the wounds? They could match the knife they got from the Campo case to Martha Renteria's wounds."

I shook my head.

"She was cremated. All they have is the descriptions and photos from the autopsy and it wouldn't be conclusive. It's not enough. Besides, I can't be seen as the guy pushing this on my own client. If I turn against a client, then I turn against all my clients. It can't look that way or I'll lose them all. I have to figure something else out."

"I think you're wrong. I think —"

"For now I go along as if I don't know any of this, you understand? But you look into it. All of it. Keep it separate from Roulet so I don't have a discovery issue. File it all under Jesus Menendez and bill the time to me on that case. You understand?"

Before Levin could answer, the waitress brought my third martini. I waved it away.

"I don't want it. Just the check."

"Well, I can't pour it back into the bottle," she said.

"Don't worry, I'll pay for it. I just don't want to drink it. Give it to the guy who makes the cheese bread and just bring me the check."

She turned and walked away, probably annoyed that I hadn't offered the drink to her. I looked back at Levin. He looked like he was pained by everything that had been revealed to him. I knew just how he felt.

"Some franchise I got, huh?"

"Yeah. How are you going to be able to act straight with this guy when you have to deal with him and meantime you're digging out this other shit on the side?"

"With Roulet? I plan to see him as little as possible. Only when it's necessary. He left me a message today, has something to tell me. But I'm not calling back."

"Why did he pick you? I mean, why would he pick the one lawyer who might put this thing together?"

I shook my head.

"I don't know. I thought about it the whole plane ride down. I think maybe he was worried I might hear about the case and put it together anyway. But if he was my client, then he knew I'd be ethically bound to protect him. At least at first. Plus there's the money."

"What money?"

"The money from Mother. The franchise. He knows how big a payday this is for me. My biggest ever. Maybe he thought I'd look the other way to keep the money coming in."

Levin nodded.

"Maybe I should, huh?" I said.

It was a vodka-spurred attempt at humor, but Levin didn't smile and then I remembered Jesus Menendez's face behind the prison Plexiglas and I couldn't even bring myself to smile.

"Listen, there's one other thing I need you to do," I said. "I want you to look at him, too. Roulet. Find out all you can without getting too close. And check out that story about the mother, about her getting raped in a house she was selling in Bel-Air."

Levin nodded.

"I'm on it."

"And don't farm it out."

This was a running joke between us. Like me, Levin was a one-man shop. He had no one to farm it out to.

"I won't. I'll handle it myself."

It was his usual response but this time it lacked the false sincerity and humor he usually gave it. He'd answered by habit.

The waitress moved by the table and put our check down without a thank you. I dropped a credit card on it without even looking at the damage. I just wanted to leave.

"You want her to wrap up your steak?" I asked.

"That's okay," Levin said. "I've kind of lost my appetite for right now."

"What about that attack dog you've got at home?"

"That's an idea. I forgot about Bruno."

He looked around for the waitress to ask for a box.

"Take mine, too," I said. "I don't have a dog."

TWENTY-ONE

Despite the vodka glaze, I made it through the slalom that was Laurel Canyon without cracking up the Lincoln or getting pulled over by a cop. My house is on Fareholm Drive, which terraces up off the southern mouth of the canyon. All the houses are built to the street line and the only problem I had coming home was when I found that some moron had parked his SUV in front of my garage and I couldn't get in. Parking on the narrow street is always difficult and the opening in front of my garage door was usually just too inviting, especially on a weekend night, when invariably someone on the street was throwing a party.

I motored by the house and found a space big enough for the Lincoln about a block and a half away. The further I had gotten from my house, the angrier I had gotten with the SUV. The fantasy grew from spitting on the windshield to breaking off the side mirror, flattening the tires and kicking in the side panels. But instead I wrote a sedate little note on a page of yellow legal paper: *This is not a parking space! Next time you will be towed.* After all, you never know who's driving an SUV in L.A., and if you threaten someone for parking in front of your garage, then they know where you live.

I walked back and was placing the note under the violator's windshield wiper when I noticed the SUV was a Range Rover. I put my hand on the hood and it was cool to the touch. I looked up above the garage to the windows of my house that I could see, but they were dark. I slapped the folded note under the windshield wiper and started up the stairs to the front deck and door. I half expected Louis Roulet to be sitting in one of the tall director chairs, taking in the twinkling view of the city, but he was not there.

Instead, I walked to the corner of the porch and looked out on the city. It was this view that had made me buy the place. Everything about the house once you went through the door was ordinary and outdated. But the front porch and the view right above Hollywood Boulevard could launch a million dreams. I had used money from the last franchise case for a down payment. But once I was in and there wasn't another franchise, I took the equity out in a second mortgage. The truth was I struggled every month just to pay the nut. I needed to get out from under it but that view off the front deck paralyzed me. I'd probably be staring out at the city when they came to take the key and foreclose on the place.

I know the question my house prompts. Even with my struggles to stay afloat with it, how fair is it that when a prosecutor and defense attorney divorce, the defense attorney gets the house on the hill with a million-dollar view while the prosecutor with the daughter gets the two-bedroom apartment in the Valley. The answer is that Maggie McPherson could buy a house of her choosing and I would help her to my maximum ability. But she had refused to move while she waited to be tapped for a promotion to the downtown office. Buying a house in Sherman Oaks or anywhere else would send the wrong message, one of sedentary contentment. She was not content to be Maggie McFierce of the Van Nuys Division. She was not content to be passed over by John Smithson or any of his young guns. She was ambitious and wanted to get downtown, where supposedly the best and brightest prosecuted the most important crimes. She refused to accept the simple truism that the better you were, the bigger threat you were to those at the top, especially if they are elected. I knew that Maggie would never be invited downtown. She was too damn good.

Every now and then this realization would seep through and she would lash out in unexpected ways. She would make a cutting remark at a press conference or she would refuse to cooperate with a downtown investigation. Or she would drunkenly reveal to a criminal defense attorney and ex-husband something about a case he shouldn't be told.

The phone started to ring from inside the house. I moved to the front door and fumbled with my keys to unlock it and get inside in time. My phone numbers and who has them could form a pyramid chart. The number in the yellow pages everybody has or could have. Next up the pyramid is my cell phone, which has been disseminated to key colleagues, investigators, bondsmen, clients and other cogs in the machine. My home phone — the land line — was the top of the pyramid. Very few had the number. No clients and no other lawyers except for one.

I got in and grabbed the phone off the kitchen wall before it went to message. The caller was that one other lawyer with the number. Maggie McPherson.

"Did you get my messages?"

"I got the one on my cell. What's wrong?"

"Nothing's wrong. I left one on this number a lot earlier."

"Oh, I've been gone all day. I just got in."

"Where have you been?"

"Well, I've been up to San Francisco and back and I just got in from having dinner with Raul Levin. Is all of that all right with you?"

"I'm just curious. What was in San Francisco?"

"A client."

"So what you really mean is you were up to San Quentin and back."

"You were always too smart for me, Maggie. I can never fool you. Is there a reason for this call?"

"I just wanted to see if you got my apology and I also wanted to find out if you were going to do something with Hayley tomorrow."

"Yes and yes. But Maggie, no apology is necessary and you should know that. I am sorry for the way I acted before I left. And if my daughter wants to be with me tomorrow, then I want to be with her. Tell her we can go down to the pier or to a movie if she wants. Whatever she wants."

"Well, she actually wants to go to the mall."

She said it as if she were stepping on glass.

"The mall? The mall is fine. I'll take her. What's wrong with the mall? Is there something in particular she wants?"

I suddenly noticed a foreign odor in the house. The smell of smoke. While standing in the middle of the kitchen I checked the oven and the stove. They were off. I was tethered to the kitchen because the phone wasn't cordless. I stretched it to the door and flicked on the light to the dining room. It was empty and its light was cast into the next room, the living room through which I had passed when I had entered. It looked empty as well.

"They have a place there where you make your own teddy bear and you pick the style and its voice box and you put a little heart in with the stuffing. It's all very cute."

I now wanted to get off the line and explore further into my house.

"Fine. I'll take her. What time is good?"

"I was thinking about noon. Maybe we could have lunch first."

"We?"

"Would that bother you?"

"No, Maggie, not at all. How about I come by at noon?"

"Great."

"See you then."

I hung the phone up before she could say good-bye. I owned a gun but it was a collector piece that hadn't been fired in my lifetime and was stored in a box in my bedroom closet at the rear of the house. So I quietly opened a kitchen drawer and took out a short but sharp steak knife. I then walked through the living room toward the hallway that led to the rear of the house. There were three doorways in the hall. They led to my bedroom, a bathroom and another bedroom I had turned into a home office, the only real office I had.

The desk light was on in the office. It was not visible from the angle I had in the hallway but I could tell it was on. I had not been home in two days but I did not remember leaving it on. I approached the open door to the room slowly, aware that this is what I may have been meant to do. Focus on the light in one room while the intruder is waiting in the darkness of the bedroom or bathroom.

"Come on back, Mick. It's just me."

I knew the voice but it didn't make me feel at ease. Louis Roulet was waiting in the room. I stepped to the threshold and stopped. He was sitting in the black leather desk seat. He swiveled it around so that he was facing me and crossed his legs. His pants rode up on his left leg and I could see the tracking bracelet that Fernando Valenzuela had made him wear. I knew that if Roulet had come to kill me, at least he would leave a trail. It wasn't all that comforting, though. I leaned against the door frame so that I could hold the knife behind my hip without being too obvious about it.

"So this is where you do your great legal work?" Roulet asked.

"Some of it. What are you doing here, Louis?"

"I came to see you. You didn't return my call and so I

wanted to make sure we were still a team, you know?"

"I was out of town. I just got back."

"What about dinner with Raul? Isn't that what you said to your caller?"

"He's a friend. I had dinner on my way in from Burbank Airport. How did you find out where I live, Louis?"

He cleared his throat and smiled.

"I work in real estate, Mick. I can find out where anybody lives. In fact, I used to be a source for the *National Enquirer*. Did you know that? I could tell them where any celebrity lived, no matter what fronts and corporations they hid their purchases behind. But I gave it up after a while. The money was good but it was so . . . tawdry. You know what I mean, Mick? Anyway, I stopped. But I can still find out where anyone lives. I can also find out whether they've maxed the mortgage value out and even if they're making their payments on time."

He looked at me with a knowing smile. He was telling me he knew the house was a financial shell, that I had nothing in the place and usually ran a month behind on the two mortgages. Fernando Valenzuela probably wouldn't even accept the place as collateral on a five-thousand-dollar bond.

"How'd you get in?" I asked.

"Well, that's the funny thing about this. It turns out I had a key. Back when this place was for sale — what was that, about eighteen months ago? Anyway, I wanted to see it because I thought I had a client who might be interested because of the view. So I came and got the key out of the realtor's combo box. I came in and looked around and knew immediately it wasn't right for my client — he wanted something nicer — so I left. And I forgot to put the key back. I have a bad habit of doing that. Isn't that strange that all this time later my lawyer would be living in this house? And by the way, I see you haven't done a thing with it. You have the view, of course, but you really need to do some updating."

I knew then that he had been keeping tabs on me since the Menendez case. And that he probably knew I had just been up to San Quentin visiting him. I thought about the man on the car-rental train. *Bad day?* I had later seen him on the shuttle to Burbank. Had he been following me? Was he working for Roulet? Was he the investigator Cecil Dobbs had tried to push onto the case? I didn't know all the answers but I knew that the only reason Roulet would be in my house waiting for me was because he knew what I knew.

"What do you really want, Louis? Are you trying to scare me?"

"No, no, I'm the one who should be scared. I assume you have a weapon of some sort behind your back there. What is it, a gun?"

I gripped the knife tighter but did not display it.

"What is it you want?" I repeated.

"I want to make you an offer. Not on the house. On your services."

"You already have my services."

He swiveled back and forth in the chair before responding. My eyes scanned the desk, checking if anything was missing. I noticed he had used a little pottery dish my daughter had made for me as an ashtray. It was supposed to be for paperclips.

"I was thinking about our fee arrangement and the difficulties the case presents," he said. "Frankly, Mick, I think you are underpaid. So I want to set up a new fee schedule. You will be paid the amount already agreed upon and you will be paid in full before the trial begins. But I am now going to add a performance bonus. When I am found by a jury of my peers to be not guilty of this ugly crime, your fee automatically doubles. I will write the check in your Lincoln as we drive away from the courthouse."

"That's nice, Louis, but the California bar refuses to allow defense attorneys to accept bonuses based on results. I couldn't accept it. It's more than generous but I can't."

"But the California bar isn't here, Mick. And we don't have to treat it as a performance bonus. It's just part of the fee schedule. Because, after all, you will be successful in defending me, won't you?"

He looked intently at me and I read the threat.

"There are no guarantees in the courtroom. Things can always go badly. But I still think it looks good."

Roulet's face slowly broke into a smile.

"What can I do to make it look even better?"

I thought about Reggie Campo. Still alive and ready to go to trial. She had no idea whom she would be testifying against.

"Nothing," I answered. "Just sit tight and wait it out. Don't get any ideas. Don't do anything. The case is coming together and we'll be all right."

He didn't respond. I wanted to get him away from thoughts about the threat Reggie Campo presented.

"There is one thing that has come up, though," I said.

"Really? What's that?"

"I don't have the details. What I know I only know from a source who can't tell me any more. But it looks like the DA has a snitch from the jail. You didn't talk to anybody about the case when you were in there, did you? Remember, I told you not to talk to anybody."

"And I didn't. Whoever they have, he is a liar."

"Most of them are. I just wanted to be sure. I'll deal with it if it comes up."

"Good."

"One other thing. Have you talked to your mother about testifying about the attack in the empty house? We need it to set up the defense of you carrying the knife."

Roulet pursed his lips but didn't answer.

"I need you to work on her," I said. "It could be very important to establish that solidly with the jury. Besides that, it could swing sympathy toward you."

Roulet nodded. He saw the light.

"Can you please ask her?" I asked.

"I will. But she'll be tough. She never reported it. She never told anyone but Cecil."

"We need her to testify and then we can get Cecil to testify and back her up. It's not as good as a police report but it will work. We need her, Louis. I think if she testifies, she can convince them. Juries like old ladies."

"Okay."

"Did she ever tell you what the guy looked like or how old he was, anything like that?"

He shook his head.

"She couldn't tell. He wore a ski mask and goggles. He jumped on her as soon as she came in the door. He had been hiding behind it. It was very quick and very brutal."

His voice quavered as he described it. I became puzzled.

"I thought you said the attacker was a prospective buyer she was supposed to meet there," I said. "He was already in the house?"

He brought his eyes up to mine.

"Yes. Somehow he had already gotten in and was waiting for her. It was terrible."

I nodded. I didn't want to go further with him at the moment. I wanted him out of my house.

"Listen, thank you for your offer, Louis. Now if you would excuse me, I want to go to bed. It's been a long day."

I gestured with my free hand toward the hallway leading to the front of the house. Roulet got up from the desk chair and came toward me. I backed into the hallway and then into the open door of my bedroom. I kept the knife behind me and ready. But Roulet passed by without incident.

"And tomorrow you have your daughter to entertain," he said.

That froze me. He had listened to the call from Maggie. I didn't say anything. He did.

"I didn't know you had a daughter, Mick. That must be nice."

He glanced back at me, smiling as he moved down the hall.

"She's beautiful," he said.

My inertia turned to momentum. I stepped into the hall and started following him, anger building with each step. I gripped the knife tightly.

"How do you know what she looks like?" I demanded.

He stopped and I stopped. He looked down at the knife in my hand and then at my face. He spoke calmly.

"The picture of her on your desk."

I had forgotten about the photo. A small framed shot of her in a teacup at Disneyland.

"Oh," I said.

He smiled, knowing what I had been thinking.

"Good night, Mick. Enjoy your daughter tomorrow. You probably don't get to see her enough."

He turned and crossed the living room and opened the front door. He looked back at me before stepping out.

"What you need is a good lawyer," he said. "One that will get you custody."

"No. She's better off with her mother."

"Good night, Mick. Thanks for the conversation."

"Good night, Louis."

I stepped forward to close the door.

"Nice view," he said from out on the front porch.

"Yeah," I said as I closed and locked the door.

I stood there with my hand on the knob, waiting to hear

his steps going down the stairs to the street. But a few moments later he knocked on the door. I closed my eyes, held the knife at the ready and opened it. Roulet raised his hand out. I took a step back.

"Your key," he said. "I figured you should have it."

I took the key off his outstretched palm.

"Thanks."

"Don't mention it."

I closed the door and locked it once again.

TWENTY-TWO

The day started better than any defense attorney could ask for. I had no courtroom to be in, no client to meet. I slept late, spent the morning reading the newspaper cover to cover and had a box ticket to the home opener of the Los Angeles Dodgers baseball season. It was a day game and a time-honored tradition among those on the defense side of the aisle to attend. My ticket had come from Raul Levin, who was taking five of the defense pros he did work for to the game as a gesture of thanks for their business. I was sure the others would grumble and complain at the game about how I was monopolizing Levin as I prepared for the Roulet trial. But I wasn't going to let it bother me.

We were in the outwardly slow time before trial, when the machine moves with a steady, quiet momentum. Louis Roulet's trial was set to begin in a month. As it was growing nearer I was taking on fewer and fewer clients. I needed the time to prepare and strategize. Though the trial was weeks away it would likely be won or lost with the information gathered now. I needed to keep my schedule clear for this. I took cases from repeat customers only — and only if the money was right and it came up-front.

A trial was a slingshot. The key was in the preparation. Pretrial is when the sling is loaded with the proper stone and slowly the elastic is pulled back and stretched to its limit. Finally, at trial you let it go and the projectile shoots forward, unerringly at the target. The target is acquittal. Not guilty. You only hit that target if you have properly chosen the stone and pulled back carefully on the sling, stretching it as far as possible.

Levin was doing most of the stretching. He had continued to dig into the lives of the players in both the Roulet and Menendez cases. We had hatched a strategy and plan we were calling a "double slingshot" because it had two intended targets. I had no doubt that when the trial began in May, we would be stretched back to the limit and ready to let go.

The prosecution did its part to help us load the slingshot, as well. In the weeks since Roulet's arraignment the state's discovery file grew thicker as scientific reports filtered in, further police investigations were carried out and new developments occurred.

Among the new developments of note was the identification of Mr. X, the left-handed man who had been with Reggie Campo at Morgan's the night of the attack. LAPD detectives, using the video I had alerted the prosecution to, were able to identify him by showing a frame taken off the video to known prostitutes and escorts when they were arrested by the Administrative Vice section. Mr. X was identified as Charles Talbot. He was known to many of the sex providers as a regular. Some said that he owned or worked at a convenience store on Reseda Boulevard.

The investigative reports forwarded to me through discovery requests revealed that detectives interviewed Talbot and learned that on the night of March 6 he left Reggie Campo's apartment shortly before ten and went to the previously mentioned twenty-four-hour convenience store. Talbot owned the business. He went to the store so that he could check on things and open a cigarette storage cabinet that only he carried the key for. Tape from surveillance cameras in the store confirmed that he was there from 10:09 to 10:51 P.M. restocking the cigarette bins beneath the front counter. The investigator's summary dismissed Talbot as having no bearing or part in the events that occurred after he left Campo's apartment. He was just one of her customers.

Nowhere in the state's discovery was there mention of Dwayne Jeffery Corliss, the jailhouse snitch who had contacted the prosecution with a tale to tell about Louis Roulet. Minton had either decided not to use him as a witness or was keeping him under wraps for emergency use only. I tended to think it was the latter. Minton had sequestered him in the lockdown program. He wouldn't have gone to the trouble unless he wanted to keep Corliss offstage but ready. This was fine with me. What Minton didn't know was that Corliss was the stone I was going to put into the slingshot.

And while the state's discovery contained little information on the victim of the crime, Raul Levin was vigorously pursuing Reggie Campo. He located a website called PinkMink.com on which she advertised her services. What was important about the discovery was not necessarily that it further established that she was engaged in prostitution but that the ad copy stated that she was "very open-minded and liked to get wild" and was "available for S&M role play — you spank me or I'll spank you." It was good ammunition to have. It was the kind of stuff that could help color a victim or witness in a jury's eyes. And she was both.

Levin also was digging deeper into the life and times of Louis Roulet and had learned that he had been a poor student who'd attended five different private schools in and around Beverly Hills as a youth. He did go on to attend and graduate from UCLA with a degree in English literature but Levin located fellow classmates who had said Roulet paid his way through by purchasing from other students completed class assignments, test answers and even a ninety-page senior thesis on the life and work of John Fante.

A far darker profile emerged of Roulet as an adult. Levin found numerous female acquaintances who said Roulet had mistreated them, either physically or mentally, or both. Two women who had known Roulet while they were students at UCLA told Levin that they suspected that Roulet had spiked their drinks at a fraternity party with a date-rape drug and then took sexual advantage of them. Neither reported their suspicions to authorities but one woman had her blood tested the day after the party. She said traces of ketamine hydrochloride, a veterinary sedative, were found. Luckily for the defense, neither woman had so far been located by investigators for the prosecution.

Levin took a look at the so-called Real Estate Rapist cases of five years before as well. Four women — all realtors — reported being overpowered and raped by a man who was waiting inside when they entered homes they believed had been vacated by their owners for a showing. The attacks went unsolved but stopped eleven months after the first one was reported. Levin spoke to an LAPD sex crimes expert who worked the cases. He said that his gut instinct had always been that the rapist wasn't an outsider. The assailant seemed to know how to get into the houses and how to draw the female sales agents to them alone. The investigator was convinced the rapist was in the real estate community, but with no arrest ever made, he never proved his theory.

Added to this branch of his investigation, Levin could find little to confirm that Mary Alice Windsor had been one of the unreported victims of the rapist. She had granted us an interview and agreed to testify about her secret tragedy but only if her testimony was vitally needed. The date of the attack she provided fell within the dates of the documented assaults attributed to the Real Estate Rapist, and Windsor provided an appointment book and other documentation showing she was indeed the realtor on record in regard to the sale of the Bel-Air home where she said she was attacked. But ultimately we only had her word for it. There were no medical or hospital records indicative of treatment for a sexual assault. And no police record.

Still, when Mary Windsor recounted her story, it matched Roulet's telling of it in almost all details. Afterward, it had struck both Levin and me as odd that Louis had known so much about the attack. If his mother had decided to keep it secret and unreported, then why would she share so many details of her harrowing ordeal with her son? That question led Levin to postulate a theory that was as repulsive as it was intriguing.

"I think he knows all the details because he was there," Levin had said after the interview and we were by ourselves.

"You mean he watched it without doing anything to stop it?"

"No, I mean I think he was the man in the ski mask and goggles."

I was silent. I think on a subliminal level I may have been thinking the same thing but the idea was too creepy to have broken through to the surface.

"Oh, man . . ." I said.

Levin, thinking I was disagreeing, pressed his case forward.

"This is a very strong woman," he said. "She built that company from nothing and real estate in this town is cutthroat. She's a tough lady and I can't see her not reporting this, not wanting the guy who did it to be caught. I view people two ways. They're either eye-for-an-eye people or they are turn-the-cheek people. She's definitely an eye-for-an-eye person and I can't see her keeping it quiet unless she was protecting that guy. Unless that guy was our guy. I'm telling you, man, Roulet is evil. I don't know where it comes from or how he got it, but the more I look at him, the more I see the devil."

All of this backgrounding was completely sub rosa. It obviously was not the kind of background that would in any way be brought forward as a means of defense. It had to be hidden from discovery, so little of what Levin or I found was put down on paper. But it was still information that I had to know as I made my decisions and set up the trial and the play within it.

At 11:05 my home phone rang as I was standing in front of a mirror and fitting a Dodgers cap onto my head. I checked the caller ID before answering and saw that it was Lorna Taylor.

"Why is your cell phone off?" she asked.

"Because I'm off. I told you, no calls today. I'm going to the ballgame with Mish and I'm supposed to get going to meet him early."

"Who's Mish?"

"I mean Raul. Why are you bothering me?"

I said it good-naturedly.

"Because I think you are going to want to be bothered with this. The mail came in a little early today and with it you got a notice from the Second."

The Second District Court of Appeal reviewed all cases emanating from L.A. County. They were the first appellate hurdle on the way to the Supreme Court. But I didn't think Lorna would be calling me to tell me I had lost an appeal.

"Which case?"

At any given time I usually have four or five cases on appeal to the Second.

"One of your Road Saints. Harold Casey. You won!"

I was shocked. Not at winning, but at the timing. I had tried to move quickly with the appeal. I had written the brief before the verdict had come in and paid extra for expedited daily transcripts from the trial. I filed the notice of appeal the day after the verdict and asked for an expedited review. Even still, I wasn't expecting to hear anything on Casey for another two months.

I asked Lorna to read the opinion and a smile widened on my face. The summary was literally a rewrite of my brief. The three-judge panel had agreed with me right down the line on my contention that the low flyover of the sheriff's surveillance helicopter above Casey's ranch constituted an invasion of privacy. The court overturned Casey's conviction, saying that the search that led to the discovery of the hydroponic pot farm was illegal.

The state would now have to decide whether to retry Casey and, realistically, a retrial was out of the question. The state would have no evidence, since the appeals court ruled everything garnered during the search of the ranch was inadmissible. The Second's ruling was clearly a victory for the defense, and they don't come that often.

"Man, what a day for the underdog!"

"Where is he, anyway?" Lorna asked.

"He may still be at the reception center but they were moving him to Corcoran. Here's what you do. Make about ten copies of the ruling and put them in an envelope and send it to Casey at Corcoran. You should have the address."

"Well, won't they be letting him go?"

"Not yet. His parole was violated after his arrest and the appeal doesn't affect that. He won't get out until he goes to the parole board and argues fruit of the poisonous tree, that he got violated because of an illegal search. It will probably take about six weeks for all that to work itself out."

"Six weeks? That's unbelievable."

"Don't do the crime if you can't do the time."

I sang it like Sammy Davis did on that old television show.

"Please don't sing to me, Mick."

"Sorry."

"Why are we sending ten copies to him? Isn't one enough?"

"Because he'll keep one for himself and spread the other nine around the prison and then your phone will start ringing. An attorney who can win on appeal is like gold in prison. They'll come calling and you're going to have to weed 'em out and find the ones who have family and can pay."

"You always have an angle, don't you?"

"I try to. Anything else happening?"

"Just the usual. The calls you told me you didn't want to hear about. Did you get in to see Glory Days yesterday at County?"

"It's Gloria Dayton and, yes, I got in to see her. She looks like she's over the hump. She's still got more than a month to go."

The truth was, Gloria Dayton looked better than over the hump. I hadn't seen her so sharp and bright-eyed in years. I'd had a purpose for going down to County-USC Medical Center to talk to her, but seeing her on the downhill side of recovery was a nice bonus.

As expected, Lorna was the doomsayer.

"And how long will it last this time before she calls your number again and says, 'I'm in jail. I need Mickey'?"

She said the last part with a whiny, nasal impression of Gloria Dayton. It was quite accurate but it annoyed me anyway. Then she topped it with a little song to the tune of the Disney classic.

"M-I-C . . . see you real soon. K-E-Y . . . why, because

you never charge me! M-O-U-T-H. Mickey Mouth ...
Mickey Mouth, the lawyer every —"

"Please don't sing to me, Lorna."

She laughed into the phone.

"I'm just making a point."

I was smiling but trying to keep it out of my voice.

"Fine. I get it. I have to get going now."

"Well, have a great time ... Mickey Mouth."

"You could sing that song all day and the Dodgers could lose twenty-zip to the Giants and I'd still have a great time. After hearing the news from you, what could go wrong?"

After ending the call I went into my home office and got a cell number for Teddy Vogel, the outside leader of the Saints. I gave him the good news and suggested that he could probably pass it on to Hard Case faster than I could. There are Road Saints in every prison. They have a communication system the CIA and FBI might be able to learn something from. Vogel said he'd handle it. Then he said the ten grand he gave me the month before on the side of the road near Vasquez Rocks was a worthy investment.

"I appreciate that, Ted," I said. "Keep me in mind next time you need an attorney."

"Will do, Counselor."

He clicked off and I clicked off. I then grabbed my first baseman's glove out of the hallway closet and headed out the front door.

Having given Earl the day off with pay, I drove myself toward downtown and Dodger Stadium. Traffic was light until I got close. The home opener is always a sell-out, even though it is a day game on a weekday. The start of baseball season is a rite of spring that draws downtown workers by the thousands. It's the only sporting event in laid-back L.A. where you see men all in stiff white shirts and ties. They're all playing hooky. There is nothing like the start of a season, before all the one-run losses, pitching breakdowns and missed opportunities. Before reality sets in.

I was the first one to the seats. We were three rows from the field in seats added to the stadium during the off-season. Levin must have busted a nut buying the tickets from one of the local brokers. At least it was probably deductible as a business entertainment expense.

The plan was for Levin to get there early as well. He had called the night before and said he wanted some private time with me. Besides watching batting practice and checking out all the improvements the new owner had made to the stadium, we would discuss my visit with Gloria Dayton and Raul would give me the latest update on his various investigations relating to Louis Roulet.

But Levin never made it for BP. The other four lawyers showed up — three of them in ties, having come from court — and we missed our chance to talk privately.

I knew the other four from some of the boat cases we had tried together. In fact, the tradition of defense pros taking in Dodgers games together started with the boat cases. Under a wide-ranging mandate to stop drug flow to the United States, the U.S. Coast Guard had taken to stopping suspect vessels anywhere on the oceans. When they struck gold — or, that is, cocaine — they seized the vessels and crews. Many of the prosecutions were funneled to the U.S. District Court in Los Angeles. This resulted in prosecutions of sometimes twelve or more defendants at a time. Every defendant got his own lawyer, most of them appointed by the court and paid by Uncle Sugar. The cases were lucrative and steady and we had fun. Somebody had the idea of having case meetings at Dodger Stadium. One time we all pitched in and bought a private suite for a Cubs game. We actually did talk about the case for a few minutes during the seventh-inning stretch.

The pre-game ceremonies started and there was no sign of Levin. Hundreds of doves were released from baskets on the field and they formed up, circled the stadium to loud cheering and then flew up and away. Shortly after, a B-2 stealth bomber buzzed the stadium to even louder applause. That was L.A. Something for everyone and a little irony to boot.

The game started and still no Levin. I turned my cell phone on and tried to call him, even though it was hard to hear. The crowd was loud and boisterous, hopeful of a season that would not end in disappointment again. The call went to a message.

"Mish, where you at, man? We're at the game and the seats are fantastic, but we got one empty one. We're waiting on you."

I closed the phone, looked at the others and shrugged.

"I don't know," I said. "He didn't answer his cell."

I left my phone on and put it back on my belt.

Before the first inning was over I was regretting what I had said to Lorna about not caring if the Giants drilled us 20–zip. They built a 5–0 lead before the Dodgers even got their first bats of the season and the crowd grew frustrated early. I heard people complaining about the prices, the renovation and the overcommercialization of the stadium. One of the lawyers, Roger Mills, surveyed the surfaces of the stadium and remarked that the place was more crowded with corporate logos than a NASCAR race car.

The Dodgers were able to bite into the lead, but in the fourth inning the wheels came off and the Giants chased Jeff Weaver with a three-run shot over the centerfield wall. I used the downtime during the pitching change to brag about how fast I had heard from the Second on the Casey case. The other lawyers were impressed, though one of them, Dan Daly, suggested that I had only received the quick appellate review because the three judges were on my Christmas list. I remarked to Daly that he had apparently missed the bar memo regarding juries' distrust of lawyers with ponytails. His went halfway down his back.

It was also during this lull in the game that I heard my phone ringing. I grabbed it off my hip and flipped it open without looking at the screen.

"Raul?"

"No, sir, this is Detective Lankford with the Glendale Police Department. Is this Michael Haller?"

"Yes," I said.

"Do you have a moment?"

"I have a moment but I am not sure how well I'll be able to hear you. I'm at the Dodgers game. Can this wait until I can call you back?"

"No, sir, it can't. Do you know a man named Raul Aaron Levin? He's a —"

"Yes, I know him. What's wrong?"

"I'm afraid Mr. Levin is dead, sir. He's been the victim of a homicide in his home."

My head dropped so low and so forward that I banged it into the back of the man seated in front of me. I then pulled back and held one hand to one ear and pressed the phone against the other. I blanked out everything around me.

"What happened?"

"We don't know," Lankford said. "That's why we are here. It looks like he was working for you recently. Is there any chance you could come here to possibly answer some questions and assist us?"

I blew out my breath and tried to keep my voice calm and modulated.

"I'm on my way," I said.

TWENTY-THREE

Raul Levin's body was in the back room of his bungalow a few blocks off of Brand Boulevard. The room had likely been designed as a sunroom or maybe a TV room but Raul had turned it into his home office. Like me he'd had no need for a commercial space. His was not a walk-in business. He wasn't even in the yellow pages. He worked for attorneys and got jobs by word of mouth. The five lawyers that were to join him at the baseball game were testimony to his skill and success.

The uniformed cops who had been told to expect me made me wait in the front living room until the detectives could come from the back and talk to me. A uniformed officer stood by in the hallway in case I decided to make a mad dash for the back room or the front door. He was in position to handle it either way. I sat there waiting and thinking about my friend.

I had decided on the drive from the stadium that I knew who had killed Raul Levin. I didn't need to be led to the back room to see or hear the evidence to know who the killer was. Deep down I knew that Raul had gotten too close to Louis Roulet. And I was the one who had sent him. The only question left for me was what was I going to do about it.

After twenty minutes two detectives came from the back of the house and into the living room. I stood up and we talked while standing. The man identified himself as Lankford, the detective who had called me. He was older, the veteran. His partner was a woman named Sobel. She didn't look like she had been investigating homicides for very long.

We didn't shake hands. They were wearing rubber gloves. They also had paper booties over their shoes. Lankford was chewing gum.

"Okay, this is what we've got," he said gruffly. "Levin was in his office, sitting in his desk chair. The chair was turned from the desk, so he was facing the intruder. He was shot one time in the chest. Something small, looks like a twenty-two to me but we'll wait on the coroner for that."

Lankford tapped his chest dead center. I could hear the hard sound of a bullet-proof vest beneath his shirt.

I corrected him. He had pronounced the name here and on the phone earlier as Levine. I said the name rhymed with heaven.

"Levin, then," he said, getting it right. "Anyway, after the shot, he tried to get up or just fell forward to the floor. He expired facedown on the floor. The intruder ransacked the office and we are currently at a loss to determine what he was looking for or what he might have taken."

"Who found him?" I asked.

"A neighbor who found his dog running loose. The intruder must have let the dog out before or after the killing. The neighbor found it wandering around, recognized it and brought it back. She found the front door open, came in and found the body. It didn't look like much of a watchdog, you ask me. It's one of those little hair balls."

"A shih tzu," I said.

I had seen the dog before and heard Levin talk about it, but I couldn't remember its name. It was something like Rex or Bronco — a name that belied the dog's small stature.

Sobel referred to a notebook she was holding before continuing the questioning.

"We haven't found anything that can lead us to next of kin," she said. "Do you know if he had any family?"

"I think his mother lives back east. He was born in Detroit. Maybe she's there. I don't think they had much of a relationship."

She nodded.

"We have found his time and hours calendar. He's got your name on almost every day for the last month. Was he working on a specific case for you?"

I nodded.

"A couple different cases. One mostly."

"Do you care to tell us about it?" she asked.

"I have a case about to go to trial. Next month. It's an attempted rape and murder. He was running down the evidence and helping me to get ready."

"You mean helping you try to backdoor the investigation, huh?" Lankford said.

I realized then that Lankford's politeness on the phone was merely sweet talk to get me to come to the house. He would be different now. He even seemed to be chewing his gum more aggressively than when he had first entered the room.

"Whatever you want to call it, Detective. Everybody is entitled to a defense."

"Yeah, sure, and they're all innocent, only it's their parents' fault for taking them off the tit too soon," Lankford said. "Whatever. This guy Levin was a cop before, right?"

He was back to mispronouncing the name.

"Yes, he was LAPD. He was a detective on a Crimes Against Persons squad but he retired after twelve years on the force. I think it was twelve years. You'll have to check. And it's Levin."

"Right, as in heaven. I guess he couldn't hack working for the good guys, huh?"

"Depends on how you look at it, I guess."

"Can we get back to your case?" Sobel asked. "What is the name of the defendant?"

"Louis Ross Roulet. The trial's in Van Nuys Superior before Judge Fullbright."

"Is he in custody?"

"No, he's out on a bond."

"Any animosity between Roulet and Mr. Levin?"

"Not that I know of."

I had decided. I was going to deal with Roulet in the way I knew how. I was sticking with the plan I had concocted — with the help of Raul Levin. Drop a depth charge into the case and make sure to get clear. I felt I owed it to my friend Mish. He would have wanted it this way. I wouldn't farm it out. I would handle it personally.

"Could this have been a gay thing?" Lankford asked.

"What? Why do you say that?"

"Prissy dog and then all around the house, he's only got pictures of guys and the dog. Everywhere. On the walls, next to the bed, on the piano."

"Look closely, Detective. It is probably one guy. His partner died a few years ago. I don't think he's been with anybody since then."

"Died of AIDS, I bet."

I didn't confirm that for him. I just waited. On the one hand, I was annoyed with Lankford's manner. On the other hand, I figured that his torch-the-ground method of investigation would preclude him from being able to tag Roulet with this. That was fine with me. I only needed to stall him for five or six weeks and then I wouldn't care if they put it together or not. I'd be finished with my own play by then.

"Did this guy go out patrolling the gay joints?" Lankford asked.

I shrugged.

"I have no idea. But if it was a gay murder, why was his

office ransacked and not the rest of the house?"

Lankford nodded. He seemed to be momentarily taken aback by the logic of my question. But then he hit me with a surprise punch.

"So where were you this morning, Counselor?"

"What?"

"It's just routine. The scene indicates the victim knew his killer. He let the shooter right into the back room. As I said before, he was probably sitting in his desk chair when he took the bullet. Looks to me like he was quite comfortable with his killer. We are going to have to clear all acquaintances, professional and social."

"Are you saying I'm a suspect in this?"

"No, I'm just trying to clear things up and tighten the focus."

"I was home all morning. I was getting ready to meet Raul at Dodger Stadium. I left for the stadium about twelve and that's where I was when you called."

"What about before that?"

"Like I said, I was home. I was alone. But I got a phone call about eleven that will put me in my house and I'm at least a half hour from here. If he was killed after eleven, then I'm clear."

Lankford didn't rise to the bait. He didn't give me the time of death. Maybe it was unknown at the moment.

"When was the last time you spoke to him?" he asked instead.

"Last night by telephone."

"Who called who and why?"

"He called me and asked if I could get to the game early. I said I could."

"How come?"

"He likes to — he liked to watch batting practice. He said we could jaw over the Roulet case a little bit. Nothing specific but he hadn't updated me in about a week."

"Thank you for your cooperation," Lankford said, sarcasm heavy in his voice.

"You realize that I just did what I tell every client and anybody who will listen not to do? I talked to you without a lawyer present, gave you my alibi. I must be out of my mind."

"I said thank you."

Sobel spoke up.

"Is there anything else you can tell us, Mr. Haller? About Mr. Levin or his work."

"Yeah, there is one other thing. Something you should probably check out. But I want to remain confidential on it."

I looked past them at the uniformed officer still standing in the hallway. Sobel followed my eyes and understood I wanted privacy.

"Officer, you can wait out front, please," she said.

The officer left, looking annoyed, probably because he had been dismissed by a woman.

"Okay," Lankford said. "What have you got?"

"I'll have to look up the exact dates but a few weeks ago, back in March, Raul did some work for me on another case that involved one of my clients snitching off a drug dealer. He made some calls, helped ID the guy. I heard afterward that the guy was a Colombian and he was pretty well connected. He could have had friends who . . ."

I left it for them to fill in the blanks.

"I don't know," Lankford said. "This was pretty clean. Doesn't look like a revenge deal. They didn't cut his throat or take his tongue. One shot, plus they ransacked the office. What would the dealer's people be looking for?"

I shook my head.

"Maybe my client's name. The deal I made kept it out of circulation."

Lankford nodded thoughtfully.

"What is the client's name?"

"I can't tell you. Attorney-client privilege."

"Okay, here we go with that bullshit. How are we going to investigate this if we don't even know your client's name? Don't you care about your friend in there on the floor with a piece of lead in his heart?"

"Yes, I care. I'm obviously the only one here who does care. But I am also bound by the rules and ethics of law."

"Your client could be in danger."

"My client is safe. My client is in lockdown."

"It's a woman, isn't it?" Sobel said. "You keep saying 'client' instead of he or she."

"I'm not talking to you about my client. If you want the name of the dealer, it's Hector Arrande Moya. He's in federal custody. I believe the originating charge came out of a DEA case in San Diego. That's all I can tell you."

Sobel wrote it all down. I believed I had now given them sufficient reason to look beyond Roulet and the gay angle.

"Mr. Haller, have you ever been in Mr. Levin's office before?" Sobel asked.

"A few times. Not in a couple months, at least."

"Do you mind walking back with us anyway? Maybe you'll see something out of place or notice something that's missing."

"Is he still back there?"

"The victim? Yes, he's still as he was found."

I nodded. I wasn't sure I wanted to see Raul Levin's body in the center of a murder scene. I then decided all at once that I must see him and I must not forget the vision. I would need it to fuel my resolve and my plan.

"Okay, I'll go back."

"Then put these on and don't touch anything while you're back there," Lankford said. "We're still processing the scene."

From his pocket he produced a folded pair of paper

booties. I sat down on Raul's couch and put them on. Then I followed them down the hallway to the death room.

Raul Levin's body was in situ — as they had found it. He was chest-down on the floor, his face turned to his right, his mouth and eyes open. His body was in an awkward posture, one hip higher than the other and his arms and hands beneath him. It seemed clear that he had fallen from the desk chair that was behind him.

I immediately regretted my decision to come into the room. I suddenly knew that the final look on Raul's face would crowd out all other visual memories I had of him. I would be forced to try to forget him, so I would not have to look at those eyes in my mind again.

It was the same with my father. My only visual memory was of a man in a bed. He was a hundred pounds tops and was being ravaged from the inside out by cancer. All the other visuals I carried of him were false. They came from pictures in books I had read.

There were a number of people working in the room. Crime scene investigators and people from the medical examiner's office. My face must have shown the horror I was feeling.

"You know why we can't cover him up?" Lankford asked me. "Because of people like you. Because of O.J. It's what they call *evidence transference.* Something you lawyers like to jump all over on. So no sheets over the body anymore. Not till we move it out of here."

I didn't say anything. I just nodded. He was right.

"Can you step over here to the desk and tell us if you see anything unusual?" Sobel asked, apparently having some sympathy for me.

I was thankful to do it because I could keep my back to the body. I walked over to the desk, which was a conjoining of three worktables forming a turn in the corner of the room. It was furniture I recognized had come from the

IKEA store in nearby Burbank. It was nothing fancy. It was simple and useful. The center table in the corner had a computer on top and a pull-out tray for a keyboard. The tables to either side looked like twin work spaces and possibly were used by Levin to keep separate investigations from mingling.

My eyes lingered on the computer as I wondered what Levin may have put on electronic files about Roulet. Sobel noticed.

"We don't have a computer expert," she said. "Too small a department. We've got a guy coming from the sheriff's office but it looks to me like the whole drive was pulled out."

She pointed with her pen under the table to where the PC unit was sitting upright but with one side of its plastic cowling having been removed and placed to the rear.

"Probably won't be anything there for us," she said. "What about the desks?"

My eyes moved over the table to the left of the computer first. Papers and files were spread across it in a haphazard way. I looked at some of the tabs and recognized the names.

"Some of these are my clients but they're old cases. Not active."

"They probably came from the file cabinets in the closet," Sobel said. "The killer could have dumped them here to confuse us. To hide what he was really looking for or taking. What about over here?"

We stepped over to the table to the right of the computer. This one was not in as much disarray. There was a calendar blotter on which it was clear Levin kept a running account of his hours and which attorney he was working for at the time. I scanned the blocks and saw my name numerous times going back five weeks. It was as they had told me, he had practically been working full-time for me.

"I don't know," I said. "I don't know what to look for. I don't see anything that could help."

"Well, most attorneys aren't that helpful," Lankford said from behind me.

I didn't bother to turn around to defend myself. He was by the body and I didn't want to see what he was doing. I reached out to turn the Rolodex that was on the table just so I could look through the names on the cards.

"Don't touch that!" Sobel said instantly.

I jerked my hand back.

"Sorry. I was just going to look through the names. I don't . . ."

I didn't finish. I was at sea here. I wanted to leave and get something to drink. I felt like the Dodger dog that had tasted so good back at the stadium was about to come up.

"Hey, check it out," Lankford said.

I turned with Sobel and saw that the medical examiner's people were slowly turning Levin's body over. Blood had stained the front of the Dodgers shirt he was wearing. But Lankford was pointing to the dead man's hands, which had not been visible beneath the body before. The two middle fingers of his left hand were folded down against the palm while the two outside fingers were fully extended.

"Was this guy a Texas Longhorns fan or what?" Lankford asked.

Nobody laughed.

"What do you think?" Sobel said to me.

I stared down at my friend's last gesture and just shook my head.

"Oh, I got it," Lankford said. "It's like a signal. A code. He's telling us that the devil did it."

I thought of Raul calling Roulet the devil, of having the proof that he was evil. And I knew what my friend's last message to me meant. As he died on the floor of his office, he tried to tell me. Tried to warn me.

TWENTY-FOUR

I went to Four Green Fields and ordered a Guinness but quickly escalated to vodka over ice. I didn't think there was any sense in delaying things. The Dodgers game was finishing up on the TV over the bar. The boys in blue were rallying, down now by just two with the bases loaded in the ninth. The bartender had his eyes glued to the screen but I didn't care anymore about the start of new seasons. I didn't care about ninth-inning rallies.

After the second vodka assault, I brought the cell phone up onto the bar and started making calls. First I called the four other lawyers from the game. We had all left when I had gotten the word but they went home only knowing that Levin was dead, none of the details. Then I called Lorna and she cried on the phone. I talked her through it for a little while and then she asked the question I was hoping to avoid.

"Is this because of your case? Because of Roulet?"

"I don't know," I lied. "I told the cops about it but they seemed more interested in him being gay than anything else."

"He was gay?"

I knew it would work as a deflection.

"He didn't advertise it."

"And you knew and didn't tell me?"

"There was nothing to tell. It was his life. If he wanted to tell people, he would have told people, I guess."

"The detectives said that's what happened?"

"What?"

"You know, that his being gay is how he got murdered."

"I don't know. They kept asking about it. I don't know what they think. They'll look at everything and hopefully it will lead to something."

There was silence. I looked up at the TV just as the winning run crossed the plate for the Dodgers and the stadium erupted in bedlam and joy. The bartender whooped and used a remote to turn up the broadcast. I looked away and put a hand over my free ear.

"Makes you think, doesn't it?" Lorna said.

"About what?"

"About what we do. Mickey, when they catch the bastard who did this, he might call me to hire you."

I got the bartender's attention by shaking the ice in my empty glass. I wanted a refill. What I didn't want was to tell Lorna that I believed I was already working for the bastard who had killed Raul.

"Lorna, take it easy. You're getting —"

"It could happen!"

"Look, Raul was my colleague and he was also my friend. But I'm not going to change what I do or what I believe in because —"

"Maybe you should. Maybe we all should. That's all I'm saying."

She started crying again. The bartender brought my fresh drink and I took a third of it down in one gulp.

"Lorna, do you want me to come over there?"

"No, I don't want anything. I don't know what I want. This is just so awful."

"Can I tell you something?"

"What? Of course you can."

"You remember Jesus Menendez? My client?"

"Yes, but what's he have —"

"He was innocent. And Raul was working on it. We were

working on it. We're going to get him out."

"Why are you telling me this?"

"I'm telling you because we can't take what happened to Raul and just stop in our tracks. What we do is important. It's necessary."

The words sounded hollow as I said them. She didn't respond. I had probably confused her because I had confused myself.

"Okay?" I asked.

"Okay."

"Good. I have to make some more calls, Lorna."

"Will you tell me when you find out about the services?"

"I will."

After closing my phone I decided to take a break before making another call. I thought about Lorna's last question and realized I might be the one organizing the services she asked about. Unless an old woman in Detroit who had disowned Raul Levin twenty-five years ago stepped up to the plate.

I pushed my glass to the edge of the bar gutter and said to the bartender, "Gimme a Guinness and give yourself one, too."

I decided it was time to slow down and one way was to drink Guinness, since it took so long to fill a glass out of the tap. When the bartender finally brought it to me I saw that he had etched a harp in the foam with the tap nozzle. An angel's harp. I hoisted the glass before drinking from it.

"God bless the dead," I said.

"God bless the dead," the bartender said.

I drank heavily from the glass and the thick ale was like mortar I was sending down to hold the bricks together inside. All at once I felt like crying. But then my phone rang. I grabbed it up without looking at the screen and said hello. The alcohol had bent my voice into an unrecognizable shape.

"Is this Mick?" a voice asked.

"Yeah, who's this?"

"It's Louis. I just heard the news about Raul. I'm so sorry, man."

I pulled the phone away from my ear as if it were a snake about to bite me. I pulled my arm back, ready to throw it at the mirror behind the bar, where I saw my own reflection. Then I stopped and brought it back.

"Yeah, motherfucker, how did you —"

I broke off and started laughing as I realized what I had just called him and what Raul Levin's theory about Roulet had been.

"Excuse me," Roulet said. "Are you drinking?"

"You're damn right I'm drinking," I said. "How the fuck do you already know what happened to Mish?"

"If by Mish you mean Mr. Levin, I just got a call from the Glendale police. A detective said she wanted to speak to me about him."

That answer squeezed at least two of the vodkas right out of my liver. I straightened up on my stool.

"Sobel? Is that who called?"

"Yeah, I think so. She said she got my name from you. She said it would be routine questions. She's coming here."

"Where?"

"The office."

I thought about it for a moment but didn't think Sobel was in any kind of danger, even if she came without Lankford. Roulet wouldn't try anything with a cop, especially in his own office. My greater concern was that somehow Sobel and Lankford were already onto Roulet and I would be robbed of my chance to personally avenge Raul Levin and Jesus Menendez. Had Roulet left a fingerprint behind? Had a neighbor seen him go into Levin's house?

"That's all she said?"

"Yes. She said they were talking to all of his recent clients and I was the most recent."

"Don't talk to them."

"You sure?"

"Not without your lawyer present."

"Won't they get suspicious if I don't talk to them, like give them an alibi or something?"

"It doesn't matter. They don't talk to you unless I give my permission. And I'm not giving it."

I gripped my free hand into a fist. I couldn't stand the idea of giving legal advice to the man I was sure had killed my friend that very morning.

"Okay," Roulet said. "I'll send her on her way."

"Where were you this morning?"

"Me? I was here at the office. Why?"

"Did anybody see you?"

"Well, Robin came in at ten. Not before that."

I pictured the woman with the hair cut like a scythe. I didn't know what to tell Roulet because I didn't know what the time of death was. I didn't want to mention anything about the tracking bracelet he supposedly had on his ankle.

"Call me after Detective Sobel leaves. And remember, no matter what she or her partner says to you, do not talk to them. They can lie to you as much as they want. And they all do. Consider anything they tell you to be a lie. They're just trying to trick you into talking to them. If they tell you I said it was okay to talk, that is a lie. Pick up the phone and call me, I will tell them to get lost."

"All right, Mick. That's how I'll play it. Thanks."

He ended the call. I closed my phone and dropped it on the bar like it was something dirty and discarded.

"Yeah, don't mention it," I said.

I drained a good quarter of my pint, then picked up the phone again. Using speed dial I called Fernando

Valenzuela's cell number. He was at home, having just gotten in from the Dodgers game. That meant that he had left early to beat the traffic. Typical L.A. fan.

"Do you still have a tracking bracelet on Roulet?"

"Yeah, he's got it."

"How's it work? Can you track where he's been or only where he's at?"

"It's global positioning. It sends up a signal. You can track it backwards to tell where somebody's been."

"You got it there or is it at the office?"

"It's on my laptop, man. What's up?"

"I want to see where he's been today."

"Well, let me boot it up. Hold on."

I held on, finished my Guinness and had the bartender start filling another before Valenzuela had his laptop fired up.

"Where're you at, Mick?"

"Four Green Fields."

"Anything wrong?"

"Yeah, something's wrong. Do you have it up or what?"

"Yeah, I'm looking at it right here. How far back do you want to check?"

"Start at this morning."

"Okay. He, uh . . . he hasn't done much today. I track it from his home to his office at eight. Looks like he took a little trip nearby — a couple blocks, probably for lunch — and then back to the office. He's still there."

I thought about this for a few moments. The bartender delivered my next pint.

"Val, how do you get that thing off your ankle?"

"You mean if you were him? You don't. You can't. It bolts on and the little wrench you use is unique. It's like a key. I got the only one."

"You're sure about that?"

"I'm sure. I got it right here on my key chain, man."

"No copies — like from the manufacturer?"

"Not supposed to be. Besides, it doesn't matter. If the ring is broken — like even if he did open it — I get an alarm on the system. It also has what's called a 'mass detector.' Once I put that baby around his ankle, I get an alarm on the computer the moment it reads that there is nothing there. That didn't happen, Mick. So you are talking about a saw being the only way. Cut off the leg, leave the bracelet on the ankle. That's the only way."

I drank the top off my new beer. The bartender hadn't bothered with any artwork this time.

"What about the battery? What if the battery's dead, you lose the signal?"

"No, Mick. I got that covered, too. He's got a charger and a receptacle on the bracelet. Every few days he's got to plug it in for a couple hours to juice it. You know, while he's at his desk or something or taking a nap. If the battery goes below twenty percent I get an alarm on my computer and I call him and say plug it in. If he doesn't do it then, I get another alarm at fifteen percent, and then at ten percent *he* starts beeping and he's got no way to take it off or turn it off. Doesn't make for a good getaway. And that last ten percent still gives me five hours of tracking. I can find him in five hours, no sweat."

"Okay, okay."

I was convinced by the science.

"What's going on?"

I told him about Levin and told him that the police would likely have to check out Roulet, and the ankle bracelet and tracking system would likely be our client's alibi. Valenzuela was stunned by the news. He might not have been as close to Levin as I had been, but he had known him just as long.

"What do you think happened, Mick?" he asked me.

I knew that he was asking if I thought Roulet was the

killer or somehow behind the killing. Valenzuela was not privy to all that I knew or that Levin had found out.

"I don't know what to think," I said. "But you should watch yourself with this guy."

"And you watch yourself."

"I will."

I closed the phone, wondering if there was something Valenzuela didn't know. If Roulet had somehow found a way to take the ankle bracelet off or to subvert the tracking system. I was convinced by the science of it but not the human side of it. There are always human flaws.

The bartender sauntered over to my spot at the bar.

"Hey, buddy, did you lose your car keys?" he said.

I looked around to make sure he was talking to me and then shook my head.

"No," I said.

"Are you sure? Somebody found keys in the parking lot. You better check."

I reached into the pocket of my suit jacket, then brought my hand out and extended it, palm up. My key ring was displayed on my hand.

"See, I tol —"

In a quick and unexpected move, the bartender grabbed the keys off my hand and smiled.

"Falling for that should be a sobriety test in and of itself," he said. "Anyway, pal, you're not driving — not for a while. When you're ready to go, I'll call you a taxi."

He stepped back from the bar in case I had a violent objection to the ruse. But I just nodded.

"You got me," I said.

He tossed my keys onto the back counter, where the bottles were lined up. I looked at my watch. It wasn't even five o'clock. Embarrassment burned through the alcohol padding. I had taken the easy way out. The coward's way, getting drunk in the face of a terrible occurrence.

"You can take it," I said, pointing to my glass of Guinness.

I picked up the phone and punched in a speed-dial number. Maggie McPherson answered right away. The courts usually closed by four-thirty. The prosecutors were usually at their desks in that last hour or two before the end of the day.

"Hey, is it quitting time yet?"

"Haller?"

"Yeah."

"What's going on? Are you drinking? Your voice is different."

"I think I might need you to drive *me* home this time."

"Where are you?"

"For Greedy Fucks."

"What?"

"Four Green Fields. I've been here awhile."

"Michael, what is —"

"Raul Levin is dead."

"Oh my God, what —"

"Murdered. So this time can you drive *me* home? I've had too much."

"Let me call Stacey and get her to stay late with Hayley, then I'll be on my way. Do not try to leave there, okay? Just don't leave."

"Don't worry, the bartender isn't gonna let me."

TWENTY-FIVE

After closing my phone I told the bartender I had changed my mind and I'd have one more pint while waiting for my ride. I took out my wallet and put a credit card on the bar. He ran my tab first, then got me the Guinness. He took so long filling the glass, spooning foam over the side to give me a full pour, that I had barely tasted it by the time Maggie got there.

"That was too quick," I said. "You want a drink?"

"No, it's too early. Let's just get you home."

"Okay."

I got off the stool, remembered to collect my credit card and phone, and left the bar with my arm around her shoulders and feeling like I had poured more Guinness and vodka down the drain than my own throat.

"I'm right out front," Maggie said. "Four Greedy Fucks, how did you come up with that? Do four people own this place?"

"No, *for*, as in *for the people*. As in Haller *for the defense*. Not the number four. Greedy fucks as in lawyers."

"Thank you."

"Not you. You're not a lawyer. You're a prosecutor."

"How much did you drink, Haller?"

"Somewhere between too much and a lot."

"Don't puke in my car."

"I promise."

We got to the car, one of the cheap Jaguar models. It was the first car she had ever bought without me holding her hand and being involved in running down the choices. She'd gotten the Jag because it made her feel classy, but anybody who knew cars knew it was just a dressed-up Ford. I didn't spoil it for her. Whatever made her happy made me happy — except the time she thought divorcing me would make her life happier. That didn't do much for me.

She helped me in and then we were off.

"Don't pass out, either," she said as she pulled out of the parking lot. "I don't know the way."

"Just take Laurel Canyon over the hill. After that, it's just a left turn at the bottom."

Even though it was supposed to be a reverse commute, it took almost forty-five minutes in end-of-the-day traffic to get to Fareholm Drive. Along the way I told her about Raul Levin and what had happened. She didn't react like Lorna had because she had never known Levin. Though I had known him and used him as an investigator for years, he didn't become a friend until after we had divorced. In fact, it was Raul who had driven me home on more than one night from Four Green Fields as I was getting through the end of my marriage.

My garage opener was in the Lincoln back at the bar so I told her to just park in the opening in front of the garage. I also realized my front door key was on the ring that had the Lincoln's key and that had been confiscated by the bartender. We had to go down the side of the house to the back deck and get the spare key — the one Roulet had given me — from beneath an ashtray on the picnic table. We went in the back door, which led directly into my office. This was good because even in my inebriated state I was pleased that we avoided climbing the stairs to the front door. Not only would it have worn me out but she would have seen the view and been reminded of the inequities between life as a prosecutor and life as a greedy fuck.

"Ah, that's nice," she said. "Our little teacup."

I followed her eyes and saw she was looking at the photo of our daughter I kept on the desk. I thrilled at the idea I had inadvertently scored a point of some kind with her.

"Yeah," I said, fumbling any chance of capitalizing.

"Which way to the bedroom?" she asked.

"Well, aren't you being forward. To the right."

"Sorry, Haller, I'm not staying long. I only got a couple extra hours out of Stacey, and with that traffic, I've got to turn around and head back over the hill soon."

She walked me into the bedroom and we sat down next to each other on the bed.

"Thank you for doing this," I said.

"One good turn deserves another, I guess," she said.

"I thought I got my good turn that night I took you home."

She put her hand on my cheek and turned my face toward hers. She kissed me. I took this as confirmation that we actually had made love that night. I felt incredibly left out at not remembering.

"Guinness," she said, tasting her lips as she pulled away.

"And some vodka."

"Good combination. You'll be hurting in the morning."

"It's so early I'll be hurting tonight. Tell you what, why don't we go get dinner at Dan Tana's? Craig's on the door now and —"

"No, Mick. I have to go home to Hayley and you have to go to sleep."

I made a gesture of surrender.

"Okay, okay."

"Call me in the morning. I want to talk to you when you're sober."

"Okay."

"You want to get undressed and get under the covers?"

"No, I'm all right. I'll just . . ."

I leaned back on the bed and kicked my shoes off. I then rolled over to the edge and opened a drawer in the night table. I took out a bottle of Tylenol and a CD that had been given to me by a client named Demetrius Folks. He was a banger from Norwalk known on the street as Lil' Demon. He had told me once that he'd had a vision one night and that he knew he was destined to die young and violently. He gave me the CD and told me to play it when he was dead. And I did. Demetrius's prophecy came true. He was killed in a drive-by shooting about six months after he had given me the disc. In Magic Marker he had written *Wreckrium for Lil' Demon* on it. It was a collection of ballads he had burned off of Tupac CDs.

I loaded the CD into the Bose player on the night table and soon the rhythmic beat of "God Bless the Dead" started to play. The song was a salute to fallen comrades.

"You listen to this stuff?". Maggie asked, her eyes squinting at me in disbelief.

I shrugged as best I could while leaning on an elbow.

"Sometimes. It helps me understand a lot of my clients better."

"These are the people who should be in jail."

"Maybe some of them. But a lot of them have something to say. Some are true poets and this guy was the best of them."

"Was? Who is it, the one that got shot outside the car museum on Wilshire?"

"No, you're talking about Biggie Smalls. This is the late great Tupac Shakur."

"I can't believe you listen to this stuff."

"I told you. It helps me."

"Do me a favor. Do not listen to this around Hayley."

"Don't worry about it, I won't."

"I've gotta go."

"Just stay a little bit."

She complied but she sat stiffly on the edge of the bed. I could tell she was trying to pick up the lyrics. You needed an ear for it and it took some time. The next song was "Life Goes On," and I watched her neck and shoulders tighten as she caught some of the words.

"Can I please go now?" she asked.

"Maggie, just stay a few minutes."

I reached over and turned it down a little.

"Hey, I'll turn it off if you'll sing to me like you used to."

"Not tonight, Haller."

"Nobody knows the Maggie McFierce I know."

She smiled a little and I was quiet for a moment while I remembered those times.

"Maggie, why do you stay with me?"

"I told you, I can't stay."

"No, I don't mean tonight. I'm talking about how you stick with me, how you don't run me down with Hayley and how you're there when I need you. Like tonight. I don't know many people who have ex-wives who still like them."

She thought a little bit before answering.

"I don't know. I guess because I see a good man and a good father in there waiting to break out one day."

I nodded and hoped she was right.

"Tell me something. What would you do if you couldn't be a prosecutor?"

"Are you serious?"

"Yeah, what would you do?"

"I've never really thought about it. Right now I get to do what I've always wanted to do. I'm lucky. Why would I want to change?"

I opened the Tylenol bottle and popped two without a chaser. The next song was "So Many Tears," another ballad for all of those lost. It seemed appropriate.

"I think I'd be a teacher," she finally said. "Grade school. Little girls like Hayley."

I smiled.

"Mrs. McFierce, Mrs. McFierce, my dog ate my homework."

She slugged me on the arm.

"Actually, that's nice," I said. "You'd be a good teacher . . . except when you're sending kids off to detention without bail."

"Funny. What about you?"

I shook my head.

"I wouldn't be a good teacher."

"I mean what would you do if you weren't a lawyer."

"I don't know. But I've got three Town Cars. I guess I could start a limo service, take people to the airport."

Now she smiled at me.

"I'd hire you."

"Good. There's one customer. Give me a dollar and I'll tape it to the wall."

But the banter wasn't working. I leaned back, put my palms against my eyes and tried to push away the day, to push out the memory of Raul Levin on the floor of his house, eyes staring at a permanent black sky.

"You know what I used to be afraid of?" I asked.

"What?"

"That I wouldn't recognize innocence. That it would be there right in front of me and I wouldn't see it. I'm not talking about guilty or not guilty. I mean innocence. Just innocence."

She didn't say anything.

"But you know what I should have been afraid of?"

"What, Haller?"

"Evil. Pure evil."

"What do you mean?"

"I mean, most of the people I defend aren't evil, Mags.

They're guilty, yeah, but they aren't evil. You know what I mean? There's a difference. You listen to them and you listen to these songs and you know why they make the choices they make. People are just trying to get by, just to live with what they're given, and some of them aren't given a damn thing in the first place. But evil is something else. It's different. It's like . . . I don't know. It's out there and when it shows up . . . I don't know. I can't explain it."

"You're drunk, that's why."

"All I know is I should have been afraid of one thing but I was afraid of the complete opposite."

She reached over and rubbed my shoulder. The last song was "to live & die in l.a.," and it was my favorite on the homespun CD. I started to softly hum and then I sang along with the refrain when it came up on the track.

> *to live & die in l.a.*
> *it's the place to be*
> *you got to be there to know it*
> *ev'ybody wanna see*

Pretty soon I stopped singing and pulled my hands down from my face. I fell asleep with my clothes on. I never heard the woman I had loved more than anyone else in my life leave the house. She would tell me later that the last thing I had mumbled before passing out was, "I can't do this anymore."

I wasn't talking about my singing.

TWENTY-SIX

I slept almost ten hours but I still woke up in darkness. It said 5:18 on the Bose. I tried to go back to the dream but the door was closed. By 5:30 I rolled out of bed, struggled for equilibrium, and hit the shower. I stayed under the spray until the hot-water tank ran cold. Then I got out and got dressed for another day of fighting the machine.

It was still too early to call Lorna to check on the day's schedule but I keep a calendar on my desk that is usually up-to-date. I went into the home office to check it and the first thing I noticed was a dollar bill taped to the wall over the desk.

My adrenaline jogged up a couple notches as my mind raced and I thought an intruder had left the money on the wall as some sort of threat or message. Then I remembered.

"Maggie," I said out loud.

I smiled and decided to leave the dollar bill taped to the wall.

I got the calendar out of the briefcase and checked my schedule. It looked like I had the morning free until an 11 A.M. hearing in San Fernando Superior. The case was a repeat client charged with possession of drug paraphernalia. It was a bullshit charge, hardly worth the time and money, but Melissa Menkoff was already on probation for a variety of drug offenses. If she took a fall for something as minor as drug paraphernalia, her probated sentence would kick in and she would end up behind a steel door for six to nine months.

That was all I had on the calendar. After San Fernando my day was clear and I silently congratulated myself for the foresight I must have used in keeping the day after opening day clear. Of course, I didn't know when I set up the schedule that the death of Raul Levin would send me into Four Green Fields so early, but it was good planning just the same.

The hearing on the Menkoff matter involved my motion to suppress the crack pipe found during a search of her vehicle after a reckless driving stop in Northridge. The pipe had been found in the closed center console of her car. She had told me that she had not given permission to the police to search the car but they did anyway. My argument was that there was no consent to search and no probable cause to search. If Menkoff had been pulled over by police for driving erratically, then there was no reason to search the closed compartments of her car.

It was a loser and I knew it, but Menkoff's father paid me well to do the best I could for his troubled daughter. And that was exactly what I was going to do at eleven o'clock in San Fernando Court.

For breakfast I had two Tylenols and chased them with fried eggs, toast and coffee. I doused the eggs liberally with pepper and salsa. It all hit the right spots and gave me the fuel to carry on the battle. I turned the pages of the *Times* as I ate, looking for a story on the murder of Raul Levin. Inexplicably, there was no story. I didn't understand this at first. Why would Glendale keep the wraps on this? Then I remembered that the *Times* put out several regional editions of the paper each morning. I lived on the Westside, and Glendale was considered part of the San Fernando Valley. News of a murder in the Valley may have been deemed by *Times* editors as unimportant to Westside readers, who had their own region's murders to worry about. I got no story on Levin.

I decided I would have to buy a second copy of the *Times* off a newsstand on the way to San Fernando Court and check again. Thoughts about which newsstand I would direct Earl Briggs to reminded me that I had no car. The Lincoln was in the parking lot at Four Green Fields — unless it had been stolen during the night — and I couldn't get my keys until the pub opened at eleven for lunch. I had a problem. I had seen Earl's car in the commuter lot where I picked him up each morning. It was a pimped-out Toyota with a low-rider profile and spinning chrome rims. My guess was that it had the permanent stink of weed in it, too. I didn't want to ride in it. In the north county it was an invitation to a police stop. In the south county it was an invitation to get shot at. I also didn't want Earl to pick me up at the house. I never let my drivers know where I live.

The plan I came up with was to take a cab to my warehouse in North Hollywood and use one of the new Town Cars. The Lincoln at Four Green Fields had over fifty thousand miles on it, anyway. Maybe breaking out the new wheels would help me get past the depression sure to set in because of Raul Levin.

After I had cleaned the frying pan and the dish in the sink I decided it was late enough to risk waking Lorna with a call to confirm my day's schedule. I went back into the home office and when I picked up the house phone to make the call I heard the broken dial tone that told me I had at least one message waiting.

I called the retrieval number and was told by an electronic voice that I had missed a call at 11:07 A.M. the day before. When the voice recited the number that the missed call had come from, I froze. The number was Raul Levin's cell phone. I had missed his last call.

"Hey, it's me. You probably left for the game already and I guess you got your cell turned off. If you don't get this

I'll just catch you there. But I've got another ace for you. I guess you —"

He broke off for a moment at the background sound of a dog barking.

"— could say I've got Jesus's ticket out of the Q. I've gotta go, lad."

That was it. He hung up without a good-bye and had used that stupid brogue at the end. The brogue had always annoyed me. Now it sounded endearing. I missed it already.

I pushed the button to replay the message and listened again and then did it three more times before finally saving the message and hanging up. I then sat there in my desk chair and tried to apply the message to what I knew. The first puzzle involved the time of the call. I did not leave for the game until at least 11:30, yet I had somehow missed the call from Levin that had come in more than twenty minutes earlier.

This made no sense until I remembered the call from Lorna. At 11:07 I had been on the phone with Lorna. My home phone was used so infrequently and so few people had the number that I did not bother to have call waiting installed on the line. This meant that Levin's last call would have been kicked over to the voicemail system and I would have never known about it as I spoke to Lorna.

That explained the circumstances of the call but not its contents.

Levin had obviously found something. He was no lawyer but he certainly knew evidence and how to evaluate it. He had found something that could help me get Menendez out of prison. He had found Jesus's ticket out.

The last thing left to consider was the interruption of the dog barking and that was easy. I had been to Levin's home before and I knew the dog was a high-strung yapper.

Every time I had come to the house, I had heard the dog start barking before I had even knocked on the door. The barking in the background on the phone message and Levin hurriedly ending the call told me someone was coming to his door. He had a visitor and it may very well have been his killer.

I thought about things for a few moments and decided that the timing of the call was something I could not in good conscience keep from the police. The contents of the message would raise new questions that I might have difficulty answering, but that was outweighed by the value of the call's timing. I went into the bedroom and dug through the pockets of the blue jeans I had worn the day before to the game. In one of the back pockets I found the ticket stub from the game and the business cards Lankford and Sobel had given me at the end of my visit to Levin's house.

I chose Sobel's card and noticed it only said *Detective Sobel* on it. No first name. I wondered why that was as I made the call. Maybe she was like me, with two different business cards in alternate pockets. One with her complete name in one, one with the more formal name in the other.

She answered the call right away and I decided to see what I could get from her before I gave her what I had.

"Anything new on the investigation?" I asked.

"Not a lot. Not a lot that I can share with you. We are sort of organizing the evidence we have. We got some ballistics back and —"

"They already did an autopsy?" I said. "That was quick."

"No, the autopsy won't be until tomorrow."

"Then how'd you get ballistics already?"

She didn't answer but then I figured it out.

"You found a casing. He was shot with an automatic that ejected the shell."

"You're good, Mr. Haller. Yes, we found a cartridge."

"I've done a lot of trials. And call me Mickey. It's funny, the killer ransacked the place but didn't pick up the shell."

"Maybe that's because it rolled across the floor and fell into a heating vent. The killer would have needed a screwdriver and a lot of time."

I nodded. It was a lucky break. I couldn't count the number of times clients had gone down because the cops had caught a lucky break. Then again, there were a lot of clients who walked because they caught the break. It all evened out in the end.

"So, was your partner right about it being a twenty-two?"

She paused before answering, deciding whether to cross some threshold of revealing case information to me, an involved party in the case but the enemy — a defense lawyer — nonetheless.

"He was right. And thanks to the markings on the cartridge, we even know the exact gun we are looking for."

I knew from questioning ballistics experts and firearms examiners in trials over the years that marks left on bullet casings during the firing process could identify the weapon even without the weapon in hand. With an automatic, the firing pin, breech block, ejector and extractor all leave signature marks on the bullet casing in the split second the weapon is fired. Analyzing the four markings in unison can lead to a specific make and model of the weapon being identified.

"It turns out that Mr. Levin owned a twenty-two himself," Sobel said. "But we found it in a closet safe in the house and it's not a Woodsman. The one thing we have not found is his cell phone. We know he had one but we —"

"He was talking to me on it right before he was killed."

There was a moment of silence.

"You told us yesterday that the last time you spoke to him was Friday night."

"That's right. But that's why I am calling. Raul called me yesterday morning at eleven-oh-seven and left me a message. I didn't get it until today because after I left you people yesterday I just went out and got drunk. Then I went to sleep and didn't realize I had a message from him till right now. He called about one of the cases he was working on for me sort of on the side. It's an appellate thing and the client's in prison. A no-rush thing. Anyway, the content of the message isn't important but the call helps with the timing. And get this, while he's leaving the message, you hear the dog start to bark. It did that whenever somebody came to the door. I know because I'd been there before and the dog always barked."

Again she hit me with some silence before responding.

"I don't understand something, Mr. Haller."

"What's that?"

"You told us yesterday you were at home until around noon before you left for the game. And now you say that Mr. Levin left a message for you at eleven-oh-seven. Why didn't you answer the phone?"

"Because I was on it and I don't have call waiting. You can check my records, you'll see I got a call from my office manager, Lorna Taylor. I was talking to her when Raul called. Without call waiting I didn't know. And of course he thought I had already left for the game so he just left a message."

"Okay, I understand. We'll probably want your permission in writing to look at those records."

"No problem."

"Where are you now?"

"I'm at home."

I gave her the address and she said that she and her partner were coming.

"Make it soon. I have to leave for court in about an hour."

"We're coming right now."

I closed the phone feeling uneasy. I had defended a dozen murderers over the years and that had brought me into contact with a number of homicide investigators. But I had never been questioned myself about a murder before. Lankford and now Sobel seemed to be suspicious of every answer I could give. It made me wonder what they knew that I didn't.

I straightened up things on the desk and closed my briefcase. I didn't want them seeing anything I didn't want them to see. I then walked through my house and checked every room. My last stop was the bedroom. I made the bed and put the CD case for *Wreckrium for Lil' Demon* back in the night table drawer. And then it hit me. I sat on the bed as I remembered something Sobel had said. She had made a slip and at first it had gone right by me. She had said that they had found Raul Levin's .22 caliber gun but it was not the murder weapon. She said it was not a Woodsman.

She had inadvertently revealed to me the make and model of the murder weapon. I knew the Woodsman was an automatic pistol manufactured by Colt. I knew this because I owned a Colt Woodsman Sport Model. It had been bequeathed to me many years ago by my father. Upon his death. Once old enough to handle it, I had never even taken it out of its wooden box.

I got up from the bed and went to the walk-in closet. I moved as if in a heavy fog. My steps were tentative and I put my hand out to the wall and then the door casement as if needing my bearings. The polished wooden box was on the shelf where it was supposed to be. I reached up with both hands to bring it down and then walked it out to the bedroom.

I put the box down on the bed and flipped open the brass latch. I raised the lid and pulled away the oilcloth covering.

The gun was gone.

PART TWO
— A WORLD WITHOUT TRUTH

TWENTY-SEVEN

The check from Roulet cleared. On the first day of trial I had more money in my bank account than I'd ever had in my life. If I wanted, I could drop the bus benches and go with billboards. I could also take the back cover of the yellow pages instead of the half page I had inside. I could afford it. I finally had a franchise case and it had paid off. In terms of money, that is. The loss of Raul Levin would forever make this franchise a losing proposition.

We had been through three days of jury selection and were now ready to put on the show. The trial was scheduled for another three days at the most — two for the prosecution and one for the defense. I had told the judge that I would need a day to put my case before the jury, but the truth was, most of my work would be done during the prosecution's presentation.

There's always an electric feel to the start of a trial. A nervousness that attacks deep in the gut. So much is on the line. Reputation, personal freedom, the integrity of the system itself. Something about having those twelve strangers sit in judgment of your life and work always jumps things up inside. And I am referring to me, the defense attorney — the judgment of the defendant is a whole other thing. I've never gotten used to it, and the truth is, I never want to. I can only liken it to the anxiety and tension of standing at the front of a church on your wedding day. I'd had that experience twice and I was reminded of it every time a judge called a trial to order.

Though my experience in trial work severely outweighed my opponent's, there was no mistake about where I stood. I was one man standing before the giant maw of the system. Without a doubt I was the underdog. Yes, it was true that I faced a prosecutor in his first major felony trial. But that advantage was evened and then some by the power and might of the state. At the prosecutor's command were the forces of the entire justice system. And against this all I had was myself. And a guilty client.

I sat next to Louis Roulet at the defense table. We were alone. I had no second and no investigator behind me — out of some strange loyalty to Raul Levin I had not hired a replacement. I didn't really need one, either. Levin had given me everything I needed. The trial and how it played out would serve as a last testament to his skills as an investigator.

In the first row of the gallery sat C. C. Dobbs and Mary Alice Windsor. In accordance with a pretrial ruling, the judge was allowing Roulet's mother to be in the courtroom during opening statements only. Because she was listed as a defense witness, she would not be allowed to listen to any of the testimony that followed. She would remain in the hallway outside, with her loyal lapdog Dobbs at her side, until I called her to the stand.

Also in the first row but not seated next to them was my own support section: my ex-wife Lorna Taylor. She had gotten dressed up in a navy suit and white blouse. She looked beautiful and could have blended in easily with the phalanx of female attorneys who descended on the courthouse every day. But she was there for me and I loved her for it.

The rest of the rows in the gallery were sporadically crowded. There were a few print reporters there to grab quotes from the opening statements and a few attorneys and citizen onlookers. No TV had shown up. The trial had not yet drawn more than cursory attention from the public, and this was good. This meant our strategy of publicity containment had worked well.

Roulet and I were silent as we waited for the judge to take the bench and order the jury into the box so that we could begin. I was attempting to calm myself by rehearsing what I wanted to say to the jurors. Roulet was staring straight ahead at the State of California seal affixed to the front of the judge's bench.

The courtroom clerk took a phone call, said a few words and then hung up.

"Two minutes, people," he said loudly. "Two minutes."

When a judge called ahead to the courtroom, that meant people should be in their positions and ready to go. We were. I glanced over at Ted Minton at the prosecution's table and saw he was doing the same thing that I was doing. Calming himself by rehearsing. I leaned forward and studied the notes on the legal pad in front of me. Then Roulet unexpectedly leaned forward and almost right into me. He spoke in a whisper, even though it wasn't necessary yet.

"This is it, Mick."

"I know."

Since the death of Raul Levin, my relationship with Roulet had been one of cold endurance. I put up with him because I had to. But I saw him as little as possible in the days and weeks before the trial, and spoke to him as little as possible once it started. I knew the one weakness in my plan was my own weakness. I feared that any interaction with Roulet could lead me into acting out my anger and desire to personally, physically avenge my friend. The three days of jury selection had been torture. Day after day I had to sit right next to him and listen to his condescending comments about prospective jurors. The only way I got through it was to pretend he wasn't there.

"You ready?" he asked me.

"Trying to be," I said. "Are you?"

"I'm ready. But I wanted to tell you something before we began."

I looked at him. He was too close to me. It would have been invasive even if I loved him and not hated him. I leaned back.

"What?"

He followed me, leaning back next to me.

"You're my lawyer, right?"

I leaned forward, trying to get away.

"Louis, what is this? We've been together on this more than two months and now we're sitting here with a jury picked and ready for trial. You have paid me more than a hundred and fifty grand and you have to ask if I'm your lawyer? Of course I'm your lawyer. What is it? What is wrong?"

"Nothing's wrong."

He leaned forward and continued.

"I mean, like, if you're my lawyer, I can tell you stuff and you have to hold it as a secret, even if it's a crime I tell you about. More than one crime. It's covered by the attorney-client relationship, right?"

I felt the low rumbling of upset in my stomach.

"Yes, Louis, that's right — unless you are going to tell me about a crime about to be committed. In that case I can be relieved of the code of ethics and can inform the police so they can stop the crime. In fact, it would be my duty to inform them. A lawyer is an officer of the court. So what is it that you want to tell me? You just heard we got the two-minute warning. We're about to start here."

"I've killed people, Mick."

I looked at him for a moment.

"What?"

"You heard me."

He was right. I had heard him. And I shouldn't have acted surprised. I already knew he had killed people. Raul Levin was among them and he had even used my gun — though I hadn't figured out how he had defeated the GPS bracelet on his ankle. I was just surprised he had decided to tell me in such a matter-of-fact manner two minutes before his trial was called to order.

"Why are you telling me this?" I asked. "I'm about to try to defend you in this thing and you —"

"Because I know you already know. And because I know what your plan is."

"My plan? What plan?"

He smiled slyly at me.

"Come on, Mick. It's simple. You defend me on this case. You do your best, you get paid the big bucks, you win and I walk away. But then, once it's all over and you've got your money in the bank, you turn against me because I'm not your client anymore. You throw me to the cops so you can get Jesus Menendez out and redeem yourself."

I didn't respond.

"Well, I can't let that happen," he said quietly. "Now, I am yours forever, Mick. I am telling you I've killed people, and guess what? Martha Renteria was one of them. I gave her just what she deserved, and if you go to the cops or use what I've told you against me, then you won't be practicing law for very long. Yes, you might succeed in raising Jesus from the dead. But I'll never be prosecuted because of your misconduct. I believe it is called 'fruit of the poisonous tree,' and you are the tree, Mick."

I still couldn't respond. I just nodded again. Roulet had certainly thought it through. I wondered how much help he had gotten from Cecil Dobbs. He had obviously had somebody coach him on the law.

I leaned toward him and whispered.

"Follow me."

I got up and walked quickly through the gate and toward the rear door of the courtroom. From behind I heard the clerk's voice.

"Mr. Haller? We're about to start. The judge —"

"One minute," I called out without turning around.

I held one finger up as well. I then pushed through the doors into the dimly lit vestibule designed as a buffer to keep hallway sounds from the courtroom. A set of double doors on the other side led to the hallway. I moved to the side and waited for Roulet to step into the small space.

As soon as he came through the door I grabbed him and spun him into the wall. I held him pressed against it with both of my hands on his chest.

"What the fuck do you think you are doing?"

"Take it easy, Mick. I just thought we should know where we both —"

"You son of a bitch. You killed Raul and all he was doing was working for you! He was trying to help you!"

I wanted to bring my hands up to his neck and choke him out on the spot.

"You're right about one thing. I am a son of a bitch. But you are wrong about everything else, Mick. Levin wasn't trying to help me. He was trying to bury me and he was getting too close. He got what he deserved for that."

I thought about Levin's last message on my phone at home. *I've got Jesus's ticket out of the Q.* Whatever it was that he had found, it had gotten him killed. And it had gotten him killed before he could deliver the information to me.

"How did you do it? You're confessing everything to me here, then I want to know how you did it. How'd you beat the GPS? Your bracelet showed you weren't even near Glendale."

He smiled at me, like a boy with a toy he wasn't going to share.

"Let's just say that is proprietary information and leave

it at that. You never know, I may have to pull the old Houdini act again."

In his words I heard the threat and in his smile I saw the evil that Raul Levin had seen.

"Don't get any ideas, Mick," he said. "As you probably know, I do have an insurance policy."

I pressed harder against him and leaned in closer.

"Listen, you piece of shit. I want the gun back. You think you have this thing wired? You don't have shit. *I've* got it wired. And you won't make it through the week if I don't get that gun back. You got that?"

Roulet slowly reached up, grabbed my wrists and pulled my hands off his chest. He started straightening his shirt and tie.

"Might I suggest an agreement," he said calmly. "At the end of this trial I walk out of the courtroom a free man. I continue to maintain my freedom, and in exchange for this, the gun never falls into, shall we say, the wrong hands."

Meaning Lankford and Sobel.

"Because I'd really hate to see that happen, Mick. A lot of people depend on you. A lot of clients. And you, of course, wouldn't want to go where they are going."

I stepped back from him, using all my will not to raise my fists and attack. I settled for a voice that quietly seethed with all of my anger and hate.

"I promise you," I said, "if you fuck with me you will never be free of me. Are we clear on that?"

Roulet started to smile. But before he could respond the door from the courtroom opened and Deputy Meehan, the bailiff, looked in.

"The judge is on the bench," he said sternly. "She wants you in here. Now."

I looked back at Roulet.

"I said, are we clear?"

"Yes, Mick," he said good-naturedly. "We're crystal clear."

I stepped away from him and entered the courtroom, striding up the aisle to the gate. Judge Constance Fullbright was staring me down every step of the way.

"So nice of you to consider joining us this morning, Mr. Haller."

Where had I heard that before?

"I am sorry, Your Honor," I said as I came through the gate. "I had an emergency situation with my client. We had to conference."

"Client conferences can be handled right at the defense table," she responded.

"Yes, Your Honor."

"I don't think we are starting off correctly here, Mr. Haller. When my clerk announces that we will be in session in two minutes, then I expect everyone — including defense attorneys and their clients — to be in place and ready to go."

"I apologize, Your Honor."

"That's not good enough, Mr. Haller. Before the end of court today I want you to pay a visit to my clerk with your checkbook. I am fining you five hundred dollars for contempt of court. You are not in charge of this courtroom, sir. I am."

"Your Honor —"

"Now, can we please have the jury," she ordered, cutting off my protest.

The bailiff opened the jury room door and the twelve jurors and two alternates started filing into the jury box. I leaned over to Roulet, who had just sat down, and whispered.

"You owe me five hundred dollars."

280

TWENTY-EIGHT

Ted Minton's opening statement was a by-the-numbers model of prosecutorial overkill. Rather than tell the jurors what evidence he would present and what it would prove, the prosecutor tried to tell them what it all meant. He was going for a big picture and this was almost always a mistake. The big picture involves inferences and suggestions. It extrapolates givens to the level of suspicions. Any experienced prosecutor with a dozen or more felony trials under his belt will tell you to keep it small. You want them to convict, not necessarily to understand.

"What this case is about is a predator," he told them. "Louis Ross Roulet is a man who on the night of March sixth was stalking prey. And if it were not for the sheer determination of a woman to survive, we would be here prosecuting a murder case."

I noticed early on that Minton had picked up a scorekeeper. This is what I call a juror who incessantly takes notes during trial. An opening statement is not an offer of evidence and Judge Fullbright had so admonished the jury, but the woman in the first seat in the front row had been writing since the start of Minton's statement. This was good. I like scorekeepers because they document just what the lawyers say will be presented and proved at trial and at the end they go back to check. They keep score.

I looked at the jury chart I had filled in the week before and saw that the scorekeeper was Linda Truluck, a homemaker from Reseda. She was one of only three women on the jury. Minton had tried hard to keep the female content to a minimum because, I believe, he feared that once it was established in trial that Regina Campo had been offering sexual services for money, he might lose the females' sympathy and ultimately their votes on a verdict. I believed he was probably correct in that assumption and I worked just as diligently to get women on the panel. We both ended up using all of our twenty challenges and it was probably the main reason it took three days to seat a jury. In the end I got three women on the panel and only needed one to head off a conviction.

"Now, you are going to hear testimony from the victim herself about her lifestyle being one that we would not condone," Minton told the jurors. "The bottom line is she was selling sex to the men she invited to her home. But I want you to remember that what the victim in this case did for a living is not what this trial is about. Anyone can be a victim of a violent crime. Anyone. No matter what someone does for a living, the law does not allow for them to be beaten, to be threatened at knifepoint or to be put in fear of their lives. It doesn't matter what they do to make money. They enjoy the same protections that we all do."

It was pretty clear to me that Minton didn't even want to use the word *prostitution* or *prostitute* for fear it would hurt his case. I wrote the word down on the legal pad I would take with me to the lectern when I made my statement. I planned to make up for the prosecutor's omissions.

Minton gave an overview of the evidence. He spoke about the knife with the defendant's initials on the blade. He talked about the blood found on his left hand. And he warned the jurors not to be fooled by the defense's efforts to confuse or muddle the evidence.

"This is a very clear-cut and straightforward case," he

said as he was winding up. "You have a man who attacked a woman in her home. His plan was to rape and then kill her. It is only by the grace of God that she will be here to tell you the story."

With that he thanked them for their attention and took his seat at the prosecution table. Judge Fullbright looked at her watch and then looked at me. It was 11:40 and she was probably weighing whether to go to a break or let me proceed with my opener. One of the judge's chief jobs during trial is jury management. The judge's duty is to make sure the jury is comfortable and engaged. Lots of breaks, short and long, is often the answer.

I had known Connie Fullbright for at least twelve years, since long before she was a judge. She had been both a prosecutor and defense lawyer. She knew both sides. Aside from being overly quick with contempt citations, she was a good and fair judge — until it came to sentencing. You went into Fullbright's court knowing you were on an even level with the prosecution. But if the jury convicted your client, be prepared for the worst. Fullbright was one of the toughest sentencing judges in the county. It was as if she were punishing you and your client for wasting her time with a trial. If there was any room within the sentencing guidelines, she always went to the max, whether it was prison or probation. It had gotten her a telling sobriquet among the defense pros who worked the Van Nuys courthouse. They called her Judge Fullbite.

"Mr. Haller," she said, "are you planning to reserve your statement?"

"No, Your Honor, but I believe I am going to be pretty quick."

"Very good," she said. "Then we'll hear from you and then we'll take lunch."

The truth was I didn't know how long I would be. Minton had been about forty minutes and I knew I would take close to that. But I had told the judge I'd be quick simply because I didn't like the idea of the jury going to lunch with only the prosecutor's side of the story to think about as they chewed their hamburgers and tuna salads.

I got up and went to the lectern located between the prosecution and defense tables. The courtroom was one of the recently rehabbed spaces in the old courthouse. It had twin jury boxes on either side of the bench. Everything was done in a blond wood, including the rear wall behind the bench. The door to the judge's chambers was almost hidden in the wall, its lines camouflaged in the lines and grain of the wood. The doorknob was the only giveaway.

Fullbright ran her trials like a federal judge. Attorneys were not allowed to approach witnesses without permission and never allowed to approach the jury box. They were required to speak from the lectern only.

Standing now at the lectern, the jury was in the box to my right and closer to the prosecution table than to the defense's. This was fine with me. I didn't want them to get too close a look at Roulet. I wanted him to be a bit of a mystery to them.

"Ladies and gentlemen of the jury," I began, "my name is Michael Haller and I am representing Mr. Roulet during this trial. I am happy to tell you that this trial will most likely be a quick one. Just a few more days of your time will be taken. In the long run you will probably see that it took us longer to pick all of you than it will take to present both sides of the case. The prosecutor, Mr. Minton, seemed to spend his time this morning telling you about what he thinks all the evidence means and who Mr. Roulet really is. I would advise you to simply sit back, listen to the evidence and let your common sense tell you what it all means and who Mr. Roulet is."

I kept my eyes moving from juror to juror. I rarely looked down at the pad I had placed on the lectern. I wanted them to think I was shooting the breeze with them, talking off the top of my head.

"Usually, what I like to do is reserve my opening statement. In a criminal trial the defense always has the option of giving an opener at the start of the trial, just as Mr. Minton did, or right before presenting the defense's case. Normally, I would take the second option. I would wait and make my statement before trotting out all the defense's witnesses and evidence. But this case is different. It's different because the prosecution's case is also going to be the defense's case. You'll certainly hear from some defense witnesses, but the heart and soul of this case is going to be the prosecution's evidence and witnesses and how you decide to interpret them. I guarantee you that a version of the events and evidence far different from what Mr. Minton just outlined is going to emerge in this courtroom. And when it comes time to present the defense's case, it probably won't even be necessary."

I checked the scorekeeper and saw her pencil moving across the page of her notebook.

"I think that what you are going to find here this week is that this whole case will come down to the actions and motivations of one person. A prostitute who saw a man with outward signs of wealth and chose to target him. The evidence will show this clearly and it will be shown by the prosecution's own witnesses."

Minton stood up and objected, saying I was going out of bounds in trying to impeach the state's main witness with unsubstantiated accusations. There was no legal basis for the objection. It was just an amateurish attempt to send a message to the jury. The judge responded by inviting us to a sidebar.

We walked to the side of the bench and the judge flipped on a sound neutralizer which sent white noise from a speaker on the bench toward the jury and prevented them from hearing what was whispered in the sidebar. The judge was quick with Minton, like an assassin.

"Mr. Minton, I know you are new to felony trial work, so I see I will have to school you as we go. But don't you ever object during an opening statement in my courtroom. This isn't evidence he's presenting. I don't care if he says your own mother is the defendant's alibi witness, you don't object in front of my jury."

"Your Hon—"

"That's it. Go back."

She rolled her seat back to the center of the bench and flicked off the white noise. Minton and I returned to our positions without further word.

"Objection overruled," the judge said. "Continue, Mr. Haller, and let me remind you that you said you would be quick."

"Thank you, Your Honor. That is still my plan."

I referred to my notes and then looked back at the jury. Knowing that Minton would have been intimidated to silence by the judge, I decided to raise the rhetoric up a notch, go off notes and get directly to the windup.

"Ladies and gentlemen, in essence, what you will be deciding here is who the real predator was in this case. Mr. Roulet, a successful businessman with a spotless record, or an admitted prostitute with a successful business in taking money from men in exchange for sex. You will hear testimony that the alleged victim in this case was engaged in an act of prostitution with another man just moments before this supposed attack occurred. And you will hear testimony that within days of this supposedly life-threatening assault, she was back in business once again, trading sex for money."

I glanced at Minton and saw he was doing a slow burn. He had his eyes downcast on the table in front of him and he was slowly shaking his head. I looked up at the judge.

"Your Honor, could you instruct the prosecutor to refrain from demonstrating in front of the jury? I did not object or in any way try to distract the jury during his opening statement."

"Mr. Minton," the judge intoned, "please sit still and extend the courtesy to the defense that was extended to you."

"Yes, Your Honor," Minton said meekly.

The jury had now seen the prosecutor slapped down twice and we weren't even past openers. I took this as a good sign and it fed my momentum. I looked back at the jury and noticed that the scorekeeper was still writing.

"Finally, you will receive testimony from many of the state's own witnesses that will provide a perfectly acceptable explanation for much of the physical evidence in this case. I am talking about the blood and about the knife Mr. Minton mentioned. Taken individually or as a whole, the prosecution's own case will provide you with more than reasonable doubt about the guilt of my client. You can mark it down in your notebooks. I guarantee you will find that you have only one choice at the end of this case. And that is to find Mr. Roulet not guilty of these charges. Thank you."

As I walked back to my seat I winked at Lorna Taylor. She nodded at me as if to say I had done well. My attention was then drawn to the two figures sitting two rows behind her. Lankford and Sobel. They had slipped in after I had first surveyed the gallery.

I took my seat and ignored the thumbs-up gesture given me by my client. My mind was on the two Glendale detectives, wondering what they were doing in the courtroom. Watching me? Waiting for me?

The judge dismissed the jury for lunch and everyone stood while the scorekeeper and her colleagues filed out. After they were gone Minton asked the judge for another sidebar. He wanted to try to explain his objection and repair the damage but not in open court. The judge said no.

"I'm hungry, Mr. Minton, and we're past that now. Go to lunch."

She left the bench, and the courtroom that had been so silent except for the voices of lawyers then erupted in chatter from the gallery and the court workers. I put my pad in my briefcase.

"That was really good," Roulet said. "I think we're already ahead of the game."

I looked at him with dead eyes.

"It's no game."

"I know that. It's just an expression. Listen, I am having lunch with Cecil and my mother. We would like you to join us."

I shook my head.

"I have to defend you, Louis, but I don't have to eat with you."

I took my checkbook out of my briefcase and left him there. I walked around the table to the clerk's station so that I could write out a check for five hundred dollars. The money didn't hurt as much as I knew the bar review that follows any contempt citation would.

When I was finished I turned back to find Lorna waiting for me at the gate with a smile. We planned to go to lunch and then she would go back to manning the phone in her condo. In three days I would be back in business and needed clients. I was depending on her to start filling in my calendar.

"Looks like I better buy you lunch today," she said.

I threw my checkbook into the briefcase and closed it. I joined her at the gate.

"That would be nice," I said.

I pushed through the g
I had seen Lankford and S
before.

They were gone.

...ts case to the jury in the ... y Ted Minton's strategy ... our witnesses were a 911 ...fficers who responded to Reg... Campo's call for help and the paramedic who treated her... she was transported to the hospital. In anticipation of the defense strategy, it was clear that Minton wanted to firmly establish that Campo had been brutally assaulted and was indeed the victim in this crime. It wasn't a bad strategy. In most cases it would get the job done.

The dispatch operator was essentially used as the warm body needed to introduce a recording of Campo's 911 call for help. Printed transcripts of the call were handed out to jurors so they could read along with a scratchy audio playback. I objected on the grounds that it was prejudicial to play the audio recording when the transcript would suffice but the judge quickly overruled me before Minton even had to counter. The recording was played and there was no doubt that Minton had started out of the gate strong as the jurors sat raptly listening to Campo scream and beg for help. She sounded genuinely distraught and scared. It was exactly what Minton wanted the jurors to hear and they certainly got it. I didn't dare question the dispatcher on cross-examination because I knew it might give Minton the opportunity to play the recording again on redirect.

The two patrol officers who followed offered different testimony because they did separate things upon arriving at the Tarzana apartment complex in response to the 911 call. One primarily stayed with the victim while the other went up to the apartment and handcuffed the man Campo's neighbors were sitting on — Louis Ross Roulet.

Officer Vivian Maxwell described Campo as disheveled, hurt and frightened. She said Campo kept asking if she was safe and if the intruder had been caught. Even after she was assured on both questions, Campo remained scared and upset, at one point telling the officer to unholster her weapon and have it ready in case the attacker broke free. When Minton was through with this witness, I stood up to conduct my first cross-examination of the trial.

"Officer Maxwell," I asked, "did you at any time ask Ms. Campo what had happened to her?"

"Yes, I did."

"What exactly did you ask her?"

"I asked what had happened and who did this to her. You know, who had hurt her."

"What did she tell you?"

"She said a man had come to her door and knocked and when she opened it he punched her. She said he hit her several times and then took out a knife."

"She said he took the knife out after he punched her?"

"That's how she said it. She was upset and hurt at the time."

"I understand. Did she tell you who the man was?"

"No, she said she didn't know the man."

"You specifically asked if she knew the man?"

"Yes. She said no."

"So she just opened her door at ten o'clock at night to a stranger."

"She didn't say it that way."

291

"But you said she told you she didn't know him, right?"

"That is correct. That is how she said it. She said, 'I don't know who he is.'"

"And did you put this in your report?"

"Yes, I did."

I introduced the patrol officer's report as a defense exhibit and had Maxwell read parts of it to the jury. These parts involved Campo saying that the attack was unprovoked and at the hands of a stranger.

"'The victim does not know the man who assaulted her and did not know why she was attacked,'" she read from her own report.

Maxwell's partner, John Santos, testified next, telling jurors that Campo directed him to her apartment, where he found a man on the floor near the entrance. The man was semiconscious and was being held on the ground by two of Campo's neighbors, Edward Turner and Ronald Atkins. One man was straddling the man's chest and the other was sitting on his legs.

Santos identified the man being held on the floor as the defendant, Louis Ross Roulet. Santos described him as having blood on his clothes and his left hand. He said Roulet appeared to be suffering from a concussion or some sort of head injury and initially was not responsive to commands. Santos turned him over and handcuffed his hands behind his back. The officer then put a plastic evidence bag he carried in a compartment on his belt over Roulet's bloody hand.

Santos testified that one of the men who had been holding Roulet handed over a folding knife that was open and had blood on its handle and blade. Santos told jurors he bagged this item as well and turned it over to Detective Martin Booker as soon as he arrived on the scene.

On cross-examination I asked Santos only two questions.

"Officer, was there blood on the defendant's right hand?"

"No, there was no blood on his right hand or I would have bagged that one, too."

"I see. So you have blood on the left hand only and a knife with blood on the handle. Would it then appear to you that if the defendant had held that knife, then he would have to have held it in his left hand?"

Minton objected, saying that Santos was a patrol officer and that the question was beyond the scope of his expertise. I argued that the question required only a commonsense answer, not an expert. The judge overruled the objection and the court clerk read the question back to the witness.

"It would seem that way to me," Santos answered.

Arthur Metz was the paramedic who testified next. He told jurors about Campo's demeanor and the extent of her injuries when he treated her less than thirty minutes after the attack. He said that it appeared to him that she had suffered at least three significant impacts to the face. He also described a small puncture wound to her neck. He described all the injuries as superficial but painful. A large blowup of the same photograph of Campo's face I had seen on the first day I was on the case was displayed on an easel in front of the jury. I objected to this, arguing that the photo was prejudicial because it had been blown up to larger-than-life size, but I was overruled by Judge Fullbright.

Then, when it was my turn to cross-examine Metz, I used the photo I had just objected to.

"When you tell us that it appeared that she suffered at least three impacts to the face, what do you mean by 'impact'?" I asked.

"She was struck with something. Either a fist or a blunt object."

"So basically someone hit her three times. Could you please use this laser pointer and show the jury on the photograph where these impacts occurred."

From my shirt pocket I unclipped a laser pointer and held it up for the judge to see. She granted me permission to carry it to Metz. I turned it on and handed it to him. He then put the red eye of the laser beam on the photo of Campo's battered face and drew circles in the three areas where he believed she had been struck. He circled her right eye, her right cheek and an area encompassing the right side of her mouth and nose.

"Thank you," I said, taking the laser back from him and returning to the lectern. "So if she was hit three times on the right side of her face, the impacts would have come from the left side of her attacker, correct?"

Minton objected, once more saying the question was beyond the scope of the witness's expertise. Once more I argued common sense and once more the judge overruled the prosecutor.

"If the attacker was facing her, he would have punched her from the left, unless it was a backhand," Metz said. "Then it could have been a right."

He nodded and seemed pleased with himself. He obviously thought he was helping the prosecution but his effort was so disingenuous that he was actually probably helping the defense.

"You are suggesting that Ms. Campo's attacker hit her three times with a backhand and caused this degree of injury?"

I pointed to the photo on the exhibit easel. Metz shrugged, realizing he had probably not been so helpful to the prosecution.

"Anything is possible," he said.

"Anything is possible," I repeated. "Well, is there any other possibility you can think of that would explain these injuries as coming from anything other than direct left-handed punches?"

Metz shrugged again. He was not an impressive witness, especially following two cops and a dispatcher who had been very precise in their testimony.

"What if Ms. Campo were to have hit her face with her own fist? Wouldn't she have used her right —"

Minton jumped up immediately and objected.

"Your Honor, this is outrageous! To suggest that this victim did this to herself is not only an affront to this court but to all victims of violent crime everywhere. Mr. Haller has sunk to —"

"The witness said anything is possible," I argued, trying to knock Minton off the soapbox. "I am trying to explore what —"

"Sustained," Fullbright said, ending it. "Mr. Haller, don't go there unless you are making more than an exploratory swing through the possibilities."

"Yes, Your Honor," I said. "No further questions."

I sat down and glanced at the jurors and knew from their faces that I had made a mistake. I had turned a positive cross into a negative. The point I had made about a left-handed attacker was obscured by the point I had lost with the suggestion that the injuries to the victim's face were self-inflicted. The three women on the panel looked particularly annoyed with me.

Still, I tried to focus on a positive aspect. It was good to know the jury's feelings on this now, before Campo was in the witness box and I asked the same thing.

Roulet leaned toward me and whispered, "What the fuck was that?"

Without responding I turned my back to him and took a scan around the courtroom. It was almost empty. Lankford and Sobel had not returned to the courtroom and the reporters were gone as well. That left only a few other onlookers. They appeared to be a disparate collection of retirees, law students and lawyers resting their feet until their own hearings began in other courtrooms. But I was counting on one of these onlookers being a plant from the DA's office. Ted Minton might be flying solo but my guess was that his boss would have a means of keeping tabs on him and the case. I knew I was playing as much to the plant as I was to the jury. By the trial's end I needed to send a note of panic down to the second floor that would then echo back to Minton. I needed to push the young prosecutor toward taking a desperate measure.

The afternoon dragged on. Minton still had a lot to learn about pacing and jury management, knowledge that comes only with courtroom experience. I kept my eyes on the jury box — where the real judges sat — and saw the jurors were growing bored as witness after witness offered testimony that filled in small details in the prosecutor's linear presentation of the events of March 6. I asked few questions on cross and tried to keep a look on my face that mirrored those I saw in the jury box.

Minton obviously wanted to save his most powerful stuff for day two. He would have the lead investigator, Detective Martin Booker, to bring all the details together, and then the victim, Regina Campo, to bring it all home to the jury. It was a tried-and-true formula — ending with muscle and emotion — and it worked ninety percent of the time, but it was making the first day move like a glacier.

Things finally started to pop with the last witness of the day. Minton brought in Charles Talbot, the man who had picked up Regina Campo at Morgan's and gone with her to her apartment on the night of the sixth. What Talbot had to offer to the prosecution's case was negligible. He was basically hauled in to testify that Campo had been in good health and uninjured when he left her. That was it. But what caused his arrival to rescue the trial from the pit of boredom was that Talbot was an honest-to-God alternate lifestyle man and jurors always loved visiting the other side of the tracks.

Talbot was fifty-five years old with dyed blond hair that wasn't fooling anyone. He had blurred Navy tattoos on both forearms. He was twenty years divorced and owned a twenty-four-hour convenience store called Kwik Kwik. The business gave him a comfortable living and lifestyle with an apartment in the Warner Center, a late-model Corvette and a nightlife that included a wide sampling of the city's professional sex providers.

Minton established all of this in the early stages of his direct examination. You could almost feel the air go still in the courtroom as the jurors plugged into Talbot. The prosecutor then brought him quickly to the night of March 6, and Talbot described hooking up with Reggie Campo at Morgan's on Ventura Boulevard.

"Did you know Ms. Campo before you met her in the bar that night?"

"No, I did not."

"How did it come about that you met her there?"

"I just called her up and said I wanted to get together with her and she suggested we meet at Morgan's. I knew the place, so I said sure."

"And how did you call her up?"

"With the telephone."

Several jurors laughed.

"I'm sorry. I understand that you used a telephone to call her. I meant how did you know *how* to contact her?"

"I saw her ad on the website and I liked what I saw and so I went ahead and called her up and we made a date. It's as simple as that. Her number is on her website ad."

"And you met at Morgan's."

"Yes, that's where she meets her dates, she told me. So I

went there and we had a couple drinks and we talked and we liked each other and that was that. I followed her back to her place."

"When you went to her apartment did you engage in sexual relations?"

"Sure did. That's what I was there for."

"And you paid her?"

"Four hundred bucks. It was worth it."

I saw a male juror's face turning red and I knew I had pegged him perfectly during selection the week before. I had wanted him because he had brought a Bible with him to read while other prospective jurors were being questioned. Minton had missed it, focusing only on the candidates as they were being questioned. But I had seen the Bible and asked few questions of the man when it was his turn. Minton accepted him on the jury and so did I. I figured he would be easy to turn against the victim because of her occupation. His reddening face confirmed it.

"What time did you leave her apartment?" Minton asked.

"About five minutes before ten," Talbot answered.

"Did she tell you she was expecting another date at the apartment?"

"No, she didn't say anything about that. In fact, she was sort of acting like she was done for the night."

I stood up and objected.

"I don't think Mr. Talbot is qualified here to interpret what Ms. Campo was thinking or planning by her actions."

"Sustained," the judge said before Minton could offer an argument.

The prosecutor moved right along.

"Mr. Talbot, could you please describe the physical state Ms. Campo was in when you left her shortly before ten o'clock on the night of March sixth?"

"Completely satisfied."

There was a loud blast of laughter in the courtroom and Talbot beamed proudly. I checked the Bible man and it looked like his jaw was tightly clenched.

"Mr. Talbot," Minton said. "I mean her physical state. Was she hurt or bleeding when you left her?"

"No, she was fine. She was okay. When I left her she was fit as a fiddle and I know because I had just played her."

He smiled, proud of his use of language. This time there was no laughter and the judge had finally had enough of his use of the double entendre. She admonished him to keep his more off-color remarks to himself.

"Sorry, Judge," he said.

"Mr. Talbot," Minton said. "Ms. Campo was not injured in any way when you left her?"

"Nope. No way."

"She wasn't bleeding?"

"No."

"And you didn't strike her or physically abuse her in any way?"

"No again. What we did was consensual and pleasurable. No pain."

"Thank you, Mr. Talbot."

I looked at my notes for a few moments before standing up. I wanted a break of time to clearly mark the line between direct and cross-examination.

"Mr. Haller?" the judge prompted. "Do you wish to cross-examine the witness?"

I stood up and moved to the lectern.

"Yes, Your Honor, I do."

I put my pad down and looked directly at Talbot. He was smiling pleasantly at me but I knew he wouldn't like me for very long.

"Mr. Talbot, are you right- or left-handed?"

"I'm left-handed."

"Left-handed," I echoed. "And isn't it true that on the night of the sixth, before leaving Regina Campo's apartment, she asked you to strike her with your fist repeatedly in the face?"

Minton stood up.

"Your Honor, there is no basis for this sort of questioning. Mr. Haller is simply trying to muddy the waters by taking outrageous statements and turning them into questions."

The judge looked at me and waited for a response.

"Judge, it is part of the defense theory as outlined in my opening statement."

"I am going to allow it. Just be quick about it, Mr. Haller."

The question was read to Talbot and he smirked and shook his head.

"That is not true. I've never hurt a woman in my life."

"You struck her with your fist three times, didn't you, Mr. Talbot?"

"No, I did not. That is a lie."

"You said you have never hurt a woman in your life."

"That's right. Never."

"Do you know a prostitute named Shaquilla Barton?"

Talbot had to think before answering.

"Doesn't ring a bell."

"On the website where she advertises her services she uses the name Shaquilla Shackles. Does that ring a bell now, Mr. Talbot?"

"Okay, yeah, I think so."

"Have you ever engaged in acts of prostitution with her?"

"One time, yes."

"When was that?"

"Would've been at least a year ago. Maybe longer."

"And did you hurt her on that occasion?"

"No."

"And if she were to come to this courtroom and say that you did hurt her by punching her with your left hand, would she be lying?"

"She damn sure would be. I tried her out and didn't like that rough stuff. I'm strictly a missionary man. I didn't touch her."

"You didn't touch her?"

"I mean I didn't punch her or hurt her in any way."

"Thank you, Mr. Talbot."

I sat down. Minton did not bother with a redirect. Talbot was excused and Minton told the judge that he had only two witnesses remaining to present in the case but that their testimony would be lengthy. Judge Fullbright checked the time and recessed court for the day.

Two witnesses left. I knew that had to be Detective Booker and Reggie Campo. It looked like Minton was going to go without the testimony of the jailhouse snitch he had stashed in the PTI program at County-USC. Dwayne Corliss's name had never appeared on any witness list or any other discovery document associated with the prosecution of the case. I thought maybe Minton had found out what Raul Levin had found out about Corliss before Raul was murdered. Either way, it seemed apparent that Corliss had been dropped by the prosecution. And that was what I needed to change.

As I gathered my papers and documents in my briefcase, I also gathered the resolve to talk to Roulet. I glanced over at him. He was sitting there waiting to be dismissed by me.

"So what do you think?" I asked.

"I think you did very well. More than a few moments of reasonable doubt."

I snapped the latches on the briefcase closed.

"Today I was just planting seeds. Tomorrow they'll sprout and on Wednesday they'll bloom. You haven't seen anything yet."

I stood up and lifted the briefcase off the table. It was heavy with all the case documents and my computer.

"See you tomorrow."

I walked out through the gate. Cecil Dobbs and Mary Windsor were waiting for Roulet in the hallway near the courtroom door. As I came out they turned to speak to me but I walked on by.

"See you tomorrow," I said.

"Wait a minute, wait a minute," Dobbs called to my back.

I turned around.

"We're stuck out here," he said as he and Windsor walked to me. "How is it going in there?"

I shrugged.

"Right now it's the prosecution's case," I answered. "All I'm doing is bobbing and weaving, trying to protect. I think tomorrow will be our round. And Wednesday we go for the knockout. I've got to go prepare."

As I headed to the elevator, I saw that a number of the jurors from the case had beaten me to it and were waiting to go down. The scorekeeper was among them. I went into the restroom next to the bank of elevators so I didn't have to ride down with them. I put my briefcase on the counter between the sinks and washed my face and hands. As I stared at myself in the mirror I looked for signs of stress from the case and everything associated with it. I looked reasonably sane and calm for a defense pro who was playing both his client and the prosecution at the same time.

The cold water felt good and I felt refreshed as I came out of the restroom, hoping the jurors had cleared out.

The jurors were gone. But standing in the hallway by

the elevator were Lankford and Sobel. Lankford was
holding a folded sheaf of documents in one hand.

"There you are," he said. "We've been looking for you."

THIRTY

The document Lankford handed me was a search warrant granting the police the authority to search my home, office and car for a .22 caliber Colt Woodsman Sport Model pistol with the serial number 656300081-52. The authorization said the pistol was believed to have been the murder weapon in the April 12 homicide of Raul A. Levin. Lankford had handed the warrant to me with a proud smirk on his face. I did my best to act like it was business as usual, the kind of thing I handled every other day and twice on Fridays. But the truth was, my knees almost buckled.

"How'd you get this?" I said.

It was a nonsensical response to a nonsensical moment.

"Signed, sealed and delivered," Lankford said. "So where do you want to start? You have your car here, right? That Lincoln you're chauffeured around in like a high-class hooker."

I checked the judge's signature on the last page and saw it was a Glendale muni-court judge I had never heard of. They had gone to a local who probably knew he'd need the police endorsement come election time. I started to recover from the shock. Maybe the search was a front.

"This is bullshit," I said. "You don't have the PC for this. I could have this thing quashed in ten minutes."

"It looked pretty good to Judge Fullbright," Lankford said.

"Fullbright? What does she have to do with this?"

"Well, we knew you were in trial, so we figured we ought to ask her if it was okay to drop the warrant on you. Don't want to get a lady like that mad, you know. She said after court was over was fine by her — and she didn't say shit about the PC or anything else."

They must have gone to Fullbright on the lunch break, right after I had seen them in the courtroom. My guess was, it had been Sobel's idea to check with the judge first. A guy like Lankford would have enjoyed pulling me right out of court and disrupting the trial.

I had to think quickly. I looked at Sobel, the more sympathetic of the two.

"I'm in the middle of a three-day trial," I said. "Any way we can put this on hold until Thursday?"

"No fucking way," Lankford answered before his partner could. "We're not letting you out of our sight until we execute the search. We're not going to give you the time to dump the gun. Now where's your car, Lincoln lawyer?"

I checked the authorization of the warrant. It had to be very specific and I was in luck. It called for the search of a Lincoln with the California license plate NT GLTY. I realized that someone must have written the plate down on the day I was called to Raul Levin's house from the Dodgers game. Because that was the old Lincoln — the one I was driving that day.

"It's at home. Since I'm in trial I don't use the driver. I got a ride in with my client this morning and I was just going to ride back with him. He's probably waiting down there."

I lied. The Lincoln I had been driving was in the courthouse parking garage. But I couldn't let the cops search it because there was a gun in a compartment in the backseat armrest. It wasn't the gun they were looking for but it was a replacement. After Raul Levin was murdered and I'd found my pistol box empty, I asked Earl Briggs to get me a gun for protection. I knew that with Earl there would be no ten-day waiting period. But I didn't know the gun's history or registration and I didn't want to find out through the Glendale Police Department.

But I was in luck because the Lincoln with the gun inside wasn't the one described in the warrant. That one was in my garage at home, waiting on the buyer from the limo service to come by and take a look at. And that would be the Lincoln that would be searched.

Lankford grabbed the warrant out of my hand and shoved it into an inside coat pocket.

"Don't worry about your ride," Lankford said. "We're your ride. Let's go."

On the way down and out of the courthouse, we didn't run into Roulet or his entourage. And soon I was riding in the back of a Grand Marquis, thinking that I had made the right choice when I had gone with the Lincoln. There was more room in the Lincoln and the ride was smoother.

Lankford did the driving and I sat behind him. The windows were up and I could hear him chewing gum.

"Let me see the warrant again," I said.

Lankford made no move.

"I'm not letting you inside my house until I've had a chance to completely study the warrant. I could do it on the way and save you some time. Or . . ."

Lankford reached inside his jacket and pulled out the warrant. He handed it over his shoulder to me. I knew why he was hesitant. Cops usually had to lay out their whole investigation in the warrant application in order to convince a judge of probable cause. They didn't like the target reading it, because it gave away the store.

I glanced out the window as we were passing the car lots on Van Nuys Boulevard. I saw a new model Town Car on a pedestal in front of the Lincoln dealership. I looked back down at the warrant, opened it to the summary section and read.

Lankford and Sobel had started out doing some good work. I had to give them that. One of them had taken a shot — I was guessing Sobel — and put my name into the state's Automated Firearm System and hit the lotto. The AFS computer said I was the registered owner of a pistol of the same make and model as the murder weapon.

It was a smooth move but it still wasn't enough to make probable cause. Colt made the Woodsman for more than sixty years. That meant there were probably a million of them out there and a million suspects who owned them.

They had the smoke. They then rubbed other sticks together to make the required fire. The application summary stated that I had hidden from the investigators the fact that I owned the gun in question. It said I had also fabricated an alibi when initially interviewed about Levin's death, then attempted to throw detectives off the track by giving them a phony lead on the drug dealer Hector Arrande Moya.

Though motivation was not necessarily a subject needed to obtain a search warrant, the PC summary alluded to it anyway, stating that the victim — Raul Levin — had been extorting investigative assignments from me and that I had refused to pay him upon completion of those assignments.

The outrage of such an assertion aside, the alibi fabrication was the key point of probable cause. The statement said that I had told the detectives I was home at the time of the murder, but a message on my home phone was left just before the suspected time of death and this indicated that I was not home, thereby collapsing my alibi and proving me a liar at the same time.

I slowly read the PC statement twice more but my

anger did not subside. I tossed the warrant onto the seat next to me.

"In some ways it's really too bad I am not the killer," I said.

"Yeah, why is that?" Lankford said.

"Because this warrant is a piece of shit and you both know it. It won't stand up to challenge. I told you that message came in when I was already on the phone and that can be checked and proven, only you were too lazy or you didn't want to check it because it would have made it a little difficult to get your warrant. Even with your pocket judge in Glendale. You lied by omission and commission. It's a bad-faith warrant."

Because I was sitting behind Lankford I had a better angle on Sobel. I watched her for signs of doubt as I spoke.

"And the suggestion that Raul was extorting business from me and that I wouldn't pay is a complete joke. Extorted me with what? And what didn't I pay him for? I paid him every time I got a bill. Man, I tell you, if this is how you work all your cases, I gotta open up an office in Glendale. I'm going to shove this warrant right up your police chief's ass."

"You lied about the gun," Lankford said. "And you owed Levin money. It's right there in his accounts book. Four grand."

"I didn't lie about anything. You never asked if I owned a gun."

"Lied by omission. Right back at ya."

"Bullshit."

"Four grand."

"Oh yeah, the four grand — I killed him because I didn't want to pay him four grand," I said with all the sarcasm I could muster. "You got me there, Detective. Motivation. But I guess it never occurred to you to see if he had even billed me for the four grand yet, or to see if I hadn't just paid an invoice from him for six thousand dollars a week before he was murdered."

Lankford was undaunted. But I saw the doubt start to creep into Sobel's face.

"Doesn't matter how much or when you paid him," Lankford said. "A blackmailer is never satisfied. You never stop paying until you reach the point of no return. That's what this is about. The point of no return."

I shook my head.

"And what exactly was it that he had on me that made me give him jobs and pay him until I reached the point of no return?"

Lankford and Sobel exchanged a look and Lankford nodded. Sobel reached down to a briefcase on the floor and took out a file. She handed it over the seat to me.

"Take a look," Lankford said. "You missed it when you were ransacking his place. He'd hidden it in a dresser drawer."

I opened the file and saw that it contained several 8 × 10 color photos. They were taken from afar and I was in each one of them. The photographer had trailed my Lincoln over several days and several miles. Each image a frozen moment in time, the photos showed me with various individuals whom I easily recognized as clients. They were prostitutes, street dealers and Road Saints. The photos could be interpreted as suspicious because they showed one split second of time. A male prostitute in mini-shorts alighting from the backseat of the Lincoln. Teddy Vogel handing me a thick roll of cash through the back window. I closed the file and tossed it back over the seat.

"You're kidding me, right? You're saying Raul came to me with that? He extorted me with that? Those are my clients. Is this a joke or am I just missing something?"

"The California bar might not think it's a joke," Lankford said. "We hear you're on thin ice with the bar. Levin knew it. He worked it."

I shook my head.

"Incredible," I said.

I knew I had to stop talking. I was doing everything wrong with these people. I knew I should just shut up and ride it out. But I felt an almost overpowering need to convince them. I began to understand why so many cases were made in the interview rooms of police stations. People just can't shut up.

I tried to place the photographs that were in the file. Vogel giving me the roll of cash was in the parking lot outside the Saints' strip club on Sepulveda. That happened after Harold Casey's trial and Vogel was paying me for filing the appeal. The prostitute was named Terry Jones and I handled a soliciting charge for him the first week of April. I'd had to find him on the Santa Monica Boulevard stroll the night before a hearing to make sure he was going to show up.

It became clear that the photos had all been taken between the morning I had caught the Roulet case and the day Raul Levin was murdered. They were then planted at the crime scene by the killer — all part of Roulet's plan to set me up so that he could control me. The police would have everything they needed to put the Levin murder on me — except the murder weapon. As long as Roulet had the gun, he had me.

I had to admire the plan and the ingenuity at the same time that it made me feel the dread of desperation. I tried to put the window down but the button wouldn't work. I asked Sobel to open a window and she did. Fresh air started blowing into the car.

After a while Lankford looked at me in the rearview and tried to jump-start the conversation.

"We ran the history on that Woodsman," he said. "You know who owned it once, don't you?"

"Mickey Cohen," I answered matter-of-factly, staring

out the window at the steep hillsides of Laurel Canyon.

"How'd you end up with Mickey Cohen's gun?"

I answered without turning from the window.

"My father was a lawyer. Mickey Cohen was his client."

Lankford whistled. Cohen was one of the most famous gangsters to ever call Los Angeles home. He was from back in the day when the gangsters competed with movie stars for the gossip headlines.

"And what? He just gave your old man a gun?"

"Cohen was charged in a shooting and my father defended him. He claimed self-defense. There was a trial and my father got a not-guilty verdict. When the weapon was returned Mickey gave it to my father. Sort of a keepsake, you could say."

"Your old man ever wonder how many people the Mick whacked with it?"

"I don't know. I didn't really know my father."

"What about Cohen? You ever meet him?"

"My father represented him before I was even born. The gun came to me in his will. I don't know why he picked me to have it. I was only five years old when he died."

"And you grew up to be a lawyer like dear old dad, and being a good lawyer you registered it."

"I thought if it was ever stolen or something I would want to be able to get it back. Turn here on Fareholm."

Lankford did as I instructed and we started climbing up the hill to my home. I then gave them the bad news.

"Thanks for the ride," I said. "You guys can search my house and my office and my car for as long as you want, but I have to tell you, you are wasting your time. Not only am I the wrong guy for this, but you aren't going to find that gun."

I saw Lankford's head jog up and he was looking at me in the rearview again.

"And why is that, Counselor? You already dumped it?"

"Because the gun was stolen out of my house and I don't know where it is."

Lankford started laughing. I saw the joy in his eyes.

"Uh-huh, stolen. How convenient. When did this happen?"

"Hard to tell. I hadn't checked on the gun in years."

"You make a police report on it or file an insurance claim?"

"No."

"So somebody comes in and steals your Mickey Cohen gun and you don't report it. Even after you just told us you registered it in case this very thing happened. You being a lawyer and all, doesn't that sound a little screwy to you?"

"It does, except I knew who stole it. It was a client. He told me he took it and if I were to report it, I would be violating a client trust because my police report would lead to his arrest. Kind of a catch-twenty-two, Detective."

Sobel turned and looked back at me. I think maybe she thought I was making it up on the spot, which I was.

"That sounds like legal jargon and bullshit, Haller," Lankford said.

"But it's the truth. We're here. Just park in front of the garage."

Lankford pulled the car into the space in front of my garage and killed the engine. He turned to look back at me before getting out.

"Which client stole the gun?"

"I told you, I can't tell you."

"Well, Roulet's your only client right now, isn't he?"

"I have a lot of clients. But I told you, I can't tell you."

"Think maybe we should run the charts from his ankle bracelet and see if he's been to your place lately?"

"Do whatever you want. He actually has been here. We had a meeting here once. In my office."

"Maybe that's when he took it."

"I'm not telling you he took it, Detective."

"Yeah, well, that bracelet gives Roulet a pass on the Levin thing, anyway. We checked the GPS. So I guess that leaves you, Counselor."

"And that leaves you wasting your time."

I suddenly realized something about Roulet's ankle bracelet but tried not to show it. Maybe a line on the trapdoor to his Houdini act. It was something I would need to check into later.

"Are we just going to sit here?"

Lankford turned and got out. He then opened my door because the inside handle had been disabled for transporting suspects and custodies. I looked at the two detectives.

"You want me to show you the gun box? Maybe when you see it is empty, you can just leave and save us all the time."

"Not quite, Counselor," Lankford said. "We're going through this whole place. I'll take the car and Detective Sobel will start in the house."

I shook my head.

"Not quite, Detective. It doesn't work that way. I don't trust you. Your warrant is bent, so as far as I'm concerned, you're bent. You stay together so I can watch you both or we wait until I can get a second observer up here. My case manager could be here in ten minutes. I could bring her up here to watch and you could also ask her about calling me on the morning Raul Levin got killed."

Lankford's face grew dark with insult and anger that he looked like he was having trouble controlling. I decided to push it. I took out my cell phone and opened it.

"I'm going to call your judge right now and see if he —"

"Fine," Lankford said. "We'll start with the car. Together. We'll work our way inside the house."

I closed the phone and put it back in my pocket.

"Fine."

I walked over to a keypad on the wall outside the garage. I tapped in the combination and the garage door started to rise, revealing the blue-black Lincoln awaiting inspection. Its license plate read NT GLTY. Lankford looked at it and shook his head.

"Yeah, right."

He stepped into the garage, his face still tight with anger. I decided to ease things a little bit.

"Hey, Detective," I said. "What's the difference between a catfish and a defense attorney?"

He didn't respond. He stared angrily at the license plate on my Lincoln.

"One's a bottom-feeding shit sucker," I said. "And the other one's a fish."

For a moment his face remained frozen. Then a smile creased it and he broke into a long and hard laugh. Sobel stepped into the garage, having not heard the joke.

"What?" she said.

"I'll tell you later," Lankford said.

THIRTY-ONE

It took them a half hour to search the Lincoln and then move into the house, where they started with the office. I watched the whole time and only spoke when offering explanation about something that gave them pause in their search. They didn't talk much to each other and it was becoming increasingly clear that there was a rift between the two partners over the direction Lankford had taken the investigation

At one point Lankford got a call on his cell phone and he went out the front door onto the porch to talk privately. I had the shades up and if I stood in the hallway I could look one way and see him out there and the other way and see Sobel in my office.

"You're not too happy about this, are you?" I said to Sobel when I was sure her partner couldn't hear.

"It doesn't matter how I am. We're following the case and that's it."

"Is your partner always like that, or only with lawyers?"

"He spent fifty thousand dollars on a lawyer last year, trying to get custody of his kids. He didn't. Before that we lost a big case — a murder — on a legal technicality."

I nodded.

"And he blamed the lawyer. But who broke the rules?"

She didn't respond and that as much as confirmed it had been Lankford who had made the technical misstep.

"I get the picture," I said.

I checked on Lankford on the porch again. He was

gesturing impatiently like he was trying to explain something to a moron. Must have been his custody lawyer. I decided to change the subject with Sobel.

"Do you think you are being manipulated at all on this case?"

"What are you talking about?"

"The photos stashed in the bureau, the bullet casing in the floor vent. Pretty convenient, don't you think?"

"What are you saying?"

"I'm not saying anything. I'm asking questions your partner doesn't seem interested in."

I checked on Lankford. He was tapping in numbers on his cell, making a new call. I turned and stepped into the open doorway of the office. Sobel was looking behind the files in a drawer. Finding no gun, she closed the drawer and stepped over to the desk. I spoke in a low voice.

"What about Raul's message to me?" I said. "About finding Jesus Menendez's ticket out, what do you think he meant?"

"We haven't figured that out yet."

"Too bad. I think it's important."

"Everything's important until it isn't."

I nodded, not sure what she meant by that.

"You know, the case I'm trying is pretty interesting. You ought to come back by and watch. You might learn something."

She looked from the desk to me. Our eyes held for a moment. Then she squinted with suspicion, like she was trying to judge whether a supposed murder suspect was actually coming on to her.

"Are you serious?"

"Yeah, why not?"

"Well, for one thing, you might have trouble getting to court if you're in lockup."

"Hey, no gun, no case. That's why you're here, right?"

She didn't answer.

"Besides, this is your partner's thing. You're not riding with him on this. I can tell."

"Typical lawyer. You think you know all the angles."

"No, not me. I'm finding out I don't know any of them." She changed the subject.

"Is this your daughter?"

She pointed to the framed photograph on the desk.

"Yeah. Hayley."

"Nice alliteration. Hayley Haller. Named after the comet?"

"Sort of. Spelled differently. My ex-wife came up with it."

Lankford came in then, talking to Sobel loudly about the call he had gotten. It had been from a supervisor telling them that they were back in play and would handle the next Glendale homicide whether the Levin case was still active or not. He didn't say anything about the call he had made.

Sobel told him she had finished searching the office. No gun.

"I'm telling you, it's not here," I said. "You are wasting your time. And mine. I have court tomorrow and need to prepare for witnesses."

"Let's do the bedroom next," Lankford said, ignoring my protest.

I backed up into the hallway to give them space to come out of one room and go into the next. They walked down the sides of the bed to where twin night tables waited. Lankford opened the top drawer of his table and lifted out a CD.

"*Wreckrium for Lil' Demon,*" he read. "You have to be fucking kidding me."

I didn't respond. Sobel quickly opened the two drawers of her table and found them empty except for a strip of condoms. I looked the other way.

"I'll take the closet," Lankford said after he had finished with his night table — leaving the drawers open in typical police search fashion. He walked into the closet and soon spoke from inside it.

"Here we go."

He stepped back out of the closet holding the wooden gun box.

"Bingo," I said. "You found an empty gun box. You must be a detective."

Lankford shook the box in his hands before putting it down on the bed. Either he was trying to play with me or the box had a solid heft to it. I felt a little charge go down the back of my neck as I realized that Roulet could have just as easily snuck back into my house to return the gun. It would have been the perfect hiding place for it. The last place I might think to check again once I had determined that the gun was gone. I remembered the odd smile on Roulet's face when I had told him I wanted my gun back. Was he smiling because I already had the gun back?

Lankford flipped the box's latch and lifted the top. He pulled back the oilcloth covering. The cork cutout which once held Mickey Cohen's gun was still empty. I breathed out so heavily it almost came out as a sigh.

"What did I tell you?" I said quickly, trying to cover up.

"Yeah, what did you tell us," Lankford said. "Heidi, you got a bag? We're going to take the box."

I looked at Sobel. She didn't look like a Heidi to me. I wondered if it was some sort of a squad room nickname. Or maybe it was the reason she didn't put her first name on her business card. It didn't sound homicide tough.

"In the car," she said.

"Go get it," Lankford said.

"You are going to take an empty gun box?" I asked. "What good does it do you?"

"All part of the chain of evidence, Counselor. You should know that. Besides, it will come in handy, since I have a feeling we'll never find the gun."

I shook my head.

"Maybe handy in your dreams. The box is evidence of nothing."

"It's evidence that you had Mickey Cohen's gun. Says it right on this little brass plaque your daddy or somebody had made."

"So fucking what?"

"Well, I just made a call while I was out on your front porch, Haller. See, we had somebody checking on Mickey Cohen's self-defense case. Turns out that over there in LAPD's evidence archive they still have all the ballistic evidence from that case. That's a lucky break for us, the case being, what, fifty years old?"

I understood immediately. They would take the bullet slugs and casings from the Cohen case and compare them with the same evidence recovered in the Levin case. They would match the Levin murder to Mickey Cohen's gun which they would then tie to me with the gun box and the state's AFS computer. I doubted Roulet could have realized how the police would be able to make a case without even having the gun when he thought out his scheme to control me.

I stood there silently. Sobel left the room without a glance at me and Lankford looked up from the box at me with a killer smile.

"What's the matter, Counselor?" he asked. "Evidence got your tongue?"

I finally was able to speak.

"How long will ballistics take?" I managed to ask.

"Hey, for you, we're going to put a rush on it. So get out there and enjoy yourself while you can. But don't leave town."

He laughed, almost giddy with himself.

"Man, I thought they only said that in movies. But there, I just said it! I wish my partner had been here."

Sobel came back in with a large brown bag and a roll of red evidence tape. I watched her put the gun box into the bag and then seal it with the tape. I wondered how much time I had and if the wheels had just come off of everything I had put into motion. I started to feel as empty as the wooden box Sobel had just sealed inside the brown paper bag.

THIRTY-TWO

Fernando Valenzuela lived out in Valencia. From my home it was easily an hour's drive north in the last remnants of rush-hour traffic. Valenzuela had moved out of Van Nuys a few years earlier because his three daughters were nearing high school age and he feared for their safety and education. He moved into a neighborhood filled with people who had also fled from the city and his commute went from five minutes to forty-five. But he was happy. His house was nicer and his children safer. He lived in a Spanish-style house with a red tile roof in a planned community full of Spanish-style houses with red tile roofs. It was more than a bail bondsman could ever dream of having, but it came with a stiff monthly price tag.

It was almost nine by the time I got there. I pulled up to the garage, which had been left open. One space was taken by a minivan and the other by a pickup. On the floor between the pickup and a fully equipped tool bench was a large cardboard box that said SONY on it. It was long and thin. I looked closer and saw it was a box for a fifty-inch plasma TV. I got out and went to the front door and knocked. Valenzuela answered after a long wait.

"Mick, what are you doing up here?"

"Do you know your garage door is open?"

"Holy shit! I just had a plasma delivered."

He pushed by me and ran across the yard to look into the garage. I closed his front door and followed him to the garage. When I got there he was standing next to his TV, smiling.

"Oh, man, you know that would've never happened in Van Nuys," he said. "That sucker woulda been long gone.

Come on, we'll go in through here."

He headed toward a door that would take us from the garage into the house. He hit a switch that made the garage door start to roll down.

"Hey, Val, wait a minute," I said. "Let's just talk out here. It's more private."

"But Maria probably wants to say hello."

"Maybe next time."

He came back over to me, concern in his eyes.

"What's up, Boss?"

"What's up is I spent some time today with the cops working on Raul's murder. They said they cleared Roulet on it because of the ankle bracelet."

Valenzuela nodded vigorously.

"Yeah, yeah, they came to see me a few days after it happened. I showed them the system and how it works and I pulled up Roulet's track for that day. They saw he was at work. And I also showed them the other bracelet I got and explained how it couldn't be tampered with. It's got a mass detector. Bottom line is you can't take it off. It would know and then I would know."

I leaned back against the pickup and folded my arms.

"So did those two cops ask where *you* were on that Saturday?"

It hit Valenzuela like a punch.

"What did you say, Mick?"

My eyes lowered to the plasma TV box and then back up to his.

"Somehow, some way, he killed Raul, Val. Now my ass is on the line and I want to know how he did it."

"Mick, listen to me, he's clear. I'm telling you, that bracelet didn't come off his ankle. The machine doesn't lie."

"Yeah, I know, the machine doesn't lie . . ."

After a moment he got it.

"What are you saying, Mick?"

He stepped in front of me, his body posture stiffening aggressively. I stopped leaning on the truck and dropped my hands to my sides.

"I'm asking, Val. Where were you on that Tuesday morning?"

"You son of a bitch, how could you ask me that?"

He had moved into a fight stance. I was momentarily taken off guard as I thought about him calling me what I had called Roulet earlier in the day.

Valenzuela suddenly lunged at me and shoved me hard against his truck. I shoved him back harder and he went backwards into the TV box. It tipped over and hit the floor with a loud, heavy *whump* and then he came down on it in a seated position. There was a sharp snap sound from inside the box.

"Oh, fuck!" he cried. "Oh, fuck! You broke the screen!"

"You pushed me, Val. I pushed back."

"Oh, fuck!"

He scrambled to the side of the box and tried to lift it back up but it was too heavy and unwieldy. I walked over to the other side and helped him right it. As the box came upright we heard small bits of material inside it slide down. It sounded like glass.

"Motherfuck!" Valenzuela yelled.

The door leading into the house opened and his wife, Maria, looked out.

"Hi, Mickey. Val, what is all the noise?"

"Just go inside," her husband ordered.

"Well, what is —"

"Shut the fuck up and go inside!"

She paused for a moment, staring at us, then closed the door. I heard her lock it. It looked like Valenzuela was sleeping with the broken TV tonight. I looked back at him. His mouth was spread in shock.

"That was eight thousand dollars," he whispered.

"They make TVs that cost eight thousand dollars?"

I was shocked. What was the world coming to?

"That was with a discount."

"Val, where'd you get the money for an eight-thousand-dollar TV?"

He looked at me and the fire came back.

"Where the fuck do you think? Business, man. Thanks to Roulet I'm having a hell of a year. But goddamn, Mick, I didn't cut him loose from the bracelet so he could go out and kill Raul. I knew Raul just as long as you did. I did not do that. I did not put the bracelet on and wear it while he went to kill Raul. And I did not go and kill Raul for him for a fucking TV. If you can't believe that, then just get the hell out of here and out of my life!"

He said it all with the desperate intensity of a wounded animal. A flash thought of Jesus Menendez came to my mind. I had failed to see the innocence in his pleas. I didn't want that to ever happen again.

"Okay, Val," I said.

I walked over to the house door and pushed the button that raised the garage door. When I turned back I saw he had taken a box cutter from the tool bench and was cutting the tape on the top of the TV box. It looked like he was trying to confirm what we already knew about the plasma. I walked past him and out of the garage.

"I'll split it with you, Val," I said. "I'll have Lorna send you a check in the morning."

"Don't bother. I'll tell them it was delivered this way."

I got to my car door and looked back at him.

"Then give me a call when they arrest you for fraud. After you bail yourself out."

I got in the Lincoln and backed out of the driveway. When I glanced back into the garage, I saw Valenzuela had stopped cutting open the box and was just standing there looking at me.

Traffic going back into the city was light and I made good time. I was just coming in through the front door when the house phone started to ring. I grabbed it in the kitchen, thinking maybe it was Valenzuela calling to tell me he was taking his business to another defense pro. At the moment I didn't care.

Instead, it was Maggie McPherson.

"Everything all right?" I asked. She usually didn't call so late.

"Fine."

"Where's Hayley?"

"Asleep. I didn't want to call until she went down."

"What's up?"

"There was a strange rumor about you floating around the office today."

"You mean the one about me being Raul Levin's murderer?"

"Haller, is this serious?"

The kitchen was too small for a table and chairs. I couldn't go far with the phone cord tether so I hoisted myself up onto the counter. Through the window over the sink I could see the lights of downtown twinkling in the distance and a glow on the horizon that I knew came from Dodger Stadium.

"I would say, yes, the situation is serious. I am being set up to take the fall for Raul's murder."

"Oh my God, Michael, how is this possible?"

"A lot of different ingredients — evil client, cop with a grudge, stupid lawyer, add sugar and spice and everything nice."

"Is it Roulet? Is he the one?"

"I can't talk about my clients with you, Mags."

"Well, what are you planning to do?"

"Don't worry, I've got it covered. I'll be okay."

"What about Hayley?"

I knew what she was saying. She was warning me to keep it away from Hayley. Don't let her go to school and hear kids talking about her father the murder suspect with a face and name splashed across the news.

"Hayley will be fine. She'll never know. Nobody will ever know if I play this thing right."

She didn't say anything and there was nothing else I could do to reassure her. I changed the subject. I tried to sound confident, even cheerful.

"How did your boy Minton look after court today?"

She didn't answer at first, probably reluctant to change the subject.

"I don't know. He looked fine. But Smithson sent an observer up because it's his first solo."

I nodded. I was counting on Smithson, who ran the DA's Van Nuys branch, having sent somebody to keep a watch on Minton.

"Any feedback?"

"No, not yet. Nothing that I heard. Look, Haller, I am really worried about this. The rumor was that you were served a search warrant in the courthouse. Is that true?"

"Yeah, but don't worry about it. I'm telling you, I have things under control. It will all come out okay. I promise."

I knew I had not quelled her fears. She was thinking about our daughter and the possible scandal. She was probably also thinking a little bit about herself and what having an ex-husband disbarred or accused of murder would do to her chances of advancement.

"Besides, if it all goes to shit, you're still going to be my first customer, right?"

"What are you talking about?"

"The Lincoln Lawyer Limousine Service. You're in, right?"

"Haller, it doesn't sound like this is a time to be making jokes."

"It's no joke, Maggie. I've been thinking about quitting.

Even before all of this bullshit came up. It's like I told you that night, I can't do this anymore."

There was a long silence before she responded.

"Whatever you want to do is going to be fine by me and Hayley."

I nodded.

"You don't know how much I appreciate that."

She sighed into the phone.

"I don't know how you do it, Haller."

"Do what?"

"You're a sleazy defense lawyer with two ex-wives and an eight-year-old daughter. And we all still love you."

Now I was silent. Despite everything I smiled.

"Thank you, Maggie McFierce," I finally said. "Good night."

And I hung up the phone.

THIRTY-THREE

The second day of trial began with a forthwith to the judge's chambers for Minton and me. Judge Fullbright wanted only to speak to me but the rules of trial made it improper for her to meet privately with me about any matter and exclude the prosecution. Her chambers were spacious, with a desk and separate seating area surrounded by three walls of shelves containing law books. She told us to sit in the seats in front of her desk.

"Mr. Minton," she began, "I can't tell you not to listen but I'm going to have a conversation with Mr. Haller that I don't expect you to join or interrupt. It doesn't concern you or, as far as I know, the Roulet case."

Minton, taken by surprise, didn't quite know how to react other than to drop his jaw a couple inches and let light into his mouth. The judge turned in her desk chair toward me and clasped her hands together on the desk.

"Mr. Haller, is there anything you need to bring up with me? Keeping in mind that you are sitting next to a prosecutor."

"No, Judge, everything's fine. Sorry if you were bothered yesterday."

I did my best to put a rueful smile on my face, as if to show the search warrant had been nothing more than an embarrassing inconvenience.

"It is hardly a bother, Mr. Haller. We've invested a lot of time on this case. The jury, the prosecution, all of us. I am hoping that it is not going to be for naught. I don't want to do this again. My calendar is already overflowing."

"Excuse me, Judge Fullbright," Minton said. "Could I just ask what —"

"No, you may not," she said, cutting him off. "What we are talking about does not concern the trial other than the timing of it. If Mr. Haller is assuring me that we don't have a problem, then I will take him at his word. You need no further explanation than that."

She looked pointedly at me.

"Do I have your word on this, Mr. Haller?"

I hesitated before nodding. What she was telling me was that there would be hell to pay if I broke my word and the Glendale investigation caused a disruption or mistrial in the Roulet case.

"You've got my word," I said.

She immediately stood up and turned toward the hat rack in the corner. Her black robe hung there on a hanger.

"Okay, then, gentlemen, let's get to it. We've got a jury waiting."

Minton and I left the chambers and entered the courtroom through the clerk's station. Roulet was seated in the defendant's chair and waiting.

"What the hell was that all about?" Minton whispered to me.

He was playing dumb. He had to have heard the same rumors my ex-wife had picked up in the halls of the DA's office.

"Nothing, Ted. Just some bullshit involving another case of mine. You going to wrap it up today?"

"Depends on you. The longer you take, the longer I take cleaning up the bullshit you sling."

"Bullshit, huh? You're bleeding to death and don't even know it."

He smiled confidently at me.

"I don't think so."

"Call it death by a thousand razor blades, Ted. One doesn't do it. They all do it. Welcome to felony practice."

I separated from him and went to the defense table. As soon as I sat down, Roulet was in my ear.

"What was that about with the judge?" he whispered.

"Nothing. She was just warning me about how I handle the victim on cross."

"Who, the woman? She actually called her a victim?"

"Louis, first of all, keep your voice down. And second, she *is* the victim in this thing. You may have that rare ability to convince yourself of almost anything, but we still — no, make that I — still need to convince the jury."

He took the rebuke like I was blowing bubbles in his face and moved on.

"Well, what did she say?"

"She said she isn't going to allow me a lot of freedom in cross-examination. She reminded me that Regina Campo is a victim."

"I'm counting on you to rip her to shreds, to borrow a quote from you on the day we met."

"Yeah, well, things are a lot different than on the day we met, aren't they? And your little scheme with my gun is about to blow up in my face. And I'm telling you right now, I'm not going down for it. If I have to drive people to the airport the rest of my life, I will do that and do it gladly if it's my only way out from this. You understand, Louis?"

"I understand, Mick," he said glibly. "I'm sure you'll figure something out. You're a smart man."

I turned and looked at him. Luckily, I didn't have to say anything further. The bailiff called the court to order and Judge Fullbright took the bench.

Minton's first witness of the day was LAPD Detective Martin Booker. He was a solid witness for the prosecution. A rock. His answers were clear and concise and given without hesitation. Booker introduced the key piece of

330

evidence, the knife with my client's initials on it, and under Minton's questioning he took the jury through his entire investigation of the attack on Regina Campo.

He testified that on the night of March 6 he had been working night duty out of Valley Bureau in Van Nuys. He was called to Regina Campo's apartment by the West Valley Division watch commander, who believed, after being briefed by his patrol officers, that the attack on Campo merited immediate attention from an investigator. Booker explained that the six detective bureaus in the Valley were only staffed during daytime hours. He said the night-duty detective was a quick-response position and often assigned cases of a pressing nature.

"What made this case of pressing nature, Detective?" Minton asked.

"The injuries to the victim, the arrest of a suspect and the belief that a greater crime had probably been averted," Booker answered.

"That greater crime being what?"

"Murder. It sounded like the guy was planning to kill her."

I could have objected but I planned to exploit the exchange on cross-examination, so I let it go.

Minton walked Booker through the investigative steps he took at the crime scene and later while interviewing Campo as she was being treated at a hospital.

"Before you got to the hospital you had been briefed by Officers Maxwell and Santos on what the victim had reported had happened, correct?"

"Yes, they gave me an overview."

"Did they tell you that the victim was engaged in selling sex to men for a living?"

"No, they didn't."

"When did you find that out?"

"Well, I was getting a pretty good sense of it when I was

in her apartment and I saw some of the property she had there."

"What property?"

"Things I would describe as sex aids, and in one of the bedrooms, there was a closet that only had negligees and clothing of a sexually provocative nature in it. There was also a television in that room and a collection of pornographic tapes in the drawers beneath it. I had been told that she did not have a roommate but it looked to me like both bedrooms were in active use. I started to think that one room was hers, like it was the one she slept in when she was alone, and the other was for her professional activities."

"A trick pad?"

"You could call it that."

"Did it change your opinion of her as a victim of this attack?"

"No, it didn't."

"And why not?"

"Because anybody can be a victim. Prostitute or pope, doesn't matter. A victim is a victim."

Spoken just as rehearsed, I thought. Minton made a check mark on his pad and moved on.

"Now, when you got to the hospital, did you ask the victim about your theory in regard to her bedrooms and what she did for a living?"

"Yes, I did."

"What did she tell you?"

"She flat out said she was a working girl. She didn't try to hide it."

"Did anything she said to you differ from the accounts of the attack you had already gathered at the crime scene?"

"No, not at all. She told me she opened the door to the defendant and he immediately punched her in the face and drove her backwards into the apartment. He assaulted her further and produced a knife. He told her he was going to rape her and then kill her."

Minton continued to probe the investigation in more detail and to the point of boring the jury. When I was not writing down questions to ask Booker during cross, I watched the jurors and saw their attention lag under the weight of so much information.

Finally, after ninety minutes of direct examination it was my turn with the police detective. My goal was to get in and get out. While Minton performed the whole case autopsy, I only wanted to go in and scrape cartilage out of the knees.

"Detective Booker, did Regina Campo explain why she lied to the police?"

"She didn't lie to me."

"Maybe not to you but she told the first officers on the scene, Maxwell and Santos, that she did not know why the suspect had come to her apartment, didn't she?"

"I wasn't present when they spoke to her so I can't testify to that. I do know that she was scared, that she had just been beaten and threatened with rape and death at the time of the first interview."

"So you are saying that under those circumstances it is acceptable to lie to the police."

"No, I did not say that."

I checked my notes and moved on. I wasn't going for a linear continuum of questions. I was potshotting, trying to keep him off balance.

"Did you catalog the clothing you found in the bedroom you said Ms. Campo used for her prostitution business?"

"No, I did not. It was just an observation I made. It was not important to the case."

"Would any of the outfits you saw in the closet have been appropriate to sadomasochistic sexual activities?"

"I wouldn't know that. I am not an expert in that field."

"How about the pornographic videos? Did you write down the titles?"

"No, I did not. Again, I did not believe that it was pertinent to the investigation of who had brutally assaulted this woman."

"Do you recall if the subject matter of any of the videos involved sadomasochism or bondage or anything of that nature?"

"No, I do not."

"Now, did you instruct Ms. Campo to get rid of those tapes and the clothing from the closet before members of Mr. Roulet's defense team could view the apartment?"

"I certainly did not."

I checked that one off my list and moved on.

"Have you ever spoken to Mr. Roulet about what happened in Ms. Campo's apartment that night?"

"No, he lawyered up before I got to him."

"Do you mean he exercised his constitutional right to remain silent?"

"Yes, that's exactly what he did."

"So, as far as you know, he never spoke to the police about what happened."

"That is correct."

"In your opinion, was Ms. Campo struck with great force?"

"I would say so, yes. Her face was very badly cut and swollen."

"Then please tell the jury about the impact injuries you found on Mr. Roulet's hands."

"He had wrapped a cloth around his fist to protect it. There were no injuries on his hands that I could see."

"Did you document this lack of injury?"

Booker looked puzzled by the question.

"No," he said.

"So you had Ms. Campo's injuries documented by photographs but you didn't see the need to document Mr. Roulet's lack of injuries, correct?"

"It didn't seem to me to be necessary to photograph something that wasn't there."

"How do you know he wrapped his fist in a cloth to protect it?"

"Ms. Campo told me she saw that his hand was wrapped right before he punched her at the door."

"Did you find this cloth he supposedly wrapped his hand in?"

"Yes, it was in the apartment. It was a napkin, like from a restaurant. It had her blood on it."

"Did it have Mr. Roulet's blood on it?"

"No."

"Was there anything that identified it as belonging to the defendant?"

"No."

"So we have Ms. Campo's word for it, right?"

"That's right."

I let some time pass while I scribbled a note on my pad. I then continued to question the detective.

"Detective, when did you learn that Louis Roulet denied assaulting or threatening Ms. Campo and that he would be vigorously defending himself against the charges?"

"That would have been when he hired you, I guess."

There was a murmur of laughter in the courtroom.

"Did you pursue other explanations for Ms. Campo's injuries?"

"No, she told me what happened. I believed her. He beat her and was going to —"

"Thank you, Detective Booker. Just try to answer the question I ask."

"I was."

"If you looked for no other explanation because you believed the word of Ms. Campo, is it safe to say that this whole case relies upon her word and what she said occurred in her apartment on the night of March sixth?"

Booker deliberated a moment. He knew I was leading him into a trap of his own words. As the saying goes, there is no trap so deadly as the one you set for yourself.

"It's not just her word," he said after thinking he saw a way out. "There is physical evidence. The knife. Her injuries. More than just her word on this."

He nodded affirmatively.

"But doesn't the state's explanation for her injuries and the other evidence begin with her telling of what happened?"

"You could say that, yes," he said reluctantly.

"She is the tree on which all of these fruits grow, is she not?"

"I probably wouldn't use those words."

"Then what words would you use, Detective?"

I had him now. Booker was literally squirming in his seat. Minton stood up and objected, saying I was badgering the witness. It must have been something he had seen on TV or in a movie. He was told to sit down by the judge.

"You can answer the question, Detective," the judge said.

"What was the question?" Booker asked, trying to buy some time.

"You disagreed with me when I characterized Ms. Campo as the tree from which all the evidence in the case grows," I said. "If I am wrong, how would you describe her position in this case?"

Booker raised his hands in a quick gesture of surrender.

"She's the victim! Of course she's important because she told us what happened. We have to rely on her to set the course of the investigation."

"You rely on her for quite a bit in this case, don't you? Victim and chief witness against the defendant, correct?"

"That's right."

"Who else saw the defendant attack Ms. Campo?"

"Nobody else."

I nodded, to underline the answer for the jury. I looked over and exchanged eye contact with those in the front row.

"Okay, Detective," I said. "I want to ask you about Charles Talbot now. How did you find out about this man?"

"Uh, the prosecutor, Mr. Minton, told me to find him."

"And do you know how Mr. Minton came to know about his existence?"

"I believe you were the one who informed him. You had a videotape from a bar that showed him with the victim a couple hours before the attack."

I knew this could be the point to introduce the video but I wanted to wait on that. I wanted the victim on the stand when I showed the tape to the jury.

"And up until that point you didn't think it was important to find this man?"

"No, I just didn't know about him."

"So when you finally did know about Talbot and you located him, did you have his left hand examined to determine if he had any injuries that could have been sustained while punching someone repeatedly in the face?"

"No, I didn't."

"Is that because you were confident in your choice of Mr. Roulet as the person who punched Regina Campo?"

"It wasn't a choice. It was where the investigation led. I didn't locate Charles Talbot until more than two weeks after the crime occurred."

"So what you are saying is that if he'd had injuries, they

337

would have been healed by then, correct?"

"I'm no expert on it but that was my thinking, yes."

"So you never looked at his hand, did you?"

"Not specifically, no."

"Did you question any coworkers of Mr. Talbot about whether they saw bruising or other injuries on his hand around the time of the crime?"

"No, I did not."

"So you never really looked beyond Mr. Roulet, did you?"

"That is wrong. I come into every case with an open mind. But Roulet was there and in custody from the start. The victim identified him as her attacker. He was obviously a focus."

"Was he *a* focus or *the* focus, Detective Booker?"

"He was both. At first he was *a* focus and later — after we found his initials on the weapon that had been held to Reggie Campo's throat — he became *the* focus, you could say."

"How do you know that knife was held to Ms. Campo's throat?"

"Because she told us and she had the puncture wound to show for it."

"Are you saying there was some sort of forensic analysis that matched the knife to the wound on her neck?"

"No, that was impossible."

"So again we have Ms. Campo's word that the knife was held to her throat by Mr. Roulet."

"I had no reason to doubt her then. I have none now."

"Now without any explanation for it, I guess you would consider the knife with the defendant's initials on it to be a highly important piece of evidence of guilt, wouldn't you?"

"Yes. Even with explanation, I would say. He brought that knife in there with one purpose in mind."

"You are a mind reader, are you, Detective?"

"No, I'm a detective. And I am just saying what I think."

"Accent on *think*."

"It's what I know from the evidence in the case."

"I'm glad you are so confident, sir. I have no further questions at this time. I reserve the right to recall Detective Booker as a witness for the defense."

I had no intention of calling Booker back to the stand but I thought the threat might sound good to the jury.

I returned to my seat while Minton tried to bandage up Booker on redirect. The damage was in perceptions and there wasn't a lot that he could do with that. Booker had only been a setup man for the defense. The real damage would come later.

After Booker stepped down, the judge called for the mid morning break. She told the jurors to be back in fifteen minutes but I knew the break would last longer. Judge Fullbright was a smoker and had already faced highly publicized administrative charges for sneaking smokes in her chambers. That meant that for her to take care of her habit and avoid further scandal, she had to take the elevator down and leave the building and stand in the entry port where the jail buses come in. I figured I had at least a half hour.

I went out into the hallway to talk to Mary Alice Windsor and work my cell phone. It looked like I would be putting on witnesses in the afternoon session.

I was first approached by Roulet, who wanted to talk about my cross-examination of Booker.

"It looked to me like it went really well for us," he said.

"Us?"

"You know what I mean."

"You can't tell whether it's gone well until you get the verdict. Now leave me alone, Louis. I have to make some calls. And where is your mother? I am probably going to

339

need her this afternoon. Is she going to be here?"

"She had an appointment this morning but she'll be here. Just call Cecil and he'll bring her in."

After he walked away Detective Booker took his place, walking up to me and pointing a finger in my face.

"It's not going to fly, Haller," he said.

"What's not going to fly?" I asked.

"Your whole bullshit defense. You're going to crash and burn."

"We'll see."

"Yeah, we'll see. You know, you have some balls trying to trash Talbot with this. Some balls. You must need a wheelbarrow to carry them around in."

"I'm just doing my job, Detective."

"And some job it is. Lying for a living. Tricking people from looking at the truth. Living in a world without truth. Let me ask you something. You know the difference between a catfish and a lawyer?"

"No, what's the difference?"

"One's a bottom-feeding, shit-eating scum sucker. The other's a fish."

"That's a good one, Detective."

He left me then and I stood there smiling. Not because of the joke or the understanding that Lankford had probably been the one to elevate the insult from defense attorneys to all of lawyerdom when he had retold the joke to Booker. I smiled because the joke was confirmation that Lankford and Booker were in communication. They were talking and it meant that things were moving and in play. My plan was still holding together. I still had a chance.

THIRTY-FOUR

Every trial has a main event. A witness or a piece of evidence that becomes the fulcrum upon which everything swings one way or the other. In this case the main event was billed as Regina Campo, victim and accuser, and the case would seem to rest upon her performance and testimony. But a good defense attorney always has an understudy and I had mine, a witness secretly waiting in the wings upon whom I hoped to shift the weight of the trial.

Nevertheless, when Minton called Regina Campo to the stand after the break, it was safe to say all eyes were on her as she was led in and walked to the witness box. It was the first time anyone in the jury had seen her in person. It was also the first time I had ever seen her. I was surprised, but not in a good way. She was diminutive and her hesitant walk and slight posture belied the picture of the scheming mercenary I had been building in the jury's collective consciousness.

Minton was definitely learning as he was going. With Campo he seemed to have arrived at the conclusion that less was more. He economically led her through the testimony. He first started with personal background before moving on to the events of March 6.

Regina Campo's story was sadly unoriginal and that was what Minton was counting on. She told the story of a young, attractive woman coming to Hollywood from Indiana a decade before with hopes of celluloid glory. There were starts and stops to a career, an appearance on a television show here and there. She was a fresh face and there were always men willing to put her in small meaningless parts. But when she was no longer a fresh face, she found work in a series of straight-to-cable films which often required her to appear nude. She supplemented her income with nude modeling jobs and slipped easily into a world of trading sex for favors. Eventually, she skipped the façade altogether and started trading sex for money. It finally brought her to the night she encountered Louis Roulet.

Regina Campo's courtroom version of what happened that night did not differ from the accounts offered by all previous witnesses in the trial. But where it was dramatically different was in the delivery. Campo, with her face framed by dark, curly hair, seemed like a little girl lost. She appeared scared and tearful during the latter half of her testimony. Her lower lip and finger shook with fear as she pointed to the man she identified as her attacker. Roulet stared right back, a blank expression on his face.

"It was him," she said in a strong voice. "He's an animal who should be put away!"

I let that go without objection. I would get my chance with her soon enough. Minton continued the questioning, taking Campo through her escape, and then asked why she had not told the responding officers the truth about knowing who the man who attacked her was and why he was there.

"I was scared," she said. "I wasn't sure they would believe me if I told them why he was there. I wanted to make sure they arrested him because I was very afraid of him."

"Do you regret that decision now?"

"Yes, I do because I know it might help him get free to do this again to somebody."

I did object to that answer as prejudicial and the judge

sustained it. Minton threw a few more questions at his witness but seemed to know he was past the apex of the testimony and that he should stop before he obscured the trembling finger of identification.

Campo had testified on direct examination for slightly less than an hour. It was almost 11:30 but the judge did not break for lunch as I had expected. She told the jurors she wanted to get as much testimony in as possible during the day and that they would go to a late, abbreviated lunch. This made me wonder if she knew something I didn't. Had the Glendale detectives called her during the mid-morning break to warn of my impending arrest?

"Mr. Haller, your witness," she said to prompt me and keep things going.

I went to the lectern with my legal pad and looked at my notes. If I was engaged in a defense of a thousand razors, I had to use at least half of them on this witness. I was ready.

"Ms. Campo, have you engaged the services of an attorney to sue Mr. Roulet over the alleged events of March sixth?"

She looked as though she had expected the question, but not as the first one out of the shoot.

"No, I haven't."

"Have you talked to an attorney about this case?"

"I haven't hired anybody to sue him. Right now, all I am interested in is seeing that justice is —"

"Ms. Campo," I interrupted. "I didn't ask whether you hired an attorney or what your interests are. I asked if you had *talked* to an attorney — any attorney — about this case and a possible lawsuit against Mr. Roulet."

She was looking closely at me, trying to read me. I had said it with the authority of someone who knew something, who had the goods to back up the charge. Minton had probably schooled her on the most important aspect of testifying: don't get trapped in a lie.

"Talked to an attorney, yes. But it was nothing more than talk. I didn't hire him."

"Is that because the prosecutor told you not to hire anybody until the criminal case was over?"

"No, he didn't say anything about that."

"Why did you talk to an attorney about this case?"

She had dropped into a routine of hesitating before every answer. This was fine with me. The perception of most people is that it takes time to tell a lie. Honest responses come easily.

"I talked to him because I wanted to know my rights and to make sure I was protected."

"Did you ask him if you could sue Mr. Roulet for damages?"

"I thought what you say to your attorney is private."

"If you wish, you can tell the jurors what you spoke to the attorney about."

There was the first deep slash with the razor. She was in an untenable position. No matter how she answered she would not look good.

"I think I want to keep it private," she finally said.

"Okay, let's go back to March sixth, but I want to go a little further back than Mr. Minton did. Let's go back to the bar at Morgan's when you first spoke to the defendant, Mr. Roulet."

"Okay."

"What were you doing at Morgan's that night?"

"I was meeting someone."

"Charles Talbot?"

"Yes."

"Now, you were meeting him there to sort of size up whether you wanted to lead him back to your place to engage in sex for hire, correct?"

She hesitated but then nodded.

"Please answer verbally," the judge told her.

"Yes."

"Would you say that practice is a safety precaution?"

"Yes."

"A form of safe sex, right?"

"I guess so."

"Because in your profession you deal intimately with strangers, so you must protect yourself, correct?"

"Yes, correct."

"People in your profession call this the 'freak test,' don't they?"

"I've never called it that."

"But it is true that you meet your prospective clients in a public place like Morgan's to test them out and make sure they aren't freaks or dangerous before you take them to your apartment. Isn't that right?"

"You could say that. But the truth is, you can never be sure about somebody."

"That is true. So when you were at Morgan's you noticed Mr. Roulet sitting at the same bar as you and Mr. Talbot?"

"Yes, he was there."

"And had you ever seen him before?"

"Yes, I had seen him there and a few other places before."

"Had you ever spoken to him?"

"No, we never talked."

"Had you ever noticed that he wore a Rolex watch?"

"No."

"Had you ever seen him drive up or away from one of these places in a Porsche or a Range Rover?"

"No, I never saw him driving."

"But you had seen him before in Morgan's and other places like it."

"Yes."

"But never spoke to him."

"Correct."

"Then, what made you approach him?"

"I knew he was in the life, that's all."

"What do you mean by 'in the life'?"

"I mean that the other times I had seen him I could tell he was a player. I'd seen him leave with girls that do what I do."

"You saw him leave with other prostitutes?"

"Yes."

"Leave to where?"

"I don't know, leave the premises. Go to a hotel or the girl's apartment. I don't know that part."

"Well, how do you know they even left the premises? Maybe they went outside for a smoke."

"I saw them get into his car and drive away."

"Ms. Campo, you testified a minute ago that you never saw Mr. Roulet's cars. Now you are saying that you saw him get into his car with a woman who is a prostitute like yourself. Which is it?"

She realized her misstep and froze for a moment until an answer came to her.

"I saw him get into a car but I didn't know what kind it was."

"You don't notice things like that, do you?"

"Not usually."

"Do you know the difference between a Porsche and a Range Rover?"

"One's big and one's small, I guess."

"What kind of car did you see Mr. Roulet get into?"

"I don't remember."

I paused a moment and decided I had milked her contradiction for all it was worth. I looked down at my list of questions and moved on.

"These women that you saw leave with Mr. Roulet,

346

were they ever seen again?"

"I don't understand."

"Did they disappear? Did you ever see them again?"

"No, I saw them again."

"Had they been beaten or injured?"

"Not that I know of but I didn't ask."

"But all of this added up to you believing that you were safe as far as approaching and soliciting him, correct?"

"I don't know about safe. I just knew he was probably there looking for a girl and the man I was with already told me he would be finished by ten because he had to go to his business."

"Well, can you tell the jury why it was that you did not have to sit with Mr. Roulet like you did with Mr. Talbot and subject him to a freak test?"

Her eyes drifted over to Minton. She was hoping for a rescue but none was coming.

"I just thought he was a known quantity, that's all."

"You thought he was safe."

"I guess so. I don't know. I needed the money and I made a mistake with him."

"Did you think he was rich and could solve your need for money?"

"No, nothing like that. I saw him as a potential customer who wasn't new to the game. Somebody who knew what he was doing."

"You testified that on prior occasions you had seen Mr. Roulet with other women who practice the same profession as yourself?"

"Yes."

"They're prostitutes."

"Yes."

"Do you know them?"

"We're acquaintances."

"And do you extend professional courtesy to these

women in terms of alerting them to customers who might be dangerous or unwilling to pay?"

"Sometimes."

"And they extend the same professional courtesy to you, right?"

"Yes."

"How many of them warned you about Louis Roulet?"

"Well, nobody did, or I wouldn't have gone with him."

I nodded and looked at my notes for a long moment before continuing. I then led her in more detail through the events at Morgan's and then introduced the video surveillance tape from the bar's overhead camera. Minton objected to it being shown to the jury without proper foundation but he was overruled. A television on an industrial stand was wheeled in front of the jury and the video was played. I could tell by the rapt attention they paid to it that they were enamored with the idea of watching a prostitute at work as well as the aspect of seeing the two main players in the case in unguarded moments.

"What did the note say that you passed him?" I asked after the television was pushed to the side of the courtroom.

"I think it just said my name and address."

"You didn't quote him a price for the services you would perform?"

"I may have. I don't remember."

"What is the going rate that you charge?"

"Usually I get four hundred dollars."

"Usually? What would make you differentiate from that?"

"Depends on what the client wants."

I looked over at the jury box and saw that the Bible man's face was getting tight with discomfort.

"Do you ever engage in bondage and domination with

your clients?"

"Sometimes. It's only role playing, though. Nobody ever gets hurt. It's just playacting."

"Are you saying that before the night of March sixth, you have never been hurt by a client?"

"Yes, that's what I am saying. That man hurt me and tried to kill —"

"Please just answer the question I ask, Ms. Campo. Thank you. Now, let's go back to Morgan's. Yes or no, at the moment you gave Mr. Roulet the napkin with your address and price on it, you were confident that he would not be a danger to you and that he was carrying sufficient cash funds to pay the four hundred dollars you demand for your services?"

"Yes."

"So, why didn't Mr. Roulet have any cash on him when the police searched him?"

"I don't know. I didn't take it."

"Do you know who did?"

"No."

I hesitated for a long moment, preferring to punctuate my shifts in questioning streams with an underscore of silence.

"Now, uh, you are still working as a prostitute, correct?" I asked.

Campo hesitated before saying yes.

"And are you happy working as a prostitute?" I asked.

Minton stood.

"Your Honor, what does this have to do with —"

"Sustained," the judge said.

"Okay," I said. "Then, isn't it true, Ms. Campo, that you have told several of your clients that your hope is to leave the business?"

"Yes, that's true," she answered without hesitation for the first time in many questions.

"Isn't it also true that you see the potential financial aspects of this case as a means of getting out of the business?"

"No, that's not true," she said forcefully and without hesitation. "That man attacked me. He was going to kill me! That's what this is about!"

I underlined something on my pad, another punctuation of silence.

"Was Charles Talbot a repeat customer?" I asked.

"No, I met him for the first time that night at Morgan's."

"And he passed your safety test."

"Yes."

"Was Charles Talbot the man who punched you in the face on March sixth?"

"No, he was not," she answered quickly.

"Did you offer to split the profits you would receive from a lawsuit against Mr. Roulet with Mr. Talbot?"

"No, I did not. That's a lie!"

I looked up at the judge.

"Your Honor, can I ask my client to stand up at this time?"

"Be my guest, Mr. Haller."

I signaled Roulet to stand at the defense table and he obliged. I looked back at Regina Campo.

"Now, Ms. Campo, are you sure that this is the man who struck you on the night of March sixth?"

"Yes, it's him."

"How much do you weigh, Ms. Campo?"

She leaned back from the microphone as if put out by what was an invasive question, even coming after so many questions pertaining to her sex life. I noticed Roulet start to sit back down and I signaled him to remain standing.

"I'm not sure," Campo said.

"On your ad on the website you list your weight at one hundred and five pounds," I said. "Is that correct?"

"I think so."

"So if the jury is to believe your story about March sixth, then they must believe that you were able to overpower and break free of Mr. Roulet."

I pointed to Roulet, who was easily six feet and outweighed her by at least seventy-five pounds.

"Well, that's what I did."

"And this was while he supposedly was holding a knife to your throat."

"I wanted to live. You can do some amazing things when your life is in danger."

She used her last defense. She started crying, as if my question had reawakened the horror of coming so close to death.

"You can sit down, Mr. Roulet. I have nothing else for Ms. Campo at this time, Your Honor."

I took my seat next to Roulet. I felt the cross had gone well. My razor work had opened up a lot of wounds. The state's case was bleeding. Roulet leaned over and whispered one word to me. *"Brilliant!"*

Minton went back in for a redirect but he was just a gnat flitting around an open wound. There was no going back on some of the answers his star witness had given, and there was no way to change some of the images I had planted in the jurors' minds.

In ten minutes he was through and I waived off a recross, feeling that Minton had accomplished little during his second effort and I could leave well enough alone. The judge asked the prosecutor if he had any further witnesses and Minton said he would like to think about it through lunch before deciding whether to rest the state's case.

Normally, I would have objected to this because I would want to know if I had to put a witness on the stand directly after lunch. But I let it go. I believed that Minton was feeling the pressure and was wavering. I wanted to push him toward a decision and thought maybe giving him the lunch hour would help.

The judge excused the jury to lunch, giving them only an hour instead of the usual ninety minutes. She was going to keep things moving. She said court would recess until 1:30 and then abruptly left the bench. She probably needed a cigarette, I guessed.

I asked Roulet if his mother could join us for lunch so that we could talk about her testimony, which I thought would come in the afternoon if not directly after lunch. He said he would arrange it and suggested we meet at a French restaurant on Ventura Boulevard. I told him we had less than an hour and that his mother should meet us at Four Green Fields. I didn't like the idea of bringing them into my sanctuary but I knew we could eat there quickly and be back to court on time. The food probably wasn't up to the standards of the French bistro on Ventura but I wasn't worried about that.

When I got up and turned from the defense table, I saw the rows of the gallery were empty. Everybody had hustled out to lunch. Only Minton was waiting by the rail for me.

"Can I talk to you for a minute?" he asked.

"Sure."

We waited until Roulet had gone through the gate and left the courtroom before either one of us spoke. I knew what was coming. It was customary for the prosecutor to throw out a low-ball disposition at the first sign of trouble. Minton knew he had trouble. The main-event witness was a draw at best.

"What's up?" I said.

"I was thinking about what you said about the thousand razors."

"And?"

"And, well, I want to make you an offer."

"You're new at this, kid. Don't you need somebody in charge to approve a plea agreement?"

"I have some authority."

"Okay, then give me what you are authorized to offer."

"I'll drop it all down to an aggravated assault with GBI."

"And?"

"I'll go down to four."

The offer was a substantial reduction but Roulet, if he took it, would still be sentenced to four years in prison. The main concession was that it knocked the case out of sex crime status. Roulet would not have to register with local authorities as a sex offender after he got out of prison.

I looked at him as if he had just insulted my mother's memory.

"I think that's a little strong, Ted, considering how your ace just held up on the stand. Did you see the juror who is always carrying the Bible? He looked like he was about to shit the Good Book when she was testifying."

Minton didn't respond. I could tell he hadn't even noticed a juror carrying a Bible.

"I don't know," I said. "It's my duty to bring your offer to my client and I will do that. But I'm also going to tell him he'd be a fool to take it."

"Okay, then, what do you want?"

"A case like this, there's only one verdict, Ted. I'm going to tell him he should ride it out. I think it's clear sailing from here. Have a good lunch."

I left him there at the gate, halfway expecting him to shout a new offer to my back as I went down the center aisle of the gallery. But Minton held his ground.

"That offer's good only until one-thirty, Haller," he called after me, an odd tone in his voice.

I raised a hand and waved without looking back. As I

went through the courtroom door, I was sure that what I had heard was the sound of desperation creeping into his voice.

THIRTY-FIVE

After we came back into court from Four Green Fields I purposely ignored Minton. I wanted to keep him guessing as long as possible. It was all part of the plan to push him in a direction I wanted him and the trial to go. When we were all seated at the tables and ready for the judge, I finally looked over at him, waited for the eye contact, and then just shook my head. No deal. He nodded, trying his best to give me a show of confidence in his case and confusion over my client's decision. One minute later the judge took the bench, brought out the jury, and Minton promptly folded his tent.

"Mr. Minton, do you have another witness?" the judge asked.

"Your Honor, at this time the state rests."

There was the slightest hesitation in Fullbright's response. She stared at Minton for just a second longer than she should have. I think it sent a message of surprise to the jury. She then looked over at me.

"Mr. Haller, are you ready to proceed?"

The routine procedure would be to ask the judge for a directed verdict of acquittal at the end of the state's case. But I didn't, fearing that this could be the rare occasion that the request was granted. I couldn't let the case end yet. I told the judge I was ready to proceed with a defense.

My first witness was Mary Alice Windsor. She was escorted into the courtroom by Cecil Dobbs, who then took a seat in the front row of the gallery. Windsor was wearing a powder blue suit with a chiffon blouse. She had a regal bearing as she crossed in front of the bench and took a seat in the witness box. Nobody would have guessed she had eaten shepherd's pie for lunch. I very quickly went through the routine identifiers and established her relationship by both blood and business to Louis Roulet. I then asked the judge for permission to show the witness the knife the prosecution had entered as evidence in the case.

Permission granted, I went to the court clerk to retrieve the weapon, which was still wrapped in a clear plastic evidence bag. It was folded so that the initials on the blade were visible. I took it to the witness box and put it down in front of the witness.

"Mrs. Windsor, do you recognize this knife?"

She picked up the evidence bag and attempted to smooth the plastic over the blade so she could look for and read the initials.

"Yes, I do," she finally said. "It's my son's knife."

"And how is it that you would recognize a knife owned by your son?"

"Because he showed it to me on more than one occasion. I knew he always carried it and sometimes it came in handy at the office when our brochures came in and we needed to cut the packing straps. It was very sharp."

"How long did he have the knife?"

"Four years."

"You seem pretty exact about that."

"I am."

"How can you be so sure?"

"Because he got it for protection four years ago. Almost exactly."

"Protection from what, Mrs. Windsor?"

"In our business we often show homes to complete

strangers. Sometimes we are the only ones in the home with these strangers. There has been more than one incident of a realtor being robbed or hurt ... or even murdered or raped."

"As far as you know, was Louis ever the victim of such a crime?"

"Not personally, no. But he knew someone who had gone into a home and that happened to them ..."

"What happened?"

"She got raped and robbed by a man with a knife. Louis was the one who found her after it was over. The first thing he did was go out and get a knife for protection after that."

"Why a knife? Why not a gun?"

"He told me that at first he was going to get a gun but he wanted something he could always carry and not be noticeable with. So he got a knife and he got me one, too. That's how I know it was almost exactly four years ago that he got this."

She held the bag up containing the knife.

"Mine's exactly the same, only the initials are different. We both have been carrying them ever since."

"So would it seem to you that if your son was carrying that knife on the night of March sixth, then that would be perfectly normal behavior from him?"

Minton objected, saying I had not built the proper foundation for Windsor to answer the question and the judge sustained it. Mary Windsor, being unschooled in criminal law, assumed that the judge was allowing her to answer.

"He carried it every day," she said. "March sixth would have been no dif —"

"Mrs. Windsor," the judge boomed. "I sustained the objection. That means you do not answer. The jury will disregard her answer."

"I'm sorry," Windsor said in a weak voice.

"Next question, Mr. Haller," the judge ordered.

"That's all I have, Your Honor. Thank you, Mrs. Windsor."

Mary Windsor started to get up but the judge admonished her again, telling her to stay seated. I returned to my seat as Minton got up from his. I scanned the gallery and saw no recognizable faces save that of C. C. Dobbs. He gave me an encouraging smile, which I ignored.

Mary Windsor's direct testimony had been perfect in terms of her adhering to the choreography we had worked up at lunch. She had succinctly delivered to the jury the explanation for the knife, yet she had also left in her testimony a minefield that Minton would have to cross. Her direct testimony had covered no more than I had provided Minton in a discovery summary. If he strayed from it he would quickly hear the deadly *click* under his foot.

"This incident that inspired your son to start carrying around a five-inch folding knife, when exactly was that?"

"It happened on June ninth in two thousand and one."

"You're sure?"

"Absolutely."

I turned in my seat so I could more fully see Minton's face. I was reading him. He thought he had something. Windsor's exact memory of a date was obvious indication of planted testimony. He was excited. I could tell.

"Was there a newspaper story about this supposed attack on a fellow realtor?"

"No, there wasn't."

"Was there a police investigation?"

"No, there wasn't."

"And yet you know the exact date. How is that, Mrs. Windsor? Were you given this date before testifying here?"

"No, I know the date because I will never forget the day I was attacked."

She waited a moment. I saw at least three of the jurors open their mouths silently. Minton did the same. I could almost hear the *click*.

"My son will never forget it, either," Windsor continued. "When he came looking for me and found me in that house, I was tied up, naked. There was blood. It was traumatic for him to see me that way. I think that was one of the reasons he took to carrying a knife. I think in some ways he wished he had gotten there earlier and been able to stop it."

"I see," Minton said, staring down at his notes.

He froze, unsure how to proceed. He didn't want to raise his foot for fear that the mine would detonate and blow it off.

"Mr. Minton, anything else?" the judge asked, a not so well disguised note of sarcasm in her voice.

"One moment, Your Honor," Minton said.

Minton gathered himself, reviewed his notes and tried to salvage something.

"Mrs. Windsor, did you or your son call the police after he found you?"

"No, we didn't. Louis wanted to but I did not. I thought that it would only further the trauma."

"So we have no official police documentation of this crime, correct?"

"That's correct."

I knew that Minton wanted to carry it further and ask if she had sought medical treatment after the attack. But sensing another trap, he didn't ask the question.

"So what you are saying here is that we only have your word that this attack even occurred? Your word and your son's, if he chooses to testify."

"It did occur. I live with it each and every day."

"But we only have you who says so."

She looked at the prosecutor with deadpan eyes.

"Is that a question?"

"Mrs. Windsor, you are here to help your son, correct?"

"If I can. I know him as a good man who would not have committed this despicable crime."

"You would be willing to do anything and everything in your power to save your son from conviction and possible prison, wouldn't you?"

"But I wouldn't lie about something like this. Oath or no oath, I wouldn't lie."

"But you want to save your son, don't you?"

"Yes."

"And saving him means lying for him, doesn't it?"

"No. It does not."

"Thank you, Mrs. Windsor."

Minton quickly returned to his seat. I had only one question on redirect.

"Mrs. Windsor, how old were you when this attack occurred?"

"I was fifty-four."

I sat back down. Minton had nothing further and Windsor was excused. I asked the judge to allow her to sit in the gallery for the remainder of the trial, now that her testimony was concluded. Without an objection from Minton the request was granted.

My next witness was an LAPD detective named David Lambkin, who was a national expert on sex crimes and had worked on the Real Estate Rapist investigation. In brief questioning I established the facts of the case and the five reported cases of rape that were investigated. I quickly got to the five key questions I needed to bolster Mary Windsor's testimony.

"Detective Lambkin, what was the age range of the known victims of the rapist?"

"These were all professional women who were pretty successful. They tended to be older than your average rape victim. I believe the youngest was twenty-nine and the oldest was fifty-nine."

"So a woman who was fifty-four years old would have fallen within the rapist's target profile, correct?"

"Yes."

"Can you tell the jury when the first reported attack occurred and when the last reported attack occurred?"

"Yes. The first was October one, two thousand, and the last one was July thirtieth of two thousand and one."

"So June ninth of two thousand and one was well within the span of this rapist's attacks on women in the real estate business, correct?"

"Yes, correct."

"In the course of your investigation of this case, did you come to a conclusion or belief that there were more than five rapes committed by this individual?"

Minton objected, saying the question called for speculation. The judge sustained the objection but it didn't matter. The question was what was important and the jury seeing the prosecutor keeping the answer from them was the payoff.

Minton surprised me on cross. He recovered enough from the misstep with Windsor to hit Lambkin with three solid questions with answers favorable to the prosecution.

"Detective Lambkin, did the task force investigating these rapes issue any kind of warning to women working in the real estate business?"

"Yes, we did. We sent out fliers on two occasions. The first went to all licensed real estate businesses in the area and the next mail-out went to all licensed real estate brokers individually, male and female."

"Did these mail-outs contain information about the rapist's description and methods?"

"Yes, they did."

"So if someone wished to concoct a story about being

attacked by this rapist, the mail-outs would have provided all the information needed, correct?"

"That is a possibility, yes."

"Nothing further, Your Honor."

Minton proudly sat down and Lambkin was excused when I had nothing further. I asked the judge for a few minutes to confer with my client and then leaned in close to Roulet.

"Okay, this is it," I said. "You're all we have left. Unless there's something you haven't told me, you're clean and there isn't much Minton can come back at you with. You should be safe up there unless you let him get to you. Are you still cool with this?"

Roulet had said all along that he would testify and deny the charges. He had reiterated his desire again at lunch. He demanded it. I always viewed the risks of letting a client testify as evenly split. Anything he said could come back to haunt him if the prosecution could bend it to the state's favor. But I also knew that no matter what admonishments were given to a jury about a defendant's right to remain silent, the jury always wanted to hear the defendant say he didn't do it. You take that away from the jury and they might hold a grudge.

"I want to do it," Roulet whispered. "I can handle the prosecutor."

I pushed my chair back and stood up.

"The defense calls Louis Ross Roulet, Your Honor."

THIRTY-SIX

Louis Roulet moved toward the witness box quickly, like a basketball player pulled off the bench and sent to the scorer's table to check into the game. He looked like a man anxious for the opportunity to defend himself. He knew this posture would not be lost on the jury.

After dispensing with the preliminaries, I got right down to the issues of the case. Under my questioning Roulet freely admitted that he had gone to Morgan's on the night of March 6 to seek female companionship. He said he wasn't specifically looking to engage the services of a prostitute but was not against the possibility.

"I had been with women I had to pay before," he said. "So I wouldn't have been against it."

He testified that he had no conscious eye contact with Regina Campo before she approached him at the bar. He said that she was the aggressor but at the time that didn't bother him. He said the solicitation was open-ended. She said she would be free after ten and he could come by if he was not otherwise engaged.

Roulet described efforts made over the next hour at Morgan's and then at the Lamplighter to find a woman he would not have to pay but said he was unsuccessful. He then drove to the address Campo had given him and knocked on the door.

"Who answered?"

"She did. She opened the door a crack and looked out at me."

"Regina Campo? The woman who testified this morning?"

"Yes, that's right."

"Could you see her whole face through the opening in the door?"

"No. She only opened up a crack and I couldn't see her. Only her left eye and a little bit of that side of her face."

"How did the door open? Was this crack through which you could see her on the right or left side?"

"As I was looking at the door the opening would have been on the right."

"So let's make sure we make this clear. The opening was on the right, correct?"

"Correct."

"So if she were standing behind the door and looking through the opening, she would be looking at you with her left eye."

"That is correct."

"Did you see her right eye?"

"No."

"So if she had a bruise or a cut or any damage on the right side of her face, could you have seen it?"

"No."

"Okay. So what happened next?"

"She saw it was me and she said come in. She opened the door wider but still sort of stood behind it."

"You couldn't see her?"

"Not completely. She was using the edge of the door as sort of a block."

"What happened next?"

"Well, it was kind of like an entry area, a vestibule, and she pointed through an archway to the living room. I went the way she pointed."

"Did this mean that she was then behind you?"

"Yes, when I turned toward the living room she was behind me."

"Did she close the door?"

"I think so. I heard it close."

"And then what?"

"Something hit me on the back of my head and I went down. I blacked out."

"Do you know how long you were out?"

"No. I think it was a while but none of the police or anybody ever told me."

"What do you remember when you regained consciousness?"

"I remember having a hard time breathing and when I opened my eyes, there was somebody sitting on me. I was on my back and he was sitting on me. I tried to move and that was when I realized somebody was sitting on my legs, too."

"What happened next?"

"They took turns telling me not to move and one of them told me they had my knife and if I tried to move or escape he would use it on me."

"Did there come a time that the police came and you were arrested?"

"Yes, a few minutes later the police were there. They handcuffed me and made me stand up. That was when I saw I had blood on my jacket."

"What about your hand?"

"I couldn't see it because it was handcuffed behind my back. But I heard one of the men who had been sitting on me tell the police officer that there was blood on my hand and then the officer put a bag over it. I felt that."

"How did the blood get on your hand and jacket?"

"All I know is that somebody put it on there because I didn't."

"Are you left-handed?"

"No, I am not."

"You didn't strike Ms. Campo with your left fist?"

"No, I did not."

"Did you threaten to rape her?"

"No, I did not."

"Did you tell her you were going to kill her if she didn't cooperate with you?"

"No, I did not."

I was hoping for some of the fire I had seen on that first day in C. C. Dobbs's office but Roulet was calm and controlled. I decided that before I finished with him on direct I needed to push things a little to get some of that anger back. I had told him at lunch I wanted to see it and wasn't sure what he was doing or where it had gone.

"Are you angry about being charged with attacking Ms. Campo?"

"Of course I am."

"Why?"

He opened his mouth but didn't speak. He seemed outraged that I would ask such a question. Finally, he responded.

"What do you mean, why? Have you ever been accused of something you didn't do and there's nothing you can do about it but wait? Just wait for weeks and months until you finally get a chance to go to court and say you've been set up. But then you have to wait even longer while the prosecutor puts on a bunch of liars and you have to listen to their lies and just wait your chance. Of course it makes you angry. I am innocent! I did not do this!"

It was perfect. To the point and playing to anybody who had ever been falsely accused of anything. There was more I could ask but I reminded myself of the rule: get in and get out. Less is always more. I sat down. If I decided there was anything I had missed I would clean it up on redirect.

I looked at the judge.

"Nothing further, Your Honor."

Minton was up and ready before I even got back to my seat. He moved to the lectern without breaking his steely glare away from Roulet. He was showing the jury what he thought of this man. His eyes were like lasers shooting across the room. He gripped the sides of the lectern so hard his knuckles were white. It was all a show for the jury.

"You deny touching Ms. Campo," he said.

"That's right," Roulet retorted.

"According to you she just punched herself or had a man she had never met before that night punch her lights out for her as part of this setup, is that correct?"

"I don't know who did it. All I know is that I didn't."

"But what you are saying is that this woman, Regina Campo, is lying. She came into this courtroom today and flat out lied to the judge and the jury and the whole wide world."

Minton punctuated the sentence by shaking his head with disgust.

"All I know is that I did not do the things she said I did. The only explanation is that one of us is lying. It's not me."

"That will be for the jury to decide, won't it?"

"Yes."

"And this knife you supposedly got for your own protection. Are you telling this jury that the victim in this case somehow knew you had a knife and used it as part of the setup?"

"I don't know what she knew. I had never shown the knife to her or in a bar where she would have been. So I don't see how she could have known about it. I think that when she went into my pocket for the money she found the knife. I always keep my knife and money in the same pocket."

"Oh, so now you have her stealing money out of your pocket as well. When does this end with you, Mr. Roulet?"

"I had four hundred dollars with me. When I was arrested it was gone. Someone took it."

Rather than try to pinpoint Roulet on the money, Minton was wise enough to know that no matter how he handled it, he would be facing a break-even proposition at best. If he tried to make a case that Roulet never had the money and that his plan was to attack and rape Campo rather than pay her, then he knew I would trot out Roulet's tax returns, which would throw serious doubt on the idea that he couldn't afford to pay a prostitute. It was an avenue of testimony commonly referred to by lawyers as a "cluster fuck" and he was staying away. He moved on to his finish.

In dramatic style Minton held up the evidence photo of Regina Campo's beaten and bruised face.

"So Regina Campo is a liar," he said.

"Yes."

"She had this done to her or maybe even did it herself."

"I don't know who did it."

"But not you."

"No, it wasn't me. I wouldn't do that to a woman. I wouldn't hurt a woman."

Roulet pointed to the photo Minton had continued to hold up.

"No woman deserves that," he said.

I leaned forward and waited. Roulet had just said the line I had told him to somehow find a way of putting into one of his answers during testimony. *No woman deserves that*. It was now up to Minton to take the bait. He was smart. He had to understand that Roulet had just opened a door.

"What do you mean by *deserves?* Do you think crimes of violence come down to a matter of whether a victim gets what they deserve?"

"No. I didn't mean it that way. I meant that no matter

what she does for a living, she shouldn't have been beaten like that. Nobody deserves to have that happen to them."

Minton brought down the arm that held the photo. He looked at it himself for a moment and then looked back up at Roulet.

"Mr. Roulet, I have nothing more to ask you."

THIRTY-SEVEN

I still felt that I was winning the razor fight. I had done everything possible to maneuver Minton into a position in which he had only one choice. It was now time to see if doing everything possible had been enough. After the young prosecutor sat down, I chose not to ask my client another question. He had held up well under Minton's attack and I felt the wind was in our sails. I stood up and looked back at the clock on the upper rear wall of the courtroom. It was only three-thirty. I then looked back at the judge.

"Your Honor, the defense rests."

She nodded and looked over my head at the clock. She told the jury to take the mid-afternoon break. Once the jurors were out of the courtroom, she looked at the prosecution table where Minton had his head down and was writing.

"Mr. Minton?"

The prosecutor looked up.

"We're still in session. Pay attention. Does the state have rebuttal?"

Minton stood.

"Your Honor, I would ask that we adjourn for the day so that the state has time to consider rebuttal witnesses."

"Mr. Minton, we still have at least ninety minutes to go today. I told you I wanted to be productive today. Where are your witnesses?"

"Frankly, Your Honor, I was not anticipating the defense

resting after only three witnesses and I —"

"He gave fair warning of that in his opening statement."

"Yes, but still the case has moved faster than anticipated. We're a half day ahead. I would beg the court's indulgence. I would be hard-pressed to get the rebuttal witness I am considering even into court before six o'clock tonight."

I turned and looked at Roulet, who had returned to the seat next to mine. I nodded to him and winked with my left eye so the judge would not see the gesture. It looked like Minton had swallowed the bait. Now I just had to make sure the judge didn't make him spit it out. I stood up.

"Your Honor, the defense has no objection to the delay. Maybe we can use the time to prepare closing arguments and instructions to the jury."

The judge first looked at me with a puzzled frown. It was a rarity that the defense would not object to prosecutorial foot dragging. But then the seed I had planted began to bloom.

"You may have an idea there, Mr. Haller. If we adjourn early today I will expect that we will go to closing statements directly after rebuttal. No further delays except to consider jury instructions. Is that understood, Mr. Minton?"

"Yes, Your Honor, I will be ready."

"Mr. Haller?"

"It was my idea, Judge. I'll be ready."

"Very well, then. We have a plan. As soon as the jurors are back I will dismiss them for the day. They'll beat the traffic and tomorrow things will run so smoothly and quickly that I have no doubt they will be deliberating by the afternoon session."

She looked at Minton and then me, as if daring one of us to disagree with her. When we didn't, she got up and left the bench, probably in pursuit of a cigarette.

Twenty minutes later the jury was heading home and I

was gathering my things at the defense table. Minton stepped over and said, "Can I talk to you?"

I looked at Roulet and told him to head out with his mother and Dobbs and that I would call him if I needed him for anything.

"But I want to talk to you, too," he said.

"About what?"

"About everything. How do you think I did up there?"

"You did good and everything is going good. I think we're in good shape."

I then nodded my head toward the prosecution table where Minton had returned and dropped my voice to a whisper.

"He knows it, too. He's about to make another offer."

"Should I stick around to hear what it is?"

I shook my head.

"No, it doesn't matter what it is. There's only one verdict, right?"

"That's right."

He patted my shoulder when he got up and I had to steady myself not to shrink away from the touch.

"Don't touch me, Louis," I said. "You want to do something for me, then give me my fucking gun back."

He didn't reply. He just smiled and moved toward the gate. After he was gone I turned to look at Minton. He now had the gleam of desperation in his eye. He needed a conviction — any conviction — on this case.

"What's up?"

"I have another offer."

"I'm listening."

"I'll drop it down further. Take it down to simple assault. Six months in county. The way they empty that place out at the end of every month, he probably won't do sixty days actual."

I nodded. He was talking about the federal mandate to

stop overcrowding in the county jail system. It didn't matter what was handed down in a courtroom; out of necessity, sentences were often drastically cut. It was a good offer but I didn't show anything. I knew the offer had to have come from the second floor. Minton wouldn't have had the authority to go so low.

"He takes that and she'll rob him blind in civil," I said. "I doubt he'll go for it."

"That's a damn good offer," Minton said.

There was a hint of outrage in his voice. My guess was that the observer's report card on Minton was not good and he was under orders to close the case out with a guilty plea. Trash the trial and the judge's and jury's time, just get that plea. The Van Nuys office didn't like losing cases and we were only two months removed from the Robert Blake fiasco. It pleaded them out when the going got rough. Minton could go as low as he needed to go, just as long as he got something. Roulet had to go down — even if it was only for sixty days actual.

"Maybe from your side of things it's a damn good offer. But it still means I have to convince a client to plead to something he says he didn't do. Then on top of that, the dispo still opens the door to civil liability. So while he's sitting up there in county trying to protect his asshole for sixty days, Reggie Campo and her lawyer are down here taking him to the cleaners. You see? It's not so good when you look at it from his angle. If it was left to me, I'd ride the trial out. I think we're winning. I know we've got the Bible guy, so we've got a hanger at minimum. But who knows, maybe we've got all twelve."

Minton slapped his hand down on his table.

"What the fuck are you talking about? You know he did this thing, Haller. And six months — let alone sixty days — for what he did to that woman is a joke. It's a fucking travesty that I'll lose sleep over, but they've been watching and think you've got the jury, so I have to do it."

I closed my briefcase with an authoritative snap and stood up.

"Then I hope you got something good for rebuttal, Ted. Because you're going to get your wish for a jury verdict. And I have to tell you, man, you're looking more and more like a guy who came naked to a razor fight. Better get your hands off your nuts and fight back."

I headed through the gate. Halfway to the doors at the back of the courtroom I stopped and looked back at him.

"Hey, you know something? If you lose sleep over this or any other case, then you gotta quit the job and go do something else. Because you're not going to make it, Ted."

Minton sat at his table, staring straight ahead at the empty bench. He didn't acknowledge what I had said. I left him there thinking about it. I thought I had played it right. I'd find out in the morning.

I went back over to Four Green Fields to work on my closing. I wouldn't need the two hours the judge had given us. I ordered a Guinness at the bar and took it over to one of the tables to sit by myself. Table service didn't start again until six. I sketched out some basic notes but I instinctively knew I would largely be reacting to the state's presentation. In pretrial motions, Minton had already asked and received permission from Judge Fullbright to use a PowerPoint presentation to illustrate the case to the jury. It had become all the rage with young prosecutors to put up the screen and flash computer graphics on it, as if the jurors couldn't be trusted to think and make connections on their own. It now had to be fed to them like TV.

My clients rarely had the money to pay my fees, let alone for PowerPoint presentations. Roulet was an exception. Through his mother he could afford to hire Francis Ford Coppola to put together a PowerPoint for him if he wanted it. But I never even brought it up. I was strictly old school. I liked going into the ring on my own. Minton could throw whatever he wanted up on the big blue screen. When it was my turn I wanted the jury looking only at me. If I couldn't convince them, nothing from a computer could, either.

At 5:30 I called Maggie McPherson at her office.

"It's quitting time," I said.

"Maybe for big-shot defense pros. Us public servants have to work till after dark."

"Why don't you take a break and come meet me for a Guinness and some shepherd's pie, then you can go back to work and finish up."

"No, Haller. I can't do that. Besides, I know what you want."

I laughed. There was never a time that she didn't think she knew what I wanted. Most of the time she was right but not this time.

"Yeah? What do I want?"

"You're going to try to corrupt me again and find out what Minton is up to."

"Not a chance, Mags. Minton is an open book. Smithson's observer is giving him bad marks. So Smithson's told him to fold the tent, get something and get out. But Minton's been working on his little PowerPoint closing and wants to gamble, take it all the way to the house. Besides that, he's got genuine outrage in his blood, so he doesn't like the idea of folding up."

"Neither do I. Smithson's always afraid of losing — especially since Blake. He always wants to sell short. You can't be that way."

"I always said they lost the Blake case the minute they passed you over. You tell 'em, Maggie."

"If I ever get the chance."

"Someday."

She didn't like dwelling on her own stalled career. She moved on.

"So you sound chipper," she said. "Yesterday you were a murder suspect. Today you've got the DA by the short hairs. What changed?"

"Nothing. It's just the calm before the storm, I guess. Hey, let me ask you something. Have you ever put a rush on ballistics?"

"What kind of ballistics?"

"Matching casing to casing and slug to slug."

"Depends on who is doing it — which department, I mean. But if they put a real rush on it, they could have something in twenty-four hours."

I felt the dull thud of dread drop into my stomach. I knew I could be on borrowed time.

"Most of the time, though, that doesn't happen," she continued. "Two or three days is what it will usually take on a rush. And if you want the whole package — casing and slug comparisons — it could take longer because the slug could be damaged and tough to read. They have to work with it."

I nodded. I didn't think any of that could help me. I knew they had recovered a bullet casing at the crime scene. If Lankford and Sobel got a match on that to the casing of a bullet fired fifty years ago from Mickey Cohen's gun, they would come for me and worry about the slug comparison later.

"You still there?" Maggie asked.

"Yeah. I was just thinking of something."

"You don't sound so chipper anymore. You want to talk about this, Michael?"

"No, not right now. But if I end up needing a good lawyer, you know who I'll call."

"That'll be the day."

"You might be surprised."

I let some more silence into the conversation. Just having her on the other end of the line was a calming comfort. I liked it.

"Haller, I should get back to my job now."

"Okay, Maggie, put those bad guys away."

"I will."

"Good night."

I closed the phone and thought about things for a few moments, then opened it up again and called the Sheraton Universal to see if they had a room available. I had decided that as a precaution I would not go home this night. There might be two detectives from Glendale waiting for me.

THIRTY-EIGHT

After a sleepless night in a bad hotel bed I got to the courthouse early on Wednesday morning and found no welcoming party, no Glendale detectives waiting with smiles and a warrant for my arrest. A flash of relief went through me as I made my way through the metal detector. I was wearing the same suit I had worn the day before but was hoping no one would notice. I did have a fresh shirt and tie on. I keep spares in the trunk of the Lincoln for summer days when I'm working up in the desert and the car's air conditioner can get overwhelmed.

When I got to Judge Fullbright's courtroom I was surprised to find I was not the first of the trial's players to arrive. Minton was in the gallery, setting up the screen for his PowerPoint presentation. Because the courtroom had been designed before the era of computer-enhanced presentations, there was no place to put a twelve-foot screen in comfortable view of the jury, the judge, and the lawyers. A good chunk of the gallery space would be taken up by the screen, and any spectator who sat behind it wouldn't get to see the show.

"Bright and early," I said to Minton.

He looked over from his work and seemed a bit surprised to see me in early as well.

"Have to work out the logistics of this thing. It's kind of a pain."

"You could always do it the old-fashioned way and just look at the jury and talk directly to them."

"No, thanks. I like this better. Did you talk to your client about the offer?"

"Yeah, no sale. Looks like we ride this one to the end."

I put my briefcase down on the defense table and wondered if the fact that Minton was setting up for his closing argument meant he had decided against mounting any kind of rebuttal. A sharp jab of panic went through me. I looked over at the state's table and saw nothing that gave me a clue to what Minton was planning. I knew I could flat out ask him but I did not want to give away my appearance of disinterested confidence.

Instead, I sauntered over to the bailiff's desk to talk to Bill Meehan, the deputy who ran Fullbright's court. I saw on his desk a spread of paperwork. He would have the courtroom calendar as well as the list of custodies bused to the courthouse that morning.

"Bill, I'm going to grab a cup of coffee. You want something?"

"No, man, but thanks. I'm set on caffeine. For a while, at least."

I smiled and nodded.

"Hey, is that the custody list? Can I take a look and see if any of my clients are on it?"

"Sure."

Meehan handed me several pages that were stapled together. It was a listing by name of every inmate that was now housed in the courthouse's jails. Following the name was the courtroom each prisoner was headed to. Acting as nonchalant as I could I scanned the list and quickly found the name Dwayne Jeffery Corliss on it. Minton's snitch was in the building and was headed to Fullbright's court. I almost let out a sigh of relief but kept it all inside. It looked like Minton was going to play things the way I had hoped and planned.

"Something wrong?" Meehan asked.

I looked at him and handed back the list.

"No, why?"

"I don't know. You look like something happened, is all."

"Nothing's happened yet but it will."

I left the courtroom and went down to the cafeteria on the second floor. When I was in line paying for my coffee I saw Maggie McPherson walk in and go directly to the coffee urns. After I paid I walked up behind her as she was mixing powder from a pink packet into her coffee.

"Sweet 'N Low," I said. "My ex-wife used to tell me that's how she liked it."

She turned and saw me.

"Stop, Haller."

But she smiled.

"Stop, Haller, or I'll holler," I said. "She used to have to say that, too. A lot."

"What are you doing? Shouldn't you be up on six getting ready to pull the plug on Minton's PowerPoint?"

"I'm not worried. In fact, you ought to come up and check it out. Old school versus new school, a battle for the ages."

"Hardly. By the way, isn't that the same suit you were wearing yesterday?"

"Yeah, it's my lucky suit. But how do you know what I was wearing yesterday?"

"Oh, I popped my head in Fullbite's court for a couple minutes yesterday. You were too busy questioning your client to notice."

I was secretly pleased that she would even notice my suits. I knew it meant something.

"So, then, why don't you pop your head in again this morning?"

"Today I can't. I'm too busy."

"What've you got?"

"I'm taking over a murder one for Andy Seville. He's

quitting to go private and yesterday they divided up his cases. I got the good one."

"Nice. Does the defendant need a lawyer?"

"No way, Haller. I'm not losing another one to you."

"Just kidding. I've got my hands full."

She snapped a top onto her cup and picked it up off the counter, using a layer of napkins as insulation against its heat.

"Same here. So I'd wish you good luck today but I can't."

"Yeah, I know. Gotta keep the company line. Just cheer up Minton when he comes down with his hat in his hand."

"I'll try."

She left the cafeteria and I walked over to an empty table. I still had fifteen minutes before the trial was supposed to start up again. I pulled out my cell and called my second ex-wife.

"Lorna, it's me. We're in play with Corliss. Are you set?"

"I'm ready."

"Okay, I'm just checking. I'll call you."

"Good luck today, Mickey."

"Thanks. I'll need it. You be ready for the next call."

I closed the phone and was about to get up when I saw LAPD Detective Howard Kurlen cutting through the tables toward me. The man who put Jesus Menendez in prison didn't look like he was stopping in for a peanut butter and sardine sandwich. He was carrying a folded document. He got to my table and dropped it in front of my coffee cup.

"What is this shit?" he demanded.

I started unfolding the document, even though I knew what it was.

"Looks like a subpoena, Detective. I would've thought you'd know what it is."

"You know what I mean, Haller. What's the game? I've got nothing to do with that case up there and I don't want to be a part of your bullshit."

"It's no game and it's no bullshit. You've been subpoenaed as a rebuttal witness."

"To rebut what? I told you and you already know, I didn't have a goddamn thing to do with that case. It's Marty Booker's and I just talked to him and he said it's gotta be a mistake."

I nodded like I wanted to be accommodating.

"I'll tell you what, go on up to the courtroom and take a seat. If it's a mistake I'll get it straightened out as soon as I can. I doubt you'll be here another hour. I'll get you out of there and back chasing the bad guys."

"How about this? I leave now and you straighten it out whenever the fuck you want."

"I can't do that, Detective. That is a valid and lawful subpoena and you must appear in that courtroom unless otherwise discharged. I told you, I will do that as soon as I can. The state's got one witness and then it's my turn and I'll take care of it."

"This is such bullshit."

He turned from me and stalked back through the cafeteria toward the doorway. Luckily, he had left the subpoena with me, because it was phony. I had never registered it with the court clerk and the scribbled signature at the bottom was mine.

Bullshit or not, I didn't think Kurlen was leaving the courthouse. He was a man who understood duty and the law. He lived by it. It was what I was counting on. He would be in the courtroom until discharged. Or until he understood why I had called him there.

THIRTY-NINE

At 9:30 the judge put the jury in the box and immediately proceeded with the day's business. I glanced back at the gallery and caught sight of Kurlen in the back row. He had a pensive, if not angry, cast to his face. He was close to the door and I didn't know how long he would last. I was figuring I would need that whole hour I had told him about.

I glanced further around the room and saw that Lankford and Sobel were sitting on a bench next to the bailiff's desk that was designated for law enforcement personnel. Their faces revealed nothing but they still put the pause in me. I wondered if I would even get the hour I needed.

"Mr. Minton," the judge intoned, "does the state have any rebuttal?"

I turned back to the court. Minton stood up, adjusted his jacket and then seemed to hesitate and brace himself before responding.

"Yes, Your Honor, the state calls Dwayne Jeffery Corliss as a rebuttal witness."

I stood up and noticed to my right that Meehan, the bailiff, had stood up as well. He was going to go into the courtroom lockup to retrieve Corliss.

"Your Honor?" I said. "Who is Dwayne Jeffery Corliss and why wasn't I told about him before now?"

"Deputy Meehan, hold on a minute," Fullbright said.

Meehan stood frozen with the key to the lockup door

poised in his hand. The judge then apologized to the jury but told them they had to go back into the deliberation room until recalled. After they filed through the door behind the box, the judge turned her focus onto Minton.

"Mr. Minton, do you want to tell us about your witness?"

"Dwayne Corliss is a cooperating witness who spoke with Mr. Roulet when he was in custody following his arrest."

"Bullshit!" Roulet barked. "I didn't talk to —"

"Be quiet, Mr. Roulet," the judge boomed. "Mr. Haller, instruct your client on the danger of outbursts in my courtroom."

"Thank you, Your Honor."

I was still standing. I leaned down to whisper in Roulet's ear.

"That was perfect," I said. "Now be cool and I'll take it from here."

He nodded and leaned back. He angrily folded his arms across his chest. I straightened up.

"I'm sorry, Your Honor, but I do share my client's outrage over this last-ditch effort by the state. This is the first we have heard of Mr. Corliss. I would like to know when he came forward with this supposed conversation."

Minton had remained standing. I thought it was the first time in the trial that we had stood side by side and argued to the judge.

"Mr. Corliss first contacted the office through a prosecutor who handled the first appearance of the defendant," Minton said. "However, that information was not passed on to me until yesterday when in a staff meeting I was asked why I had never acted on the information."

This was a lie but not one I wanted to expose. To do so would reveal Maggie McPherson's slip on St. Patrick's Day and it might also derail my plan. I had to be careful. I needed to argue vigorously against Corliss taking the stand but I also needed to lose the argument.

I put my best look of outrage on my face.

"This is incredible, Your Honor. Just because the DA's office has a communication problem, my client has to suffer the consequences of not being informed that the state had a witness against him? This man should clearly not be allowed to testify. It's too late to bring him in now."

"Your Honor," Minton said, jumping in quickly. "I have had no time to interview or depose Mr. Corliss myself. Because I was preparing my closing I simply made arrangements for him to be brought here today. His testimony is key to the state's case because it serves as rebuttal to Mr. Roulet's self-serving statements. To not allow his testimony is a serious disservice to the state."

I shook my head and smiled in frustration. With his last line Minton was threatening the judge with the loss of the DA's backing should she ever face an election with an opposing candidate.

"Mr. Haller?" the judge asked. "Anything before I rule?"

"I just want my objection on the record."

"So noted. If I were to give you time to investigate and interview Mr. Corliss, how much would you need?"

"A week."

Now Minton put on the fake smile and shook his head.

"That's ridiculous, Your Honor."

"Do you want to go back and talk to him?" the judge asked me. "I'll allow it."

"No, Your Honor. As far as I'm concerned all jailhouse snitches are liars. It would do me no good to interview him because anything that comes out of his mouth would be a lie. Anything. Besides, it's not what he has to say. It's what others have to say about him. That's what I would need time for."

"Then I am going to rule that he can testify."

"Your Honor," I said. "If you are going to allow him into this courtroom, could I ask one indulgence for the defense?"

"What is that, Mr. Haller?"

"I would like to step into the hallway and make a quick phone call to an investigator. It will take me less than a minute."

The judge thought for a moment and then nodded.

"Go ahead. I will bring the jury in while you do it."

"Thank you."

I hurried through the gate and down the middle aisle. My eyes caught those of Howard Kurlen and he gave me one of his best smirks.

In the hallway I speed-dialed Lorna Taylor's cell phone and she answered right away.

"Okay, how far away are you?"

"About fifteen minutes."

"Did you remember the printout and the tape?"

"Got it all right here."

I looked at my watch. It was a quarter to ten.

"Okay, well, we're in play here. Don't delay getting here but then I want you to wait out in the hall outside the courtroom. Then at ten-fifteen come into court and give it to me. If I'm crossing the witness, just sit in the first row and wait until I notice you."

"Got it."

I closed the phone and went back into the courtroom. The jury was seated and Meehan was leading a man in a gray jumpsuit through the lockup door. Dwayne Corliss was a thin man with stringy hair that wasn't getting washed enough in the lockdown drug program at County-USC. He wore a blue plastic hospital ID band on his wrist. I recognized him. He was the man who had asked me for a business card when I interviewed Roulet in the holding cell my first day on the case.

Corliss was led by Meehan to the witness box and the court clerk swore him in. Minton took over the show from there.

"Mr. Corliss, were you arrested on March fifth of this year?"

"Yes, the police arrested me for burglary and possession of drugs."

"Are you incarcerated now?"

Corliss looked around.

"Um, no, I don't think so. I'm just in the courtroom."

I heard Kurlen's coarse laugh behind me but nobody joined in.

"No, I mean are you currently being held in jail? When you are not here in court."

"I'm in a lockdown drug treatment program in the jail ward at Los Angeles County–USC Medical Center."

"Are you addicted to drugs?"

"Yes. I'm addicted to heroin but at the moment I am straight. I haven't had any since I got arrested."

"More than sixty days."

"That's right."

"Do you recognize the defendant in this case?"

Corliss looked over at Roulet and nodded.

"Yes, I do."

"Why is that?"

"Because I met him in lockup after I got arrested."

"You are saying that after you were arrested you came into close proximity to the defendant, Louis Roulet?"

"Yes, the next day."

"How did that happen?"

"Well, we were both in Van Nuys jail but in different wards. Then, when we got bused over here to the courts, we were together, first in the bus and then in the tank and then when we were brought into the courtroom for first appearance. We were together all of that time."

"When you say 'together,' what do you mean?"

"Well, we sort of stuck close because we were the only white guys in the group we were in."

"Now, did you talk at all while you were together for all of that time?"

Corliss nodded his head and at the same time Roulet shook his. I touched my client's arm to caution him to make no demonstrations.

"Yes, we talked," Corliss said.

"About what?"

"Mostly about cigarettes. We both needed them but they don't let you smoke in the jail."

Corliss made a what-are-you-going-to-do gesture with both hands and a few of the jurors — probably smokers — smiled and nodded.

"Did you reach a point where you asked Mr. Roulet what got him into jail?" Minton asked.

"Yes, I did."

"What did he say?"

I quickly stood up and objected but just as quickly was overruled.

"What did he tell you, Mr. Corliss?" Minton prompted.

"Well, first he asked me why I was there and I told him. So then I asked him why he was in and he said, 'For giving a bitch exactly what she deserved.'"

"Those were his words?"

"Yes."

"Did he elaborate further on what he meant by that?"

"No, not really. Not on that."

I leaned forward, waiting for Minton to ask the next obvious question. But he didn't. He moved on.

"Now, Mr. Corliss, have you been promised anything by me or the district attorney's office in return for your testimony?"

"Nope. I just thought it was the right thing to do."

"What is the status of your case?"

"I still got the charges against me, but it looks like if I complete my program I'll be able to get a break on them. The drugs, at least. I don't know about the burglary yet."

"But I have made no promise of help in that regard, correct?"

"No, sir, you haven't."

"Has anyone else from the district attorney's office made any promises?"

"No, sir."

"I have no further questions."

I sat unmoving and just staring at Corliss. My pose was that of a man who was angry but didn't know exactly what to do about it. Finally, the judge prompted me into action.

"Mr. Haller, cross-examination?"

"Yes, Your Honor."

I stood up, glancing back at the door as if hoping a miracle would walk through it. I then checked the big clock on the back door and saw it was five minutes after ten. I noticed as I turned back to the witness that I had not lost Kurlen. He was still in the back row and he still had the same smirk on his face. I realized that it might have been his natural look.

I turned to the witness.

"Mr. Corliss, how old are you?"

"Forty-three."

"You go by Dwayne?"

"That's right."

"Any other names?"

"People called me D.J. when I was growing up. Everybody called me that."

"And where did you grow up?"

"Mesa, Arizona."

"Mr. Corliss, how many times have you been arrested before?"

Minton objected but the judge overruled. I knew she was going to give me a lot of room with this witness since I was the one who had supposedly been sandbagged.

"How many times have you been arrested before, Mr. Corliss?" I asked again.

"I think about seven."

"So you've been in a number of jails in your time, haven't you?"

"You could say that."

"All in Los Angeles County?"

"Mostly. But I got arrested over in Phoenix before, too."

"So you know how the system works, don't you?"

"I just try to survive."

"And sometimes surviving means ratting out your fellow inmates, doesn't it?"

"Your Honor?" Minton said, standing to object.

"Take a seat, Mr. Minton," Fullbright said. "I gave you a lot of leeway bringing this witness in. Mr. Haller gets his share of it now. The witness will answer the question."

The stenographer read the question back to Corliss.

"I suppose so."

"How many times have you snitched on another inmate?"

"I don't know. A few times."

"How many times have you testified in a court proceeding for the prosecution?"

"Would that include my own cases?"

"No, Mr. Corliss. For the prosecution. How many times have you testified against a fellow inmate for the prosecution?"

"I think this is my fourth time."

I looked surprised and aghast, although I was neither.

"So you are a pro, aren't you? You could almost say your occupation is drug-addicted jailhouse snitch."

"I just tell the truth. If people tell me things that are bad, then I feel obligated to report it."

"But you try to get people to tell you things, don't you?"

"No, not really. I guess I'm just a friendly guy."

"A friendly guy. So what you expect this jury to believe is that a man you didn't know would just come out of the blue and tell you — a perfect stranger — that he gave a bitch exactly what she deserved. Is that correct?"

"It's what he said."

"So he just mentioned that to you and then you both just went back to talking about cigarettes after that, is that right?"

"Not exactly."

"Not exactly? What do you mean by 'not exactly'?"

"He also told me he did it before. He said he got away with it before and he would get away with it now. He was bragging about it because with the other time, he said he killed the bitch and got away with it."

I froze for a moment. I then glanced at Roulet, who sat as still as a statue with surprise on his face, and then back at the witness.

"You . . ."

I started and stopped, acting like I was the man in the minefield who had just heard the *click* come from beneath my foot. In my peripheral vision I noticed Minton's body posture tightening.

"Mr. Haller?" the judge prompted.

I broke my stare from Corliss and looked at the judge.

"Your Honor, I have no further questions at this time."

FORTY

Minton came up from his seat like a boxer coming out of his corner at his bleeding opponent.

"Redirect, Mr. Minton?" Fullbright asked.

But he was already at the lectern.

"Absolutely, Your Honor."

He looked at the jury as if to underline the importance of the upcoming exchange and then at Corliss.

"You said he was bragging, Mr. Corliss. How so?"

"Well, he told me about this time he actually killed a girl and got away with it."

I stood up.

"Your Honor, this has nothing to do with the case at hand and it is rebuttal to no evidence previously offered by the defense. The witness can't —"

"Your Honor," Minton cut in, "this is information brought forward by defense counsel. The prosecution is entitled to pursue it."

"I will allow it," Fullbright said.

I sat down and appeared dejected. Minton plowed ahead. He was going just where I wanted him to go.

"Mr. Corliss, did Mr. Roulet offer any of the details of this previous incident in which he said he got away with killing a woman?"

"He called the girl a snake dancer. She danced in some joint where she was like in a snake pit."

I felt Roulet wrap his fingers around my biceps and squeeze. His hot breath came into my ear.

"What the fuck is this?" he whispered.

I turned to him.

"I don't know. What the hell did you tell this guy?"

He whispered back through gritted teeth.

"I didn't tell him anything. This is a setup. You set me up!"

"Me? What are you talking about? I told you, I couldn't get to this guy in lockdown. If you didn't tell him this shit, then somebody else did. Start thinking. Who?"

I turned and looked up at Minton standing at the lectern and continuing his questioning of Corliss.

"Did Mr. Roulet say anything else about the dancer he said he murdered?" he asked.

"No, that's all he really told me."

Minton checked his notes to see if there was anything else, then nodded to himself.

"Nothing further, Your Honor."

The judge looked at me. I could almost see sympathy on her face.

"Any recross from the defense with this witness?"

Before I could answer, there was a noise from the rear of the courtroom and I turned to see Lorna Taylor entering. She hurriedly walked down the aisle toward the gate.

"Your Honor, can I have a moment to confer with my staff?"

"Hurry, Mr. Haller."

I met Lorna at the gate and took from her a videotape with a single piece of paper wrapped around it with a rubber band. As she had been told to do earlier, she whispered in my ear.

"This is where I act like I am whispering something very important into your ear," she said. "How is it going?"

I nodded as I took the rubber band off the tape and looked at the piece of paper.

"Perfect timing," I whispered back. "I'm good to go."

"Can I stay and watch?"

"No, I want you out of here. I don't want anybody talking to you after this goes down."

I nodded and she nodded and then she left. I went back to the lectern.

"No recross, Your Honor."

I sat down and waited. Roulet grabbed my arm.

"What are you doing?"

I pushed him away.

"Stop touching me. We have new information we can't bring up on cross."

I focused on the judge.

"Any other witnesses, Mr. Minton?" she asked.

"No, Your Honor. No further rebuttal."

The judge nodded.

"The witness is excused."

Meehan started crossing the courtroom to Corliss. The judge looked at me and I started to stand.

"Mr. Haller, surrebuttal?"

"Yes, Your Honor, the defense would like to call D.J. Corliss back to the stand as surrebuttal."

Meehan stopped in his tracks and all eyes were on me. I held up the tape and the paper Lorna had brought me.

"I have new information on Mr. Corliss, Your Honor. I could not have brought it up on cross."

"Very well. Proceed."

"Can I have a moment, Judge?"

"A short one."

I huddled with Roulet again.

"Look, I don't know what is going on but it doesn't matter," I whispered.

"What do you mean it doesn't matter? Are you —"

"Listen to me. It doesn't matter because I can still destroy him. Doesn't matter if he says you killed twenty women. If he's a liar, he's a liar. If I destroy him, none of it counts. You understand?"

Roulet nodded and seemed to calm as he considered this.

"Then destroy him."

"I will. But I have to know. Is there anything else he knows that could come out? Is there anything I need to stay away from?"

Roulet whispered slowly, as if explaining something to a child.

"I don't know because I never talked to him. I'm not that stupid as to have a discussion about cigarettes and murder with a total fucking stranger!"

"Mr. Haller," the judge prompted.

I looked up at her.

"Yes, Your Honor."

Carrying the tape and the paper that came with it, I stood up to go back to the lectern. On the way I took a quick glance across the gallery and saw that Kurlen was gone. I had no way of knowing how long he had stayed and what he had heard. Lankford was gone as well. Only Sobel remained and she averted her eyes from mine. I turned my attention to Corliss.

"Mr. Corliss, can you tell the jury exactly where you were when Mr. Roulet supposedly made these revelations to you about murder and assault?"

"When we were together."

"Together where, Mr. Corliss?"

"Well, on the bus ride we didn't talk because we were in different seats. But when we got to the courthouse, we were in the same holding cell with about six other guys and we sat together there and we talked."

"And those six other men all witnessed you and Mr. Roulet talking, correct?"

"They woulda had to. They were there."

"So what you are saying is that if I brought them in here one by one and asked them if they observed you and Mr. Roulet talking, they would confirm that?"

"Well, they should. But . . ."

"But what, Mr. Corliss?"

"It's just that they probably wouldn't talk, that's all."

"Is it because nobody likes a snitch, Mr. Corliss?"

Corliss shrugged.

"I guess so."

"Okay, so let's make sure we have all of this straight. You didn't talk with Mr. Roulet on the bus but you did talk to him when you were in the holding cell together. Anywhere else?"

"Yeah, we talked when they moved us on out into the courtroom. They stick you in this glassed-in area and you wait for your case to be called. We talked some in there, too, until his case got called. He went first."

"This is in the arraignment court where you had your first appearance before a judge?"

"That's right."

"So you two were talking in the court and this is where Mr. Roulet would have revealed his part in these crimes you described."

"That's right."

"Do you remember specifically what he told you when you were in the courtroom?"

"No, not really. Not specifics. I think that might have been when he told me about the girl who was a dancer."

"Okay, Mr. Corliss."

I held the videotape up, described it as video of Louis Roulet's first appearance, and asked to enter it as a defense exhibit. Minton tried to block it as something I had not produced during discovery, but that was easily and quickly shot down by the judge without my having to argue the point. He then objected again, citing the lack of authentication of the tape.

"I am just trying to save the court some time," I said. "If needed I can have the man who took the film here in about an hour to authenticate it. But I think that Your Honor will be able to authenticate it herself with just one look."

"I am going to allow it," the judge said. "Once we see it the prosecution can object again if so inclined."

The television and video unit I had used previously was rolled into the courtroom and placed at an angle viewable by Corliss, the jury and the judge. Minton had to move to a chair to the side of the jury box to fully see it. The tape was played. It lasted twenty minutes and showed Roulet from the moment he entered the courtroom custody area until he was led out after the bail hearing. At no time did Roulet talk to anyone but me. When the tape was over I left the television in its place in case it was needed again. I addressed Corliss with a tinge of outrage in my voice.

"Mr. Corliss, did you see a moment anywhere on that tape where you and Mr. Roulet were talking?"

"Uh, no. I —"

"Yet, you testified under oath and penalty of perjury that he confessed crimes to you while you were both in the courtroom, didn't you?"

"I know I said that but I must have been mistaken. He must have told me everything when we were in the holding cell."

"You lied to the jury, didn't you?"

"I didn't mean to. That was the way I remembered it but I guess I was wrong. I was coming off a high that morning. Things got confused."

"It would seem that way. Let me ask you, were things confused when you testified against Frederic Bentley back in nineteen eighty-nine?"

Corliss knitted his eyebrows together in concentration but didn't answer.

"You remember Frederic Bentley, don't you?"

Minton stood.

"Objection. Nineteen eighty-nine? Where is he going with this?"

"Your Honor," I said. "This goes to the veracity of the witness. It is certainly at issue here."

"Connect the dots, Mr. Haller," the judge ordered. "In a hurry."

"Yes, Your Honor."

I picked up the piece of paper and used it as a prop during my final questions of Corliss.

"In nineteen eighty-nine Frederic Bentley was convicted, with your help, of raping a sixteen-year-old girl in her bed in Phoenix. Do you remember this?"

"Barely," Corliss said. "I've done a lot of drugs since then."

"You testified at his trial that he confessed the crime to you while you were both together in a police station holding cell. Isn't that correct?"

"Like I said, it's hard for me to remember back then."

"The police put you in that holding cell because they knew you were willing to snitch, even if you had to make it up, didn't they?"

My voice was rising with each question.

"I don't remember that," Corliss responded. "But I don't make things up."

"Then, eight years later, the man who you testified had told you he did it was exonerated when a DNA test determined that the semen from the girl's attacker came from another man. Isn't that correct, sir?"

"I don't . . . I mean . . . that was a long time ago."

"Do you remember being questioned by a reporter for the *Arizona Star* newspaper following the release of Frederic Bentley?"

"Vaguely. I remember somebody calling but I didn't say anything."

"He told you that DNA tests exonerated Bentley and

asked you whether you fabricated Bentley's confession, didn't he?"

"I don't know."

I held the paper I was clutching up toward the bench.

"Your Honor, I have an archival story from the *Arizona Star* newspaper here. It is dated February ninth, nineteen ninety-seven. A member of my staff came across it when she Googled the name D.J. Corliss on her office computer. I ask that it be marked as a defense exhibit and admitted into evidence as a historical document detailing an admission by silence."

My request set off a brutal clash with Minton about authenticity and proper foundation. Ultimately, the judge ruled in my favor. She was showing some of the same outrage I was manufacturing, and Minton didn't stand much of a chance.

The bailiff took the computer printout to Corliss, and the judge instructed him to read it.

"I'm not too good at reading, Judge," he said.

"Try, Mr. Corliss."

Corliss held the paper up and leaned his face into it as he read.

"Out loud, please," Fullbright barked.

Corliss cleared his throat and read in a halting voice.

"'A man wrongly convicted of rape was released Saturday from the Arizona Correctional Institution and vowed to seek justice for other inmates falsely accused. Frederic Bentley, thirty-four, served almost eight years in prison for attacking a sixteen-year-old Tempe girl. The victim of the assault identified Bentley, a neighbor, and blood tests matched his type to semen recovered from the victim after the attack. The case was bolstered at trial by testimony from an informant who said Bentley had confessed the crime to him while they were housed together in a holding cell. Bentley always maintained his innocence during the trial and even after his conviction. Once DNA testing was accepted as valid evidence by courts in the state, Bentley hired attorneys to fight for such testing of semen collected from the victim of the attack. A judge ordered the testing earlier this year, and the resulting analysis proved Bentley was not the attacker.

"'At a press conference yesterday at the Arizona Biltmore the newly freed Bentley railed against jailhouse informants and called for a state law that would put strict guidelines on police and prosecutors who wish to use them.

"'The informant who claimed in sworn testimony that Bentley admitted the rape was identified as D.J. Corliss, a Mesa man who had been arrested on drug charges. When told of Bentley's exoneration and asked whether he fabricated his testimony against Bentley, Corliss declined comment Saturday. At his press conference, Bentley charged that Corliss was well known to the police as a snitch and was used in several cases to get close to suspects. Bentley claimed that Corliss's practice was to make up confessions if he could not draw them out of the suspects. The case against Bentley —'"

"Okay, Mr. Corliss," I said. "I think that is enough."

Corliss put the printout down and looked at me like a child who has opened the door of a crowded closet and sees everything about to fall out on top of him.

"Were you ever charged with perjury in the Bentley case?" I asked him.

"No, I wasn't," he said forcefully, as if that fact exonerated him of wrongdoing.

"Was that because the police were complicit with you in setting up Mr. Bentley?"

Minton objected, saying, "I am sure Mr. Corliss would have no idea what went into the decision of whether or not to charge him with perjury."

Fullbright sustained it but I didn't care. I was so far ahead on this witness that there was no catching up. I just moved on to the next question.

"Did any prosecutor or police officer ask you to get close to Mr. Roulet and get him to confide in you?"

"No, it was just luck of the draw, I guess."

"You were not told to get a confession from Mr. Roulet?"

"No, I was not."

I stared at him for a long moment with disgust in my eyes.

"I have nothing further."

I carried the pose of anger with me to my seat and dropped the tape box angrily down in front of me before sitting down.

"Mr. Minton?" the judge asked.

"I have nothing further," he responded in a weak voice.

"Okay," Fullbright said quickly. "I am going to excuse the jury for an early lunch. I would like you all back here at one o'clock sharp."

She put on a strained smile and directed it at the jurors and kept it there until they had filed out of the courtroom. It dropped off her face the moment the door was closed.

"I want to see counsel in my chambers," she said. "Immediately."

She didn't wait for any response. She left the bench so fast that her robe flowed up behind her like the black gown of the grim reaper.

FORTY-ONE

Judge Fullbright had already lit a cigarette by the time Minton and I got back to her chambers. After one long drag she put it out against a glass paperweight and then put the butt into a Ziploc bag she had taken out of her purse. She closed the bag, folded it and replaced it in the purse. She would leave no evidence of her transgression for the night cleaners or anyone else. She exhaled the smoke toward a ceiling intake vent and then brought her eyes down to Minton's. Judging by the look in them I was glad I wasn't him.

"Mr. Minton, what the fuck have you done to my trial?"

"Your —"

"Shut up and sit down. Both of you."

We did as we were told. The judge composed herself and leaned forward across her desk. She was still looking at Minton.

"Who did the due diligence on this witness of yours?" she asked calmly. "Who did the background?"

"Uh, that would have — actually, we only did a background on him in L.A. County. There were no cautions, no flags. I checked his name on the computer but I didn't use the initials."

"How many times had he been used in this county before today?"

"Only one previous time in court. But he had given information on three other cases I could find. Nothing about Arizona came up."

"Nobody thought to check to see if this guy had been anywhere else or used variations of his name?"

"I guess not. He was passed on to me by the original prosecutor on the case. I just assumed she had checked him out."

"Bullshit," I said.

The judge turned her eyes to me. I could have sat back and watched Minton go down but I wasn't going to let him try to take Maggie McPherson with him.

"The original prosecutor was Maggie McPherson," I said. "She had the case all of about three hours. She's my ex-wife and she knew as soon as she saw me at first apps that she was gone. And you got the case that same day, Minton. Where in there was she supposed to background your witnesses, especially this guy who didn't come out from under his rock until after first appearance? She passed him on and that was it."

Minton opened his mouth to say something but the judge cut him off.

"It doesn't matter who should have done it. It wasn't done properly and, either way, putting that man on the stand in my opinion was gross prosecutorial misconduct."

"Your Honor," Minton barked. "I did —"

"Save it for your boss. He's the one you'll need to convince. What was the last offer the state made to Mr. Roulet?"

Minton seemed frozen and unable to respond. I answered for him.

"Simple assault, six months in county."

The judge raised her eyebrows and looked at me.

"And you didn't take it?"

I shook my head.

"My client won't take a conviction. It will ruin him. He'll gamble on a verdict."

"You want a mistrial?" she asked.

I laughed and shook my head.

"No, I don't want a mistrial. All that will do is give the prosecution time to clean up its mess, get it all right and then come back at us."

"Then what do you want?" she asked.

"What do I want? A directed verdict would be nice. Something with no comebacks from the state. Other than that, we'll ride it out."

The judge nodded and clasped her hands together on the desk.

"A directed verdict would be ridiculous, Your Honor," Minton said, finally finding his voice. "We're at the end of trial, anyway. We might as well take it to a verdict. The jury deserves it. Just because one mistake was made by the state, there is no reason to subvert the whole process."

"Don't be stupid, Mr. Minton," the judge said dismissively. "It's not about what the jury deserves. And as far as I am concerned, one mistake like you have made is enough. I don't want this kicked back at me by the Second and that is surely what they will do. Then I am holding the bag for your miscon —"

"I didn't know Corliss's background!" Minton said forcefully. "I swear to God I didn't know."

The intensity of his words brought a momentary silence to the chambers. But soon I slipped into the void.

"Just like you didn't know about the knife, Ted?"

Fullbright looked from Minton to me and then back at Minton.

"What knife?" she asked.

Minton said nothing.

"Tell her," I said.

Minton shook his head.

"I don't know what he's talking about," he said.

"Then you tell me," the judge said to me.

"Judge, if you wait on discovery from the DA, you might as well hang it up at the start," I said. "Witnesses disappear, stories change, you can lose a case just sitting around waiting."

"All right, so what about the knife?"

"I needed to move on this case. So I had my investigator go through the back door and get reports. It's fair game. But they were waiting for him and they phonied up a report on the knife so I wouldn't know about the initials. I didn't know until I got the formal discovery packet."

The judge formed a hard line with her lips.

"That was the police, not the DA's office," Minton said quickly.

"Thirty seconds ago you said you didn't know what he was talking about," Fullbright said. "Now suddenly you do. I don't care who did it. Are you telling me that this did in fact occur?"

Minton reluctantly nodded.

"Yes, Your Honor. But I swear, I didn't —"

"You know what this tells me?" the judge said, cutting him off. "It tells me that from start to finish the state has not played fair in this case. It doesn't matter who did what or that Mr. Haller's investigator may have been acting improperly. The state must be above that. And as evidenced today in my courtroom it has been anything but that."

"Your Honor, that's not —"

"No more, Mr. Minton. I think I've heard enough. I want you both to leave now. In half an hour I'll take the bench and announce what we'll do about this. I am not sure yet what that will be but no matter what I do, you aren't going to like what I have to say, Mr. Minton. And I am directing you to have your boss, Mr. Smithson, in the courtroom with you to hear it."

I stood up. Minton didn't move. He still seemed frozen to the seat.

"I said you can go!" the judge barked.

FORTY-TWO

I followed Minton through the court clerk's station and into the courtroom. It was empty except for Meehan, who sat at the bailiff's desk. I took my briefcase off the defense table and headed toward the gate.

"Hey, Haller, wait a second," Minton said, as he gathered files from the prosecution table.

I stopped at the gate and looked back.

"What?"

Minton came to the gate and pointed to the rear door of the courtroom.

"Let's go out here."

"My client is going to be waiting out there for me."

"Just come here."

He headed to the door and I followed. In the vestibule where I had confronted Roulet two days earlier Minton stopped to confront me. But he didn't say anything. He was putting words together. I decided to push him even further.

"While you go get Smithson I think I'll stop by the *Times* office on two and make sure the reporter down there knows there'll be some fireworks up here in a half hour."

"Look," Minton sputtered. "We have to work this out."

"We?"

"Just hold off on the *Times,* okay? Give me your cell number and give me ten minutes."

"For what?"

"Let me go down to my office and see what I can do."

"I don't trust you, Minton."

"Well, if you want what's best for your client instead of a cheap headline, you're going to have to trust me for ten minutes."

I looked away from his face and acted like I was considering the offer. Finally, I looked back at him. Our faces were only two feet apart.

"You know, Minton, I could've put up with all your bullshit. The knife and the arrogance and everything else. I'm a pro and I have to live with that shit from prosecutors every day of my life. But when you tried to put Corliss on Maggie McPherson in there, that's when I decided not to show you any mercy."

"Look, I did nothing to intentionally —"

"Minton, look around. There's nobody here but us. No cameras, no tape, no witnesses. Are you going to stand there and tell me you never heard of Corliss until a staff meeting yesterday?"

He responded by pointing an angry finger in my face.

"And you're going to stand there and tell me you never heard of him until this morning?"

We stared at each other for a long moment.

"I may be green but I'm not stupid," he said. "The strategy of your whole case was to push me toward using Corliss. You knew all along what you could do with him. And you probably got it from your ex."

"If you can prove that, then prove it," I said.

"Oh, don't worry, I could ... if I had the time. But all I've got is a half hour."

I slowly raised my arm and checked my watch.

"More like twenty-six minutes."

"Give me your cell number."

I did and then he was gone. I waited in the vestibule for fifteen seconds before stepping through the door. Roulet was standing close to the glass wall that looked down at the plaza below. His mother and C. C. Dobbs were sitting on a bench against the opposite wall. Further down the hallway I saw Detective Sobel lingering in the hallway.

Roulet noticed me and started walking quickly toward me. Soon his mother and Dobbs followed.

"What's going on?" Roulet asked first.

I waited until they were all gathered close to me before answering.

"I think it's all about to blow up."

"What do you mean?" Dobbs asked.

"The judge is considering a directed verdict. We'll know pretty soon."

"What is a directed verdict?" Mary Windsor asked.

"It's when the judge takes it out of the jury's hands and issues a verdict of acquittal. She's hot because she says Minton engaged in misconduct with Corliss and some other things."

"Can she do that? Just acquit him."

"She's the judge. She can do what she wants."

"Oh my God!"

Windsor brought one hand to her mouth and looked like she might burst into tears.

"I said she is considering it," I cautioned. "It doesn't mean it will happen. But she did offer me a mistrial already and I turned that down flat."

"You turned it down?" Dobbs yelped. "Why on earth did you do that?"

"Because it's meaningless. The state could come right back and try Louis again — this time with a better case because they'll know our moves. Forget the mistrial. We're not going to educate the prosecution. We want something with no comebacks or we ride with this jury to a verdict today. Even if it goes against us we have solid grounds for appeal."

"Isn't that a decision for Louis to make?" Dobbs asked. "After all, he's —"

"Cecil, shut up," Windsor snapped. "Just shut up and stop second-guessing everything this man does for Louis. He's right. We're not going through this again!"

Dobbs looked like he had been slapped by her. He seemed to shrink back from the huddle. I looked at Mary Windsor and saw a different face. It was the face of the woman who had started a business from scratch and had taken it to the top. I also looked at Dobbs differently, realizing that he had probably been whispering sweet negatives about me in her ear all along.

I let it go and focused on what was at hand.

"There's only one thing the DA's office hates worse than losing a verdict," I said. "That's getting embarrassed by a judge with a directed verdict, especially after a finding of prosecutorial misconduct. Minton went down to talk to his boss and he's a guy who is very political and always has his finger in the wind. We might know something in a few minutes."

Roulet was directly in front of me. I looked over his shoulder to see that Sobel was still standing in the hallway. She was talking on a cell phone.

"Listen," I said. "All of you just sit tight. If I don't hear from the DA, then we go back into court in twenty minutes to see what the judge wants to do. So stay close. If you will excuse me, I'm going to go to the restroom."

I stepped away from them and walked down the hallway toward Sobel. But Roulet broke away from his mother and her lawyer and caught up to me. He grabbed me by the arm to stop me.

"I still want to know how Corliss got that shit he was saying," he demanded.

"What does it matter? It's working for us. That's what matters."

Roulet brought his face in close to mine.

"The guy calls me a murderer on the stand. How is that working for us?"

"Because no one believed him. And that's why the judge is so pissed, because they used a professional liar to get up there on the stand and say the worst things about you. To put that in front of the jury and then have the guy revealed as a liar, that's the misconduct. Don't you see? I had to heighten the stakes. It was the only way to push the judge into pushing the prosecution. I am doing exactly what you wanted me to do, Louis. I'm getting you off."

I studied him as he computed this.

"So let it go," I said. "Go back to your mother and Dobbs and let me go take a piss."

He shook his head.

"No, I'm not going to let it go, Mick."

He poked a finger into my chest.

"Something else is going on here, Mick, and I don't like it. You have to remember something. I have your gun. And you have a daughter. You have to —"

I closed my hand over his hand and finger and pushed it away from my chest.

"Don't you ever threaten my family," I said with a controlled but angry voice. "You want to come at me, fine, then come at me and let's do it. But if you *ever* threaten my daughter again, I will bury you so deep you will never be found. You understand me, Louis?"

He slowly nodded and a smile creased his face.

"Sure, Mick. Just so we understand each other."

I released his hand and left him there. I started walking toward the end of the hallway where the restrooms were and where Sobel seemed to be waiting while talking on a cell. I was walking blind, my thoughts of the threat to my daughter crowding my vision. But as I got close to Sobel I shook it off. She ended her call when I got there.

"Detective Sobel," I said.

"Mr. Haller," she said.

"Can I ask why you are here? Are you going to arrest me?"

"I'm here because you invited me, remember?"

"Uh, no, I don't."

She narrowed her eyes.

"You told me I ought to check out your trial."

I suddenly realized she was referring to the awkward conversation in my home office during the search of my house on Monday night.

"Oh, right, I forgot about that. Well, I'm glad you took me up on it. I saw your partner earlier. What happened to him?"

"Oh, he's around."

I tried to read something in that. She had not answered the question about whether she was going to arrest me. I gestured back up the hallway toward the courtroom.

"So what did you think?"

"Interesting. I wish I could have been a fly on the wall in the judge's chambers."

"Well, stick around. It ain't over yet."

"Maybe I will."

My cell phone started to vibrate. I reached under my jacket and pulled it off my hip. The caller ID readout said the call was coming from the district attorney's office.

"I have to take this," I said.

"By all means," Sobel said.

I opened the phone and started walking back up the hallway toward where Roulet was pacing.

"Hello?"

"Mickey Haller, this is Jack Smithson in the DA's office. How's your day going?"

"I've had better."

"Not after you hear what I'm offering to do for you."

"I'm listening."

FORTY-THREE

The judge did not come out of chambers for fifteen minutes on top of the thirty she had promised. We were all waiting, Roulet and I at the defense table, his mother and Dobbs behind us in the first row. At the prosecution table Minton was no longer flying solo. Next to him sat Jack Smithson. I was thinking that it was probably the first time he had actually been inside a courtroom in a year.

Minton looked downcast and defeated. Sitting next to Smithson, he could have been taken as a defendant with his attorney. He looked guilty as charged.

Detective Booker was not in the courtroom and I wondered if he was working on something or simply if no one had bothered to call him with the bad news.

I turned to check the big clock on the back wall and to scan the gallery. The screen for Minton's PowerPoint presentation was gone now, a hint of what was to come. I saw Sobel sitting in the back row, but her partner and Kurlen were still nowhere to be seen. There was nobody else but Dobbs and Windsor, and they didn't count. The row reserved for the media was empty. The media had not been alerted. I was keeping my side of the deal with Smithson.

Deputy Meehan called the courtroom to order and Judge Fullbright took the bench with a flourish, the scent of lilac wafting toward the tables. I guessed that she'd had a cigarette or two back there in chambers and had gone heavy with the perfume as cover.

"In the matter of the state versus Louis Ross Roulet, I understand from my clerk that we have a motion."

Minton stood.

"Yes, Your Honor."

He said nothing further, as if he could not bring himself to speak.

"Well, Mr. Minton, are you sending it to me telepathically?"

"No, Your Honor."

Minton looked down at Smithson and got the go-ahead nod.

"The state moves to dismiss all charges against Louis Ross Roulet."

The judge nodded as though she had expected the move. I heard a sharp intake of breath behind me and knew it was from Mary Windsor. She knew what was going to happen but had held her emotions in check until she had actually heard it in the courtroom.

"Is that with or without prejudice?" the judge asked.

"Dismiss with prejudice."

"Are you sure about that, Mr. Minton? That means no comebacks from the state."

"Yes, Your Honor, I know," Minton said with a note of annoyance at the judge's need to explain the law to him.

The judge wrote something down and then looked back at Minton.

"I believe for the record the state needs to offer some sort of explanation for this motion. We have chosen a jury and heard more than two days of testimony. Why is the state doing this at this stage, Mr. Minton?"

Smithson stood. He was a tall and thin man with a pale complexion. He was a prosecutorial specimen. Nobody wanted a fat man as district attorney and that was exactly what he hoped one day to be. He wore a charcoal gray suit with what had become his trademark: a maroon bow tie with matching handkerchief peeking from the suit's breast pocket. The word among the defense pros was that a political advisor had told him to start building a recognizable media image so that when the time came to run, the voters would think they already knew him. This was one situation where he didn't want the media carrying his image to the voters.

"If I may, Your Honor," he said.

"The record will note the appearance of Assistant District Attorney John Smithson, head of the Van Nuys Division. Welcome, Jack. Go right ahead, please."

"Judge Fullbright, it has come to my attention that in the interest of justice, the charges against Mr. Roulet should be dropped."

He pronounced Roulet's name wrong.

"Is that all the explanation you can offer, Jack?" the judge asked.

Smithson deliberated before answering. While there were no reporters present, the record of the hearing would be public and his words viewable later.

"Judge, it has come to my attention that there were some irregularities in the investigation and subsequent prosecution. This office is founded upon the belief in the sanctity of our justice system. I personally safeguard that in the Van Nuys Division and take it very, very seriously. And so it is better for us to dismiss a case than to see justice possibly compromised in any way."

"Thank you, Mr. Smithson. That is refreshing to hear."

The judge wrote another note and then looked back down at us.

"The state's motion is granted," she said. "All charges against Louis Roulet are dismissed with prejudice. Mr. Roulet, you are discharged and free to go."

"Thank you, Your Honor," I said.

"We still have a jury returning at one o'clock,"

Fullbright said. "I will gather them and explain that the case has been resolved. If any of you attorneys wish to come back then, I am sure they will have questions for you. However, it is not required that you be back."

I nodded but didn't say I would be back. I wouldn't be. The twelve people who had been so important to me for the last week had just dropped off the radar. They were now as meaningless to me as the drivers going the other way on the freeway. They had gone by and I was finished with them.

The judge left the bench and Smithson was the first one out of the courtroom. He had nothing to say to Minton or me. His first priority was to distance himself from this prosecutorial catastrophe. I looked over and saw Minton's face had lost all color. I assumed that I would soon see his name in the yellow pages. He would not be retained by the DA and he would join the ranks of the defense pros, his first felony lesson a costly one.

Roulet was at the rail, leaning over to hug his mother. Dobbs had a hand on his shoulder in a congratulatory gesture, but the family lawyer had not recovered from Windsor's harsh rebuke in the hallway.

When the hugs were over, Roulet turned to me and with hesitation shook my hand.

"I wasn't wrong about you," he said. "I knew you were the one."

"I want the gun," I said, deadpan, my face showing no joy in the victory just achieved.

"Of course you do."

He turned back to his mother. I hesitated a moment and then turned back to the defense table. I opened my briefcase to return all the files to it.

"Michael?"

I turned and it was Dobbs reaching a hand across the railing. I shook it and nodded.

"You did good," Dobbs said, as if I needed to hear it from him. "We all appreciate it greatly."

"Thanks for the shot. I know you were shaky about me at the start."

I was courteous enough not to mention Windsor's outburst in the hallway and what she had said about him backstabbing me.

"Only because I didn't know you," Dobbs said. "Now I do. Now I know who to recommend to my clients."

"Thank you. But I hope your kind of clients never need me."

He laughed.

"Me, too!"

Then it was Mary Windsor's turn. She extended her hand across the bar.

"Mr. Haller, thank you for my son."

"You're welcome," I said flatly. "Take care of him."

"I always do."

I nodded.

"Why don't you all go out to the hallway and I'll be out in a minute. I have to finish up some things here with the clerk and Mr. Minton."

I turned back to the table. I then went around it and approached the clerk.

"How long before I can get a signed copy of the judge's order?"

"We'll enter it this afternoon. We can send you a copy if you don't want to come back."

"That would be great. Could you also fax one?"

She said she would and I gave her the number to the fax in Lorna Taylor's condominium. I wasn't sure yet how it could be used but I had to believe that an order to dismiss could somehow help me get a client or two.

When I turned back to get my briefcase and leave I noticed that Detective Sobel had left the courtroom. Only

Minton remained. He was standing and gathering his things.

"Sorry I never got the chance to see your PowerPoint thing," I said.

He nodded.

"Yeah, it was pretty good. I think it would have won them over."

I nodded.

"What are you going to do now?"

"I don't know. See if I can ride this out and somehow hold on to my job."

He put his files under his arm. He had no briefcase. He only had to go down to the second floor. He turned and gave me a hard stare.

"The only thing I know is that I don't want to cross the aisle. I don't want to become like you, Haller. I think I like sleeping at night too much for that."

With that he headed through the gate and strode out of the courtroom. I glanced over at the clerk to see if she had heard what he had said. She acted like she hadn't.

I took my time following Minton out. I picked up my briefcase and turned backwards as I pushed through the gate. I looked at the judge's empty bench and the state seal on the front panel. I nodded at nothing in particular and then walked out.

FORTY-FOUR

Roulet and his entourage were waiting for me in the hallway. I looked both ways and saw Sobel down by the elevators. She was on her cell phone and it seemed as though she was waiting for an elevator but it didn't look like the down button was lit.

"Michael, can you join us for lunch?" Dobbs said upon seeing me. "We are going to celebrate!"

I noticed that he was now calling me by my given name. Victory made everybody friendly.

"Uh . . ." I said, still looking down at Sobel. "I don't think I can make it."

"Why not? You obviously don't have court in the afternoon."

I finally looked at Dobbs. I felt like saying that I couldn't have lunch because I never wanted to see him or Mary Windsor or Louis Roulet again.

"I think I'm going to stick around and talk to the jurors when they come back at one."

"Why?" Roulet asked.

"Because it will help me to know what they were thinking and where we stood."

Dobbs gave me a clap on the upper arm.

"Always learning, always getting better for the next one. I don't blame you."

He looked delighted that I would not be joining them. And for good reason. He probably wanted me out of the way now so he could work on repairing his relationship with Mary Windsor. He wanted that franchise account just to himself again.

I heard the muted bong of the elevator and looked back down the hall. Sobel was standing in front of the opening elevator. She was leaving.

But then Lankford, Kurlen and Booker stepped out of the elevator and joined Sobel. They turned and started walking toward us.

"Then we'll leave you to it," Dobbs said, his back to the approaching detectives. "We have a reservation at Orso and I'm afraid we're already going to be late getting back over the hill."

"Okay," I said, still looking down the hall.

Dobbs, Windsor and Roulet turned to walk away just as the four detectives got to us.

"Louis Roulet," Kurlen announced. "You are under arrest. Turn around, please, and place your hands behind your back."

"No!" Mary Windsor shrieked. "You can't —"

"What is this?" Dobbs cried out.

Kurlen didn't answer or wait for Roulet to comply. He stepped forward and roughly turned Roulet around. As he made the forced turn, Roulet's eyes came to mine.

"What's going on, Mick?" he said in a calm voice. "This shouldn't be happening."

Mary Windsor moved toward her son.

"Take your hands off of my son!"

She grabbed Kurlen from behind but Booker and Lankford quickly moved in and detached her, handling her gently but strongly.

"Ma'am, step back," Booker commanded. "Or I will put you in jail."

Kurlen started giving Roulet the Miranda warning. Windsor stayed back but was not silent.

"How dare you? You cannot do this!"

Her body moved in place and she looked as though unseen hands were keeping her from charging at Kurlen again.

"Mother," Roulet said in a tone that carried more weight and control than any of the detectives.

Windsor's body relented. She gave up. But Dobbs didn't.

"You're arresting him for what?" he demanded.

"Suspicion of murder," Kurlen said. "The murder of Martha Renteria."

"That's impossible!" Dobbs cried. "Everything that witness Corliss said in there was proven to be a lie. Are you crazy? The judge dismissed the case because of his lies."

Kurlen broke from his recital of Roulet's rights and looked at Dobbs.

"If it was all a lie, how'd you know he was talking about Martha Renteria?"

Dobbs realized his mistake and took a step back from the gathering. Kurlen smiled.

"Yeah, I thought so," he said.

He grabbed Roulet by an elbow and turned him back around.

"Let's go," he said.

"Mick?" Roulet said.

"Detective Kurlen," I said. "Can I talk to my client for a moment?"

Kurlen looked at me, seemed to measure something in me and then nodded.

"One minute. Tell him to behave himself and it will all go a lot easier for him."

He shoved Roulet toward me. I took him by one arm and walked him a few paces away from the others so we would have privacy if we kept our voices down. I stepped close to him and began in a whisper.

"This is it, Louis. This is good-bye. I got you off. Now you're on your own. Get yourself a new lawyer."

The shock showed in his eyes. Then his face clouded over with a tightly focused anger. It was pure rage and I realized it was the same rage Regina Campo and Martha Renteria must have seen.

"I won't need a lawyer," he said to me. "You think they can make a case off of what you somehow fed to that lying snitch in there? You better think again."

"They won't need the snitch, Louis. Believe me, they'll find more. They probably already have more."

"What about you, Mick? Aren't you forgetting something? I have —"

"I know. But it doesn't matter anymore. They don't need my gun. They've already got all they need. But whatever happens to me, I'll know that I put you down. At the end, after the trial and all the appeals, when they finally stick that needle in your arm, that will be me, Louis. Remember that."

I smiled with no humor and moved in closer.

"This is for Raul Levin. You might not go down for him but make no mistake, you are going down."

I let that register for a moment and then stepped back and nodded to Kurlen. He and Booker came up on either side of Roulet and took hold of his upper arms.

"You set me up," Roulet said, somehow maintaining his calm. "You aren't a lawyer. You work for them."

"Let's go," Kurlen said.

They started moving him but he shook them off momentarily and put his raging eyes right back into mine.

"This isn't the end, Mick," he said. "I'll be out by tomorrow morning. What will you do then? Think about it. What are you going to do then? You can't protect everybody."

They took a tighter hold of him and roughly turned him toward the elevators. This time Roulet went without a struggle. Halfway down the hall toward the elevator, his mother and Dobbs trailing behind, he turned his head to look back over his shoulder at me. He smiled and it sent something right through me.

You can't protect everybody.

A cold shiver of fear pierced my chest.

Someone was waiting for the elevator and it opened just as the entourage got there. Lankford signaled the person back and took the elevator. Roulet was hustled in. Dobbs and Windsor were about to follow when they were halted by Lankford's hand extended in a stop signal. The elevator door started to close and Dobbs angrily and impotently pushed on the button next to it.

My hope was that it would be the last I would ever see of Louis Roulet, but the fear stayed locked in my chest, fluttering like a moth caught inside a porch light. I turned away and almost walked right into Sobel. I hadn't noticed that she had stayed behind the others.

"You have enough, don't you?" I said. "Tell me you wouldn't have moved so quickly if you didn't have enough to keep him."

She looked at me a long moment before answering.

"We won't decide that. The DA will. Probably depends on what they get out of him in interrogation. But up till now he's had a pretty smart lawyer. He probably knows not to say a word to us."

"Then why didn't you wait?"

"Wasn't my call."

I shook my head. I wanted to tell her that they had moved too fast. It wasn't part of the plan. I wanted to plant the seed, that's all. I wanted them to move slowly and get it right.

The moth fluttered inside and I looked down at the floor. I couldn't shake the idea that all of my machinations had failed, leaving me and my family exposed in the hard-eyed focus of a killer. *You can't protect everybody.*

It was as if Sobel read my fears.

"But we're going to try to keep him," she said. "We have what the snitch said in court and the ticket. We're working on witnesses and the forensics."

My eyes came up to hers.

"What ticket?"

A look of suspicion entered her face.

"I thought you had it figured out. We put it together as soon as the snitch mentioned the snake dancer."

"Yeah. Martha Renteria. I got that. But what ticket? What are you talking about?"

I had moved in too close to her and Sobel took a step back from me. It wasn't my breath. It was my desperation.

"I don't know if I should tell you, Haller. You're a defense lawyer. You're *his* lawyer."

"Not anymore. I just quit."

"Doesn't matter. He —"

"Look, you just took that guy down because of me. I might get disbarred because of it. I might even go to jail for a murder I didn't commit. What ticket are you talking about?"

She hesitated and I waited, but then she finally spoke.

"Raul Levin's last words. He said he found Jesus's ticket out."

"Which means what?"

"You really don't know, do you?"

"Look, just tell me. Please."

She relented.

"We traced Levin's most recent movements. Before he was murdered he had made inquiries about Roulet's parking tickets. He even pulled hard copies of them. We inventoried what he had in the office and eventually compared it with what's on the computer. He was missing one ticket. One hard copy. We didn't know if his killer took it that day or if he had just missed pulling it. So we

423

went and pulled a copy ourselves. It was issued two years ago on the night of April eighth. It was a citation for parking in front of a hydrant in the sixty-seven-hundred block of Blythe Street in Panorama City."

It all came together for me, like the last bit of sand dropping through the middle of an hourglass. Raul Levin really had found Jesus Menendez's salvation.

"Martha Renteria was murdered two years ago on April eighth," I said. "She lived on Blythe in Panorama City."

"Yes, but we didn't know that. We didn't see the connection. You told us that Levin was working separate cases for you. Jesus Menendez and Louis Roulet were separate investigations. Levin had them filed that way, too."

"It was a discovery issue. He kept the cases separate so I wouldn't have to turn over anything on Roulet that he came up with on Menendez."

"One of your lawyer angles. Well, it stopped us from putting it together until that snitch in there mentioned the snake dancer. That connected everything."

I nodded.

"So whoever killed Raul Levin took the hard copy?"

"We think."

"Did you check Raul's phones for a tap? Somehow somebody knew he found the ticket."

"We did. They were clear. Bugs could have been removed at the time of the murder. Or maybe it was someone else's phone that was tapped."

Meaning mine. Meaning it might explain how Roulet knew so many of my moves and was even conveniently waiting for me in my home the night I had come home from seeing Jesus Menendez.

"I will have them checked," I said. "Does all of this mean I am clear on Raul's murder?"

"Not necessarily," Sobel said. "We still want to see what

comes back from ballistics. We're hoping for something today."

I nodded. I didn't know how to respond. Sobel lingered, looking like she wanted to tell me or ask me something.

"What?" I said.

"I don't know. Is there anything you want to tell me?"

"I don't know. There's nothing to tell."

"Really? In the courtroom it seemed like you were trying to tell us a lot."

I was silent a moment, trying to read between the lines.

"What do you want from me, Detective Sobel?"

"You know what I want. I want Raul Levin's killer."

"Well, so do I. But I couldn't give you Roulet on Levin even if I wanted to. I don't know how he did it. And that's off the record."

"So that still leaves you in the crosshairs."

She looked down the hall at the elevators, her implication clear. If the ballistics matched, I could still have a problem on Levin. They would use it as leverage. Give up how Roulet did it or go down for it myself. I changed the subject.

"How long do you think before Jesus Menendez gets out?" I asked.

She shrugged.

"Hard to say. Depends on the case they build against Roulet — if they have a case. But I know one thing. They can't prosecute Roulet as long as another man is in prison for the same crime."

I turned and walked over to the glass wall. I put my free hand on the railing that ran along the glass. I felt a mixture of elation and dread and that moth still batting around in my chest.

"That's all I care about," I said quietly. "Getting him out. That and Raul."

She came over and stood next to me.

"I don't know what you are doing," she said. "But leave the rest for us."

"I do that and your partner will probably put me in jail for a murder I didn't commit."

"You are playing a dangerous game," she said. "Leave it alone."

I looked at her and then back down at the plaza.

"Sure," I said. "I'll leave it alone now."

Having heard what she needed to, she made a move to go.

"Good luck," she said.

I looked at her again.

"Same to you."

She left then and I stayed. I turned back to the window and looked down into the plaza. I saw Dobbs and Windsor crossing the concrete squares and heading toward the parking garage. Mary Windsor was leaning against her lawyer for support. I doubted they were still headed to lunch at Orso.

FORTY-FIVE

By that night the word had begun to spread. Not the secret details but the public story. The story that I had won the case, gotten a DA's motion to dismiss with no comebacks, only to have my client arrested for a murder in the hallway outside the courtroom where I had just cleared him. I got calls from every other defense pro I knew. I got call after call until my cell phone finally died. My colleagues were all congratulating me. In their eyes, there was no downside. Roulet was the ultimate franchise. I got schedule A fees for one trial and then I would get schedule A fees for the next one. It was a double-dip most defense pros could only dream about. And, of course, when I told them I would not be handling the defense of the new case, each one of them asked if I could refer him to Roulet.

It was the one call that came in on my home line that I wanted the most. It was from Maggie McPherson.

"I've been waiting for your call all night," I said.

I was pacing in the kitchen, tethered by the phone cord. I had checked my phones when I had gotten home and found no evidence of bugging devices.

"Sorry, I've been in the conference room," she said.

"I heard you were pulled in on Roulet."

"Yes, that's why I'm calling. They're going to cut him loose."

"What are you talking about? They're letting him go?"

"Yes. They've had him for nine hours in a room and he hasn't broken. Maybe you taught him too well not to talk,

427

because he's a rock and they got nothing and that means they don't have enough."

"You're wrong. There is enough. They have the parking ticket and there have to be witnesses who can put him in The Cobra Room. Even Menendez can ID him there."

"You know as well as I do that Menendez is a scratch. He'd identify anybody to get out. And if there are other wits from The Cobra Room, then it's going to take some time to run them down. The parking ticket puts him in the neighborhood but it doesn't put him inside her apartment."

"What about the knife?"

"They're working on it but that's going to take time, too. Look, we want to do this right. It was Smithson's call and, believe me, he wanted to keep him, too. It would make that fiasco you created in court today a little more palatable. But it's just not there. Not yet. They're going to kick him loose and work the forensics and look for the witnesses. If Roulet's good for this, then we will get him, and your other client will get out. You don't have to worry. But we have to do it right."

I swung a fist impotently through the air.

"They jumped the gun. Damn it, they shouldn't have made the move today."

"I guess they thought nine hours in interrogation would do the trick."

"They were stupid."

"Nobody's perfect."

I was annoyed by her attitude but held my tongue on that. I needed her to keep me in the loop.

"When exactly will they let him go?" I asked.

"I don't know. This all just went down. Kurlen and Booker came over here to present it and Smithson just sent them back to the PD. When they get back, I assume they'll kick him loose."

"Listen to me, Maggie. Roulet knows about Hayley."

There was a horribly long moment of silence before she answered.

"What are you saying, Haller? You let our daughter into —"

"I didn't let anything happen. He broke into my house and saw her picture. It doesn't mean he knows where she lives or even what her name is. But he knows about her and he wants to get back at me. So you have to go home right now. I want you to be with Hayley. Get her and get out of the apartment. Just play it safe."

Something made me hold back on telling her everything, that I felt that Roulet had specifically threatened my family in the courthouse. *You can't protect everybody.* I would only use that if she refused to do what I wanted her to do with Hayley.

"I'm leaving now," she said. "And we're coming to you."

I knew she would say that.

"No, don't come to me."

"Why not?"

"Because *he* might come to me."

"This is crazy. What are you going to do?"

"I'm not sure yet. Just go get Hayley and get somewhere safe. Then call me on your cell, but don't tell me where you are. It will be better if I don't even know."

"Haller, just call the police. They can —"

"And tell them what?"

"I don't know. Tell them you've been threatened."

"A defense lawyer telling the police he feels threatened ... yeah, they'll jump all over that. Probably send out a SWAT team."

"Well, you have to do something."

"I thought I did. I thought he was going to be in jail for the rest of his life. But you people moved too fast and now you have to let him go."

"I told you, it wasn't enough. Even knowing now about the possible threat to Hayley, it's still not enough."

"Then go to our daughter and take care of her. Leave the rest to me."

"I'm going."

But she didn't hang up. It was like she was giving me the chance to say something more.

"I love you, Mags," I said. "Both of you. Be careful."

I closed the phone before she could respond. Almost immediately I opened it again and called Fernando Valenzuela's cell phone number. After five rings he answered.

"Val, it's me, Mick."

"Shit. If I'd known it was you I wouldn't have answered."

"Look, I need your help."

"My help? You're asking for my help after what you asked me the other night? After you accused me?"

"Look, Val, this is an emergency. What I said the other night was out of line and I apologize. I'll pay for your TV, I'll do whatever you want, but I need your help right now."

I waited. After a pause he responded.

"What do you want me to do?"

"Roulet still has the bracelet on his ankle, right?"

"That's right. I know what happened in court but I haven't heard from the guy. One of my courthouse people said the cops picked him up again so I don't know what's going on."

"They picked him up but he's about to be kicked loose. He'll probably be calling you so he can get the bracelet taken off."

"I'm already home, man. He can find me in the morning."

"That's what I want. Make him wait."

"That ain't no favor, man."

"This is. I want you to open your laptop and watch him. When he leaves the PD, I want to know where he's going. Can you do that for me?"

"You mean right now?"

"Yeah, right now. You got a problem with that?"

"Sort of."

I got ready for another argument. But I was surprised.

"I told you about the battery alarm on the bracelet, right?" Valenzuela said.

"Yeah, I remember."

"Well, I got the twenty percent alarm about an hour ago."

"So how much longer can you track him until the battery's dead?"

"Probably about six to eight hours' active tracking before it goes on low pulse. Then he'll come up every fifteen minutes for another five hours."

I thought about all of this. I just needed to make it through the night and to know that Maggie and Hayley were safe.

"The thing is, when he is on low pulse he beeps," Valenzuela said. "You'll hear him coming. Or he'll get tired of the noise and juice the battery."

Or maybe he'll pull the Houdini act again, I thought.

"Okay," I said. "You told me that there were other alarms that you could build into the tracking program."

"That's right."

"Can you set it so you get an alarm if he comes near a specific target?"

"Yeah, like if it's on a child molester you can set an alarm if he gets close to a school. Stuff like that. It's got to be a fixed target."

"Okay."

I gave him the address of the apartment on Dickens in Sherman Oaks where Maggie and my daughter lived.

"If he comes within ten blocks of that place you call me. Doesn't matter what time, call me. That's the favor."

"What is this place?"

"It's where my daughter lives."

There was a long silence before Valenzuela responded.

"With Maggie? You think this guy's going to go there?"

"I don't know. I'm hoping that as long as he's got the tracker on his ankle he won't be stupid."

"Okay, Mick. You got it."

"Thanks, Val. And call my home number. My cell is dead."

I gave him the number and then was silent for a moment, wondering what else I could say to make up for my betrayal two nights earlier. Finally, I let it go. I had to focus on the current threat.

I moved from the kitchen and down the hallway to my office. I rolled through the Rolodex on my desk until I found a number and then grabbed the desk phone.

I dialed and waited. I looked out the window to the left of my desk and noticed for the first time that it was raining. It looked like it was going to come down hard and I wondered if the weather would affect the satellite tracking of Roulet. I dropped the thought when my call was answered by Teddy Vogel, the leader of the Road Saints.

"Speak to me."

"Ted, Mickey Haller."

"Counselor, how are you?"

"Not so good tonight."

"Then I am glad you called. What can I do for you?"

I looked out the window at the rain before answering. I knew that if I continued I would be indebted to people I never wanted to be on the hook with.

But there was no choice.

"You happen to have anybody down my way tonight?" I asked.

There was a hesitation before Vogel answered. I knew he had to be curious about his lawyer calling him for help. I was obviously asking about the kind of help that came with muscles and guns.

"Got a few guys watching things at the club. What's up?"

The club was the strip bar on Sepulveda, not too far from Sherman Oaks. I was counting on that.

"There's a threat to my family, Ted. I need some warm bodies to put up a front, maybe grab a guy if needed."

"Armed and dangerous?"

I hesitated but not too long.

"Yeah, armed and dangerous."

"Sounds like our kind of move. Where do you want them?"

He was immediately ready to act. He knew the value of having me under his thumb instead of on retainer. I gave him the address of the apartment on Dickens. I also gave him a description of Roulet and what he had been wearing in court that day.

"If he shows up at that apartment, I want him stopped," I said. "And I need your people to go now."

"Done," Vogel said.

"Thank you, Ted."

"No, thank you. We're glad to help you out, seeing as how you've helped us out so much."

Yeah, right, I thought. I hung the phone up, knowing I had just crossed one of those lines you hope to never see let alone have to step across. I looked out the window again. Outside, the rain was now coming down hard off the roof. I had no gutter in the back and it was coming down in a translucent sheet that blurred the lights out there. Nothing but rain this year, I thought. Nothing but rain.

I left the office and went back to the front of the house. On the table in the dining alcove was the gun Earl Briggs had given me. I contemplated the weapon and all the moves I had made. The bottom line was I had been flying blind and in the process had endangered more than just myself.

Panic started to set in. I grabbed the phone off the kitchen wall and called Maggie's cell. She answered right away. I could tell she was in her car.

"Where are you?"

"I'm just getting home now. I'll get some things together and we'll get out."

"Good."

"What do I tell Hayley, that her father put her life in danger?"

"It's not like that, Maggie. It's him. It's Roulet. I couldn't control him. One night I came home and he was sitting in my house. He's a real estate guy. He knows how to find places. He saw her picture on my desk. What was I —"

"Can we talk about this later? I have to go in now and get my daughter."

Not *our* daughter. *My* daughter.

"Sure. Call me when you're in a new place."

She disconnected without further word and I slowly hung the phone back on the wall. My hand was still on the phone. I leaned forward until my forehead touched the wall. I was out of moves. I could only wait on Roulet to make the next one.

The phone's ring startled me and I jumped back. The phone fell to the floor and I pulled it up by the cord. It was Valenzuela.

"You get my message? I just called."

"No, I've been on the phone. What?"

"Glad I called back, then. He's moving."

"Where?"

I shouted it too loud into the phone. I was losing it.

"He's heading south on Van Nuys. He called me and said he wanted to lose the bracelet. I told him I was already home and that he could call me tomorrow. I told him he had better juice the battery so he wouldn't start beeping in the middle of the night."

"Good thinking. Where's he now?"

"Still on Van Nuys."

I tried to build an image of Roulet driving. If he was going south on Van Nuys that meant he was heading directly toward Sherman Oaks and the neighborhood where Maggie and Hayley lived. But he could also be headed right through Sherman Oaks on his way south over the hill and to his home. I had to wait to be sure.

"How up to the moment is the GPS on that thing?" I asked.

"It's real time, man. This is where he's at. He just crossed under the one-oh-one. He might be just going home, Mick."

"I know, I know. Just wait till he crosses Ventura. The next street is Dickens. If he turns there, then he's not going home."

I stood up and didn't know what to do. I started pacing, the phone pressed tightly to my ear. I knew that even if Teddy Vogel had immediately put his men in motion they were still minutes away. They were no good to me now.

"What about the rain? Does it affect the GPS?"

"It's not supposed to."

"That's comforting."

"He stopped."

"Where?"

"Must be a light. I think that's Moorpark Avenue there."

That was a block before Ventura and two before Dickens. I heard a beeping sound come over the phone.

"What's that?"

"The ten-block alarm you asked me to set."

The beeping sound stopped.

"I turned it off."

"I'll call you right back."

I didn't wait for a response. I hung up and called Maggie's cell. She answered right away.

"Where are you?"

"You told me not to tell you."

"You're out of the apartment?"

"No, not yet. Hayley's picking the crayons and coloring books she wants to take."

"Goddamn it, get out of there! Now!"

"We're going as fast as —"

"Just get out! I'll call you back. Make sure you answer."

I hung up and called Valenzuela back.

"Where is he?"

"He's now at Ventura. Must've caught another light, because he's not moving."

"You're sure he's on the road and not just parked there?"

"No, I'm not sure. He could — never mind, he's moving. Shit, he turned on Ventura."

"Which way?"

I started pacing, the phone pressed so hard against my ear that it hurt.

"Right — uh, west. He's going west."

He was now driving parallel to Dickens, one block away, in the direction of my daughter's apartment.

"He just stopped again," Valenzuela announced. "It's not an intersection. It looks like he's in the middle of the block. I think he parked it."

I ran my free hand through my hair like a desperate man.

"Fuck it, I've gotta go. My cell's dead. Call Maggie and tell her he's heading her way. Tell her to just get in the car and get out of there!"

I shouted Maggie's number into the phone and dropped it as I headed out of the kitchen. I knew it would take me a minimum of twenty minutes to get to Dickens — and that was hitting the curves on Mulholland at sixty in the Lincoln — but I couldn't stand around shouting orders on the phone while my family was in danger. I grabbed the gun off the table and went to the door. I was shoving it into the side pocket of my jacket as I opened the door.

Mary Windsor was standing there, her hair wet from the rain.

"Mary, what —"

She raised her hand. I looked down to see the metal glint of the gun in it just as she fired.

FORTY-SIX

The sound was loud and the flash as bright as a camera's. The impact of the bullet tearing into me was like what I imagine a kick from a horse would feel like. In a split second I went from standing still to moving backwards. I hit the wood floor hard and was propelled into the wall next to the living room fireplace. I tried to reach both hands to the hole in my gut but my right hand was hung up in the pocket of my jacket. I held myself with the left and tried to sit up.

Mary Windsor stepped forward and into the house. I had to look up at her. Through the open door behind her I could see the rain coming down. She raised the weapon and pointed it at my forehead. In a flash moment my daughter's face came to me and I knew I wasn't going to let her go.

"You tried to take my son from me!" Windsor shouted. "Did you think I could allow you to do that and just walk away?"

And then I knew. Everything crystallized. I knew she had said similar words to Raul Levin before she had killed him. And I knew that there had been no rape in an empty house in Bel-Air. She was a mother doing what she had to do. Roulet's words came back to me then. *You're right about one thing. I am a son of a bitch.*

And I knew, too, that Raul Levin's last gesture had not been to make the sign of the devil, but to make the letter *M* or *W,* depending on how you looked at it.

Windsor took another step toward me.

"You go to hell," she said.

She steadied her hand to fire. I raised my right hand, still wrapped in my jacket. She must have thought it was a defensive gesture because she didn't hurry. She was savoring the moment. I could tell. Until I fired.

Mary Windsor's body jerked backwards with the impact and she landed on her back in the threshold of the door. Her gun clattered to the floor and I heard her make a high-pitched whining noise. Then I heard the sound of running feet on the steps up to the front deck.

"Police!" a woman shouted. "Put your weapons down!"

I looked through the door and didn't see anyone.

"Put your weapons down and come out with your hands in full view!"

This time it was a man who had yelled and I recognized the voice.

I pulled the gun out of my jacket pocket and put it on the floor. I slid it away from me.

"The weapon's down," I called out, as loud as the hole in my stomach allowed me to. "But I'm shot. I can't get up. We're both shot."

I first saw the barrel of a pistol come into view in the doorway. Then a hand and then a wet black raincoat containing Detective Lankford. He moved into the house and was quickly followed by his partner, Detective Sobel. Lankford kicked the gun away from Windsor as he came in. He kept his own weapon pointed at me.

"Anybody else in the house?" he asked loudly.

"No," I said. "Listen to me."

I tried to sit up but pain shot through my body and Lankford yelled.

"Don't move! Just stay there!"

"Listen to me. My fam —"

Sobel yelled a command into a handheld radio,

ordering paramedics and ambulance transport for two people with gunshot wounds.

"One transport," Lankford corrected. "She's gone."

He pointed his gun at Windsor.

Sobel shoved the radio into her raincoat pocket and came to me. She knelt down and pulled my hand away from my wound. She pulled my shirt out of my pants so she could lift it and see the damage. She then pressed my hand back down on the bullet hole.

"Press down as hard as you can. It's a bleeder. You hear me, hold your hand down tight."

"Listen to me," I said again. "My family's in danger. You have to —"

"Hold on."

She reached inside her raincoat and pulled a cell phone off her belt. She flipped it open and hit a speed-dial button. Whoever she called answered right away.

"It's Sobel. You better bring him back in. His mother just tried to hit the lawyer. He got her first."

She listened for a moment and asked, "Then, where is he?"

She listened some more and then said good-bye. I stared at her as she closed her phone.

"They'll pick him up. Your daughter is safe."

"You're watching him?"

She nodded.

"We piggy-backed on your plan, Haller. We have a lot on him but we were hoping for more. I told you, we want to clear Levin. We were hoping that if we kicked him loose he'd show us his trick, show us how he got to Levin. But the mother sort of just solved that mystery for us."

I understood. Even with the blood and life running out of the hole in my gut I was able to put it together. Releasing Roulet had been a play. They were hoping that he'd go after me, revealing the method he had used to defeat the GPS ankle bracelet when he had killed Raul Levin. Only he hadn't killed Raul. His mother had done it for him.

"Maggie?" I asked weakly.

Sobel shook her head.

"She's fine. She had to play along because we didn't know if Roulet had a tap on your line or not. She couldn't tell you that she and Hayley were safe."

I closed my eyes. I didn't know whether just to be thankful that they were okay or to be angry that Maggie had used her daughter's father as bait for a killer.

I tried to sit up.

"I want to call her. She —"

"Don't move. Just stay still."

I leaned my head back on the floor. I was cold and on the verge of shaking, yet I also felt as though I were sweating. I could feel myself getting weaker as my breathing grew shallow.

Sobel pulled the radio out of her pocket again and asked dispatch for an ETA on the paramedics. The dispatcher reported back that the medical help was still six minutes away.

"Hang in there," Sobel said to me. "You'll be all right. Depending on what the bullet did inside, you should be all right."

"Gray . . ."

I meant to say *great* with full sarcasm attached. But I was fading.

Lankford came up next to Sobel and looked at me. In a gloved hand he held up the gun Mary Windsor had shot me with. I recognized the pearl grips. Mickey Cohen's gun. My gun. The gun she shot Raul with.

He nodded and I took it as some sort of signal. Maybe that in his eyes I had stepped up, that he knew I had done their work by drawing the killer out. Maybe it was even the offering of a truce and maybe he wouldn't hate lawyers so much after this.

Probably not. But I nodded back at him and the small movement made me cough. I tasted something in my mouth and knew it was blood.

"Don't flatline on us now," Lankford ordered. "If we end up giving a defense lawyer mouth-to-mouth, we'll never live it down."

He smiled and I smiled back. Or tried to. Then the blackness started crowding my vision. Pretty soon I was floating in it.

PART THREE

— POSTCARD FROM CUBA

FORTY-SEVEN

It has been five months since I was in a courtroom. In that time I have had three surgeries to repair my body, been sued in civil court twice and been investigated by both the Los Angeles Police Department and the California Bar Association. My bank accounts have been bled dry by medical expenses, living expenses, child support and, yes, even my own kind — the lawyers.

But I have survived it all and today will be the first day since I was shot by Mary Alice Windsor that I will walk without a cane or the numbing of painkillers. To me it is the first real step toward getting back. The cane is a sign of weakness. Nobody wants a defense attorney who looks weak. I must stand upright, stretch the muscles the surgeon cut through to get to the bullet, and walk on my own before I feel I can walk into a courtroom again.

I have not been in a courtroom but that does not mean I am not the subject of legal proceedings. Jesus Menendez and Louis Roulet are both suing me and the cases will likely follow me for years. They are separate claims but both of my former clients charge me with malpractice and violation of legal ethics. For all the specific accusations in his lawsuit, Roulet has not been able to learn how I supposedly got to Dwayne Jeffery Corliss at County-USC and fed him privileged information. And it is unlikely he ever will. Gloria Dayton is long gone. She finished her program, took the $25,000 I gave her and moved to Hawaii to start life again. And Corliss, who probably knows better than anyone the value of keeping one's mouth shut, has divulged nothing other than what he testified to in court — maintaining that while in custody Roulet told him about the murder of the snake dancer. He has avoided perjury charges because pursuing them would undermine the case against Roulet and be an act of self-flagellation by the DA's office. My lawyer tells me Roulet's lawsuit against me is a face-saving effort without merit and that it will eventually go away. Probably when I have no more money to pay my lawyer his fees.

But Menendez will never go away. He is the one who gets to me at night when I sit on the deck and watch the million-dollar view from my house with the million-one mortgage. He was pardoned by the governor and released from San Quentin two days after Roulet was charged with Martha Renteria's murder. But he only traded one life sentence for another. It was revealed that he contracted HIV in prison and the governor doesn't have a pardon for that. Nobody does. Whatever happens to Jesus Menendez is on me. I know this. I live with it every day. My father was right. There is no client as scary as an innocent man. And no client as scarring.

Menendez wants to spit on me and take my money as punishment for what I did and didn't do. As far as I am concerned he is entitled. But no matter what my failings of judgment and ethical lapses were, I know that by the end, I bent things in order to do the right thing. I traded evil for innocence. Roulet is in because of me. Menendez is out because of me. Despite the efforts of his new attorneys — it has now taken the partnership of Dan Daly and Roger Mills to replace me — Roulet will not see freedom again. From what I have heard from Maggie McPherson, prosecutors have built an impenetrable case against him for the Renteria murder. They have also followed Raul Levin's steps and connected Roulet to another killing: the follow-home rape and stabbing of a woman who tended bar in a Hollywood club. The forensic profile of his knife was matched to the fatal wounds inflicted on this other woman. For Roulet, the science will be the iceberg spotted too late. His ship will founder and go down. The battle for him now lies in just staying alive. His lawyers are engaged in plea negotiations to keep him from a lethal injection. They are hinting at other murders and rapes that he would be willing to clear up in exchange for his life. Whatever the outcome, alive or dead, he is surely gone from this world and I take my salvation in that. It is what has mended me better than any surgeon.

Maggie McPherson and I are attempting to mend our wounds, too. She brings my daughter to visit me every weekend and often stays for the day. We sit on the deck and talk. We both know our daughter will be what saves us. I can no longer hold anger for being used as bait for a killer. I think Maggie no longer holds anger for the choices I have made.

The California bar looked at all of my actions and sent me on a vacation to Cuba. That's what defense pros call being suspended for conduct unbecoming an attorney. CUBA. I was shelved for ninety days. It was a bullshit finding. They could prove no specific ethical violations in regard to Corliss, so they hit me for borrowing a gun from my client Earl Briggs. I got lucky there. It was not a stolen or unregistered gun. It belonged to Earl's father, so my ethical infraction was minor.

I didn't bother contesting the bar reprimand or appealing the suspension. After taking a bullet in the gut, ninety days on the shelf didn't look so bad to me. I served the suspension during my recovery, mostly in a bathrobe while watching Court TV.

Neither the bar nor the police found ethical or criminal violation on my part in the killing of Mary Alice Windsor.

She entered my home with a stolen weapon. She shot first and I shot last. From a block away Lankford and Sobel watched her take that first shot at my front door. Self-defense, cut and dried. But what has not been so clear-cut are the feelings I have for what I did. I wanted to avenge my friend Raul Levin, but I didn't want to see it done in blood. I am a killer now. Being state sanctioned only tempers slightly the feelings that come with that.

All investigations and official findings aside, I think now that in the whole matter of Menendez and Roulet I was guilty of conduct unbecoming myself. And the penalty for that is harsher than anything the state or the bar could ever throw at me. No matter. I will carry all of it with me as I go back to work. My work. I know my place in this world and on the first day of court next year I will pull the Lincoln out of the garage, get back on the road and go looking for the underdog. I don't know where I will go or what cases will be mine. I just know I will be healed and ready to stand once again in the world without truth.

ACKNOWLEDGMENTS

This novel was inspired by a chance meeting and conversation with attorney David Ogden many years ago at a Los Angeles Dodgers baseball game. For that, the author will always be grateful. Though the character and exploits of Mickey Haller are fictitious and wholly of the author's imagination, this story could not have been written without the tremendous help and guidance of attorneys Daniel F. Daly and Roger O. Mills, both of whom allowed me to watch them work and strategize cases and were tireless in their efforts to make sure the world of criminal defense law was depicted accurately in these pages. Any errors or exaggerations in the law or the practice of it are purely the fault of the author.

Superior Court Judge Judith Champagne and her staff in Department 124 in the Criminal Courts Building in downtown Los Angeles allowed the author complete access to her courtroom, chambers and holding cells and answered any question posed. To the judge, Joe, Marianne, and Michelle a great debt of thanks is owed.

Also of great help to the author and contribution to the story were Asya Muchnick, Michael Pietsch, Jane Wood, Terrill Lee Lankford, Jerry Hooten, David Lambkin, Lucas Foster, Carolyn Chriss, and Pamela Marshall.

Last but not least, the author wishes to thank Shannon Byrne, Mary Elizabeth Capps, Jane Davis, Joel Gotler, Philip Spitzer, Lukas Ortiz, and Linda Connelly for their help and support during the writing of this story.

PERMISSIONS

A case that survived against all odds.
Was the flame kept burning?
Or was the secret meant to be snuffed out?

THE NIGHT FIRE

Renée Ballard & Harry Bosch will be back.
'The Lincoln Lawyer' Mickey Haller will join them.

Read on for an exclusive early sneak peek at the new
blockbuster thriller from the crime writing genius
that is Michael Connelly . . .

Bosch

1

Bosch arrived late and had to park on a cemetery lane far from the gravesite. Careful not to step on anybody's grave, he limped through two memorial sections, his cane sinking into the soft ground, until he saw the gathering for John Jack Thompson. It was standing room only around the old detective's gravesite and Bosch knew that wouldn't work with his knee only three weeks post-op. He retreated to the nearby Garden of Legends section and sat on a concrete bench that was part of Tyrone Power's tomb. He assumed it was okay since it was clearly a bench. He remembered his mother taking him to see Power in the movies when he was a kid. Old stuff they would run in the revival theaters on Beverly. He remembered the handsome actor as Zorro and as the accused American in *Witness for the Prosecution*.

The service for Thompson lasted a half hour. Bosch was too far away to hear what was said but he knew what was said. John Jack—he was always called that— was a good man who gave forty years of service to the Los Angeles Police Department in uniform and as a detective. He put many bad people away and taught generations of detectives how to do the same.

One of them was Bosch—paired with the legend as a newly minted homicide detective in Hollywood Division more than three decades earlier. Among other things, John Jack had taught Bosch how to read the tells of a liar in an interrogation room. John Jack knew when somebody was lying. He always did.

Their pairing had lasted two years only because Bosch trained well and John Jack was needed to break in the next new homicide man, but the mentor and student had stayed in touch through the years. Bosch spoke at Thompson's retirement party, recounting the time they were working a murder case and John Jack pulled over a bakery delivery truck when he saw it turn right at a red light without first coming to a complete stop. Bosch questioned why they were stopping their search for a murder suspect for a minor traffic infraction and John Jack said it was because he and his wife, Margaret, were having company for dinner that night and he needed to bring home a dessert. He got out of their city ride, approached the truck, and badged the driver. He told him he had just committed a two-pie traffic offense. But being a fair man, John Jack cut a deal for one cherry pie and he came back to the city car with that night's dessert.

Those kinds of stories and the legend of John Jack Thompson dimmed in the twenty years since his retirement but the gathering around his grave was thick and Bosch recognized many of the men and women he had worked with himself during his own time with an LAPD badge. He suspected that the reception at John

Jack's house after the service was going to be equally crowded and might last into the night.

After the casket was lowered and people started heading back to their cars, Bosch made his way across the lawn to where Margaret remained seated, a folded flag in her lap. She smiled at Bosch as he approached.

"Harry, you got my message," she said. "I'm glad you came."

"Wouldn't miss it," Bosch said.

He leaned down and kissed her cheek and squeezed her hand.

"He was a good man, Margaret," he said.

"He was," she said. "And you were one of his favorites. He took great pride in all of the cases you closed."

Bosch turned and looked down into the grave. John Jack's box appeared to have been made of stainless steel.

"He picked it," Margaret said. "He said it looked like a bullet."

Bosch smiled.

"I'm sorry I didn't get over to see him," he said. "Before the end."

"It's okay, Harry," she said. "You had your knee. How is it doing?"

"Better every day. I won't need this cane much longer."

"When John Jack had his knees done, he said it was a new lease on life. That was fifteen years ago."

Bosch just nodded. He thought a new lease on life was a little optimistic.

"Are you coming back to the house?" Margaret asked. "There is something there for you. From him."

Bosch looked at her.

"From him?"

"You'll see. Something I would give only to you."

Bosch saw members of the family gathered by a stretch limo in the parking lane. It looked like two generations of children.

"Can I walk you over to the limo?" Bosch asked.

"That would be nice, Harry," Margaret said.

2

Bosch had picked up a cherry pie that morning at Gelson's and that was what had made him late to the funeral. He carried it into the bungalow on Orange Grove, where John Jack and Margaret Thompson had lived for more than fifty years. He put it on the dining room table, where there were other plates and trays of food.

The house was crowded. Bosch said hellos and shook a few hands as he pushed his way through the knots of people, looking for Margaret. He found her in the kitchen, oven mitts on and getting a hot pan out of the oven. Keeping busy.

"Harry," she said. "Did you bring the pie?"

"Yes," he said. "I put it on the table."

She opened a drawer and gave Bosch a spatula and a knife.

"What were you going to give me?" Bosch asked.

"Just hold your horses," Margaret said. "First cut the pie, then go back to John Jack's office. Down the hall, on the left. It's on his desk and you can't miss it."

Bosch went into the dining room and used the knife she had given him to cut the pie into eight slices that were equal to the width of the triangular spatula. He then made his way through the people crowded in the living room to a hallway that he remembered led back to John Jack's home office. The door was closed and for some reason he knocked, even though he knew no one should be in there.

He opened the door and entered a small, cluttered office with shelves on two walls and a desk pushed up against a third under a window. Sitting on a green blotter was a blue plastic binder that was thick with three inches of documents inside.

It was a murder book.

Ballard

3

Ballard studied what she could see of the remains with an unflinching eye. The smell of kerosene mixed with burned flesh was overpowering this close, but she stood her ground. She was in charge of the scene until the fire experts arrived. The nylon tent had melted and collapsed on the victim. It tightly shrouded the body in places where the fire had not completely burned through. The body was broad-shouldered and large. She assumed the victim was a male. He seemed to be in repose and she wondered how he could have slept through it. She also knew that toxicity tests would determine his alcohol and drug levels.

Ballard knew it would not be her case but she pulled out her phone and took photos of the body and the scene, including close-ups of the overturned camping heater, the presumed source of the blaze. She then opened the temperature app on the phone and noted that the current temperature listed for Hollywood was 52 degrees. That would go in her report and be forwarded to the fire department's arson unit.

She stepped back and looked around. It was 3:15 a.m. and Cole Avenue was largely deserted, except for the homeless people who had come out of the tents and cardboard shanties that lined the side-walk running alongside the Hollywood Recreation Center. They stared both wide-eyed and addled as the investigation into the death of one of their own proceeded.

"How'd we get this?" Ballard asked.

Stan Dvorek, the patrol sergeant who had called her out, stepped over.

"FD called us," he said. "They got it from coms. Somebody driving by saw the flames and called it in as a fire."

"They get a name on the PR?" Ballard asked.

"He didn't give one. Called it in, kept driving."

"Nice."

There were two fire trucks still on scene, having made the journey just three blocks down from Station 27 to douse the tent fire. The crews were standing by to be questioned.

"I'm going to take the fire guys," Ballard said. "Why don't you have your guys talk to some of these people, see if anybody saw anything."

"Isn't that arson's job?" Dvorek asked. "They're just going to have to re-interview if we find anybody worth talking to."

"First on scene, Stan. We need to do this right."

Ballard walked away, ending the debate. Dvorek might be the patrol supervisor, but Ballard was in charge of the crime scene. Until it was determined that the fatal fire was an accident, she would treat it as a crime scene.

She walked over to the waiting firefighters and asked which of the two crews were first on scene. She then asked the six firefighters assigned to the first truck what they saw. The information she received from them was thin. The tent fire had almost burned itself out by the time the fire-rescue team was on scene. Nobody saw anyone around the blaze. No witnesses, no suspects. A fire extinguisher from the truck was used to douse the remaining flames, and the victim was determined to be dead and therefore was not transported to a hospital.

From there Ballard took a walk up and down the block, looking for cameras. The homeless encampment ran along the city park's outdoor basketball courts, where there were no security cameras. On the west side of Cole was a line of one-story warehouses inhabited by prop houses and equipment-rental houses catering to the film and television industry. Ballard saw a few cameras but on closer inspection they turned out to be either dummies or set at angles that would not be helpful to the investigation.

When she got back to the scene, she saw Dvorek conferring with two of his patrol officers. Ballard recognized them from the morning-watch roll call at Hollywood Division.

"Anything?" Ballard asked.

"About what you'd expect," Dvorek said. "'I didn't see nothin', I didn't hear nothin', I don't know nothin'.' Waste of time."

Ballard nodded.

"Had to be done, D.," she said.

"So where the fuck is arson?" Dvorek asked. "I need to get my people back out."

"Last I heard, in transit. They don't run twenty-four hours, so they had to roust a team from home."

"Jesus, we'll be waiting out here all night. Did you roll the M.E. out yet?"

"On the way. You can probably clear half your guys and yourself. Just leave one car here."

"You got it."

Dvorek went off to issue new orders to his officers. Ballard walked back to the immediate crime scene and looked at the tent that had melted over the dead man like a shroud. She was staring down at it when peripheral movement caught her eye. She looked up to see a woman and a girl climbing out of a shelter made of a blue plastic tarp tied to the fence that surrounded the basketball court. Ballard moved quickly to them and redirected them away from the body.

"Honey, you don't want to go over there," she said. "Come this way."

They walked down the sidewalk to the end of the encampment.

"What happened?" the woman asked.

Ballard studied the girl as she answered.

"Somebody got burned," she said. "Did you see anything? It happened about an hour ago."

"We were sleeping," the woman said.

The girl had still not said anything.

"Why aren't you in a shelter?" Ballard asked. "This is dangerous out here. That fire could've spread."

She looked from the mother to the daughter.

"How old are you?"

The girl had large brown eyes and brown hair and was slightly overweight. The woman stepped in front of her and answered Ballard.

"Please don't take her from me."

Ballard saw the pleading look in the woman's brown eyes.

"I'm not here to do that. I just want to make sure she's safe. You're her mother?"

"Yes. My daughter."

"What's her name?"

"Amanda—Mandy."

"How old?"

"Fourteen."

Ballard leaned down to talk to the girl. She had her eyes cast down.

"Mandy? Are you okay?"

She nodded.

"Would you want me to try to get you and your mother into a shelter for women and children? It might be better than being out here."

Mandy looked up at her mother when she answered.

"No. I want to stay here with my mother."

"I'm not going to separate you. I will take you and your mother if you want."

The girl looked up at her mother again for guidance.

"You put us in there, and they will take her away," the mother said. "I know they will."

"No, I'll stay here," the girl said.

"Okay," Ballard said. "I won't do anything, but I don't think this is where you should be. It's not safe out here for either of you."

"The shelters aren't safe either," the mother said. "People steal all your stuff."

Ballard pulled out a business card and handed it to her.

"Call me if you need anything," she said. "I work the midnight shift. I'll be around if you need me."

The mother took the card. Ballard's thoughts returned to the case. She turned and nodded toward the crime scene.

"Did you know him?" she asked.

"A little," the mother said. "He minded his own business."

"Had he been here a long time?"

"A couple months. He said he had been over at Blessed Sacrament but it was too crowded."

Ballard knew that Blessed Sacrament over on Sunset allowed the homeless to camp on the front portico. She drove by it often and knew it to be heavily crowded at night with tents and makeshift shelters.

"Did he have any trouble with anybody here?" she asked.

"Not that I saw," said the mother.

Ballard looked at Amanda to see if she had a response but was interrupted by a voice from behind.

"Detective?"

Ballard turned around. It was one of Dvorek's officers. His name was Rollins.

"What?"

"The guys from arson are here."

"Okay. I'll be right there."

MEDIA AND SOCIETY IN THE TWENTIETH CENTURY

A Historical Introduction

LYN GORMAN AND DAVID McLEAN

350 Main Street, Malden, MA 02148-5018, USA
108 Cowley Road, Oxford OX4 1JF, UK
550 Swanston Street, Carlton South, Melbourne, Victoria 3053, Australia
Kurfürstendamm 57, 10707 Berlin, Germany

First published 2003 by Blackwell Publishers Ltd, a Blackwell Publishing company

Library of Congress Cataloging-in-Publication Data

Gorman, Lyn.
Media and society in the twentieth century : a historical introduction / Lyn Gorman and David McLean.
    p.   cm.
Includes bibliographical references and index.
ISBN 0–631–22234–0 (hard : alk. paper) – ISBN 0–631–22235–9 (pbk. : alk. paper)
1. Mass Media – History – 20th century.   I. McLean, David.   II. Title.
P90 .G577 2003
302.23′09′04–dc21

                                                                        2002004242

A catalogue record for this title is available from the British Library.

Set in 10/12.5pt Photina
by Graphicraft Limited, Hong Kong
Printed and bound in the United Kingdom
by TJ International Ltd, Padstow, Cornwall

For further information on
Blackwell Publishing, visit our website:
http://www.blackwellpublishing.com

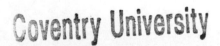

CONTENTS

ACKNOWLEDGMENTS

We would like to acknowledge the importance of our experience in developing and teaching subjects in media history to students at Charles Sturt University. Such experience provided the incentive to write this book, because no single work provided a satisfactorily comprehensive and up-to-date history of mass media.

We thank Ross McKibbin, Neville Meaney, and Therese Taylor for reading the manuscript and providing constructive criticism. We are very grateful to family, friends, and colleagues for their understanding during the writing process. Lyn Gorman would like to thank David Levine for access to a very special library; Bill Fitzwater for constructive critique of the final two chapters and some "gems" on British television history; and Caroline for the support and inspiration only a daughter can give. David McLean would like to thank Wendy, Jessica, and Simon for their patience and support.

1

INTRODUCTION

The pervasiveness of media at the beginning of the twenty-first century and the controversial question of the role of media in shaping today's world point to the need for an accurate historical perspective on media and society. Here, as in all other aspects of human experience, the benefits of historical understanding include an awareness of alternatives (a reminder "that the choices open to us are often more varied than we might have supposed" if we were to focus exclusively on the present situation); the exposure of myths – of misleading and sometimes dangerous beliefs based on a distorted view of the past; and a clear appreciation of "what is enduring and what is ephemeral in our present circumstances."[1] Discussion of the role of the media in society has too often been characterized by assumptions that present-day media arrangements are somehow natural and unavoidable, by too limited an awareness of the range of possibilities for media structure, content, and influence, and by questionable and erroneous ideas about the "lessons" of media history.

In the last two decades a burgeoning scholarly literature has provided the basis for a sound historical perspective on media and society. It is true, as Kevin Williams has observed in a fine recent survey of the history of mass communications in Britain, that the "historical development of the mass media, and how media forms and representations have changed over time, have been traditionally of less interest in the growing amount of research, writing and musing on the mass media and modern society and culture."[2] Nonetheless, there is now a substantial body of works on aspects of media history, with newspapers, the film industry, radio, television, advertising, and propaganda the subjects of first-rate works by historians and other scholars. Yet with the exception of Ken Ward's 13-year-old *Mass*

Communications and the Modern World,[3] we have lacked a survey that brings together the findings of specialized research on media history in a number of countries, attempts to make sense of developments over the whole course of the twentieth century, and provides an introduction for readers unfamiliar with the field. This book is designed to meet that need. As a successor to Ward, it draws on the considerable body of historical writing on media published since 1989, as well as providing historical perspective on the rapid and extensive developments in media and communications since the 1980s.

The book begins with the emergence of the mass press in the late nineteenth century and ends with media and globalization in the early twenty-first century. Within that broad framework it takes up various themes. These include the importance of the context – political, social, cultural, economic – in which mass media have developed and been adopted; the interaction between technological and social change; the relationships between media institutions and the state; and the interrelationships of different media. Our main focus is on the development of newspapers, film, radio, television, and the new media that arose at the end of the century; on their use for purposes of information, persuasion, and entertainment; and on their cultural and political impact. Chapters 2, 3, and 4 examine the emergence and development of the three main mass media before World War II. Chapters 5, 6, and 7 deal with the use of media for purposes of economic and political persuasion through advertising and propaganda. The post-1945 history of television and older media is the subject of chapters 8 and 9. Chapters 10, 11, and 12 are concerned with crucial late twentieth-century developments concerning the role of media in war and international relations, the rise of new media, and globalization. The study does not claim to be comprehensive. Limits on length have not allowed a fuller treatment of magazines and book publishing, or of links between media and the popular music industry, for example. We hope nonetheless that the final choice of media to be covered and themes to be pursued satisfies readers in relation to the dominant mass media and the major issues that have arisen concerning their role in society.

The study is comparative as well as historical: it is based on the firm conviction that an understanding of media and society requires not only an analysis of change over time but a comparison of the experience of different societies. Evidence is presented from a range of countries, but particular attention is given to the United States and the United Kingdom. Limitations of space partly account for this emphasis, but it is justified also by the global influence of US and British media developments and by the fact that most work in the field has concerned these two societies.

The role of the media in society has been contentious since the beginning of the mass-circulation press and the film industry in the 1890s. It is a controversy that has been evident both in popular discussion and in various theoretical approaches that have emerged. These provide a backdrop to this work. "Mass society" approaches have been especially influential. The term "mass" gained currency just as communication possibilities were expanding rapidly at the end of the nineteenth century. As Williams notes, "The history of mass communication is in one sense a history of the fear of the masses . . . [who became] increasingly visible with the growth of the media and communication industries."[4] The concept of a "mass society" created by the products of the mass media was part of the pessimistic assessment of the impact of industrialization that developed early in the twentieth century. This approach dominated critical thinking for a long time. Writers such as T. S. Eliot and F. R. Leavis drew negative conclusions about the effects of mass media. They distinguished high from low culture, considered "packaged" popular culture inferior, and deplored the undermining of individual cultural experience by media products.[5]

Members of the Marxist "Frankfurt school," including Theodor Adorno, Max Horkheimer, and Herbert Marcuse (who left Nazi Germany for the United States in the 1930s), developed another version of mass society theory in their efforts to explain why capitalism had survived. Extending Marx's theory, which he had developed before the advent of mass communications, they suggested that the mass media had encouraged the working class to be passive, thereby diminishing the likelihood of proletarian revolution to overthrow capitalism. According to this view, capitalist society maintained social control and cohesion through ideology; the culture industry reproduced the values necessary to maintain capitalist society; and the mass media made people passive recipients of the dominant ideology.

There have been other variants of this "ideological control" thesis, which depict media messages or particular media as supporting those in power and subordinating working people. Thus television is portrayed as a tool of capitalism, a means of maintaining ideological control. It gives a false view of reality, makes viewers unquestioningly accept existing social conditions; its programs reduce critical consciousness and encourage hypnotic passivity. Louis Althusser and other theorists developed these views in the 1960s, arguing that the maintenance of capitalism depended on manipulation of the ruling ideology so that workers would submit to it.

Questions about the relative importance of "mass culture," of the influences that shape the products of mass media, and of the impact of media messages – whether associated with political ideology or with the values and aspirations of consumer culture – remain very relevant. An opposing view of the media has also been influential: the idea that they are important in ensuring freedom and democratic rights, and in providing channels for popular participation. This was especially influential in relation to newspapers as they developed on a mass scale. The press was seen as "the fourth estate," playing a watchdog role as a check on government. Similar views feature in contemporary discussion of the potential of new media, such as the Internet, to offer citizens means of active participation and unrestrained access to information.

This study advocates a skeptical view of extreme conceptualizations of the role of mass media – either as means of social control, or as ensuring democratic freedoms. The emphasis here is on the need to examine the broad range of factors that influence both the particular medium and its role in society during a specific period. The corollary of this is that relations between media and society do not remain static. This is pertinent not only to discussion of new media, when technological change has facilitated rapid developments, but to the entire period studied here.

2

THE PRESS AS A MASS MEDIUM

Newspapers had existed long before the press developed as a mass medium. However, social and economic change in the late nineteenth century, together with various technological developments, led to the emergence of newspapers directed to, and attracting, a mass readership. Powerful owners emerged – the "press barons" – of whom Stanley Baldwin said, "What proprietorship of these papers is aiming at is power, and power without responsibility – the prerogative of the harlot throughout the ages."[1] The press barons were responsible for substantial changes in the economic organization of the press from the late nineteenth century into the early decades of the twentieth. Their mass-circulating newspapers also attracted attention during wartime, as vehicles for propaganda and means of sustaining national morale. Thus the history of the press in this period sheds light on some central questions regarding the role of the media in society.

This chapter concentrates on British and American experiences. In Britain "the Northcliffe revolution" of the late nineteenth and early twentieth centuries exemplified significant changes in the economic organization of the press. American experiences illustrate both the growth of a national mass press and of changes in journalism that continued to influence twentieth-century mass media.

Early Newspaper Development

The earliest predecessors of the modern newspaper appeared soon after the invention of the printing press. In the mid-fifteenth century there were forms of printed material carrying news of events. In the seventeenth century small publications called "corantoes" (news sheets) contained items of news for a given period; gazettes commented on public affairs; and newsbooks and almanacs appeared. The first daily newspaper to be published in Europe was the *Leipziger Zeitung* in 1660. During this period the term "newspaper" came into common use, denoting a publication carrying recent news and appearing regularly. The first English newspaper appeared in 1665 – the *London Gazette* – and in America *Publick Occurrences* in Boston in 1690, although it did not last beyond its first issue. The first daily newspaper in London began in 1702, the *Daily Courant*. By the mid-eighteenth century there were five daily and five weekly papers in London. These were popular in the coffee houses that developed from the mid-seventeenth century. In both the seventeenth and eighteenth centuries, when few individuals could afford to buy a newspaper, locations such as coffee houses, public houses, and barbers' shops provided access to newspapers to an increasingly literate public. Greater access was also provided by English provincial newspapers which increased in numbers from 24 in 1723 to about 50 in 1782.[2] By the late eighteenth century there were daily newspapers in America too, such as the *Pennsylvania Packet*, and the *Daily Advertiser* in Philadelphia.

None of these publications had a wide circulation, and the significance of the eighteenth-century press should not be exaggerated. While it "is probable that during the century the press became for some groups a more significant source of information and even of opinion," the English press "developed far less and was substantially less influential than is commonly believed."[3] Nonetheless, the growth of newspaper publishing attracted official attention, and governments took steps to limit the emerging press lest it become a means of spreading radical or revolutionary sentiments that might undermine established authority. In England the Stamp Act of 1712 provided that a newspaper proprietor had to pay one penny per sheet printed and one shilling for every advertisement inserted. These rates increased during the period to 1836.

In the nineteenth century social and economic change created circumstances conducive to the growth of newspapers of wider circulation. Increasing industrialization and urbanization, technological innovation, and changes in transportation and in education all had an impact. In England, for example, the Education Act of 1870, and subsequent reforms that made elementary schooling compulsory and progressively raised the school leaving age, created a wider reading public. Opportunities to read increased with the invention of the kerosene lamp. The extension of the franchise led to a growing demand for information, and the growth of cities also tended to increase demand for information in urban areas. In the 1830s and 1840s passenger trains carried London newspapers to provincial English towns; by the 1870s special newspaper trains were operating, making possible more rapid circulation of metropolitan papers in the provinces.

The establishment of international news agencies in the 1830s and 1840s – Havas in Paris, Reuter in London, Wolff in Berlin – extended news gathering internationally and provided to newspapers previously inaccessible content. These companies became increasingly important as mass-circulation newspapers developed and public demand for news increased. They themselves reflected the trends toward big business and commercialization that came to characterize the newspaper industry. News agencies also had an effect on journalism and reporting, placing greater emphasis on objectivity and on "facts" rather than opinion.

Technological developments also had an impact on nineteenth-century news gathering. In 1844 Morse transmitted the first telegraph message, thus establishing for reporters a means of transmitting news quickly. In the 1850s the first transatlantic cable was laid, also providing a new means of more rapid communication between Europe and North America, and from the 1870s telephone communication became possible. In the 1890s Guglielmo Marconi's experiments with wireless telegraphy and the transmission of radio signals laid the foundations for a worldwide radio telegraph network (see chapter 4).

Other technological changes influenced newspaper production, with advances in papermaking techniques and in printing being particularly important. Previously paper had been made mainly from rags; but from the 1850s a new process based on wood pulp was introduced, making mass production of paper simpler. Steam power was applied to the printing press, and the cylinder press was developed. The change from the pre-1850s flatbed printing press to the cylinder press meant that many more newspapers could be printed quickly. The typewriter also came into common use in newspaper offices after the 1860s, while the Linotype machine revolutionized typesetting with the use of keyboards and other typographical improvements in newspaper page composition.

Finally, the abolition of previous restrictions on the press had a considerable impact. In England the eighteenth-century imposition of duties had restricted newspaper circulation, keeping prices high enough to limit sales and acting as a disincentive to advertisers. In 1853 the advertisement duty was abolished, followed by the stamp duty in 1855 and the paper duty in 1861. (Freedom from such restrictions had been considered fundamental in America. Taxes on newspapers were resisted at the time of the American

Revolution, and the First Amendment to the Constitution, ratified in 1791, ensured freedom of the press.) The result of the removal of duties in nineteenth-century England was

> something of a revolution. Daily papers sprang up for the first time in the provinces, reducing their price to twopence, and then to one penny. In London appeared the *Daily Telegraph*, soon priced at a penny. It was aimed at "the million" and heralded in what was to become known as "the New Journalism," with its lighter style, its spirited crusades, and the absence of the former heavy emphasis on politics. By 1880 its daily sale was 250,000.[4]

Thus social and economic change had produced conditions conducive to the development of newspapers to satisfy larger literate audiences. Various technological developments made it possible for news stories to be transmitted more rapidly and for newspapers to be produced more easily and in greater numbers. Policy changes removed obstacles and disincentives to relatively cheap newspaper production. Finally, changes in economic organization were crucial to the emergence of a mass press in the late nineteenth century.

Changes in the Economic Organization of the Press

Two changes in economic organization, specific to the press industry, were crucial to the growth of newspapers that appealed to, and were accessible to, much broader audiences than earlier publications. The first was the rise of advertising – which made it possible to sustain a cheap popular press; the second was the development of newspaper and magazine chains – which produced a different pattern of newspaper ownership, led to the emergence of "press barons" at the turn of the century, and made it possible to achieve "economies of scale." These newspaper owners were less interested in elite opinion and political leaders than in reaching larger groups in society, providing content that appealed to mass audiences, who in turn would attract advertisers whose expenditure would ensure the profitability of the publishing companies.

The popular press in Britain expanded rapidly at the turn of the century. New national papers were published such as *People* in 1881, the *Daily Mail* in 1896, the *Daily Express* in 1900, and the *Daily Mirror* in 1903. Dailies, weeklies, and Sunday papers became more numerous, many aiming at a large middle market. Whereas in 1850 in Britain the number of copies per capita sold to people over the age of 14 was six, by 1920 the figure was 182; annual newspaper sales rose from 85 million in 1851 to 5,604 million in 1920.[5]

Most of these new ventures differed from previous newspaper publishing in the relative importance of commercial concerns. Earlier newspapers had been run mainly as small family businesses or by a proprietor who was also interested in writing as editor, perhaps putting forward opinions on a range of political or social issues, but generally not expecting to reach a very wide audience. In the late nineteenth century the popular press was commercialized, and newspapers became large businesses whose owners were essentially interested in making a profit.

While technological change enabled mass production of daily newspapers, increasingly this was only possible with large capital investment. Whereas it was possible to start a London daily in the 1850s with approximately £20,000 sterling, the capital required for the buildings, machinery, etc. for the *Daily Mail* in 1896 was approximately half a million pounds.[6] National newspapers became substantial enterprises with large staffs and significant capital investment and operating costs.

Nonetheless, although these costs were rising, the cost of daily newspapers to the public fell. A key factor was the growth of advertising; this was central to the development of a cheap mass-circulation press. Advertising provided the revenue without which these late-nineteenth-century newspapers, printed on a large scale, could not have continued. The rise in advertising had begun after the repeal of the advertisement duty in 1853. Increasingly, in an era of mass production and the development of surpluses of goods, it became important for manufacturers to bring their products to the attention of potential consumers. From the advertiser's point of view it became more and more attractive to advertise in newspapers as their circulation increased; the newspaper press provided an ideal means of promoting goods aimed at a popular market. Advertisers were interested in reaching not only a wide audience but also an audience with sufficient spending power to be able to respond to their advertisements by buying.

Linked with these changes were the rise of advertising agencies and the emergence of major national advertisers. Relationships of dependence developed: of manufacturers on advertising agencies to prepare attractive material to be placed in newspapers; of advertisers on the newspaper press as a means of promoting products; of newspaper proprietors on advertisers for the finance which enabled them to run their large enterprises yet at the same time reduce the price of their newspapers to the public. These developments were fostered in Britain by the practice of newspaper proprietors such as Alfred Harmsworth – who became Lord Northcliffe in 1904 – of making available statistics on circulation. With these, advertisers knew how widely their product would be promoted. Northcliffe certified circulation numbers and fixed advertising rates according to the number of readers. By 1907 advertising expenditure in Britain was of the order of 20 million pounds annually.[7]

The greater volume of advertising in newspapers was one important component of what came to be called "the Northcliffe revolution." The second significant change was the development by increasingly powerful owners of chains of newspapers (and often magazines). Northcliffe was the pioneering figure in these developments in British press history. He was the proprietor of what became the most extensive British newspaper "empire" during this period; and he and his brother Harold (who became Lord Rothermere in 1910) came to own numerous mass-circulation daily newspapers, Sunday papers, and magazines.

In the late nineteenth century Alfred Harmsworth had developed a number of small magazines for specific audiences – including *Answers, Comic Cuts, Halfpenny Marvel, Boy's Friend, Bicycling News* – and by the mid-1890s his journals were enjoying a circulation of more than 2 million. In 1894 he moved into the larger arena with his acquisition of the London *Evening News*, a paper that exemplified the new popular style of journalism of the 1890s, with concise and lively stories, simplified news reporting, greater use of illustrations and more varied typography, and a women's column to enhance the paper's appeal to a wider audience. In May 1896 Harmsworth began publication of the *Daily Mail*, a morning newspaper published in London and selling for a halfpenny.

The *Daily Mail*, "the first truly national newspaper,"[8] emphasized human interest stories, was easily read, and was intended to appeal to "the person in the street." It rapidly became popular with a mass audience, and sales exceeded those of other British newspapers. It attracted advertisers because of its mass clientele, and its proprietor encouraged this by publicizing the scale and nature of his audience. The success of the *Daily Mail* was due to Harmsworth's understanding of the interaction between circulation and advertising, linked with efficient production and distribution, plus the generally populist political outlook of the newspaper.[9] Harmsworth established overseas offices in New York and Paris, taking advantage of cable transmission to convey news rapidly; he made effective use of railway distribution so that the morning paper was widely available throughout the United Kingdom; and by the late 1890s his printing operations had expanded to more rotary presses than any other newspaper (making possible economies of scale in newspaper printing). By 1899 the *Daily Mail* had a circulation of approximately 1 million, its sales having been boosted in particular by the public appetite for news during the Boer War. In 1905 three Northcliffe publications, the *Daily Mail*, the *Evening News*, and the *Weekly Dispatch*, were incorporated as Associated Newspapers Ltd, and shares in this public company sold rapidly.

The Harmsworth brothers also invested in provincial papers and continued to publish magazines. In 1908 Northcliffe fulfilled a long-held ambition when he acquired *The Times*, a newspaper that could trace its lineage back to the 1780s. *The Times* had dominated British newspapers in the mid-nineteenth century under the "astute commercial policy and editorial flair" of John Thadeus Delane. It acquired a reputation for objectivity and independence and was referred to as "the Thunderer" for its willingness to challenge politicians and policy. Still strongly identified with the governing classes and enjoying considerable prestige, *The Times* had, nonetheless, by the early twentieth century suffered from competition from cheaper newspapers and the expanding provincial press, and from a decline in political patronage. As Ken Ward points out, when Northcliffe acquired the newspaper there was apprehension about "what he might do to a paper which was seen as a national institution;" but the fears were unjustified, and *The Times*'s importance as a voice in public affairs only grew.[10]

By the early twentieth century Northcliffe's newspaper empire was an outstanding example of the concentration of ownership – the second main feature of the immense changes constituting the Northcliffe revolution. By 1921, the year prior to his death, Lord Northcliffe controlled the *Daily Mail*, *The Times*, the *Weekly/Sunday Dispatch*, and the London *Evening News*. His brother, Lord Rothermere, controlled the *Daily Mirror*, the *Sunday Pictorial*, the *Daily Record*, the *Glasgow Evening News*, and the *Sunday Mail*. They jointly owned the magazine group, Amalgamated Press. Another brother, Sir Lester Harmsworth, had a chain of papers in southwest England. Together, the Harmsworth brothers owned newspapers with an aggregate circulation of more than 6 million.[11]

Thus by the early years of the twentieth century newspaper publishing in Britain had become a major industry, paralleling more general developments in business and industry. (Lord Northcliffe was well aware of similar developments in the United States; he met newspaper proprietors Hearst and Pulitzer there during a visit in 1900 and subsequently made numerous trips to the United States.) The press industry was an important part of the economic system because of its considerable reliance on advertising; and the concentration of ownership had brought about a change in the relationship between the London newspaper industry and the provincial press, with increasing dominance of the center over the provinces. Lord Northcliffe and his brothers had brought about substantial change in the economic organization of the press, establishing newspapers on a mass scale.

Northcliffe was also important in British media history as a "media baron" who demonstrated the power of the press. Political leaders of the time attributed considerable influence to the popular press, and they took care to court media owners. Northcliffe's biographer draws attention to the "intimate relationship between British politics and journalism during the First World War" (see below), and points out that there can be "no doubt as to the influence of Northcliffe in the calculations and policy decision of the nation's leadership."[12]

Developments in Popular Journalism and Newspaper Mass Appeal

In Britain the Northcliffe revolution accomplished the significant changes in economic organization that underpinned the emergence of the mass press. The importance of advertising as a source of revenue was linked with appeal to a predominantly middle-class readership with sufficient spending power to be attractive to advertisers. However, although Lord Northcliffe is credited with the "invention" of the mass press, in fact a popular press had flourished in America for more than fifty years before he established the *Daily Mail* in Britain in 1896.[13]

Newspaper expansion had been rapid in the United States, linked with the growth of American society. After the brief appearance of *Publick Occurrences* in 1690 a *Boston News-Letter* was published weekly from 1704 and distributed through the postal service to subscribers. Colonial newspapers developed during the eighteenth century, and the first daily, the *Pennsylvania Evening Post*, was established in 1783. The burgeoning press was guaranteed freedom in the First Amendment to the US Constitution ratified in 1791.

Early nineteenth-century American newspapers tended to support particular parties or deal with mercantile matters (shipping, business, finance); they were sold by subscription and appealed mainly to the economic and political elites. The mercantile papers began taking advertisements and expanding in size, but they had only low circulations. In the 1830s and 1840s technological change, "coupled with an emerging middle class and a skilled labor class . . . suggested the possibility of a popular newspaper which could attain large circulations with a lower price and a broader appeal than the political and mercantile papers offered." Popular cheap newspapers developed, sold for 1 or 2 cents by street vendors; in New York papers such as the *Sun* (1833), the *Herald* (1835), the *Tribune* (1841), and *Times* (1851) were founded. By about 1860 some had daily circulations of 50,000, with the New York *Herald* having probably the largest daily circulation at that time of 77,000.[14]

American newspapers and news-related organizations took advantage of the technical advances referred to previously. In the late 1840s Associated Press was established, a confederation of local and regional news-gathering organizations using the new telegraph system to disseminate a daily telegraphic news report to association members. This meant that smaller newspapers were able to afford access to reasonably comprehensive reports. (In 1851 Julius Reuter set up his London office, providing a similar news service to British newspapers.)

The public hunger for news during the American Civil War (1861–5) stimulated further development of American newspapers, particularly the northern press. Between the end of the Civil War and 1900 urbanization and rising literacy increased the demand for newspapers. As in Britain, major newspapers became big business, relying on advertising revenue and aiming for mass circulation. However, American journalism was not concentrated in one city, as in Britain. New York certainly had more newspapers than any other city, but there were flourishing newspapers in Washington, Philadelphia, Boston, Chicago, and elsewhere. These were aimed at a mass readership (rather than the essentially middle-class audiences of London and the British provincial dailies). Also significant in nineteenth-century America was the growth of the black press, reflecting the growth of urban black communities. The ethnic press also grew, reaching a numerical peak in 1917 (1,323 newspapers in various languages including German, Spanish, and Italian).[15]

While Northcliffe was a dominant figure of late nineteenth-century and early twentieth-century British newspaper history, in the United States key protagonists were Joseph Pulitzer and William Randolph Hearst. Not only did they become proprietors of large-scale press enterprises; they were also associated with styles of journalism that played an important role in the popular appeal of their newspapers.

By the 1880s Joseph Pulitzer had acquired various newspapers, including the *New York World* (a forerunner of modern tabloids). His papers exemplified the "new journalism" of the late nineteenth century. They were low-priced (and increasingly dependent on advertising for revenue) and easily read, designed to appeal to a mass audience with their popular content, appealing layout, and illustrations. Hearst became a competitor to Pulitzer in the 1890s. He had taken over the *San Francisco Examiner* from his father in 1887, in 1895 acquired the *New York Morning Journal*, and in the following year established the *Evening Journal*. His papers were associated with the style of writing and reporting referred to as "yellow journalism," characterized by sensationalist reporting and a heavy emphasis on human interest stories. He went on to establish a national chain of newspapers and periodicals (and inspired Orson Welles's 1941 film, *Citizen Kane*). Another important figure in American newspaper publishing was Adolph Ochs. He took over the *New York Times* in 1896 and over the next 20 years oversaw its growth as a leading newspaper.

In the United States the *New York Times* and in Britain *The Times* represented a type of newspaper – the broadsheet – that would remain important throughout the twentieth century, noted for their authoritativeness and comprehensive news coverage, and serving as newspapers of record. They were to be distinguished from the cheap, mass-appeal newspapers of slightly smaller format that emerged at the end of the nineteenth century and were to hold a significant place in twentieth-century newspaper history – the tabloids, designed to appeal to a broad readership, making considerable use of photographs, and relying on popular journalism or sensationalist reporting to achieve mass circulation.

It is worth noting that, alongside the mass press, magazine publishing developed in the nineteenth century, also satisfying mass audiences. Magazines had come into existence in the previous century (in England in 1709 Daniel Defoe's *Review*, in 1711 Richard Steele's *Tatler* and Steele and Joseph Addison's *Spectator*, and in America in 1741 Andrew Bradford's *American Magazine* and Benjamin Franklin's *General Magazine*). These early magazines were directed at the literate elite, with short stories and poems, essays on philosophy, religion, and natural science, and political and social commentary. In the economic and social circumstances of the nineteenth century in which mass-circulating newspapers began to emerge, magazines also flourished, offering affordable and varied content, some of them addressed to particular markets. The first women's magazine, *Godey's Lady's Book*, was published in 1830, with content on fashion, taste, manners, and household matters. There was a boom in magazine sales in the United States in the period from 1865 to 1900 for magazines such as the *Saturday Evening Post*, *Harper's* and *Atlantic Monthly*, *Collier's*, *Cosmopolitan*, and *McClure's*. These were sold cheaply, attracted large readerships, proved attractive to advertisers, and provided models for a type of publishing that would continue throughout the following century. Cheaper than books, magazines were an early popular entertainment medium. In the twentieth century they proved to be adaptable, offering a medium for innovations such as photo-journalism and in-depth personality profiles, and a means of developing content in an easily accessible form for niche markets.

The Popular Press and War

The growth of widely circulating newspapers in the context of more literate and urbanized populations raised questions about the power of the press in relation to public opinion, especially at times of national emergency. In turn the role of war correspondents became more important. The war correspondent has long been recognized in literature. Those who reported battles in classical and medieval times (for example, Xenophon, Caesar, Homer) are sometimes referred to as forerunners of the war reporters of modern times. The development of mass-circulation media was, of course, critical to any broader impact of reporting from battlefronts.

The period between ca. 1865 and the outbreak of World War I in 1914 is sometimes referred to as a "golden age" for war correspondents because of the rise of the popular press, technological developments leading to use of the telegraph, the lack of censorship, and the popularity with popular press readers of stories of wartime "adventures" abroad. One early war correspondent was William Howard Russell who wrote for *The Times* in England during the Crimean War of 1854–6. In his reports he drew attention to British bungling, to the inadequacies of the British command, and the appalling conditions in which wounded British troops suffered. Russell's "revelations about the conduct of the war, backed up by the editorials written by Delane himself [John Thadeus Delane, editor at *The Times*], aroused public opinion to such an extent that it led to the fall of the Aberdeen government in 1855,"[16] showing how damaging press revelations could be, and how political/military and media interests could diverge significantly. After the Crimean War governments tried, with varying degrees of success, to control newspapermen during war.

In other wars in the second half of the nineteenth century war reporters played roles of some significance. In the American Civil War they released information of value to the enemy. In various imperialistic wars and expeditions of the late nineteenth and early twentieth centuries war correspondents helped stimulate jingoistic and nationalistic sentiments. The Spanish–American War of the late 1890s provided an example of the manner in which mass-circulation newspapers, particularly the New York newspapers owned by Pulitzer and Hearst, could be used to influence opinion during war, encouraging nationalist and pro-war sentiments.

In 1897 these papers waged a campaign for the United States to go to war against Spain over Cuba, when Cuban nationalists staged a rebellion against Spain. For the New York press the Spanish–American War was a convenient one – it was not too close; it was relatively short (April–December 1898); it made limited demands on men and materials; and for the United States there were no defeats, no stalemates, and a relatively low casualty rate (385 dead and 1,662 wounded).

One of the main questions about the role of the newspapers in this conflict is whether their reporting did contribute substantially to American involvement. The traditional view is that powerful newspaper proprietors provoked American intervention by promoting national hysteria, and that this was an early example of media involvement in military matters. Hearst and Pulitzer certainly encouraged war; they stirred up xenophobia, publishing violently anti-Spanish stories (some apparently completely fabricated), and indulging in newspaper jingoism. Hearst is said to have sent the artist Frederick Remington to Havana to provide illustrations of the war. When Remington reported that everything was quiet and expressed a wish to return to New York, Hearst reportedly advised him, "Please remain. You furnish the pictures and I'll furnish the war."[17] The reporting by the New York papers also had a potentially widespread impact, as other regional newspapers took many stories from them.

The US Congress voted for war on April 19, 1898. However, the impact of the press should not be exaggerated, as other factors were important. The United States wanted to end Spanish and European colonialism on the American continent, and war was likely regardless of the role of Hearst or Pulitzer.[18] The question about newspaper influence might be put in another way: were the Hearst and Pulitzer papers reflecting existing national extremism and pro-war sentiment, or were they leading and shaping public opinion? The relationship between mass media and public attitudes has been a continuing theme in histories of the mass media in the twentieth century. In general it seems safe to say that views expressed in newspapers are unlikely to strike a chord in readers unless there are pre-existing dispositions or attitudes favorable to their reception.

In the history of the mass-circulation press the Spanish–American War was significant for reasons additional to proprietors' use of the medium to express bellicose and nationalist sentiments. The result of the sensationalist reporting was that circulations of New York papers increased dramatically to more than 1 million per day. The war also encouraged more extensive reporting of foreign affairs by the large American newspapers and wire services (although reporting costs were so high that proprietors failed to make a profit).[19] Through arousing interest in war reporting, the Spanish–American War set the scene for newspaper reporting of World War I. Even before active American involvement in the Great War, by 1915 there were about 500 American correspondents in Europe, and many more joined them after the United States declared war against Germany in April 1917. The public thirst for news during wartime contributed to growing demand for newspapers.

The popular press continued to thrive in the United States during and after World War I. Hearst established an "empire" comparable to that of the Harmsworths in Britain. After World War I he owned 31 newspapers, 6 magazines, and 2 wire services, as well as having interests in the film industry. In the early years of the twentieth century the American newspaper press as a whole was at a peak numerically. By 1910 there were 2,433 daily newspapers with an aggregate daily circulation of 24.2 million, and by 1918 some 2,600 dailies.[20]

At the turn of the century, reporting of the Boer War in the English press also illustrated the importance of mass media during war. New media technologies and growth of the mass press enabled reporting of this colonial war of 1899–1902 in a manner and on a scale previously not possible. The press helped create a climate of public opinion for war and was used for propagandist purposes. Stephen Badsey notes that "Another common theme which found its first expression in the Boer War was the military belief that recent changes to press behaviour, public sensibilities and media technology posed a new and dangerous threat to their ability to carry out military operations." However, he concludes cautiously:

> it is not necessary to overdraw parallels, nor to project back onto a previous age the obsessions of our own, to show beyond dispute that the role of the mass news media in the Boer War was, and was recognized at the time to be, of central importance to its conduct. The Boer War was a media war, just as much as it was a political war, or a soldier's war, or a people's war.[21]

Just over a decade later the media assumed greater significance during war, as entire populations became involved in "the Great War."

The Mass Press and Total War

The large-scale control and presentation of information became vital during World War I, when civilians, as well as the military, were critical to the conduct of "total war." The manipulation of information was directed to two main ends: first, to maintain morale among the home front population; and, second, to influence opinion in neutral and enemy countries. Censorship and propaganda were central in these efforts.

There is debate about the role of the mass press during the lead-up to war. One view is that the press created a climate of opinion favorable to war. Some of the British newspapers conducted campaigns that were anti-German, highly patriotic, and jingoistic. Some journalists encouraged militarism and promoted an unreasoning hatred of Germany, contributing to the highly charged pre-1914 international atmosphere. Northcliffe's *Daily Mail*, with its own foreign news service and wide coverage of international affairs, was anti-German and "scaremongering."[22] When Northcliffe acquired *The Times* in 1907, it is said that he left the newspaper a large degree of independence, promising no editorial interference, but with one proviso: the editor would have unrestricted control unless he should fail to warn the British people of the coming German peril. Northcliffe insisted "upon that duty being discharged."[23]

An opposing view is that the press was merely reflecting dominant views rather than leading public opinion. Moreover, even if one could prove the link between mass public opinion and the views expressed in the daily press, the relative significance of public opinion in the decision to go to war – compared with the decisions of politicians, diplomats, and military leaders – should not be exaggerated.

While the contemporary consensus is that the role of the media in the lead-up to World War I should be assessed within the broader context of politics and foreign policy-making, it is worth noting that at the time many politicians and journalists shared an exaggerated belief in the abilities of the press to shape public opinion. As a result, the mass press did wield considerable influence: wartime magnified the power of journalists, and Lord Northcliffe was influential in his campaigns on censorship, recruitment, conscription, munitions supply, war strategy, air power, propaganda, and peace terms, among other things.[24]

During World War I "the national news and propaganda media, recognized as potent war weapons, indispensable for manipulating the truth so as to sustain Home Front morale and influence neutral opinion, were . . . rigorously harnessed."[25] In Britain legislation gave the government more powers to intervene in communication. A Press Bureau was set up to monitor telegrams and dispatches in 1914, to issue to newspapers the official war news supplied by the War Office and Admiralty, and to censor war news obtained independently by the newspapers. The Defence of the Realm Act gave the government powers to limit press freedom. As the war dragged on, as the need for fighting manpower increased, and as conscription became an issue, civilian morale and active contributions to the war effort assumed greater importance. Here the popular press played a role in encouraging enlistment, carrying advertisements for munitions workers, encouraging food economy, and so on.

While the maintenance of morale at home was one important function of the press during wartime, propaganda was another. In Britain a War Propaganda Bureau was established in 1914 and placed under the general direction of the Foreign Office in 1916. While contemporary opinion considered propaganda in neutral countries to be vital to the war effort, historians debate just how much it achieved. Some say that British propaganda in the United States during the early years of the war and until US entry in 1917 stimulated sympathy for the Allied cause and broke down American isolationism. Others question its impact: appeals to informed American opinion may have reinforced pro-British sentiment, but Ward maintains that the key factor was the cutting of the telegraphic cable between Germany and the United States in August 1914.[26] This meant that war news from Europe was routed through London to the United States and was subject to censorship under the Defence of the Realm Act regulations. Thus the United States received its European war news with a British slant.

In relation to this debate it is evident that a decision to go to war is always based on many factors in a complex situation, and that any explanation that relies solely on a single reason, such as the impact of propaganda, is likely to be too simple. The United States went to war for various reasons, including unwillingness to see Britain replaced by Germany as a major power, the impact of German submarine warfare on US interests, and the evolution of opinion concerning American involvement, but not simply because of British propaganda.

Nonetheless, at the time propaganda continued to be considered important. In Britain a new Department of State, responsible directly to Prime Minister Lloyd George, was established in London to deal with propaganda in early 1917. In the following year Lord Beaverbrook, the owner of the *Daily Express* from 1917, was appointed Minister of Information. Thus a press baron was given an important wartime portfolio, with responsibility for propaganda at home and in the United States, France, and other neutral countries.

As well as propaganda directed at neutrals, propaganda directed at the enemy began to be organized more methodically when Lord Northcliffe was appointed Director of Propaganda in Enemy Countries in 1918. (His brother, Lord Rothermere, served as Secretary of State for the Air during the war.) Northcliffe too enjoyed direct access to the prime minister. He initiated a stream of propaganda, engaging in psychological warfare by leaflet. By October 1918 Britain was dropping 167,000 leaflets per day over enemy lines to spread Allied propaganda and to raise hopes among German troops of a just peace for a democratized Germany. The importance attributed at the time to such psychological warfare can be gauged by a comment in the German press in 1918: "Had we shown the same activity in our propaganda, perhaps many things would have been different now. But in this, we regret to say, we were absolutely unprepared."[27] Thus the expertise of press magnates – Lords Northcliffe, Rothermere, and Beaverbrook – and of the popular press in Britain was harnessed to the government's wartime propaganda efforts. Lloyd George appears to have had considerable faith in the power of press barons to stimulate and maintain popular support for the war effort.

Similar measures were taken in the United States: a Committee of Public Information was set up within a week of the declaration of war in 1917 to "sell the war to the American people." This was accompanied by censorship and other measures, including the Espionage Act (June 1917), the Trading with the Enemy Act (October 1917), and the Sedition Act (May 1918). The cumulative impact of such measures was considerably to restrict the freedom of US media during wartime.

In summary, during total war, when psychological warfare supplemented active military engagement, the mass press was seen as an ideal vehicle for stimulating nationalist sentiment, maintaining home front morale, attempting to win over neutrals, and spreading disenchantment among enemy soldiers. It is worth noting that journalists were largely in sympathy with government policy during the war, and there was little conflict between the mass circulation newspapers and political and military intentions: "controls were largely unnecessary, since the overwhelming patriotism and sense of duty among the media in the field resulted in total commitment to the government's war aims." More negatively, the part played by the media in total war has been described as the "beginnings of a great conspiracy," with media conscripted to the purposes of the state, and news treated as a strategic commodity.[28] Although film was not yet widely available, World

War I also saw the beginnings of its use for patriotic and propagandist purposes. In Britain *The Battle of the Somme* was shown to mass audiences, contributing to patriotic sentiment concerning the losses in the battle of 1916. In subsequent conflicts other media – radio, film, television – would be used for similar purposes.

Concentration and Competition

In the early twentieth century "the familiar modern newspaper industry structure with mass-circulation tabloids and broadsheets, populars and qualities and with chain ownership was established."[29] During the two decades after World War I there were minor rather than major changes in the mass press: first, although there was a growth in circulation, there was a contraction in the number of national dailies in both Britain and the United States; second, the trend toward concentration of ownership continued, with the interwar years described as the "era of the press barons;"[30] and, third, the commercial nature of the newspaper enterprise was confirmed, with growing dependence on a substantial proportion of revenue coming from advertising. During this period newspapers, the oldest of the mass media, began to face competition from other emerging popular media, radio broadcasting and the film industry.

The growth in newspaper circulation can be illustrated from British statistics: in 1918 the total circulation of national dailies was 3.1 million; by 1926 this had risen to 4.7 million, and by 1939 to 10.6 million. National dailies such as the *Mail*, the *Express*, and the *Daily Herald* engaged in "circulation wars," using gimmicks and the services of door-to-door salesmen to increase circulation. However, during the same period the number of newspaper titles declined, with 30 daily and Sunday newspapers in Britain ceasing publication between 1921 and 1937.[31]

Similarly in the United States, which experienced considerable population growth and urbanization between 1910 and 1930, daily newspaper circulation increased from 22.4 million copies a day in 1910 to 39.6 million copies in 1930, with Sunday newspaper circulation more than doubling in the same period. Yet there too there was a net loss of 258 daily newspapers over those 20 years.[32]

Concentration of ownership came to dominate the national publishing scene. In Britain Northcliffe's death in 1922 was followed by various changes in ownership. For the remainder of that decade and into the 1930s five main companies controlled newspaper production: Associated Press,

Amalgamated Press, Westminster Press, and the Beaverbrook and Cadbury groups. A major factor in the concentration of ownership was the cost of establishing and maintaining newspapers as large-scale industrial concerns.

What the Northcliffe revolution had begun in relation to advertising was consolidated during this period, with the press dependent on advertising revenue for a substantial proportion of income, supplemented by large circulations based on low prices. In the United States total newspaper advertising revenue tripled in the period 1915–29 from approximately $275 million to $800 million.[33] This predominantly commercial aspect of newspaper enterprises had an impact on the nature of much of the popular press, with entertainment values dominating over news and information.

Tabloids, of which early examples had been published by Hearst and Northcliffe at the end of the nineteenth century, came to enjoy great popularity in the 1920s and 1930s, finding expanding audiences among the less well educated. In New York in the 1920s, for example, three new tabloids, the *New York Daily News*, the *Daily Mirror*, and the *Daily Graphic*, circulated to more than 1.5 million readers without making any significant impact on existing daily newspaper circulation statistics. These small-format newspapers relied on sensationalist journalism (the "jazz journalism" of the 1920s) and "gossip, sin, and scandal." Their use of photographs to enhance their appeal did much to encourage photojournalism in the 1920s.[34] The bleaker environment of the Depression decade saw a decline in popularity of the tabloids. Nonetheless, this newspaper format was to retain varying degrees of popularity throughout the twentieth century.

Finally, during this period newspapers faced competition from radio broadcasting and from the emerging film industry as media of information and entertainment. In particular the press had to compete with commercial radio for advertising revenue. Twentieth-century media history would demonstrate that there was scope for diverse mass media to emerge and flourish, without extinguishing earlier forms; but there was concern in the 1920s about the likely impact of competition on the newspaper press, and in the 1930s newspapers tended to be overshadowed by radio, which was by then enjoying its "golden age."

By the beginning of the twentieth century, therefore, the main characteristics of the modern press had been established. Development over several decades of cheap, mass-circulating, advertising-supported newspapers, many in chains owned by a single proprietor, and the experience of newspaper reporting in the lead-up to, and during, war, had also raised fundamental questions about the role and influence of media in modern societies. These included the relationship between media and public opinion, the power of media to influence policy-making, the links between the press and commercial concerns, and the role of media owners whose power was seen to derive from a concentration of ownership of many media outlets. These remained important considerations in the history of mass media throughout the twentieth century and beyond.

Further reading

Black, Jeremy. *The English Press in the Eighteenth Century.* London: Croom Helm, 1987.

Boyce, George, James Curran, and Pauline Wingate (eds.). *Newspaper History from the Seventeenth Century to the Present Day.* London: Constable, 1978.

Cranfield, Geoffrey Alan. *The Press and Society: From Caxton to Northcliffe.* London: Longman, 1978.

Curran, James, and Jean Seaton. *Power Without Responsibility: The Press and Broadcasting in Britain,* 5th edn. London: Routledge, 1997.

Douglas, George H. *The Golden Age of the Newspaper.* Westport, CT: Greenwood Press, 1999.

Emery, Michael, Edwin Emery, and Nancy L. Roberts. *The Press and America: An Interpretive History of the Mass Media.* Boston, MA: Allyn and Bacon, 1996.

Morris, A. J. Anthony. *The Scaremongers: The Advocacy of War and Rearmament 1896–1914.* London: Routledge and Kegan Paul, 1984.

Nasaw, David. *The Chief: The Life of William Randolph Hearst.* Boston, MA: Houghton Mifflin, 2000.

Schwarzlose, Richard A. *Newspapers: A Reference Guide.* Westport, CT: Greenwood Press, 1987.

Thompson, J. Lee. *Northcliffe: Press Baron in Politics 1865–1922.* London: John Murray, 2000.

— *Politicians, the Press and Propaganda: Lord Northcliffe and the Great War, 1914–1919.* Kent, OH: Kent State University Press, 2000.

Ward, Ken. *Mass Communications and the Modern World.* Basingstoke: Macmillan Education, 1989.

3

THE DEVELOPMENT OF THE FILM INDUSTRY

The economic and social transformations that underlay the development of the mass press in the late nineteenth century also formed the context for the emergence of film as a mass medium. Significantly, mass-circulation newspapers and cinema began at the same time; the 1890s, the decade of "yellow journalism" in New York and the publication of the first mass-circulation daily newspaper in Britain, saw the first commercial screenings of motion pictures in a number of countries. Both film and the mass press catered to the need for cheap entertainment for the vast audiences created by urbanization. But while the reach of newspapers was confined to city, region, or nation, film crossed cultural and national boundaries and created the basis for a global mass culture with the United States at its center. "Far more people today are reached by the moving picture than by the daily press," a reporter observed in 1908, "and while we read the newspaper only in parts, the moving picture we see complete."[1] Firmly established by 1914 as the most popular medium of mass entertainment, it remained so until the late 1940s. From the outset, and continuing to the present day, film was controversial; and anxieties about its social and political influence frequently led to attempts to exert political control over the medium.

This chapter examines film's emergence as the most successful form of mass entertainment. The economics and organization of the US film industry before the 1950s, and the international ascendancy of that industry, are considered. The chapter also examines the efforts of politicians and middle-class reformers to censor and control film content, and the effects of these campaigns. Finally, the question of the ideological influence of American movies is discussed.

Origins and Early Development

Film emerged in the 1890s as the culmination of experiments and inventions which took place through the nineteenth century in the United States, France, Germany, and Britain. Techniques of projecting moving images had existed as early as the seventeenth century in such forms as popular "magic lantern" shows, involving the use of a candle or lamp, lens, and glass slides with pictures to simulate movement. The crucial new development was the projection of photographed moving images. Advances in the application of electricity, the development of photography and celluloid film, and the invention of the motion picture camera and new techniques of projection laid the foundation for the technology of film. The American inventor and entrepreneur Thomas Edison exploited some of these innovations when between 1891 and 1894 he and his assistants invented the "kinetoscope," a "peepshow" machine which ran a 50-foot loop of film past a light source, to be viewed in a piano-sized box in penny arcades. The next step, the projection of motion pictures to be seen by large audiences rather than one person at a time, was the work of a number of inventors. The brothers Auguste and Louis Lumière developed a combined camera and projector, the *cinématographe*, which they used for the first presentation of a motion picture for the general public on December 28, 1895 at the Grand Café on the Boulevard des Capucines in Paris. The *cinématographe* was a commercial success internationally. Within weeks the Lumières had taken their machinery to Britain, other parts of Europe, and the United States. Within a year the *cinématographe* had been used for public motion picture screenings in Egypt, India, Japan, and Australia.[2] Meanwhile film projectors were developed by Max and Emil Skladanowsky in Germany, Birt Acres in Britain, and Charles Frances Jenkins and Thomas Armat in the United States. Armat's invention, the vitascope, was used by Edison for the first public screening of a motion picture in the United States at Koster and Bial's Music Hall in New York on April 23, 1896.

Development of the technology of moving pictures occurred despite the absence of clear and generally accepted ideas on the purpose for which these inventions might be used. That film became above all a form of popular entertainment was the work not of scientists or inventors but of small entrepreneurs who saw its profit-making potential. Often these were disreputable characters with backgrounds in vaudeville theater, music halls, or fairs; and it was in these settings that film screenings usually took place. For ten years after 1895 films were rarely more than a minute in length; the idea of building a whole evening's entertainment around the new medium was scarcely feasible. Instead, films were normally screened during intervals on vaudeville or music hall programs, as sideshows at fairgrounds, or as features in traveling shows. The appeal of these early films lay mainly in the novelty of moving images. Their content was simple, consisting of actual footage or reenactment of scenes relating to public events – including Kaiser Wilhelm reviewing his troops, President McKinley taking the oath of office, troops marching off to war – or scenes from everyday life, typically trains arriving at stations, trains going into tunnels, and men playing cards. In many cases the early filmmakers used subjects which drew directly on the entertainment tradition of the fairground and vaudeville, especially boxing matches, slapstick comedy, cockfights, and belly dancing.

Throughout the world, film was mainly an urban phenomenon, and audiences were drawn overwhelmingly from the urban working class. Film provided these people an affordable and easily understood escape from the reality of their harsh lives. Even language was no barrier to enjoyment during the era of silent film, an observation that has particular significance for the rise of cinema in the United States. Between 1890 and 1914, 18 million immigrants entered the United States, most of them from Southern and Eastern Europe. In the formative years of the film industry, therefore, the American working class was an ethnically diverse, predominantly immigrant community, the members of which often had little grasp of English. The role of film in presenting American myths and customs to immigrant audiences demonstrated the new medium's potential as a force for cultural integration.

Between 1905 and World War I film rose above its down-market origins and established itself as a respectable form of mass entertainment, extending its appeal to middle-class audiences. This development, which would be consolidated in the 1920s, was made possible by major innovations in film production and exhibition. The first step was the simultaneous development in a number of countries of film as a medium for telling stories. Between 1896 and 1906 a French magician, Georges Méliès, made over 500 narrative films that were innovative in their use of professional actors, trick photography, animation, and detailed story lines. His pioneering work pointed to the potential of narrative film and provided a foundation for other filmmakers. In the United States Edwin S. Porter's *The Great Train Robbery* (1903) moved beyond the constraints of Méliès's fixed-camera approach, employing realistic plots, tight editing, and shots from different locations. Similar techniques were used in Britain in Cecil Hepworth's seven-minute film *Rescued by Rover* (1905). These filmmakers established film's claim to be an art form in its own right rather than a mere extension of vaudeville, the fairground, or the theater. From the mid-1900s until the late-1910s, the one-reel film of about 10–15 minutes' duration was the staple of cinema.

Important changes in exhibition accompanied the increasing sophistication of film production. In the middle of the first decade of the century the first permanent movie theaters were established; they quickly replaced the primitive means of screening films that had prevailed since the 1890s. In the United States a proliferation of cinemas began in June 1905 when a Pittsburgh vaudeville magnate, Harry Davis, converted a store for the purpose of continuous daily film screenings and, charging a nickel for admission, called it a "nickelodeon."[3] By 1910 there were 10,000 moving-picture theaters throughout the United States, and 26 million people in a population of 92 million attended the movies each week. In Western Europe, too, the conversion of stores into cinemas proceeded at a rapid rate. In Germany there were 2,446 theaters by 1914; in Britain there were nearly 4,000 with a weekly attendance of 7 to 8 million. Worldwide, there are estimated to have been 60,000 theaters by 1913.[4] Meanwhile, modern methods of distribution were introduced, replacing the system by which exhibitors bought films directly from producers. Now the producers sold or leased prints to distributors who in turn rented them to exhibitors, allowing a rapid turnover in cinema programs.

The trend towards permanent theaters for film exhibition arose from pressures from two opposite parts of the social order.[5] For the working class, including the immigrant population in the United States, cinema attendance for as little as 5 cents offered a more affordable form of entertainment than a music hall or vaudeville theater. In 1907 a writer in the *Saturday Evening Post* observed of nickelodeons that "in cosmopolitan city districts the foreigners attend in larger proportions than the English speakers," with "the Latin races" particularly prominent.[6] At the same time the movement towards permanent cinemas was an essential step in the effort to gain the new medium respectability and attract middle-class audiences. Film could be freed, to a large extent, of its early association with disreputable forms of entertainment, and film screenings could take place in better neighborhoods, away from the world of the fairground, vaudeville, and the music hall. The next step, from around 1908, was an attempt to increase film's middle class appeal by building more comfortable and sumptuous theaters, some equipped with full orchestras. The trend would culminate in the construction of ornate, luxurious "picture palaces" in the 1920s.[7]

Coinciding with these changes in exhibition and distribution, developments in filmmaking confirmed film's status as both a unique artistic form and a highly successful commercial product that could attract middle-class as well as lower-class audiences. A more sophisticated approach to narrative film paved the way. The great American director D. W. Griffith worked within the limitations of the one-reel film to bring together a number of advances in narrative technique pioneered by other American and European directors. Rapid cutting from one location to another, flashbacks, close-ups of characters' faces, fade-ins and fade-outs, shooting on location, and a more natural acting style were all part of this new "language" of film. From 1908 Griffith directed over 400 films for the Biograph company. His resignation from Biograph in 1913, in protest at the company's refusal to allow him to make longer films, was symptomatic of the growing desire of filmmakers, supported by public demand, to move beyond the one-reel format.

Two and three-reelers, and eventually feature-length films, became increasingly common. The world's first feature film, *The Story of the Kelly Gang*, of more than an hour in length, had been made by the Australian director Charles Tait in 1906. More influential internationally were a one-hour French film, *Queen Elizabeth* (1912), starring the famous actress Sarah Bernhardt, and three Italian epics: Mario Caserini's *The Last Days of Pompeii* (1913), Enrico Guazzoni's *Quo Vadis?* (1912), and Giovanni Pastrone's *Cabiria* (1914). Inspired by the success of these European features, Griffith set out to make his own epic. *Birth of a Nation* (1915), Griffith's best-known film, is the story of a southern family during the Civil War and Reconstruction periods. The film is informed by stereotypes that reflect Griffith's own southern background: it presents Ku Klux Klansmen as heroes, blacks as brutes, their white allies from the north as corrupt and rapacious. A controversial film because of its racial and political assumptions, it was also a great commercial success. Nearly three hours long, it featured on a large scale those narrative techniques that Griffith had developed in his years at Biograph. More than anyone else, as Robert Sklar has written, Griffith made these techniques "the norms of filmmaking practice and spectator expectation."[8]

By 1920 other principles of the film industry had also been established. Audiences had come to expect films to be organized into separate genres – categories or styles of film – such as comedy, melodrama, and Western. Public interest in the films themselves came to be closely associated with fascination with the lives of film stars. The star system, initiated in the United States, was carefully manufactured by film proprietors as a means of promoting their films. The stars "acted as known quantities; like brand names they guaranteed the quality of the product."[9] By as early as 1915, film stars – Mary Pickford, Douglas Fairbanks, Charlie Chaplin, Theda Bara, and William S. Hart were the most prominent – were not simply actors but public personalities. Both the stars and their films were supported by mass publicity. Meanwhile, major organizational changes had begun in the American industry that had far-reaching implications for the development of cinema internationally.

The Hollywood Studio System

In the United States the important developments in production and exhibition of the decade from 1908 coincided with intense competition in the film industry. As the profit-making potential of the medium became clear, many new production companies were established. An early attempt to create a monopoly over the industry was made in 1908 when Edison formed the Motion Picture Patents Company (MPPC) to pool patents on cameras, projectors, and celluloid film, aiming to control film production, distribution, and exhibition. The MPPC waged war against independent producers and foreign imports, but by 1915, when a federal court ordered its dissolution for violation of anti-trust laws, the company was already a spent force.

Yet the MPPC's defeat did not assure the triumph of market forces. The same pressures towards consolidation and concentration that were evident throughout the American economy, including the newspaper industry, proved irresistible. Large amounts of capital were required to exploit the new technologies. The introduction of the expensive technology of sound to American movies between 1927 and 1930 accentuated that requirement. Enormous advantages were to be gained from economies of scale and the elimination of competition. There was an inescapable logic in concentrating film production, distribution, and exhibition in the same hands: production companies wanted to guarantee distribution and exhibition of the films they made, while exhibitors needed a guaranteed supply of good films to screen.

By 1920 the more successful of the independents had laid the foundation for domination of the film industry through a cartel far more successful than the MPPC. Almost all the men who created these companies were Jews of Eastern European or German origins: Carl Laemmle, Adolph Zukor, Jesse Lasky, Samuel Goldwyn, Marcus Loew, Louis B. Mayer, William Fox, the Warner brothers (Harry, Albert, Jack, and Samuel). Most of them began their careers in film as small cinema owners, when the industry was shunned by Anglo-Americans, and they developed a keen appreciation of audience tastes.[10] These men established the principles of the "Hollywood studio system." Oligopoly (control of the market by a small number of firms) and vertical integration (the undertaking by a single firm of all stages in the process of production, distribution, and retail) were central to the success of this system. Consolidated by 1930, it prevailed through the golden age of Hollywood in the 1930s and 1940s.

The shift of film production from the east coast to southern California was part of this development. By the early 1920s most production activity was centered in or around Hollywood, on the outskirts of Los Angeles. The area offered a number of attractions: a sunny climate for outside filming, space for expansion, geographical variety – especially useful for filming Westerns – and a large pool of non-unionized labor. Yet the term "Hollywood studio" is misleading. The "studios" were in fact large corporations, with headquarters not in Hollywood but in New York. Company executives in New York decided annually on the number of films to be made and the budget for each. Moreover, these organizations depended heavily on financial support from Wall Street banks, a dependence that was increased by the large costs of converting to sound after Warner Bros. produced the first "talkie," *The Jazz Singer*, in 1927, and by additional financial pressures created by the Great Depression from 1929.

Film production was only one part of the major companies' activities; distribution and exhibition were also of central importance to the success of the eight corporations that dominated the industry in this period. The five largest, the "Big Five," were fully integrated, involved in film production, distribution, and exhibition: Paramount Pictures, 20th Century-Fox, Warner Bros., Loew's Inc. (parent company of the production subsidiary Metro-Goldwyn-Mayer), and Radio-Keith-Orpheum (RKO). Of the others – the "Little Three" – Universal and Columbia were involved in production and distribution, while United Artists, formed in 1919 by Mary Pickford, Douglas Fairbanks, Charlie Chaplin, and D. W. Griffith, played the unique role of providing a distribution network for independent producers. These eight companies accounted for the production of about three-quarters of all feature films made in the United States during the 1930s and 1940s.[11] Through collusion, these firms minimized the risk of significant competition entering the industry.

The Big Five's control of exhibition was of particular importance. Ownership of 2,600 first-run theaters in the main cities accounted for 94 percent of investment by these companies during the studio era, production a mere

5 percent.[12] Although these theaters comprised only 16 percent of the total in the United States, they consistently took in three-quarters of box office revenues.[13] For purposes of exhibition the Big Five divided the country into spheres of influence: Paramount dominated first-run theater ownership in the south, New England and the upper midwest, 20th Century-Fox controlled the far west, RKO and Loew's shared New York, New Jersey, and Ohio, and Warner Bros. controlled the mid-Atlantic states. Of the 100 feature films screened in first-run theaters each year, a Big Five company would screen 40 to 60 of its own films in the cinemas it owned and make up the rest with the best films from the other four companies. Independent exhibitors depended on the cooperation of the major firms. Through their employment on long-term contract of the biggest stars and the best producers, directors, and writers, the majors provided the films that most Americans wanted to see. Control of the first-run theaters also gave them crucial leverage: independent exhibitors were reluctant to rent films that had not had a first run, with the free advance publicity that this involved. The system of "block-booking," by which independents were obliged to rent packages of films, including the worst as well as the successful, assured the major companies of a return on every film made. Similarly, independent producers depended on the majors' willingness to distribute and exhibit their films.

Douglas Gomery, the leading economic historian of American film, has placed the film industry in the context of developments in the broader American economy. Approaches to film exhibition employed by the Big Five were derived from retailing techniques developed by the leading chain stores of the period. Large chains of theaters, with centralized management, accounting, and advertising, could spread fixed costs over a large number of operations, ensuring economies of scale. The Big Five adapted these techniques to the changing economic circumstances of the interwar period. The ornate picture palaces built during the 1920s – theaters in which film screenings were accompanied by lavish stage show presentations – gave way, with the onset of the Depression, to simpler theaters. To reduce costs further, the major firms employed fewer ushers and introduced double features as an enticement to the public. The sale of in-house refreshments, especially popcorn and soft drinks, became a significant source of revenue from the 1930s. By the 1940s the double-bill program, with an intermission for the sale of food and drink, was the norm in American movie exhibition. Along with the successful exploitation of sound technology, adaptation of the Big Five's exhibition practices to new economic circumstances assisted the American industry to survive the Depression.[14]

The International Dominance of American Film

The full measure of the success of the major American firms is that their domination of film markets extended well beyond the borders of the United States. Year after year in the interwar period, US firms produced 75–85 percent of all films shown in the world. This international phenomenon, which began in the mid-1910s, continued to have a profound effect on international cinema and mass culture for the remainder of the century. So pervasive was American influence on filmmaking styles and on public expectations of feature films that the very terms "Hollywood" and "the movies" came to be synonymous globally.[15]

American ascendancy in world cinema was established at such an early stage that it is easy to overlook the fact that it did not always exist. Before World War I, France dominated international film markets. In 1908 one French company, Pathé, sold twice as many films in the United States as all American production companies put together. By 1910 up to 70 percent of all films exported worldwide were produced in France.[16] Historians have identified a number of reasons for the success of the major American companies in overtaking the French lead in a very short period and in establishing a long-term domination of world film. The most immediate reason can be found in the effects of World War I. From the outbreak of war in August 1914 European film production was severely reduced, as personnel and resources were diverted to the war effort. With the United States remaining neutral until April 1917, American film exporters took full advantage of the war by moving into markets in South America, Australia, and Europe itself – markets previously dominated by French and Italian companies. The American majors capitalized on this advantage by opening offices in each of the main foreign markets, instead of selling through agents in London as they had done before. An effective global distribution network was established that would serve American film exporters well after the war's end in 1918.[17]

The effects of World War I and the implementation of global distribution procedures account for the American industry's international expansion from 1915 but not for its long-term ascendancy. In themselves these factors formed no insurmountable obstacle to a postwar European recovery and challenge to United States hegemony. The American companies' dominant position stemmed from important advantages over the film industries of other countries. The most fundamental was the large American domestic market. Unlike their foreign competitors, the US majors were assured of a profit from domestic exhibition. They could afford the high levels of investment necessary to make feature films of the highest quality. In smaller national markets, investment in film production was more fraught with risk.

Superior production values, made possible by lavish expenditure, largely account for the universal appeal of American film. Also the complexity of American society, with its ethnic, religious, and regional diversity, prepared Hollywood filmmakers to cater for a wide range of audiences. The ability of American movies to cross ethnic and class lines was a great advantage in world film markets. Moreover, the American studios' international ascendancy was self-reinforcing: starting in the 1920s, some of the most talented foreign film professionals, including art directors and cinematographers as well as actors and directors, were drawn to Hollywood. Greta Garbo, Marlene Dietrich, Pola Negri, Sonja Henie, Errol Flynn, Basil Rathbone, Maurice Chevalier, Charles Boyer, Charles Laughton, Joseph von Sternberg, and Erich von Stroheim were among the wave of foreign talent that helped to make Hollywood not only the center of American film production but the capital of international filmmaking. Year after year a wide range of American films – Westerns, gangster movies, comedies, melodramas, mysteries, historical dramas, horror films, adaptations of literary classics and, with the advent of sound, musicals – proved enormously popu lar throughout the world, as did the stars who featured in them. By contrast, the productions of other film industries usually enjoyed a narrower appeal. Constrained by limited budgets and characterized by inferior production values, they often dealt with pessimistic themes that undermined their popularity even with home audiences. The British documentary maker John Grierson identified the problem when he observed in 1928 that American films were optimistic in outlook and characterized by a "spirit of bubbling vigour and unchastened self-confidence," while British films were marked by a pessimism and "drabness" which "do not serve them well in the larger cinema market."[18]

Any prospect of European film industries challenging the postwar American domination of international film markets hinged on their capacity to offset the American majors' domestic advantage with exports to the United States. This had been the basis of the prewar success of French and Italian firms: by 1908 over three-quarters of leading European film producers' profits came from the American market.[19] A return to such access after 1918 proved impossible. The same oligopoly that, through its control of distribution and exhibition, placed huge obstacles in the path of independent American production companies, also ensured that few foreign films were imported. In the 1920s, with the crucial American market denied them, a group of German, French, and Swedish companies planned

"Film Europe," a cartel intended to break down national barriers to film distribution throughout Europe. By treating Europe as one market, it was hoped to offset the advantage enjoyed by the American majors through control of their large domestic market. An ambitious proposal in any circumstances, Film Europe was effectively killed by the coming of sound. Language barriers that could be ignored while films remained silent now created an insurmountable obstacle to hopes for a European equivalent of the American film market.

The American film industry's international dominance aroused widespread concern and resentment in many countries, not only from film industries threatened by American competition but from others who worried about the content and influence of Hollywood films. Concerns were frequently expressed about Hollywood's treatment of sex and violence, its unflattering depiction of particular national and racial groups, and "product placement," the use of movies to advertise American consumer products, especially cars, furniture, and clothes. These anxieties were often subsumed under a more general fear of "Americanization." An English writer, Arthur Weigall, lamented as early as 1921 that the world "is being trained to see life as it is seen by a certain group of kinema producers and writers congregated in a corner of the United States. The world is being Americanized by the photoplay."[20] In 1927 an article in the London *Daily Express* expressed similar fears and could well have spoken for many newspaper editors and politicians throughout the world: "the bulk of picturegoers are Americanized to an extent that makes them regard a British film as a foreign film . . . They talk America, think America, and dream America. We have several million people, mostly women, who, to all intent and purpose, are temporary American citizens."[21]

The American industry's business interests required it to portray its products abroad as non-ideological, to downplay their American features, and to portray them as an entertainment medium emphasizing universal themes. Throughout the interwar period, the eight majors obtained an average of 35 percent of their gross revenue from foreign trade.[22] They saw it as vital to cultivate export markets; and they sought to assuage foreign anxieties about Hollywood movies. The formation of the Motion Picture Producers and Distributors of America (MPPDA) in 1922, to protect the common interests of the eight majors, was partly prompted by an action of the Mexican government. In that year Mexico banned the import of films from American companies deemed guilty of making Westerns that featured Mexican villains, invariably depicted as violent, treacherous, and temperamental "greasers."[23] Since the whole industry stood to suffer in such cases, the MPPDA during the 1920s developed procedures for over-seeing movie content, negotiating with studios to eliminate material likely to give offence to foreign audiences. Particular attention was given to the sensitivities of crucial markets.[24] By the mid-1920s, therefore, German heroes started to appear in Hollywood films, while Russian villains replaced the sinister "Huns" who had flourished in 1918, a reflection of the relative import-ance of Germany and the Soviet Union as sources of foreign revenue for the American industry. After the Nazi regime gained power in 1933, the MPPDA continued to treat the German market with the utmost respect. Hollywood movies before World War II avoided any hint of sympathy for Jews or criticism of Hitler's Germany.[25]

During the 1920s European governments attempted to protect their film industries from American competition by imposing quotas on film imports. These measures had only limited success. To a large extent American firms were able to circumvent protectionist legislation by the production of "quota quickies" – inferior films made for the sole purpose of meeting quota requirements – through US production subsidiaries abroad. Moreover, such legislation was often built upon shaky political foundations, for exhibitors and the movie-going public tended not to share the producers' opposition to American imports. The fate of a French quota of 1929 highlighted this weakness. In response to a proposal to reduce the ratio of imported to domestically produced films to three to one, the American majors imposed a total boycott on the French market. After six months the French backed down, and an older ratio of seven to one was restored.[26]

With the limitations of protectionist legislation apparent by the end of the 1920s, the introduction of sound to film from 1927 nonetheless raised foreign hopes of ending American hegemony. European companies centering on the German consortium Tobis-Klangfilm used patents over sound systems to delay the entry of American "talkies" into European markets. While language posed no barrier to the American industry's inter-national expansion during the silent era, the introduction of sound raised the prospect that US domination might be restricted to English-speaking countries. Yet by 1931 the US majors had largely overcome the threat that sound had posed to their domination of world film markets. Satisfactory techniques of subtitling and dubbing had been developed, the sound pat-ents struggle had been resolved, and Film Europe was dead. The Holly-wood studios made such effective use of sound technology, for music and effects as much as for dialogue, that in the long term the advent of sound accentuated the superiority of the American product. The years 1927–31 were the last period in which the US industry's foreign opponents seriously entertained hopes of ending its global preeminence. In the decades that followed, American hegemony in cinema would for the most part be taken for granted as a fact of international cultural life.

Censorship and Control

International anxieties about the effects of American movies reflected a common assumption that film is a particularly persuasive medium. In this vein the Russian Bolshevik leader Leon Trotsky noted film's peculiar power as a medium "which is accessible to everyone, which is attractive, which cuts into the memory."[27] Similarly, in Britain in 1916 the National Council of Public Morals observed that films "are having a profound influence upon the mental and moral outlook of millions of our young people – an influence the more subtle in that it is subconsciously exercised."[28] Fear of film's influence being used for harmful purposes was as widely held in the United States as elsewhere. With regard to sex and crime, international and American concerns about the influence of Hollywood movies overlapped. The overwhelming dominance of the United States in world film markets ensured that American controversies about the moral content of Hollywood's products shaped the kinds of films that the rest of the world saw.

Concerns about film's moral influence are virtually as old as the medium itself. A belief in film's persuasive qualities, the fact that cinema bypassed the traditional authority sources of family, school, and church, its early image as a working-class and, in the United States, immigrant form of entertainment, and the early discovery by filmmakers and exhibitors of the great value of violence and sexual titillation in attracting audiences, all led middle-class reformers from the first years of the twentieth century to decry the harmful effects of film, especially on the behavior of children and youth. The first three decades of the century saw the adoption of more liberal attitudes to sexual behavior and the removal of much of the traditional taboo that had surrounded discussion or artistic depiction of sexual themes. Since films reflected these changing values and helped define new forms of personal and social behavior, many concluded that film was responsible for a wholesale decline in moral standards.

In some countries this reaction led to film censorship at the national level, but in the United States, Britain, and France municipal authorities implemented censorship, supplemented in America by some state government bodies. For the American and British film industries, self-regulation was an attractive alternative to such systems. The British Board of Film

Censors was set up by the industry in 1912 and issued certificates to companies that chose to submit their films for scrutiny. Although producers were not obliged to gain the Board's approval and local authorities were not prevented from imposing their own censorship standards, this approach came to be accepted not only by the industry but also by the British government and most local governments. In the United States a 1909 experiment in self-censorship by a National Board of Censorship (later the National Board of Review) proved less successful. The National Board's critics claimed that it too often erred on the side of leniency towards filmmakers. Its existence failed to stem the expansion of local and state censorship during the 1910s or demands for censorship at the federal level.

Pressures for governmental control of the movies were a response to developments during the silent era. The pre-World War I tendency of filmmakers to portray and exploit the breaking down of older moral values, especially where sex was concerned, was more fully developed in the 1920s. The leading female stars of the postwar decade – Pola Negri, Clara Bow (the "It Girl"), Gloria Swanson, and Greta Garbo – played characters who embodied the period's liberal attitudes to sexual pleasure. Among male stars, none was more popular than Rudolph Valentino and Erich von Stroheim, who exuded sexuality in their screen roles as exotic foreign lovers. The most successful director of the period, Cecil B. DeMille, based a series of comedies on the general message that consumption, fun, and sexual passion can strengthen marriage, giving his films suitably suggestive titles: *Old Wives for New* (1918), *Male and Female* (1919), *Don't Change Your Husband* (1919), *Why Change Your Wife?* (1920), *Forbidden Fruit* (1921), and *The Affairs of Anatol* (1921). He followed these with two biblical epics that afforded ample opportunity to exploit the box-office appeal of violence, orgies, and female nudity: *The Ten Commandments* (1923) and *King of Kings* (1927).

The hostility of the film industry's critics to such movies was exacerbated by Hollywood's reputation for extravagance and debauchery. Based initially on the palatial homes, conspicuous consumption, and glamorous images of the stars, such impressions were encouraged by a series of scandals in 1922. The trial of comedian Roscoe "Fatty" Arbuckle for manslaughter after the death of an actress during a wild party, the murder of a director in circumstances which implicated two actresses, the death of an actor from drug abuse, and public disapproval of Mary Pickford's divorce and quick remarriage, all highlighted to industry leaders the need to create an effective form of self-regulation if calls for federal government intervention were to be silenced.

It was chiefly for this purpose that the MPPDA was established in 1922 with Will Hays, a prominent Republican Party figure, as president. Hays introduced measures to improve the industry's public image and resist federal censorship. Lobby groups were invited to advise the MPPDA on film content, signaling the industry's apparent readiness to listen to public concerns. Producers were encouraged to submit films to the "Hays Office" for scrutiny before their release. In 1927 a set of guidelines for studios, the "Don'ts and Be Carefuls," was introduced. By 1928 the MPPDA was playing an active role in negotiating with filmmakers over synopses and scripts before films reached the production stage. Yet at the end of the 1920s state and local censors were as active as ever and pro-censorship groups still vocal. The problem lay in the lack of enforcement machinery. Studios were neither obliged to submit scripts and films for review nor, if they did so, to accept MPPDA recommendations.

The coming of sound to the movies accentuated the problem. Risqué and profane dialogue, and on-screen discussion of love affairs and criminal behavior, gave the censors and industry critics additional reasons to object to Hollywood's products. Yet sound movies, while more vulnerable to censorship than silent films, were also far more expensive to modify. This was a time, moreover, when the costs of conversion to sound, emerging competition from commercial radio, and, from 1929, the Depression placed the industry under serious economic pressure. By the end of the 1920s, therefore, it was more than ever in the industry's interest to make censor-proof movies. In 1930 the MPPDA revised its guidelines to take account of the introduction of sound, producing a formal Production Code. The Code listed in detail those subjects or forms of behavior that were forbidden (including prostitution, homosexuality, miscegenation, obscenity "in word, gesture, reference, song, joke, or by suggestion," nudity, "excessive and lustful kissing," profane language) or were to be treated carefully (including murder, bedroom scenes, and adultery). From 1931 the studios were compelled to submit scripts to the MPPDA's Studio Relations Committee (SRC) for approval before production. But provision for the studios to appeal SRC decisions to a panel of producers undermined the new Code's effectiveness. As the impact of the Depression became clear, with weekly attendances falling from an all-time high of 90 million in 1930 to 60 million in 1932, and with profits dropping sharply in 1931 and continuing to fall in 1932–3, producers explored all avenues to bring in revenue.[29]

Between 1930 and 1934, despite the Code, American filmmakers exploited even more than before the box-office appeal of sex and violence. A wave of gangster movies included the highly successful *Little Caesar* (1930),

Public Enemy (1931), and *Scarface* (1932). The former Broadway star Mae West reached the peak of her movie career in *She Done Him Wrong* (1933) and *I'm No Angel* (1933), films that abounded in ribald humor and flaunted female sexuality. Cecil B. DeMille returned to the biblical epic genre with *Sign of the Cross* (1932), a film which surpassed even his own previous efforts to cram as much violence, nudity, and salaciousness as possible into a feature film. Hollywood's two leading foreign female stars were cast as prostitutes: Marlene Dietrich in *Blonde Venus* (1932), Greta Garbo in *Anna Christie* (1930), *Susan Lennox (Her Fall and Rise)* (1931), and *As You Desire Me* (1931). Many other films dealt with adultery, promiscuity, and prostitution in ways that often proved popular but attracted the ire of Hollywood's critics.

A series of studies sponsored by the Payne Fund and based on social science research conducted between 1929 and 1933 gave ammunition to these critics. The Payne Fund studies' cautious conclusions – that movies, along with other cultural factors, did influence children's behavior – were themselves a source of concern. The distortion of those findings in Henry James Forman's alarmist bestseller *Our Movie-Made Children* (1935) lent plausibility to the view that the movie industry posed a direct threat to public morals – a threat so great that Hollywood was "subversive to the best interests of society . . . nothing less than an *agent provocateur*, a treacherous and costly enemy let loose at the public expense."[30]

In addition to renewed threats of federal government intervention and the strengthening of local and state censorship, the industry faced the growth of Catholic opposition, culminating in the formation of the Catholic Legion of Decency in 1934. More than anything else, the threat of a movie boycott by 20 million American Catholics persuaded the MPPDA to give teeth to its Code. In 1934 it replaced the SRC with a Production Code Administration (PCA) under the direction of Joseph Breen, a conservative Catholic who took as his guiding star the conviction that most moviegoers were not only young but mostly "nit-wits, dolts and imbeciles."[31] Studios were obliged to submit both scripts and completed films to Breen's office. Heavy fines, exclusion from the Big Five's theaters, and condemnation by the Legion of Decency were the penalties for release of a film without a PCA seal of approval.

From 1934 until the 1950s the Production Code, enforced by the PCA, heavily influenced the content of American films. Studios took it as axiomatic that in the movies sexual relations outside marriage were never justified and vice and crime must always be punished. Filmmakers were careful to exclude offensive language and accepted strict limits on displays of bare flesh on the screen. The sexual suggestiveness that had flourished in the movies between 1930 and 1934 became a thing of the past. Yet while film-makers often complained about these restrictions, they did retain the freedom to deal with sexual themes, though these now had to be approached obliquely. In the form of "romance," sexuality remained a staple of Holly-wood cinema.[32] Despite the impact of the Code, Hollywood continued to make films that were extremely popular among both American and foreign audiences – films that were often artistic as well as commercial successes.

Ideology and Influence

Although the censorship movement in the United States was motivated mainly by anxieties about Hollywood's treatment of sex and crime, both the scope of the MPPDA's activities and the range of community com-plaints about film content were far more varied. The SRC and PCA con-sidered objections from professions, trade associations, and other groups, each of which asserted that its image or interests had been harmed by particular films or the movies in general. Thus social workers resented their portrayal as heartless and interfering. Anthracite coal producers organized a boycott of Fox because of a comedy showing a householder's troubles with his coal furnace. A circus tent fire in one film led circus operators to threaten legal action. Businessmen in Atlantic City objected to the depic-tion of their city as "the place to take one's secretary for a week-end." The men's undershirt business complained of a drastic drop in sales after Clark Gable removed his shirt and revealed a bare chest in *It Happened One Night* (1934).[33]

The industry sought to mollify aggrieved groups and preempt organized opposition by removing potential causes of offense. In 1938 the PCA codi-fied this approach in a statement of policy on handling sensitive issues not covered by the Code. One result was that Hollywood films tended to fea-ture a utopian social background in which, as Ruth Vasey has written, "doctors, lawyers, and bank managers were motivated by altruism, and the police force pursued wrongdoers largely untroubled by graft and cor-ruption."[34] By the mid-1920s it became less common for the movies to adopt a sympathetic view of radical politics or take a pro-labor position on relations between workers and employers. If financial dependence on Wall Street bankers and the predispositions of company executives and studio bosses were not in themselves enough to ensure the triumph of conservat-ive political views, the commercial imperative of obtaining the approval of state, local, and foreign censors, supported by the MPPDA's role in the production process, reinforced the tendency.[35]

Ideological assumptions about nationality, ethnicity, and race were also embedded in Hollywood's products. Films that featured foreign villains or gave unflattering views of other countries were frequent causes of complaint from representatives of foreign governments. As products of mass culture, American movies expressed cultural stereotypes that were highly influential in the English-speaking world during the first decades of the twentieth century. Brutal and treacherous Mexicans, inscrutable and cunning "Orientals," and emotional and undisciplined Europeans, all found their way into motion pictures and all generated protests. The MPPDA worked to persuade the studios to remove offensive stereotypes, but success depended on the importance of the market in question for the distribution of particular films. Not all films were made for international distribution, and of those that were, some markets were more significant sources of revenue than others, as the contrast between Germany and the Soviet Union shows. Despite the MPPDA's efforts, cultural stereotypes remained. Moreover, even when Hollywood responded to foreign pressures by avoiding an explicit association of such stereotypes with particular national groups, the effect was not to achieve a more sophisticated view of the world but to present a universe populated by "Americans" and "foreigners," the former governed by middle-class values, the latter an undifferentiated mass characterized by their adherence to alien customs – often quaint or exotic, sometimes sinister, but always different from the American norm.[36]

In another way, too, the universe of Hollywood movies diverged from reality. While the pressures of international film distribution led the MPPDA to work to reduce the role of cultural stereotypes in the movies, the entrenched racial prejudice of US society had a very different effect where the portrayal of the American black population was concerned. The treatment of race in American movies in the interwar period is a two-part story. In these years independent black filmmakers sought to express "the colored man's viewpoint"[37] in movies that screened in black neighborhood theaters. Chronically hamstrung by limited funding, these "race movies" nonetheless included such works of artistic value as *Body and Soul* (1925), made by Oscar Micheaux, the most successful African-American director, and featuring the famous black singer and actor Paul Robeson.[38] These films gave a prominence to the depiction of black life that stood in stark contrast to the content of mainstream American cinema.

In its approach to race, as in the treatment of sex and crime, the MPPDA saw its primary task as eliminating controversial film content likely to antagonize state and local censorship boards. A policy of not offending white sentiment, including that of the segregated south, governed Hollywood's approach. In an era when the African-American population of the southern states endured a system of apartheid, when black men were frequently lynched by white mobs, and blacks throughout the United States lived in a condition of social and economic inferiority, the MPPDA steered Hollywood clear of stories and characters that seemed subversive of the status quo in race relations. In pre-World War II movies African Americans were seldom persecuted, and miscegenation did not occur. It was unusual for blacks to appear outside the traditional roles of servant, railway porter, or entertainer, and strong black characters were seldom portrayed. The "sambo" stereotype – the black as servile, childlike, and happy – was as much a part of Hollywood's universe as the Mexican bandit and the evil Chinese villain.[39]

Although, therefore, the Hollywood bosses insisted that their films were intended merely to entertain – "If you want to send a message, call Western Union," Samuel Goldwyn is reputed to have said – the movies did present a coherent worldview, based on distinctive attitudes to politics, race, ethnicity, and "Americanism." They did, in other words, send "messages." How much this mattered – to what extent audiences were influenced by these messages – is a central problem concerning film's role in society. Early twentieth-century critics saw the media as enormously powerful institutions with an unlimited capacity to shape public attitudes (see chapter 1). Even today, this view of the media as a determinant of "mass society" continues to influence popular attitudes. Yet the history of the film industry points to the limitations of such a view. Even the world's most successful film industry – the oligopoly of eight major US firms – was in one perspective merely the mirror of its society. The adoption and implementation of the Production Code, following years of controversy over the moral content of films, highlights the extent to which Hollywood was vulnerable to societal pressures. Moreover, the cultural stereotypes that abounded in American movies were not invented by Hollywood or employed for the purpose of indoctrinating the public. Rather they pre-dated the invention of film and appealed to filmmakers partly because these people were themselves products of time and place, partly because such images drew upon attitudes and beliefs that were widely shared and therefore easily appreciated by audiences. Nor should it be assumed that audiences passively absorbed on-screen messages. Continuing objections to film content from many sources, both in the United States and abroad, underline the power of moviegoers to accept or reject the ideas conveyed by films.

Yet it would be wrong to conclude that film did no more than mirror society and that anxieties concerning the medium's influence were entirely misconceived. At the very least, American films exerted a powerful influence on language, fashion, and consumer behavior. Moreover, the US industry's global dominance ensured that this influence extended to most parts of the world. Within the United States, it is true that the movies did not create prevailing attitudes towards race and class. Nor did they create the national myth of American exceptionalism – the idea that America is a unique nation, the embodiment of liberty, entrusted with a providential mission to carry the benefits of democracy to all peoples. Yet the movies' mass appeal ensured their importance in sustaining and disseminating these attitudes. By World War II film had established itself not only as the most successful medium of mass entertainment but also as a social force of fundamental significance. In the context of total war, national governments of diverse political complexions would acknowledge this phenomenon as they attempted to exploit film's potential as a medium of mass persuasion.

Further reading

Basinger, Jeanine. *American Cinema: One Hundred Years of Filmmaking*. New York: Rizzoli, 1994.

Black, Gregory D. *Hollywood Censored: Morality Codes, Catholics, and the Movies*. Cambridge: Cambridge University Press, 1994.

Cripps, Thomas. *Hollywood's High Noon: Moviemaking and Society before Television*. Baltimore, MD: Johns Hopkins University Press, 1997.

Doherty, Thomas. *Pre-Code Hollywood: Sex, Immorality, and Insurrection in American Cinema, 1930–1934*. New York: Columbia University Press, 1999.

Gomery, Douglas. *The Hollywood Studio System*. New York: St Martin's Press, 1986.

Jarvie, Ian. *Hollywood's Overseas Campaign: The North Atlantic Movie Trade, 1920–1950*. Cambridge: Cambridge University Press, 1992.

Jowett, Garth. *Film: The Democratic Art*. Boston, MA: Little, Brown, 1976.

Koszarski, Richard. *An Evening's Entertainment: The Age of the Silent Feature Picture, 1915–1928*. New York: Scribner, 1990.

May, Lary. *Screening Out the Past: The Birth of Mass Culture and the Motion Picture Industry*. Chicago, IL: University of Chicago Press, 1983.

Parkinson, David. *History of Film*. London: Thames and Hudson, 1995.

Puttnam, David. *The Undeclared War: The Struggle for Control of the World's Film Industry*. London: HarperCollins, 1997.

Rhode, Eric. *A History of the Cinema from Its Origins to 1970*. New York: Hill and Wang, 1976.

Ross, Steven J. *Working-Class Hollywood: Silent Film and the Shaping of Class in America*. Princeton, NJ: Princeton University Press, 1998.

Shindler, Colin. *Hollywood in Crisis: Cinema and American Society 1929–1939*. London: Routledge, 1996.

Sklar, Robert. *Film: An International History of the Medium*. New York: H. N. Abrams, 1993.

— *Movie-Made America: A Cultural History of American Movies*. New York: Vintage Books, 1994.

Vasey, Ruth. *The World According to Hollywood, 1918–1939*. Madison: University of Wisconsin Press, 1997.

4

THE GROWTH OF RADIO BROADCASTING

In the 1920s radio developed as a mass medium, and radio broadcasting evolved as a means of bringing entertainment into private homes. According to Herbert Hoover, the radio boom was "one of the most astounding things that [has] come under my observation of American life."[1] Like other "inventions," radio drew on a range of earlier technological developments, on the pioneering work of individuals in various countries, and in this case on enthusiastic experimentation by amateurs. The 1930s and 1940s are considered to have been radio's "golden age," when it became an integral part of the domestic environment, a key supplier of entertainment, and a trusted source of information. During these decades radio enjoyed a popularity that was only challenged by the advent of another mass entertainment medium, television, in the 1950s.

During this time institutional forms evolved in the United States and Britain – commercially based network broadcasting and public service broadcasting respectively – that provided models for the development of radio broadcasting elsewhere. A variety of program formats evolved, some drawing on earlier forms of entertainment, others developing to take advantage of the special qualities of the new medium. During this period radio's relationship with other mass media stabilized after initial suspicion, antagonism, and competition. On the eve of World War II not only was radio poised to play an important wartime role as a source of information and entertainment and as a powerful tool for propaganda, but the manner in which radio broadcasting had developed provided a basis for the development of an equally pervasive medium in the second half of the twentieth century – television.

Early Radio Development

Radio as a means of mass communication, broadcasting to sizeable audiences, developed in the 1920s, but technological developments during earlier decades, experimentation by pioneering individuals, and rather different uses of the technology formed an important background to the relatively quick take-up of radio after World War I.

Radio communication had existed for more than twenty years before radio broadcasting on a large scale began. It began as wireless telegraphy, using Morse code as a means of communication, with each letter of the alphabet represented by a series of dots and dashes signaled by electrical impulses. One of the pioneers of radio development was the Italian Gugliemo Marconi. In the 1890s he carried out experiments at his father's estate in Italy, transmitting wireless messages using Morse code. He moved to Britain in the mid-1890s and established the Marconi Wireless Telegraph Company, then in 1899 set up the Marconi Wireless Company of America. In 1901 the first transatlantic wireless signal was sent from England to Newfoundland. Marconi began to use wireless telegraphy in ship-to-ship and ship-to-shore communication (with Marconigrams), and the British Navy became interested in his work.

Across the Atlantic Lee De Forest (who claims in his autobiography that he was the "father of radio") made an important advance with the "audion," a three-electrode vacuum tube used to amplify voice transmissions. He interested the United States Navy in his work on wireless telegraphy. In 1903 the US Signal Corps became involved in experiments, in 1905 President Theodore Roosevelt used wireless on the warship *West Virginia*, and in 1908 De Forest's radiotelephone equipment was installed on ships of the North Atlantic Fleet. In the same year De Forest broadcast phonograph records from the Eiffel Tower in Paris, and two years later he was responsible for a live opera broadcast from the Metropolitan, New York, drawing attention to the entertainment potential of radio. In 1912 the sinking of the *Titanic* had some significance for wireless development, as the rescue operation was coordinated by Marconi wireless telegraphy.[2] The work of pioneers in the United States such as De Forest, Reginald Fessenden, and Frank Conrad was important in moving beyond wireless telegraphy and the transmission of information through the use of Morse code to wireless telephony and the transmission of voice and music.

During the early years of the new century enthusiastic amateurs began to focus attention on radio as a technology with potential for entertainment purposes. From about 1906 in the United States there was an amateur radio boom, with enthusiasts building their own crystal sets, locally broadcasting brief items such as weather reports, using Morse code, or making occasional or weekly broadcasts of news bulletins and music. In some instances music stores provided phonograph records in return for advertising, but this practice was stopped in 1922 when a clause in amateur radio licenses prohibited the broadcasting of "entertainments."

The outbreak of war in 1914 temporarily halted any development of radio as a source of entertainment or as a means of mass communication. (The armed services took over Marconi's American operations, and a ban was imposed on amateur radio.) However, technical progress during the war years (for example, in the production of valves) contributed to improvements in the quality of radio broadcasting in the 1920s. After the war radio became more popular. In Britain, where the Post Office had control over radio communication and issued licenses to users, the growing popularity of amateur radio was evident from the number of licenses issued: by 1921 in Britain 150 amateurs were licensed to transmit and 4,000 to receive radio broadcasts.[3]

In the postwar years commercial interests became involved in radio broadcasting. In England in 1920 the Marconi Company began transmitting speech from Chelmsford to test radio telephony. An early example of cross-media collaboration occurred in June that year when Northcliffe's *Daily Mail* sponsored a half-hour recital by opera singer Dame Nellie Melba. In the United States the Westinghouse Corporation took out licenses and began broadcasting regularly with a published weekly schedule. These early programs drew on newspaper and magazine publishers, music publishing houses, and dance orchestras in New York hotels.

By the 1920s radio had moved from being primarily a means of maritime communication to a medium capable of providing entertainment to large audiences in their homes. No longer just the concern of amateurs, it was increasingly attracting commercial attention.

Technology and Society

A key question regarding developments in radio, and indeed in any other mass medium, concerns the relationship between technological and social change. Does technology shape society or cause social change; or is the main determinant the way in which society uses technology or controls technological change?

Technological determinism is the view that technology is the agent of social change; it implies that technological change occurs autonomously. The opposing view is that social forces shape technology. For example, corporate decisions to finance research and development may have a crucial impact on technological change, or state decisions concerning the form in which a technology is to be developed may be critical.

With respect to radio development it is insufficient to focus simply on technology. Rather, the interrelation between technology and society is important. It is evident that various technological developments in the late nineteenth and early twentieth centuries were essential in enabling the transmission of messages by wireless telegraphy or telephony. However, the development of radio broadcasting as a mass medium depended on other factors as well as technological change.

For example, wireless sets had to be produced on a large scale and marketed. This became possible partly because of expertise developed during World War I, but a changing social context was also important in increasing public receptiveness of radio as a new medium. Increasing urbanization and mobility created a need for more efficient communication systems, and there was considerable emphasis on the private sphere, on the family home, as a center of social life in societies such as Britain and the United States. Thus a suitable social context existed for a medium that brought news and entertainment into the home. Context was also important for the institutional models of radio broadcasting that developed. In Britain attitudes to the role of the state, influenced by the recent experience of war, favored some state involvement, but there were also strong public service ideals. In the United States commercial concerns and support for free enterprise affected the way in which radio broadcasting developed.

Thus it is important to consider the development of radio in its broad socioeconomic–cultural context. According to Hugh G. J. Aitken, "broadcasting did not result from the inexorable unfolding of a technological imperative latent in radio technology; it burst on the scene when continuous wave radio finally found a mass market." Susan Douglas has extended the social analysis of radio broadcasting by looking at broadcasting "prehistory" between 1899 and 1922. She points not only to technological but also to social, economic, ideological, and cultural frameworks that influenced the enduring shape of American radio broadcasting, for example, the role of the business community and large corporate concentrations.[4]

Susan Smulyan, examining the commercialization of American broadcasting, argues that a range of factors influenced the choice of a particular technology to provide radio broadcasting services: "Wired networks had a deciding influence on the development of broadcast radio because network radio brought expensive charges to rent wires and thus the need for broadcasting, as well as receiver sales, to make money." Programming had to be centralized to save money and to attract advertisers who wished to appeal to a national audience. The attempt by the developing networks to attract advertisers affected the form and content of radio broadcasting and was fundamental to the American commercial broadcasting model: "Radio became a way to sell products, and most programs merely filled the time between commercials."[5]

During the early decades other socioeconomic changes were important; for example, the spread of electricity in rural areas in 1930s in the United States made feasible the purchase of radios, which became the center of family entertainment. The emergence of radio as a mass medium illustrates well the importance of contextual as well as technological factors. The institutional forms that emerged in different countries illustrate how different contexts and values shaped radio broadcasting. The contrasts between the United States and Britain exemplify the impact of specific socio-political–cultural environments on the development of this mass medium in the 1920s and 1930s.

Institutional Models

Two contrasting institutional forms of radio broadcasting emerged in the United States and Britain after World War I: commercial broadcasting and public service broadcasting (on totalitarian models of radio broadcasting see chapter 6). These provided not only models for the development of sound broadcasting elsewhere, but also frameworks for the establishment of television as a mass medium in later decades of the twentieth century.

The commercial model

The institutional arrangements for radio broadcasting that developed in the United States reflected the needs of commercial groups that saw radio broadcasting primarily as a means of profit-making.

In 1919, partly to consolidate patents needed for further development, the Radio Corporation of America (RCA) was formed, comprising the companies General Electric, Westinghouse, and American Telephone and Telegraph (AT&T). Another reason for establishing RCA was to avoid foreign control of the emerging industry via the British Marconi Company.[6]

The formation of RCA set a pattern for American radio broadcasting, one in which commercial entrepreneurs dominated, with the main stakeholders in the company being wireless equipment manufacturers and cable owners.

The Westinghouse company had been involved in developing transmission equipment and crystal sets. In 1920 it had made the first scheduled, non-experimental public radio broadcast from KDKA station in Pittsburgh, a broadcast of the US presidential election results. After this experiment the members of RCA acquired or established stations in many major cities. In 1922 AT&T withdrew from RCA and established the first advertising-supported station, WEAF in New York. The first paid radio advertisement, for property from a Long Island real estate firm, went to air on WEAF that year.

The number of broadcasting stations in the United States grew swiftly in the early 1920s. By 1922, 30 licenses to broadcast on the bandwidth designated by the Secretary of Commerce had been issued to businesses, institutions, and wealthy individuals. By the following year there were more than 550 stations, with at least one in every state. Crystal sets and early model radios, most requiring headphones, became available. Within two years of the KDKA broadcast it is estimated that there were 1.5 million radio sets in the United States.[7] There were problems as a result of this rapid expansion, as competition for limited wavelengths for broadcasting developed. This American experience had an impact in Britain, where there was a desire to avoid such chaos and impose greater regulation.

One important innovation was the use of telephone lines to broadcast across large distances. AT&T had a monopoly of US telephone lines in the early 1920s. It proposed to link selected radio stations into a network, allowing members to use the system on payment of a "toll." Station owners then let out time to sponsors who organized program content. This opened the way to creating chains or networks of stations, simultaneously broadcasting the same program. The networks became the characteristic institutions of American radio – and subsequently television – broadcasting. In addition, advertising revenue became the means of financing radio broadcasting, with a lasting impact on the content of programming.

In 1926 the first of the networks was formed, the National Broadcasting Company (NBC). Led by David Sarnoff, president of RCA, the parent company of NBC, this network began broadcasting with 24 stations. By 1931 it had expanded to 61 stations for each of its two components, the "Red" and "Blue" networks. NBC took over AT&T broadcasting facilities and used AT&T landlines.

In 1927 the US Congress established the Federal Radio Commission to regulate radio, to ensure that stations operated in the public interest and that monopolistic control was avoided. In 1934 this became the Federal Communications Commission (FCC), with powers extended to include telephone as well as radio. Ken Ward points out that the FCC was unable to interfere in the basic organization of broadcasting in the United States, network control, and that there was no real government intention of interfering in sound business practice. Smulyan demonstrates how these developments in broadcasting occurred in a society already accustomed to integrating new technologies such as the railroad, the telegraph, and telephone. Precedents such as these helped to shape the relationship between radio and the federal government, and existing forms of economic organization influenced radio development. After patent issues were resolved, private control of radio technology production and private control of broadcasting itself – seemed "normal" in the American context.[8]

A second network emerged in 1927, the Columbia Broadcasting System (CBS), initially with 47 stations but by 1931 comprising 79 affiliates.[9] The networks continued to expand throughout the 1930s, making national radio programming possible. Another was added in 1934, the Mutual Broadcasting System (MBS), which, by the mid-1940s, had more than 300 affiliate stations. In 1943 NBC, after charges of monopolistic practices, sold off the stations of its "Blue" network and these formed the American Broadcasting Company. NBC, CBS, and the ABC remained the dominant American network broadcasters for the remainder of the twentieth century.

A key aspect of the emergence of radio in the United States is the manner in which broadcasting was financed. The essential characteristic of US broadcasting was that financially the networks relied on selling time to advertisers, who made or sponsored programs. The impact of commercial sponsors on radio programming content in turn became an important issue in the interwar period (and later). As radio became an increasingly lucrative business, advertising agencies established radio departments and supplied radio programs. They took over responsibility for developing, writing, and packaging complete programs and series for sponsors, and they sold program packages to the networks as part of sponsorship arrangements.

The amounts spent on advertising increased substantially. In 1935 NBC had a net income from advertising of US$3.7 million and CBS of $3.2 million; five years later the respective figures were $5.8 million and $7.4 million. By 1944 CBS customers included 13 who bought more than $1 million of time each, and three who spent more than $4 million on advertising.[10]

The development of audience rating services in the 1930s (at a time when market research and public relations were assuming greater importance in industrialized societies) increased the power of sponsors and agencies. In the 1930s the Crossley ratings and the Hooperatings (succeeded in the late 1940s by ratings research by the A. C. Nielsen Company) provided data to prospective advertisers on listening audiences. If a program did not rate well, it was highly likely that the sponsor would withdraw and the network drop the program. Thus the commercial environment, and more specifically radio advertisers, were powerful influences in the history of American broadcasting, having considerable impact on program content (see also chapter 5).[11]

Because the networks relied financially on selling time to advertisers, the pressure to commercialization was apparently irresistible. J. Fred MacDonald supports the argument that American radio could not have escaped commercialism: "It was an instrument of electrical entertainment aimed at a commercial democracy – a world of independent, average people who preferred an occasional advertising announcement to the implications of a broadcasting system fully regulated by governmental bureaucrats."[12] Smulyan, in her detailed analysis of the commercialization of American broadcasting between 1920 and 1934, does not accept "commercial inevitability" but rather notes the range of economic, organizational, and cultural factors that shaped American broadcasting.[13] In contrast to Britain these factors included a less stratified society, the dominance of economic considerations, and greater diversity rather than a tendency to elite national cultural leadership.

In summary, the broad context in which radio broadcasting became technically possible and in which radio was adopted on a mass scale was important. The lack of agreement in the 1920s about using radio for advertising purposes (see chapter 5) indicates that there was, indeed, no "inevitability" about commercial broadcasting being the norm. Rather, factors such as the relative power of commercial interests during the early decades of radio development, the strength of American consumer culture, and public reluctance to support high levels of government intervention were important in favoring a commercial model. The different history of radio development in Britain illustrates the impact of contrasting contextual socioeconomic–political circumstances.

The public service broadcasting model

In Britain a public service broadcasting model was adopted. In the 1920s the British Post Office, responsible for such matters, authorized the Marconi Company to broadcast to wireless enthusiasts, first locally (at Chelmsford), then more widely from a London station, 2LO, in 1922. As in the United States, pressure from amateur radio enthusiasts (who in 1922 established a Radio Society of Great Britain) encouraged this decision. However, the British Postmaster General, aware of developments in the United States and fearful of chaos and congestion on the wavelengths, declined to license other wireless manufacturers to conduct broadcasts. Instead he proposed a consortium of leading manufacturers (including Marconi, Metropolitan-Vickers, Western Electric, and General Electric). This resulted in the formation of the British Broadcasting Company, which received a license from the Post Office and began transmissions in November 1922 from 2LO (London), followed by transmissions from other stations in major centers of population such as Manchester and Birmingham.

In contrast to the situation in the United States, in Britain finance for radio broadcasting came from royalties on wireless sets sold by the companies, plus part of the revenue from broadcast receiving licenses, that is a license fee.[14] Advertising revenue was not the financial basis for British broadcasting.

By October 1923 the British Broadcasting Company was operating eight stations, and about half the population could pick up a signal strong enough to operate a crystal set, with this rising to about 85 percent by 1925.[15] After some financial problems, and after investigations by the Sykes and Crawford committees in 1923 and 1925, the company became a corporation, the British Broadcasting Corporation (BBC), established on January 1, 1927 by a royal charter, effectively avoiding domination by either commercial and manufacturing interests or by government, and emerging as a national institution, promoting the national interest and culture.

The responsibilities of the BBC, as set out in its charter, were to "inform, educate and entertain." It was neither to advertise nor to editorialize. It was promised a guaranteed income from licenses, and it enjoyed editorial independence. The situation was, therefore, in marked contrast to that in the United States. In Britain the BBC had a monopoly; it was publicly funded; it was not dependent on advertising or sponsorship; and it had "public service" responsibilities under its charter. If there were any constraints on its independence, they did not come from advertisers or program sponsors but rather from parliament, where the level of license fees was determined.

There is debate about the origin of public service broadcasting concepts in Britain. Ward contrasts Britain with the United States, arguing that the development of public service broadcasting in the former showed that greater consideration was given to political and social needs. Paddy Scannell and David Cardiff put a rather different view: "Public service was a concept grafted onto an initial pragmatic set of arrangements between the Post Office and the British radio industry to establish a broadcasting service that would create a market for radio-receiving apparatuses; the definition of broadcasting as a public utility to be developed as a national service in the public interest came from the state."[16]

As in the United States, so too in Britain, a range of factors explains the adoption of this particular institutional model of radio broadcasting. The creation of the BBC, a public corporation with public funding and a monopoly over radio broadcasting, was understandable in the interwar period. World War I had led to higher levels of government intervention and centralized control. This continued to have an impact in the 1920s. "The development of the public corporation depended on the rejection of both market forces and politics in favour of efficiency and planned growth controlled by experts . . . There was a widespread dissatisfaction with the *ad hoc* nature of industrial competition." In the British context there was less support for market forces, capitalist competition, and unrestrained commercialism; there was greater support for traditions of public service; and there were many precedents for public corporations to be established under royal charter, free from both private control and direct state management.[17]

In addition to these broad influences on British broadcasting, one individual stands out for his impact on the developing character and ethos of the BBC and for his imprint on public service radio broadcasting. John Reith was appointed managing director of the British Broadcasting Company in 1922, general manager of the newly created British Broadcasting Corporation in 1926, and its director general between 1927 and 1938. Reith (knighted in 1927 to become Sir John Reith) considered that broadcasting carried with it a high moral responsibility. Rather than seeing radio as a commercial enterprise, he led the BBC during its first decade as a respectable national institution providing a public service. He believed that the BBC should lead and shape rather than follow public taste; and he stressed the educative function of the public broadcaster. Reith's approach reflected the confidence of an upper class in a stratified society, where there was support for national institutions and cultural leadership.

The public service model did not go unchallenged in the 1930s. Rather than serving British society generally (as suggested by Ward), the BBC came to be identified with the "establishment" as an authoritative institution whose programming captured state and royal events rather than catering to all social classes and conveying more comprehensive images of British society during the Depression decade.[18] Discontent with the BBC monopoly and with Reith's leadership became apparent, and pressure mounted for the BBC to be more responsive to audience demands. Reith's resignation and then the war years ushered in substantial change in BBC programming, although the public service ethos remained strong for decades thereafter.

In summary, by the 1930s two different models for radio broadcasting had emerged in the United States and Britain. Competing networks were the basis of commercial radio in the United States; they depended on income from advertising and sponsorship, and provided programming designed to appeal to mass audiences and emphasizing entertainment values. The BBC had a monopoly over radio broadcasting in Britain. This public service broadcaster was publicly funded, did not take advertising, and enjoyed considerable independence within broad charter obligations to provide news, information, and entertainment, but with considerable emphasis on educational rather than entertainment values. These models – or combinations of the two – provided frameworks for radio broadcasting in other countries, and in the second half of the twentieth century for the development of television broadcasting.

Radio Programming in the "Golden Years"

In both the United States and Britain radio spread rapidly and was taken up with enthusiasm in the interwar period. In the former, whereas access to radio in the 1920s had been confined to a few densely populated areas, by 1938 more than 90 percent of urban households and 70 percent of rural households contained at least one radio set. In Britain by the mid-1920s some 85 percent of the population was able to receive national or regional programs, and by the end of the 1930s approximately 9 million radio sets were licensed. In both countries the extension of electricity was an important factor in making possible the take-up of radio in private homes.

When radio broadcasting began, listening involved using crystal sets with headphones and was, therefore, a solitary activity. Technological change and experimentation during World War I led to developments that resulted in valve receivers with loudspeakers being available in the post-war years. This made group and family listening the most common means of enjoying radio. Development of cheap utility sets made radio more widely accessible. During the "golden years" radio listening was, therefore, most commonly a feature of the home, with radio sets as large pieces of furniture dominating living areas. During the Depression years radio fulfilled an important role in cultural and social life in both countries, as many people found themselves with hours of involuntary leisure time and a desire for escapism. Polls in the United States in the late 1930s found that radio listening was overwhelmingly preferred (over reading and movie-going, for example) as an inexpensive leisure activity.[19]

For these expanding audiences, a rich variety of radio programs was developed during the 1920s and 1930s. Some accounts of these "golden years" nostalgically celebrate particular programs and the contributions made by individual radio personalities: *The Jack Benny Program*, *Amos 'n' Andy*, *Fibber McGee and Molly*, Orson Welles's *Mercury Theater of the Air*, *The Bob Hope Show*, *The Lux Radio Theater*, among many in the United States; *Music Hall*, *In Town Tonight*, *Band Waggon*, and *The Children's Hour* were among BBC programs during this time. In the field of entertainment, early radio tended to draw on existing forms such as vaudeville and theater, broadcasting stage plays, variety shows, public lectures, and concerts, without any significant adaptation to take advantage of the features of radio as a medium. This borrowing was not without problems. For example, theater owners initially saw radio as a competitor and refused to cooperate, putting pressure on actors not to work on radio. Broadly speaking, one can contrast the greater "seriousness" of BBC programming, with its educative and informing intentions, with American programs dominated by entertainment values, exemplified by radio serials, soap opera, "sitcoms" and the like.

One type of programming that was relatively uncontroversial, and that played an important role in early radio, was music. In the 1920s the foundations were laid for an enduring relationship between radio and the music industry. Music not only became an important component of radio programs, but radio in turn had considerable impact on music, making it possible for music to be heard at a distance and by a theoretically limitless number of listeners. It became "both a unique popularizer of minority music (including classical music) and by far the most powerful means for selling records. Radio did not change music, but the role of music in contemporary life is inconceivable without it."[20]

Initially music was important partly because of a lack of other types of program, and partly because of the idea that radio programming should flow, be continuous, without breaks or silences. Music was easily incorporated into programming; it was uncontroversial; it did not have to be adapted (unlike drama, for example); it was not subject to the sorts of pressures exerted by theater owners. It also offered opportunities for mutually satisfactory arrangements in the commercial environment of early American radio. De Forest refers to the first sponsored radio program in 1916, when recordings from the Columbia Gramophone Company were broadcast.[21] Radio and music seemed to be obvious partners in the 1920s: early radio broadcasting coincided with the craze for dancing, and dance music became a very popular component of radio programs.

In the 1930s the American networks featured dance music (including "swing" and "jitterbug"); big band leaders had regular series; and a weekly program featured the top ten in record sales. In Britain the BBC's use of music was partly driven by Reith's paternalistic approach, preferring "high culture" to popular taste, and aiming to raise levels of musical appreciation among the listening public. Classical music formed an important part of British broadcasting. The BBC established its own Music Department in 1927, took over sponsorship of the Henry Wood Promenade Concerts (the "Proms"), and in 1930 established its own symphony orchestra.

However, the BBC repertoire did extend beyond classical works. Music such as comic and light opera and light orchestral works, other popular forms such as military band music, musical comedy, revue numbers, and ballads, as well as the music of popular dance bands, helped to fill BBC airtime. In the 1920s British radio reached agreements with large hotels such as the Savoy in London to broadcast dance band music directly; the success of bands such as the Savoy Orpheus led to their recording with companies such as His Master's Voice and helped to popularize this type of music. In 1928 the Corporation established its own dance orchestra.

Stephen Barnard has argued that the BBC exerted pressure as a major contractor of bands, influencing the form, content, and repertoire of dance-band music and legitimizing this type of music to the exclusion of other contemporary forms of popular music such as accordion playing and community singing.[22] In the 1930s the BBC came under pressure to broaden its programming in music and other areas. British listeners began to have access to American-style music programs when, in 1931, Radio Normandie started to operate from the north coast of France; and in 1933 Radio Luxembourg opened an unauthorized wavelength, playing light music and operating on the American model. This gave impetus to demands for the BBC to be more responsive to audience tastes.

Radio's use of music for entertainment had an immense impact on the music industry. The demand for sheet music increased as radio popularized particular songs and dances. Radio came to be a major factor in the spread of particular styles of music beyond their regional sources, including country and western music, gospel music, and jazz. Developments in recorded music led to higher quality recordings in the 1930s. During the war years, 1939–45, broadcasters increasingly relied on gramophone records as conscription limited the number of bands and musicians available, and as music came to play a large part in wartime programming as a means of bolstering morale.

In addition to music other program formats evolved during the "golden years." Sporting events became important, sports commentating for radio developed, and sport provided both a popular and relatively cheap form of content (as it would continue to do in later decades). Radio drama developed, particularly as radio's special power to stimulate the imagination came to be appreciated. The most striking example of the power of radio drama in the 1930s was the broadcast by Orson Welles of his *War of the Worlds* in 1938. Welles's "clever manipulation of the various conventions of radio was responsible for inciting a nationwide panic" that Martians had landed, as listeners mistook drama for factual reporting.[23]

In addition to music, drama, and sport, American radio programming in particular offered a rich offering of comedy and variety shows, Westerns and detective programs, soap operas (so called after the soap companies that were major sponsors of this format), and quiz shows. Radio was also used for political purposes by Presidents Harding and Coolidge in the 1920s, and by other political leaders subsequently, including President Roosevelt in the 1930s (see below).[24]

By the end of the 1930s radio was an established and popular medium. Program formats had been developed to take advantage of its particular qualities. It was also a serious competitor for the newspaper press as a source of news, and for the film industry as a source of entertainment.

Radio and Other Media

As radio developed in the 1920s, its relationship with the newspaper press and with another mass medium, the film industry, evolved. Information programming, specifically news broadcasting, illustrates one aspect of the relationship between established and emerging mass media.

In Britain in the 1920s newspaper owners were hostile toward radio, which was seen as a competitor in providing news to the public. The Newspaper Proprietors' Association attempted to prevent the broadcasting of news bulletins before 7.00 p.m. to protect newspaper sales and to prevent radio comment on public events. However, particular events helped to establish radio as a news medium. One was the General Strike of 1926 in Britain. Because of the strike very few newspapers were published, so audiences nationwide received news from the radio, showing the potential of the medium for news broadcasting. As a consequence, the BBC developed its own news service. In the following decade a particular event is noted in radio histories as highlighting the advantages of the medium in terms of immediacy and impact. In 1936 during the Crystal Palace fire the BBC reporter Richard Dimbleby gave an on-the-spot telephone report, complete with background sound of firebells and the crackle of flames. The fire occurred after the evening papers had gone to press, so timing gave radio an advantage in this instance.

In the United States newspaper interests played an important part in early radio development. Michele Hilmes cites examples of newspapers in Chicago and Detroit, for example, that used radio to advertise and enhance their profile with the public. Hilmes points to the complementarity of these media, with radio being used to draw readers to newspapers for schedules, promotions, comics, and advertising tied to popular radio features. However, by the 1930s cooperation had given way to competition, as a long-running battle developed between the newspaper press and radio over control of news distribution channels.

The economic depression of the early 1930s added to growing journalistic concerns about radio as a competing source of news, as the press began to lose advertising revenue to radio. In the United States the Biltmore Agreement of 1933 attempted to prevent the supply of news to radio by the newspaper press and wire services. Under the terms of this agreement the radio networks were to dismantle their news divisions and receive just two brief news bulletins from a Press–Radio Bureau. This was to be established after the Biltmore Conference to take wire service news bulletins from press associations and provide copy to be read over the air. News bulletins were only to be broadcast at certain times of day when they would not provide serious competition for newspapers, and news services were to be broadcast without sponsorship. However, the agreement broke down, and the Press–Radio Bureau was disbanded in 1938.

Gwenyth L. Jackaway argues that this period of "media warfare" came to an end for a number of reasons. In the mid-to-late 1930s some newspaper proprietors, rather than continuing to treat radio as a competitor, decided to take a stake in the new medium and gained an interest in radio stations. There was also increasing pressure to use sponsorship not only for entertainment programs but also for news broadcasts because they too represented a potentially lucrative source of advertising income. The agreement collapsed partly because it did not have comprehensive support from broadcasters, as some independent radio stations had not participated and were able to take news from other wire services and engage in sponsored news bulletins. Thus by about 1937 newspapers had abandoned their antagonism toward radio and accepted it as an established institution. In the late 1930s the networks reestablished their own news divisions.[25]

Between radio and the film industry mutually supportive arrangements developed in the 1930s. For example, in the United States popular radio drama programs such as *Lux Radio Theater* used Hollywood stars. The program was based on Hollywood movies, and the broadcasting site was even moved from New York to Hollywood. Thus for mass audiences new media expanded the range of information and entertainment programming available, and new and emerging media found ways of working together.

The Impact and Significance of Radio

There was relatively little serious historical study of the significance of radio as a mass medium before the 1990s. Hilmes in 1997 claimed that no other medium had been "more thoroughly forgotten by the public, historians, and media scholars alike." Television had been the subject of many studies, but radio had attracted little scholarly attention.[26] Douglas too noted that, "radio as an invention, and a cultural force, is regarded as mattering very little now in the grand scheme of things, especially in the face of cable TV, blockbuster movies, and the Internet. It is low-tech, unglamorous, and taken for granted."[27] The work of Hilmes, Douglas, and others has done much to advance historical understanding of radio broadcasting beyond earlier studies of technological changes that made radio broadcasting possible and celebratory accounts of early program genres. Recent studies have indicated the broader significance of radio by the late 1930s. This can be illustrated by reference to three areas: politics, consumerism, and national and cultural identity.

Very early radio broadcasts included political messages: the 1920 pioneering broadcast by KDKA, Pittsburgh, covered the results of the US presidential election. As national networks developed in the 1920s and 1930s political candidates could reach national rather than local audiences. The relationship between the media and politicians became increasingly important throughout the twentieth century, with the amounts of money spent on political campaigning increasing exponentially. President Franklin D. Roosevelt made effective use of radio in the 1930s with his "fireside chats." He used radio as a political instrument to win elections, silence opponents, and sell his domestic and foreign policy measures to the American public, including the New Deal agenda at home and anti-isolationist messages concerning American involvement abroad.[28]

The development of radio as a commercial mass medium in the United States was also intertwined with expanding consumerism in the twentieth century. Advertising and sponsorship provided the financial basis of American radio broadcasting, and audiences received "free-to-air" services as a result. Advertisers reached huge national markets by way of the broadcasting networks. The fact that the institutional framework developed for American radio also applied to television in the second half of the twentieth century meant that broadcasting was an extraordinarily powerful tool for commercial and corporate interests, with the audience as potential consumers. Douglas claims that radio hastened "the shift away from identifying oneself – and one's social solidarity with others – on the basis of location and family ties, to identifying oneself on the basis of consumer and taste preferences."[29] The increasing importance of commercialism has been a recurring theme in the history of mass media in the twentieth century and beyond (see chapter 5).

Finally, radio exercised a powerful influence socially and culturally at the national level and for particular groups. Douglas, writing of the American context, states:

> Radio played a pivotal role, especially in the first half of the century, in helping us imagine ourselves and our relationships to other Americans differently. It constructed imagined communities . . . and thus cultivated both a sense of nationhood and a validation of subcultures . . . Radio did indeed . . . bring the country together . . . [and] the radio networks cemented New York City's role as the cultural capital of the nation.[30]

Similar arguments could be made for the role of radio in other national settings. Historians have highlighted the role of radio in catering to specific audiences such as women, for example in daytime programs including the popular serials and soap opera that developed in the 1930s.[31] Radio has also been important at the local level in fostering and sustaining community identity; community radio has retained widespread popularity even as new media have emerged.

In addition to these areas – politics, consumerism, national and cultural identity – Douglas notes more generally:

> Radio is arguably the most important electronic invention of the century. Cognitively, it revolutionized the perceptual habits of the nation. Technically, culturally, and economically, it set the stage for television. It forever blurred the boundaries between the private domestic sphere and public,

commercial, and political life. It made listening to music a daily requirement for millions of Americans. For the entire span of the twentieth century, listening to radio – first introduced to America as "wireless telegraphy" in 1899 – has been a major cultural pastime. Even with the advent of television, which was supposed to make radio obsolete, radio has remained a thriving cultural and political force.[32]

By the late 1930s radio had revolutionized home entertainment, introducing to the domestic environment a hitherto unknown variety of entertainments. A mutually beneficial relationship between radio and music had been established that would continue for decades, and previously unimagined audiences had access to whatever styles of music broadcasters chose to include in their programming. Arrangements for commercial broadcasting – and the role of advertisers and sponsors – provided easy access to vast markets of listeners as consumers. The existence of national networks had made possible an "intimacy" between political leaders and electorates impossible in previous periods. As a source of information, radio offered an immediacy and scope in terms of audience reach unmatched by any other medium at that time. World War II would enhance the reputation of radio as a source of information and entertainment.

Further reading

Aitken, Hugh G. J. *The Continuous Wave: Technology and American Radio, 1900–1932*. Princeton, NJ: Princeton University Press, 1985.

Barfield, Ray E. *Listening to Radio, 1920–1950*. Westport, CT: Praeger, 1996.

Barnard, Stephen. *On the Radio: Music Radio in Britain*. Milton Keynes: Open University Press, 1989.

Barnouw, Erik. *A History of Broadcasting in the United States*, 3 vols. New York: Oxford University Press, 1966–70.

Briggs, Asa. *The BBC: The First Fifty Years*. Oxford: Oxford University Press, 1985.

— *The History of Broadcasting in the United Kingdom*, 4 vols. Oxford: Oxford University Press, 1961–79.

Brown, Robert J. *Manipulating the Ether: The Power of Broadcast Radio in Thirties America*. Jefferson, NC: McFarland, 1998.

De Forest, Lee. *Father of Radio: The Autobiography of Lee de Forest*. Chicago, IL: Wilcox and Follett, 1950.

Douglas, Susan J. *Inventing American Broadcasting, 1899–1922*. Baltimore, MD: Johns Hopkins University Press, 1987.

— *Listening In: Radio and the American Imagination*. New York: Random House, 1999.

Geddes, Keith, with Gordon Bussey. *The Setmakers: A History of the Radio and Television Industry.* London: British Radio and Electronic Equipment Manufacturers' Association, 1991.

Hilmes, Michele. *Radio Voices: American Broadcasting, 1922–1952.* Minneapolis: University of Minnesota Press, 1997.

Jackaway, Gwenyth L. *Media at War: Radio's Challenge to the Newspapers, 1924–1939.* Westport, CT: Praeger, 1995.

MacDonald, J. Fred. *Don't Touch That Dial: Radio Programming in American Life, 1920–1960.* Chicago, IL: Nelson Hall, 1982.

Scannell, Paddy, and David Cardiff. *A Social History of British Broadcasting. Vol. 1, 1922–1939, Serving the Nation.* Oxford: Blackwell, 1991.

Shingler, Martin, and Cindy Wieringa. *On Air: Methods and Meanings of Radio.* London: Hodder, 1998.

Smulyan, Susan. *Selling Radio: The Commercialization of American Broadcasting 1920–1934.* Washington, DC: Smithsonian Institution Press, 1994.

Ward, Ken. *Mass Communications and the Modern World.* Basingstoke: Macmillan Education, 1989.

5

THE RISE OF ADVERTISING

"When the historian of the Twentieth Century shall have finished his narrative, and comes searching for the sub-title which shall best express the spirit of the period," commented *Printer's Ink* in May 1915, "we think it not at all unlikely that he may select 'The Age of Advertising' for the purpose."[1] Those developments in media and society that were the cause of such observations are the subject of this chapter. It examines the emergence of modern advertising from the late nineteenth century. Changes in the techniques and content of advertising after World War I, including the application of "psychology" and use of the new medium of radio, are then considered. Finally, the chapter discusses the question of advertising's influence, giving particular attention to the problem of advertising's role in the creation of consumer culture and its effects on consumer behavior.

The Origins and Development of Advertising

Modern advertising is a product of the late nineteenth century; its origins are to be found in broader changes in the economy and communication that occurred at that time. A response to the Industrial Revolution, advertising's early development was inextricably linked to that of the mass-circulation press. Its chief characteristics are best understood by looking at forms of advertising that existed before the late nineteenth century. British and American newspapers had published paid advertisements since the seventeenth century, but these were mostly short, closely printed factual notices of the kind now called "classified" advertising. Some of these early advertisements had a persuasive element, especially in the case of patent medicines. As early as 1758 Samuel Johnson complained of the exaggerated claims of advertisers: "Advertisements are now so numerous that they are very negligently perused, and it is therefore become necessary to gain attention by magnificence of promises and by eloquence sometimes sublime and sometimes pathetick. Promise, large promise, is the soul of an advertisement."[2] Yet most advertisements in this period were intended simply to inform potential customers of the availability of goods and services. This remained the case for newspaper and magazine advertising well into the second half of the nineteenth century. Display advertising – non-classified advertisements with a visual appeal – became increasingly common from mid-century, but in outdoor forms: posters, billboards, sandwich boards, and eventually advertisements on streetcars, buses and trains, and electric signs. Display advertising at first lacked respectability, being associated with circuses and sellers of patent medicines, men whose reputation was akin to that of used car salesmen in later years. Usually, therefore, the reputable press shunned this kind of advertising.

The situation changed in the last two decades of the nineteenth century. In these years, throughout the West, the press was transformed, with the emergence of mass-circulation newspapers and magazines supported by advertising revenue (see chapter 2). In these publications small factual notices gave way to larger advertisements – incorporating large print, pictures, even color – to the point where full-page advertisements became common. Such a fundamental change in the physical appearance of advertisements reflected a major shift in intention: the main purpose of advertising was now to persuade buyers, rather than simply provide information.

The readiness of the press at the end of the nineteenth century to embrace forms of advertising once regarded as disreputable arose from major changes in economic life. Department stores, which began in the United States and Europe in the 1860s and 1870s, expanded their operations in the following two decades and advertised extensively in newspapers.[3] In the same period large national manufacturing companies emerged and began to advertise directly to the public. Previously consumer goods had been in chronic short supply; there had therefore been a ready market for such goods. A vast increase in productivity, made possible by the mechanization of manufacturing, fundamentally altered older patterns of production and distribution. Periods of depression between the mid-1870s and mid-1890s highlighted the new problem of overproduction, which industrialists began to define as one of underconsumption. To minimize their risks, they sought to control the market, partly by advertising to ensure demand for their products.[4]

Some of the goods advertised in this way were new inventions, such as bicycles, typewriters, sewing machines, and photographic film and equipment. Advertising was also used extensively where there was little difference between the products of different manufacturers. This was true of soaps, breakfast cereals, beverages, cigarettes, and electric light bulbs. Not surprisingly, manufacturers of such products figured prominently in the ranks of advertisers at the turn of the century: Pear's, Ivory, Sapolio, Colgate-Palmolive, Kellogg, Quaker Oats, Bovril, Nestlé, Cadbury, American Tobacco Company, General Electric. Where competing products were more or less identical, distinctions had to be planted in the minds of consumers by advertisements that said little about the products' intrinsic merits. In the 1880s brand names started to be used for this purpose. Brand name advertising aimed to persuade the public to regard a particular brand as synonymous with quality, even to regard the brand as synonymous with the product. Slogans or catch-phrases served the same purpose. "Good morning! Have you used Pears' Soap?," Ivory soap's "It floats," and National Biscuit's "Lest you forget, we say it yet, Uneeda Biscuit," provide early examples of how effective slogans could be in creating popular awareness of a particular product which, to all intents and purposes, differed little from the products of the manufacturer's competitors.[5]

The transformation of the purpose and content of advertising brought with it the emergence of a modern advertising industry. The period 1890–1914 saw the development of fully-fledged advertising agencies, which employed specialist copywriters and designed and prepared advertisements rather than simply buying space in the press as earlier agencies had done. Advertising campaigns were introduced, involving the careful coordination of newspaper and magazine advertisements with outdoor advertising and storefront displays. Advertising overcame much of its previous lack of respectability and was increasingly seen as an attractive profession for ambitious young men and women.[6] The total annual volume of advertising in the United States grew rapidly from an estimated $682 million in 1914 to $1,409 million in 1919 and $2,987 million in 1929.[7]

The rise of advertising was closely intertwined with the development of consumer culture. In the United States between the 1880s and the 1920s the vast expansion in consumer goods and their greater affordability, along with a steady reduction in working hours and the increased availability of inexpensive entertainments, transformed attitudes to consumption and leisure. The rapid growth of the film industry was one aspect of this development; increased expenditure on a wide variety of consumer products was another. The decade from 1919 saw a huge growth in Americans' ownership of cars, radios, telephones, washing machines, vacuum cleaners, refrigerators, silk stockings, and other goods.[8] In this context a traditional emphasis on the virtues of self-denial, frugality, and hard work was increasingly challenged by a preoccupation with acquisition, material comfort, individual indulgence, and pleasure as the way to happiness. The term "consumer culture" refers to this new set of values and beliefs. (The terms "consumerism," "consumer society," and "consumption ethic" are also used by writers on the subject.) The advertising industry that expanded so quickly from the last two decades of the nineteenth century aimed on one level to persuade the public to purchase the goods that industry was now capable of producing in vast numbers. On another level its aims were more ambitious, involving no less than the overturning of traditional values of self-denial and simplicity and the promotion of consumption as a way of life.

This important historical development was not as straightforward as has sometimes been claimed. In recent years historians have shown that the origins of consumer culture can be found well before the 1880s. Even by the eighteenth century, in Britain and the North American colonies, a fondness for commercially marketed clothing, furniture, and other consumer goods was widespread among the middle classes and even those below them in the social order. Yet even in the 1920s, despite the general prosperity of the decade, many Americans remained too poor to take advantage of the expansion of consumer products, while others, even among the affluent, resisted the values of consumer culture. The final triumph of these values in the United States occurred only after World War II. Nonetheless, there can be no doubt that the 40 years from 1880 saw a major change in American patterns of consumption, and that in these years a shift towards the values of consumerism, although incomplete, also took place.[9] These changes were most fully developed in the United States; similar trends would occur in other countries at different stages of the twentieth century. The relationship between the emergence of consumer culture and the growth of mass advertising is a central historical problem.

The Techniques and Content of Advertising

Just as significant as the rapid expansion of advertising after World War I were changes in advertising techniques. In these years "psychological advertising" was fully developed, inspired by wartime propaganda and by the influence of behavioral psychology, with its claims to hold the key to the manipulation of human desires. The rise of the mass media seemed to confirm the lessons of psychology: advertisers looked to the popular appeal of movies, tabloid newspapers, and confessional magazines as evidence that consumers were best reached through emotional appeals rather than reason.[10] In the 1920s the main trends in twentieth-century advertising were firmly established. Advertisements, especially in the United States, increasingly focused on the consumer rather than the product. They moved beyond prewar reliance on brand names, slogans, and catch-phrases as methods of persuasion and aimed to convince consumers that health, social success, sex appeal, and marital happiness would result from the use of Ipana toothpaste, Palmolive soap, Chesterfield cigarettes, and countless other mass-produced goods. The advertiser took on the role of the consumer's friend, confidant, or adviser. Many advertisements invoked the advice of fictional or real-life "experts" on medical matters, home economics, child rearing, interpersonal relations, interior decoration, and dress sense. Consumers were encouraged to distrust their own inexpert judgment and to welcome the advertiser's assistance in dealing both with sources of discontent inherent in the human condition – illness, loneliness, frustration – and with many other causes of unhappiness identified by the advertising industry, including wrinkled skin, body odor, dandruff, "halitosis" (bad breath), "intestinal fatigue" (constipation), and "homotosis" (poor home furnishings). Central to this approach was the aim to create a perpetually insecure, dissatisfied consumer, anxious about status and personal well-being and ready to embrace consumption as the solution to life's problems.[11]

These approaches were first developed in the traditional advertising media of magazines and newspapers. From the late 1920s American advertisers increasingly supplemented their use of the printed press by exploiting the new medium of radio. They did so after initial hesitation. In its early years radio was viewed as a dignified, culturally uplifting medium, presenting a stark contrast to the downmarket appeal of the movies and tabloid press – a perception that stemmed largely from the affluence of radio's initial audience. Even the leaders of the advertising industry shared Secretary of Commerce Herbert Hoover's belief in 1922 that it was inconceivable that "we should allow so great a possibility for service, for news, for entertainment, for education, and for vital commercial purposes, to be drowned in advertising chatter, or used for commercial purposes." Advertisers feared that the intrusion of commercial messages into such a lofty medium would breed audience resentment towards all kinds of advertising.[12]

But radio's advantages as a vehicle for persuasion proved irresistible, all the more so when the medium gained nationwide coverage with the creation of broadcasting networks (see chapter 4). In 1928 the American

Tobacco Company drew attention to this potential when it increased sales of Lucky Strike cigarettes by 47 percent in two months after a radio advertising campaign.[13] With growing concerns that the public was becoming saturated with advertisements, and with fears of overproduction that came to a head with the beginning of the Depression in 1929, radio provided a new way to try to grab the consumer's attention. Its advantages included intrusiveness: the radio listener, unlike the magazine reader, could not easily ignore advertisements. More than print advertising, radio allowed the commercial to be blended easily with entertainment. Product names could easily be interwoven into the plots of radio drama and comedy programs or mentioned in passing in musical variety shows. Dramatized commercials – commercials in the form of brief mini-dramas, of the kind now familiar from television – also appeared. By the 1930s, as the radio audience expanded, advertisers revised their earlier view of listeners' elevated tastes and discarded many of their reservations about the medium's suitability for salesmanship. Radio advertising became more direct, hard-hitting, and ubiquitous. Radio "personalities" – whether announcers, comedians, or singers – took on the combined roles of showman and salesman, their effectiveness accentuated by the ability to seem to speak personally to each listener. Radio advertising was now so closely integrated with entertainment that the newly created radio departments of advertising agencies scripted and produced both the commercials and the shows.[14]

American advertisers were attracted to radio partly because they were persuaded of its value as a means to reach women through daytime programs. They had long been convinced, correctly, that consumers were overwhelmingly female.[15] Advertisements designed for a mainly female audience highlight advertisers' adeptness in exploiting social change. In an era of major advance in women's rights – women gained the vote in the United States in 1920 – advertising portrayed consumption as the expression of female freedom and autonomy and as the path to fulfillment. Through their purchasing decisions and loyalty to the brands of their choice, women were told, they would exercise their sovereign rights. Through the purchase of new home appliances they would be freed from the slavery of domestic labor. Cigarette advertisements portrayed these products as symbols of female emancipation.[16]

Advertisements often combined an emphasis on progress with appeals to traditional values of domesticity. Thus a widely distributed General Electric advertisement of 1925 presented an image of a mother reading to her two children, accompanied by a text which explained that electrification had freed mothers to do more important things than housework. It was, the advertisement insisted, a mother's duty to delegate to electricity as much household labor as possible: "Human lives are in her keeping, their future is molded by her hands and heart. No lesser duties should interfere with the supreme duty of having plenty of time with the children."[17] In American advertisements generally in the interwar period the "modern" woman remained above all a homemaker. The chief benefit of the vast array of consumer goods now available, advertisements suggested, was that they would assist women to become "better wives and mothers." A woman's "duty" was to make full use of advertised products to run the household efficiently and stay beautiful.[18]

The treatment of women's role in society is a good example of ideological messages conveyed through advertising. Another concerns questions of social class. American advertising of the 1920s and 1930s, in marked contrast to European advertising, appealed to middle-class values and aspirations.[19] To reach as large an audience as possible, American advertising obscured class differences and portrayed an affluent, classless society. Advertisements conveyed a clear message, reflected in such catch-phrases as "any woman can" and "every home can afford": those who purchased the advertised product, regardless of occupation or means, would assert their equality in a middle-class world through possession of the same products as the very rich. A young housewife's inability to afford a $780-a-year maid like her neighbor, Ivory Soap declared in a typical advertisement of the kind, could not deny her the possession of "nice hands" by using Ivory.[20] Class resentment and proposals to redistribute wealth were to be frowned on, since "equality," it was asserted, already existed in the form of a general availability of inexpensive consumer goods. In the advertisements of the 1920s, therefore, could be seen the beginnings of an idea that reached its peak in the 1950s: America as a middle-class consumer society.[21] Outside the United States, too, the identification of ordinary people as "consumers" rather than "citizens" became increasingly common in the four decades after 1920.[22]

The Influence of Advertising

In the depiction of women as subservient to men and of US society as classless, advertisements presented as self-evident and permanent what were in reality historically conditioned and questionable assumptions. The effects on cultural values and attitudes of such portrayals of social relations represent one of the most important forms of advertising's influence. As in the case of cultural stereotypes in the movies, the ideological messages conveyed by advertisements reinforced prevailing views on social roles and helped to perpetuate forms of behavior favored by dominant groups.

Also important was the far-reaching influence that advertising exerted throughout the twentieth century by virtue of its central role in the economics of the media. By 1900 advertising provided the bulk of revenue for newspapers and magazines. By 1930 it provided almost 100 percent of the revenue for radio in the United States; this would later be the case also for television. The importance of these facts of economic life is difficult to overstate: in a fundamental way the print media and commercial broadcasting shaped their content with a view to maximizing advertising revenue, usually by seeking mass appeal. At the very least, the result was media content that differed markedly from that of public service and government-controlled media systems. Viewed optimistically, advertising's dominant role generated programs and publications that responded to popular taste and were free of political interference. Yet in some respects the results were clearly deleterious, although often in ways that involved sins of omission rather than commission. Above all, media dependence on advertising has threatened freedom of expression, by fostering reluctance on the part of media firms to publish articles or broadcast programs seen as likely to offend some members of the audience and therefore deter advertisers, and by encouraging an unwillingness to criticize companies with advertising money to spend. Significantly, for many years *Reader's Digest* was the only mainstream American publication to campaign against the tobacco industry on the basis of steadily mounting evidence of the lethal consequences of smoking. As the one popular magazine that did not accept advertising, *Reader's Digest* was not deterred by fear of losing revenue from cigarette advertising.[23]

Equally contentious is the question of advertising's influence on consumer behavior. The advertisers of the 1920s and conservative critics of "mass society" had in common a belief in the passive nature of the mass audience. The public, they assumed, was easily manipulated by advertising, as it was by movies and other forms of mass culture.[24] The apparent success of advertising campaigns was taken as proof that the public accepted at face value the emotional appeals of advertisements. Particularly instructive, it was thought, was the Lambert Company's marketing of Listerine antiseptic. After 1920 Listerine achieved a spectacular increase in sales, apparently as a result of a series of advertisements that persuaded the public to discover a new need: to use a mouthwash to combat "halitosis." Lambert capitalized on this success by inventing other uses for the same product: a cure for dandruff, an after-shave lotion, a cure for colds and sore throats, and a deodorant. The Listerine advertisements, which included such famous lines as "She was often a bridesmaid but never a bride" and "Even your best friend won't tell you," were models of the new advertising approach with its association of the product with love, social success, and happiness.[25]

After World War II the same assumptions about the power of advertising formed the basis of a liberal critique of the institution. Especially influential in the 1950s and 1960s, and most clearly stated by the historian David M. Potter and the economist John Kenneth Galbraith, this view maintained that the industry had been central to the creation of consumer culture in the early twentieth century. It lamented the allegedly powerful influence of advertising in the United States (and, by implication, in other Western countries). So convinced was Potter of the all-important role of advertising in building a consumer culture that he identified it as one of those institutions which wields immense influence in American society, comparable in this respect to the church, the education system, and business. Unlike these other institutions, however, Potter maintained that "advertising has in its dynamics no motivation to seek the improvement of the individual or to impart qualities of social usefulness, unless conformity to material values may be so characterized."[26] In particular, liberal critics condemned two aspects of advertising's economic role. First, they argued that advertising raises the prices of products – because manufacturers need to recoup the costs of advertising – and that it works against rational consumer choice and the efficient use of resources. Consumers, they maintained, choose products not on the basis of quality and price, as should be the case in an efficient economy, but because of the persuasiveness or manipulative influence of advertisements. Second, these critics accused advertising of creating "false needs," of persuading consumers that they need products which, in any objective view of things, they do not.

Marxist writers, notably the social philosopher Herbert Marcuse, also made the distinction between real and false needs.[27] Like the liberal critics, Marxists emphasized the powerful and manipulative nature of advertising. For the Marxists advertising was essential to the survival of capitalism. Without advertising, they argued, the problem of overproduction would have led to a state of permanent depression, causing the collapse of the capitalist system. Marxist critics also argued that advertising has functioned as a mechanism for control of the working class by the capitalist ruling class. By instilling in the masses a preoccupation with the illusory attractions of consumption, advertising was intended to turn workers' minds away from the exploitative nature of capitalism and the oppressive conditions in which they live and work, and in this way to protect the capitalist system from working-class unrest and revolution.[28]

Since the 1960s the liberal and Marxist critiques have been increasingly questioned by other scholars, who have argued that advertising is not as powerful as previous writers had believed, that advertising did not create consumer culture, and that the influence of advertising can only be understood by examining its interaction with other developments. An appraisal of advertising's role in the history of the twentieth century must take these recent perspectives into account.

That advertising undermines efficiency by often rewarding persuasiveness, at the expense of price and quality, is undeniable. On the other side of the ledger, advertising may well contribute to economies of scale. In the final analysis the long-standing debate as to whether advertising's overall economic impact is harmful or beneficial probably cannot be resolved. By contrast, the view that advertising affects brand choice is largely uncontested. As early as the 1880s the successful campaigns of major soap manufacturers demonstrated that advertisements could indeed persuade consumers to purchase a particular brand rather than another brand or a generic (and equally effective) product. In the early twentieth century the history of the cigarette reinforced the point: the success of the R. J. Reynolds brand Camel, the American Tobacco Company's Lucky Strike brand, and Liggett and Myers's Chesterfield in the 1920s owed much to effective advertising.[29] The history of advertising provides many such examples of the impact of advertising campaigns on brand choice.

Whether advertising's influence extends to the primary demand for products – whether many people buy, say, cigarettes at all only because of advertising – is a more controversial question. Although the Listerine campaigns of the 1920s suggest that in that period at least advertising may well have had the power to persuade consumers to purchase products which otherwise they would not have considered, the case of cigarette marketing highlights the complexity of the issue. Between 1910 and 1930 cigarette sales in the United States increased tenfold. The increase coincided with heavy investment in advertising by the major tobacco firms, leading many observers at the time and since to conclude that advertising had caused the jump in sales. But it is more likely that the growth in cigarette retailing resulted from the interaction of advertising with social and cultural changes, assisted by the production of milder forms of cigarette than those available before World War I. The war encouraged many young men to take up smoking as a means of relief from the horrors and tedium of warfare. After the war the cigarette was linked to the movement towards greater social and civic equality for women: cigarettes became a cheap and convenient symbol of equality. Michael Schudson points out that tens of thousands of women began smoking in the 1920s before any cigarette advertisements were directed specifically at women. He concludes that it would be "more accurate to observe that cigarette smoking among women led tobacco companies to advertise toward the female market than to suggest that advertising created the market in the first place." For Schudson, the example of cigarette advertising illustrates a broader truth: "That advertising has played a role since the late 1920s in promoting smoking among women should not blind us to the fact that this change in consumption patterns, like many others, had roots deep in cultural change and political conflict that advertising often responds to but rarely creates."[30]

Other evidence supports the suggestion that cigarettes had an appeal independent of the influence of advertising. While American advertisers made far-reaching claims for their ability to manipulate human emotions, their normal practice was first to determine who was likely to buy the product and then tailor an advertising campaign accordingly. At the outset they excluded from their calculations between 30 and 65 percent of the population; this was the range of estimates of those who were not sufficiently well-off to achieve consumer status. Invariably, before the late 1940s, the potential market was viewed as affluent, white, and of north and west European origins. Blacks and other ethnic minorities never appeared in advertisements as consumers – as opposed to servants and menial workers – because these groups were not seen as part of the market. By targeting those who were viewed as predisposed to buy, advertisers implicitly recognized the limitations of manipulation.[31]

A predisposition to purchase consumer goods was often based on the intrinsic merits of those products. Whatever the role of advertising in increasing sales of electrical appliances, it was also the case that, as David E. Nye reminds us, "Electric stoves were far cleaner than coal and wood stoves; electric washing machines eliminated a backbreaking chore; electric irons made ironing faster and cooler work in the summer."[32] Many low-priced, packaged goods – soaps, breakfast cereals, biscuits, canned food, and similar products – offered the advantage of convenience. Yet in other cases – cosmetics and such multipurpose products as Listerine are good examples – the utility of consumer goods was questionable. In such cases the suspicion arises that sales depended on the success of advertising in manipulating the emotions of the audience. The issue of advertising as the creator of "false needs" therefore arises.

Here, too, recent scholarship has questioned one of the central ideas of older critiques of advertising. Where Potter, Galbraith, and Marcuse assumed that there is a useful distinction between "real" needs, which can somehow be determined objectively, and false needs, artificially whipped up by advertising or some other social influence, subsequent writers have emphasized the difficulty of establishing objective, generally accepted criteria which might be used to determine which needs are "real" and which "false," which products are necessary and which not. Beyond the most basic biological requirements, they argue, all human needs are socially constructed: the needs of people in one society differ from those in another. To show that a particular need has been stimulated by advertising is therefore not to demonstrate that it is false; it simply shows that advertising has contributed to a redefinition of needs.[33]

These insights do not amount to an apologia for advertising. Thus Schudson, one of the leading critics of older interpretations, nonetheless regards advertising as "the art form of bad faith," claiming that "it features messages that both its creators and its audience know to be false and it honors values they know to be empty." Whether it sells products or not, it "often promotes bad values."[34] But Schudson argues that advertising's liberal and Marxist critics, in emphasizing its central role in the creation of consumer culture and in the stimulation of "false needs," have underestimated the complexity of the historical process. Both advertising and consumer culture, he suggests, had their origins in changes in the market in the late nineteenth century. It was not a matter of advertising causing consumer culture; rather, both developments were part of a more fundamental social transformation. Seen in this light, advertising "is but one factor among many in shaping consumer choice and human values."[35] Such conclusions are consistent with those of recent scholarship on the history of the press, film, and radio, replacing earlier assumptions about the all-powerful impact of media content on public attitudes and values with a more complex picture – one which emphasizes the need to understand media influence as the product of interaction with broader cultural factors.

Further reading

Fox, Stephen. *The Mirror Makers: A History of American Advertising and Its Creators.* New York: Vintage, 1985.

Lears, Jackson. *Fables of Abundance: A Cultural History of Advertising in America.* New York: Basic Books, 1994.

Leiss, William, Stephen Kline, and Sut Jhally. *Social Communication in Advertising: Persons, Products, and Images of Well-Being.* Toronto: Methuen, 1986.

Marchand, Roland. *Advertising the American Dream: Making Way for Modernity, 1920–1940.* Berkeley: University of California Press, 1985.

Nye, David E. *Image Worlds: Corporate Identities at General Electric, 1890–1930.* Cambridge, MA: MIT Press, 1985.

Pope, Daniel. *The Making of Modern Advertising.* New York: Basic Books, 1983.

Potter, David M. "The Institution of Abundance: Advertising," in *People of Plenty: Economic Abundance and the American Character.* Chicago, IL: University of Chicago Press, 1954 (pp. 166–88).

Schudson, Michael. *Advertising, The Uneasy Persuasion: Its Dubious Impact on American Society.* London: Routledge, 1993.

Smulyan, Susan. *Selling Radio: The Commercialization of American Broadcasting 1920–1934.* Washington, DC: Smithsonian Institution Press, 1994.

Williams, Raymond. "Advertising: The Magic System," in *Problems in Materialism and Culture: Selected Essays.* London: Verso, 1980 (pp. 170–95).

6

PROPAGANDA IN PEACE AND WAR

The word "propaganda" was originally used with a religious connection. In the seventeenth century Pope Gregory XV established the Sacred Congregation for the Propagation of the Faith ("de Propaganda Fide"), a body with a missionary role. In subsequent centuries the word was used to describe not only religious proselytizing but also the dissemination of political beliefs. The development of media of mass communication from the end of the nineteenth century provided new and vastly expanded channels for propagandists. As demonstrated in chapter 2, World War I showed how modern media could be used on a large scale for propagandist purposes. Governments in the belligerent countries used the media to bolster patriotic and nationalist sentiment, to sustain morale at home, and to wage psychological warfare against the enemy.

In the twentieth century the exploitation of media for political purposes became commonplace. Totalitarian states such as the Soviet Union and Nazi Germany provided striking examples, but propaganda was by no means absent from democratic societies. A major difference in official approaches to use of propaganda was willingness as opposed to reluctance to "label" activities aimed at persuading or influencing the minds and political behavior of others. In Germany in the 1930s, for example, the Nazis viewed propaganda in a very positive light and made no effort to disguise the fact that it was to be employed as a tool of the regime. When Hitler came to power in 1933, he established a Ministry for Popular Enlightenment and Propaganda. By contrast, in the democracies during the same period and subsequently there was reluctance to admit to the use of propagandist activities and these tended to be described as "information," "education," or, rather more aggressively, "psychological warfare."

Whatever terms proved most acceptable in specific political contexts, propaganda does involve an effort to persuade, to manipulate opinion. Therefore, it is likely to be most effective if people do not have access to multiple sources of information and if they are discouraged from thinking critically. Michael Balfour has suggested that the "best touchstone for distinguishing propaganda from science is whether a plurality of sources of information and of interpretations is being discouraged or fostered." David Welch has noted that, although propaganda is often seen as the art of persuasion, more often than not it reinforces existing trends and beliefs. Furthermore, according to a common view of propaganda, it appeals to irrational instincts; but Welch notes that, to be effective, propaganda must also appeal to rational elements.[1] Most importantly in relation to modern media, historians have pointed to the importance of technological developments for twentieth-century propagandists. Jacques Ellul in the 1960s drew attention to propaganda as a sociological phenomenon in technological societies, stressing the importance of mass media in the psychological manipulation characteristic of propaganda. Garth S. Jowett and Victoria O'Donnell defined propaganda as "the deliberate and systematic attempt to shape perceptions, manipulate cognitions, and direct behavior to achieve a response that furthers the desired intent of the propagandist," emphasizing the importance of propaganda as communication, and persuasion as part of propaganda.[2] Modern media of mass communication provided channels for the dissemination of content intended to influence, persuade, convert, and harness populations to particular political causes on a scale unknown before the twentieth century.

This chapter examines the use by both totalitarian and democratic regimes of modern media for propagandist purposes. Bolshevik and Stalinist activities between 1917 and 1945 illustrate the positive use of propaganda within the highly centralized political system of the Soviet Union, where visual media were particularly important in a society with a high level of illiteracy. The propagandist activities of the Nazi regime in Germany from 1933 to 1945 illustrate a systematic effort to control and exploit modern media to disseminate political and ideological messages. The use of propaganda by democratic governments such as those of Britain and the United States during World War II demonstrates that propaganda should by no means be seen as confined to single-party, centralized, totalitarian political regimes.

The Context of Soviet Propaganda

Much of the writing on propaganda has concentrated on its use in the Soviet Union under Lenin and Stalin and in Germany under Hitler. In both countries propaganda was important as these regimes set out to politicize vast areas of life.

After the Bolshevik Party seized power in Russia in 1917, mass indoctrination was an important means of transforming society along communist lines. Institutions of mass mobilization and propaganda became central to the Soviet system. The Bolsheviks paid great attention to persuasion, using new symbols, rituals, and visual imagery to instruct Soviet citizens and to transform popular attitudes and beliefs.[3] Under Vladimir Ilich Lenin, Bolshevik revolutionary leaders set out to manage the revolution through a highly centralized and disciplined party structure and to educate the proletariat. They were ruthless in not tolerating opposition and in manipulating opinion for the sake of the revolution. Propaganda was of central importance to the Bolshevik Party (subsequently the Communist Party), particularly simple forms of propaganda that conveyed easily understood messages to a population with a high level of illiteracy.

The main aims of Soviet propaganda evolved with changing circumstances between 1917 and 1945. The revolution of 1917 was followed by a period of civil war, lasting to 1922, when the regime struggled for survival against various enemies both internal and external (including the supporters of the deposed tsar – the Whites – national groups seeking independence, and armies of the Western powers that sought to influence events in Russia). The Bolsheviks triumphed in the civil war, but the regime was still insecure. The New Economic Policy of 1921–9, which allowed for a degree of moderation and for a mixed economy, was intended to reconcile to the regime various alienated groups, especially the peasants who comprised a substantial part of the population. Throughout the 1920s a main task of propaganda was to persuade the unconverted and remind those loyal to the new regime that the revolution and its results were legitimate and that sacrifices should be endured for the sake of a better future.

From the power struggle following Lenin's death in 1924 Joseph Stalin emerged as the dominant figure in the Communist Party and leader of the Soviet Union. His policy of building "socialism in one country" and modernizing the Soviet economy included the collectivization of agriculture and rapid industrialization. Stalin's Five-Year Plans, beginning in 1929, resulted in extraordinary hardship for Soviet citizens and were only implemented with the brutal use of force.

The peasantry resisted collectivization. There was a full-scale military campaign and virtual civil war in the Soviet countryside from 1929 to 1933. Millions died from the fighting, in executions and mass deportations, and as a result of artificially created famine, especially in the Ukraine in the winter of 1932–3. In this context the role of propaganda was to persuade the peasants to accept a new, state-controlled agricultural order, and to portray to urban populations what was happening in the countryside in a positive manner. Despite falling living standards, rationing, the devastation of agriculture, and the upheaval created by massive migration to urban areas, propaganda had to convey the message that the regime was responsible for significant accomplishments.

Industrialization, implemented by means of the Five-Year Plans that imposed virtually unachievable objectives on heavy industry, led to deplorable living standards in the rapidly expanding urban areas and involved rigid labor discipline, enforced by the People's Commissariat of Internal Affairs, the NKVD or secret police (which, by the end of the 1930s, employed some 366,000 people). Propaganda was used in conjunction with coercion to persuade workers and their families that the great hardships of the Five-Year Plans were a necessary cost in building a strong, modern country capable of defending itself against powerful external enemies. Stories popularized by the regime in the 1930s included ideas of a "radiant future" (holding out the hope that sacrifice and hardship in the present would lead to a future socialist state of abundance) and "out of backwardness" (with the regime overcoming the legacy inherited from tsarist Russia and becoming a modern, industrialized economy).

In the 1930s coercion and terror, along with Stalin's cult of personality, became dominant aspects of Soviet life. Hundreds of thousands were executed and millions sent to labor camps in northern Russia and Siberia. The victims, depicted as "class enemies," included surviving leaders of the revolution of 1917, wealthy peasants ("kulaks"), priests, private businessmen from the New Economic Policy years, party officials who had fallen out of favor with the Stalinist administration, and the bulk of the officer corps of the Red Army and Navy. The culmination of the terror came with the show trials of 1936–8 involving high-profile public and military figures such as Zinoviev, Kamenev, Bukharin, and Marshal Tukhachevsky, when some of Stalin's victims "confessed" to conspiring with foreign powers to overthrow the Soviet state.

Part of the context for these developments was the rise of Nazi Germany, stimulating fear that Hitler's regime posed a threat to the survival of the Soviet Union and raising the possibility of another war. Thus propaganda emphasized the need for vigilance and personal sacrifice to defend the Soviet Union against fascism or Nazism; it attempted to convince the public that the Soviet Union was surrounded by enemies; that these enemies were assisted by traitors within the country; and that the most extreme measures were necessary to destroy them. In August 1939 a dramatic adjustment was required when Hitler and Stalin signed the Nazi–Soviet Non-Aggression Pact. However, less than two years later, in June 1941, Hitler turned against his ally and invaded the Soviet Union. The central function of propaganda then became the harnessing of the total population to a single-minded war effort against the Nazi aggressors. Russian nationalism and the fight against fascism were central themes during what was referred to as "the great patriotic war."

Media and Methods of Soviet Propaganda

After the revolution of 1917 the Bolsheviks moved quickly to exploit existing media for propagandist purposes, nationalizing the publishing industry in 1917, taking control of the main newspapers *Pravda* and *Izvestia*, banning private advertisements, nationalizing the Petrograd Telegraph Agency, taking over news production by establishing the All-Russian Telegraph Agency (ROSTA) in 1918, and establishing press censorship. Newspapers played a dominant role in Soviet propaganda. According to Jeffrey Brooks, "party leaders shaped all modes of expression through the central press, and local publishers reproduced the Party's message."[4]

Lenin also attempted to use radio. As an emerging mass medium, it had propagandist potential, especially because of high levels of illiteracy (by 1926, despite Bolshevik efforts at education, some 50 percent of the rural and 20 percent of the urban population of the Soviet Union were still basically without literacy skills). The Bolsheviks used radio broadcasts to spread party political messages from 1922, but the potential of radio as a propaganda tool remained limited by its relative expense in a poor economy. In the 1930s the regime used loudspeakers to broadcast in factories, clubs, and collective farms to reach wider audiences. However, the print media remained more important than radio: whereas there were some 7 million radio sets in the Soviet Union by 1940, newspaper circulation figures were of the order of 38 million.[5]

The problem of illiteracy and the expense of other forms of communication in a vast and poor country meant that mass meetings and "agitation" were important methods of Soviet propaganda. In the 1920s, under the supervision and tight control of the Agitational-Propaganda Section of the Central Committee of the Communist Party (Agitprop), party "agitators" went from the city to the countryside to "sell the revolution," and special "agit-trains" and ships were used for propagandist purposes. Party-controlled groups such as the trade unions and the Komsomol, the Young Communist League, the party's main youth organization, provided a means of mobilizing mass support for the party's goals and were a source of active propagandists. Forms of mass mobilization and propaganda included carnivals and parades, and in the 1930s the "public theater" of the show trials. Sheila Fitzpatrick has pointed out that the show trials were given intensive media coverage as public theatrical performances used by the Central Committee of the Communist Party as entertainment-cum-agitational tools.[6]

Posters were an important form of visual propaganda in the Soviet state. They were simple in form and suited a society with a highly visual traditional culture and low literacy levels; they could be produced in long print runs; and messages could be changed to respond quickly to a changing political context. Poster art stressed conflict and opposition: good and evil, worker and capitalist, peasant and landowner, revolutionary and counter-revolutionary. Early posters depicted revolutionaries as breaking all ties with the old bourgeois world, as bold and heroic defenders of the revolution. They disseminated the Bolshevik slogan of "peace, land and bread" and the theme of class war. They exhorted the people to fight and work harder, and they exposed and ridiculed foreign and domestic enemies. During the civil war posters circulated on a massive scale, and during the Five-Year Plans they depicted the new era of collectivization and industrialization. In the 1930s poster production was centralized under the State Publishing House. Dominant images included Stalin as uncontested and all-powerful leader, and the overachieving worker promoted under the Stakhanovite campaign (named after a coalminer who far exceeded his quota for coalmining shifts and became a national hero). They conveyed the atmosphere of threat and fear during the purges, as Stalin became increasingly paranoid about potential opposition. They emphasized the need for vigilance to detect enemies at a time when denunciation became commonplace during the show trials and the great purge.

The Bolsheviks also valued film as a propaganda tool. As another visual medium, film promised to surmount the problems of widespread illiteracy and differences of language and culture in the Soviet Union. Unlike theater, it allowed the central government to exert tight control over political messages that could be reproduced and exhibited in all parts of the country.

The Bolsheviks aimed to harness cinema to the purposes of the state, using it to persuade and educate rather than to entertain.

In practice the Bolsheviks were not able to exploit film's propaganda potential extensively in the 1920s. The production and exhibition of feature films throughout such a huge country was very expensive, so resources were largely devoted to making newsreels or brief films with acted parts called "agitki." During the period of the New Economic Policy much film production, distribution, and exhibition remained privately controlled, and the party was not sufficiently in control to impose complete film censorship. Imported films were permitted from 1924 as a revenue-making measure, and until 1927 most full-length films shown in Soviet cinemas were foreign, especially American. Furthermore, cinema remained a predominantly urban form of entertainment during the 1920s.

Nonetheless, some feature films were made by directors such as Sergei Eisenstein and Alexander Dovzhenko that are now considered classics of the Soviet period, including *Battleship Potemkin*, *October*, *Arsenal*, and *Earth*. These sought to legitimize the revolution and the Soviet regime, portraying a contest between good and evil in a world in which historical forces, rather than individuals, were all-important. Richard Taylor observes that the Soviet worldview "led to a hero who fell clearly into an ideologically respectable category, be he worker, peasant, soldier, sailor, revolutionary or Party worker, while the villain included all potential sources of dissent or opposition, being characterized (and frequently caricatured) as capitalist, bourgeois, landowner, kulak, priest, officer, spy or counter-revolutionary."[7]

Soviet filmmakers of the 1920s worked under political constraints; nonetheless, within these limits they were allowed considerable artistic freedom. They developed innovative techniques such as montage, the juxtaposition of images to elicit a specific emotional response from the viewer, which had an impact beyond the Soviet Union. In the case of directors such as Eisenstein and Dovzhenko their "propaganda" was also the product of conviction rather than compulsion, as they were committed Bolsheviks. Yet their films, although containing politically sound communist messages, lost favor with the regime. They appear not to have been popular with Soviet audiences, who preferred good stories and recognizable characters. The films therefore presented the Party with a dilemma: it wanted films to provide both entertainment (and revenue) and propaganda. Films that ordinary Russians could not understand or did not enjoy were unlikely to be effective in either respect. At the end of the 1920s the films of the great directors were increasingly criticized within the Party for being artistically advanced, which prompted the accusation that such films were tainted with bourgeois ideas.

Under Stalin there was greater restriction on artistic freedom in the film industry, reflecting growing centralization and ideological rigidity, and leading to artistic sterility. Film did become more accessible, as collectives acquired film projectors; but choice was limited in the 1930s, there were virtually no foreign imports, and the number of domestically produced films fell from about 130 per annum in the late 1920s to 35 in 1933. The 308 films made in Soviet studios between 1933 and 1940 were subject to increasing control and censorship. Stalin personally viewed and approved films for exhibition, maintaining tight control over distribution. In 1932 Soviet authorities decreed that "socialist realism" was the only acceptable style for artists and writers, an extreme example of the state attempting to dictate the purpose and form of creativity and resulting in much literature that was propagandist. There was great emphasis on Stalin's cult of personality. Pictorial representations of Stalin's political opponents were altered, as Stalin manipulated the photographic record to erase the memory of his victims. Airbrushing and cropping techniques were used to obliterate all traces of those who fell out of favor or disappeared during the purges of the 1930s; and techniques such as photomontage were used to magnify Stalin's image and importance.[8]

With the beginning of World War II propaganda served the purposes of the state during another total war. After the Nazi invasion of the Soviet Union in 1941 all Soviet media were mobilized to support the struggle against Germany. An example of the blatant use of film for propagandist purposes was *Alexander Nevsky*. In 1938, when Germany's foreign policy was increasingly threatening, Sergei Eisenstein had produced this historical epic, intended to rouse patriotic Russian sentiment against the German danger. When Soviet policy changed in 1939 with the Nazi–Soviet Non-Aggression Pact, Stalin banned the film; but it was rereleased in 1941 after the Nazis invaded the Soviet Union. This film – as did other media, press, and radio – emphasized themes of patriotism, national unity, and the despicable nature of the enemy. As the war went on, newsreels and documentaries attempted to persuade Soviet citizens that the German army was not invincible. Soviet wartime propaganda from 1941 depicted the struggle against Nazi Germany as a clash between two ideologies, with the Soviet people united in a struggle for a no-compromise victory.

Thus the Soviet Union in the Stalinist period provided an example of the mass media being used as tools of the state, with the regime having achieved an effective monopoly on public expression. Newspapers, radio, and film were used to spread propagandist messages about the cult of the leader, the successes of a progressive and modernizing policy at home, and, insofar as they gave attention to events beyond Soviet borders, the dangers of enemies abroad.

Nazi Propaganda and Control of the Media

As in the Soviet Union under Stalin, so too in Germany under Hitler and the Nazi Party between 1933 and 1945 the mass media were vital to the regime's propagandist activities. Propaganda – again supplemented by repression and terror – was highly valued by the Nazis, although in the very different context of an industrialized and more literate society than the Soviet Union.

Before becoming chancellor of Germany in 1933, Adolf Hitler had written about the importance of propaganda and employed it to facilitate the rise to power of the *National soczialistiche Deutsche Arbeiterparte* (National Socialist German Workers' Party, NSDAP, abbreviated to Nazi Party). In his political manifesto, *Mein Kampf*, completed in 1925 during a period of imprisonment, he discussed the aims and means of propaganda. Hitler considered the task of propaganda was to bring certain subjects to the attention of the masses. Propaganda should be simple, concentrating on a few key essentials, expressed in stereotyped formulas and repeated persistently. (His assumptions about the audience and his views on propagandist methods and messages were not unlike those of American advertisers – see chapter 5.)

Hitler began to implement his ideas about propaganda at party functions in the 1920s. He was a skillful public speaker, adept at establishing rapport with his audience and appealing to listeners' emotions. The Nazis organized extremely effective mass meetings. The first of the Nuremberg party rallies was held in 1926, and the emotive torchlight parades and night events became a feature of this annual event. The party experimented with techniques of political agitation and adopted what became powerful symbols (the swastika, the eagle, the *Horst Wessel Lied* as a "theme song").[9] When Nazi meetings ended in violence, this only enhanced their propaganda value and attracted more publicity. Examples occurred when the *Sturmabteilungen* (the SA, storm troops) or the *Schutzstaffel* (the SS, Hitler's personal bodyguard) broke up communist or socialist meetings, especially in Berlin.

In their rise to power the Nazis attempted to make use of established media. The party acquired a Bavarian newspaper in the early 1920s but did not succeed in establishing a wide circulation, and during this period failed to attract many journalists or writers. The mass meeting seemed more effective in spreading the Nazi message. Z. E. B. Zeman has noted: "until 1929 the technical equipment at the disposal of Nazi propagandists was rather primitive. The means of mass communication – large-circulation press, films, radio, and television – . . . were usually absent during the rise to power." However, by the 1930s Nazi leaders were able to take advantage of new techniques of mass communication: "the technical means for propaganda had been developed, and they became available to Hitler at a time when he disposed of adequate financial resources and when a highly receptive audience existed."[10] This is not to say that the Nazis did not use older forms of propaganda. Even in this country with a much higher literacy rate than the Soviet Union, posters, for example, were used extensively to propagate slogans and publicize the values of the party.

Propagandist activities at the local level helped to establish Nazi control. William S. Allen, in a detailed study of the central German town of Northeim, undertaken to shed light on how Nazi activities at this level contributed to the establishment of the regime, showed how the party gained control of the press, developed a newspaper, and in the first six months after coming to power subjected the town "to a veritable barrage of propaganda." The Weimar flag was burned and replaced by the Imperial flag, the swastika, and other Nazi symbols; there were mass demonstrations, parades, speeches, a celebration of Hitler's birthday, the Day of German Labor, a book-burning day, various SA and SS events, Hitler Youth meetings, plays, and movies. The Nazis were so successful in orchestrating events that popular energy in Northeim for other activities was diminished.[11]

While Hitler emphasized the importance of propaganda as a tool in the Nazi rise to power, he thought that the need for it would decline once the party had gained control of the German state, and that organization would be more important than propaganda. In fact Nazi Germany was very much a propaganda state, and Joseph Goebbels was a key figure in making it so. Goebbels had been entrusted with responsibility for the emerging party's propaganda from the late 1920s. He adopted a very organized approach, creating sections to look after every aspect of propaganda, with directors at various levels of the party hierarchy. In March 1933 Hitler appointed Goebbels Minister for Popular Enlightenment and Propaganda. The importance of propagandist activities to the party can be gauged not only by the establishment of the ministry – and the overt reference to propaganda in its title – but also by the fact that by 1934 more than 14,000 people were involved in the party propaganda apparatus.[12] Goebbels "felt that propaganda should continue to play an important role even after the Nazis had come to power. Propaganda would be necessary to mobilize the masses in support of the new state and its ideological foundations."[13] Thus propaganda was a vital means of converting citizens to Nazi ideology, and, as in the Soviet Union, when propaganda failed to achieve its objectives, terror was used as an additional instrument of the state.

Goebbels had specific ideas on the role of different media. The press was a means of informing and instructing the German people about reasons for government policy; radio provided a link between the individual citizen and the nation. These media were vehicles for propaganda designed to win active commitment, to mobilize total support for the Nazi state. Propaganda was "at the heart of all contact between Government and people, indeed at the heart of all political activity." The fundamental aim of Nazi propaganda, to mobilize the German people behind Nazi policies, implied a restructuring of values, and truth was only important insofar as it served the interests of the state. Old loyalties had to be replaced with selfless service to the national community; racial purity had to be recognized as indispensable; the German people had to develop a hatred of Germany's enemies, while unquestioningly trusting German leadership.[14]

Party control of German media was a necessity, given Nazi propaganda ambitions. Goebbels, as Minister for Popular Enlightenment and Propaganda, had considerable power to implement measures to align the media with Nazi priorities, supervising radio, film, the press, and theater, as well as organizing propaganda abroad. In relation to the press he did not attempt to achieve instant "coordination" (*Gleichschaltung*) with Nazi objectives, but he set about gradually eroding the independence of German newspapers. He banned or suppressed communist and social democratic papers. He instituted official press conferences to convey government views to journalists. A 1933 law ended editorial independence, specifying who could be appointed as an editor and how they should act. By the end of the decade Goebbels had imposed Nazi control over much of German publishing.[15]

With respect to radio, it was relatively easy for the Nazi Party to take control over the broadcasting system that had been state-run before 1933. However, whereas prior to 1933 German broadcasting had relied on a network of regional companies loosely controlled by the German Broadcasting Company, from 1933 the Nazis centralized control and Goebbels began to use radio as a tool for political purposes and ideological education. He developed political broadcasts, transmitting some fifty of Hitler's speeches in 1933 alone. He encouraged the production and distribution of cheap and more powerful radio sets so that by 1939 70 percent of German households had wireless receivers. Goebbels also used shortwave broadcasting to reach German minority populations beyond German borders. For example, in the Saar cheap receivers were distributed to Germans and used for propaganda broadcasting. Foreign-language broadcasting, using short wave to the United States and medium wave to the United Kingdom, was also developed in the 1930s. Horst J. P. Bergmeier and Rainer E. Lotz have demonstrated how music, including popular music, swing, and jazz, was exploited in Nazi-controlled radio broadcasting to attract listeners to propaganda broadcasts.[16]

Goebbels also experimented with television broadcasting in Germany in the 1930s. Rather than using television sets as a domestic medium, the Nazis made sets available in public places, initially in Berlin, using them to broadcast party messages to viewers. However, television did not become a mass medium under the Nazis.

The film industry was important to Nazi propaganda efforts, and both Hitler and Goebbels were obsessed with cinema. Goebbels placed great importance on film as a means of entertainment, while also considering entertainment as a very effective means of propaganda. For him the cinema was a tool to reinforce existing values and beliefs as well as moving people's thinking toward key aspects of Nazi ideology. Films of the Nazi period included themes such as German nationalism, the supremacy of the Aryan race, the Volk community, and militarism.

Even before 1933 film had been important for the Nazi Party. A film had been made of the 1927 Nuremberg party rally and screened to closed party gatherings, and in the early 1930s Goebbels had established a film distribution unit in Berlin. Once in power, he began to establish control over previously independent companies. A Nazi nominee was appointed head of the Cinema Owners' Association in 1933, the official film industry trade union was dissolved, and in July a *Reichsfilmkammer* (Reich Film Chamber) was established. This enabled Goebbels and his ministry to exert control over filmmakers and the industry, as the *Reichsfilmkammer* had power to license films, decide on the release of completed films, on film financing and tax concessions.[17]

Another law in February 1934 enabled Goebbels to supervise films from the early stages of production, with compulsory script censorship centralized in Berlin. The Nazis established a film finance bank; and the bank could stop production of undesirable films simply by refusing credit. Jews and other "degenerate" artists were removed from German cultural life. Art criticism and film reviews (other than purely descriptive) were banned in 1936, and critics needed a special license from the *Reichsfilmkammer*.

Not surprisingly, few foreign films were imported. Nazi organizations distributed films for Hitler Youth organizations, with mobile film units traveling to rural areas and providing a mixture of entertainment and indoctrination to German youth. Between 1937 and 1942 nationalization of the German film industry was achieved, with the state taking over remaining film companies under an umbrella organization, *Ufa-Film*. The result was "enormous concentration of a mass medium in the hands of the National Socialist State and, more specifically, the minister for popular enlightenment and propaganda."[18]

Film historians have provided detailed analyses of specific Nazi films, demonstrating how they disseminated elements of Nazi ideology. For example, *Hitler Youth Quex*, an early Nazi film first shown in Munich in September 1933 and estimated to have reached an audience of 10 million, influenced young Germans with ideas of heroism, comradeship, sacrifice, and the notion of the hero-martyr. The brilliant "documentaries" of Leni Riefenstahl demonstrate the power of Nazi propaganda. *Triumph of the Will*, commissioned by Hitler and released in 1935, portrayed the Nuremberg rally as a Nazi propaganda spectacular, with its themes of leadership and the Führer cult, the national community, the submergence of individual will in the will of the German nation, the triumph of a strong Germany, as well as its powerful use of symbols – the swastika, eagles, and banners. Hitler also commissioned Riefenstahl to record the 1936 Olympic Games in Berlin, and the film was released in 1938. While documenting the games, it was also a powerful advertisement for the achievements of the "new Germany."[19]

Historians have pointed to the significance of propaganda in explaining the great tenacity of the German home front during World War II. Goebbels's achievement was to create a mentality of struggle and endurance. He made special use of film to sustain home front morale and fighting spirit. Even towards the end of the war, as Germany's military situation deteriorated, Goebbels continued to commission films. For the historical drama *Kolberg*, about German resistance to Napoleon's army, he diverted 187,000 soldiers and 4,000 sailors from active duty to act as extras.[20] Such an extraordinary action was a measure of the importance of propaganda for the Nazi regime. Blatantly racist films were also produced in an attempt to win support for this component of Nazi ideology and policy. Hitler initiated *Der Ewige Jude* (*The Eternal Jew*), a crude effort that was a box office disaster. Goebbels's anti-Jewish film, *Jud Suss*, had more success, and Himmler ordered all under his command, including guards in the extermination camps, to see the film.

As well as feature films, Goebbels and his ministry coordinated the production of newsreels. From 1938 legislation made it compulsory to show a newsreel with all film programs, and newsreels were widely and cheaply distributed. During World War II newsreels were used to instill obedience and encourage belief in German victory. By 1940 all other newsreel production companies had been dissolved, and production of the war newsreels was centralized in the *Deutsche Wochenschau*. The films were used not only within Germany but also in efforts to intimidate populations in countries about to be attacked by German armies, showing resistance to the German forces as futile.

From 1941 it became more and more difficult for German newsreels to be successful, as their effectiveness depended on being able to report military victories. Rather than providing factual war reporting, they became unrealistic and increasingly reliant on irrational themes. Despite Goebbels's view of the importance of newsreels, German audiences responded negatively. Crowds lingered outside cinemas until the newsreels (first on cinema programs) had finished. Goebbels attempted to enforce attendance by closing cinema box offices during the showing of the newsreel so that patrons were obliged to watch the newsreel if they wanted to see the feature. However, newsreel content did nothing to encourage attendance or combat growing German disillusionment. After the German invasion of the Soviet Union newsreels played on fear as a means of maintaining German fighting spirit and contained threats of "subhuman Bolsheviks." As Allied bombing of Germany caused increasing destruction, Goebbels attempted to stir up hatred of the enemy and anti-defeatism among the German people. However, despite Goebbels's unremitting efforts, Welch argues that the war newsreels finally failed to produce a suspension of disbelief. Once German military successes came to an end, Germans tended to associate the newsreels with myth rather than reality.[21]

In Germany under Hitler, as in the Soviet Union under Lenin and Stalin, control of the media was centralized, and newspapers, radio, and film were used by the regime for propagandist purposes. While it is evident that both regimes exploited the media, it is more difficult to assess just how effective these propagandist efforts were.

The Effectiveness of Propaganda

Totalitarian states regarded propaganda as of central importance in mobilizing mass support and establishing total control over society. Because of this emphasis, and because of the sheer extent of totalitarian propaganda, it is tempting to conclude that it must have been successful.

In the case of the Soviet Union the Bolsheviks and subsequently the Communist Party were successful in consolidating the revolution, extending political control throughout a vast area, and surviving the turmoil of the 1930s and the crisis of the German invasion in 1941. The Nazis in Germany of the 1930s have been viewed as masters of modern propaganda techniques, employing them in an ambitious bid to reeducate the German people for a new society and new value system.

However, closer analysis indicates that it is too simplistic to point to propaganda as a single-factor explanation of political "success." In both of these totalitarian systems propaganda was accompanied by terror and repression. It could be argued that "success" was due less to effective propaganda than to Stalinist and Nazi readiness to resort to repression and terror to destroy opposition or force opponents into submission.

Nor is it easy to establish that loyalty to a regime attested to the success of propaganda; some loyalty may well have existed for reasons independent of the influence of propaganda. There were certainly instances of the failure of policy and propaganda: Stalin's collectivization campaign and famine created enormous hostility to the Communist Party in the Ukraine, to the point where the German invaders were at first welcomed as liberators in 1941. Moreover, although official mass culture had a monopoly of the mass media, James von Geldern and Richard Stites have argued that in the Soviet Union the makers of mass culture could not entirely ignore popular tastes. They point out that unofficial popular cultural forms continued to flourish beneath the surface, that the apparatus of cultural control had to compromise with audience tastes. Authorities could not force consumers to read material they found dull, or force them to interpret it as officials intended.[22]

Similarly, Fitzpatrick, in her study of urban Russian life in the heyday of Stalinism in the 1930s, concludes that, despite the regime's promises of future abundance and massive propaganda about its achievements, a degree of popular skepticism remained and it is likely that the regime was relatively unpopular in Russian towns. There is evidence that the regime had its active supporters – among Soviet youth, the privileged, office-holders, party members, beneficiaries of affirmative action policies, and favored groups such as the Stakhanovites – but the attitudes of the majority of urban citizens in the 1930s are more difficult to ascertain. Furthermore, the working class had changed so much that its coherence as a class and any workers' sense of special connection with the regime must be called into question.[23]

Ian Kershaw's conclusion about the effectiveness of propaganda is applicable to both the Soviet Union and Nazi Germany: the effectiveness of propaganda "was heavily dependent upon its ability to build on an existing consensus, to confirm existing values, to bolster existing prejudices."[24] In the Soviet Union propaganda was most likely to be successful when it built on existing fears and prejudices such as memories of tsarist and aristocratic oppression in pre-revolutionary days and fears of Russia's vulnerability to foreign invasion. These were used as a basis for propaganda to persuade citizens of the legitimacy of the regime, the need for hard work and rigid labor discipline, even for brutality towards the peasants and other alleged enemies. In Germany propaganda that built on existing values – anti-Marxism, anti-leftism, hostility to the Weimar Republic and the postwar settlement, support for a strong leader (encouraging personal loyalty to Hitler and belief in the Führer myth) – was also largely successful.

Where a consensus did not exist, propaganda tended to be less successful. Kershaw cites the Nazi attempt to promote the idea of a national community; this was not achieved, as social and class divisions did not disappear. Furthermore, propaganda "in a vacuum," such as Nazi racial propaganda, while it succeeded in creating a "Jewish question" and in depersonalizing the Jew, failed to strike a chord with many Germans. Indeed, the main "successes" of Nazi policy against the Jews were not the result of propaganda but of terror and legal discrimination. The regime hid, rather than publicized, the "final solution" to the "Jewish problem," showing the failure of Nazi propaganda on racial ideology. Both anti-Slav/Russian propaganda and propaganda in support of a racial–eugenic policy of euthanasia in Germany were also largely unsuccessful. Finally, as the war went on and the gap between propaganda and the realities of war widened, disbelief set in among German citizens. In its final years the Nazi regime resorted to terroristic repression when propaganda failed.[25]

One important factor in relation to use of the media for propagandist purposes was the extent to which absolute control could be exercised and opportunities for the presentation of alternative views denied. In the Soviet Union, particularly in the 1930s, the propaganda machinery was largely successful in denying access to other points of view. Kenez argues that, as a result, the Soviet people "ultimately came not so much to believe the Bolsheviks' world view as to take it for granted." With other points of view suppressed, "the distinction between belief and nonbelief and truth and untruth is washed away."[26] Yet even when such control was possible, terror was also applied. Both the Soviet Union and Nazi Germany experienced widespread terror and repression as well as extensive official propaganda.

Wartime Propaganda in Liberal Democratic Societies

The Soviet and Nazi regimes, because they aimed to politicize all aspects of society, afforded propaganda a central role in political and social life. Governments in liberal democratic countries also engaged in propaganda; indeed, if propaganda is viewed simply as the attempt to influence political attitudes and behavior, it can be understood as a normal part of the activities of government. But the need for systematic propaganda comparable to that of the totalitarian regimes was recognized by the democracies only in wartime. During World War I they employed propaganda to mobilize the domestic mass support essential for the prosecution of total war and to influence opinion in neutral and enemy countries. For the same purposes, at the start of World War II Allied governments established propaganda agencies: these included the Office of War Information (OWI) in the United States and the Ministry of Information (MOI) in Britain. Use of the euphemism "information" in these cases reflected the negative view of propaganda prevailing in liberal democratic societies: it was regarded as something that could be justified only in extreme circumstances and only as a necessary evil.

The reluctance of officials in Allied governments to admit that their "information" activities were indistinguishable from propaganda went hand in hand with a highly influential view of how propaganda should be conducted. Propagandists in Western countries agreed that the most effective propaganda is that which is subtle, indirect and, indeed, invisible. In other words, it was believed that people are more likely to accept a propaganda message if they are unaware that they are being propagandized. A restrained approach, presenting factual information in a rational way and avoiding lies and highly emotional appeals, was thought more likely to produce that effect. Allied propagandists therefore aimed to achieve a "strategy of truth" or "propaganda with facts." British propaganda in the war with Germany represented the most successful example of this approach. Yet a "strategy of truth," although generally accepted in principle at the time as the most effective approach, did not always prevail. At the other extreme was propaganda that sought to demonize and generate hatred towards the enemy; it came to the fore especially in the war with Japan.

US Propaganda in World War II

Whereas in Nazi Germany and Soviet Russia the content of propaganda was directly controlled by the regime, in liberal democratic societies the propagandist's task was more complicated. Democratic governments did not usually enjoy the benefits of direct control of the media but relied instead on censorship and regulation, on such other pressures as they could bring to bear, and on appeals to the good sense and patriotism of media owners and personnel. In such societies, too, not all propaganda was government propaganda. People who controlled and worked in media organizations often had their own ideas as to what messages were best calculated to encourage public support for the war. These aspects of the relationship between media and society in time of total war are exemplified by the experience of the United States between 1941 and 1945.

Those officials given responsibility for US wartime propaganda enjoyed potential advantages. By the 1940s the American press, radio, and film had achieved a degree of penetration of the population that was unequalled in any other country, providing the means by which the propaganda message could be broadcast readily to a mass audience. On the other hand, these institutions were entirely in private hands; there was no system of public service broadcasting, susceptible to direct government influence in times of national crisis, as in Britain. Censorship was employed to some extent, but it had only negative uses (denying news and information), and the practical need for media cooperation, congressional oversight of the executive arm of government, and a powerful tradition of freedom of the press counselled against its overuse: information was regulated to a lesser extent in the United States than in Britain.[27]

Moreover, US industrial strength and geographical isolation, and a tradition of isolationism in world affairs, created powerful obstacles to the mobilization of mass support for the war. Unlike Britain, the United States did not face a direct German threat to its physical survival; nor was it threatened in any plausible way by the prospect of Japanese invasion, notwithstanding the attack on Pearl Harbor. In 1940–1 the America First movement, supported by many influential Americans, campaigned strongly against US involvement in the war. Its appeal was shattered by the Pearl Harbor bombing and Germany's subsequent declaration of war on the United States in December 1941. Yet even so, government and military leaders worried about the effects on morale of lingering doubts about the extent of America's interest in the European conflict. Providing the American public and servicemen with a clear rationale for the nation's involvement in the war, especially the war in Europe, was one of the main aims of US propaganda.

Race relations within the United States also posed problems for propaganda officials. Lack of enthusiasm for the war among America's black population, 13 million strong in a total population of 132 million in 1940, caused concern for US leaders both because it threatened to undermine the war effort and because such disunity provided food for enemy propaganda. In the context of entrenched discrimination and prejudice against blacks, including institutionalized segregation in the southern states, many African Americans felt uneasy about a war with another non-white people, the Japanese. This was especially the case since that war seemed to hold little promise of improvement in the position of America's black population and was often justified by white Americans in racial terms. An early 1942 survey, which asked blacks whether they would be better off under Japanese rule, indicated that 18 percent of respondents thought the Japanese would treat them better than did American whites, 31 percent thought their treatment would be the same, and only 28 percent believed they would be worse off.[28] Horace Cayton, a Chicago black leader, put succinctly the dilemma facing many blacks: "Am I a Negro first and then a policeman or soldier second, or should I forget in any emergency situation the fact that . . . my first loyalty is to my race?"[29]

The OWI was the principal government agency responsible for overcoming such doubts and marshaling mass support for the war effort, as well as ensuring that domestic disunity and disaffection did not harm America's image abroad. Created in June 1942, the OWI sought to harness the media to the purposes of government propaganda. Its attempts to do so often led to antagonism on the part of media organizations, which were often supported by congressmen suspicious of liberal elements in the OWI and of President Roosevelt's administration in general. As a result the OWI was only partly successful in securing media cooperation with its requests.

Much of the US government's propaganda effort was directed towards the use of film. Government propagandists understood well the advantages to be gained from harnessing the resources of the world's leading film industry. Filmmakers, for their part, contributed willingly to the war effort, convinced of the power of their medium to mobilize public support. They did so out of conviction, but it was also the case that such collaboration served the film industry's interests. For the studios not to be seen pulling their weight in support of the war effort would have jeopardized the support of the public – and therefore cinema attendances – and of the banks on which film companies depended for financial backing. Another incentive for collaboration lay in the need for the cooperation of the US military, which often assisted the studios by giving access to its facilities and equipment. Moreover, the OWI, although lacking powers of direct censorship, controlled film exhibition in liberated areas and enjoyed considerable influence with the Office of Censorship, which issued export licenses for films. Since exports accounted for a large part of the industry's profits, government officials held significant bargaining power with the film companies. Overall the major film companies profited from their part in the war effort: despite wartime shortages, the number of movies produced during the war was only slightly below the peacetime level.[30]

Hollywood's contribution to wartime propaganda took a number of forms. Five of the major studios – Paramount, 20th Century-Fox, RKO, MGM, and Universal – produced newsreels (usually around eight minutes long) which played a vital role in satisfying the public's demand for visual information about the war and therefore in sustaining morale. Newsreels took on a new importance in the appeal of cinema.[31] The major film companies also gave assistance to government agencies in making propaganda films. Some of Hollywood's leading directors enlisted in the armed services for this purpose. John Huston, while in the army, made a celebrated trilogy of documentaries dealing with the behavior of American soldiers in battle and the emotional impact of war on these men: *Report from the Aleutians* (1943), *The Battle of San Pietro* (1945), and *Let There Be Light* (1946) (the latter film was so graphic that the War Department withheld it from public exhibition). John Ford served as a commander in the navy and made *The Battle of Midway* (1942), in which the American forces "seem to achieve victory because of their moral strength expressed in Ford's folksy style, not because of their superior tactics or armaments."[32] Frank Capra served in the army's signal corps and supervised production of the important *Why We Fight* series, seven orientation films designed to give recruits a clear rationale for American participation in the war (and influenced by Leni Riefenstahl's *Triumph of the Will*). The first of these films, *Prelude to War* (1943), was also released for civilian viewing in cinemas throughout the United States. Capra also played a major role in the production of the army documentary *The Negro Soldier* (1944), released both to military and – at OWI's urging – civilian audiences. The film aimed to promote racial unity and black support for the war by celebrating the contribution of blacks to American history and the war effort.[33]

In the United States, as elsewhere, feature films were widely assumed to offer the most effective means of mass persuasion, a consequence of their visual appeal and facility for blending political messages with entertainment. Many Hollywood feature films dealt with war-related themes, typically celebrating the bravery of American fighting men. The OWI prepared an "Information Manual" for Hollywood in 1942, giving guidelines on how to present the war. It reviewed film scripts from all the major studios except Paramount. The OWI's role was not unwelcome to many writers and some directors, who shared the liberal political views that tended to prevail in that organization; but it was often resented by proprietors and producers. While happy to assist the government in making films for propaganda purposes, they were never reconciled to the idea of government agencies telling Hollywood how to make movies. Their suspicions were fueled by an anti-trust suit filed by the Roosevelt administration in 1938 – suspended in 1940 but revived in 1944 – against the eight major companies for violation of laws on restraint of trade. Above all, the studios were wary of any OWI interference that called for departures from their entrenched practice, reinforced by the 1930 Production Code, of avoiding controversial political and social subjects. They were especially wary on the subject of race relations, where they feared that compliance with the OWI's attempts to improve the portrayal of black people in the movies would produce an adverse reaction from censorship boards in the south. On this question the film companies were supported by southern congressmen and other conservatives in Congress.

Such resistance imposed limitations on the OWI's achievement. That agency did succeed in bringing about minor changes to many scripts. At the OWI's urging, the studios made films which portrayed the United States as a harmonious, unified nation, in which its diverse ethnic groups were as one in their devotion to American ideals of liberty and their determination to defeat fascism. Combat films, accordingly, made a point of presenting ethnically diverse battle units, with, say, Italian, Irish, and Jewish Americans fighting side by side. In a few films the principle was even extended to blacks: in *Bataan*, *Sahara*, and *Crash Dive*, all released in 1943, black characters appeared in racially integrated combat units (in real life the American armed forces – including supplies of blood plasma – were racially segregated until 1948, and black units were usually limited to noncombat roles). However, in general the OWI had only modest success in persuading Hollywood to move beyond the stereotyped portrayal of blacks which had always prevailed in the movies. Only a handful of World War II films – including *Casablanca* (1942) and Alfred Hitchcock's *Lifeboat* (1944) – featured strong black characters.[34] For the most part American feature films continued, as the writer Dalton Trumbo put it, to make "tarts of the Negro's daughters, crap shooters of his sons, obsequious Uncle Toms of his fathers, superstitious and grotesque crones of his mothers, strutting peacocks of his successful men, psalm-singing mountebanks of his priests, and Barnum and Bailey side-shows of his religion."[35]

The historian Thomas Cripps has identified two separate impulses behind the treatment of race in American wartime propaganda films. First, blacks and their white liberal allies (including those in Hollywood) saw the war as an opportunity to bring about radical change in the position of blacks in American society and regarded film as a vehicle for that purpose. Second, the main concern of government officials was to encourage black support for the war. On the whole, Cripps argues, World War II propaganda films satisfied the latter group rather than the former. Only after the war, from 1949, were the ideas of the "Hollywood conscience-liberals" realized in a general way with a series of films which depicted black characters integrated into mainstream American society.[36]

The American case highlights a dilemma which confronted all propagandists: that of striking a balance between messages which engender hatred of the enemy and those which are so graphic in their treatment of the horrors of war as to undermine morale. American military and civilian officials, usually with the full support of the media, played an active role in restricting the release to the public of photographs and film footage depicting war casualties, as well as evidence of racial conflict on military bases and conflict between American servicemen and those from Allied nations. These restrictions were eased from 1943, when political and military leaders began to worry about public complacency about the war. American newspapers, magazines, and films in 1943–5 therefore tended to give a more vivid portrayal of wartime horrors than those in the earlier stage of the war. Publications in 1944–5, for example, were permitted to give much fuller coverage of Japanese atrocities.[37]

Great Britain and the "Strategy of Truth"

A reluctance to exploit Nazi atrocities for propaganda purposes was one aspect of Britain's wartime "strategy of truth." Here the lessons of World War I were important. As a result of the earlier conflict, British propaganda had gained a reputation for exaggeration and lies in the form of anti-German atrocity stories. In their determination to live down this reputation, the officials of the MOI were careful to avoid any suggestion of fabrication. Therefore, although Britain was now at war with one of the most barbaric regimes in modern history, the subject of Nazi atrocities was handled cautiously. The full scale of Nazi barbarism, including the genocide against the Jews, was not clearly understood until the end of the war, but the determination of propaganda officials not to risk inviting public disbelief, either at home or abroad, was an important influence on British propaganda.

The techniques of a successful strategy of truth were not at first obvious to British officials. In the early stages of the war the principle that no news is good news was allowed to prevail; the needs of military secrecy were taken to extremes and allowed to override the demands of good propaganda. Thus in 1939 newsreels were prevented from showing scenes of British troops leaving for France, and newspapers were confiscated for reporting the arrival of British troops in France, so that opportunities to combat impressions of the invincibility of the German army were lost.[38] Incorporation of the censorship machinery of the Press and Censorship Bureau into the Ministry of Information (MOI) in April 1940 was an important organizational reform which reflected recognition of the need to integrate the control of news with the generation of positive propaganda. In working to mobilize the press, broadcasting, and the film industry behind the war effort, the MOI gave top priority to news – "the shocktroops of propaganda," as Sir John Reith described it.[39] Britain's propaganda officials applied three main principles. The first was that it is not enough to suppress news; the public demands news, especially in wartime, and to deprive it is bad for morale. Second, the news must be true and accurate: propaganda "with facts, if not *the* facts, truth, if not the *whole* truth." Otherwise the public are bound to learn that they are being manipulated and will therefore trust neither government nor the media. Third, it was taken as axiomatic that censorship is best when invisible and that, therefore, precensorship (control of the news at the point of generation) is far more valuable than post-censorship.[40]

These principles were implemented so successfully that, as Nicholas Pronay states, "the press, the BBC and other organs of 'news' managed to maintain the trust of the British public at home and gained a reputation for Britain abroad for having even in wartime an honest, free and truthful media, yet which gave practically nothing of significance away to an ever-vigilant enemy."[41] Goebbels himself paid tribute to the British approach, observing of a MOI booklet "The Battle of the Atlantic" that "it does so much justice to the German point of view that you get the impression of it having been written by a Swedish Professor who is on the side of neither England nor Germany but only of truth."[42] The BBC, especially, although it worked closely with the MOI and was central to the operation of British propaganda, gained a reputation both at home and abroad for the accuracy and reliability of its news services. As George Orwell observed, "The BBC as far as its news goes has gained enormous prestige since about

1940 . . . 'I heard it on the radio' is now almost equivalent to 'I know it must be true'."[43] A comparison with Germany's wartime propaganda, which increasingly lost credibility in the eyes of the German public, highlights the effectiveness of the British approach to propaganda.

Propaganda and the Pacific War

Where Britain's war with Germany epitomized a moderate, truthful form of propaganda, the war with Japan often involved a very different approach, one which sought to mobilize popular support for the war by emphasizing differences between Us and the Other, by portraying the enemy as the devil's disciples or as subhuman. In Allied propaganda of the Pacific war this approach was reflected in the frequent use of racial stereotypes. In cartoons, films, magazines, newspapers, posters, and radio broadcasts the Japanese were commonly depicted as apes (typically as savage, buck-toothed monkeys or menacing gorillas), vermin, or subhuman monsters. This tendency to dehumanize the Japanese – to treat them as not only politically but biologically separate from the people of Allied countries – found no parallels in anti-German propaganda, in which the Germans were invariably portrayed as human beings, even if evil, and distinctions were sometimes made between good Germans and Nazis.[44] The racial aspect of Allied propaganda in the Pacific war raises complex issues concerning the effects of propaganda and the relationship between propaganda and society.

Demonization of the Japanese was sometimes the purpose of official propaganda. In early 1942 the Australian government's Department of Information launched its "Know Your Enemy" drive, a "multi-media package of posters, radio broadcasts, newspaper articles and community-based speeches" which departmental memos referred to openly as a "hate campaign."[45] Drawing on the services of journalists, academics, and commercial advertising agencies, and enlisting the cooperation of the press and radio, it was characterized by highly emotional appeals and crude racial stereotypes. One radio script, for example, referred to the Japanese as "a despicable, ape-like race that lent colour to the theory of evolution," and as "the little monkey-men of the North."[46] Such virulent propaganda attracted a strong public backlash. Criticisms included the charge that "Know Your Enemy" was blatant, and therefore poor, propaganda, that it was "unchristian," that it encouraged a "fear complex," and that it would endanger Australian prisoners of war.[47]

The same criticisms of crude racial propaganda were common in the United States, but with the significant difference that the main official propaganda agency, the OWI, generally sought to restrain, rather than generate, such extremism. In addition to the reasons that motivated Australian critics of the "Know Your Enemy" campaign, OWI officials were concerned about the effects of racially based propaganda on African Americans' support for the war and on attitudes to Asian peoples other than the Japanese. These officials also feared, with good reason, that such blatant evidence of white American racism would be exploited by Japanese propaganda. Hoping to steer hatred of the enemy into "properly directed" channels, the OWI tried, with only limited success, to persuade the Hollywood studios to produce films which promoted hatred of totalitarian and militaristic systems rather than individual leaders or the German and Japanese peoples. On the question of Japanese atrocities, the OWI's advice revealed a tension between the desire to restrain excessively hostile treatment of the enemy and the aim of deterring public complacency in the last two years of the war.[48]

That crude, racially based propaganda thrived as it did, despite official qualms, is evidence of the peculiar nature of Western public attitudes towards Japan. While Australian criticisms of the "Know Your Enemy" campaign serve to remind us of the complexity of public attitudes, it remains the case that, in those Western countries involved in the Pacific war, the media both reflected and helped bring about a degree of hatred of the Japanese that even surpassed hostility towards Germany. Scholars such as John Dower have documented the extent of these hatreds and have pointed to the savagery of the conflict in the Pacific, evidenced for example by the ruthless determination of Allied soldiers not to take prisoners. Dower, in a controversial interpretation, argues that the hatreds, and the racial imagery in which they found expression, stemmed from longstanding racist attitudes, established well before 1941 and reflected before World War II in fears of the "Yellow Peril," restrictions on Asian immigration in the United States and Australia, and discrimination against Japanese (and other Asian) immigrants in those countries. These attitudes were matched by a Japanese sense of superiority to Westerners, reflected in images of foreign demons, depicted as impure, decadent, arrogant, and barbaric.[49]

The value of Dower's work is to remind us that propaganda cannot succeed in a vacuum. Western racial images of the Japanese were appealing in part because they fed upon preexisting stereotypes. A belief in white superiority to non-Europeans had prevailed in the West since at least the fifteenth century. It received pseudo-scientific support from Social Darwinism in the late nineteenth century. The anti-Japanese racial stereotypes that flourished in World War II grew out of these beliefs; they were not invented during the war itself. Nonetheless, Dower underestimates the extent to which the experience of the Pacific war, as opposed to preexisting racial prejudices, caused hatred towards the Japanese and led to crude Allied propaganda. To a large extent American, Australian, and British hostility to the Japanese was a response to Japan's actions since 1937: its aggression and atrocities in China, its attack on Pearl Harbor in 1941, and its subsequent brutality and cruelty towards Allied prisoners of war and civilian internees. To the extent that the Japanese were more the target of Western hatred than the Germans, this experience, at least as much as racism, provides the explanation. Of course, during World War II Germany committed acts of barbarism on an even greater scale than Japan. However, it was crucial to Western attitudes that German atrocities involved mainly Jews and Eastern Europeans, whereas Allied servicemen and civilians were among the victims of Japanese atrocities (although not on the same scale as Chinese, Indians, Koreans, Indonesians, and other Asians).

The more convincing conclusion, therefore, is that racial propaganda directed at Japan appealed to many Americans, Australians, and Britons because it fed both on longstanding prejudices, reflected in stereotyped wartime portrayal of the Japanese as apes and vermin, and on the experience of the war itself. This kind of propaganda contributed to wartime hatreds, but only in a secondary way. To a greater extent such propaganda should be seen as mirroring, rather than causing, anti-Japanese hostility.

These examples of the use of propaganda in peace and war, by both totalitarian and democratic regimes, illustrate the importance of mass media when exploited in the interests of the state. As media evolved during the twentieth century, they were used for the purposes of persuasion both at home and abroad. However, the effectiveness of such propagandist use of the newspaper press, radio, and film varied not only according to the extent of media penetration but also with other factors such as preexisting attitudes and beliefs, the extent to which propagandist messages confirmed or diverged from social "realities," and the degree to which the state resorted to other measures such as terror and repression to supplement propaganda to realize official purposes.

Further reading

Balfour, Michael. *Propaganda in War 1939–1945: Organisations, Policies and Publics in Britain and Germany.* London: Routledge and Kegan Paul, 1979.

Brooks, Jeffrey. *Thank You, Comrade Stalin! Soviet Public Culture from Revolution to Cold War*. Princeton, NJ: Princeton University Press, 2000.

Carruthers, Susan L. *The Media at War: Communication and Conflict in the Twentieth Century*. London: Macmillan, 2000.

Cuomo, Glenn R. (ed.). *National Socialist Cultural Policy*. New York: St. Martin's Press, 1995.

Doherty, Thomas. *Projections of War: Hollywood, American Culture, and World War II*. New York: Columbia University Press, 1999.

Dower, John. *War Without Mercy: Race and Power in the Pacific War*. New York: Pantheon, 1986.

Ellul, Jacques. *Propaganda: The Formation of Men's Attitudes*. New York: Knopf, 1965.

Fitzpatrick, Sheila. *Everyday Stalinism: Ordinary Life in Extraordinary Times: Soviet Russia in the 1930s*. New York: Oxford University Press, 1999.

Jowett, Garth S. and Victoria O'Donnell. *Propaganda and Persuasion*, 3rd edn. Newbury Park, CA: Sage, 1999.

Kenez, Peter. *The Birth of the Propaganda State: Soviet Methods of Mass Mobilization 1917–1929*. Cambridge: Cambridge University Press, 1985.

Koppes, Clayton R., and Gregory D. Black. *Hollywood Goes to War: How Politics, Profits, and Propaganda Shaped World War II Movies*. New York: Free Press, 1987.

Roeder, George H., Jr. *The Censored War: American Visual Experience during World War Two*. New Haven, CT: Yale University Press, 1993.

Short, K. R. M. (ed.). *Film and Radio Propaganda in World War II*. Knoxville: University of Tennessee Press, 1983.

Taylor, Philip M. *Munitions of the Mind: A History of Propaganda from the Ancient World to the Present Era*. Manchester: Manchester University Press, 1995.

Taylor, Richard. *Film Propaganda: Soviet Russia and Nazi Germany*. London: Croom Helm, 1979.

Taylor, Richard, and Derek Spring (eds.). *Stalinism and Soviet Cinema*. London: Routledge, 1993.

Welch, David (ed.). *Nazi Propaganda: The Power and the Limitations*. London: Croom Helm, 1983.

— *Propaganda and the German Cinema 1933–1945*. Oxford: Oxford University Press, 1983.

— *The Third Reich: Politics and Propaganda*. London: Routledge, 1993.

7

COLD WAR AND COMMUNICATION

The defeat of Nazi Germany and Imperial Japan was soon followed by the start of a conflict which President Harry S. Truman described in 1950 as a "struggle, above all else, for the minds of men," one in which the American people would eventually prevail by getting "the real story across to people in other countries" – in other words, by propaganda.[1] His successor, President Dwight D. Eisenhower, shared this view, identifying America's "aim in the Cold War" as "to get the world, by peaceful means, to believe the truth." The means by which this was to be done, he explained, were summed up by the term "psychological warfare," which he defined as "the struggle for the minds and wills of men."[2] Like World War II, this struggle for hearts and minds demonstrated again the inextricable links between media and politics at both domestic and international levels.

The Cold War dominated international politics for four decades. Its violent rhetorical clashes, the reluctance of the United States and the Soviet Union to negotiate their differences, and above all their engagement in a highly dangerous nuclear arms race, encouraged a widespread fear that the conflict would lead to total annihilation. The Cold War was at its height from 1947 to 1962, and especially, within that period, until Stalin's death in 1953. But tensions between Washington and Moscow were renewed in the 1980s, and the whole period from 1945 to 1989 was one of US–Soviet rivalry. The era ended with the disintegration in 1989 of the empire acquired by Moscow in Eastern Europe at the end of World War II, and the collapse of the Soviet Union itself in 1991.

Although the Cold War had important political, strategic, and economic dimensions, an ideological clash between Soviet communism and American nationalism was central to the conflict. The universalistic nature of the conflicting ideologies was crucial: each claimed to represent the aspirations of humanity, regarded the other as the devil's disciple, and allowed no room for compromise with its rival. This aspect of communism is well known: the communists asserted that the masses of the world aspired to rid themselves of the chains of feudalism and capitalism and to embrace communism, and that only the wicked designs of the class enemies of ordinary people could prevent the realization of this utopia. The importance of ideology in American attitudes and policies is not generally recognized, yet it stood at the very core of American nationalism.[3] The American national myth saw the United States as destined to play the role of redeemer to the rest of humanity, guiding the peoples of the world to liberal democracy and modernity, and protecting them from the selfish ambitions of the other great powers. America's selflessness and affinity with the peoples of the world (as opposed to the governments that ruled them), and the universal relevance of American values and institutions, were the central assumptions of an ideology that shaped Americans' understanding of the Cold War. Thus Eisenhower regarded the US Cold War effort as one "conducted in the belief that if there is no war, if two systems of government are allowed to live side by side, that ours, because of its greater appeal to men everywhere, to mankind, in the long run will win out."[4] In the same vein Senator John F. Kennedy, speaking in 1957 on the problem of winning the support of Arab, African, and Asian peoples for the United States, insisted that "The strength of our appeal to these key populations – and it is rightfully our appeal, and not that of the Communists – lies in our traditional and deeply felt philosophy of freedom for all peoples everywhere."[5]

The central role of communication followed from this view of the Cold War as a psychological contest. Both sides gave a high priority to the use of media for persuasion: to mobilize their domestic populations, and to win the support of public opinion internationally. As a result the Cold War had a major impact on media content, while at the same time the media significantly affected development of the conflict. This chapter first examines the nature and effectiveness of Soviet propaganda during the Cold War, then the role of privately owned commercial media in the United States. For a number of reasons the US media gave wholehearted support to anti-Soviet and anti-communist positions. The far-reaching impact of the Cold War on the American press, and especially on film and broadcasting, was reflected in the blacklisting of alleged communist sympathizers and in media content. Finally, the chapter examines the West's international propaganda – in the form of both psychological warfare and cultural diplomacy – and assesses its role in the Cold War.

The Soviet Union: Media as Servants of the State

The story of communication in the Soviet Union during the Cold War was one of media in the service of government. The propaganda apparatus developed in the early years of the Soviet regime was adapted to Cold War purposes. The Soviet leadership, untroubled by the negative connotations evoked by the word "propaganda" in liberal democratic societies, viewed the role of the media primarily as mobilizing public support for the regime. The Department of Agitation and Propaganda (Agitprop) of the Central Committee of the Communist Party fed government propaganda to media and other organizations. Government control over the appointment and training of media personnel, close scrutiny by the censors, and habits of self-censorship which were a consequence of the severe punishment meted out to "deviationists" under Stalin's rule, helped ensure that the media served the regime's purposes and that political content in newspapers and magazines, film, radio, and television closely followed official policy.

Outside the Soviet Union Stalin's creation of the Communist Information Bureau (Cominform) in September 1947 marked the start of a systematic campaign, masterminded by Agitprop, to marshal international support for Moscow against the Western powers. A network of "front" organizations was established, including the World Peace Council, the World Federation of Trade Unions, and the International Union of Students, that followed Moscow's positions on international issues, while giving the appearance of independence from Soviet control and influence. Sympathetic Western journalists and academics were encouraged to act as Soviet "agents of influence," gaining privileged access to Soviet sources of information and financial rewards in return for their willingness to advocate the communist cause. Various agencies of the Soviet government and Communist Party, including the state-owned news agency Tass and the Ministry of Foreign Affairs, provided information to media throughout the world. The Cominform itself, from the late 1940s, published in many languages a weekly magazine, *For a Lasting Peace, For a People's Democracy!*, and similar magazines were produced subsequently. These overt forms of propaganda were supplemented by covert "black" propaganda – based on falsehoods and deception – orchestrated by the Committee for State Security (KGB).

The purpose of this vast propaganda effort was to win domestic and international support both for Moscow's stance on particular Cold War issues and for the general Soviet worldview. Simple juxtapositions of good and evil – worker and capitalist, revolutionary and counter-revolutionary, communist and fascist – had always been central to the Soviet mentality.

Now the West, especially the United States, was given the demonic role in Soviet imagery that had recently been reserved for Nazi Germany. In Soviet rhetoric the United States was portrayed as "imperialist" and war-minded, while the Soviet Union championed "peace," "disarmament," "democracy," "liberation," and the world's "progressive" forces.[6]

Crude abuse of the Western powers followed logically from this emotionally charged view of the world. Violent anti-Western language reached its peak during the late 1940s and early 1950s, but for many years after Stalin's death such epithets as "criminal regime" and "racist government" were commonplace in Soviet news broadcasts.[7] Images of American society emphasized capitalist exploitation of the workers, extremes of wealth and poverty, high unemployment, persecution of unions, racism, and the trashiness of popular culture. The fat banker with cigar and the Ku Klux Klansman were common cartoon stereotypes. By contrast the Soviet Union was portrayed in positive, often utopian, fashion as a model society in which the Soviet people should take pride and which the rest of the world should emulate. At their most critical the Soviet media dealt with those social problems – such as alcoholism, poor workmanship, corruption, a high divorce rate – on which the regime tolerated public discussion. Yet for the most part emphasis was given to the alleged prosperity of domestic life, to scientific, technological, and cultural achievement, and to the might of the Soviet armed forces.[8]

Even taking into account the difficulties of assessing the influence of propaganda on public attitudes in a closed society, some conclusions can be drawn about the effectiveness of Soviet propaganda during the Cold War. These offer no support for alarmist fears held in the West about the communists' skill as propagandists. The belief that totalitarian regimes had found the key to manipulation of the human mind, and that the populations of communist countries were held in slavery partly by terror, partly by "brainwashing," was encouraged by a commonly held but mistaken belief that Chinese techniques of indoctrination had persuaded large numbers of American and British prisoners of war to collaborate with the enemy during the Korean War.[9] Yet the very characteristics which many in the West regarded as the keys to the alleged success of communist propaganda – monotonous stress on a few simple ideas, exaggeration and distortion, crude abuse of opponents – were its weakest points, for they strained credibility, especially among audiences of any sophistication.[10] The Soviet regime, despite its control of the media, never succeeded in winning an uncritical acceptance of communist ideology or of the communist system among the Soviet population. Large-scale jamming of Western radio broadcasts was symptomatic of the weakness of Moscow's position: the regime itself was convinced that it could not afford to expose the public to alternative views on international affairs.[11] Public indifference or hostility to government propaganda was all the more common when it challenged deep-seated convictions and customs. Religious beliefs and practices survived seven decades of communist rule despite systematic persecution and anti-religious propaganda.[12] The extent of prosperity and progress in Soviet society also affected public trust in government. By the 1980s problems of economic decay, low living standards, and official corruption and incompetence were so pervasive that the shrewdest propaganda could not overcome Soviet citizens' alienation from the regime.

It would, however, be wrong to conclude that propaganda had no significant impact on public attitudes and beliefs. In the 1950s and to a lesser extent the 1960s, with invasion and victory over Nazi Germany a recent memory, with an impressive performance in some areas of industry, and with the launch in 1957 of Sputnik, the first artificial satellite, propaganda enjoyed a fertile field in which to work by appealing to the public's patriotism and expectations of economic growth. Interviews with Soviet émigrés in the 1950s found acceptance of "many of the regime's values" even among these opponents of the communist government.[13] The first scholarly surveys of public opinion in the Soviet Union, conducted in the late 1960s, showed that the great majority of respondents accepted the regime's critical views of the United States and its international behavior.[14] These attitudes cannot be accounted for entirely as the product of propaganda, but the images and interpretations of international events that the Soviet media disseminated in support of Moscow's Cold War policies were bound to have an impact on public attitudes, all the more so because alternative views were not presented.

Outside the Soviet Union a similarly complex picture emerged – one which underscores the extent to which propaganda's effectiveness depends on its success in tapping into people's existing beliefs and direct experience. In the Soviet client states of Eastern Europe a propaganda barrage as thorough as that experienced by the citizens of the Soviet Union made little headway in overcoming popular resentment that stemmed from Moscow's imposition of communist regimes on these countries between 1945 and 1948. The Soviet Union's failure to create any viable basis for its Eastern European empire other than coercion was highlighted by the Red Army's brutal suppression of reformist movements in Hungary in 1956 and Czechoslovakia in 1968 and by the eventual unraveling of Soviet power in the 1980s. By contrast, Soviet denunciation of "American imperialism" found a receptive audience in much of Asia, Africa, and Latin America, in countries where a history of colonization and exploitation at the hands of Western powers lent plausibility to the Soviet Union's claim to be the champion of anti-imperialist forces. Even so, Third World governments were wary of Moscow's embrace, and most were determined to remain apart from both the Soviet and Western camps. Many were happy to accept economic or military aid from the Soviets. However, the main inducement was not ideological sympathy for Moscow but a rational desire to exploit the Cold War for their own purposes, and to play off the Soviet Union against the United States, later the Soviets against China, accepting assistance from the highest bidder. In the Third World Soviet propaganda succeeded in promoting and reinforcing negative images of the United States but failed to win a long-term victory in the contest for hearts and minds.

In the West such success as Soviet propaganda enjoyed outside the ranks of communist parties depended on its alignment with causes – "peace," nuclear disarmament, opposition to American military intervention in Vietnam – which had widespread appeal for reasons more deep-rooted than the effects of communist propaganda. Few of the many people who supported these causes between the 1950s and 1980s looked upon the Soviet Union with loyalty or admiration. In the 1930s and 1940s many Western intellectuals had embraced communism as an attractive alternative to the evils of capitalism. After the late 1940s it enjoyed little such support: too much was known about the realities of Stalinism and the stagnant, repressive system that survived Stalin's death.

The United States: Commercial Media as Instruments of Propaganda

If government control of the Soviet media ensured their uncritical support for Moscow's policies, the media of major Western powers, while not usually subject to direct political control, for the most part cooperated with their governments and voiced support for their international policies during the Cold War. Contrary to the view commonly held in the West that only totalitarian regimes engaged in propaganda, Western media, including privately owned media organizations, played their part in the Cold War struggle. Nowhere in liberal democratic societies was enlistment of the media in the global contest with communism more important than in the United States – the country in which government controls over the media were weakest.

From 1947 the American media disseminated images of communism and the Soviet Union, and interpretations of international events, that derived from Cold War ideology. The central assumptions were that communism was a monolithic movement with its headquarters in Moscow, and that a messianic ideology compelled international communism to embark on a virtually limitless drive for world domination. The Cold War, therefore, as the authors of the important policy statement NSC 68 declared in the months before the outbreak of the Korean War, was "a basic conflict between the idea of freedom under a government of laws, and the idea of slavery under the grim oligarchy of the Kremlin." At stake was no less than "the fulfillment or destruction not only of this Republic but of civilization itself."[15] Only firm action by the United States against communism in all parts of the world could save the "free world" from the relentless ambitions of this sinister form of totalitarianism. A strategy of "containment" of Soviet power followed from these beliefs.

The media were central to the mobilization of public support for the foreign and defense policies of the US government. Newspapers, radio, and television provided presidents, secretaries of state, and other officials with the means of communicating directly to the public, by giving generous coverage to their speeches, statements, and press conferences and their "off-the-record" background briefings. Journalists relied heavily on official sources of information, giving government agencies considerable influence over media coverage of the news. From 1947 dissenting views of the Cold War were rarely given exposure in news coverage and political commentary. The national television networks even collaborated with federal government information agencies in the production of news and public affairs programs. Until the mid-1950s many of these were produced or scripted by the Department of Defense and other government agencies.[16]

The international realities of this period were more complex than the US government and Cold War orthodoxy allowed. US policymakers were justified in concerning themselves with the possible political and military consequences of a failure to contain Russian power on the European continent. Large-scale economic aid to Western Europe through the Marshall Plan of 1947, and American leadership of the North Atlantic Treaty Organization (NATO) from 1949, were constructive responses to the circumstances of the time. But some of the assumptions underlying American policy were questionable, as the disastrous experience of US military intervention in Vietnam in the 1960s would make clear. The Cold War framework within which American policymakers operated underestimated the importance of tensions between Soviet and Chinese communism and the nationalist character of non-European communist parties, overstated the extent of Moscow and Beijing's influence over Asian communism, greatly exaggerated the role of ideologically driven expansionism in Chinese and Vietnamese communism, and overestimated the Western powers' ability to influence events in the Third World. At the height of the Cold War a small number of officials, academics, journalists, and others made these criticisms, but it was rare to find them expressed in mainstream media. Journalists and commentators who expressed unconventional views were edged aside or restricted to uncontroversial subjects.

Yet the American media were no mere mouthpiece for government propaganda. Often they followed a more extreme version of Cold War orthodoxy than the White House would have liked. Between 1948 and 1950 much of media and public opinion started to run ahead of government policy, demanding extreme and simplistic approaches to international problems. Demands for increased US intervention in the Chinese civil war on behalf of Chiang Kai-shek's Nationalist forces in 1948–9, intense hostility to the new communist regime in Beijing from 1949, demands for extreme solutions to the Korean War (including the use of nuclear weapons), and a refusal to contemplate any form of *rapprochement* with Russia through the 1950s and 1960s, all severely limited the US government's freedom of action in foreign policy.[17]

The fact that media responses to the Cold War were not identical to those of the executive arm of the US government is a reflection of the range of influences at work in the American media. These included pressures from Congress, which was a major center of anti-communist sentiment and maintained constant surveillance of perceived communist influence in the media, as in other areas of American life. Commercial pressures were also important. Withdrawal of advertising, and in the case of the film industry withdrawal of financial support from Wall Street, were effective sanctions for business and the banks to employ against media organizations that failed to measure up to the test of political correctness; fear of such penalties gave media organizations every incentive to assert their anti-communist loyalties. Also important were the beliefs of media proprietors and personnel, who often had firm convictions on how to deal with the communist threat. Nor should the role of the public be discounted. It is impossible to say with certainty to what extent the media created, rather than simply reflected, simplistic and inflexible public attitudes to the Soviet Union and communism. It is likely that at times the media were driven to adopt extreme anti-communist positions by fear of adverse public reaction to any suggestion of moderation in dealings with communists.[18] The origins of these attitudes lay ultimately in a deep-rooted American antipathy to communism and radicalism that pre-dated the Cold War and stemmed from a nationalist preoccupation with "Americanism" (and rejection of "un-American" ideologies). However, elements of the media played a major role in lending credibility to these extreme views and in extending their influence among the American public.

This generalization holds true even more for the domestic Cold War than in matters of foreign and defense policy. The most extreme forms of American anti-communism were manifest less in ideas on external policy than in the paranoid approach to internal affairs associated with Senator Joseph McCarthy of Wisconsin: in the deeply felt conviction that American society was riddled with spies and traitors, many holding positions of influence in the US government and other institutions, and in the belief that radical measures were required to root out these subversives. The Soviet Union did have considerable success in the 1930s and 1940s in penetrating the US government with its agents, but the victims of McCarthy's witchhunts were seldom the real witches. Few Soviet spies were ever caught. McCarthy's targets were the strongly anti-communist Democratic Party administration of President Truman and hundreds of other people who were innocent of any connection with Soviet espionage.[19]

Sections of the media played a major part in the growth of domestic anti-communist extremism. Not only did the effectiveness of McCarthy and other red-baiters depend on adept use of television and the press to attract maximum publicity. The broadcasting media and many newspapers (including those of the Hearst organization and Robert McCormick's *Chicago Tribune*) also connived in the witchhunts of the period. This was partly because their owners, executives, and editors supported McCarthy's views, partly because of a cynical refusal to let the facts stand in the way of newsworthy stories, and partly because of a misplaced sense of "objectivity," which counseled against close examination of the veracity of politicians' assertions. Some major newspapers and magazines (including the *New York Times* and the *New York Post*) and leading columnists (including the popular Drew Pearson and the eminent Walter Lippmann) consistently opposed McCarthy. Nonetheless, the overall record of the media in their handling of anti-communist demagoguery was a sorry one.[20]

The United States: Film, Broadcasting, and the Cold War

The impact of the Cold War was especially far-reaching in American film and broadcasting. In the context of global ideological conflict, the film industry was widely perceived to have a central role. Any suggestion that

Hollywood's output might be tainted by ideological impurity demanded close scrutiny. In 1947 the House Committee on Un-American Activities (HUAC), a committee of the US House of Representatives, opened an investigation into allegations of communism in Hollywood. It did so at the urging of conservative elements within the industry, organized in the Motion Picture Alliance for the Preservation of American Ideals, in the aftermath of bitter labor disputes which had affected the major studios and led to charges of "red" infiltration. In closed hearings in Los Angeles in May, "friendly" witnesses testified to the prevalence of communist activity, especially in the Screen Writers' Guild and the Screen Actors' Guild. In Washington in October the allegations were repeated at public hearings by studio heads Walt Disney and Jack Warner and by such celebrities as Gary Cooper, Robert Taylor, Robert Montgomery, Lela Rogers (the mother of Ginger), Ronald Reagan, and Adolphe Menjou. Nineteen "unfriendly" witnesses – those suspected of communist subversive activity or at least of communist sympathies – were subpoenaed to appear before the Washington hearings. Ten (seven writers, two directors, and one producer) agreed among themselves to plead their constitutional right to free speech and refused to answer the question, "Are you now or have you ever been a member of the Communist Party?" For their refusal the "Hollywood Ten" were indicted for contempt of Congress and sent to prison for up to one year. HUAC conducted further investigations of communist influence in the film industry in 1951–2.

The HUAC investigations occurred at a time when the film industry was especially vulnerable to outside pressure. A longstanding anti-trust action by the federal government against the major firms (resolved against the studios in 1948), and the prospect of intense competition from the new medium of television, undermined the industry's capacity to ward off political intervention. Although industry leaders declared their determination not to "accept dictation on hiring or editorial policies," their actions belied their words. At a meeting at the Waldorf-Astoria Hotel in New York on November 24, 1947, film executives agreed to "suspend without pay," in effect to fire, the Hollywood Ten. They declared that the industry would no longer "knowingly employ a Communist or member of any party or group which advocates the overthrow of the government of the United States by force or illegal constitutional methods."[21] The studios moved immediately to deny employment to writers, directors, producers, and actors whose political affiliations were deemed unacceptable. Expanded after the second round of HUAC investigations in 1951–2, the Hollywood blacklist affected around 300 people in the film industry and remained in operation until the early 1960s. A ritual of humiliation and conversion, by which HUAC demanded that former communists give up the names of party comrades as proof that they had renounced their past sins and embraced the secular faith of Americanism, awaited many of those who tried to avoid blacklisting.

Less well known than the Hollywood blacklist was the blacklisting of alleged communist sympathizers in the radio and television industries. Broadcasting was the main target of *Counterattack: The Newsletter of Facts on Communism*, a weekly newsletter started in 1947 by three ex-FBI agents with the assistance of Alfred Kohlberg, a businessman prominent in anti-communist causes. *Counterattack*, which set out to expose communist front organizations and demanded that action be taken against individuals associated with them, quickly built up a profitable subscription list among business firms and government offices. American Business Consultants, the publishers of *Counterattack*, also did loyalty investigations, for a fee, for broadcasting executives wishing to check the anti-communist bona fides of entertainers, writers, directors, announcers, producers, and other employees. The company had already acquired considerable influence over the hiring policies of radio and television companies when, in June 1950, it published *Red Channels: The Report of Communist Influence in Radio and Television*. Claiming that "the Cominform and the Communist Party USA now rely more on radio and TV than on the press and motion pictures as 'belts' to transmit pro-Sovietism to the American public," the book listed 151 people – mostly writers, directors, and performers – as alleged subversives within the broadcasting industry. *Red Channels*, soon followed by other lists, was the starting point for a broadcasting blacklist comparable in its impact to the film industry's blacklist.[22]

The blacklists ruined the careers of hundreds of people. Many victims, including the Hollywood Ten, were or had been communists in the formal sense of membership of the Communist Party. But in their communist allegiances they had committed no crimes: the Communist Party was not an illegal organization, and there was no suggestion that any of them had plotted violent revolution or engaged in espionage for Soviet Russia. They were Stalinists, but not in the sense that they approved of Stalin's crimes; rather they denied that these had taken place.[23] Their greatest sins were those of *naïveté* or stupidity, not treason. Their political views have to be understood against the background of the 1930s, when the Depression, the rise of fascism, and the sorry record of the Western powers in contending with Hitler's expansionism had encouraged a highly idealized view of the USSR and an interest in communism as an alternative to capitalism.

Moreover, many of the blacklists' victims had never been communists but were targeted simply because of a past association with liberal causes: support for the New Deal, condemnation of lynching of blacks in the south, opposition to General Franco's reactionary forces in the Spanish Civil War, support for cooperation between America and Russia.

The political and commercial pressures reflected in the introduction of blacklists also shaped film and broadcasting content. In their efforts to find evidence of communist influence in the film industry, HUAC's invest-igators could identify at most three films that might be described as pro-communist or pro-Soviet, all products of Hollywood's wartime effort to marshal public support for America's Soviet ally: *Mission to Moscow* (1943), *The North Star* (1943), and *Song of Russia* (1944). That there were so few is not surprising: whatever the political sympathies of writers and directors, the industry's entrenched policy of refusing to touch politically or socially controversial subjects virtually guaranteed that radical points of view would seldom be aired in feature films. By the end of the decade, with the industry under close scrutiny from HUAC and its supporters, the major firms had adopted an even more restrictive definition of what was controversial. In the late 1930s and early 1940s the films of Frank Capra (*Meet John Doe*, *Mr Deeds Goes to Town*, *Mr Smith Goes to Washington*) and John Ford (*The Grapes of Wrath*, *Tobacco Road*) had shown that it was possible to make successful films which criticized businessmen, politicians, and injustices in American society. In 1946 the head of the Motion Picture Producers' Association, Eric Johnston, heralded the start of a less tolerant era, telling screenwriters: "We'll have no more *Grapes of Wrath*, we'll have no more *Tobacco Roads*, we'll have no more films that deal with the seamy side of American life. We'll have no more films that treat the banker as a villain."[24] The late 1940s did see a spate of Hollywood movies with a social or political message, but Johnston's remarks highlighted the dangers faced by filmmakers involved in these productions. In 1947 widespread condem-nation of Universal's *The Senator Was Indiscreet*, a satire about a corrupt senator, demonstrated that such themes were now taboo. Controversy sur-rounding Edward Dmytryk's *Crossfire*, in which a Jew is murdered by an anti-semitic war veteran, suggested that an inclination to examine the darker side of American life could give rise to charges of communist sub-version. Dmytryk was one of the Hollywood Ten, and it is likely that *Crossfire* fueled his accusers' antagonism to him.[25]

From the end of the 1940s Hollywood usually steered clear of such themes and concentrated on the production of musicals, Westerns, and other un-controversial genres. Criticism of the political status quo did not disappear from the screen, but subtlety was now essential. *High Noon* (1952) presented such an oblique attack on anti-communist conformity that the film's star, Gary Cooper – one of HUAC's "friendly" witnesses of 1947 – probably did not grasp the message.[26] Subtlety was not a feature of Hollywood's anti-communist propaganda films, which included *The Iron Curtain* (1948), *The Woman on Pier 13* (originally *I Married a Communist*) (1949), *The Red Menace* (1949), *I Was a Communist for the FBI* (1951), *My Son John* (1952), and *Big Jim McClain* (1952). Giving full expression to McCarthyite obsessions, these films portrayed a world in which ruthless, corrupt, and cynical communist bosses, virtually indistinguishable from the central characters of gangster movies, plotted the overthrow of American democracy and exploited the gullibility of teachers, intellectuals, trade unionists, and blacks to gain recruits to their cause. If any doubts remained about the film industry's willingness to play its part in the Cold War, the studios cooperated with the State Department and other federal government agencies to ensure that unsuitable films were not exported. They took advice on film content from representatives of the Joint Chiefs of Staff and from agents of the Central Intelligence Agency (CIA) placed in Hollywood for that purpose.[27] Cold War politics also exerted a major influence on television entertainment, with images of East–West conflict and warnings of communism's menace to the United States frequently conveyed in a number of television genres.[28]

The Cold War's influence on the US media took its most extreme forms in the 1950s. In the early 1960s, and especially after the Cuban missile crisis of October 1962, a relaxation of Cold War tensions occurred and was matched by a tempering of domestic anti-communism. The media were affected by this change. The blacklists in film and broadcasting ceased to operate, while the release of such films as *The Manchurian Candidate* (1962) and *Dr Strangelove* (1964) showed that it was possible to criticize or ridicule American institutions, leaders, and policies in an overt way that had been out of the question ten years earlier.

Yet the most important effects of media involvement in the Cold War were more longlasting. Even taking into account the limitations to media influence on public opinion, it remains a persuasive argument that by failing for so long to examine critically US government policies, and by denying the public access to unorthodox views of international affairs, the media helped lay the groundwork for the foreign policy disaster of American military involvement in Vietnam (see chapter 10).[29] Moreover, as late as the 1980s Cold War imagery still prevailed in American film and television depictions of the Soviet Union, with the Soviets portrayed "as inhumane, vicious torturers who enjoy inflicting pain and murdering children."[30] The effects of decades of anti-Soviet propaganda could still be seen in an opinion poll which suggested that 25 percent of US college students believed the Soviets had invented the atomic bomb; while 28 percent of respondents to a *New York Times* survey in November 1985 believed that in World War II the Soviet Union had fought against the United States.[31] While it would be wrong to attribute such ignorance wholly to the effects of media manipulation, the media nonetheless had contributed greatly, over four decades, to the dissemination of the attitudes and images from which these flawed impressions were derived.

International Propaganda: Psychological Warfare and Cultural Diplomacy

While the US government relied on commercially based media organizations to mobilize domestic support for the Cold War, the conduct of international propaganda required direct state involvement. Washington created its own agencies to influence international opinion, including public opinion inside the Soviet Union and the satellite states of Eastern Europe. From 1947 the United States invested heavily in "psychological warfare" and "cultural diplomacy." The latter refers to the dissemination of cultural products – such as films, magazines, radio and television programs, art exhibitions – to enhance the nation's image among the populations of other countries, with a view to influencing the policies of their governments through pressure of public opinion. "Psychological warfare" is more difficult to define. After 1945, US officials usually employed the term to refer to strategies that linked the use of communication systems for propaganda to the selective use of violence in, for example, sabotage, assassinations, and counter-insurgency operations. Among communication scholars no clear consensus emerged on the meaning of "psychological warfare," and often it was used simply as a synonym for propaganda. Generally it implied propaganda of a particularly aggressive kind; and in this respect it reflects the purpose of US propaganda operations against countries behind the Iron Curtain.[32]

An intensive effort to shape world opinion had bipartisan support within the United States. Despite rhetorical differences between Democrats who favored containment policies and Republicans who insisted that the free world must not simply contain but "roll back" communism and deliver "liberation" to the captive peoples behind the Iron Curtain, both Democrat and Republican administrations worked to bring about the collapse of communist regimes in Eastern Europe and the Soviet Union. Propaganda was a means to this end.

By 1948 alarm at the seeming effectiveness of Soviet propaganda had created support for the Smith–Mundt Act, which created the legal framework for a permanent overseas information program, using the media, exchange programs, and exhibitions to combat the Soviets' "campaign of vilification and misrepresentation" against the United States.[33] The responsibility for clandestine psychological warfare and "black" propaganda – as well as such other covert tasks as sabotage, subversion, and assassinations – was given to a lavishly funded, secret branch of the newly formed CIA: the Office of Policy Coordination. By the spring of 1950 the stage was set for what Edward Barrett, the *Newsweek* editor appointed assistant secretary of state for public affairs, called "an all-out effort to penetrate the Iron Curtain with our ideas." With NSC 68 warning of a grave deterioration in the world situation and recommending a vast increase in defense expenditure and other measures to protect US security, Truman launched an aggressive international propaganda campaign, the "Campaign of Truth." Calling for a "sustained, intensified program to promote the cause of freedom against the propaganda of slavery," Truman declared that the Cold War was "a struggle, above all else, for the minds of men," one which the forces of "imperialistic communism" were currently winning.[34] Responding to the president's appeal, Congress increased by $80 million the normal appropriation of $32 million for the overseas information program. To coordinate the government's psychological warfare strategy, the Truman administration in 1951 created the Psychological Strategy Board (PSB). In 1953 the Eisenhower administration replaced the PSB with the Operations Coordinating Board and separated government information activities from the State Department, creating an independent United States Information Agency (USIA) with a director who reported to the president and the National Security Council (NSC). Eisenhower "planned to elevate psychological warfare to the center of Cold War strategy."[35]

Although the United States led the free world's campaign of psychological warfare against the communist regimes, the propaganda and intelligence agencies of other Western governments also played a part. The most influential was the Information Research Department (IRD), a secret branch of the British Foreign Office which fed non-attributable anti-communist propaganda to the BBC and other media organizations in Britain and abroad, as well as to British politicians and diplomatic missions throughout the world.[36]

By the early 1950s, therefore, the Western powers attached high priority to psychological warfare and were employing propaganda measures to win international opinion to support the free world and, ultimately, to bring about the disintegration of communist regimes. US overseas information centers and libraries, documentary films and newsreels, and material fed to newspapers and magazines by a US press service and Britain's IRD, all played a part in this campaign.

As a means of disseminating propaganda within the Soviet Union and its Eastern European empire, radio was the most effective weapon available to the West's psychological warriors. With powerful radio transmitters in Central Europe and the Mediterranean it proved possible to penetrate the Iron Curtain, despite Moscow's systematic jamming of Western broadcasts. In the vanguard of this campaign was the Voice of America (VOA). Established in 1942 as a wartime expedient, the VOA was quickly adapted in the postwar years to the purposes of US international propaganda. State-funded, operated first by the State Department then by the USIA from 1953, it has "always been used and recognized as an instrument of US foreign policy."[37] By 1953 it broadcast in 46 languages, with more than half its budget devoted to programming behind the Iron Curtain. Its broadcasts featured aggressive, often crude, anti-communist propaganda. Making heavy use of the words of refugees from communist regimes and of US and other Western leaders, VOA programming, according to a State Department internal study of 1950, contrasted "the virtues of democracies with the vices of communist regimes," emphasized "the inevitability of our ultimate triumph," and depicted the USSR as "the scheming villain," the United States as the country which "stands up against the powers of evil." For fear of inducing "propaganda fatigue" among listeners, the propaganda message was softened by other programs – straight news, features, and music.[38]

The VOA's development as an effective broadcasting arm of US propaganda was far from trouble-free. In 1953 Senator McCarthy turned his attention to the organization. In an episode which underlined the irrationality of the period's anti-communist extremism, McCarthy's brutal interrogation of VOA staff uncovered no evidence of communist influence but destroyed the careers of several employees, undermined morale within the organization, and probably affected its funding. In that year "Song of India" was temporarily removed from the VOA's music library, on the grounds that "it's by Rimsky-Korsakov, and we're not supposed to use anything by Russians."[39] The VOA also suffered from its status as the voice of the US government, and comparisons with the BBC brought into question internationally its journalistic independence.

The BBC, formally independent of the British government although state-funded, continued during the Cold War to enjoy its wartime reputation for objectivity, accuracy, and trustworthiness. A 1953 study of English language radio services observed that the BBC "sounded like a news service almost self-consciously trying to make everything come out 50 percent on each side," in contrast to Radio Moscow, which "sounded like a propaganda agency using news to illustrate themes," and the VOA, which "sounded like the news service of one of the great protagonists of the cold war . . . neither as neutral as the BBC nor as carefully propagandistic as Radio Moscow."[40] Nonetheless, the BBC functioned as an instrument of international propaganda, its effectiveness enhanced by its credibility as an independent broadcasting service. Like the VOA, its overseas broadcasting reflected government priorities, established not by direct government control but by formal and informal ties with the British Foreign Office. The BBC's external services were legally obliged to broadcast in languages determined by the Foreign Office, to accept information from it, and to seek its advice on countries to which to broadcast. Both BBC executives and Foreign Office officials shared the common outlook on world affairs of the British establishment.[41]

The external operations of the BBC and the VOA were supplemented by broadcasts of the West German service Deutsche Welle and by two German-based US radio stations, ostensibly private but covertly funded by the CIA: Radio Free Europe (RFE) began broadcasting in 1950, Radio Liberation (from 1964 Radio Liberty, RL) in 1953. Staffed largely by anti-Soviet émigrés, RFE broadcast anti-communist propaganda to the populations of the Eastern European satellite states, RL to the Soviet Union.

The evidence suggests that the VOA, the BBC, RFE, RL, and Deutsche Welle developed a large audience behind the Iron Curtain. The success of their broadcasts as an influence on public attitudes is more difficult to gauge. Interviews with Soviet and Eastern European defectors – by definition an unrepresentative group – form the main part of rudimentary audience research suggesting that Western radio propaganda was successful. What is clear is that both the Western powers and the Soviet regime believed radio propaganda to be effective: the former demonstrated this by large-scale investment in broadcasting behind the Iron Curtain, the latter by its desperate attempts to counter the broadcasts, through jamming and vehement criticism of Western programs in the Soviet media. Two conclusions seem persuasive. One is that Soviet leaders were less concerned by propaganda attacks on communism than by images of Western affluence that invited comparison with the low living standards of communist countries. Another is that Soviet leaders were more anxious about Western broadcasts in the Eastern European satellite states than in the Soviet Union itself. In the former the impact of foreign propaganda was not to create disaffection with communism – such attitudes were already inherent in the relationship between Moscow and the peoples of Eastern Europe – but to sustain hopes for eventual liberation and a determination to work towards that end.[42]

Events in Hungary in 1956 encouraged charges that in this last respect the Western broadcasts were too successful. When an uprising against Soviet domination was brutally suppressed by the Red Army, international radio propaganda was widely accused of raising false expectations of Western intervention, thus encouraging the revolt and contributing to the Hungarians' suffering. Such charges had most substance in the case of RFE, least with the BBC, which emerged from the crisis with its credibility intact.[43] For the VOA, criticisms arising from the Hungarian episode encouraged a shift away from the use of strident anti-communist propaganda towards an attempt to emulate the BBC's "objective" approach. This change reflected the declining importance of psychological warfare in American Cold War propaganda from the mid-1950s and an increasing emphasis on cultural infiltration of the communist bloc. Radio remained an important weapon in the West's Cold War arsenal, and the Cuban missile crisis of October 1962 underlined the medium's value as a tool of superpower diplomacy, as well as a means of disseminating propaganda. During the crisis both Washington and Moscow used radio to communicate with each other, supplementing traditional diplomatic channels.[44] But increasingly, broadcasting was seen less as the chief medium for waging psychological warfare against the Soviets and more as one of a range of means by which the United States might win hearts and minds throughout the world through the gradualist approach of cultural diplomacy.[45]

The universal appeal of American mass culture had been clear as early as the 1920s, with the enormous success of American movies, music, and other mass-produced goods. The Cold War, widely perceived as a conflict between opposing ways of life, gave this attraction added political significance. From the mid-1950s US policymakers believed that cultural diplomacy would complement psychological warfare and that in the long term it might prove more effective. Between the 1950s and the 1980s the export of American culture was heavily subsidized by the US government and coordinated by the USIA. Cultural exchange programs, international trade fairs and exhibitions, and the distribution of Hollywood movies, documentary films, books, magazines, and music were all means by which the United States extracted propaganda value from the appeal of America's way of life, especially its popular culture and material prosperity. From the mid-1950s VOA programmers exploited the popularity of jazz and later rock 'n' roll among audiences behind the Iron Curtain, using music programs to boost the image of the United States. Before the end of the Cold War the worldwide popularity of such symbols of "Americanization" as blue jeans, Coca-Cola, and McDonald's testified to the success of this approach to the confrontation with America's ideological rival.[46]

Also central to the cultural Cold War was the mobilization of Western intellectuals in the anti-communist cause. While CIA agents in Hollywood sought to exploit media influence on mass opinion, much of the organization's propaganda activity was aimed not at the general public but at "opinion leaders." From the late 1940s the CIA developed an extensive network of cultural front organizations, the most important of which was the Congress for Cultural Freedom (CCF). Founded in 1950 and based in Paris, the CCF's aims were to combat communist and neutralist sentiment among the intelligentsia, especially in Western Europe, and to advocate the virtues of the American way of life. The CCF sponsored liberal, anti-communist magazines throughout the world, including *Encounter* (Britain), *Preuves* (France), *Der Monat* (Germany), *Quest* (India), and *Quadrant* (Australia). It sponsored the publication of hundreds of books and organized conferences, concerts, and art exhibitions. The CIA covertly funded these activities on a generous scale, with private foundations used to disguise the source of the money. Many writers and artists collaborated, unwittingly or otherwise, in the US government's Cold War propaganda campaign. They included eminent intellectuals of the period: Arthur Koestler, Raymond Aron, Sidney Hook, Bertrand Russell, Isaiah Berlin, Daniel Bell, Julian Huxley, W. H. Auden, Robert Penn Warren.[47] Britain's IRD also made a major contribution to the cultural Cold War, paying trusted academics and journalists to write articles and books with anti-communist content and covertly subsidizing the publication and worldwide distribution of works by approved authors.[48]

The exposure from the late 1960s of CIA backing of the CCF led to a varied response. Some of the beneficiaries of CIA largesse saw no harm in an intelligence organization's underwriting of culture. Like Yehudi Menuhin, they thought "much more of the CIA" for associating with "people like us."[49] According to this defense, the very fact that writers and artists were unaware of the CIA's involvement in funding proves that no political strings were attached to the process. Yet if the CIA had operated merely as a generous facilitator of independent intellectual and artistic activity, there would have been no need for secrecy about its involvement. CIA support did, of course, come at a price, even if the ties that bound it to such organizations as the CCF were more subtle and complex than those at work in Moscow's control of its many fronts. The purpose of CIA subsidies for cultural activity was to inculcate favorable attitudes to American culture and society and to US policies. The result was interference in and corruption of the process of intellectual inquiry. The publisher Jason Epstein summed up the problem well:

> What most irritated us was that the government seemed to be running an underground gravy train whose first-class compartments were not always occupied by first-class passengers: the CIA and the Ford Foundation, among other agencies, had set up and were financing an apparatus of intellectuals selected for their correct cold-war positions, as an alternative to what one might call a free intellectual market where ideology was presumed to count for less than individual talent and achievement, and where doubts about established orthodoxies were taken to be the beginning of all inquiry.[50]

The ability of the CIA and IRD to disguise their sponsorship of cultural activity for many years – until the late 1960s for the former, the late 1970s for the latter – highlights the key to the success of Western propaganda: so much of it was not generally recognized as propaganda. The IRD, like the BBC, gained credibility from an emphasis on a factual, balanced approach to its material. Similarly, American political messages were often presented in the form of information and entertainment. The CIA encouraged its front organizations to preserve their appearance of independence from the US government by not slavishly following every aspect of US policy. In this respect they contrasted markedly with their Soviet counterparts. Moreover, particular care was taken to cultivate intellectuals of the non-communist left; it was reasoned that anti-communist messages would be all the more credible when voiced by left-wing figures.

The complicity of intellectuals in the West's propaganda campaigns also affected some academic disciplines, especially in the United States. Thus US government psychological warfare programs funded the growth of mass communication research as a scholarly field in American universities between 1945 and 1960. The financial support came at a price, ensuring that priority was given to development of the discipline as the study of techniques by which elites could persuade, manipulate, and dominate target groups. Similar patterns were evident in social psychology and sociology.[51]

The most far-reaching claim for the effectiveness of the West's propaganda is that psychological warfare and cultural infiltration, by exposing populations behind the Iron Curtain to a highly attractive alternative way of life, played "a major, perhaps decisive, role in the collapse of the Soviet and East European regimes."[52] Yet the circumstances of this collapse suggest the need for a more cautious assessment. The main causes of Soviet decline are to be found in deep-seated economic and social problems, the causes of which lay not in the impact of US foreign policy or Western propaganda but in the inherent weaknesses of the Soviet political and economic system. Nonetheless, in the context of a deteriorating economy and social decay, the West's propaganda campaigns highlighted the deficiencies of the Soviet system and therefore exacerbated the crisis facing the regime. In the Eastern European satellite countries the effects of the West's psychological warfare and cultural diplomacy were to reinforce existing antagonism towards the Soviet Union, to help sustain hopes of eventual liberation, and to encourage resistance to Moscow's domination. Beyond the Soviet bloc, American mass culture and material abundance had a universal appeal that the Soviets could not match. The US government's exploitation of that appeal was the most successful aspect of the West's Cold War propaganda.

Further reading

Bernhard, Nancy E. *U.S. Television News and Cold War Propaganda, 1947–1960.* Cambridge: Cambridge University Press, 1999.

Dennis, Everette E., George Gerbner, and Yassen N. Zassoursky (eds.). *Beyond the Cold War: Soviet and American Media Images.* Newbury Park, CA: Sage, 1991.

Hixson, Walter L. *Parting the Curtain: Propaganda, Culture, and the Cold War, 1945–1961.* New York: St. Martin's Press, 1997.

Lashmar, Paul, and James Oliver. *Britain's Secret Propaganda War.* Stroud: Sutton, 1998.

MacDonald, J. Fred. *Television and the Red Menace: The Video Road to Vietnam.* New York: Praeger, 1985.

May, Lary. *The Big Tomorrow: Hollywood and the Politics of the American Way.* Chicago, IL: University of Chicago Press, 2000 (chapter 5).

Nelson, Michael. *War of the Black Heavens: The Battles of Western Broadcasting in the Cold War.* London: Brassey's, 1997.

Pells, Richard. *Not Like Us: How Europeans Have Loved, Hated, and Transformed American Culture since World War II.* New York: Basic Books, 1997.

Rawnsley, Gary D. *Radio Diplomacy and Propaganda: The BBC and VOA in International Politics, 1956–64.* New York: St. Martin's Press, 1996.

— (ed.). *Cold-War Propaganda in the 1950s.* New York: St. Martin's Press, 1999.

Saunders, Frances Stonor. *Who Paid the Piper?: The CIA and the Cultural Cold War.* London: Granta, 1999. Published in the United States as *The Cultural Cold War: The CIA and the World of Arts and Letters.* New York: Free Press, 1999.

Simpson, Christopher. *Science of Coercion: Communication Research and Psychological Warfare 1945–1960.* New York: Oxford University Press, 1994.

Taylor, Philip M. *Munitions of the Mind: A History of Propaganda from the Ancient World to the Present Era*. Manchester: Manchester University Press: 1995 (chapter 24).

Urban, George R. *Radio Free Europe and the Pursuit of Democracy: My War Within the Cold War*. New Haven, CT: Yale University Press, 1997.

Wagnleitner, Reinhold. *Coca-Colonization and the Cold War: The Cultural Mission of the United States in Austria after World War II*. Chapel Hill: University of North Carolina Press, 1994.

Whitfield, Stephen J. *The Culture of the Cold War*. Baltimore, MD: Johns Hopkins University Press, 1991.

8

TELEVISION AND CONSUMER SOCIETIES

Television, a 1962 report on broadcasting in Britain claimed, was "one of the major long-term factors that would shape the moral and mental attitudes, and the values of our society." With this assertion the Pilkington committee both gave expression to a view of television's influence that has remained widespread and highlighted the importance of understanding the medium's role in society.[1] In the second half of the twentieth century the rise of television transformed the media. The popularity of cinema, newspapers, magazines, and radio declined, while television became the dominant medium. Television was central to the rise of consumer societies.

After a brief discussion of the origins of television, this chapter examines postwar growth of the medium in the United States and Britain and the development of contrasting organizational arrangements – commercial and public service – in those countries. Further expansion from the 1970s, the proliferation of channels, and increasing commercialization of television are then discussed, along with the implications of those developments for programming. The chapter also examines US domination of international television markets, developments in public affairs programming, the influence of television on politics, and the question of television's general impact on society.

Origins

The invention of television was based on "a complex of inventions and developments in electricity, telegraphy, photography and motion pictures, and radio," many of them not specifically aimed at television development.[2]

By the 1920s the work of a number of individuals had demonstrated the feasibility of using radio waves to carry visual images. In Germany, Paul Nipkow had developed a mechanical scanning dish in the 1880s. Others, such as Boris Rosing in Russia and A. A. Campbell Swinton in Britain, had experimented with a cathode-ray tube to scan objects electronically. A key figure in early television development in Britain was John Logie Baird, who energetically promoted experiments based on a mechanical scanning device. In experimental transmissions Baird televised objects in outline in 1924, recognizable human faces in 1925, and moving objects in 1926. He even, quite remarkably, demonstrated a rudimentary form of color television in 1928. But his system proved inferior to electronic scanning.

In the 1920s and 1930s the work of Manfred von Ardenne in Germany and the Russian-born Vladimir Zworykin in the United States led to further technical progress on the problem of electronic scanning. In 1929 Zworykin joined Radio Corporation of America (RCA), which put resources into research and development and the purchase of relevant patents. In 1931 RCA acquired part-ownership of Electric and Musical Industries (EMI), which itself had resulted from the merger of two British companies involved in the music recording industry. EMI, with direct access to American research, adopted the sophisticated electronic scanning system based on Zworykin's work and pressed for its use by the British Broadcasting Corporation (BBC). Although Baird secured a short-term agreement with the BBC for test transmissions using his mechanical device between 1932 and 1934, it was the RCA system that formed the basis for the beginning of television broadcasting in both the United States and Britain.

Limited television services began in Germany in March 1935, in Britain in November 1936, and in the United States in April 1939. In Nazi Germany television was used entirely for propagandist purposes and reception was restricted to special halls in Berlin. The British service was closed from the outbreak of war in September 1939; the war also delayed development of television in the United States. In each of these countries the major expansion would take place in the more favorable conditions of the postwar years. Television's development would be shaped in part by technology but also by political and social systems and by the institutional arrangements already established for radio broadcasting. The influence of existing forms of entertainment was also important. Like radio, television was a parasitical medium: it borrowed much of its content from existing events – sport, royal weddings, and political conventions, for example – and developed genres that owed much to vaudeville, theater, radio, and cinema.

Eventually the medium would be organized almost universally on the basis of television sets in individual homes. This development was not determined by the technology of television. In some cases – including Nazi Germany, China before the 1970s, and Italy in the early years of television – receivers were placed not in homes but in public places. Indeed, before the 1950s some observers believed that television was most likely to develop in cinemas, in direct competition with the movies, rather than on a domestic basis.[3] These examples remind us that aspects of television often assumed to be inherent in the medium are instead the product of interaction between technology and society.[4]

Postwar Growth: Television from the 1940s to the 1960s

The United States and commercial television

In the United States the prosperity of the 1950s encouraged a rapid growth in television. The number of households with television sets jumped from under 4 million in 1950 to 44 million in 1959, an increase from 9 percent to 86 percent of total households. The number of stations on air increased from 69 in 1949 to 609 in 1959.[5] That US television would develop along the lines of the distinctive American system of broadcasting pioneered by radio in the 1920s was scarcely questioned. The main features of that system – privately owned broadcasting companies funded by the sale of advertising, with limited government regulation through the Federal Communications Commission (FCC) – were established at the outset of the new medium's development. By the mid-1950s the structure of US commercial television had been consolidated. The two original broadcasting networks, the National Broadcasting Company (NBC) and the Columbia Broadcasting System (CBS), along with the younger and weaker American Broadcasting Company (ABC), formed an oligopoly that owed its privileged economic position to the FCC's decision to restrict television services initially to the Very High Frequency (VHF) portion of the electromagnetic spectrum, severely limiting the number of channels in each population center and therefore the possibility of competition. A fourth network, DuMont, struggled and went out of business in 1955.

In the 1950s and 1960s almost all local television stations were affiliated with one of the networks and devoted over 60 percent of their air time, including evenings, to national programming.[6] Despite the high costs of television production, a rapid growth in advertising revenue from the early 1950s ensured high profits for station owners.[7] The decade from 1945 saw a vast increase in the availability of consumer goods in the United States, and in the early 1950s advertisers quickly appreciated the advantages of national television for mass marketing. Television's share of advertising agencies' business expanded enormously as they established new departments to exploit the qualities of the medium. Combining the visual appeal of magazines with the sound and intrusiveness of radio, television seemed to many advertisers to offer special powers of persuasion.[8]

Television advertising at first took the form of sponsorship. As in radio, program development was controlled not by a broadcasting network but by an advertising agency, usually working for a single sponsor. Sponsorship came at a price. In paying to sponsor entire programs, companies felt entitled to have the last word on content, as when the agency representing Camel cigarettes, the sponsor of the *Man Against Crime* series, instructed that scripts were not to "have the heavy or any disreputable person smoking a cigarette."[9] More pervasive than this kind of interference with program details was pressure on producers to avoid controversy, for fear of jeopardizing the sponsor's image. Sponsors' concerns and Cold War political pressures had the same effect: television's early growth coincided with the implementation of the blacklist, and the inclination to tread warily with political and social matters influenced television entertainment as well as its coverage of news and public affairs (see chapter 7).

Yet the early 1950s is often called the "golden age" of American television. Ideological conservatism did not stand in the way of programs which were sometimes of a quality that would later be considered rare in US network television. Interference by sponsors was not the rule; some valued the prestige to be gained from association with programs of high quality and for this reason allowed producers considerable creative freedom.[10] One result was an exploration of the possibilities of television drama. Sponsored anthology series such as Kraft Television Theater, Philco Playhouse, and General Electric Theater presented live plays from New York each week and launched the careers of many distinguished dramatists and actors. Raymond Williams has pointed to the value of such television plays as *Marty* (1953), *Twelve Angry Men* (1954), and *Days of Wine and Roses* (1958): "In substance and in method – the exploring 'eye of the camera', the feel for every-day ordinary life, the newly respected rhythms of the speech of work and the streets and of authentic privacy . . . this new television drama stimulated similar work elsewhere."[11]

The golden age lasted no longer than the mid-1950s. The rapid growth of television in working-class households in itself encouraged a shift from studio drama to lighter entertainment. Moreover, the heyday of anthology drama was a period of network dependence on live broadcasts. It ended with the introduction of videotape and the forging of a new collaborative arrangement with the Hollywood film studios. From the mid-1950s the Hollywood majors began to make their feature film libraries available to television. In the next decade movies became a staple of prime-time programming. At this time, too, the major film studios became convinced of the profits to be made from telefilm production. The way had been shown by the ratings success in 1952 of *I Love Lucy* and *Dragnet*, weekly series produced in independent Hollywood studios. In 1954 ABC's negotiations with Walt Disney, then with Warner Bros., led to production of two highly successful weekly filmed series, *Disneyland* and the Western *Cheyenne*. The other majors followed. By the late 1950s, with live drama all but extinct, prime-time television was dominated by filmed series produced in Hollywood. Westerns were most common (including *Have Gun Will Travel*, *Rawhide*, *Gunsmoke*, and *Bonanza*). Other successful genres of the late 1950s and early 1960s were private detective series (such as *77 Sunset Strip*, *Surfside 6*, and *Hawaiian Eye*), and drama series about doctors (*Ben Casey*, *Dr Kildare*) and lawyers (*Perry Mason*). For the networks, filmed series offered the advantages of being both popular and, by comparison with live drama, cheaper to produce. Advertisers also saw advantages in these programs. Their glamorous settings, attractive stars, and happy endings promised to put viewers in the right mood for the sales pitch of the commercials; while the series form, by creating viewer attachment to particular stars, characters, and situations, allowed advertisers more easily to predict the size and nature of a program's audience.[12]

A fundamental change in the role of advertisers accompanied the shift from live to filmed production. As production costs rose, and as demand for airtime increased advertising charges, it became difficult for one company to sponsor an entire program. Single sponsorship gave way to joint sponsorship and, increasingly, advertising in the form of short "spot" commercials inserted within and between programs. The networks acquired the control over production that had previously been the preserve of sponsors, licensing independent production companies to make programs and selling spots to advertisers. A rigid preoccupation with ratings was the consequence. With advertising spots priced according to the number of people watching a program, networks aimed to maximize profits by attracting the largest possible audience. In the early 1950s a program's viability had depended on the availability of a sponsor. By the end of the decade this was no longer sufficient. Networks cancelled sponsored programs that were well regarded but low rating, fearing that they would adversely affect audience "flow" to the next program. The search for high ratings accentuated the conservative bias of network television. Fear of offending or excluding any significant part of the potential audience reinforced an unwillingness to touch controversial themes and bred a creative caution that was reflected in slavish reliance on proven formulas.

By the end of the decade it was a common view that the networks had betrayed the promise of television's early years. The public interest, critics charged, had been sacrificed to commercial interests, a view fueled by the 1959 revelation of "fixing" in the popular prime-time quiz programs. In 1961 Newton Minow, President J. F. Kennedy's appointment as chairman of the FCC, spoke for these critics when he condemned network television as "a vast wasteland":

> You will see a procession of game shows, violence, audience participation shows, formula comedies about totally unbelievable families, blood and thunder, mayhem, violence, sadism, murder, western badmen, western good men, private eyes, gangsters, more violence, and cartoons. And endlessly, commercials – many screaming, cajoling, and offending.[13]

In the early 1960s the networks sought to appease such high-placed critics and assert their public service bona fides with increased prime-time programming of documentaries and news. The concession was enough to suppress calls for greater government regulation. For all the critics' concerns, there was little evidence of public dissatisfaction with the status quo.[14] News programs aside, the networks defended their programs by appealing to a view of the public interest expressed by CBS president Frank Stanton: "a program in which a large part of the audience is interested is by that very fact . . . in the public interest."[15] In the 1960s the networks provided a steady diet of formulaic situation comedies ("sitcoms") and drama series and increasingly large doses of sports programming.[16]

The contention of the networks' critics that American television should provide for a different view of the public interest found expression in the Public Broadcasting Act of 1967, which established the Public Broadcasting Service (PBS). The country's many non-profit "educational" television stations, permitted on the Ultra High Frequency (UHF) band since 1952, were brought together in a system that was to be partly funded by the federal government. Supporters of the new service hoped that it would provide a successful alternative to commercial television.

Great Britain and public service television

In Britain, too, television grew rapidly in the context of a consumer boom in the 1950s. The proportion of the adult population who owned a television set increased from 4 percent in 1950 to 40 percent in 1955 and 80 percent in 1960.[17] As in the United States, British television developed within an organizational framework inherited from radio. The BBC was at first granted a national monopoly over television. Forbidden to advertise, it was funded by the sale of annual licenses for television and radio receivers. Though state-funded and state-regulated, the BBC was not subject to direct government control. However, this independence was qualified by the government's power to appoint the corporation's board of governors, which in turn appointed the director general and senior staff. It also owed much to an expectation that the BBC would not depart from the orthodoxies of the British establishment. The difficulty of defining the public interest clearly in a way that distinguished it from the state interest, and the tendency for political leaders to assume that the two were synonymous,[18] were highlighted by tensions between the corporation and both major political parties when in power.

The BBC's approach to television programming was heavily influenced by Sir John Reith's definition of broadcasting as a public service – by the idea that broadcasting has a cultural and educative role and is not merely a means of entertainment. In the first postwar decade the corporation's critics blamed the Reithian ethos for television programs that were often cautious, conservative, and, they claimed, dull. The limitations were typified by an avoidance of domestic political discussion, for fear of upsetting the political parties, and by news bulletins that relied heavily on still photographs and, until 1955, did not show the faces of newsreaders. These criticisms were often misplaced. The BBC needed to maintain a broad audience to justify its funding by annual license fee. Even before the start of its postwar television operations, it had moved beyond the narrow interpretation of broadcasting's role that had prevailed in the early years of radio (see chapter 4). The BBC's public service mission and its broadcasting monopoly did contribute to conservative programming, but just as important were a bias towards radio, in a period when the corporation's senior managers were men whose careers had developed in the older medium, and, especially, the austerity of the early postwar years, which limited both the ownership of television sets and the BBC's scope for expenditure on television production.[19]

The advent of general prosperity was bound to bring changes to programming, but widespread dissatisfaction with the BBC's monopoly led to more far-reaching reforms to British television. In 1951 a committee of inquiry on broadcasting chaired by Lord Beveridge criticized the BBC for "the four scandals of monopoly: bureaucracy, complacency, favouritism and inefficiency."[20] Beveridge, nonetheless, recommended that the BBC's monopoly and funding by license fee should continue, on the grounds that commercial television, to judge by the American experience, would be worse. A dissenting report by one of the committee members, Conservative parliamentarian Selwyn Lloyd, urged the establishment of a commercial alternative to the BBC and was welcomed by commercial interests, centered on the entertainment and advertising industries. They successfully lobbied the Conservative government elected in 1951. The Television Act of 1954 established a commercial television service, Independent Television (ITV), administered by an Independent Television Authority (ITA) that owned transmission facilities and granted licenses to 14 companies based in different regions, a provision which responded to the Beveridge report's criticism of centralization under the BBC. The companies were funded by sales of advertising spots, limited to six minutes per hour, with sponsorship ruled out on the grounds that it would give advertisers too much influence on programs. Such restrictions underlined a determination to avoid the worst abuses of American network television. Indeed, the British version of commercial television, far from emulating the US model, represented a distinctively British application of "public service" principles to a commercial broadcasting service. Members of the ITA – and from 1972 its successor, the Independent Broadcasting Authority (IBA) – were government-appointed, like the BBC board of governors. The ITA enjoyed extensive regulatory powers, designed to ensure that ITV companies maintained "balance," "impartiality," and high programming standards. Thus the state-funded BBC and the "independent" commercial companies existed side by side as separate arms of a public service television system.[21]

Nonetheless, to attract large audiences – the key to advertising revenue and profitability – ITV did introduce new kinds of programs to British television, including soap operas, variety shows, quiz programs produced according to American formats, imported American series, and an innovative news service. Inevitably, these programs made inroads into the BBC's audience. The extent to which they did so is difficult to measure and was probably exaggerated both by ITV and within the BBC.[22] But the rise of commercial television did generate criticism of what was perceived to be a lowering of cultural standards and an excessive reliance on imported American programs. These anxieties informed the report of the Pilkington committee of inquiry into broadcasting in 1962. Pilkington criticized ITV for crass commercialism and the alleged triviality and sensationalism of its programs. His report insisted that "winning the largest number of viewers . . . is not the only, and by no means the most important, test of good broadcasting."[23] In the tradition of Reith, the Pilkington report insisted that programs of a high cultural standard should be presented to the broad population rather than confined to an educated minority. As a result of its recommendations, the powers of the ITA were strengthened and a second BBC channel, BBC 2, was established in 1964.

Encouraged by the Pilkington report, the BBC in the 1960s adopted a more innovative approach to programming. Competition between the BBC and ITV proved beneficial for British television. The prosperity of the 1960s provided economic security for both systems and allowed greater investment in production. ITV attracted high levels of advertising revenue, while the BBC's income benefited from an increase in license fees with the introduction of color on BBC 2 in 1967. The existence of a rival television system prevented the BBC from becoming dull or complacent, while the ITA's regulatory powers kept ITV aware of its public service responsibilities and deterred it from seeking to satisfy the lowest common denominator in public taste. Both systems enjoyed about half the viewing audience. British television was responsible for outstanding programs of various kinds: drama, comedy, documentaries, and public affairs programs. If the early 1950s were the golden age of American television, the 1960s were Britain's equivalent.

State television

In the quarter century after 1945, therefore, the development of the medium in Britain and the United States highlighted two contrasting principles, commercial and public service, that might govern television systems. As organizational models, both American and British television were influential internationally, the American system especially in Latin America, the British in the Federal Republic of Germany and, most directly, in those Commonwealth countries – Canada, Australia, New Zealand – where public broadcasters modeled on the BBC coexisted with commercial networks influenced by the US example. Yet neither the British nor the American system was typical of television's institutional arrangements in other countries: direct state control of television services was more common than either. This was true not only of authoritarian regimes such as the Soviet Union and China but also of such Western European democracies as France and Italy. In these cases public service objectives were paramount, but, by comparison with Britain, the public interest was less insulated from the interests of government. State-controlled systems did not necessarily produce bad programs,[24] but pronounced limitations on television's political independence were an incongruous feature of democratic societies. The next three decades would see continuing tension between commercial and public service objectives and marked changes in the roles of governments in the world's television systems.

The Triumph of Commercialism: Television since the 1970s

The United States

The 1970s saw the American networks at the height of their power and profitability. At the end of that decade they enjoyed a 90 percent share of the television audience. Their total revenues increased from $1 billion to $3 billion despite apparent setbacks in the early 1970s. A Congressional ban on cigarette advertising on television from January 1971 cost the networks a lucrative source of revenue. The FCC's Prime Time Access Rule, designed to assist local stations, limited the networks to three hours of prime time nightly from October 1971. The restriction had the unintended effect of increasing demand for limited network advertising time, and this, as well as the new interest in network advertising of such major companies as McDonald's and Coca-Cola, allowed CBS, NBC, and ABC to increase advertising rates steadily through the decade.[25] A preoccupation with ratings continued to govern programming, with the networks' news services the one remaining concession to the idea of broadcasting as public service.

By now, however, the search for high ratings was complicated by a concern for the demographic characteristics of viewers. Research into television audiences taught advertisers to value not large audiences in themselves but large numbers of those viewers most likely to buy the advertised product. For this reason CBS cancelled such high-rating prime-time programs as *The Beverly Hillbillies* and *The Andy Griffith Show*: their popularity was based too much on an appeal to elderly, low-income, and rural viewers, rather than the young, affluent urban-dwellers most prized by advertisers.[26]

Both the advertising industry's preoccupation with "demographics" and broader cultural change shaped programming in the 1970s. Beginning with CBS, the networks sought to exploit the changing attitudes and values that resulted from the Vietnam War, the black civil rights movement, women's liberation, and the 1960s sexual revolution. The previously monoracial world of network programs gradually disappeared, as black characters and images of ethnic togetherness became common.[27] Sitcoms of the early 1970s reflected the new willingness of CBS to deal with controversial subjects – bigotry, abortion, the role of women in society – in order to shift its audience appeal from rural and small-town America, perceived as culturally conservative, to liberal urban and suburban audiences. Such series as *All in the Family*, *Maude*, *The Mary Tyler Moore Show*, *M*A*S*H*, and *Rhoda* won critical acclaim as well as enjoying high ratings. Less sophisticated, and more based on a simple appeal to voyeurism, were the programs that in the second half of the decade lifted ABC from its perennial status as third network to ratings leader. The highly successful sitcoms *Three's Company* and *Soap* relied heavily on sexual situations and dialogue. The action-adventure series *Charlie's Angels*, the mini-series *Roots*, and the movies featured on ABC also owed much of their popularity to sexual content. Such programs were intended to attract a younger audience; their success in doing so could not be ignored by CBS and NBC. As James L. Baughman has written, "ABC had shamelessly played to the broadest taste and, by winning the ratings wars so conclusively, set the terms of battle of its rivals . . . Successfully cultivating the twelve-year-old's cultural preferences, ABC made life more difficult for those producers who proposed series that would appeal to an older, more mature sensibility."[28]

These were the very concerns that had led to the establishment of a public broadcasting alternative to the networks in 1967, but the weakness of PBS soon became apparent. From the outset PBS proved vulnerable to political influence. Members of the Corporation for Public Broadcasting (CPB), which distributes federal funds through the system, are presidential appointees, and all too often appointments were made purely on the basis of political allegiance. The Nixon and Reagan administrations, in particular, were out of sympathy with public broadcasting, regarding PBS as a hotbed of left-wing ideology. Such hostility was reflected both in the nature of appointments to the CPB and in pressure on funding. Republican control of Congress in the late 1990s posed another threat: federal funds for PBS were cut from $312 million in 1996 to $250 million in 1998.[29]

Funding of PBS has always been precarious. Thus in 1993, while Britain spent US$38.99 per citizen on public television and Canada $31.05, the United States spent $6.83 per citizen; and of that amount a mere $1.09 came from the federal government.[30] For the balance of its revenues PBS had to look to a number of sources, including state and local governments, corporate sponsors, and subscribers. The fundraising appeals that have formed a frequent and tedious part of PBS programming underline the extent of the problem. Moreover, revenues are diluted by the decentralized structure of public broadcasting. PBS is a loose federation of many local stations throughout the United States – 347 in 2001 – each with its own transmission equipment, studios, offices, and bureaucracy. Whatever its responsiveness to local needs, the inefficiency of such a system has severely limited the amount of money available for making programs.

PBS has presented some very successful programs. They include the Ken Burns documentary series *The Civil War*, the *MacNeil–Lehrer NewsHour*, and some children's programs, notably *Sesame Street*. But not surprisingly, in view of the chronic shortage of money, many of PBS's best programs have been imported British products, especially from the BBC. In the 1990s that source, too, began to dry up, as the BBC increasingly favored cable channels at the expense of PBS. A chronic fear of antagonizing corporate sponsors, the White House, Congressmen, and anyone else whose displeasure might threaten PBS stations' funding, encouraged bland, cautious programming, reflected in a paucity of good documentaries, of strong coverage of politics, of original drama and comedy, and in programs which were often indistinguishable from the content of commercial television (they often included reruns of old network programs).[31] Yet these concessions to commercialism did not win PBS popularity: its ratings remained consistently at around 2 percent of the total viewing audience. PBS, therefore, suffered the worst of both worlds, failing as both a public service and a commercial broadcaster.

While PBS posed no threat to the oligopoly of CBS, NBC, and ABC, the rapid rise of cable television from the late 1970s, made possible by the use of satellite technology, followed by growth in the number of independent stations in the 1980s and the creation of Rupert Murdoch's Fox network in 1986, caused the established networks far greater concern. These new forms of competition greatly eroded the three networks' audience share, from around 90 percent in prime time in the late 1970s, to 60 percent in 1990, to around 50 percent in 2000. A boom in video cassette recorder (VCR) ownership and video rentals during the 1980s further undermined the networks' dominance. The use of VCRs for "time shifting," and the growing popularity of remote control devices, interfered with careful calculations of audience flow and, by allowing viewers more easily to avoid commercials, further reduced the attraction of network television to advertisers (see chapter 11).[32]

In this fiercely competitive market all three networks were taken over by conglomerates which, in their insistence that every division be profitable, heightened the preoccupation with ratings and desperation to please advertisers. The scope to do so was extended by the triumph of an ideology of "deregulation" in the FCC in the 1980s – the body's chairman during the Reagan administration defined the public interest simply as "that which interests the public"[33] – effectively eliminating public service concerns as an obstacle to commercial interests in broadcasting. The networks' subservience to advertisers was evident in three ways. First, the removal of FCC restrictions led to an increase in the amount of advertising time on television.[34] Second, the lines between commercials and programs were blurred. Since the 1950s television programs had served "to naturalize the world of consumer goods by turning even domestic dramas into de facto fashion shows and shopping catalogues."[35] From the mid-1980s the commercial purpose of programs was even more blatant, with product placement, long a feature of movies, becoming increasingly common in television entertainment.[36] Third, a desire to maximize advertising revenues and profits encouraged network complicity in the growth of "trash television" – programs characterized by tabloid journalism of a particularly sensationalist kind, by a frequent blurring of the lines between reality and fiction, and by a preoccupation with sleaze. The term embraces a number of kinds of programs, including daytime "talk shows," "news magazine" programs such as *Hard Copy* and *A Current Affair*, and "reality" shows which purport to examine the lives of real people – all programs that were both popular and cheap to produce.[37] Meanwhile the quality of television news and public affairs programming – as measured by willingness to allow journalistic values to prevail over the conventions of television entertainment – declined. In the last years of the century, therefore, competitive pressures and the end of regulation led to programming trends that seemed to vindicate the worst fears of commercial television's critics.[38]

Great Britain

Commercial considerations became more important in British television from the 1970s. The period did see one important development in Britain's public service broadcasting system with the creation of Channel 4, which began transmission in 1982. A commercial channel but heavily regulated by the IBA, it was intended to cater for minority audiences, who were thought not to be well served by ITV. It was funded by an annual levy imposed on the ITV companies, which were allowed to sell advertising on the new channel. It also differed from the existing ITV stations in that it did not produce programs, taking them instead from independent production companies. Channel 4 was generally greeted as a valuable addition to Britain's television system. However, other forms of public broadcasting faced new difficulties. Starting in the 1970s, the BBC encountered increasing financial difficulties when revenue from the license fee failed to keep pace with rising production costs. ITV, for its part, responded to the growing costs of programming by raising the price of advertising, a solution which led advertisers to be more critical of restrictions on the nature and amount of advertising on ITV and to press for the creation of new channels. The rise of cable, satellite, and VCR technology in the 1980s increased pressure on both ITV and the BBC: on the former by creating competition for advertisers' expenditure on television, on the latter by threatening the BBC's audience share and therefore its case for an increase in the license fee.[39]

Growing ideological opposition to public service broadcasting, one aspect of the neoliberal economic ideas that gained influence after the 1960s, found a powerful political voice in Margaret Thatcher, prime minister from 1979 to 1990. Thatcher's government showed scant respect for the conventions of BBC independence from the state, filling the board of governors with government sympathizers who tended to view the corporation as a center of left-wing bias, unpatriotic attitudes, and loose morals, and who did not hesitate to interfere in its management. The BBC's revenues were severely cut by the simple expedient of not increasing the license fee in a period of inflation. Staff numbers were reduced, the powers of the board of governors were increased, the corporation was required after 1990 to draw more of its programs from independent production houses, and morale was further eroded by a restructuring that reflected some of the excesses of late-twentieth-century "managerialism." Yet the corporation survived these trials: it resisted political pressure to introduce advertising, retained a large audience share, and continued to make programs of high quality. It remained the world's preeminent public service broadcaster. Nonetheless, the public service ethos of BBC programmers continued to be under threat, and the corporation stood accused of abandoning "its commitment to enlighten and inform" by presenting "a distinctively English mix of gardening, cooking, quiz shows, home improvement, and low-end comedy, interspersed with nostalgic recollections from its better days."[40]

The extent of the threat to public service broadcasting was highlighted by the 1990 Broadcasting Act, which reorganized ITV. Franchises for television companies were to be auctioned, and the IBA was replaced by the weaker Independent Television Commission, which lacked its predecessor's powers to control program quality. Deregulation and the pressures of a competitive television market led to reduced spending on production, a greater reliance on imports, and increased emphasis on the pursuit of ratings and, therefore, the lowest common denominator in popular taste.

A steady diet of "pop, chat, soap, and sport," on ITV as well as cable and satellite stations, seemed the likely result.[41] Public service responsibilities, once central to the purpose of British commercial television, were pushed to the background.

International developments

The 1970s saw the start of a vast expansion of the television audience outside its initial strongholds in the developed world. In the last three decades of the century there took place a huge increase in the number of television sets in the Soviet Union, China, and developing countries. By the 1990s the majority of the world's television audience lived in the Third World, with the largest audience in China.[42] During the same period major institutional and technological changes occurred. From the 1980s commercial interests took on a greater importance in television throughout the world. The growth of consumer societies, the ready availability of advertising revenue, financial pressures on state-funded television systems, growing ideological support for deregulation, and the undermining of political regulations by a vast proliferation of cable and satellite stations, often transmitting programs that could be received by viewers in more than one country, weakened state television monopolies in many countries. The creation of new commercial stations, the privatization of some state-owned channels, and an easing of restrictions on advertising on state networks were the results. In Western Europe, where state television monopolies were the rule in the 1970s, the effect of the growing commercialization of the medium was to increase the number of terrestrial stations from 38 in 1980 to 125 in 1991, while by the early 1990s there were more than 140 satellite channels. The extent of change is also underlined by the growing importance of advertising even in the television system of the world's one remaining major communist power.[43]

In the 1990s, therefore, public broadcasters in many countries came under pressure. To maintain audience share in the face of new forms of competition, and to justify continuation of their public funding, they increasingly resorted to programs that were indistinguishable from those shown on commercial television; and in this way they brought into question the very reason for their existence. The new technologies lent plausibility to the argument that minority audiences, formerly dependent on public service broadcasting, could be catered for by cable television rather than subsidized by the taxpayer. By the end of the century the future of public service broadcasting systems, and of the ethos that had supported them, was uncertain. The triumph of commercial television, meanwhile, presented a fundamental paradox. While the 20 years from 1980 saw a huge increase in the number of television stations globally, and in this sense a far more competitive medium, real program choice had been greatly circumscribed. Competition for advertising revenue had created a universal trend to follow the path pioneered by US commercial television: to emphasize formulaic light entertainment at the expense of alternative program forms.[44]

Global television

During the 1950s the American networks built upon their domestic ascendancy by selling programs abroad. By the end of the decade US companies dominated international television markets, and they have continued to do so. American programs have enjoyed a prominent place in prime-time television throughout the world, accounting for almost half of all imported programs worldwide, far more in Canada and Latin America.[45] Even locally produced programs have often been made according to American formats. Indeed, American genres were so influential that they came to be thought of as natural to the medium.[46]

Also important were two other aspects of US preeminence in international program sales. One is that from the early 1960s, as the expense of telefilm production increased, the American industry concluded that foreign sales were essential if profits were to be made. The other is that the United States has been almost the only country not to import a large proportion of its television programs. Moreover, its tiny percentage of imports, mainly from Britain, has been limited to PBS and cable. The commercial networks have preferred to remake foreign series for American audiences (thus *Sanford and Son*, *All in the Family*, and *Three's Company* were based on the British sitcoms *Steptoe and Son*, *Till Death Us Do Part*, and *Man About the House*). The implications for public attitudes of this peculiarity of American television, in a country in which a tendency towards parochialism is already encouraged by the sense of exceptionalism central to American nationalism, and by a decline in overseas reporting in television news programs, are likely to be far-reaching.

The causes of American dominance of international markets lay in the expense of television production, which gave a strong economic incentive to import programs, and in the American industry's capacity to respond to international demand for popular and relatively cheap entertainment. The international advantages of US television were the same as those of the US film industry; and, of course, the lines between the two were blurred when

Hollywood involved itself in telefilm production. Control of a large domestic market permitted high levels of investment in production, while American filmmakers proved adept at creating entertainment – including television sitcoms, drama series, Westerns, soap operas, and cartoons – that enjoyed worldwide appeal. From the 1980s the proliferation of cable, satellite, and terrestrial television channels throughout the world and consequent short-age of programming, pressure to cut costs in a new competitive market, growing dependence on advertising revenue, and increased pressure on state media systems to be responsive to audience tastes all increased inter-national demand for American programs.[47]

From the 1950s American preeminence in global television led to a renewal of the widespread fears of "Americanization" that American film exports had generated since the 1920s. In the 1970s these anxieties were expressed in communication scholars' warnings of "cultural imperialism." From the mid-1980s the concerns of European intellectuals and politicians focused more on their own countries than on the Third World. Denunci-ation of the melodrama *Dallas* by the French minister of culture, Jack Lang, in 1983 gave expression to growing fears that the American way of life was being imposed on European countries through the impact of American mass culture. In response to these fears the European Community imposed quotas on non-European programs permitted into Western Europe, restric-tions which became an issue in trade negotiations with the United States.[48] At the end of the 1990s concerns about the harmful cultural effects of American media exports continued in the form of criticisms of "globaliza-tion." Yet simple images of a one-way flow of American programs, estab-lishing US economic, political, and social control over the rest of the world, do not do justice to the complexities of global television (see chapter 12).

Public Affairs Programming

As a source of news and discussion of public affairs, national television networks have commanded larger audiences than newspapers and radio stations. From the 1960s a majority of respondents to opinion polls in the United States have claimed to rely mainly on television for news.[49] Whether this apparent trust is justified is a question of central importance to an understanding of the role of television in society.

The US networks' news divisions enjoyed a special status for two decades from the early 1960s. In September 1963 CBS and NBC extended their evening news bulletins from 15 to 30 minutes (followed by ABC in 1967) and freed their news divisions from the commercial considerations that governed other programs. By respecting the professional autonomy of good journalists, the networks sought to regain prestige and protect themselves from government regulators such as FCC chairman Minow.[50] In Britain, meanwhile, the development of strong news services was one of the benefits of competition between the BBC and ITV. Raymond Williams, writing during the early 1970s after systematically watching both British and American television news bulletins, commented on the high journalistic standards of television, noting that "the selection and relative priority of news items" were similar to those of quality newspapers and far removed from those of the tabloid press.[51] Moreover, the advantages of the visual element in television news have often been made clear – for example, in reporting on the civil rights marches and demonstrations in the United States in the early 1960s, the student demonstrations and massacre in Beijing's Tiananmen Square in 1989, the downfall of Eastern European communist regimes in the same year, and the terrorist attacks on New York and Washington on September 11, 2001.

Televised public proceedings also demonstrated the medium's value as a source of information; especially important was coverage of national political party conventions and Congressional hearings in the United States, and of parliamentary sessions in Britain and other countries. As early as 1951 Edward R. Murrow's weekly public affairs program See It Now, on the CBS network, underlined the potential of the medium for investigative journalism. In Britain the golden age of the 1960s and early 1970s included the production of outstanding documentaries and public affairs discussion and interview programs. With these in mind Williams observed, "broadcasting as a whole, and television especially, has markedly broadened the forms of public argument and discussion."[52]

Often, however, television news and public affairs programming has been marked by superficiality; a temptation to emphasize the visual at all costs, placing the demands of entertainment above journalistic criteria, has accentuated this.[53] Political timidity and an unthinking conservatism, arising from television's relationship with society and the state, have also been apparent. This characteristic is most obvious in state-controlled media, especially in closed societies such as the Soviet Union and China, but it has also been evident in democracies, such as France, where political interference was a feature of television's development. Even the BBC, although not subject to direct government control, limited its news service and domestic political discussion during its period of television monopoly in the early 1950s, partly out of fear of offending the political parties.

On commercial television, too, news and public affairs programming has proved vulnerable to political pressures. The example of television in Russia since 1991 highlights the potential abuse of privately owned television outside the framework of a stable democracy: in the 1996 presidential election television was used as a weapon to attack opponents of the incumbent, Boris Yeltsin. In the United States television's postwar development was shaped by the Cold War and the blacklisting of alleged communist sympathizers in broadcasting. In the 1950s television news and political commentary reflected the industry's collaboration with the US government and whole-hearted engagement in the anti-communist cause (see chapter 7).

It is often pointed out that television contributed to Senator Joseph McCarthy's downfall. A series of documentaries by Edward Murrow on *See It Now* in 1953–4 exposed McCarthy as an unscrupulous bully. Televised Senate hearings between McCarthy and the Army in 1954 further undermined his credibility and helped bring about his censure by the Senate. Yet it is significant that the Murrow exposé was not only late in coming (four years after McCarthy's rise to national prominence) but that it received only minimal support from CBS and *See It Now*'s sponsor, Alcoa. In the aftermath of McCarthy's downfall neither CBS nor the other networks showed any enthusiasm for the investigative journalism with which Murrow was identified. *See It Now* was axed in 1958, after several years of difficulty in maintaining adequate sponsorship, and was not replaced by anything similar. Its decline was symptomatic of the priorities of American television, as was the fact that the Army–McCarthy hearings were televised only on the weaker ABC and DuMont networks, with CBS and NBC preferring to fill their daytime schedules with entertainment.[54]

Even in the 1960s, when the networks elevated public affairs to a more prestigious role in their programming, news and documentaries still reflected an uncritical view of US government policy.[55] A more critical approach did develop in the late 1960s and early 1970s in the context of the failure of US military intervention in Vietnam and the Watergate scandal involving the administration of President Richard Nixon. Tensions emerged between the media and political leaders, with Vice-President Spiro Agnew attacking network television for alleged ideological bias and excessive power. Yet a new willingness to interrogate or criticize politicians – especially unpopular politicians – did not alter the fundamental tendency of the networks to avoid programs that were likely to alienate any significant part of the mass audience that is crucial to the medium's appeal to advertisers. The need to remain in step with majority opinion discouraged critical examination of the policies of political leaders who, like President

Ronald Reagan in the 1980s, were skilled in exploiting popular sentiment. In the last years of the Cold War, as in the 1950s, network news and public affairs programs aligned themselves with the strident American nationalism that flourished in that period.[56]

From the 1970s the protection of network news from commercial pressures weakened. Deregulation and fierce competition in the 1980s had a major impact on television journalism. The importance of network news bulletins for nightly audience flow exposed them to pressure to be more conscious of ratings. So too did the success of new forms of competition in the provision of national news. The Cable News Network (CNN) began in 1980. A vogue for "news magazine" programs – which defined the news as "what's got good pictures, what's got sex appeal"[57] – began with such programs as *60 Minutes* and *48 Hours* and culminated in the popularity of *A Current Affair*, *Hard Copy*, and similar tabloid programs. From the 1970s, too, the profitability of local news services, in which journalistic content was minimal, demonstrated to network executives the benefits to be gained from redefining the news as entertainment. As a result, the journalistic standards once important in network news were eroded. The consequences were a greater emphasis on visual imagery, ten second soundbites, and "human interest" stories. Reporting on national politics was reduced and increasingly trivialized. International affairs received little attention at all.

Equally disturbing was the fragmentation of the news audience: with the rise of cable, an increasing proportion of American viewers either avoided news programs altogether or received their "news" in the distorted forms of tabloid television journalism. With newspaper circulations in decline, the prospect that the audience for serious coverage of public affairs would be restricted to an educated minority has disturbing implications for democratic society. These trends, moreover, have not been limited to the United States, although they have been most fully developed there.[58]

Television and Politics

Television's role in politics has been the focus of much of the discussion of the medium's influence. From the 1950s television increasingly played a central role in the conduct of political campaigns. It enabled political candidates to reach large audiences quickly, without the time-consuming travel that had previously characterized campaigning. Also attractive to politicians and their advisers were the opportunities that television provided to "package" a candidate's presentation to the public without the mediation of journalists. As early as the 1952 US presidential election campaign an advertising agency prepared a series of short television commercials for the Republican candidate, Dwight D. Eisenhower. Vice-presidential candidate Richard Nixon used his Checkers speech, an emotional television appeal to the public, to defend himself from charges of financial impropriety.

Of course, television sometimes played a more constructive role than facilitating politicians' manipulation of voters. Where public affairs programming was well developed, as in Britain in the 1960s and 1970s, political leaders submitted themselves to "more open and public questioning of their policies than has ever been the case in any comparable communications system."[59] Nonetheless, the idea that the key to political success lay in the skillful use of television to create a politician's image came increasingly to be taken for granted. It received a major boost from the political career of the telegenic John F. Kennedy. A televised "debate" between Kennedy and Nixon in the 1960 presidential election campaign soon became the centerpiece in a store of commonly accepted wisdom on the crucial role of television image in politics. Kennedy appeared fit, tanned, and well-groomed; Nixon, showing the effects of a recent illness, was pale, underweight, and haggard. Polls indicated that a majority of viewers believed Kennedy had won, while among the radio audience most thought Nixon the winner. Two decades later, the political success of President Ronald Reagan was widely believed to stem from clever management of image, especially through television. In such cases the effects of media manipulation were too readily assumed rather than subjected to analysis; it is questionable whether voters were so easily swayed by slick media presentation of politicians and their policies.[60] Yet the belief that this was the case acquired the status of a truism among political parties and their public relations consultants, and not only in the United States. In Britain a preoccupation with political leaders' television image began with Conservative Prime Minister Harold Macmillan in the late 1950s and culminated in the tightly controlled television appearances of Margaret Thatcher between 1979 and 1990.[61] The trend was virtually universal.

In the United States the politicians' fondness for media packaging converged with television's blurring of the lines between public affairs and entertainment. The result was television treatment of politics as a kind of sporting contest, preoccupied with who is winning, who is losing, and with image and personality at the expense of issues and policies. Since the 1980s the central role of journalism in television reporting on presidential campaigns has more and more been superseded by "infotainment" programs. In 1992 Democrat candidate Bill Clinton set the tone for this approach, making 47 appearances on television talk shows.[62] In 2000 coverage of the national party conventions by the three broadcasting networks, once a normal part of presidential elections, was greatly reduced, but appearances on the late-night comedy talk shows of Jay Leno and David Letterman were regarded as essential for both George W. Bush and Al Gore. An almost complete absence of discussion of issues was the hallmark of television coverage of the 2000 elections.[63] In such cases television reflected and reinforced the shallowness of Western culture at the start of the twenty-first century. In the United States, too, the huge cost of television advertising, the main means by which political candidates get their message across to voters, has restricted political office to those who are either personally wealthy or who receive "campaign contributions" from the wealthy.[64] It is hard to avoid the conclusion that, on balance, television has played a deleterious role in politics in recent years, especially in the United States.

The Impact of Television

The impact of television in the second half of the twentieth century was in some ways clearcut. Television became the most popular form of mass entertainment and affected the development of other media. It quickly became a global medium. As the chief vehicle for national and international advertising, it was central to the growth of consumer economies. The influence of television changed the nature of political campaigning; it also led to changes in media–military relations (see chapter 10).

Changes in the world of sport provide one illustration of television's impact. Television provided the possibility of huge national and international audiences for sporting events, as well as enormous advertising potential through sports sponsorship. Links between television, sport, and sponsorship progressively tightened. Television stimulated greater professionalization of sport. Television led to new game formats, rule changes, and game modifications, in some cases specifically to allow advertising breaks during games to satisfy sponsors. Sports sponsorship grew exponentially. The interrelationship between television and sport is illustrated in the enormous amounts now paid by television networks for rights to televise major international events such as the Olympic Games and the soccer World Cup.[65]

However, the complexity of the question of television's impact becomes clear when we move beyond such straightforward examples and raise more contentious questions about television's effects, some of them already discussed in this chapter: has television been a vehicle for US or Western

political and economic domination of other countries; has television enabled politicians to influence voters through image management; has television assisted advertisers to manipulate consumer behavior; have television
programs fostered violence or anti-social behavior among youth? There is
no scholarly consensus on such issues, but there is now little support for
claims that television has the power easily to manipulate popular attitudes
and values. Such views exaggerate the passivity of audiences and, by attrib-
uting to television too central a role, underestimate the complexity of cultural change. On the effects of television advertising, for example, recent
studies emphasize the problem posed for advertisers by "clutter:" the vast
number of commercials on television reduces the likelihood that any particular advertisement will be noticed, let alone have its intended effect.[66]
On the controversial subject of the effects on children of television depictions of violence, the weight of evidence suggests that watching television
programs is unlikely to lead to violent or anti-social behavior except in
cases where a predisposition to such behavior exists.[67]

Yet while the more far-reaching claims for television's influence may be
rejected, it remains indisputable that images and ideas conveyed by television can shape and reinforce popular attitudes. Television's influence on
behavior, ideas, language, and fashion has derived from its power to suggest what is normal, desirable, and important. Sometimes its influence can
be exerted in surprisingly positive ways. Thus the late 1970s American
drama *Holocaust*, when shown on West German television, confronted German audiences with aspects of their history that many of them had not
known or thought about, prompting the journalist Heinz Hohne to write:

> An American television series, made in a trivial style, produced more for
> commercial than moral reasons, more for entertainment than for enlighten-
> ment, accomplished what hundreds of books, plays, films, and television pro-
> grams, thousands of documents, and all the concentration camp trials have
> failed to do in the more than three decades since the end of the war: to
> inform Germans about crimes against Jews committed in their name so that
> millions were emotionally touched and moved.[68]

Often, however, the influence of television gave grounds for concern.
Racial and gender stereotyping in television programs, the increasing tendency of television to condescend to its audience, and the decline of news
and public affairs programming, were all causes of well-founded criticism.
Moreover, the development of television as above all a commercial medium,

with advertising and the celebration of consumer culture at the center of its programming, has had consequences which have undoubtedly been profound, although not yet fully examined. In the United States the post-war growth of commercial television reinforced those tendencies, promoted by advertising since the 1920s, to view American society as prosperous and classless – as one in which the only significant differences were those of freely chosen "lifestyle." The rise of television consolidated the tendency in commercial popular culture to distract attention from economic and social inequalities and to undermine support for political measures to deal with them.[69] The growing global influence of the US commercial broad-casting model in the late twentieth century suggested that television would have similar effects in other affluent societies. In poor countries, mean-while, it seemed likely that television had created new levels of dissatis-faction among people whose own living standards were far removed from those depicted on screen.[70]

An image of society as classless need not encourage tolerance or coop-eration. Beginning in the mid-1970s, driven by the rise of cable television, American advertisers developed a vision of America as a fragmented popu-lation of selfish, suspicious individuals whose ties extended no further than people who share the same "lifestyle." Target markets, in which advertisers and media companies divide the population into narrow segments accord-ing to such distinctions as age, gender, income, and marital status, replaced the mass marketing of the past. The consequences for social cohesion, most immediately in the United States but by implication in other countries affected by similar developments in media and advertising, constitute one of the central problems concerning the role of media in society today.[71]

An examination of television in historical and comparative perspect-ive highlights the range of cultural possibilities presented by the medium. The commercial organization of television and an emphasis on popular entertainment programs, although often assumed to be a natural outgrowth of the technology, are in reality a product of political and economic arrange-ments in particular societies. The prominence of public service television in some countries, especially before the 1980s, and the attention given to cultural and journalistic criteria in some broadcasting systems, serve as a reminder that the technology itself is neutral, and that the uses to which it can be put are varied. "What are the effects of television?" is a useful question only when the role of television is viewed in historical context, with full regard to the interests and ideas that have shaped the uses of the medium.[72]

Further reading

Barker, Chris. *Global Television: An Introduction.* Oxford: Blackwell, 1997.

Barnouw, Erik. *Tube of Plenty: The Evolution of American Television.* Oxford: Oxford University Press, 1982.

Baughman, James L. *The Republic of Mass Culture: Journalism, Filmmaking, and Broadcasting in America since 1941.* Baltimore, MD: Johns Hopkins University Press, 1992.

Buscombe, Edward (ed.). *British Television: A Reader.* Oxford: Oxford University Press, 2000.

Curran, James, and Jean Seaton. *Power Without Responsibility: The Press and Broadcasting in Britain,* 5th edn. London: Routledge, 1997.

Donovan, Robert J., and Ray Scherer. *Unsilent Revolution: Television News and American Public Life.* Cambridge: Cambridge University Press, 1992.

Hallin, Daniel C. *We Keep America on Top of the World: Television Journalism and the Public Sphere.* London: Routledge, 1994.

Hong, Junhao. *The Internationalization of Television in China: The Evolution of Ideology, Society, and Media Since the Reform.* Westport, CT: Praeger, 1998.

Ledbetter, James. *Made Possible By . . . : The Death of Public Broadcasting in the United States.* London: Verso, 1997.

Rose, Brian G. (ed.). *TV Genres: A Handbook and Reference Guide.* Westport, CT: Greenwood Press, 1985.

Seymour-Ure, Colin. *The British Press and Broadcasting Since 1945,* 2nd edn. Oxford: Blackwell, 1996.

Smith, Anthony, with Richard Paterson (eds.). *Television: An International History,* 2nd edn. Oxford: Oxford University Press, 1998.

Turow, Joseph. *Breaking Up America: Advertisers and the New Media World.* Chicago, IL: University of Chicago Press, 1997.

Watson, Mary Ann. *The Expanding Vista: American Television in the Kennedy Years.* Durham, NC: Duke University Press, 1994.

Williams, Kevin. *Get Me a Murder a Day! A History of Mass Communication in Britain.* London: Arnold, 1998 (chapters 8–9).

Williams, Raymond. *Television: Technology and Cultural Form.* New York: Schocken Books, 1975.

9

MEDIA, INFORMATION, AND ENTERTAINMENT

The impact of television on older media was difficult to foresee in the early postwar years. Samuel Goldwyn was more prescient than most when he suggested that Hollywood was about to enter a new stage in its development – after the silent period and the sound era, the film industry now faced the "Television Age."[1] The same might have been said of the print media and radio. At the end of World War II there was, as James L. Baughman has written, "a rough equality among the mass media."[2] Television upset this equilibrium and established its dominance to such an extent that fears were held for the survival of cinema, newspapers, magazines, and radio. Yet by coming to terms with television's supremacy and accepting a secondary role in the provision of information and entertainment, these media adjusted well to the altered circumstances of the second half of the century. In each case the adjustment involved major changes in the medium's structure and content. In considering the development of these media, this chapter looks first at changes in the US film industry and its relationship with cinema in other countries. In examining the experience of the press and radio, the chapter continues the American and British case studies begun in chapters 2 and 4.

The End of the Hollywood Studio System

The world's dominant film industry prospered from its wartime collaboration with the US government's propaganda campaigns (see chapter 6). At the end of the war, with the oligopoly of eight major firms still intact, Hollywood appeared to be at the height of its success. In 1946 average weekly movie attendances in the United States reached 90 million, a level not seen since 1930. At the same time pent-up demand for American films in postwar Europe provided a rich source of profits for the US industry. Yet such signs of health were misleading. There followed a rapid decline both in the fortunes of the major film companies and in the status of cinema as a mass entertainment medium. By 1956 American weekly movie attendances had fallen to around half their level of a decade earlier; while weekly attendance per household declined rapidly from a postwar peak of 2.35 in 1946 to 1.38 in 1950 and 0.76 in 1960. One of the Big Five, RKO, went out of business in 1955, while the other majors suffered a steady decline in box-office receipts and profits.[3]

Competition from television, which grew rapidly from 1948, provides a large part of the explanation for film's decline, but other factors also contributed. As a result of the postwar growth of suburbs – with theaters still concentrated in downtown areas – and of the financial commitments of young families with the start of the "baby boom," cinema-going became less convenient and less affordable. More difficult to assess is the long-term impact on the US film industry of the HUAC investigations and the black-listing that followed (see chapter 7). But it is clear that this episode both encouraged extreme caution towards movie content and deprived the industry of a large pool of talented actors, directors, writers, and technicians at a time when it could least afford to lose them.

Another cause of the US industry's problems is also clear. In 1948 the majors were dealt a severe blow when the Supreme Court ruled on *United States vs. Paramount*, the federal government's long-standing anti-trust case against the film industry. Accepting the Justice Department's argument that vertical integration constituted an illegal restraint of trade, the court ordered the Big Five to divest themselves of their theater chains. They therefore relinquished the most profitable part of their activities – exhibition – and became chiefly production and distribution companies. Moreover, all eight majors were affected by the court's prohibition of the practice of "block booking," which had obliged exhibitors to rent films in blocks rather than individually and had guaranteed the film companies a return on every film made. With the loss of their control over exhibition and with profits less certain, the majors cut production, concentrated on making films that seemed most likely to succeed at the box office, and relied more on distribution as a source of revenue. The films they distributed were increasingly made by independent production companies: unburdened by high studio overheads, independents received a boost from the Supreme Court ruling. The decline of the Hollywood studio system – by which stars, producers, directors, writers, and all the technical staff involved in film production were employed on long-term contracts by the studios, each run by a powerful "movie mogul" – was hastened by the *Paramount* decision. By 1960 that system had collapsed. Film production was now based on deals negotiated by freelance producers, directors, or stars; the majors acted chiefly as distributors and financiers.

While seeking to adjust to these fundamental structural changes, the film industry adopted two main strategies to meet the challenge of television. One involved forging a cooperative relationship with the television networks. During the 1950s the majors recognized that in some respects the success of the new medium could be turned to their advantage. Production of television programs, the sale of old movies to television, and, by the late 1960s, the production of movies for television, became important sources of revenue for the major film companies. Another strategy was to exploit film's relative advantages. With television viewing confined mainly to small, black-and-white sets, technological innovation offered one solution. An experiment with three-dimensionality was short-lived, but a move from black-and-white to color films (with color the norm by the 1960s) and development of stereophonic sound and widescreen projection had a long-term impact.

In the 1950s the majors looked to exploit these innovations with big-budget, prestige films, relying on lavish production values and spectacular visual appeal to entice audiences away from their television sets. Westerns, musicals, and epics – *Quo Vadis* (1951), *The Robe* (1953), *The Ten Commandments* (1956), *Ben Hur* (1959) – lent themselves especially well to this approach and were also politically uncontroversial, an important consideration at the height of the Cold War. At the same time, drive-in theaters appealed to suburban and teenage audiences: the number of drive-ins in the United States increased from 820 in 1948 to over 4,000 ten years later.[4]

These strategies enabled the US film industry to survive the immediate challenge from television but did not provide a long-term solution to the problem of Hollywood's decline. In 1962 box-office receipts fell to a postwar low of $903 million.[5] The studios continued to look to the production of big-budget prestige films as the surest road to profitability. Vindication of this approach seemed to come with the commercial success of *Lawrence of Arabia* (1962), *Doctor Zhivago* (1965), and a number of musicals: *West Side Story* (1961), *Mary Poppins* (1964), *My Fair Lady* (1964), and the highly successful *The Sound of Music* (1965). But the huge risks of this "blockbuster" approach were highlighted by the failure of *Cleopatra* (1963) – the film that almost bankrupted 20th Century-Fox – and of a string of musicals with which the studios attempted to emulate the success of *The Sound of Music*. In 1969 most of the major firms incurred losses, and big-budget musicals were thought to be largely to blame.[6] A series of takeovers between 1967 and 1969 highlighted the majors' financial vulnerability. Paramount was purchased by Gulf and Western, a conglomerate chiefly involved in steel and mining; Warner Bros. by Kinney National Services, a funeral home, car rental, and parking lot company; United Artists by TransAmerica, a banking and insurance company; and MGM by Kirk Kerkorian, a Las Vegas hotel magnate.

The limited success of the prestige films of the 1960s emphasized the costs of Hollywood's persistence in trying to produce movies with universal appeal. Such an approach had worked well in the 1930s and 1940s but was far less appropriate when television became the dominant medium of mass entertainment. Above all, it ignored the cinema-going potential of 18–25-year-olds. This group had little interest in musicals, regardless of their lavish production values; but its patronage of foreign "art house" and independent films suggested an interest in movies that contained more adult content – particularly movies that demonstrated a more open attitude to sex – than could be found in most Hollywood products. The majors' capacity to exploit this market was hamstrung by their attempt to make movies suitable for all age groups and, related to that, by their insistence on retaining the 1930 Production Code, even though it lived on in an increasingly watered-down form in the 1950s and 1960s and was challenged by adventurous filmmakers such as Otto Preminger in *The Moon Is Blue* (1953), *The Man with the Golden Arm* (1955), and *Advise and Consent* (1962), Elia Kazan in *Baby Doll* (1956), and Stanley Kubrick in *Lolita* (1962). In contrast to the 1920s, when Hollywood had reflected and helped define changing cultural values, the US film industry was slow to respond to the changes of the 1960s.[7]

The box office success of two films produced in 1967, Arthur Penn's *Bonnie and Clyde* and Mike Nichols's *The Graduate*, the former characterized by graphic depiction of violence, the latter by its direct approach to sex, marked the end of this approach. The Code, now regarded as untenable, was abolished in 1968 and replaced by a ratings system. Freed from the Code's constraints, the studios in 1969 released films that proved popular with the "baby boom" generation: *Easy Rider*, *Midnight Cowboy*, *The Wild Bunch*, *Alice's Restaurant*, and *Goodbye, Columbus*. A new generation of American directors demonstrated that it was possible to make low-budget films that were both commercially and artistically successful. The first half of the 1970s saw the release of movies generally regarded as representing one of the most impressive periods of American filmmaking. They included Martin Scorsese's *Mean Streets* (1973), *Alice Doesn't Live Here Any More* (1974), and *Taxi Driver* (1976), Peter Bogdanovich's *The Last Picture Show* (1971), Robert Altman's *M*A*S*H* (1970), *McCabe and Mrs Miller* (1971), and *Nashville* (1975), Francis Ford Coppola's *The Godfather* (1972) and *The Conversation* (1974), George Lucas's *American Graffiti* (1973), and Roman Polanski's *Chinatown* (1974).

International Cinema

Following the disruption of wartime, the US film industry was quick to reestablish its main export markets. It did so with support from US government agencies, which regarded Hollywood as vital to Cold War cultural diplomacy. With the decline in domestic box-office takings, foreign sales became more important than ever to the major US firms. By the 1960s more than half Hollywood's income came from exports, especially to Western Europe.[8] The American industry's international dominance was not affected by its domestic problems. The Italian, French, and British film industries each enjoyed a brief postwar "golden age," but Hollywood's competitive advantage was as clear as it had been in the interwar years.[9] With few exceptions – Japan, India, the protected markets of communist countries – film industries outside the United States have struggled to maintain economic viability.

Nonetheless, the postwar period saw significant changes in the relationship between the United States and cinema in the rest of the world. Although few national film industries could compete with Hollywood, even in their home markets, the US industry's postwar cuts in production allowed a larger number of imported foreign films to be exhibited in American theaters, to the point where, between 1961 and 1965, imports accounted for more than two-thirds of films screened in the United States.[10] Above all, the postwar rise of "art house" cinemas in the United States and Europe, and the establishment of international film festivals at Venice and Cannes, enabled many European and Asian directors to achieve international success, especially among young, middle-class, educated filmgoers who saw cinema as an art form as well as entertainment. Filmmakers who rose to international prominence between the 1940s and 1970s – not least in the United States – included Akira Kurosawa (Japan), Satyajit Ray (India), Carol Reed (Britain), Ingmar Bergman (Sweden), Luis Buñuel (Spain), and Miloš Forman (Czechoslovakia). They included also the main figures of late-1940s

Italian Neo-Realism (Roberto Rossellini, Vittorio De Sica, Luchino Visconti, Giuseppe De Santis) and subsequent cinematic revivals in Italy (Federico Fellini, Michelangelo Antonioni, Bernardo Bertolucci), France (the New Wave of François Truffaut, Jean-Luc Godard, Claude Chabrol, Jacques Rivette, Eric Rohmer, Alain Resnais, Louis Malle), Britain (the New Cinema of Tony Richardson and John Schlesinger), and Germany (the New German Cinema of Rainer Werner Fassbinder and Wim Wenders). Similarly, many European actors – including Brigitte Bardot, Sophia Loren, Jeanne Moreau, Marcello Mastroianni, Yves Montand – achieved international stardom without the need to emigrate to Hollywood or star in American films.

From the 1960s the lines between Hollywood and foreign cinema became increasingly blurred. This was partly because foreign cinema, especially the films of the French New Wave, influenced the new generation of American directors who came to prominence in the late 1960s and early 1970s (these French filmmakers, in turn, acknowledged a debt to such Hollywood directors as Alfred Hitchcock, John Ford, Howard Hawks, and Nicholas Ray). Moreover, film production became increasingly internationalized. In the 1950s Hollywood discovered the advantages of film production in Europe. At a time of economic pressure on the film industry at home, European government subsidies, cheap labor, and lower production costs offered a powerful incentive to make movies abroad. Hollywood's increased dependence on exports afforded an additional motive: foreign locations and European casts could enhance a movie's appeal to international audiences. Foreign funding was another advantage; by the 1960s the US studios drew on overseas financial sources for a substantial part of the costs of production abroad. This "runaway" production reached a peak in that decade: in 1969 183 films, 60 percent of Hollywood's output, were made abroad.[11] As a shorthand name for the US film industry, the term "Hollywood" has always been misleading. In relation to the period from the 1920s to the late 1940s it had failed to reflect the central roles of distribution and exhibition for film companies that were directed not from Los Angeles but from New York. From the 1950s the term ceased to convey accurately even the nature of US film production, which was increasingly carried out not in Hollywood but on location, and more and more outside the United States.

At the same time, in the 1950s American companies, including the majors, started to invest heavily in European cinema, taking advantage of the growing demand for foreign movies among American exhibitors resulting from the reduction of Hollywood's own production. Some of

Europe's leading directors benefited from American funding as well as the support of US distributors. United Artists financed both Truffaut and Bergman for some of their films. Two British directors were involved in highly successful co-productions: David Lean in *The Bridge on the River Kwai* (1957), *Lawrence of Arabia* (1962), and *Doctor Zhivago* (1965); Tony Richardson in *Tom Jones* (1963), and *Far from the Madding Crowd* (1967). In the following years Italian directors figured prominently in co-productions: Michelangelo Antonioni in *Blowup* (1966), *Zabriskie Point* (1970), and *The Passenger* (1975); and Bernardo Bertolucci in *Last Tango in Paris* (1972) and *The Last Emperor* (1987). American investment played a crucial part in European film production in this period.[12]

Co-production has continued to be central to international cinema. For filmmakers outside the United States it constituted one of two main ways (the other is collaboration with television) to compensate for the absence of self-sufficient national film industries. It maximizes the prospects of a movie gaining international appeal and facilitates entry to the all-important US market. Since 1980 many foreign films have been successful at the US box office, even beyond the art house circuit. They include *Chariots of Fire, Gandhi, The Killing Fields, Crocodile Dundee, Cry Freedom, Cinema Paradiso, The Crying Game, Howard's End, The Remains of the Day, The Piano, Four Weddings and a Funeral, Shine, The English Patient, Life Is Beautiful*, and *Crouching Tiger, Hidden Dragon*. American companies have been involved in the financing and distribution of most of these films, and many have involved American actors.

Such films are typically made with an eye to international markets and, in particular, to the tastes of US audiences; their content is influenced by this consideration. This influence does not make them "American" films, but nor can a film that results from international co-production easily be described as, say, British, French, or Italian. Identification of such films with particular national cultures has become increasingly problematic. Baz Luhrmann, the Australian director of the 2001 blockbuster *Moulin Rouge* – a film made in Sydney with a largely Australian cast but a Scottish male lead, set in Paris, and financed by 20th Century-Fox – insisted on the film's Australian character by claiming that his own "artistic sensibility" is "particularly Australian."[13] Such comments are interesting as a director's perception of his work, but they say little about the realities of international filmmaking.

If the independence of Australian, British, and Italian film industries was threatened by the internationalization of film production, developments in the 1980s and 1990s also raised questions about the extent to which

Hollywood's products could still be regarded as "American." With movie making an increasingly precarious financial undertaking, the studios were receptive to the promise of financial stability that came with takeover bids by large corporations. With the exception of Disney (which had joined the ranks of the majors after 1945), all the surviving major firms were purchased by conglomerates that sought to take advantage of "synergies" between movies and other media products (see chapter 12). Two of these corporations were US-based: Warner Bros. merged with Time Inc. in 1990 to form Time Warner Inc.; Paramount was acquired by Viacom in 1994. The other four were acquired by foreign conglomerates: 20th Century-Fox by the Australian newspaper magnate Rupert Murdoch's News Corporation in 1985; Columbia by the Japanese electronics firm Sony in 1990; MCA-Universal by another Japanese electronics corporation, Matsushita, in 1990; and MGM-United Artists by an Italian concern financed by a French bank in the same year.

Foreign ownership was not reflected in the content of Hollywood movies: the newly acquired studios did not proceed to produce or distribute films that were in any meaningful sense Australian, Japanese, or Italian. Yet although the heterogeneous character of American society has always compelled Hollywood filmmakers to cater for a wide range of audiences, and the studios have long employed directors, actors, and technical staff drawn from many countries, in the late twentieth century it was arguably less common for the most popular US-produced films, regardless of studio ownership, to present a distinctively American cultural outlook. Some movies did reflect American values; thus films as diverse as the Rambo trilogy (1982–8) and Steven Spielberg's *Saving Private Ryan* (1998) were expressions of American nationalism. Far more pervasive, however, was the influence of commercial values that demanded that Hollywood movies be easily understood by audiences around the globe.

The takeovers of the late 1980s occurred during a period which, as David Parkinson has stated, the US film industry had spent largely "in pursuit of commercial success, to the point that its main preoccupation seems to be making money rather than movies."[14] More than ever, and despite the failure of the big-budget musicals of the late 1960s, the majors were governed by a blockbuster mentality. The enormous commercial success of *The Towering Inferno* (1974), *Jaws* (1975), and *Star Wars* (1977) convinced studio heads that their best course was to make fewer films and concentrate on "megahits," lavishly produced films supported by expensive publicity campaigns. Such films gave minimal attention to plot and characterization but fully exploited the movies' advantages over television with the use of superstars and the technology of special effects. The trend was firmly established in the 1970s and 1980s. Especially popular were action-adventure and science fiction-fantasy films, including *Close Encounters of the Third Kind* (1977), *Superman* (1978), *Star Trek* (1979), *E.T.* (1982), two *Star Wars* sequels (1980 and 1983), *Back to the Future* (1985), *Batman* (1989), Spielberg's Indiana Jones trilogy (1981–9), and the films of Arnold Schwarzenegger and Sylvester Stallone. Comedy and pop-musicals were other successful genres: box-office successes included *Beverly Hills Cop* (1984), *Ghostbusters* (1984), *Saturday Night Fever* (1977), *Fame* (1980), *Flashdance* (1983), and *Dirty Dancing* (1987). The blockbuster trend continued in the 1990s with *Jurassic Park* (1993), *The Lion King* (1994), *Independence Day* (1996), and *Titanic* (1997), and in the next decade with *Pearl Harbor* (2001) and the Harry Potter movies (2001–2).

The blockbuster strategy was aimed especially at young audiences: children, teenagers, and adults with juvenile tastes. It was designed to exploit fully the money-making potential of product placement, which from the early 1980s became more important than ever, and of other "cross-promotional" deals. These movies did not stand alone but formed part of marketing packages that included film-related toys, games, books, clothing, soundtrack albums, and fast food.[15] Opportunities for cross-promotion were enhanced when the film companies were absorbed into media conglomerates (see chapter 12).

Cinema therefore defied the predictions of those who, at various times since the advent of the television age, had questioned its chances of survival. Technological developments ensured that film production, distribution, and exhibition continued to be very profitable activities. These developments included color and widescreen projection in the 1950s and, in the 1980s and 1990s, the special effects that characterized blockbuster movies and the rise of VCRs and cable television. Home video sales and rentals and cable television rights are major sources of revenue for the Hollywood studios; like the studios' involvement in telefilm production and sales of movies to television, they highlight the success of the US film industry in coming to terms with the rival medium. During the second half of the century the organization of film was greatly altered. The internationalization of much film production, the end of the Hollywood studio system, the US industry's concentration on making fewer films with bigger budgets, and multi-million dollar payments to stars were all aspects of this transformation. Ownership of that industry had changed hands. Yet ownership remained highly concentrated. In this respect film had much in common with other media industries at the beginning of the twenty-first century.

The Press

The United States

Newspapers, like cinema, experienced a marked audience decline after World War II. In the United States circulation fell steadily from 1.25 newspapers per household in 1953 to 0.97 in 1973, 0.84 in 1977, and 0.68 in 1990. In 1967 73 percent of Americans reported reading a newspaper every day; by 1991 the proportion had fallen to 51 percent. The trend was most pronounced among young people, despite the postwar expansion of both high school and college education. In 1990 a mere 24 percent of those under 35 years reported reading a newspaper on the previous day, compared to 52 percent in a similar survey in 1965. Not surprisingly, many papers did not survive. Many closed in the 1960s and 1970s, leaving large cities with just one or two daily newspapers. New York, a city with seven dailies in 1960, lost four of them by 1966, including the *Herald Tribune*, once the main rival of the *New York Times*, and the *New York Mirror*, despite sales of almost a million copies a day when it closed in 1963. Boston, a city with seven newspapers and a total circulation of 1,552,000 in 1950, had only two newspapers with a combined circulation of 857,876 by 1987 (despite a 67 percent growth in the city's population in the same period).[16]

The rise of television helps explain the decline of the press, but as in the case of cinema other factors were also involved. One of these was increased production costs, caused by rising newsprint expenses, the wage demands of unionized printers, and the disruption that arose from industrial disputes. Publishers faced a choice between higher newspaper prices – with the likely loss of readers – and reduced profits. This problem remained until the introduction of new technology in the 1970s and 1980s transformed the press from a labor-intensive to a capital-intensive industry. The postwar expansion of suburbs also undermined the economic viability of many publications, especially afternoon city newspapers: delivery problems were exacerbated by traffic congestion around the major population centers. The related growth in car ownership and the decline of public transport reduced opportunities for newspaper reading: commuters could not read a daily paper while driving, as they could on a train or trolley.

Yet, of those papers that survived, most did well. Newspapers remained the most popular vehicle for local advertising; those that did not suffer the problems of the big-city dailies, particularly papers that established a monopoly and exploited new technology, often made spectacular profits.

Prominent among these were suburban and small-city newspapers, especially those owned by chains. The degree of concentration in the American press increased after 1960, as companies such as Gannett, Knight-Ridder, Times Mirror, and Newhouse, possessing the capital essential for exploitation of new technology, extended their ownership of the more profitable publications.

Institutional developments encouraged changes in newspaper content. In the first half of the century it was common for proprietors to regard their papers as forums for their own political views. William Randolph Hearst and Colonel Robert McCormick, publisher of the *Chicago Tribune*, are two notable examples of highly opinionated owners who used their publications in this way. Gradually this approach gave way to an acceptance of the separation of ownership and the editorial function, a change that was accompanied by the professionalization of journalism. It was increasingly believed that journalists should be guided by a professional ethos of objectivity; in this way they would serve the public interest rather than the political or commercial interests of their employers. Such views prevailed by the 1950s; a symbolic milestone occurred when the *Los Angeles Times*, traditionally a strongly pro-Republican paper, adopted a neutral stance in the 1960 presidential elections.

"Objective journalism" represented an advance on the partisan newspaper content of the early twentieth century, yet it did not always serve the public well. Characterized by a heavy dependence on official sources of information, respect for political authority, and an uncritical acceptance of the statements of government officials, it restricted analysis to questions of strategy and tactics – whether a policy was successful rather than whether it was right or wrong. The consequences of this approach included an avoidance of the problems of entrenched poverty and racial inequality in American society, a neutral stance towards the activities of Joseph McCarthy, and unquestioning support for US foreign policy during the Cold War and military intervention in Vietnam.[17]

The ethos of objective newspaper journalism, along with the related view that newspapers should present "hard" news as it happened, was eroded during the 1960s and 1970s. The first challenge came from the television network news bulletins, which increasingly took over the role of "breaking" the news; simply reporting on events could no longer be the newspaper's role. Another challenge came from political and cultural change – from the breakdown of political consensus during the years of the Vietnam War, the Watergate affair, and conflict over black civil rights and women's rights. The decline of objective journalism was underlined by the decision of the

New York Times in June 1971 to defy the federal government and publish the "Pentagon Papers," a top-secret Defense Department study of the history of US involvement in Vietnam; and by the prominent role played by the *Washington Post* in investigating the Nixon administration's involvement in the June 1972 break-in at the Democratic Party's offices in the Watergate building. The extent of change in journalistic practice should not be exaggerated. Notwithstanding the experience of the Vietnam War and Watergate, American journalists continued to rely heavily on official sources and to be governed by a "need to appear strictly objective." This approach encouraged an inclination to "focus on questions of strategy, effectiveness, and technique, questions that did not touch directly on conflicts of interest or clashes over the ends and values of political life." Nonetheless, as a result of the changes of the 1960s and 1970s an emphasis on presentation of the news increasingly gave way to analysis and interpretation, with the journalist's subjective judgment given far greater scope. Opinionated columnists increasingly became a feature of print journalism.[18]

By the 1980s commercial pressures ensured that a trend away from "hard" news and information was followed by a general reduction in coverage of public affairs. The struggle to attract advertising revenue in the context of an overall decline in newspaper readership, and the increasing importance in the US press of "publicly" owned companies beholden to Wall Street (as opposed to the family-owned companies that had once dominated the industry), led to a greater emphasis on marketing at the expense of journalistic values.[19] Especially important was the attempt to attract younger readers – the "demographic" that was at once highly valued by advertisers and most resistant to reading newspapers. The result was that American papers increasingly followed the model of Gannett's daily *USA Today*, which began national publication in 1982 and, its critics claimed, did for the news what McDonald's had done for food. Short and simple stories, heavy use of color and graphics, and much attention to celebrities, sport, fashion, and "lifestyle" characterized this approach to newspaper publication. At the other end of the scale the prestige American dailies continued to provide serious coverage of domestic and international public affairs, but even they made concessions to readers whose expectations had been conditioned by the television age. In the 1990s the *New York Times* embraced color, graphics, and bigger headlines and extended its coverage of local news and sport. "The trick," a senior editor commented, "is how to do [all] this and still be the *New York Times*."[20]

If the effects of television largely account for postwar changes in the US newspaper industry, television's impact on magazines was even more direct. Because the United States did not possess national newspapers, magazines and network radio had been the main forums for national advertising. The efficiency of network television as a means of reaching audiences across the country therefore posed a direct threat to the advertising revenue of general-interest magazines. The country's great weekly mass-circulation magazines did not survive this threat; competition from television undermined both their attractiveness to advertisers and their sense of immediacy and visual appeal to readers. *Collier's* collapsed as early as 1956. The *Saturday Evening Post*, *Look*, and *Life* ceased publication between 1969 and 1972. They were revived as monthlies in the 1970s, but only *Life* lasted for long, and since 2000 it has been published only on a limited basis. The fate of these periodicals demonstrated that, in order to prosper in the television age, magazines had to specialize – to "help specialized advertisers reach specialized audiences." On this basis many magazines have been successful, with *TV Guide* the most profitable. Meanwhile those magazines which most resembled newspapers in their content – *Time*, *Newsweek*, and *U.S. News & World Report* – retained large circulations. Assisted by the high proportion of tertiary-educated readers in the US population, these publications had no equivalent in other English-speaking countries. But from the 1970s they underwent significant changes. With daily newspapers increasingly providing news analysis of the kind once characteristic of the news magazines, and with the *Washington Post*, the *New York Times*, and the *Wall Street Journal* publishing national editions, the magazines gave less attention to public affairs and more to show business, celebrities, and lifestyle features.[21] Their changing content mirrored developments in newspapers and in television programming.

Great Britain

The experience of the press in Britain in the second half of the century in many ways resembled that of the United States, with newspapers experiencing a steady decline in circulations and readership. Until 1956 the press was insulated from competition by the extension of wartime rationing of newsprint. With a consequent shortage of advertising space, even papers with weaker circulations had no trouble attracting sufficient advertising to remain profitable. The removal of this protection exposed the press to commercial television's threat to advertising revenue and to the same problem of rising production costs that troubled US newspapers. A number of famous national dailies, including the *News Chronicle* and the *Daily Herald*, did not survive. Medium-circulation dailies, unable to deliver advertisers either the affluent readership of the broadsheet "quality" press or the mass circulation of the tabloids, were prominent among those papers that closed between 1960 and the early 1970s.[22]

The British press, like its American counterpart, was marked by increasing economic concentration. A series of takeovers and mergers left nearly 60 percent of the national daily and Sunday newspapers in the hands of three chains by 1988, with a high degree of concentration also characteristic of the regional and local markets.[23] The introduction of new technology, inaugurated by Rupert Murdoch's removal of his printing operations from Fleet Street to Wapping in East London in 1986, consolidated the position of the leading chains.

Murdoch, who extended his Australian newspaper empire to acquire the *News of the World* in 1968 and subsequently the *Sun*, *The Times*, and the *Sunday Times*, is the most controversial of a new generation of press barons who came to dominate the British press after the 1960s. As in the United States, the postwar years saw a decline in political partisanship in British newspapers, with proprietors less willing to impose their own political views on their publications and more prepared to accept the professional autonomy of editors and journalists. But to a far greater extent than in the American press, this trend was reversed with the arrival of powerful owners – Murdoch, Victor Matthews, Robert Maxwell, Conrad Black – who did not hesitate to use their newspapers to promote their own conservative political views and to further their business interests. "I did not come all this way," Murdoch declared at the *News of the World*, "not to interfere." These proprietors selected their senior staff according to political criteria, gave detailed instructions on the content of editorials, and did not hesitate to express strong approval or disapproval of particular articles, columns, and headlines.[24]

Unlike the press magnates of the interwar period, proprietors such as Murdoch were not concerned primarily with newspapers; they were instead the heads of global corporations with other media and commercial interests. They were not wedded to political parties in the fashion of the previous generation of interventionist proprietors. Thus Murdoch in the mid-1990s withdrew his support from the Conservative Party and threw the weight of his newspaper empire behind the Labour Party of Tony Blair, having first satisfied himself that a Blair government would be well disposed towards the interests of Murdoch's News Corporation.

With control of the British press in few hands, the tendency of newspaper proprietors to treat their publications as tools for their own commercial and political interests was hardly compatible with the diversity of opinion that is vital to the health of democratic politics. Also disturbing was the lowering of journalistic standards that occurred, as commercial concerns were increasingly pushed to the foreground. As in the US press, fierce competition for advertising revenue led to a decline in political coverage and a greater emphasis on entertainment, sport, human interest, and lifestyle features aimed at particular markets. In the popular British press these developments saw the triumph of forms of tabloid journalism more extreme than could usually be found in other countries. The chief impetus came from a circulation war that began in 1969 when Murdoch acquired the *Sun* and recast the paper in a way that was soon emulated by other popular newspapers. As Kevin Williams has written: "The amount of news and information in the popular press has as a result declined, to be replaced by an endless spewing out of sex, nudity, exposés of the private lives of people (and not only those in the public eye) and countless stories about the comings and goings of the Royal Family and the characters of soap operas."[25]

There was much similarity between the history of the press in Britain and the United States in the late twentieth century, and these common features typified the experience of newspapers and magazines in Western countries. The alignment of the press with big business, economic concentration, a tendency to favor market forces over journalistic standards, and the attempt to entice younger readers with an emphasis on celebrity, fashion, and lifestyle, characterized the adjustment of the press to the television age.

Radio

The postwar growth of television immediately affected American radio broadcasting. Large radio receivers were replaced by television sets, and leading radio stars were lured to the new medium. Even Bob Hope, the most popular radio performer, saw his rating drop from 23.9 in 1949 to 5.4 in 1954.[26] Network radio declined rapidly: local stations took less and less network programming, and hundreds disaffiliated from the networks. Yet radio continued to thrive in a greatly altered form. The development of transistor radios and car radios, both of which became enormously popular in the 1950s and 1960s, sustained the medium: typically people now listened to their radio receivers individually, in the bedroom, kitchen, or car, rather than with the family. Public demand for radio remained high, but local stations, not the networks, now dominated the medium. The number of stations increased from 996 in 1945 to 2,819 in 1950, 4,086 in 1960, and 6,745 in 1970.[27] Most of them filled their airtime relatively cheaply by playing recorded music. Instead of trying to reach a mass audience as the networks had done, they specialized in particular formats – country and western, rhythm and blues, mainstream popular, and "easy listening" were common – and attracted advertising on the basis of their appeal to niche audiences, distinguished by characteristics of age, region, class, or gender. Especially lucrative, as the postwar baby boom generation grew into adolescence, was the teenage market. Its expansion persuaded many stations from the mid-1950s to adopt a Top 40 rock 'n' roll format, presenting a steady diet of rock music accompanied by the patter of a disk jockey. Format radio encouraged rigid and cautious programming: fear of alienating listeners, and therefore advertisers, discouraged any departure from tried and tested formulas. A willingness to experiment and greater openness to diversity in music programming marked the beginnings of a boom in FM radio in the late 1960s and early 1970s; but there, too, commercial pressures eventually prevailed. "By the 1980s," Susan Douglas has written, "much of FM, once so vibrant and experimental, had been sliced up into predictable, homogenized formats that offered little surprise and no interaction."[28]

As in other media, deregulation and growing economic concentration shaped the development of American radio in the last two decades of the twentieth century. In the 1980s the Federal Communications Commission began to lift restrictions on ownership of radio stations, in a process that culminated in the Telecommunications Act of 1996. New national radio companies were formed. By 1997 a number of companies owned between 200 and 300 stations each. One, Chancellor Media Corporation, controlled 463 stations by 1998, with an estimated audience of 65 million. At the same time satellite technology, by allowing instant and inexpensive transmission of syndicated programs, led to the re-networking of radio, but with many more networks than in the pre-television age and with many of those dedicated to a single format, such as talk, "beautiful music," or "music from the eighties and nineties." Unlike the old networks, the corporations that now dominated American radio did not distribute uniform programming for a national audience. Rather they took advantage of their ownership of multiple stations in major markets to broadcast a range of formats, each designed to appeal to a "demographic" highly prized by advertisers. In this sense each of the major companies controlled a number of different networks. Thus the new forms of networking and concentration, while undermining localism, did not reverse that fragmentation of the national radio audience that had characterized radio broadcasting since the advent of television.[29]

Deregulation encompassed content as well as ownership and control. In radio as in television, during the 1980s the FCC abolished the public service regulations that had previously applied to American broadcasting. Station licensing periods were extended from three to seven years, restrictions on advertising time were relaxed, and requirements that stations provide a balance of views and devote a proportion of their programming to news and public affairs were removed. Freed of political regulation, the radio corporations recognized no responsibility other than that of maximizing their profits. As in the case of television, public affairs programs were the main casualty: on all but a small minority of stations, such programs gave way to even larger doses of music, selected to comply with rigid formats, and to even more commercials.

Douglas has argued that the growing popularity in the 1980s and 1990s of talk radio and National Public Radio (NPR) – the radio arm of public broadcasting – stemmed from public discontent with these developments. By the mid-1990s talk radio was second only to country music as a popular format. Combined with the re-networking of radio, it made national figures of such "shock jocks" as Don Imus, Howard Stern, and Rush Limbaugh. The rise of NPR was surprisingly successful, especially by comparison with its ailing television cousin, PBS. By 1995 NPR's morning and evening news programs, *Morning Edition* and *All Things Considered*, commanded an audience of 10 to 11 million in a typical week. Large numbers of Americans also tuned into NPR's documentaries and public interest programs and its live coverage of Congressional hearings and debates, as well as its drama programs and Garrison Keillor's affectionate send up of small-town America and old-time radio, *A Prairie Home Companion*. Talk radio and NPR appealed to very different listeners: the former was politically right-wing and its audience predominantly working-class and lower-middle-class males; the latter was more liberal and its listeners tended to be more highly educated. Both offered a more detailed coverage of public affairs than could be found elsewhere on radio or in other media. They both spoke to "a profound sense of public exclusion from and increasing disgust with the mainstream media in general and TV news in particular."[30]

The post-1945 development of radio in Britain in some ways paralleled the American experience. The central role of a public service broadcaster, not dependent on advertising revenue, worked against the degree of fragmentation of the radio audience that occurred in the United States. But even the BBC, in seeking to retain its audience in the face of a challenge from offshore "pirate" stations, expanded to four networks by 1967 and began local radio operations. Moreover, the Sound Broadcasting Act of 1972 created additional radio services in the form of independent commercial radio. Independent Broadcasting Authority regulations required each of these stations to provide a range of programs, including news services. In this way the public interest was protected, but the regulatory framework undermined the ability of these stations to appeal to specialized audiences and provide advertisers with niche markets. The lifting of most of these restrictions by the Broadcasting Act of 1990 allowed independent radio to become more profitable and led to the creation of additional stations. However, the promise that audience needs would be better served through greater diversity in programming has not been vindicated. In Britain, as in the United States, radio companies have embraced rigid formats as the surest way to attract advertising revenue.[31] In both countries a balance between commercial interests and public service considerations proved elusive.

Radio, the press, and cinema remained major media by accepting secondary roles within an environment dominated by television. A common feature of their adjustment to the television age was the attempt to capture specialized audiences, having relinquished to television the role of providing entertainment and information to a mass audience. Yet, as chapter 8 showed, fragmentation of the audience characterized television too, with the rise of cable and satellite in the 1980s and 1990s. Before World War II the media – movies, mass-circulation newspapers and magazines, national radio – had been forces for cultural integration. Now they were increasingly involved in a process of cultural segregation, with different groups of the population receiving different kinds of media content. This development was inextricably linked with the predominance of commercial forces at the expense of public service values, and with the tendency to favor entertainment over information. These were general features of media history in the late twentieth century.

Further reading

Baughman, James L. *The Republic of Mass Culture: Journalism, Filmmaking, and Broadcasting in America since 1941.* Baltimore, MD: Johns Hopkins University Press, 1992.

Bogart, Leo. *Press and Public: Who Reads What, When, Where, and Why in American Newspapers,* 2nd edn. Hillsdale, NJ: Lawrence Erlbaum Associates, 1989.

Curran, James, and Michael Gurevitch (eds.). *Mass Media and Society*, 3rd edn. London: Arnold, 2000.

Curran, James, and Jean Seaton. *Power Without Responsibility: The Press and Broadcasting in Britain*, 5th edn. London: Routledge, 1997.

Donovan, Robert J., and Ray Scherer. *Unsilent Revolution: Television News and American Public Life*. Cambridge: Cambridge University Press, 1992.

Douglas, Susan J. *Listening In: Radio and the American Imagination*. New York: Random House, 1999.

Hallin, Daniel C. *We Keep America on Top of the World: Television Journalism and the Public Sphere*. London: Routledge, 1994.

Jowett, Garth. *Film: The Democratic Art*. Boston, MA: Little, Brown, 1976.

MacDonald, J. Fred. *Don't Touch That Dial! Radio Programming in American Life, 1920–1960*. Chicago, IL: Nelson-Hall, 1979.

Parkinson, David. *History of Film*. London: Thames and Hudson, 1995.

Puttnam, David. *The Undeclared War: The Struggle for Control of the World's Film Industry*. London: HarperCollins, 1997.

Rhode, Eric. *A History of the Cinema from Its Origins to 1970*. New York: Hill and Wang, 1976.

Sklar, Robert. *Film: An International History of the Medium*. New York: H. N. Abrams, 1993.

— *Movie-Made America: A Cultural History of American Movies*. New York: Vintage Books, 1994.

Williams, Kevin. *Get Me a Murder a Day! A History of Mass Communication in Britain*. London: Arnold, 1998.

10

MEDIA, WAR, AND INTERNATIONAL RELATIONS

Since the development of a mass press at the end of the nineteenth century and through the following hundred years, with the growth of other mass and communications media – radio, film, television, the Internet – the media have played an increasingly controversial role during war. Attention was given to mass media, particularly television, during the Vietnam War in the 1960s and 1970s, as efforts were made to explain the American defeat in that Southeast Asian conflict. The BBC broadcaster Robin Day expressed a particularly influential view when he observed: "One wonders if in future a democracy which has uninhibited television coverage in every home will ever be able to fight a war, however just . . . The full brutality of the combat will be there in close up and colour, and blood looks very red on the colour television screen."[1] In subsequent "limited wars" and in peacekeeping operations in the final decades of the twentieth century, especially as "global media" emerged, the relationship between the military and the media has received increasing attention. An examination of the role of media in war in this period highlights the nature of the relationship between media and state, media and public opinion.

The term "media war" is now commonplace, but it is of relatively recent origin, having come into common usage during the Gulf War in 1991. Stephen Badsey notes: "diplomatic and military historians have adopted the term 'media war' to a long-standing belief that mass news media coverage has been a missing or misunderstood element in the wider understanding of war."[2] As indicated above (see chapters 2 and 6), the advent of total war in the twentieth century led to use of the media for political purposes, to disseminate official information, to sustain home front morale, to persuade and spread propagandist messages. Between 1939 and 1945 both totalitarian regimes and democracies imposed wartime controls over information and used the media for their own purposes in a war of competing ideologies. Journalists and news agencies in both World War I and World War II tended to cooperate willingly with governments, acceding to censorship requirements, and collaborating in the war effort. With relatively little conflict between the mass media and political and military leaderships, with journalists largely supporting nationalist and patriotic causes, war reporting was often less concerned with accuracy than with impact. Phillip Knightley's frequently cited work on war and the media uses the phrase derived from Hiram Johnson's statement to the United States Senate in 1917 to describe war reporting: "The first casualty when war comes is truth."[3] Censorship and restrictions had been largely accepted as part of the impositions of wartime. In the latter part of the twentieth century such cooperation was not to last.

The Media and War in Korea and Vietnam

The spread of television as a mass medium in the decades after World War II opened up possibilities of a different level of exposure of civilian populations to the "realities" of war. Television broadcasting was becoming established in the 1950s just as the United States became involved in active engagement in a Cold War conflict in Korea in 1950–3. However, television was not sufficiently widespread to be considered a genuinely mass medium; it had not achieved saturation coverage of American homes, and it was not technically or professionally sophisticated enough to report the war thoroughly, or to exploit the possibilities of integrating sound and moving images. Television news was still modeled on radio, and the networks relied on the established newsreels for footage or on film supplied by the US Army Signal Corps. Thus Korea was not a television war. It was a war in which the military imposed formal censorship and in which war journalists, typical of media cooperation with government during the Cold War (see chapter 7), tended to be complicit with governments and the military in not posing fundamental questions about war aims and objectives, in not questioning Western interventionist foreign policies in what were essentially civil wars.[4]

In the following two decades the relationship between the media and the state during wartime (especially in the United States) underwent considerable change. The high level of nationalist and patriotic support that prevailed during the Korean War was eroded; in the 1960s older values of uncritical loyalty to the state were questioned, and there was greater willingness to consider "victims" of US foreign policy (see chapters 8 and 9 on changing cultural values in the United States in the 1960s). The Vietnam War of the 1960s and 1970s ended in defeat for the United States and its allies, and in the search for explanations for this outcome, conservatives drew attention to the importance of the mass media, with television a particular target. Influential politicians and others credited the media with exerting great influence on public opinion, leading to a withdrawal of support for American foreign policy in Southeast Asia. What came to be a popular orthodoxy emerged that in this war, in which no formal censorship was imposed, "the media lost the war." Television brought images of war into American living rooms, turned the American public against the war, and made continuing US involvement in the Southeast Asian conflict impossible.

Such conclusions about the war were possible because of technological changes and because of the establishment of television broadcasting on a large scale. By the 1960s, when American and allied forces became involved in Vietnam, almost all American homes had a television set. It became easier for reporters and cameramen to cover the war because of technical improvements in lightweight sound cameras, and because of easier transport and communications. Moreover, the extension of network evening news bulletins from 15 minutes to half an hour in 1963 allowed more detailed coverage of American military operations. Thus it was argued that the American people, tuning in to nightly television news, saw the full horrors of the war in their living rooms. Because this was the first war in which the United States suffered a decisive defeat, a simple cause-and-effect argument developed: this was "the first television war," this was America's first defeat; therefore the first "caused" the second. The orthodox view was that this was the first modern war in which the outcome had been determined on the television screen rather than on the battlefield.

President Lyndon Johnson supported this view; he maintained that America was defeated because the war was televised; regular public exposure to the awful realities of war turned the public against the war, forced the withdrawal of US troops, and left the way open for a communist victory in Vietnam. Similarly, President Nixon maintained that the American news media came to dominate domestic opinion about the purpose and conduct of the Vietnam War; they showed suffering and sacrifice and led to serious demoralization on the home front, which resulted in withdrawal of American support from the South Vietnamese and the final victory of the communist North. American generals expressed similar views; and even beyond the political and military establishment there was support for "the oppositional media thesis." Robert Elegant, himself a correspondent in Vietnam, blamed the media, referring to the collective policy of the news media to seek "the victory of the enemies of the correspondents' own side" by "graphic and unremitting distortion" of the facts.[5]

It was easy to move from this interpretation to a view that no televised war can long retain political support at home. According to this, the media – especially television – exercise a profound influence on the conduct of foreign policy during war. By means of television, viewers are exposed nightly to images of the brutality of war; the immediacy and horror of these images cannot fail to have an impact; the public, alerted to the costs of war, will not tolerate continued hostilities.

This orthodoxy, so influential among political and military leaders and the general public, was soon challenged by scholars. By the 1980s media historians were questioning the "oppositional media thesis." Broadly, their argument was that the United States failed in Vietnam for a number of reasons, especially the costs of prosecuting the war, and that the media merely mirrored preexisting attitudes, following rather than leading public opinion. Daniel C. Hallin's conclusion was:

> The collapse of America's "will" to fight in Vietnam resulted from a political process of which the media were only one part. And that process was deeply rooted in the nature and course of the war – the fact that it was a limited war, not only in its tactics but in its relevance to vital American interests; and also the fact that it was an unsuccessful limited war.[6]

These critics – or "revisionists" – also examined the arguments about media impact. They pointed out that it was not clear what proportion of the population actually watched television news at the time it was supposedly influencing public opinion against the war. They also referred to lack of evidence about the proportion of those watching who actually paid attention or remembered items from nightly broadcasts. They cited polls and surveys that showed less television viewing and lower recall than the orthodox view implied. They argued that battle scenes on television lost any sense of reality or danger; real battles in Vietnam were seen as "just another Hollywood drama;" and this induced apathy or rendered the war trivial. Much of the television coverage was dominated by combat footage that showed less violence than the orthodox view implied. Also, by presenting groups of American soldiers engaged against a faceless enemy in apparently successful but unspecified battles, it could be argued that television conveyed a misleading impression of the war and created unfounded optimism, rather than stimulating opposition to the war.

One much cited statistic was that American acceptance of the conflict consistently declined in step with the rise in American casualties, falling some 15 percentage points each time total American killed and wounded rose by a factor of 10. Thus, when total casualties from all causes went from 1,000 to 10,000 or from 10,000 to 100,000, public regret grew by about 15 percent. This reaction occurred regardless of whether the war appeared to be going well or poorly, and in spite of favorable or unfavorable press or television coverage. A similar parallel between casualties and public opinion occurred during the Korean War, when television news was still in its infancy.[7]

As well as arguing that American losses in Vietnam were more important than media coverage, revisionists questioned the links between television and public attitudes. For example, television coverage may have merely reinforced existing attitudes rather than changed them; or television may have encouraged support rather than opposition by stirring viewers' patriotism and backing for the American soldiers they saw fighting on the screen. Furthermore, there was deep-seated anti-war sentiment in the United States before television and before Vietnam, and, although this was the first televised war, it was not the first unpopular war.

Scholars tend to agree that, even if other factors were more important than media in explaining the American defeat, the role of the media changed over time, becoming more important in the late 1960s. Television reporting of the Tet offensive in 1968, when communist forces seemed to make significant gains (although interpreted after the event as more important in psychological than military terms), showed the contradiction between political and military optimism in the United States (maintaining that the United States was winning the war) and the "real happenings" in South Vietnam (including communist advances into the grounds of the American Embassy in Saigon).

Hallin summed up the impact of media coverage of the Tet offensive as follows:

> The conventional wisdom is that the Tet coverage, and television pictures of the battles of Khe Sanh that followed, were the last straw for the American public. There is little doubt that these actions played an important part in strengthening opposition to the war, but it is apparent that the tide of public opinion had already turned. All the media did was confirm the widespread public view held well before Tet, that the people had been the victims of a massive deception . . . Tet was less a turning point than a crossover point, a

moment where trends that have been in motion for some time reach balance
and began to tip the other way.[8]

Subsequent media revelations in the United States, such as the breaking
of the story of the My Lai massacre (when American soldiers, reportedly
under orders from their platoon commander, massacred more than 200
civilians – including women and children – in March 1968, an event that
was not reported until late 1969), confirmed the impression of adversarial
media. However, the My Lai story broke at a time when American public
opinion was prepared to believe it, partly because of the shock caused by
news of the Tet offensive and the blow to the credibility of the Johnson
administration, partly because of growing frustration with a war in which
massive American efforts were failing to achieve victory. By the early 1970s
media opposition was even more apparent when the *New York Times*, in
defiance of the government, supported publication of the Pentagon Papers,
the classified history of the war. By this time President Nixon and his administration were facing growing war weariness and disillusionment; and the
media were one among other factors contributing to opposition to the war.
It should be noted, moreover, that there were limits to the adversarial role
of the media. At this time media editors and producers, apparently judging
that the war in Vietnam was almost over and that public interest was
declining, began to give it less attention despite public disillusionment and
questioning of foreign policy. Moreover, American journalists tended to
continue to identify with "their side," to revert to "consensus journalism,"
and to privilege the administration rather than the anti-war movement
in relation to news. According to Hallin, the "constraints of ideology and
of journalistic routines tying news coverage to Washington perspectives"
excluded basic questions from the news agenda (including the wisdom of
US intervention in Vietnam, and the outcomes of the war for the people of
Indochina), containing the extent to which the media could be genuinely
oppositional.[9]

The debate over the role of television in the Vietnam War is important in
media history in focusing attention on links between public opinion and
media, and in raising the fundamental question about the extent of television's influence. In the case of the Vietnam War it is important to acknowledge the complexities of that conflict, the enormous problems facing
successive US administrations in their prosecution of the war, the impact
on American society of continuing losses in a prolonged conflict, and the
complex reasons for the emergence of the anti-war movement. No single-
cause explanation of the war's outcome can be satisfactory, and certainly

not an explanation in terms of media influence that singles out one mass medium – television – for blame. While media may have served as communication channels for the growing anti-war movement and facilitated heightened awareness of the war, they did not "lose the war."

The Media and Limited Conflicts in the 1980s

Scholarly debate on the role of media in the US defeat in Vietnam had little effect on military and political leaders in the United States and elsewhere. In post-Vietnam conflicts they acted as if television – or the media more generally – had indeed lost the war. One legacy of American involvement in Southeast Asia in the 1960s and early 1970s (an aspect of the so-called "Vietnam syndrome") was the desire to avoid any protracted military involvement abroad, and, in the event of US involvement, to keep any engagement short and to control media reporting so that public opinion at home did not have time – or the basis for informed decision-making afforded by detailed media coverage – to become disenchanted and to withdraw support from American foreign policy.

A key issue in post-Vietnam conflicts was the extent of official control over journalists. In the Vietnam War there had been no formal censorship, and large numbers of reporters had gone to Vietnam, unconstrained by strict military controls (although often, by necessity, dependent on the military for transport and communications). In limited wars of the 1980s governments acted to limit such media freedom.

Britain took account of the perceived lessons of Vietnam during war with Argentina in the Falklands War of 1982. This was Britain's "first taste of a campaign fought in the full glare of modern media attention."[10] The remoteness of this war in the south Atlantic facilitated media management. Places on Royal Navy taskforce ships were limited, and the government and military leadership were able to decide which organizations should be allowed to report the war at first hand, and to exclude non-British correspondents and control communications from the war zone. Correspondents relied on the Navy to transmit copy, and reports were subject to delays and censorship.

The Falklands War highlighted the conflict between, on the one hand, the perceived public right in any democratic system to be informed and, on the other, government and military needs to withhold information for reasons of operational security. The British government and military leadership practiced a policy of "deception, misinformation, disinformation and media manipulation through denial of access, control of communications and politically based censorship."[11] Because this was a short and limited war in a remote area, it was relatively easy for the government and military to employ these restrictive tactics.

British media management during the Falklands War provided a model for American military–media relations during other limited conflicts. When US forces went into Grenada in 1983 (in a commando raid operation to rescue Americans supposedly held by a government friendly with Cuba), the US defense secretary excluded journalists during the initial landing. Media reports were largely accounts after the event, based on officially released information. Following this operation, and at the request of the chairman of the Joint Chiefs of Staff, General Vessy Jr., a commission was set up to make recommendations on press–military relations in any future operations. The Sidle commission report provided for public affairs planning alongside operational planning. It recommended that media compliance with military guidelines should be voluntary, and that sufficient military personnel should be available to assist correspondents to cover operations adequately.

In another limited American operation in Panama in 1989 (against General Noriega), the media were again excluded initially. Once journalists were allowed access, they were dependent on the military for transport and access to transmission facilities, and their reports were censored by the military. A "pool" system was used in Grenada, with reporters assigned to military units and accompanied by military escorts. Those journalists who were not part of the pool could only operate on the fringe of the war without access to the action.[12]

Media historians see the experiences of Grenada and Panama as stages in a process of increasingly rigid media management by the military. They "reinforced the post-Vietnam model of military operations: use overwhelming force, do the job quickly, keep casualties to a minimum . . . and attempt to control what the public sees."[13] Military–media relations in these limited conflicts of the 1980s were based on the traditional view, derived from the experience of the Vietnam War, that attributed power to the media during war, and they became a model for further restrictive media management.

Media Management during the Gulf War

When the Gulf War began in 1991 the US military had taken to heart the lessons of Vietnam and subsequent experiences of tight media management in Grenada and Panama. The Gulf War provided an even more striking example of military restraint of media.

After the Iraqi invasion of Kuwait in 1990 and unsuccessful United Nations (UN) attempts to bring about a solution through sanctions and an embargo, a United States-led coalition began Operation Desert Storm against Iraq on February 24, 1991. The war lasted 42 days, and included a heavy allied bombardment, defeat of the Iraqi air force, and a brief ground offensive. It resulted in the defeat of Iraq and the liberation of Kuwait, although Saddam Hussein remained in power in Iraq.

The role of the media in the Gulf War was largely determined by the idea that the United States would, by means of this short, sharp, victorious war, put the Vietnam War behind it. President George Bush even said, "we've kicked the Vietnam syndrome once and for all." The Gulf War was seen as a surrogate for wars the United States could not win in Southeast Asia. Americans needed a victory, and the supposed "mistakes" of Vietnam could not be allowed to recur. Television had to serve the interests of the state and the military once war began.[14]

Technological change (enabling real-time television broadcasting) and the advent of the 24-hour global television news service, Cable News Network (CNN), made the Gulf War of 1991 a media event on a grand scale with extensive and virtually instantaneous coverage. The American, Iraqi, and other leaders used CNN to send messages to one another, bypassing traditional routes via embassies and foreign ministries. Television coverage of the conflict was extensive in terms of airtime devoted to it. Yet analysts depict the war as one of the worst reported because of military management of the media. To a large extent this view reflected journalists' and media organizations' expectations rather than reality; it could be argued that in some respects the Gulf War was more comprehensively reported than previous conflicts (several high-profile television correspondents from CNN, the BBC, and ITN ignored attempts to regiment Western media, went to Baghdad and filed vivid reports "from the other side," showing the results of Allied bombing of Iraq).

However, the majority of journalists found themselves subject to restrictions. The pool system, used earlier in the limited conflict in Grenada, was again used to limit media "intrusion," and the military imposed specific guidelines on reporting. Journalists were not permitted into the war zone except as part of a designated pool and could not move freely in combat areas; non-pool reporters were forbidden access to forward areas. Military escorts were provided for journalists, and all copy was subject to military security review. US Defense Department rules banned publication or broadcast of specific information such as numbers of troops, aircraft, weapons, equipment and supplies, future plans and operations, locations of forces, and tactics. In addition, military briefings set out the official viewpoint for reporters, and official footage filmed from US combat aircraft was supplied to television broadcasters.

Such restrictions resulted in "sanitized coverage" of a "clean war" in which images of "smart," high-tech weaponry dominated. There was little footage of casualties (and certainly none of casualties from "friendly fire"). There was overwhelming emphasis on the air war rather than the ground war. Much of the television coverage consisted of interviews, reporters talking to cameras, still photographs, graphics, and maps. The military press conference was the most frequently portrayed single event in the Gulf War.

Much of the media coverage during the Gulf War was devoted to propaganda, presenting a politically acceptable war. On the Allied side reporting tended to demonize Saddam Hussein, and there was little serious analysis of longer-term reasons for the conflict. Similarly the government of Iraq attempted to manipulate the media in presenting a view of the war favorable to Saddam Hussein. The level of analysis of the issues at stake was low, and sources of information were restricted. Journalists assigned to the pools not only showed how memories of Vietnam shaped attitudes and actions during the US-led Western coalition's war against Saddam Hussein and Iraq, but also depicted themselves as "hotel warriors," covering the war from hotel rooms, reliant on information from televised briefings, pool reports, and CNN coverage for their own copy, rather than first-hand experience of the conflict on the ground or in the air.[15]

At a time when sophisticated technologies offered the possibility of immediate and extensive reporting to a global audience from the war zone in the Middle East, and when CNN might have provided a public channel to the traditionally largely secret world of diplomacy, the scope of media coverage of the conflict in 1991 was restricted by an active policy of containment. More fundamentally, historians of this and other recent conflicts have argued that the very nature of television as a medium impeded reflection and interpretation, instead valuing speed over judgment and accuracy.[16]

Much of the writing on the media and the Gulf War expressed concerns about journalistic independence and the freedom of contemporary media: there was criticism of high levels of political influence over the media, and of the power of the US military to dictate to American media how wars should be covered. There was a widely shared view that governments and the military had realized the importance of public opinion during war and developed policies of containment and control to harness the media and enlist and maintain public support.[17] Yet a review of the relationship of the media and government during other wars of the twentieth century serves as a reminder that in most cases media cooperated with governments, complied with measures such as censorship, implemented to protect the national interest in wartime, or indeed acted in such a way that regulation was unnecessary (see chapters 2, 4, 6, and 7). From this perspective the adversarial stance of some media during the late 1960s and 1970s was an aberration rather than the norm.

Global Media in the Post-Cold War Era

The debate about the political significance of the media during the Vietnam War, and about links between media coverage and shifts in public opinion, in any case seemed to have been of academic importance only. Although critics of the orthodox view that television "lost the war" developed a convincing case in the 1980s, in fact, in conflicts in the same and subsequent decade the "powers that be" acted precisely as if the media were indeed to blame. When the US military implemented policies of media management during the Gulf War's Operation Desert Storm in January 1991, their objectives reflected lessons based on the orthodox view of the role of the media in the Vietnam War: never again should the media enjoy the freedom of Vietnam; never again should they have the opportunity to turn public opinion against US foreign policy in time of war.

In the post-Cold War years technological and political developments made media management more difficult. The extension of satellite broadcasting, developments in cable and direct broadcasting, the rise of a 24-hour, dedicated global news network such as CNN, and the rapid growth of Internet use opened up possibilities of immediate and global coverage of trouble spots virtually anywhere in the world. The strength of globalizing influences, with media that are part of larger transnational corporate interests and capable of broadcasting across national boundaries, highlighted the difficulties for nation-states of controlling channels of news and information during war.

The orthodox view of the power of television in the 1960s was paralleled in the 1990s by emphasis on "the CNN factor" during global crises. CNN had gained prominence as the main source of news worldwide during the Gulf War, and "the CNN factor" referred to the power of the media, particularly global television broadcasting across national boundaries, to influence public opinion and have an impact on policy. It was argued that certain global crises were constituted by global media and the responses that media coverage evoked in civil societies; that television had moved from being a managed medium during the Gulf War to representing the victims of violence (as in the Kurdish refugee crisis of 1991). One of the more extreme versions of the CNN effect was that it resulted in a loss of policy control on the part of government officials, with media and public opinion constituting the key players in foreign policy-making.[18]

It was suggested that pervasive media images of famine-ravaged populations could stimulate public support for multinational humanitarian efforts coordinated through United Nations agencies; or that images of the impact of civil war could boost popular demand for peacekeeping operations in parts of the world that had negligible strategic interest for the peacekeepers. Various events seemed to illustrate the CNN factor at work, suggesting a causal connection between global media portrayals of crises and international action: sending US and then UN troops to establish security for humanitarian relief efforts in Somalia between 1991 and 1995; peace operations following the civil wars in the former Yugoslavia between 1991 and 1995; US and then UN intervention in Haiti in 1994 to restore the elected government of President Jean-Bertrand Aristide; international intervention in Rwanda in 1993–4 following ethnic strife, mass slaughter, and the refugee crisis; NATO intervention in Kosovo and Serbia in 1999 in another Balkan war.

During this period relationships between the media and the military were further complicated by the importance placed on psychological operations (PSYOPS), the use of targeted information to help achieve political and military objectives (on psychological warfare during the Cold War see chapter 7). According to Philip M. Taylor, "infowar and PSYOPS," the use of communications technologies to aid military and other operations, has become as important as traditional military, economic, and diplomatic aspects of international relations.[19] They are crucial instruments of policy for international bodies such as the United Nations and for nation-states in their attempts to influence attitudes and behavior before, as well as during, war.

The role of global media during crises was demonstrated with extraordinary impact on and after September 11, 2001. The strength of support for media to reflect patriotic and nationalist values, even at the expense of providing comprehensive information, also became evident during this period. Stunning images of the terrorist attacks on the twin towers of the World Trade Center in New York and the Pentagon in Washington were disseminated to global audiences with immense speed. In the American-led "war against terror" that followed, directed at the man assumed responsible for the attacks, Osama bin Laden, and his al-Qaeda network, based in Afghanistan, conventional and new media revealed to the world aspects of the war with immediacy and saturation coverage.

In the months following the September attacks most American media were largely complicit with government, demonstrating a consensus about the national interest and agreement about American values reminiscent of earlier periods (see chapter 7). They conveyed American outrage and justified military intervention in Afghanistan. The leading television networks agreed to a Bush administration request to stop broadcasting live Osama bin Laden's words and to omit his more inflammatory oratory, because this was considered as aiding the enemy and disseminating his propaganda. The administration also limited media access to information on military operations. Both the Hollywood film industry and the commercial networks imposed their own self-censorship, removing advertisements and providing commercial-free programming immediately after the terrorist attacks, and withdrawing content (such as movies with a terrorist theme) that might have been offensive.

Contradictory expectations of the media during the war against terrorism were evident. On the one hand, they were criticized for confusing patriotism with traditional obligations concerning free speech, information, and objectivity, and for being too deferential to the Bush administration and the war effort. On the other, they were accused of irresponsibility and treasonable behavior by providing coverage that helped the enemy.[20] Media responses to the events of September 11 – and public reactions to media coverage of the terrorist attacks and the ensuing "assault on terrorism" – therefore highlight the complexities of the role of the media in a liberal democracy.

Other aspects of media coverage of this crisis were noteworthy. One was the importance of non-Western media, particularly the Qatar-based, 24-hour satellite news channel, al-Jazeera, broadcasting widely in Arabic and offering perspectives different from those of CNN. Western media reactions to al-Jazeera were inconsistent: they drew on its news and footage from the war zone, but they also questioned the credibility of this pan-Arab news outlet. American responses to al-Jazeera indicated underlying tensions in contemporary views of media responsibilities. When US representatives complained to the Emir of Qatar that al-Jazeera was providing terrorism with a platform and should be curtailed, it was ironic that the Emir had to remind them that a free press is essential to democratic life. There was also a suggestion – denied by the US military – that the Kabul offices of al-Jazeera television were targets for US bombing. If confirmed, such reports would suggest a readiness to deny a genuinely global flow of information.[21]

Another significant element – apparent in conflicts of the 1990s but magnified in 2001 because of the pervasiveness of the medium – was use of the Internet (see chapter 11) as a rapid communication medium in time of war (whether conventional or terrorist). There was massive traffic to news sites within an hour of the terrorist attacks on September 11. The Internet played a vital role in providing information, in conveying messages, and sharing experiences about the tragedy. New York companies directly affected by the attacks used corporate websites to keep employees, families, and customers informed. To cope with demand, news sites stripped web pages of large graphics and multimedia features and posted simple text reports. It was reported that the terrorists too had used the Internet, particularly email, prior to the September attacks. As a result, the US Senate passed laws in October 2001 giving intelligence agencies extensive surveillance powers to monitor web users, and to pass on information to government departments.[22]

The role of contemporary media during war, or in relation to peacekeeping, is therefore complex, with relationships among policy-makers, public opinion, and the media difficult to disentangle. Warren P. Strobel, in his study of media in peace operations, noted that

> the news media's impact is almost invariably due to the conditions that officials themselves (or other policy actors) create . . . when deciding whether to send US military forces into harm's way or whether to withdraw them, officials look far beyond the realm of portable satellite dishes, laptop computers, handheld videocameras, and the like. The evidence strongly suggests that they examine the same constellation of factors they always have: the risks of intervention, the likely benefits of the mission, the stakes for the country, the depth of congressional support, the state of public opinion. The public, for its part, continues to weigh the real costs of a military mission against the perceived US interests. If those costs – chiefly American combat casualties – are shown on television, it may have a temporal effect, speeding the end of a mission that already lacks public support. But television has little effect on the public's basic calculation of costs and interests.[23]

Reactions to the events of September 2001 indicate not only government and military but also extensive public support for media that respond to crises with patriotism and national interest at the forefront, rather than traditional journalistic values of free speech, free flow of information, and independence. While new communications technologies have made it more difficult to censor or block transmission of content, it may be that the pressure of opinion will achieve a similar result.

Further reading

Adams, Valerie. *The Media and the Falklands Campaign*. Basingstoke: Macmillan, 1986.

Bennett, W. Lance, and David L. Paletz (eds.). *Taken by Storm: The Media, Public Opinion, and US Foreign Policy in the Gulf War*. Chicago, IL: University of Chicago Press, 1994.

Carruthers, Susan L. *The Media at War: Communication and Conflict in the Twentieth Century*. London: Macmillan, 2000.

Denton, Robert E., Jr. *The Media and the Persian Gulf War*. Westport, CT: Praeger, 1993.

Fialka, John J. *Hotel Warriors: Covering the Gulf War*. Washington, DC: Woodrow Wilson Center Press, 1991.

Gow, James, Richard Paterson, and Alison Preston (eds.). *Bosnia by Television*. London: British Film Institute, 1996.

Hallin, Daniel C. *The "Uncensored War": The Media and Vietnam*. New York: Oxford University Press, 1986.

Hammond, William M. *Reporting Vietnam: Media and Military at War*. Modern World Studies. Lawrence: University Press of Kansas, 1998.

Hudson, Miles, and John Stanier. *War and the Media: A Random Searchlight*. Stroud: Sutton, 1997.

Knightley, Phillip. *The First Casualty: The War Correspondent as Hero and Myth Maker from the Crimea to Kosovo*. London: Prion, 2000.

Mercer, Derrik, Geoff Mungham, and Kevin Williams. *The Fog of War: The Media on the Battlefield*. London: Heinemann, 1987.

Mermin, Jonathan. *Debating War and Peace: Media Coverage of US Intervention in the Post-Vietnam Era*. Princeton, NJ: Princeton University Press, 1999.

Strobel, Warren P. *Late-Breaking Foreign Policy: The News Media's Influence on Peace Operations*. Washington: United States Institute of Peace Press, 1997.

Taylor, Philip M. *War and the Media: Propaganda and Persuasion in the Gulf War*. Manchester: Manchester University Press, 1992.

Young, Peter, and Peter Jesser. *The Media and the Military: From the Crimea to Desert Strike*. Basingstoke: Macmillan, 1997.

11

NEW MEDIA

From the late nineteenth century to approximately the 1970s various mass media had developed – the newspaper press, radio broadcasting, the film industry, television broadcasting – that could conveniently be labeled "traditional media" from a late twentieth-century perspective. As each of these grew on a mass scale, initial competition and uncertainty about the extent to which older media might survive gave way not only to accommodation but in many instances to mutually beneficial relationships. From the 1970s technological change made possible, and socioeconomic, political, and ideological contexts provided opportunities for, the emergence of "new media." These new media also presented challenges, but again new accommodations have proved possible, traditional media have adapted, and global changes have produced a complex "mediascape" in the early twenty-first century.

Traditional Media, Convergence, and New Media

The idea of "new media" is still sufficiently recent to require some definition, particularly as technological changes have blurred boundaries between previously separate areas. A key concept here is "convergence." Peter Forman and Robert W. Saint John describe convergence and its possible outcomes as follows:

> . . . the union of audio, video and data communications into a single source, received on a single device, delivered by a single connection . . . We will be able to enjoy movies, TV shows, Internet video, and music on our home

theater, computer or wristwatch wherever we are, whenever we want . . . The big convergence is made up of three subsidiary convergences: content (audio, video and data); platforms (PC, TV, Internet appliance, and game machine); and distribution (how the content gets to your platform).[1]

Convergence has blurred distinctions between different kinds of media delivery technologies; broadcasting, communications, electronics, computing, and publishing technologies and industries have merged. As a result of media mergers, single corporations own what were formerly separate media interests, and giant corporations with media interests now embrace many other areas. There are new relationships among media industries, Internet service providers, and telecommunications companies in relation to production and delivery of content and to institutional linkages. Previously the term "mass media" had a clear meaning; now mass media are sometimes subsumed under other terms such as "information and communication technologies," the product of convergence. As chapter 12 demonstrates, technological changes and policy preferences in industrialized countries for deregulation have led to greater internationalization. New strategic alliances cross earlier media "borders." As a result, traditional media can no longer be understood in isolation.

The emergence of new media has presented a challenge for media theorists. One collection of theoretical writing emphasizes the need to approach digital media and technoculture with a sense of historical perspective and to pose basic questions that have run through traditional media theorizing. These include questions about technology and society (reviving earlier debates about technological determinism, and about information technologies and democratic values); about media content, delivery, and audiences (including cultural studies emphases on consumers and users of media products); about complex interrelationships relevant to media technologies, including modes of production, professional practices, the political economy and regulatory systems; and more "grand theory" philosophical speculation about ideology and experiential effects.[2]

In the final decades of the twentieth century "new media" embraced many innovations. Video technologies evolved, home video spread, and new methods of delivering television broadcasting emerged. In 1994 Wilson Dizard included the following among the new, computer-based, media: high-definition television (HDTV), digital radio broadcasting, multimedia computers, CD-ROMs, laser discs, advanced facsimile machines, handheld databanks, electronic books, videotext networks, intelligent telephones, direct-to-home broadcasting satellites (DBS), and portable electronic newspapers. Since the mid-1990s the rapid growth of the Internet and the World Wide Web has revolutionized global media. By the year 2000 definitions of "new media" added to Dizard's list the Internet, palmtop computers, wireless communications, videodiscs, consumer computer networks, and online news services.[3]

This chapter does not attempt to cover the entire range of new media. Rather, it concentrates on selected developments with mass potential and implications for traditional media. It focuses on video, pay television via cable and satellite, direct broadcasting by satellite, multimedia, the Internet, and emerging technologies that provide access to online content. Chapter 12 provides more detail on the global context of these new media and the institutional frameworks within which they operate.

Video

Video recordings, home videotape players, and video rentals were taken up on a mass scale in the 1980s. Video was important for its impact on the way consumers accessed and experienced existing mass media, particularly film and television. It also removed some predictability about the way audiences experienced the products of the film and television industries, and this had implications for advertisers.

Home video made it possible to use video cassette players/recorders and television sets to play rented tapes or to record movies and other programs. For consumers, video offered a convenient and relatively inexpensive technology; it freed them from the programming schedules of traditional broadcasters, and it was not easily subject to control or intervention. Video technology provided a means of "decentralizing and democratizing the media and placing content distribution, exhibition, and to some extent production, in a wider range of hands," with community video and video use by otherwise disenfranchised groups providing examples.[4]

Video both challenged and offered opportunities to existing media interests. To audiences it offered greater choice and control. It represented a step toward convergence of different media and separate types of entertainment. Video made it possible for film industry products to be "consumed" in a more flexible way in the domestic environment, encouraging linkages between cinema and broadcast television – and cinema and cable/pay television in the 1980s. In the early years of video there was considerable delay between box-office and video release of new films. When it became apparent how lucrative and popular the home video rental business was in the 1990s, film studios began almost simultaneous release of new films in cinemas and on video.

This was part of the attempt by the film industry to recoup its position after the initial impact of home video. In countries such as the United States and Australia video penetration in television-owning homes had exceeded 80 percent by the mid-1990s. In the former there had been a dramatic decline in the relative value of ticket sales to the Hollywood film industry. Whereas in 1980 approximately 80 percent of film industry revenue had been from box-office takings, by 1991 this had fallen to 20 percent, with remaining income coming from home video and product sales to television. In Australia video quickly achieved a high level of penetration, and video rental became "big business." By the mid-1990s annual turnover of home video outlets far exceeded both cinema box-office takings and the advertising revenues of the commercial television networks.[5]

The established film studios compensated for the decline in cinema audiences and retained their high profile as entertainment providers by becoming major providers for the home video entertainment industry. The Hollywood studios did this not only in the United States but also abroad, as video spread in both industrialized and developing countries in the 1980s and 1990s. Corporations with large stakes in the American entertainment industry and links to the Hollywood studios – Fox, Warner, CIC, Columbia-Tristar – were prominent in video production and distribution. Video cassettes provided an important source of revenue even as they had eroded cinema ticket sales.

The film industry reached accommodation with, and came to reap significant financial benefit from, the spread of home video, again illustrating how traditional media have adapted to emerging competition. There were other spin-offs for the film industry; the popularity of video helped to revive interest in cinema. In the decades when television was spreading as a mass medium, many cinemas had closed down, but in the 1980s new multiplexes, housing numerous cinemas, were built in major centers of population, cinema admissions increased, and public and media interest in film-related events such as festivals revived.

However, for advertisers video technology was problematic. Advertisers and advertising agencies had previously worked on the assumption that commercial television viewers continued to watch during "ad breaks." The advent of video and the time shifting that it made possible – combined with the development of the "remote control" – introduced uncertainty about viewing habits and about viewer exposure to the commercial messages that punctuated entertainment programming. The remote control gave viewers greater control, making "channel surfing" easy during advertising breaks. The video recorder enabled users to pause recording to cut out advertisements, or to "fast forward" during "ad breaks" when watching recorded programs. Time shifting played havoc with the carefully planned strategies of broadcasters. Evening television schedules are planned to entice viewers early in the evening, and to hold them through the remainder of the scheduled program, thus ensuring audiences for advertisers. The changes in viewing patterns and the flexibility afforded by video technology and time shifting upset such careful planning.

Other problems associated with video included an increase in video piracy and the loss to producers of revenue to which they should have been entitled. The possibility of recording off-air and making multiple copies from an original video recording was an enormous threat to copyright. One estimate put the cost of video piracy to the Hollywood studios in the late 1980s at US$1.5 billion annually.[6]

Pay Television via Cable and Satellite

There is a tendency to associate cable television with developments in the 1970s in fiber-optic and coaxial cable, but cable television has an earlier history. As early as the 1930s in Britain the Rediffusion company developed twisted pair cable to carry television signals to subscribers' homes beyond the London area and continued to use similar technology in the 1950s. However, large-scale use of the technology was a later phenomenon. The development of fiber-optic cables allowed the transmission of voice, video, and other data over beams of laser light via very thin cable strands of glass that were lighter, took up less space, and carried much more data than the older coaxial cable. Cable television, unlike traditional free-to-air broadcasting, has been used to deliver television services to home viewers on a payment-for-service basis. Its advantages include more channels and therefore greater consumer choice.

The fact that cable services depended initially on the physical laying of cable meant that, where populations were thinly spread over large geographical areas, cable delivery was not economically attractive. What made cable delivery viable on a larger scale was its combination with satellite, enabling television communication across vast distances. In the United States this combination "redefined the US media environment" between the 1970s and 1990s.[7]

American media interests began to use satellite services in conjunction with cable in the 1970s, transmitting to a particular locality by satellite, then by cable to individual households, even in small towns. Ted Turner bought a failing television station in Atlanta, Georgia, and transformed it into the first "superstation," WTBS, by transmitting low-cost sports and entertainment programs via satellite to cable systems throughout the country, accelerating the spread of cable television nationwide. Turner went on to develop Cable News Network and Turner Network Television in the 1980s. Gerald Levin of Time Inc. also did much to spread cable services, with Home Box Office being particularly popular in disseminating film as home entertainment via cable services.

US cable companies enjoyed growing profits through the 1980s, challenging the free-to-air national networks by offering multi-channel services, catering to particular audience tastes, and providing greater choice than network programming. Satellite and cable-delivered programs in the 1990s included dominant names in the entertainment industries, such as Home Box Office, the Movie Channel, the Disney Channel, MTV for music entertainment, Nickelodeon for children's television, and Arts and Entertainment. News and information were delivered by cable, and cable sports services were very popular. In the early 1990s the CompuServe data service began using cable television networks to deliver interactive games, databanks, and services such as electronic banking.

In news delivery the great success story of the 1990s was Cable News Network (CNN). Ted Turner founded CNN in 1980 as an advertising-supported,24-hour television service devoted entirely to news broadcasts. It offered live coverage of events as well as regular programming devoted to international news, business and sports news, health issues, and entertainment news. CNN sprang into prominence as an influential global news provider during the Gulf War of 1991 (see chapter 10) and then grew rapidly. By 1992 it was reaching a global audience of some 53 million viewers in 138 nations and 60 million in the United States. It has remained important as a source of information for global audiences and as an influential news provider for other media and political and policy-making circles. C-SPAN, another US cable service, provided public affairs broadcasts and, from the 1970s, covered the proceedings of the US Congress and other public affairs forums.

The development of cable services has been uneven. By the mid-1990s it was estimated that at the global level about 23 percent of television households had cable services. The United States had the most extensive penetration, with about 70 percent (ca. 189 million) of television households accessing cable. In Europe, where Sky Channel began in 1982 as a satellite-delivered television service to European cable systems and enjoyed some success, overall about 23 percent of European television households accessed cable. Percentages were lower in Asia (some 20 percent) and in South America (as low as 7 percent).[8]

As occurred with video, the development of cable and pay television services drew the attention of advertisers, particularly as different cable networks offered access to different markets. In the United States advertising revenue for cable television increased from approximately $230 million in the early 1980s to $3 billion a decade later. Traditional broadcasters such as the national networks felt the combined impact of home video and cable/pay television. Although network television was still the most pervasive of the mass media in the United States at the end of the twentieth century, it had lost audiences and revenue to competitors. The number of viewers watching prime-time programs declined in absolute terms (from 36.9 million in 1975 to 32.7 million in 1990), as did the networks' share of advertising revenue.[9]

The networks were themselves experiencing change from the 1980s – influenced partly by the decline in advertising profits and partly by the more general economic climate. The three long-established networks were taken over by larger corporate interests (ABC by Capital Cities Communications, NBC by General Electric, CBS by Loews Corporation), and all faced problems related to economic recession, staff cuts, and rising program production costs. Cable television was a competitor, attracting not only advertising revenue but also particular programs away from the networks. CNN provided news to local or affiliate stations that had previously taken network services. CNN's global coverage and the immediacy of its news broadcasts gave it a competitive advantage, particularly as audiences became accustomed to instantaneous international news coverage. By the 1990s CNN was supplying news services not only to many local stations in the United States but also to hundreds of television distributors internationally. The networks also suffered from cable competition in areas such as sport, compounded by the greater prices that sports organizations were asking for sporting events broadcasting rights.

Although cable/pay and satellite-delivered television has challenged traditional broadcasters, the extent of its success continues to depend on provision of physical infrastructure. Its spread has been uneven, with lower penetration outside densely populated and predominantly metropolitan areas. Britain exemplifies the limits of pay television penetration, with around one-third of television households subscribing to pay services, an unspectacular rate compared with other technologies such as video.

One of the criticisms of pay television is the degree to which content is dominated by American, and to a lesser extent British, programs. In Australia, for example, cable news programs are supplied primarily by American CNN or British BBC news services, movie channels show predominantly Hollywood fare, and many sporting programs are imported. The proportion of local programming is extremely low. (See chapter 12 on cultural and media imperialism.)

Direct broadcasting by satellite (DBS) to viewers' homes, using receiving dishes purchased by individual households, is another alternative to the free-to-air broadcasting of traditional networks and independent television stations. DBS became available in the United States in the 1970s, in Europe in the 1980s, and in other parts of the world in the 1990s. It has been less successful than cable services as an alternative to conventional broadcasting transmission, because of inadequate technology, weak financing, and poor marketing strategies.[10] There have been exceptions, particularly the direct broadcasting ventures of News Corporation through BSkyB in Britain and Europe. Efforts by Rupert Murdoch in 2001 to buy into DirecTV in the United States indicated that News Corporation retained an interest in this technology and its potential profitability as a means of television broadcasting (see chapter 12).

Multimedia

Multimedia have emerged from the convergence of various technologies and of the broadcasting, communications, electronics, computing, and publishing industries. Digital technology made possible this integration, as well as the manipulation and combined storage of video, audio, text, and graphics. Examples of multimedia products include CD-ROM discs, online multimedia databases, and video conferencing facilities. A feature of convergent multimedia is that there is the capacity for interactivity, with users able to "navigate through the material in a non-linear way, actively engaging with the content for diverse purposes."[11]

The emergence of multimedia drew on various developments, including the growing popularity of personal computers, the production of electronic books, the growth of desktop publishing, the development of software (such as Hypercard and Toolbox) that enabled interactivity, and software (such as QuickTime) that made possible the compression of large quantities of data including video, music, voice, and text, as well as the use of television sets and set-top players and handheld video devices for the delivery of games (embodying interactivity).

The CD-ROM, a major form of multimedia, is inexpensive and durable, providing high-quality sound and images and able to hold large volumes of data. From the mid-1990s CD-ROMs became increasingly popular, offering an expanding range of video games, "edutainment," electronic books, and music video; and they became easier to access as more personal computers were manufactured to include CD-ROM players. Video games have continued to be a popular multimedia product, as the list of other multimedia products has grown.

Digital Video Discs (DVDs) became available in the late 1990s, offering greater storage capacity than the CD-ROM, and capable of bringing high-quality, large-screen images and superior sound to film viewers in the home environment. Films released on DVD not only had better sound and picture quality; many came with "extras" such as scenes deleted from the original version, documentaries on how the film was made, or commentaries from writers, directors, and actors, all of these providing more than the simple video experience. Home video rental chains began offering DVDs. Although DVD players were relatively expensive when they appeared in the 1990s, this is an expanding market.

While multimedia are very much a feature of the twenty-first century "mediascape," forms of delivery such as CD-ROMs seem likely to give way increasingly to online services available via the Internet. However, until sufficient bandwidth becomes available to carry large volumes of integrated and interactive services, some multimedia may continue to supplement online delivery.

The Internet and the World Wide Web

One of the most significant developments for media in recent decades has been the emergence of the Internet and the World Wide Web. The Internet cannot be defined as a single, independent or tangible entity; it is not owned by a particular business but is, rather, a global collection of networks that link smaller computer networks. By the year 2000 private companies and computer centers in universities and research organizations owned a large proportion of the equipment associated with Internet use; Internet communication used existing telephone lines owned by private companies and public utilities; and Internet service providers (ISPs) had become the main "property owners of cyberspace," managing or renting physical assets and controlling access to the system. The economics of the Internet had evolved considerably from its beginnings, from a relatively free resource to a medium more and more dominated by commercial interests.[12] Use of the Internet increased dramatically from the late 1990s, as personal computer use grew, and as Internet service provision expanded; but the history of the Internet goes back to the 1950s.

As with other mass media, development of the Internet depended on a range of technological advances, including remote access to, and operation of, computers by telephone wires, the creation of programming protocols to allow users to share the computing power of a single machine with maximum efficiency, and the breaking up of continuous messages into smaller "packages" of information to maximize efficiency within an electronic network.

In 1957, against the Cold War background of heightened tension between the United States and the Soviet Union, particularly Soviet success in the space race with its launch of the first satellite, Sputnik, the US Department of Defense established the Advanced Research Projects Agency. The project involved designing a communications system capable of surviving nuclear attack. The intention was to create a decentralized system of linked computers so that information could be rerouted if any part of the network was damaged or ceased to function. The first network was named the Advanced Research Program Agency Network (ARPANET) and was used initially by computer experts in various research centers associated with the US Department of Defense. Thus the origins of the Internet lay in a national security project based on military and strategic concerns. This can be considered the first phase of Internet development.[13]

Over the following decades the Internet emerged as a means of linking research centers and academic institutions, its growing use linked closely with the spread of computers. Electronic mail – email – was used for communication purposes, and mail lists were created to disseminate information. Use expanded considerably as more host computers were linked to the network. In 1969 only four host computers were connected; by 1980 there were 213.

In the 1980s the network moved further from its original military strategic purpose and into a second phase of development. In the United States the National Science Foundation took over the Department of Defense role, established five supercomputing centers around the country, linked them with its own high-speed network, NSFNet, and encouraged research institutions to form regional networks, thus producing the basic structure of the Internet with its multiple layers of networks. As use of the network expanded, it became necessary to introduce various organizational principles and practices. In 1986 domain names were introduced (for example, "edu." for educational institutions, "com." for commercial enterprises, and "mil." for military forces).

Arrangements to extend and provide reliable access to the Internet were important in the 1980s and 1990s. Academic networks negotiated with telecommunications companies and stimulated the emergence of Internet service providers. Thus commercially based companies began to provide Internet services, and what was originally a tax-funded enterprise was handed over to the private sector. CompuServe started in 1979 and by the mid-1980s claimed 3.2 million users in 120 countries. America Online also emerged, with commercial relationships with the German group Bertelsmann and the French group Hachette. The National Science Foundation in 1995 handed over the backbone of the system and its management to private telecommunications companies Sprint, Ameritech, and Pacific Bell.

There was rapid growth in use, and by the end of the 1990s the Internet was a mass medium. By the late 1980s some 90,000 computers were linked to the Internet, and the numbers expanded from 1.3 million in 1993 to 9.5 million (estimated to be linking some 40 million people) in 1996, to 19.5 million host computers with registered IP addresses in 1997. Internet use grew as personal computer ownership increased. By 1998 more than 100 million email messages were being sent daily. By early 1999 there were 52,000 new Internet users every day in the United States. Estimates of use showed dramatic growth from 153.3 million users worldwide in 1999 to 447.4 million in 2001.[14]

The network developed as a means not only of communicating and transferring information but also of providing new and alternative modes of expression. New terms such as "cyberspace" gained currency – from William Gibson's 1989 novel, *Neuromancer*. Users established new conventions – for example, the use of symbols and punctuation to convey "emotion" in text messages and the descriptive term "emoticons" in 1979. The Internet Society was established in 1992. Groups of users with shared interests used electronic news groups and bulletin boards for information-sharing and ideas exchange, and the notion of "virtual communities" emerged, with geographical distance apparently irrelevant. Throughout the 1990s regional and international organizations, including the European Commission and the World Trade Organization, encouraged growth of the Internet as a vehicle for mass communication.

New ways of accessing information via the network were created: the Mosaic web browser, made freely available in 1993, followed by the Netscape browser. Tim Berners Lee's work at the European Laboratory for Particle Physics (CERN) was important in establishing a new protocol for distributing information via the Internet based on hypertext and in introducing the World Wide Web in 1991–2.

From the mid-1990s there was another shift in emphasis, as the Internet entered its third phase of development, with greater commercialization, and a shift from educational to commercial use, from e-communication to e-commerce. As mass use of the Internet developed, it became obvious to advertisers that this was a new vehicle for marketing products and a potentially important player in consumer societies. Web-based advertising became attractive, new features such as banner advertisements were included on websites, and small and large businesses began to develop a presence in the electronic world via their own websites, with the number of commercial sites rising rapidly. By 1996 Internet advertising revenue was estimated at $300 million, compared with advertising revenue going to traditional broadcast television of some $38 billion.[15]

Powerful corporations became involved in commercial exploitation of the Internet. The outstanding example of a giant corporation of the information and communication technologies (ICT) age is Microsoft. Microsoft was established by Bill Gates in the 1970s. It developed computer languages such as BASIC, FORTRAN, COBOL, and Pascal, and in 1980 entered into an agreement with IBM to supply software for IBM's first personal computer, as well as developing the disk operating system (DOS). In the 1980s Microsoft went on to develop software and operating systems that became virtually the universal standards. The company went public in 1986, and by the 1990s it was showing massive profits. In 1998, with the release of Windows 98, the company took advantage of the growth of the Internet when it integrated the Microsoft browser into desktop computers. Microsoft's importance in relation to the Internet lay not only in providing software for the personal computers that were essential to widespread Internet take-up but also in its expanding stake in Internet use through Microsoft Network, an Internet service provider. Microsoft's business practices attracted attention in the 1990s, and legal suits were brought against the company for monopolistic practices, and for stifling competition. These dragged on into the next century, without a definitive outcome. Given the ubiquity of Microsoft products on computers worldwide and the global reach and power of this giant corporation, it was questionable whether likely penalties – such as the separation of components of the

Microsoft "empire" – would really lead to any decline in the influence of the company.

Other companies that had previously been involved in traditional media met the challenge of the Internet by themselves becoming involved, developing a web presence to reach new audiences, promote their more traditional products, and participate in developing content for the e-environment. One successful "industry" on the Internet has been pornography. Pornography and sex sites have generated billion-dollar profits and account for some of the most visited sites. Lack of regulation of the medium, and the degree of privacy available to users, have contributed to pornography flourishing on the Internet – and to public concern about some types of use of this mass medium.

By the end of the twentieth century, with the withdrawal of the United States government and with greater private company involvement, the nature of the Internet had changed substantially since its beginnings. Internet service providers such as America Online, Yahoo!, and Microsoft Network had become important players, managing or renting physical assets and enabling access to the system via connections provided to subscribers. ISPs were exercising a degree of control by setting charging policies and playing a "gatekeeper" role, using portals to structure or customize content, categorize web pages, and direct users to particular resources. Power with respect to the Internet had shifted "to commercial entities, to multinational businesses and mass media conglomerates as well as to small businesses, small media, and small non-government organizations."[16]

For a period there was great optimism about the future of the Internet. Speculation on a grand scale saw millions of dollars invested in "dotcom" ventures. The stock exchange established specifically to deal with high-technology stocks and shares, the Nasdaq, reflected both the buoyancy and volatility of the e-world market. After earlier dramatic rises, from March 2000 the Nasdaq began falling, venture capitalists became cautious about investment in Internet startup companies, and companies began laying off staff. This marked a turning point in the economic importance of the Internet, with greater caution prevailing after the boom period of the late 1990s.

Nonetheless, at the beginning of the twenty-first century the Internet appeared to offer advantages and to have wrought significant change. It had revolutionized communication at the global level. This was especially evident in relation to war and to peacekeeping operations – not simply as a means of disseminating information during operations but also by international agencies and governments for psychological operations and by terrorist groups as an easy channel of communication (see chapter 10). In everyday communication, services such as email facilitated instantaneous and easy contact between individuals; listservs, synchronous chat services, and asynchronous online forums linked users in inexpensive and user-friendly ways.

These opportunities for electronic networking encouraged some advocates of the e-world to make large claims for the Internet. It was suggested that Marshall McLuhan's idea (dating from the 1960s) of a "global village" was achievable: the Internet removed the limitations of time and place, enabling global interaction; it potentially empowered groups and individuals on the socioeconomic and geographical margins because of interactivity and independence of existing power structures. Its decentralization would, it was argued, have a democratizing impact. Against these claims, especially with increasing commercialization, others argued that use of the Internet is really determined by the economics of production and distribution, and that arguments about empowerment and its democratizing potential ignore enormous inequalities of access to the medium.

There is considerable inequality in Internet access and use. The industrialized countries of the Organization for Economic Cooperation and Development (OECD) have the majority of Internet hosts, whereas developing countries have few, and some of the poorest Third World countries (for example, in central Africa) have none. African countries are falling further behind the world in relation to Internet use. In July 2000 Somalia only had around 200 Internet users; and South Africa had almost 60 percent (1.8 million) of all African Internet users. Fewer than 0.2 percent of the 760 million people in the rest of Africa had Internet access, and there were probably as few as 12,000 Internet hosts. By the year 2001, although more than one-third of people in the world's richest nations had access to the Internet, the figure in poor countries was less than 0.1 percent.

These problems of access in countries such as those in Africa are not easily overcome. Financial difficulties and structural barriers impede the development of an efficient Internet, since most African countries rely on their former colonizers to provide the main links. This means that neighboring countries have different access and that there are few opportunities for economies of scale. Moreover, there is an important relationship between existing telecommunications infrastructure and access to the online world. In industrialized countries with highly developed telecommunications systems it is relatively easy to provide capacity both to Internet service providers and to domestic users, whereas this is not the case in many developing countries. The Internet is usually only available where phone lines exist, although experiments in Asian countries such as Cambodia have brought Internet access to villagers in remote regions without telephones or electricity using desktop computers, solar panels, and a satellite dish.[17]

Even within the developing world there are considerable differences in access and Internet take-up. Unlike Africa, Latin American countries have experienced more rapid Internet growth. By the year 2000 in Latin America 13–16 million people were online, although this only represented 3–4 percent of the region's 500,000 million people compared with more than 50 percent being Internet users in the United States. However, the user rate in Latin America was more than doubling each year, but mainly representing greater take-up by relatively well-off residents of South American megacities. There were programs in Argentina, Chile, and Brazil to provide personal computers, to offer Internet access in public schools, and to establish computer courses; and the advent of cellular phones that offer Internet access via "wireless application protocol" (WAP) technology (see below) seemed likely to lead to greater Internet use. However, continuing problems relating to infrastructure and low literacy levels in rural areas meant that inequalities within and among Latin American countries were likely to remain for some considerable time.[18]

A further factor contributing to inequality is that connection bandwidth varies across the globe and with it the speed of data transmission via the Internet. The United States is in the most favorable position in relation to bandwidth, with other countries lagging behind. Thus, even if online content is developed in "marginalized" areas, this is useless without bandwidth to transmit it. Finally, the cost of Internet access varies according to financial development and geographical position, again resulting in considerable inequality.

Commercialization of the Internet is aggravating the impact of inequalities of access by leading to greater emphasis on different types of content. Seen from this perspective, the Internet is predominantly a vehicle to strengthen existing patterns of conglomeration in the global communications industry and to emphasize the values of consumer societies rather than providing a means of freedom of expression and debate. The Internet has become a "commodified medium," generating billions of dollars of revenue annually, and attracting large amounts for advertising (also the Internet service provision market was worth US$8.4 billion by the end of the twentieth century, and Internet navigation tools and search engines were worth large sums – Yahoo!, for example, had an income of some $30 million in the first quarter of 1998).[19]

It is likely that increasing commercialization, linked with corporate dominance, will limit opportunities to exploit the online environment in the service of "global village" ideals:

> one of the reasons the Internet has become so ubiquitous is not because it is an impressive piece of technology, but because of its potential for big business, and with more and more companies relocating to cyberspace, it seems increasingly unlikely that the present haphazard, unregulated environment, which has seen the Net thrive, can continue indefinitely.[20]

It remains to be seen if governments, rather than commercial interests, will direct future Internet development. Governments have found it difficult to regulate the electronic environment, sometimes simply arguing that converging technologies make regulation obsolete. Moreover, lack of regulation accords with what has became the dominant Western ideology since the 1980s. Yet, while lack of regulation is desirable in the interests of freedom of expression, regulation should not be abandoned in relation to matters such as copyright and privacy.

The test case of online music drew attention to problems of protecting copyright in new media environments. The music industry instigated legal action against the online venture Napster in an effort to prevent the free exchange of music files among Internet users. After the likelihood of a commercial solution being found in 2000, when the German media corporation Bertelsmann purchased a major stake in Napster and it seemed that the music site would evolve into a fee-based downloading service, it closed in mid-2001. However, the Internet continues to offer possibilities of circumventing copyright provisions and trading in pirated music, video, and software files.

Another area for concern, as new media expand, is privacy. Internet databases hold growing banks of personal information derived from various online transactions, and control over misuse of such information is difficult to achieve.

Developments in new media such as the Internet have substantially changed the context in which traditional media operate. However, this is still a transitional period. Until the late 1990s, as Internet company stocks boomed and as Internet use grew dramatically, many traditional media became involved in the online environment. By 2001 the difficulties of making a profit in the e-environment, the end of the dotcom boom, and declining Internet advertising revenue compelled media groups to reassess their online strategies and to value more traditional practices. Major media businesses, including newspaper groups such as the New York Times, television networks such as NBC, the music channel MTV, and Time Warner's CNN, scaled back their online operations. The future remains uncertain and the relative importance of traditional and new media difficult to predict.

Emerging New Media

At the beginning of the twenty-first century some emerging media, although not yet adopted on a mass scale, appear to have the potential to influence how consumers access traditional media products, partly because of increasing convergence, partly because traditional media players are adapting to deliver their "products" in diverse ways. These new media include personal digital assistants and associated handheld devices, as well as cellular or mobile phones, including those that use WAP technology to access information electronically.

Devices such as the Palm Pilot have become popular, offering "personal organizer" tools – calendaring services, address books, electronic calculators – as well as synchronized electronic access via a personal computer to email. Audio or text-based books can be downloaded from the Internet via a personal computer to a handheld device such as the eBookMan, which might come complete with encryption software developed to deal with copyright issues. Web PC cameras and MP3 (music) players have become readily available. It was forecast that worldwide sales of handheld computing devices would jump from 7.1 million by the end of 2001 to 19.1 million by the end of 2004. Moreover, a growing range of add-ons may make handheld devices increasingly popular.[21] The significance of these handheld devices for mass media is that they provide ways of accessing both information and entertainment from online sources, considerably extending consumer choice but also creating greater demand for content.

One of the fastest growing sectors in the telecommunications area since the 1980s has been mobile or cellular phones. The mobile phone, which frees users from reliance on wired networks, has been adopted with great enthusiasm in both developed and developing countries, in information-preoccupied societies where mobility and easy communication are at a premium. In addition, the development of WAP has made it possible to use mobile phones to deliver content (data and images), and to provide Internet and email access to handheld devices. WAP, as an emerging digital technology, has advantages over other communication and delivery mechanisms including portability (users can send email messages when away from their desks and personal computers) and immediacy (users can, for example, access Internet sites carrying breaking news with a WAP-enabled mobile phone).[22]

Another increasingly popular service that involves the application of WAP is the "short messaging service" (SMS), with the mobile phone pad serving as a keyboard for entering a message, and messages being transmitted to the receiver's mobile phone screen. Vodafone, the telecommunications company, introduced SMS in 1995. It was rapidly taken up by a mass market, as cheap pre-paid phone usage grew, as service providers promoted new mobile phone uses, and as companies linked their networks so that messages could cross to any cellular phone. At a global level use of SMS grew exponentially. A survey in December 2000 put the number of SMS messages sent at 100 billion, up from 5.4 billion two years previously.

A principal advantage of this technology is cost, as text messaging is cheaper than standard telephone call charges. Initially the service was used so that telephone users could send each other quick text messages. Another feature is its multimedia potential, supplying not only text but also digital pictures or video clips. Companies began to develop commercial applications, sending users news headlines, stock market updates, sports scores, and movie listings. This has implications for traditional media, offering competition to newspapers and radio in particular. However, the extent to which users will tolerate the limitations imposed by the small size of the technology remains to be seen.[23]

Another possible impact of these new devices and services is that they will attract advertising dollars that would otherwise have gone to traditional media. For example, mobile phones using WAP to access online information have considerable appeal for advertisers because of the size of the market. There were an estimated 75 million cell phone users in the United States in mid-2000, compared with 35 million households with Internet access via a personal computer. Use of these devices and protocols for commercial purposes does raise questions about consumer privacy. While advertisers were considering ways of marketing via mobile phones, consumer groups were expressing concern that wireless service providers might infringe privacy by tracking users via their phones.[24]

Traditional and New Media in the Twenty-First Century

For the traditional media that had dominated the provision of information and entertainment to mass audiences during earlier decades of the twentieth century, developments in new media since the 1970s have had important implications. This chapter concludes by extending the analysis of chapters 8 and 9 to consider the relationships of traditional and new media at a time when there is greater commercialization, when more media are competing for advertising and sponsorship, and there is growing demand for media content.

Newspapers have responded to the challenge of new media, in particular the Internet but also potentially other WAP-enabled technologies, by moving into the online environment. Traditional publishing companies launched online newspapers from the mid-1990s. Newspaper websites are capable of providing breaking news with an immediacy impossible in hardcopy formats; they also offer enhanced services such as online archives, searchable databases, and extensive links to other services of potential interest to readers.

While the production of electronic versions has provided newspapers with a presence in the online environment, there have been perhaps fewer benefits than anticipated. Newspapers appear to have attracted existing users to their websites without extending their readership significantly by enticing new audiences, particularly the "youth demographic." Younger consumers, accustomed to using the Internet but not to reading printed newspapers, seem largely not to be developing the newspaper-reading habit. There have also been costs of website news delivery, especially the effects on traditional editorial and journalistic practice. Editors tend to lose control of the agenda in online journalism; because the Internet provides rapid access to "breaking news," there is a tendency for editors and journalists to abandon caution and publish stories quickly without confirming that they are true by checking more than one source. Furthermore, boundaries tend easily to become blurred in the electronic environment, as marketing and advertising merge with news, and as distinctions between opinion and factual information are lost.

These issues aside, newspaper organizations (with other established news providers) remain important in the Internet context:

> The Web sites which command the most respect for their content are the established wire services, the print-based offshoots of major newspapers and magazines, and the sites offering text versions of radio and television items. Not only do these established sources provide an unflagging stream of paragraphs for content-hungry sites, they do so with the priceless added ingredient of longstanding credibility.[25]

While newspapers continue to benefit from their reputations and the credibility of news reports from their journalists, they have lost their advantage with respect to some types of news. An example is corporate press releases. These had previously been sent first to traditional media before being distributed elsewhere. From October 2000 the main distributors, PR Newswire and Businesswire, decided to make them available to websites at the same time as they were sent to financial news organizations. Wire services have also become more readily accessible via websites (by mid-2000 Reuters news agency stories could be read on about 1,000 websites),[26] offering users an alternative means of rapid access.

It remains to be seen how enthusiastic users will be on any mass scale about accessing online news and information services via handheld devices and mobile phones. Customized services that deliver news on topics of interest to the user may be valuable in their selectivity and immediacy, but the small screens of these technologies are not very "user-friendly." Nonetheless, it is likely that, as electronic news and information services proliferate, traditional media will lose readers and viewers. A 2000 survey found that 15 percent of the sample took their daily news from the Internet compared with 6 percent two years previously; and 30 percent watched network television newscasts regularly compared with 38 percent two years previously. Particular groups – younger consumers and the better educated – were spending more time using the Web for news and watching less network television news (although cable television news from CNN and MSNBC appeared to be immune from the shift to the Internet).[27]

In the face of such trends some traditional news providers have formed alliances that offer novel ways of providing news and information, including sharing news stories across media. An example is the link between the Washington Post company (owner of the *Washington Post* newspaper and of *Newsweek*, America's second-biggest-selling news magazine) and MSNBC and NBC News (which jointly produce two cable television channels and two websites). In this case a well established newspaper company chose not to rely on its own website but rather to provide enhanced content for MSNBC.com, an online news site.[28]

In the same way that some newspapers have responded to change, radio has shown adaptability in relation to new media. Increasing media convergence, developments in digital audio broadcasting, and radio websites have provided new means of delivering radio programs. By 2000 more than 1,500 radio stations were available online. This made it possible to access, via the Internet, radio programs from around the world, thus overcoming the limitations of short-wave reception. Websites developed by radio broadcasters provided opportunities for audience interaction, supplementing more traditional interactivity such as talkback radio. It is likely that there will be increasing use of digital Internet stations. This means of "broadcasting" has advantages such as low cost and simplicity compared with the expense and unwieldiness of traditional radio transmitters. It is also attractive for local or small-scale operators in that they do not have to compete for frequency allocation on AM or FM bands.[29]

In the history of radio broadcasting the relationship between radio and the music industry has been important, with the former providing a means of disseminating live and recorded music to mass audiences, and the latter offering a wealth of programming material to radio (see chapter 4). Use of the Internet for the dissemination of music has created problems, with implications for this relationship. Legal battles over issues of copyright, arising because web-based services such as Napster made possible the free exchange of music files among users, have raised questions about the future of music on the Internet, making it difficult to predict the effect on the radio–music industry relationship. Certainly radio broadcasting survived earlier competition for music after the advent in the 1980s of music television (MTV).

New media and prospects of media convergence are also significant for traditional television broadcasting. The audience share of free-to-air broadcasters, the commercial networks, independent stations, and public service broadcasters, has declined as choice has expanded with cable and satellite pay television (see chapter 8), and with Internet delivery of video-like content.[30] Moreover, media convergence has enabled the use of the television set for interactive purposes rather than merely reception of scheduled programs.

Television, too, has adapted in response to new technologies. Broadcasters have moved into the Internet environment and established alliances in the online world, attempting to expand their audiences, and to take up opportunities for interactivity. Television publicizes Internet and computer use; television commercials refer viewers to websites; and television viewers are encouraged to use email for communication about program content. Material derived from traditional broadcasters is now combined with original web material, and with gateways to other related sites; and such interactivity is in turn having an effect on traditional broadcasting activities. For example, audience contributions on a website for a particular show may contribute to further plot development for a television series.[31]

Traditional television broadcasters are likely to lose advertising revenue in the face of competition from advertising via the Internet and media such as WAP-enabled devices. The growth in Internet use has provided advertisers with an enormous potential market to be reached online. Advertisers are likely to find the very precise information that is available about the electronic environment an incentive to use the Internet. They can, for instance, access online real-time reporting showing how many banner advertisements are being served on various sites, how many people are clicking on them and following links, and, using post-click tracking, monitor how people came to the advertising site initially. Such specific data enable advertisers to target desirable audiences as potential consumers.

Media convergence and the possibility of delivering television-type content via the Internet and, conversely, online content via the television set present a challenge to traditional media. Some companies have begun to develop content specifically for online delivery and not simply as repackaged segments from traditional media programming. Development of content for broadband services may hinge on the extension of user-pays principles, as audience demand for online video grows, and as video-streaming technology becomes more accessible.

The film industry's response to new media has also shown adaptability and resilience. Cinema met various challenges from the 1950s onward – the rise of television, the boom in home video, the expansion of pay television services, the advent of the Internet – although the industry has changed substantially in the process (see chapter 9). The main players of the traditional film industry, the Hollywood studios, were able to increase their income by capitalizing on the impact of changing technologies and audience demand as home video became popular.[32] Older film companies have been submerged in the process of media mergers; the resulting corporations now promote and use film studio product across various media. Such corporate activities, combined with the revival of interest in cinema, indicate that film will continue to play an important part in entertainment. For the film industry, change in the near future is likely to include direct satellite transmission to movie theaters, expansion of production for high-definition television, and possibly the direct delivery of movies to home television screens on a pay-per-view basis.

The rate of technological change and the take-up of new media have been rapid, but the extent of enduring social impacts is difficult to determine. In one respect new media have effected remarkable change – in the area of communication via email and mobile telephony – and this has implications for delivery of content. However, extravagant claims about more general effects of the Internet will not be realized while access remains so uneven globally, regionally, and in many societies locally. That traditional media have remained and continue to flourish, particularly in delivering diverse forms of entertainment, also indicates a less than revolutionary impact.

If the relationship between media and politics is taken as an example, the potential of new media – particularly the Internet – to stimulate significant change, even in Western societies where adoption has been on a large scale, should not be exaggerated. James Fallows, having analyzed the US presidential election of 2000, noted several areas in which change might have been expected if the Internet were having any significant impact on the conduct of American politics. One indication would have been that political candidates could compete without requiring enormous resources; yet that election was the most expensive to that time. Another likely effect would have been that new political candidates would use the novel communications channels to get their message to voters – but this did not occur. Nor did candidates use the medium to address virtual constituencies, "united mainly through electronic means, rather than dealing state-by-state and bloc-by-bloc in traditional machine politics." More generally, an important indicator of the impact of new media on domestic politics would have been a decline in the importance of old media, particularly television, in national elections. In fact, the 2000 election in the United States only confirmed the continuing importance of traditional television coverage.[33]

The early twenty-first-century "mediascape" is significantly different from 50 years previously. Traditional media have shown resilience in adapting to a changing environment and in utilizing new technologies. For mass media consumers the result is greater variety and expanding choice in the ways they access information and entertainment. This expansion and varied means of delivery have stimulated demand for content development for new media. A key question about converging, and increasingly interactive, media is whether users will gain access to genuinely novel and more varied forms of content – or whether there will merely be "more of the same." The pressures of commercialism suggest that innovation and experimentation will be circumscribed by profit-making imperatives.

Further reading

Barker, Chris. *Global Television: An Introduction.* Oxford: Blackwell, 1997.

— *Television, Globalization and Cultural Identities.* Buckingham: Open University Press, 1999.

Barr, Trevor. *newmedia.com.au: The Changing Face of Australia's Media and Communications.* St. Leonards: Allen and Unwin, 2000.

Cunningham, Stuart, and Graeme Turner (eds.). *The Media in Australia,* 2nd edn. St. Leonards: Allen and Unwin, 1997.

Curran, James (ed.). *Media Organisations in Society*. London: Arnold, 2000.

Dizard, Wilson, Jr. *Old Media/New Media: Mass Communications in the Information Age*. London: Longman, 1994.

Downing, John, Ali Mohammedi, and Annabelle Sreberny-Mohammadi. *Questioning the Media: A Critical Introduction*, 2nd edn. London: Sage, 1995.

Hearn, Greg, Tom Mandeville, and David Anthony. *The Communication Superhighway: Social and Economic Change in the Digital Age*. St. Leonards: Allen and Unwin, 1998.

Held, David, and Anthony McGrew (eds.). *The Global Transformations Reader: An Introduction to the Globalization Debate*. Cambridge: Polity Press, 2000.

Herman, Edward S. *The Global Media: The New Missionaries of Corporate Capitalism*. London: Cassell, 1997.

Hiebert, Ray Eldon, and Sheila Jean Gibbons. *Exploring Mass Media for a Changing World*. London: Lawrence Erlbaum, 2000.

Negrine, Ralph. *Satellite Broadcasting: The Politics and Implications of the New Media*. London: Routledge, 1988.

— (ed.). *Television and the Press since 1945*. Manchester: Manchester University Press, 1998.

Owen, Bruce M. *The Internet Challenge to Television*. Cambridge, MA: Harvard University Press, 1999.

Winston, Brian. *Media Technology and Society: A History; From the Telegraph to the Internet*. London: Routledge, 1998.

12

GLOBALIZATION AND MEDIA

The term "globalization" came into common usage in the late 1990s. It describes changes in international relationships, particularly in economics and international trade, but also increasingly with respect to society and culture, including media and communications. It gained currency after the end of the Cold War in a world where the relationship between the United States and the Soviet Union no longer dominated international affairs. This chapter examines the impact of globalization on mass media and communications. After outlining the main features of globalization, it focuses on the relationship between changes in global communications networks and the media, and on the emergence of global media institutions. It provides examples of "mega-media corporations" and discusses problems they pose in relation to more traditional conceptions of the role of media in society. It considers the debate about media or cultural imperialism in the context of globalization; this debate has subsumed concerns about the worldwide influence of US cinema and television during earlier periods. Finally, it summarizes the nature of media at the end of the twentieth century and questions contemporary expectations and assumptions about their role in society.

Definitions of Globalization

Analysts have emphasized different reasons for, and effects of, globalization. According to Jeremy Hardie, globalization derived from post-1945 policies aimed at freedom for investment and open trade in goods and services.

It is amplified by cheaper transport and communications generally, including, but not primarily, the Internet; by standardization of English as the lingua franca of business and popular culture; by the development of international finance; and by the general belief that free trade is the ideologically correct strategy to achieve prosperity and self-improvement.

One manifestation of globalization is the integration of financial markets and the traffic through stock exchanges. Changes in information technology have enabled huge financial transactions to be carried out almost instantaneously, with "extraordinary shifts of financial information around the world's capital markets." More complex global interconnections have developed, relying on vast computer networks. The role of information in a more global world economy has become central.[1]

Apart from easier travel and communication, changing trade and investment patterns, globalization has had an impact on culture and modes of thought. Frank J. Lechner and John Boli refer to post-World War II developments in communication and transportation infrastructure, with satellite broadcasts that brought events to an increasingly global audience and the Internet that linked "interest groups of educated users" as "the raw material of globalization." They note that

democracy gains strength as a global model for organizing nation-states; numerous international organizations take on new responsibilities in addressing issues of common concern . . . The world is becoming a single place, in which different institutions function as parts of one system and distant peoples share a common understanding of living together on one planet. This world society has a culture . . . To links and institutions we therefore add culture and consciousness. Globalization is the process that fitfully brings these elements of world society together.[2]

Central to globalization is the notion that local and national economies and societies will become integrated into a more unified political, economic, and cultural order. This has important implications for the "old order:" in a globalized world, nation-states, it is suggested, enjoy diminished power relative to global corporations, whose influence in turn derives from globalized industrial processes, trade, and communication. A related aspect of globalization is that international agencies such as the United Nations, the World Bank, the North Atlantic Treaty Organization, and the European Union, as well as regional trading blocs such as ASEAN (the Association of South East Asian Nations) and NAFTA (the North Atlantic Free Trade Association), play larger roles relative to nation-states not only in economic matters but also in other areas such as peacekeeping.

While the idea of globalization has gained currency, and as academic works on the subject multiply, it is important to note that claims about globalization have also provoked skepticism. Jean Seaton notes that orthodox "globalization" theories "are far too wide to be able to describe many of the things that are actually happening. Huge changes are gathering speed, but in order to deal with these, we need evidence not speculation."[3] By the year 2000 it was apparent not just from academic discussion but also from the activism of disparate groups in various locations that there was not a consensus about globalization, its desirability, or its significance. Protesters at international meeting venues opposed aspects of globalization such as world trade. In examining the relationship between the processes described as "globalization" and the media, it is important to question discrepancies between the ideas and the reality.

Global Communications and the Media

Technological developments and the rise of new media (discussed in chapter 11) have facilitated global communication. The extension of fiber-optic cable systems, of satellite links, of Internet communication networks, and the deregulation of telecommunications systems have theoretically made it possible to bypass the borders of nation-states that have traditionally exercised regulatory powers over media institutions. The trend appears to be toward greater internationalization of media systems.

However, recent developments have not occurred in isolation, and late nineteenth- and early twentieth-century innovations were important for the emergence of global communication networks. One such development was the extension of underwater cable systems by the European great powers from the 1850s. By 1900 this had produced "a global system of communication in which the capacity to transmit messages was clearly separated from the time-consuming processes of transportation." Another was the establishment of international news agencies. Charles Havas established the first in Paris in 1835; this was followed by Paul Julius Reuter's agency in London and by the Berlin agency of Bernard Wolff in the 1840s. International news agencies, particularly Reuters, Associated Press and United Press International (both American), and Agence France Presse (which succeeded Havas as the French international news agency), have retained an important global role in collecting and distributing news. At the international level the formation of organizations (such as the International Telecommunication Union in 1865) to introduce order into the allocation of the electromagnetic spectrum, and radio spectrum in the twentieth century, was important for global communication.[4]

In more recent times new technologies have facilitated global communication and the global spread of media. Telecommunications satellites made possible greater geographical reach and distribution, enabling virtually instantaneous global communication without microwave relays and coaxial cable. Satellites in turn became integrated into wider telecommunications networks (for telephone, fax, electronic mail, and so on). Telecommunications satellites act as relay stations and distribution points for both traditional network systems and cable television systems nationally and internationally, while at the same time serving other communications functions. The global spread of media services has also been driven by the large corporations that emerged as key players in the global system of communication and information diffusion. Examples include News Corporation's Star Television, which broadcasts to more than 50 countries in Asia with an audience of 220 million viewers, and the Cable News Network (CNN) – part of the huge AOL-Time Warner conglomerate since 2000 – that provides news services to more than 200 countries.[5]

The reduction or elimination of traditional institutional and legal barriers – or the capability simply to bypass them – has facilitated the spread of global media. At the end of the twentieth century there was support, among Western governments in particular, for free market policies that provided for minimal government intervention in many areas, for the reduction or elimination of barriers to free trade, for deregulation and the privatization of previously public services. New technologies and laissez-faire policies opened up media markets to highly integrated global corporations.

As an example of deregulation, policy changes in the United States in the 1980s and 1990s stimulated greater competition in telecommunications, produced a less regulated broadcasting environment, enabled greater consolidation in media industries, and greater integration into global media markets. AT&T, which had previously controlled nationwide telephone services, lost its monopoly, opening the way to competition. It also diversified into other areas, buying a cable television company and an Internet company, and extended its international operations, contributing to greater convergence and to global expansion.

There were other indications of lighter regulation in American broadcasting. Limits on advertising time were relaxed, as were guidelines that had encouraged news, public affairs, and local programming. The easing of rules that had restricted cross-media ownership opened the way to greater concentration of media ownership. Thus a single global corporation such as News Corporation (see below) was able to accumulate extensive interests in newspapers, the film industry, and both network and cable television. In the United Kingdom similarly the privatization of British Telecom and the deregulation of telecommunications industries led British Telecom to seek new global partners and to enter other markets such as cable television.[6]

While changes in national policies have contributed to globalization, international organizations, too, have encouraged commercial media at the global level. In a world where information exchange is considered vital, the media are seen as central to the world economy. Organizations such as the International Monetary Fund (IMF) and the World Trade Organization (WTO) have supported global media in the service of the market economy. One implication is that national governments face difficulties in retaining control over vital areas of communication.[7] Furthermore, global media operate increasingly in a world where commercialization has triumphed (see chapters 8 and 9).

Giant Media Corporations

In the 1990s the growth of giant media corporations exploited the possibilities of multiple media ownership and of commercial concerns that transcended national boundaries. Media companies, responding to the market situation, moved toward being larger, global, and vertically integrated so that they could achieve cost savings and take advantage of cross-selling and cross-promotion opportunities. Many media businesses became part of global conglomerates producing entertainment and media products, and computing software, with global distribution networks. Some large media concerns in turn became part of even larger corporations whose interests extended far beyond media. By the late 1990s seven huge corporations – Time Warner, Walt Disney, Bertelsmann, Viacom, News Corporation, Seagram, and Sony – dominated the world's publishing and entertainment business.[8] In Europe large corporations such as Bertelsmann, Havas, and Matra-Hachette expanded and became involved in complex cross-ownership arrangements; Bertelsmann in particular became an important global player.

Giant media corporations enjoyed advantages of scale and integration; they exploited opportunities for cross-promotion (see chapter 9). A Disney film could be shown on pay cable and commercial network television, the company could produce and sell soundtracks based on the film, create spin-off television series, establish related amusement park events, produce

CD-ROMs, books, comics, and merchandise to be sold in Disney retail stores, and promote the film and related material across its media properties. "The profit whole for the vertically integrated firm can be significantly greater than the profit potential of the individual parts in isolation." With increasing media convergence it was important for corporations to encompass distribution as well as production operations. The size and market power of the media giants also made it possible to develop exclusive agreements for cross-promotion with other marketing and retailing corporations. For example, a 1996 deal between Disney and the McDonald's fast food chain gave exclusive global rights to McDonald's to promote Disney products. Such alliances enhanced the profitability and competitive position of the largest global corporations.[9]

The development of giant media corporations poses questions about the role and responsibilities of media in contemporary societies. Three examples illustrate some of the issues. In Italy the emergence of Fininvest, with substantial media holdings and controlled by Silvio Berlusconi, drew attention to concentration of media ownership, conflicts of interest, and the role of the media in modern societies. The expansion of Rupert Murdoch's News Corporation provoked concern about cross-media ownership and the power of transnational media. The establishment of the giant AOL-Time Warner conglomerate at the beginning of 2000 raised questions about the impact of converging technologies and about possibilities for media giants to operate in a largely unregulated "global space." The power of individual media magnates again became topical, as it had been in the era of the "press barons" a century earlier.

Fininvest

The Italian media magnate and politician Silvio Berlusconi and his company provide a case study of the concentration of media ownership and of potential conflict of interest. European and global attention was drawn to Fininvest in 2001 when May elections in Italy resulted in a win for Silvio Berlusconi and his conservative party. Berlusconi was noted not only for a previous brief period in Italian politics in 1994 but also as a media magnate. He and his family owned 96 percent of Fininvest, which had extensive media and other interests, including a large stake in three television networks in Italy – Canale 5, Italia 1, Retequattro – through the company Mediaset. These networks carried 60 percent of Italian television advertising. Berlusconi had a 48 percent stake in Mondadore, Italy's largest publishing group and publisher of the leading newspaper *Il Giornale*, and of the influential weekly magazine *Panorama*, and he owned Medusa Video, a film production and distribution company, as well as having a 51 percent stake in the video rental chain Blockbuster Italia.

With this dominant role in Italy's communications industries and the potential to exercise considerable influence over public opinion, Berlusconi used the media in his political campaign prior to the election. As prime minister, he also gained *de facto* control over the state television network, RAI, bringing the total audience share of enterprises in which he had an interest (state television and his private commercial channels) to greater than 90 percent. This substantial concentration of media ownership and Berlusconi's political role raised questions about conflict of interest. Berlusconi was both Italian prime minister and the country's dominant media figure; this led to anxiety about the consequent destruction of media independence and opportunities for free expression via the press and broadcasting. After the Italian election European media referred to such power heralding "a new form of totalitarianism."[10]

News Corporation

Another giant media corporation that has provoked concern about the power and influence of media and of media magnates in the twenty-first century is News Corporation.

Since the 1950s Rupert Murdoch had been a dominant figure in News Corporation as it expanded from a local company involved only in newspaper publication to a giant global corporation with diverse media and other interests. Murdoch inherited an Australian newspaper, the *Adelaide News*, from his father in 1954. In the 1960s he acquired papers in other Australian state capital cities, and he established a national newspaper, *The Australian*, in 1964. He bought into the British press in the late 1960s with *News of the World* and the *Sun*, and then in the 1980s the prestigious *Times* and *Sunday Times*. He modernized British newspaper publishing practices, in the process taking on the powerful print unions and breaking with tradition by moving his newspaper offices away from Fleet Street.

In the 1980s Murdoch expanded his media interests to the United States. He was permitted by the Federal Communications Commission (FCC) to acquire a television station in New York, where he also owned a daily newspaper, the *New York Post*. In 1985 he renounced his Australian nationality and became an American citizen so that he could purchase US television stations, avoiding US laws that restricted foreign ownership of television assets. In 1985 he launched Fox Broadcasting Company as a fourth network, competing against the long-standing three national networks, CBS, NBC, and ABC. In addition to substantial media holdings in the United States and the United Kingdom, his media company, News Corporation, owned newspapers in Australia and New Zealand, book and magazine publishing companies in Britain, and the 20th Century-Fox movie studio based in the United States. It had a major stake in BSkyB, which had been at the forefront of digital television services via satellite in the United Kingdom, and a controlling interest in Star Television, based in Hong Kong and broadcasting extensively in Asia. In 2001 its total assets were approximately US$39 billion and total annual revenue of the order of $14 billion. News Corporation's diversified global operations included the production and distribution of motion pictures and television programming; television, satellite and cable broadcasting; the publication of newspapers, magazines, and books; the production and distribution of promotional and advertising products and services; the development of digital broadcasting; and the creation and distribution of online programming.

The power and influence of a global media corporation such as News Corporation can be illustrated not only by its assets and income but also by its market share in a particular country. In the United Kingdom Murdoch's media conglomerate had the following share of media markets: of national newspapers it owned the bestselling daily and Sunday tabloids as well as important broadsheets such as *The Times*, with a market share of 26 percent of daily and 33 percent of Sunday readerships; in television BSkyB accounted for approximately 4 percent of all television viewers, and Fox TV also supplied terrestrial channels; in cinema 20th Century-Fox had over 20 percent of the film distribution market; in video Fox Guild had 14 percent of the video rental market and 6.2 percent of video retail; News Corporation also had a share in book publishing through HarperCollins and in the specialist education press with *The Times Educational Supplement*, *The Times Higher Education Supplement*, and *The Times Literary Supplement*; finally, News Corporation was involved in Internet services through LineOne.[11]

With the growth of new media and increasing media convergence, News Corporation sought ways of extending its traditional assets. A senior News Corporation executive in early 2000 noted:

> there is a tremendous sense of urgency throughout News Corp to transform our platforms and our content to exploit the lucrative opportunities of this new digital age . . . At each of our platforms, at each of our content businesses, we are furiously reviewing old business plans against the new reality

of broadband technology, interactivity, e-commerce and an exploding world-wide web and constantly asking ourselves one simple question: "How can we derive more value from our assets within this new reality using these new technologies?"[12]

News Corporation became involved in some Internet projects from mid-1999, but by mid-2000 there were cutbacks in the News Digital Media division. In the more cautious environment of 2001, after the failure of many dotcom businesses and the end of the boom period for Internet stocks, Murdoch appeared to be concentrating on the established media interests of News Corporation while also trying to expand operations in the United States.

In 2001 he was negotiating to purchase DirecTV, a satellite television system in the United States, part of Hughes Electronics, a division of General Motors. DirecTV was already available in approximately 10 million American homes and was the third largest provider of subscription television in the United States (behind AT&T with more than 15 million subscribers and AOL-Time Warner with 13 million). The addition of DirecTV to the Murdoch media empire, with its already extensive holdings in national network, local television, and cable services, would enhance News Corporation's position in the United States, allowing it to compete more effectively with existing cable systems in a market where it had tended previously to operate in the shadow of companies such as AOL and Time-Warner. However, the proposed takeover provoked reaction from the FCC and from consumer groups opposing such a concentration of media ownership. One senator warned that it could result in "a consolidation of power the likes of which this country has not seen since William Randolph Hearst," drawing a parallel between Murdoch and a newspaper proprietor of a century earlier.[13]

Critics of News Corporation maintain that it represents an enormous concentration of power in the hands of one man – and Murdoch has openly proclaimed his interventionist style (see chapter 9). This undermines the capacity for media within this giant corporation to fulfill traditional expectations about objectivity in news and information delivery, and for untrammeled journalistic independence. Furthermore, the extent of News Corporation control over certain media markets has reduced diversity and limited the variety of information available to the public. Policy decisions about media content have been based purely on commercial considerations: in response to protests about news services delivered by Star Television, News Corporation conceded to the wishes of Chinese political authorities and modified its programming (see below). This raises questions about the main forces driving global media in the twenty-first century. Given the strength of commercialization and of profit-making considerations, do traditional expectations retain any relevance?

AOL-Time Warner

The merger of America Online (AOL) and Time Warner at the beginning of 2000 was the most striking example to that time of an institutional partnership between old and new media. The combination of the traditional media company, Time Warner, itself a merger of two long-established media organizations, and America Online, an online company and the world's fourth largest corporation (after Microsoft, General Electric, and Cisco Systems), produced a media giant valued at US$525 billion. This example of converging media provided institutional confirmation that the barrier between television and personal computers was disappearing, and that old and new media convergence could make available content from traditional media (newspapers, television, and film) to leading companies of the information age.

Time Warner brought with it the various components of Turner Entertainment (the CNN news group, Home Box Office, Warner Bros. and New Line Cinema, Time Warner Cable); Time Inc., with a long tradition of radio, film, and television involvement dating back to series such as *The March of Time* (1935–51), and of publishing such as *Time, Sports Illustrated, People, Fortune,* and *Entertainment Weekly,* as well as Time-Life books; the Warner Music Group (including record labels Warner Music International, Atlantic, Elektra, Rhino, Sire and affiliates). AOL customers gained access to Time Warner media and entertainment, while AOL opened to Time Warner the world's largest online and e-commerce platform (including AOL.com, CompuServe, Netscape Communications, and ICQ), giving the media company a means of delivering its products over the Internet in a comprehensive way. For one of Time Warner's components, CNN, the media merger meant that the cable news service could integrate its news operations amid converging technologies. No longer relying only on cable and satellite delivery, CNN journalists and technicians in the field were able to send image and sound files via satellite phones instantaneously to the CNN.com website.[14]

The scale and reach of AOL-Time Warner operations highlight the impact of trends to convergence on traditional media. In many cases publishing or broadcasting operations have been absorbed into very large corporations. While these may provide opportunities for commercialization and profitability, questions arise about the extent to which media in these contexts can exercise any real independence. Will media any longer fulfill their traditionally critical role in society, contributing to, or reflecting, national culture? In relation to the information-providing function of media, as news becomes just another product sold by big media companies, it is regarded simply as a commodity. It tends to be more entertainment-based, and traditional values such as objectivity and regard for accuracy are lost. The possibility of an operation such as AOL-Time Warner exercising monopoly power has raised concerns about its control over cable television in the United States and about its power to deny access to competing Internet sites or services. Concerns about the decline of nationally based media have also revived discussion of media or cultural imperialism.

Global Media and Imperialism

The impact of globalization on the media has revived interest in the notion of cultural or media imperialism. The expansion of corporate ownership of media and related industries and the strong global influence of American programming suggest that globalized media are subject to predominantly American influences in the same way that national film and television industries in earlier periods were subject to US ascendancy in international markets.

Resentment and concern at US domination of media content were recurring themes in the twentieth century, provoked initially by the powerful international position of the US film industry in the 1920s. In the postcolonial era such concern was expressed in ideas of cultural or media imperialism. Theories of dependence emerged in the 1960s, especially in Latin America; these were applied not only to political and economic relations between the former colonial powers and the newly independent, developing nations but also to culture. Newly independent countries saw themselves as victims of cultural colonialism, with the media playing an important role in the transmission and imposition of ideas and values.

In 1973 representatives of non-aligned countries at a summit in Algiers called for a "new international economic order." This was endorsed by the United Nations General Assembly in 1974, and at a meeting in Tunis in 1976 a similar resolution called specifically for a "new information and communication order," with a free and balanced flow of information among all countries. In 1976 UNESCO appointed an International Commission for the Study of Communications Problems whose report, entitled *Many Voices, One World*, was known as the MacBride report (named after Sean MacBride, who chaired the commission).[15]

The MacBride report – and other critics of media imperialism – criticized Western news agencies for their monopoly of news and the one-way news flow between industrialized and developing countries. Agencies such as Associated Press, Reuters, United Press International, and Agence France Presse tended to transmit information to developing countries while bringing back relatively little. Moreover, much of what little Western coverage there was of events in developing countries presented stereotyped views and emphasized dramatic events such as war, natural disasters, and political instability.

In the 1980s US domination of the film and television industries in particular continued to provoke dismay at the lack of balance in distribution and programming flow, but not only with respect to Third World countries. In Europe, too, there was concern about the harmful effect on national, regional, and local cultures of US media exports and American mass culture (see chapter 8). The power of the US film industry and broadcasting networks was such that it was difficult for other film and television industries to compete. The result was that production elsewhere was limited, and imported values dominated what local cultural product there was.

Advertising appeared to exemplify striking inequities, particularly with respect to developing countries. There was a predominantly one-way flow in advertising that emphasized Western consumer culture, and encouraged people elsewhere to respond to, and conform with, the requirements of predominantly US-based transnational consumer goods manufacturers. The success of global brands such as Coca-Cola, Levi's, and McDonald's seemed to confirm the power and influence of transnational corporations and of capitalist values. The advent of new technologies, with communications satellites and telecommunications networks facilitating transborder data flows, created additional challenges to states in relation to regulating or controlling media and content. There were also imbalances between developed and developing countries as spectrum frequencies and orbital slots for satellites were assigned.

The inequalities in media and communications were reflected in concepts that supplemented older approaches to media imperialism. "North–South" relations described the relationship between the predominantly highly industrialized and developed countries of the Northern hemisphere and the less developed countries of the South. The "core–periphery" thesis conceived of industrialized countries as the core or center of the global system, with less developed countries marginalized in the periphery. This idea of "peripheral players" was applied to non-US media industries in the 1990s.[16]

During the 1980s UNESCO conferences continued to support the idea of a new information and communication order, but unity among the non-aligned nations declined, and attention shifted to the growing trends to deregulation of media and privatization of public sector enterprises that gained momentum in that decade. Problems about international flows of information remained, particularly given the significance of information and communication in modern societies, but there was little prospect that these would be priority concerns of Western governments supportive of free market ideologies or of giant media corporations operating globally.

Yet, while global corporations expanded and inequalities persisted, the real impact of cultural or media imperialism at national and local levels was questioned in the 1990s. Increasingly, it was suggested that there were limits to US dominance and that the spread of American influences has been, and continues to be, uneven. Nor could it be assumed that all American programs simply conveyed the values of Western capitalism; not all exported US media content supported capitalist society or consumer culture. Audiences interpret American content in their own contexts, and they understand film and television programs in diverse ways. Moreover, various non-American media industries have developed and flourished, confirming that too much emphasis should not be placed on American influence or on the importance of imported products.

In the complex "international mediascapes" of the 1990s new conceptions of media relationships suggested that any simple model of media imperialism was inadequate to capture the many factors that influence cultural exchange. These include leisure traditions and viewers' attitudes and perceptions, decisions by "gatekeepers" about what should or should not be imported, when programs should be scheduled, and what the balance between local and imported programming should be; the regulatory frameworks of particular countries; and perceptions of difference between national and imported programs. Audiences receive global media products and interpret them in many and varied ways; and different cultures are resilient in transforming and absorbing foreign influences and putting "mass culture" to local use. Rather than seeing global mass culture as replacing local culture, it is more appropriate to consider the two as coexisting. Research in Asia, for example, has shown that in seven of nine countries, more hours of domestic television programs were broadcast than of imported programs, and the share of imported programs in total national television supply was often low. Recent work on globalization supports the acceptance of cultural and political differences, with global culture itself embracing the idea that people and countries are entitled to their particularity or distinctiveness. As Trevor Barr has indicated,

> a key paradox of the new media is institutional consolidation on the one hand, yet user diversification on the other. Corporations search for economies of scale as a result of globalization, yet find that their markets are more fragmented and complex culturally than ever before. Diversity is alive and well in the world's many global villages.[17]

Catering to these diverse audiences are film and television industries – there are examples from Australia, Canada, India, Mexico, Brazil, and Egypt – whose successes illustrated the inadequacy of the concept of US media imperialism to describe relationships in regional and global markets in the 1990s. In the Indian subcontinent, for instance, Bombay became a center of media production and trade for the Hindi film industry, exporting film on video to the UK, Singapore, Hong Kong, the United Arab Emirates, and elsewhere where large Indian minority populations ensured strong demand for Hindi films. Hong Kong and Taiwan exported film and television programs to Chinese-speaking populations in other Asian countries, as did Egypt to other Arabic speakers. In Mexico and Brazil local media entrepreneurs reversed earlier trends. Using videotapes, Mexican producers developed programs for export and, with the advent of satellite, Mexican Televisa broadcast Spanish-language programs to some 15 million Hispanic households in the United States from the late 1980s. Brazil's TV Globo built up a thriving export industry, marketing its telenovelas or soap operas in Portugal and in more than 100 other countries. Other examples of "contra-flow," reversing the directions in which media content had historically moved, were successful film and television exports from Australia and Canada to the United States and the United Kingdom.[18]

It was necessary to extend the media imperialism thesis to incorporate conceptions of media at the global level that acknowledged national and regional difference and modified views of US dominance. Nonetheless, continuing media convergence and corporate mergers suggest that global media will remain subject to strong influences from a few giant corporations. Just how pervasive is American influence within these media giants is debatable, given the extent of non-US interests in the major global media conglomerates, as well as increasingly common practices such as co-productions (see chapter 9).

In the early twenty-first century the relevance of discussion about media imperialism can itself be questioned, as media convergence continues, and as Internet use expands. When audiences are not confined within national boundaries, as geographical boundaries seem to lose their relevance to "virtual" or "imagined" communities, it becomes more difficult to ascertain how media products are received and, therefore, just how influential are content developers. A simple model of US media imperialism is inadequate in the contemporary world of giant global media corporations and diverse national media industries.

Global Media and Politics

One of the claims made for global media – especially television and the Internet – is that they have the potential to spread democratic values and opportunities, to empower and encourage participation by marginalized groups, to challenge governments whose power and authority have depended on the control of information. The Internet is seen as a means for promoting democratic ideals and for distributing information rapidly in times of political crisis. Related to this is the view that globalization and developments in global media have led to a decline in the power of nation-states. The capacity for control by the nation-state, given an increasingly globalized economy and media culture and greater transborder information flows, has been reduced; it is argued that state control can be "bypassed by global flows of capital, goods, services, technology, communication and information."[19]

The People's Republic of China provides an interesting case study. Coverage of the Chinese government clampdown on the pro-democracy movement in Tiananmen Square in 1989 appeared to exemplify the potential of global media. International satellite television showed the use of force against pro-democracy demonstrators to a global audience, stimulating widespread condemnation of Chinese government and military actions. Chinese students successfully used Western media to further their cause, bearing banners with American symbols and written in English for the wider television audience. The scope of global television seemed to have been redefined, showing its power to affect political events within national boundaries, to influence world diplomacy and international public opinion.[20]

However, relations between Chinese governments and Western media have not been one-sided. Tension between News Corporation and the Chinese government four years after the Tiananmen Square incidents led to a backdown by the media corporation. In 1993 Rupert Murdoch commented in a well publicized speech that "Advances in technology of tele-communications have proved an unambiguous threat to totalitarian regimes everywhere. Satellite broadcasting makes it possible for information hungry residents of many closed societies to by-pass state controlled television channels."

Chinese authorities had earlier objected to foreign coverage of the events of 1989 and reacted to Murdoch's statement in 1993, threatening to prevent News Corporation, in particular its Star Television service, from gaining access to the Chinese market. Murdoch took steps to placate China, and News Corporation removed the BBC World Television Service from its Asian satellite service. In another incident in 1997 Murdoch appeared to take heed of pressure from China when the News Corporation publishing company, HarperCollins, repudiated an agreement to publish a controversial book by the former governor of Hong Kong, Chris Patten, to whom the Chinese government was hostile.[21]

Growth of the Internet has created a dilemma for Chinese authorities. On the one hand information technology, access to information, and developments in e-commerce are considered important to China's economic future. On the other, freedom of information could threaten Chinese Communist Party authority and pose a challenge in a society where tight political control over information has been the norm. Exercising such control became difficult in the face of rapid popular take-up of new media. Chinese Internet use surged from just over 2 million in December 1998, to approximately 9 million a year later, to 26 million by mid-2001.

Unwilling to allow free access to global information and entertainment sources, Chinese authorities blocked access to foreign websites, particularly news organizations (the BBC, CNN, the *New York Times*, the *Washington Post*) and human rights sites critical of Chinese policy. In January 2000 new regulations forbade the release, discussion, or transfer of "state secret information" on bulletin boards, chat rooms, or in Internet newsgroups. Websites were required to undergo security checks; and those that failed to implement safeguards against security breaches could be shut down. China-based Internet service providers were barred from running foreign news on websites, instead having to use reports from official Chinese news outlets. However, it was difficult to enforce these restrictions as users found ways to evade them. By May 2000 there seemed to be some easing of the Chinese attitude when authorities allowed China's first website to go public overseas, with Sina.com being listed on the Nasdaq exchange. However, the practice of blocking selected foreign websites, including those of high-profile Western newspapers, continued. In 2001 there were reports of plans by US agencies (the International Broadcasting Bureau, parent agency of the Voice of America) to finance a computer network designed to thwart Chinese government attempts to censor or block websites.[22]

In other countries, too, where traditional media had been subject to control, the Internet has provided opportunities for free expression and been used by opposition groups to call for political reform. In some cases authorities have acted to restrict or prohibit use, in extreme cases banning the Internet, and in others implementing censorship measures or requiring Internet service providers to be licensed. Perhaps even more so than in relation to political censorship, the Internet has subverted moral censorship everywhere, with easy access to pornographic and similar websites. The nature of the medium continues to make censorship or regulatory measures difficult to implement, as users bypass censors or gain access via direct satellite links or Internet service providers in other countries. One limitation on the potential of new media such as the Internet to be used for "democratic purposes" is that access remains highly unequal, with striking discrepancies between rich and poor countries (see chapter 11).

The Chinese and other examples illustrate difficulties for nation-states in regulating or controlling media, given technological and institutional change. Certainly the communications revolution is posing new challenges, making it possible for interest groups to ignore the constraints of time and of geography. Some of these groups are unsympathetic to globalization and see new media as means of exerting pressure.

> Huge networks of public interest, environment, human rights, consumer development, religious and umbrella civil society groups, drawing in local, national and international organizations, are beginning to emerge. For the first time they are able to respond immediately to international events, counter state propaganda or bring concerted pressure to bear on governments, companies or international bodies.[23]

Examples of action by these new coalitions have been the "netwars" waged against world trade talks, against world debt, against landmines, and against genetically modified foods. Such action via the Internet, it is suggested, may pose a threat to capitalism and to neoliberal economies, as loyalties shift from the nation-state to the transnational level of global civic society. It could also be argued that if the virtual world of the Internet becomes overly preoccupying, it threatens the "real lived worlds" of individuals in communities.

Such claims should not be accepted at face value. It is unwise to move from discussion of the potential of new communications technologies and global media to the statement that globalization has "killed the nation-state." Some assertions about the impact of globalized media on domestic or foreign policy-making in nation-states have been exaggerated (see chapters 9, 10, and 11). As Seaton argues, "Nations still exist . . . National preferences still exist, national patterns of media use and habit still exist. Policies about resources and distribution, though more difficult to get right and in some areas beyond the control of individual nation-states, matter more, not less."[24]

Media and Society in a New Century

The rise of global media conglomerates at the end of the twentieth century highlighted a central paradox in the history of communications. The advocates of global communication forecast the breaking down of national and ethnic differences and the growth of international understanding, all to be achieved through the influence of media operating on a global scale. But the promise is hard to reconcile with the realities of media development since the 1980s. Far from creating a unified world, commercial media organizations have increasingly fostered a fragmentation of audiences and a strengthening of social barriers. Where big-city newspapers and national radio and television programs once reached mass audiences, the tastes of specialized groups, distinguished by different "lifestyles" and perceived as niche markets for advertising revenue, shape media content to an unprecedented degree. Far from fostering international understanding, the same organizations have presided over a marked reduction in serious coverage of public affairs in both broadcasting and print media, and not least in treatment of international affairs. The world has in some respects become more globalized, but in the United States, in particular, an increasing emphasis on entertainment at the expense of information, the growing tendency for the American public to receive their news as "infotainment," or to receive no news at all, and the downplaying of world news on network television, on radio, and in the press have resulted in media content that is more parochial than at any stage at least since the interwar period. With the United States the one remaining superpower, it is less and less the case that the media perform the vital role of helping to develop an informed public as an influence on US international policies.

This failing points to another paradox. The rise of new media – the expansion of cable television and the Internet in particular – has presented the world with an unprecedented number of media outlets and new ways to gain access to information. But in two respects the potential created by new technology has not been fulfilled. The decline of news and public affairs content is one: by the end of the century it was less the case that mainstream media saw an important part of their role as providing members of the public with the information they need to act as citizens in democratic societies. Moreover, the growing diversity of media outlets stood in curious contrast with the reality of circumscribed content. The decline of news and public affairs coverage underlined the problem: rigid formulas, calculated to maximize advertising revenue, encouraged a global trend to rely on similar forms of entertainment as the basis for profitability.

These developments reflected the triumph of commerce and the decline of a public service ethos in media generally at the end of the century, assisted by a greater unwillingness of governments to regulate media content. Such trends highlight one of the central issues in the study of the media: in what ways are the public best served by their media or, to put it another way, what should a democracy expect of its media? One version of "democracy," favored by the media corporations, is to point to the vast audiences commanded by modern media as a source of legitimacy. In this view the very popularity of programs and publications demonstrates that they serve the public interest. Thus media products are treated as commodities; their success or failure is determined by the market. This view is now so deeply ingrained that it has come to be regarded by many as common sense. It attributes no political or cultural importance to the media. Yet the study of the history of media in a number of societies in the twentieth century reminds us that there are other possibilities for media organization and content. The "mass society" and Marxist critics who were for so long influential in the study of communications vastly exaggerated the power of media to determine attitudes and values. Nonetheless, their views had the virtue of drawing attention to the cultural and political importance of media, an importance increasingly overlooked in a globalized media world. Historical understanding of the emergence of modern media provides a basis for envisaging alternatives in a commercialized, globalized era.

Further reading

Barker, Chris. *Global Television: An Introduction.* Oxford: Blackwell, 1997.
— *Television, Globalization and Cultural Identities.* Buckingham: Open University Press, 1999.

Barr, Trevor. *newmedia.com.au: The Changing Face of Australia's Media and Communications*. St. Leonards: Allen and Unwin, 2000.

Branston, Gill, and Roy Stafford. *The Media Student's Book*, 2nd edn. London: Routledge, 1999.

Cunningham, Stuart, and Elizabeth Jacka. *Australian Television and International Mediascapes*. Cambridge: Cambridge University Press, 1996.

Cunningham, Stuart, and Graeme Turner (eds.). *The Media in Australia*, 2nd edn. St. Leonards: Allen and Unwin, 1997.

Curran, James (ed.). *Media Organisations in Society.* London: Arnold, 2000.

Downing, John, Ali Mohammadi, and Annabelle Sreberny-Mohammadi. *Questioning the Media: A Critical Introduction*, 2nd edn. London: Sage, 1995.

Held, David, and Anthony McGrew (eds.). *The Global Transformations Reader: An Introduction to the Globalization Debate*. Cambridge: Polity Press, 2000.

Held, David, Anthony McGrew, David Goldblatt, and Jonathan Perraton. *Global Transformations: Politics, Economics and Culture*. Cambridge: Polity Press, 2000.

Lechner, Frank J., and John Boli. *The Globalization Reader*. Oxford: Blackwell, 2000.

Owen, Bruce M. *The Internet Challenge to Television*. Cambridge, MA: Harvard University Press, 1999.

Sinclair, John, Elizabeth Jacka, and Stuart Cunningham (eds.). *New Patterns in Global Television: Peripheral Vision*. Oxford: Oxford University Press, 1996.

Wheeler, Mark. *Politics and the Mass Media*. Oxford: Blackwell, 1997.

Winston, Brian. *Media Technology and Society: A History; From the Telegraph to the Internet*. London: Routledge, 1998.

NOTES

1 Introduction

1 John Tosh, *The Pursuit of History: Aims, Methods and New Directions in the Study of Modern History*, 2nd edn. (London: Longman, 1991), pp. 15–22. The quotations are from pages 16 and 18.
2 Kevin Williams, *Get Me a Murder a Day! A History of Mass Communication in Britain* (London: Arnold, 1998), p. vii.
3 Ken Ward, *Mass Communications and the Modern World* (Basingstoke: Macmillan, 1989).
4 Williams, *Get Me a Murder a Day!*, p. 2.
5 Ward, *Mass Communications and the Modern World*, p. 9.

2 The Press as a Mass Medium

1 James Curran and Jean Seaton, *Power Without Responsibility: The Press and Broadcasting in Britain*, 5th edn. (London: Routledge, 1997), p. 42.
2 Jeremy Black, *The English Press in the Eighteenth Century* (London: Croom Helm, 1987), p. 304.
3 Ibid, pp. 291, 301, 306.
4 Curran and Seaton, *Power Without Responsibility*, p. 26; Geoffrey Alan Cranfield, *The Press and Society: From Caxton to Northcliffe* (London: Longman, 1978), p. 226.
5 Ibid, pp. 37–8.
6 Ibid, pp. 31–2.
7 Francis Williams, *The Right to Know: The Rise of the World Press* (London: Longman, 1969), p. 79; Curran and Seaton, *Power Without Responsibility*, p. 50.

8 J. Lee Thompson, *Northcliffe: Press Baron in Politics, 1865–1922* (London: John Murray, 2000), p. 35.

9 Ken Ward, *Mass Communications and the Modern World* (Basingstoke: Macmillan Education, 1989), pp. 41–3.

10 Ibid, pp. 41–2; Williams, *The Right to Know*, pp. 32–6.

11 Curran and Seaton, *Power Without Responsibility*, p. 43.

12 Ward, *Mass Communications and the Modern World*, p. 42; Stefan Collini, "Lament for a Lost Culture," *Times Literary Supplement*, January 19, 2001, p. 4; J. Lee Thompson, *Politicians, the Press, and Propaganda: Lord Northcliffe and the Great War, 1914–1919* (Kent, OH: Kent State University Press, 1999), p. 238; Thompson, *Northcliffe*, p. xiv.

13 Richard Allen Schwarzlose, *Newspapers: A Reference Guide* (Westport, CT: Greenwood Press, 1987), pp. xvii–xxv.

14 Ibid, p. xxiii; Williams, *The Right to Know*, ch. 4; Michael Emery, Edwin Emery, and Nancy L. Roberts, *The Press and America: An Interpretive History of the Mass Media* (Boston, MA: Allyn and Bacon, 1996), p. 103.

15 Ibid, p. 230.

16 Peter Young and Peter Jesser, *The Media and the Military: From the Crimea to Desert Strike* (South Melbourne: Macmillan Education, 1997), p. 23.

17 Williams, *The Right to Know*, p. 60; Ward, *Mass Communications and the Modern World*, p. 34.

18 Williams, *The Right to Know*, p. 63.

19 Ward, *Mass Communications and the Modern World*, p. 34.

20 Schwarzlose, *Newspapers: A Reference Guide*, pp. xxix–xxx.

21 Stephen Badsey, "The Boer War as a Media War," in *The Boer War: Army, Nation and Empire*, ed. Peter Dennis and Jeffrey Grey (Canberra: Army History Unit, Department of Defence, 2000), pp. 79, 83.

22 A. J. Anthony Morris, *The Scaremongers: The Advocacy of War and Rearmament 1896–1914* (London: Routledge and Kegan Paul, 1984).

23 Thompson, *Northcliffe*, p. 146.

24 See, for example, Morris, *The Scaremongers*, pp. 365, 380–1; Ward, *Mass Communications and the Modern World*, pp. 58–9; R. Davenport-Hines, review of Thompson, *Northcliffe* and *Politicians, the Press and Propaganda* in *Times Literary Supplement* (June 2, 2000), p. 36.

25 John Williams, *The Home Fronts: Britain, France and Germany 1914–1918* (London: Constable, 1972), p. 24.

26 Ward, *Mass Communications and the Modern World*, pp. 69–70.

27 Williams, *The Home Fronts*, pp. 258, 283. The quotation is from the *Rheinische-Westfalische Zeitung*.

28 Young and Jesser, *The Media and the Military*, p. 33; Phillip Knightley, *The First Casualty: The War Correspondent as Hero and Myth Maker from the Crimea to Kosovo* (London: Prion, 2000); Miles Hudson and John Stanier, *War and the Media: A Random Searchlight* (Stroud: Sutton, 1997).

29   Peter J. S. Dunnett, *The World Newspaper Industry* (London: Croom Helm, 1988), p. 6.
30   Graham Murdock and Peter Golding, "The Structure, Ownership and Control of the Press, 1914–76," in *Newspaper History from the Seventeenth Century to the Present Day*, ed. George Boyce, James Curran, and Pauline Wingate (London: Constable, 1978), p. 136.
31   Ibid, p. 130.
32   Emery, Emery, and Roberts, *The Press and America*, p. 293.
33   Ibid.
34   Ibid, p. 274; George H. Douglas, *The Golden Age of the Newspaper* (Westport, CT: Greenwood Press, 1999), p. 229.

3 The Development of the Film Industry

1   Quoted in Steven J. Ross, *Working-Class Hollywood: Silent Film and the Shaping of Class in America* (Princeton, NJ: Princeton University Press, 1998), p. 5.
2   Eric Rhode, *A History of the Cinema from Its Origins to 1970* (New York: Hill and Wang, 1976), p. 16.
3   Charles Musser, *The Emergence of Cinema: The American Screen to 1907* (New York: Charles Scribner's, 1990), pp. 418–20.
4   Eileen Bowser, *The Transformation of Cinema 1907–1915* (New York: Charles Scribner's, 1990), p. 6; Russell Merritt, "Nickelodeon Theaters 1905–1914: Building an Audience for the Movies," in *The American Film Industry*, ed. Tino Balio (Madison: University of Wisconsin Press, 1985), p. 86; Ken Ward, *Mass Communications and the Modern World* (Basingstoke: Macmillan, 1989), p. 50; Kevin Williams, *Get Me a Murder a Day! A History of Mass Communication in Britain* (London: Arnold, 1998), p. 70; Klaus Kreimeier, *The Ufa Story: A History of Germany's Greatest Film Company, 1918–1945* (Berkeley: University of California Press, 1999), p. 15.
5   Robert Sklar, *Film: An International History of the Medium* (New York: H. N. Abrams, 1993), pp. 47–8.
6   Quoted in Bowser, *Transformation of Cinema*, p. 3.
7   Lary May, *Screening Out the Past: The Birth of Mass Culture and the Motion Picture Industry* (New York: Oxford University Press, 1980), pp. 147–66.
8   Sklar, *Film: An International History*, p. 63.
9   Victoria de Grazia, "Mass Culture and Sovereignty: The American Challenge to European Cinemas, 1920–1960," *Journal of Modern History*, 61 (1989), p. 61.
10   May, *Screening Out the Past*, pp. 169–79; Neal Gabler, *An Empire of Their Own: How the Jews Invented Hollywood* (New York: Doubleday, 1988).
11   Douglas Gomery, *The Hollywood Studio System* (New York: St Martin's Press, 1986), p. 9.

12   Ibid, p. 8.

13   Ibid, pp. 2, 12.

14   Ibid, pp. 14–23; Douglas Gomery, "Film and Business History: The Development of an American Mass Entertainment Industry," *Journal of Contemporary History*, 19, 1 (1984), pp. 89–103.

15   Kristin Thompson, *Exporting Entertainment: America in the World Film Market 1907–34* (London: British Film Institute, 1985), pp. ix, 170; Ian Jarvie, *Hollywood's Overseas Campaign: The North Atlantic Movie Trade, 1920–1950* (Cambridge: Cambridge University Press, 1992), p. 18.

16   Susan Hayward, *French National Cinema* (London: Routledge, 1993), p. 20.

17   Thompson, *Exporting Entertainment*, pp. x, 100, 169.

18   John Grierson, "Notes for English Producers," quoted in Ian Jarvie and Robert L. Macmillan, "John Grierson on Hollywood's Success, 1927," *Historical Journal of Film, Radio and Television*, 9, 3 (1989), p. 315.

19   Ibid, p. 20.

20   Quoted in Garth Jowett, *Film: The Democratic Art* (Boston, MA: Little, Brown, 1976), p. 203.

21   Quoted in Jeffrey Richards, *The Age of the Dream Palace: Cinema and Society in Britain 1930–1939* (London: Routledge and Kegan Paul, 1984), p. 63.

22   Ruth Vasey, *The World According to Hollywood, 1918–1939* (Madison: University of Wisconsin Press, 1997), p. 7.

23   Ibid, p. 19.

24   Ibid, passim.

25   Ibid, pp. 51–5; Thomas Doherty, *Pre-Code Hollywood: Sex, Immorality, and Insurrection in American Cinema, 1930–1934* (New York: Columbia University Press, 1999), pp. 93–102; Thomas Cripps, *Hollywood's High Noon: Moviemaking and Society before Television* (Baltimore, MD: Johns Hopkins University Press, 1997), p. 87.

26   Vasey, *World According to Hollywood*, pp. 89–90; Thompson, *Exporting Entertainment*, p. 121.

27   Quoted in Peter Kenez, *The Birth of the Propaganda State: Soviet Methods of Mass Mobilization, 1917–1929* (Cambridge: Cambridge University Press, 198), p. 219.

28   Quoted in Garth S. Jowett, "Extended Images," in *Contact: Human Communication and Its History*, ed. Raymond Williams (London: Thames and Hudson, 1981), p. 193.

29   Jowett, *Film: The Democratic Art*, p. 475; Gregory D. Black, *Hollywood Censored: Morality Codes, Catholics, and the Movies* (Cambridge: Cambridge University Press, 1994), pp. 53–4; Frank Walsh, *Sin and Censorship: The Catholic Church and the Motion Picture Industry* (New Haven, CT: Yale University Press, 1996), p. 70.

30   Quoted in Doherty, *Pre-Code Hollywood*, p. 322. On the Payne Fund studies and the surrounding controversy, see Garth S. Jowett, Ian C. Jarvie, and

Kathryn H. Fuller, *Children and the Movies: Media Influence and the Payne Fund Controversy* (Cambridge: Cambridge University Press, 1996); Jowett, *Film: The Democratic Art*, pp. 220–9; Robert Sklar, *Movie-Made America: a Cultural History of American Movies* (New York: Vintage Books, 1994), pp. 134–40; and Black, *Hollywood Censored*, pp. 151–5.

31   Quoted in Black, *Hollywood Censored*, p. 39.

32   See Vasey, *World According to Hollywood*, pp. 195, 205–10.

33   Ibid, pp. 197–8; Jowett, *Film: The Democratic Art*, pp. 272–3.

34   Vasey, *World According to Hollywood*, p. 196.

35   Ibid, pp. 202–6; Ross, *Working-Class Hollywood*, pp. 194–211.

36   Vasey, *World According to Hollywood*, pp. 49–62, 115–22, 140–93, 210–19; Allen L. Woll, "Hollywood Views the Mexican-American: From *The Greaser's Revenge* to *The Milagro Beanfield War*," in *Hollywood as Mirror: Changing Views of "Outsiders" and "Enemies" in American Movies*, ed. Robert Brent Toplin (Westport, CT: Greenwood Press, 1993), pp. 41–52; Gina Marchetti, *Romance and the "Yellow Peril": Race, Sex, and Discursive Strategies in Hollywood Fiction* (Berkeley: University of California Press, 1993).

37   Emmett J. Scott, quoted in Thomas Cripps, *Slow Fade to Black: The Negro in American Film, 1900–1942* (New York: Oxford University Press, 1977), p. 74.

38   See ibid, esp. pp. 170–202.

39   Ibid; Vasey, *World According to Hollywood*, pp. 137–40.

4 The Growth of Radio Broadcasting

1   Susan Douglas, *Listening In: Radio and the American Imagination* (New York: Random House, 1999), pp. 64–5.

2   Martin Shingler and Cindy Wieringa, *On Air: Methods and Meanings of Radio* (London: Hodder, 1998), p. 4.

3   Keith Geddes, with Gordon Bussey, *The Setmakers: A History of the Radio and Television Industry* (London: British Radio and Electronic Equipment Manufacturers' Association, 1991), pp. 12–13.

4   Hugh G. J. Aitken, *The Continuous Wave: Technology and American Radio, 1900–1932* (Princeton, NJ: Princeton University Press, 1985), p. 362; Susan J. Douglas, *Inventing American Broadcasting, 1899–1922* (Baltimore, MD: Johns Hopkins University Press, 1987), p. xxi. Geddes and Bussey, *The Setmakers*, provide a detailed account of the technical aspects of radio and television manufacturing, accompanied by excellent illustrative material; examples of analyses of social, commercial, and cultural aspects include works by Douglas, Hilmes, and Smulyan.

5   Susan Smulyan, *Selling Radio: The Commercialization of American Broadcasting 1920–1934* (Washington, DC: Smithsonian Institution Press, 1994), pp. 8–9, 63.

6   Ken Ward, *Mass Communications and the Modern World* (Basingstoke: Macmillan Education, 1989), p. 81.

7   L. White, "The Growth of American Radio" and "Ragtime to Riches," in *Mass Communications*, 2nd edn., ed. Wilbur L. Schramm (Urbana: University of Illinois Press, 1969); J. Fred MacDonald, *Don't Touch That Dial! Radio Programming in American Life, 1920–1960* (Chicago, IL: Nelson Hall, 1982), p. 4.

8   Ward, *Mass Communications and the Modern World*, pp. 84–5; Smulyan, *Selling Radio*.

9   MacDonald, *Don't Touch That Dial!*, p. 63.

10   Ibid, p. 31.

11   Ibid, pp. 76–7.

12   Ibid, pp. 2, 25.

13   Smulyan, *Selling Radio*.

14   James Curran and Jean Seaton, *Power Without Responsibility: The Press and Broadcasting in Britain*, 5th edn. (London: Routledge, 1997), pp. 111ff.

15   Geddes and Bussey, *The Setmakers*, p. 16.

16   Ward, *Mass Communications and the Modern World*, p. 87; Paddy Scannell and David Cardiff, *A Social History of British Broadcasting. Vol. 1, 1922–1939, Serving the Nation* (Oxford: Blackwell, 1991), pp. 5–6.

17   Curran and Seaton, *Power Without Responsibility*, pp. 119, 120.

18   Ibid, p. 123.

19   Ward, *Mass Communications and the Modern World*; Curran and Seaton, *Power Without Responsibility*; Robert J. Brown, *Manipulating the Ether: The Power of Broadcast Radio in Thirties America* (Jefferson, NC: McFarland, 1998), p. 3.

20   Eric Hobsbawm, *Age of Extremes: The Short Twentieth Century 1914–1991* (London: Abacus, 1994), p. 197.

21   Alice Goldfarb Marquis, "Written on the Wind: The Impact of Radio During the 1930s," *Journal of Contemporary History*, 19 (1984), pp. 403–4; Lee De Forest, *Father of Radio: The Autobiography of Lee de Forest* (Chicago: Wilcox and Follett, 1950).

22   Stephen Barnard, *On the Radio: Music Radio in Britain* (Milton Keynes: Open University Press, 1989).

23   Brown, *Manipulating the Ether*, p. 225.

24   MacDonald, *Don't Touch That Dial!*, p. 10.

25   Michele Hilmes, *Radio Voices: American Broadcasting, 1922–1952* (Minneapolis: University of Minnesota Press, 1997), p. 68; Gwenyth L. Jackaway, *Media at War: Radio's Challenge to the Newspapers, 1924–1939* (Westport, CT: Praeger, 1995).

26   Hilmes, *Radio Voices*, p. xiv.

27   Douglas, *Listening In*, p. 9.

28   Brown, *Manipulating the Ether*, p. 1.

29   Douglas, *Listening In*, p. 5.

30   Ibid, p. 11.

31   Hilmes, *Radio Voices*, chs 5–6.
32   Douglas, *Listening In*, p. 9.

5 The Rise of Advertising

1   Quoted in Daniel Pope, *The Making of Modern Advertising* (New York: Basic Books, 1983), p. 17.
2   Quoted in Raymond Williams, "Advertising: The Magic System," in *Problems in Materialism and Culture: Selected Essays* (London: Verso, 1980), p. 172.
3   See Susan Strasser, *Satisfaction Guaranteed: The Making of the American Mass Market* (New York: Pantheon, 1989), pp. 206–11.
4   Pope, *Making of Modern Advertising*, pp. 18–61; Williams, "Advertising," pp. 177–8; Olivier Zunz, *Why the American Century?* (Chicago, IL: University of Chicago Press, 1998), pp. 80–5; Strasser, *Satisfaction Guaranteed*, p. 18.
5   Pope, *Making of Modern Advertising*, pp. 48–61; Williams, "Advertising," pp. 175–6; Strasser, *Satisfaction Guaranteed*, pp. 29–57; Michael Schudson, *Advertising, The Uneasy Persuasion: Its Dubious Impact on American Society* (London: Routledge, 1993), passim.
6   Pope, *Making of Modern Advertising*, pp. 112–83; Stephen Fox, *The Mirror Makers: A History of American Advertising and Its Creators* (New York: Vintage, 1985), pp. 19–77; Strasser, *Satisfaction Guaranteed*, pp. 93–5.
7   Pope, *Making of Modern Advertising*, p. 26.
8   See Steven J. Ross, *Working-Class Hollywood: Silent Film and the Shaping of Class in America* (Princeton, NJ: Princeton University Press, 1998), p. 178; William E. Leuchtenburg, *The Perils of Prosperity, 1914–32* (Chicago, IL: University of Chicago Press, 1958), p. 195.
9   Daniel Horowitz, *The Morality of Spending: Attitudes Toward the Consumer Society in America, 1875–1940* (Baltimore, MD: Johns Hopkins University Press, 1985); William Leach, *Land of Desire: Merchants, Power, and the Rise of a New American Culture* (New York: Pantheon, 1993).
10   Roland Marchand, *Advertising the American Dream: Making Way for Modernity, 1920–1940* (Berkeley: University of California Press, 1985), pp. 52–87; Jackson Lears, *Fables of Abundance: A Cultural History of Advertising in America* (New York: Basic Books, 1994), pp. 206–34; Zunz, *Why the American Century?*, pp. 57–62; Strasser, *Satisfaction Guaranteed*, pp. 155–9; Williams, "Advertising," pp. 179–80.
11   Marchand, *Advertising the American Dream*, passim, esp. pp. 9–24, 349–52; Lears, *Fables of Abundance*, pp. 162–95; Fox, *The Mirror Makers*, pp. 86–101; Williams, "Advertising," pp. 179–81, 184–5; Susan Smulyan, *Selling Radio: The Commercialization of American Broadcasting 1920–1934* (Washington, DC: Smithsonian Institution Press, 1994), pp. 88–91.

12 Marchand, *Advertising the American Dream*, pp. 88–94, 105–8; Smulyan, *Selling Radio*, pp. 68–71. The quotation is from ibid, p. 70.

13 Fox, *The Mirror Makers*, p. 154.

14 Ibid, pp. 150–62; Marchand, *Advertising the American Dream*, pp. 94–116; Smulyan, *Selling Radio*, passim; Susan Douglas, *Listening In: Radio and the American Imagination, From Amos 'n' Andy and Edward R. Murrow to Wolfman Jack and Howard Stern* (New York: Times Books, 1999), pp. 120–2.

15 Smulyan, *Selling Radio*, pp. 86–92; Marchand, *Advertising the American Dream*, pp. 66–9, 72; Charles McGovern, "Consumption and Citizenship in the United States, 1900–1940," in *Getting and Spending: European and American Consumer Societies in the Twentieth Century*, ed. Susan Strasser, Charles McGovern, and Matthias Judt (Cambridge: Cambridge University Press, 1998), pp. 45–6.

16 Ibid, p. 46; Marchand, *Advertising the American Dream*, pp. 167–79, 186–8; David E. Nye, *Image Worlds: Corporate Identities at General Electric, 1890–1930* (Cambridge, MA: MIT Press, 1985), p. 129; Schudson, *Advertising: The Uneasy Persuasion*, pp. 182–97; Richard Kluger, *Ashes to Ashes: America's Hundred-Year Cigarette War, the Public Health, and the Unabashed Triumph of Philip Morris* (New York: Alfred A. Knopf, 1996), pp. 64–6.

17 Quoted in Nye, *Image Worlds*, pp. 130–1. See also Marchand, *Advertising the American Dream*, pp. 167–79.

18 Marchand, *Advertising the American Dream*, pp. 167–79; Lears, *Fables of Abundance*, pp. 183–92.

19 On the comparison with Europe, see Victoria de Grazia, "Changing Consumption Regimes in Europe, 1930–1970: Comparative Perspectives on the Distribution Problem," in Strasser, McGovern, and Judt, *Getting and Spending*, pp. 67–9.

20 Marchand, *Advertising the American Dream*, p. 218.

21 Ibid, pp. 63–83, 194–201, 217–22, 291–3; McGovern, "Consumption and Citizenship," pp. 47–8; Zunz, *Why the American Century?*, pp. 60–1, 94.

22 See Williams, "Advertising," p. 187.

23 Kluger, *Ashes to Ashes*, pp. 112, 129–31, 152.

24 See Lears, *Fables of Abundance*, pp. 206–10, 223–33.

25 Marchand, *Advertising the American Dream*, pp. 18–21; Fox, *The Mirror Makers*, pp. 97–8.

26 David M. Potter, *People of Plenty: Economic Abundance and the American Character* (Chicago, IL: University of Chicago Press, 1954), pp. 166–88. The quotation is from p. 177. For critiques of the Potter thesis on advertising, see Jackson Lears, "Reconsidering Abundance: A Plea for Ambiguity," in Strasser, McGovern, and Judt, *Getting and Spending*, pp. 454–5; and Schudson, *Advertising: The Uneasy Persuasion*, pp. 246–50. Galbraith's criticisms of advertising are set out in *The New Industrial State* (Boston, MA: Houghton Mifflin, 1967), esp. pp. 203–10, 272–3.

27 Marcuse's argument on needs is developed in his *One Dimensional Man: Studies in the Ideology of Advanced Industrial Society* (London: Routledge and Kegan Paul, 1964).

28 For a clear statement of a Marxist interpretation of the history of advertising, see Stuart Ewen, *Captains of Consciousness: Advertising and the Social Roots of the Consumer Culture* (New York: McGraw-Hill, 1976).

29 Kluger, *Ashes to Ashes*, pp. 57–8, 60–2, 71–2, 76–9, 81–2, 85–8, 90–1.

30 Ibid, pp. 62–6; Schudson, *Advertising: The Uneasy Persuasion*, pp. 178–204. The quotations are from ibid, pp. 183, 197.

31 Marchand, *Advertising the American Dream*, pp. 63–6, 191–4; Zunz, *Why the American Century?*, pp. 59–62.

32 Nye, *Image Worlds*, p. 129.

33 See Patricia Springborg, *The Problem of Human Needs and the Critique of Civilisation* (London: George Allen and Unwin, 1981); and Schudson, *Advertising: The Uneasy Persuasion*, passim.

34 Schudson, *Advertising: The Uneasy Persuasion*, pp. 11, 240.

35 Ibid, p. 241.

6 Propaganda in Peace and War

1 Michael Balfour, *Propaganda in War 1939–1945: Organisations, Policies and Publics in Britain and Germany* (London: Routledge and Kegan Paul, 1979), pp. 421–2; David Welch (ed.), *Nazi Propaganda: The Power and the Limitations* (London: Croom Helm, 1983), p. 2.

2 Jacques Ellul, *Propaganda: The Formation of Men's Attitudes* (New York: Knopf, 1965); Garth S. Jowett and Victoria O'Donnell, *Propaganda and Persuasion*, 2nd edn. (Newbury Park, CA: Sage, 1992), p. 4.

3 Peter Kenez, *The Birth of the Propaganda State: Soviet Methods of Mass Mobilization 1917–1929* (Cambridge: Cambridge University Press, 1985), pp. 4, 8; Victoria E. Bonnell, *Iconography of Power: Soviet Political Posters under Lenin and Stalin* (Berkeley: University of California Press, 1997), pp. 1–3.

4 Jeffrey Brooks, *Thank You, Comrade Stalin! Soviet Public Culture from Revolution to Cold War* (Princeton, NJ: Princeton University Press, 2000), p. 5.

5 Ibid, p. 5.

6 Sheila Fitzpatrick, *Everyday Stalinism: Ordinary Life in Extraordinary Times; Soviet Russia in the 1930s* (New York: Oxford University Press, 1999), p. 21.

7 Richard Taylor, *Film Propaganda: Soviet Russia and Nazi Germany* (London: Croom Helm, 1979), p. 71.

8 Richard Taylor and Derek Spring (eds.), *Stalinism and Soviet Cinema* (London: Routledge, 1993), pp. 55, 63, 71; David King, *The Commissar Vanishes: The Falsification of Photographs and Art in Stalin's Russia* (New York: Metropolitan Books/Henry Holt, 1997).

9   Z. A. B. Zeman, *Nazi Propaganda*. 2nd edn. (Oxford: Oxford University Press, 1973).

10   Ibid, pp. 24, 30.

11   William Sheridan Allen, *The Nazi Seizure of Power: The Experience of a Single German Town 1922–1945*, revd. edn. (New York: Franklin Watts, 1984), esp. ch. 13.

12   Zeman, *Nazi Propaganda*, p. 38.

13   Richard Taylor, *Film Propaganda*, p. 157.

14   Richard Taylor, "Goebbels and the Function of Propaganda," in Welch, *Nazi Propaganda*, pp. 29–44; Ian Kershaw, "How Effective Was Nazi Propaganda?" in Welch, *Nazi Propaganda*, pp. 180–205.

15   Zeman, *Nazi Propaganda*, pp. 44–5.

16   Ibid, p. 49; Robert Jackall (ed.), *Propaganda* (New York: New York University Press, 1995), p. 188; Horst J. P. Bergmeier and Rainer E. Lotz, *Hitler's Airwaves: The Inside Story of Nazi Radio Broadcasting and Propaganda Swing* (New Haven, CT: Yale University Press, 1997), p. 136.

17   See David Welch, "Nazi Film Policy: Control, Ideology, and Propaganda," in *National Socialist Cultural Policy*, ed. Glenn R. Cuomo (New York: St. Martin's Press, 1995), pp. 100–7; David Welch, *Propaganda and the German Cinema 1933–1945* (Oxford: Oxford University Press, 1983).

18   Welch, "Nazi Film Policy," p. 107; Welch, *Propaganda and the German Cinema*, pp. 30–8; Klaus Kreimeier, *The Ufa Story: A History of Germany's Greatest Film Company 1918–1945*, trans. Robert and Rita Kimber (New York: Hill and Wang, 1996).

19   See, for example, Linda Deutschmann, *Triumph of the Will: The Image of the Third Reich* (Wakefield: Longwood Academic, 1991).

20   Welch, *Propaganda and the German Cinema*, p. 234.

21   David Welch, "Nazi Wartime Newsreel Propaganda," in *Film and Radio Propaganda in World War II*, ed. K. R. M. Short (Knoxville: University of Tennessee Press, 1983), pp. 201–19.

22   James von Geldern and Richard Stites (eds.), *Mass Culture in Soviet Russia: Tales, Poems, Songs, Movies, Plays and Folklore 1917–1953* (Bloomington: Indiana University Press, 1995), p. xxvii.

23   Fitzpatrick, *Everyday Stalinism*, p. 224.

24   Kershaw, "How Effective Was Nazi Propaganda?" p. 200.

25   Ibid, pp. 180–205.

26   Kenez, *The Birth of the Propaganda State*, p. 253.

27   See George H. Roeder, Jr., *The Censored War: American Visual Experience during World War Two* (New Haven, CT: Yale University Press, 1993), p. 2.

28   Richard Polenberg, *One Nation Divisible: Class, Race, and Ethnicity in the United States since 1938* (Harmondsworth: Penguin Books, 1980), p. 69.

29   Quoted in Clayton R. Koppes and Gregory D. Black, "Blacks, Loyalty, and Motion-Picture Propaganda in World War II," *Journal of American History*, 73, 2 (1986), p. 383.

30 Garth Jowett, *Film: The Democratic Art* (Boston, MA: Little, Brown, 1976), p. 310; Robert Sklar, *Movie-Made America: A Cultural History of American Movies* (New York: Vintage Books, 1994), p. 250.

31 On newsreels in the US during World War II, see Thomas Doherty, *Projections of War: Hollywood, American Culture, and World War II*, 2nd edn. (New York: Columbia University Press, 1999), pp. 227–50.

32 Quoted in William T. Murphy, "The United States Government and the Use of Motion Pictures during World War II," in *The Japan/America Film Wars: World War II Propaganda and Its Cultural Contexts*, ed. Abe Mark Nornes and Fukushima Yukio (Chur, Switzerland: Harwood, 1994), p. 61. See especially David Culbert, "'Why We Fight': Social Engineering for a Democratic Society at War," in Short, *Film and Radio Propaganda in World War II*, pp. 173–91.

33 See Thomas Cripps, *Making Movies Black: The Hollywood Message Movie from World War II to the Civil Rights Era* (New York: Oxford University Press, 1993), pp. 102–25.

34 Ibid, passim; Koppes and Black, "Blacks, Loyalty, and Motion-Picture Propaganda," pp. 383–406; Clayton R. Koppes and Gregory D. Black, *Hollywood Goes to War: How Politics, Profits, and Propaganda Shaped World War II Movies* (New York: Free Press, 1987), pp. 84–90, 178–84; Doherty, *Projections of War*, pp. 205–26.

35 Koppes and Black, *Hollywood Goes to War*, p. 179.

36 Thomas Cripps, "Racial Ambiguities in American Propaganda Movies," in Short, *Film and Radio Propaganda in World War II*, pp. 125–45.

37 Roeder, *The Censored War*, pp. 7–25.

38 Nicholas Pronay, "The News Media at War," in *Propaganda, Politics and Film, 1918–45*, ed. Nicholas Pronay and D. W. Spring (London: Macmillan, 1982), p. 183; Philip M. Taylor, *Munitions of the Mind: A History of Propaganda from the Ancient World to the Present Era* (Manchester: Manchester University Press, 1995), p. 212.

39 Quoted in Pronay, "The News Media at War," p. 182.

40 Ibid, pp. 186–96.

41 Ibid, p. 174.

42 Quoted in Balfour, *Propaganda in War 1939–1945*, p. 432.

43 Quoted in Paul Lashmar and James Oliver, *Britain's Secret Propaganda War* (Stroud: Sutton, 1998), p. 19.

44 See John Dower, *War Without Mercy: Race and Power in the Pacific War* (New York: Pantheon, 1986); and Michael Renov, "Warring Images: Stereotype and American Representations of the Japanese, 1941–1991," in Nornes and Yukio, *The Japan/America Film Wars*, pp. 104–8.

45 Lynette Finch, "Knowing the Enemy: Australian Psychological Warfare and the Business of Influencing Minds in the Second World War," *War and Society*, 16, 2 (1998), pp. 72, 83.

46 Quoted in Kay Saunders, "'An Instrument of Strategy': Propaganda, Public Policy and the Media in Australia during the Second World War," *War and Society*, 15, 2 (1997), pp. 85–6.

47 Ibid, pp. 86–7; Finch, "Knowing the Enemy," pp. 72, 83.

48 Koppes and Black, *Hollywood Goes to War*, pp. 100, 248–82; Doherty, *Projections of War*, pp. 122–48.

49 Dower, *War Without Mercy*.

7 Cold War and Communication

1 Quoted in Walter L. Hixson, *Parting the Curtain: Propaganda, Culture, and the Cold War, 1945–1961* (New York: St. Martin's Press, 1997), p. 14.

2 Quoted in Frances Stonor Saunders, *Who Paid the Piper?: The CIA and the Cultural Cold War* (London: Granta, 1999), p. 148.

3 On ideology and US Cold War foreign policy, see Michael H. Hunt, *Ideology and U.S. Foreign Policy* (New Haven, CT: Yale University Press, 1987), esp. pp. 125–98; W. Scott Lucas, "Beyond Diplomacy: Propaganda and the History of the Cold War," in *Cold-War Propaganda in the 1950s*, ed. Gary D. Rawnsley (New York: St. Martin's Press, 1999), pp. 11–30; and Scott Lucas, "Campaigns of Truth: The Psychological Strategy Board and American Ideology, 1951–1953," *International History Review*, 18 (1996), pp. 279–302.

4 Quoted in Hixson, *Parting the Curtain*, p. 24.

5 Quoted in Robert J. McMahon, *Colonialism and Cold War: The United States and the Struggle for Indonesian Independence, 1945–49* (Ithaca, NY: Cornell University Press, 1981), p. 43.

6 Richard Stites, "Heaven and Hell: Soviet Propaganda Constructs the World," in Rawnsley, *Cold-War Propaganda in the 1950s*, pp. 85–103; Martin Ebon, *The Soviet Propaganda Machine* (New York: McGraw-Hill, 1987), pp. 3–16.

7 Ellen Mickiewicz, "Images of America," in *Beyond the Cold War: Soviet and American Media Images*, ed. Everette E. Dennis, George Gerbner, and Yassen N. Zassoursky (Newbury Park, CA: Sage, 1991), p. 28.

8 Stites, "Heaven and Hell," pp. 91–8.

9 Susan L. Carruthers, "'Not Just Washed but Dry-Cleaned': Korea and the 'Brainwashing' Scare of the 1950s," in Rawnsley, *Cold-War Propaganda in the 1950s*, pp. 47–66; Abbott Gleason, *Totalitarianism: The Inner History of the Cold War* (New York: Oxford University Press, 1995), pp. 89–107.

10 See Mark W. Hopkins, *Mass Media in the Soviet Union* (New York: Pegasus, 1970), p. 339; and Reinhold Wagnleitner, *Coca-Colonization and the Cold War: The Cultural Mission of the United States in Austria after the Second World War* (Chapel Hill: University of North Carolina Press, 1994), pp. 60–1.

11 Michael Nelson, *War of the Black Heavens: The Battles of Western Broadcasting in the Cold War* (London: Brassey's, 1997); Hixson, *Parting the Curtain*, pp. 32–7,

46–52; Ellen Propper Mickiewicz, *Media and the Russian Public* (New York: Praeger, 1981), pp. 137–42.

12 Hopkins, *Mass Media in the Soviet Union*, pp. 336–7.

13 Stites, "Heaven and Hell," p. 101.

14 Larissa Fedotova, "The Image of the United States in the Soviet Mass Media: The Results of Sociological Surveys," in Dennis, Gerbner, and Zassoursky, *Beyond the Cold War*, p. 61.

15 US Department of State, *Foreign Relations of the United States, 1950*, Vol. 1 (Washington, DC: US Government Printing Office, 1977), pp. 238–9.

16 See, for example, Stephen J. Whitfield, *The Culture of the Cold War* (Baltimore, MD: Johns Hopkins University Press, 1991), pp. 154–63; Mark H. Van Pelt, "The Cold War on the Air," *Journal of Popular Culture*, 18 (1984), pp. 97–110; J. Fred MacDonald, *Television and the Red Menace: The Video Road to Vietnam* (New York: Praeger, 1985), pp. 58–100; and Nancy E. Bernhard, *U.S. Television News and Cold War Propaganda, 1947–1960* (Cambridge: Cambridge University Press, 1999).

17 See Walter LaFeber, "American Policy-Makers, Public Opinion, and the Outbreak of the Cold War, 1945–50," in *The Origins of the Cold War in Asia*, ed. Yonosuke Nagai and Akira Iriye (New York: Columbia University Press, 1977), pp. 55–6.

18 The point is well made in the context of the 1980s by Daniel C. Hallin, "Images of Self and Others in American Television Coverage of the Reagan–Gorbachev Summits," in Dennis, Gerbner, and Zassoursky, *Beyond the Cold War*, p. 58; and Daniel C. Hallin, *We Keep America on Top of the World: Television Journalism and the Public Sphere* (London: Routledge, 1994), pp. 105–8.

19 See Thomas Powers, "The Plot Thickens," *New York Review of Books* (May 11, 2000), pp. 53–60.

20 Whitfield, *Culture of the Cold War*, pp. 163–4; Ken Ward, *Mass Communications and the Modern World* (Basingstoke: Macmillan, 1989), pp. 158–9; James L. Baughman, *The Republic of Mass Culture: Journalism, Filmmaking, and Broadcasting in America since 1941* (Baltimore, MD: Johns Hopkins University Press, 1992), pp. 64–5; David Halberstam, *The Fifties* (New York: Ballantine Books, 1994), p. 55; Bernhard, *U.S. Television News*, pp. 156–77.

21 Quoted in Erik Barnouw, *A History of Broadcasting in the United States*, 3 vols. (New York: Oxford University Press, 1966–70), Vol. 2: *The Golden Web, 1933–1953*, p. 251; and Lary May, *The Big Tomorrow: Hollywood and the Politics of the American Way* (Chicago, IL: University of Chicago Press, 2000), p. 197.

22 Barnouw, *A History of Broadcasting*, Vol. 2, pp. 253–73. The quotation is from p. 265.

23 See Thom Andersen, "Red Hollywood," in *Literature and the Visual Arts in Contemporary Society*, ed. Suzanne Ferguson and Barbara Groseclose (Columbus: Ohio State University Press, 1985), pp. 156–7.

24 Quoted in May, *The Big Tomorrow*, p. 177.

25 Whitfield, *Culture of the Cold War*, pp. 132–3; Bernard F. Dick, *Radical Innocence: A Critical Study of the Hollywood Ten* (Lexington: University Press of Kentucky, 1989), pp. 5–7; Ian Hamilton, *Writers in Hollywood 1915–1951* (New York: Harper and Row, 1990), pp. 284, 290.

26 Whitfield, *Culture of the Cold War*, pp. 146–9.

27 May, *The Big Tomorrow*, pp. 175–80, 202–4; Saunders, *Who Paid the Piper?*, pp. 284–95. Valuable studies of the Cold War's impact on Hollywood film content include May, *The Big Tomorrow*; Whitfield, *Culture of the Cold War*; Andersen, "Red Hollywood"; Les K. Adler, "The Politics of Culture: Hollywood and the Cold War," in *The Specter: Original Essays in the Cold War and the Origins of McCarthyism*, ed. Robert Griffith and Athan Theoharis (New York: New Viewpoints, 1974), pp. 242–60; and Daniel J. Leab, "Hollywood and the Cold War, 1945–1961," in *Hollywood as Mirror: Changing Views of 'Outsiders' and 'Enemies' in American Movies*, ed. Robert Brent Toplin (Westport, CT: Greenwood Press, 1993), pp. 117–37.

28 See MacDonald, *Television and the Red Menace*, pp. 101–45.

29 Ibid, p. 145; and Whitfield, *Culture of the Cold War*, pp. 162–3.

30 Brett Silverstein, quoted in George Gerbner, "The Image of Russians in American Media and The 'New Epoch'," in Dennis, Gerbner, and Zassoursky, *Beyond the Cold War*, p. 31.

31 Ibid, pp. 31–2.

32 On the concept of psychological warfare, see Christopher Simpson, *Science of Coercion: Communication Research and Psychological Warfare 1945–1960* (New York: Oxford University Press, 1994), esp. pp. 3–14, 31–51, 87–93; and Hixson, *Parting the Curtain*, pp. 2–4.

33 Hixson, *Parting the Curtain*, p. 10.

34 Quoted in ibid, pp. 13–14.

35 Ibid, p. 21.

36 Paul Lashmar and James Oliver, *Britain's Secret Propaganda War* (Stroud: Sutton, 1998).

37 Gary D. Rawnsley, *Radio Diplomacy and Propaganda: The BBC and VOA in International Politics, 1956–64* (New York: St. Martin's Press, 1996), p. 14.

38 Hixson, *Parting the Curtain*, pp. 37–46. The quotations are from p. 38.

39 Quoted in Nelson, *War of the Black Heavens*, p. 60.

40 Ibid, p. 37.

41 Rawnsley, *Radio Diplomacy and Propaganda*; Lashmar and Oliver, *Britain's Secret Propaganda War*, pp. 57–65.

42 For discussion of this question, see Hixson, *Parting the Curtain*, pp. 32–7, 46–52; Rawnsley, *Radio Diplomacy and Propaganda*, pp. 67–108, 166–82; Nelson, *War of the Black Heavens*, pp. 62–6; and Mickiewicz, *Media and the Russian Public*, pp. 137–42.

43 On the role of Western radio in the Hungarian uprising, see Rawnsley, *Radio Diplomacy and Propaganda*, pp. 67–108; Gary D. Rawnsley, "The BBC External

Services and the Hungarian Uprising, 1956," in Rawnsley, *Cold-War Propaganda in the 1950s*, pp. 165–81; George R. Urban, *Radio Free Europe and the Pursuit of Democracy: My War Within the Cold War* (New Haven, CT: Yale University Press, 1997), pp. 211–44, 281–91; Hixson, *Parting the Curtain*, pp. 79–86; and Nelson, *War of the Black Heavens*, pp. 69–84.

44 Rawnsley, *Radio Diplomacy and Propaganda*, pp. 109–43.
45 On the fundamental shift in US propaganda approaches from the mid-1950s, see Hixson, *Parting the Curtain*.
46 Major studies of US cultural diplomacy during the Cold War include Hixson, *Parting the Curtain*; Wagnleitner, *Coca-Colonization and the Cold War*; Richard Pells, *Not Like Us: How Europeans Have Loved, Hated, and Transformed American Culture since World War II* (New York: Basic Books, 1997); and Robert H. Haddow, *Pavilions of Plenty: Exhibiting American Culture Abroad in the 1950s* (Washington, DC: Smithsonian Institution Press, 1997).
47 Saunders, *Who Paid the Piper?*
48 Lashmar and Oliver, *Britain's Secret Propaganda War*.
49 Quoted in Saunders, *Who Paid the Piper?*, p. 408.
50 Quoted in ibid, p. 409. On responses to the exposure of CCF links with the CIA, and on the ethical issues involved, see ibid, pp. 4–5, 367–416.
51 Simpson, *Science of Coercion*.
52 Hixson, *Parting the Curtain*, p. 223. See also Nelson, *War of the Black Heavens*.

8 Television and Consumer Societies

1 Quoted in James Curran and Jean Seaton, *Power Without Responsibility: The Press and Broadcasting in Britain*, 5th edn (London: Routledge, 1997), p. 175.
2 Raymond Williams, *Television: Technology and Cultural Form* (New York: Schocken Books, 1975), pp. 14–15.
3 Susan Briggs, "Television in the Home and Family," in *Television: An International History*, ed. Anthony Smith with Richard Paterson, 2nd edn (Oxford: Oxford University Press, 1998), p. 110.
4 See Williams, *Television*, passim.
5 Nancy E. Bernhard, *U.S. Television News and Cold War Propaganda, 1947–1960* (Cambridge: Cambridge University Press, 1999), pp. 5, 47.
6 Les Brown, "The American Networks," in Smith with Paterson, *Television: An International History*, p. 147; James L. Baughman, *The Republic of Mass Culture: Journalism, Filmmaking, and Broadcasting in America Since 1941* (Baltimore, MD: Johns Hopkins University Press, 1992), pp. 44, 92.
7 Ibid, p. 46.
8 Stephen Fox, *The Mirror Makers: A History of American Advertising and Its Creators* (New York: Vintage, 1985), pp. 210–11; William Leiss, Stephen Kline, and

Sut Jhally, *Social Communication in Advertising: Persons, Products, and Images of Well-Being* (Toronto: Methuen, 1986), pp. 80, 86, 115.

9   Quoted in Erik Barnouw, *A History of Broadcasting in the United States*, 3 vols. (New York: Oxford University Press, 1966–70), Vol. 3: *The Image Empire*, p. 23.

10 Fox, *The Mirror Makers*, p. 213; Baughman, *Republic of Mass Culture*, p. 45.

11 Williams, *Television*, pp. 57–8.

12 Leiss, Kline, and Jhally, *Social Communication in Advertising*, pp. 88–9; Matthew P. McAllister, *The Commercialization of American Culture: New Advertising, Control and Democracy* (Thousand Oaks, CA: Sage, 1996), pp. 47–50; George Lipsitz, "Consumer Spending as State Project: Yesterday's Solutions and Today's Problems," in *Getting and Spending: European and American Consumer Societies in the Twentieth Century*, ed. Susan Strasser, Charles McGovern, and Matthias Judt (Cambridge: Cambridge University Press, 1998), pp. 144–5.

13 Quoted in Barnouw, *The Image Empire*, pp. 197–8.

14 See Baughman, *Republic of Mass Culture*, p. 93.

15 Quoted in Stephen J. Whitfield, *The Culture of the Cold War* (Baltimore, MD: Johns Hopkins University Press, 1991), p. 166.

16 Baughman, *Republic of Mass Culture*, pp. 98–107; Brown, "The American Networks," pp. 153–5; Mary Ann Watson, *The Expanding Vista: American Television in the Kennedy Years* (Durham, NC: Duke University Press, 1994), pp. 36–54.

17 Kevin Williams, *Get Me a Murder a Day! A History of Mass Communication in Britain* (London: Arnold, 1998), p. 156.

18 See Williams, *Television*, pp. 33–4, 38–9.

19 Curran and Seaton, *Power Without Responsibility*, pp. 163–5; Williams, *Get Me a Murder a Day!*, pp. 151–4.

20 Quoted in ibid, p. 162.

21 Curran and Seaton, *Power Without Responsibility*, pp. 167–8, 171–2, 182.

22 See ibid, pp. 166–7.

23 Quoted in Williams, *Get Me a Murder a Day!*, p. 166.

24 See Anthony Smith, "Television as a Public Service Medium," in Smith with Paterson, *Television: An International History*, p. 44.

25 Baughman, *Republic of Mass Culture*, pp. 143–4; Brown, "The American Networks," pp. 157–8.

26 Leiss, Kline, and Jhally, *Social Communication in Advertising*, p. 88; McAllister, *Commercialization of American Culture*, pp. 45–7; Baughman, *Republic of Mass Culture*, p. 145.

27 Fath David Ruffins, "Reflecting on Ethnic Imagery in the Landscape of Commerce, 1945–1975," in Strasser, McGovern, and Judt, *Getting and Spending*, pp. 401–5.

28 Baughman, *Republic of Mass Culture*, p. 155.

29 James Ledbetter, *Made Possible By . . . : The Death of Public Broadcasting in the United States* (London: Verso, 1997), pp. 3–4.

30 Ibid, p. 4.

31 Ibid, passim.

32 McAllister, *Commercialization of American Culture*, pp. 18–36.

33 Quoted in Daniel C. Hallin, "Commercialism and Professionalism in the American News Media," in *Mass Media and Society*, 3rd edn., ed. James Curran and Michael Gurevitch (London: Arnold, 2000), p. 234.

34 McAllister, *Commercialization of American Culture*, pp. 24–5.

35 Lipsitz, "Consumer Spending as State Project," p. 139. See also Leiss, Kline, and Jhally, *Social Communication in Advertising*, p. 89; and Williams, *Television*, pp. 70–1.

36 McAllister, *Commercialization of American Culture*, p. 110.

37 Michael Tracey, "Non-Fiction Television," in Smith with Paterson, *Television: An International History*, pp. 82–4; Daniel C. Hallin, *We Keep America on Top of the World: Television Journalism and the Public Sphere* (London: Routledge, 1994), pp. 178–9.

38 See, for example, Robert Hughes, "Why Watch It, Anyway?," *New York Review of Books* (February 16, 1995), pp. 37–42; Godfrey Hodgson, "The End of the Grand Narrative and the Death of News," *Historical Journal of Film, Radio, and Television*, 20, 1 (2000), pp. 23–31; Jürgen Kronig, "Elite versus Mass: The Impact of Television in an Age of Globalization," ibid, pp. 43–9.

39 Curran and Seaton, *Power Without Responsibility*, pp. 187–205, 303–4; Williams, *Get Me a Murder a Day!*, pp. 171–5.

40 Curran and Seaton, *Power Without Responsibility*, pp. 203–36; Williams, *Get Me a Murder a Day!*, pp. 185–90; David Welch, "News into the Next Century: Introduction," *Historical Journal of Film, Radio, and Television*, 20, 1 (2000), pp. 5–13; Hodgson, "End of the Grand Narrative;" Kronig, "Elite versus Mass." The quotation is from Tony Judt, "'Twas a Famous Victory," *New York Review of Books* (July 19, 2001), p. 27. On prospects for the BBC, see Jeremy Tunstall and David Machin, *The Anglo-American Connection* (Oxford: Oxford University Press, 1999), pp. 174–85.

41 Curran and Seaton, *Power Without Responsibility*, p. 204. On the problem of "dumbing down" on UK television, see Welch, "News into the Next Century;" Hodgson, "End of the Grand Narrative;" and Kronig, "Elite versus Mass."

42 Dietrich Berwanger, "The Third World," in Smith with Paterson, *Television: An International History*, p. 188; Junhao Hong, *The Internationalization of Television in China: The Evolution of Ideology, Society, and Media since the Reform* (Westport, CT: Praeger, 1998), p. 87.

43 Ibid, pp. 14–15, 82–6, 96–8, 120.

44 See Curran and Seaton, *Power Without Responsibility*, pp. 312–14.

45 Chris Barker, *Global Television: An Introduction* (Oxford: Blackwell, 1997), p. 49; Hong, *Internationalization of Television in China*, p. 18.

46 Anthony Smith, "Introduction," in Smith with Paterson, *Television: An International History*, p. 4.

47 Richard Pells, *Not Like Us: How Europeans Have Loved, Hated, and Transformed American Culture Since World War II* (New York: Basic Books, 1997), pp. 207–9, 230–2, 259–62; Hong, *Internationalization of Television in China*, pp. 12–19, 89, 119.

48 Barker, *Global Television*, pp. 28, 119; Pells, *Not Like Us*, pp. 259, 273–4.

49 For a skeptical view of such claims, see Baughman, *Republic of Mass Culture*, pp. 160–2; and Hallin, *We Keep America on Top of the World*, p. 100.

50 Ibid, pp. 97–8; Baughman, *Republic of Mass Culture*, pp. 93–8.

51 Williams, *Television*, p. 46.

52 Ibid, p. 49.

53 See Hallin, *We Keep America on Top of the World*, pp. 91, 98, 100–1, 105, 136; Baughman, *Republic of Mass Culture*, pp. 98, 162; Williams, *Television*, pp. 46–8.

54 Daniel J. Leab, *"See It Now*: A Legend Reassessed," in *American History/American Television: Interpreting the Video Past*, ed. John E. O'Connor (New York: Frederick Ungar, 1983), pp. 1–32; Thomas Rosteck, See It Now *Confronts McCarthyism: Television Documentary and the Politics of Representation* (Tuscaloosa: University of Alabama Press, 1994); J. Fred MacDonald, *Television and the Red Menace: The Video Road to Vietnam* (New York: Praeger, 1985), pp. 54–7; Whitfield, *Culture of the Cold War*, pp. 164–6; Barnouw, *The Image Empire*, pp. 46–56; Robert J. Donovan and Ray Scherer, *Unsilent Revolution: Television News and American Public Life* (Cambridge: Cambridge University Press, 1992), pp. 23–34.

55 Baughman, *Republic of Mass Culture*, pp. 95–6.

56 Hallin, *We Keep America on Top of the World*, pp. 87–92, 102–10.

57 Don Hewitt, quoted in Baughman, *Republic of Mass Culture*, p. 165.

58 Baughman, *Republic of Mass Culture*, pp. 216–18, 220; Hallin, *We Keep America on Top of the World*, pp. 176–80; Hallin, "Commercialism and Professionalism in the American News Media," pp. 218–37; S. Elizabeth Bird, "Audience Demands in a Murderous Market: Tabloidization in U.S. Television News," in *Tabloid Tales: Global Debates over Media Standards*, ed. Colin Sparks and John Tulloch (Lanham, MD: Rowman and Littlefield, 2000), pp. 213–28; Curran and Seaton, *Power Without Responsibility*, p. 206; Williams, *Get Me a Murder a Day!*, pp. 249–50; Welch, "News into the Next Century;" Hodgson, "End of the Grand Narrative;" and Kronig, "Elite versus Mass."

59 Williams, *Television*, p. 125.

60 See Elliot King and Michael Schudson, "The Myth of the Great Communicator," *Columbia Journalism Review*, 26 (1987), pp. 37–9; Baughman, *Republic of Mass Culture*, pp. 211–12; and Hallin, *We Keep America on Top of the World*, p. 105.

61 Williams, *Get Me a Murder a Day!*, pp. 251–4.

62 Tracey, "Non-Fiction Television," p. 81.

63   Mark Danner, "The Shame of Political TV," *New York Review of Books* (September 21, 2000), pp. 101–2; James Fallows, "Internet Illusions," *New York Review of Books* (November 16, 2000), pp. 29–30.

64   Danner, "The Shame of Political TV;" Lars-Erik Nelson, "Democracy for Sale," *New York Review of Books* (December 3, 1998), pp. 8–10.

65   See, for example, Steven Barnett, *Games and Sets: The Changing Face of Sport on Television* (London: British Film Institute, 1990); Garry Whannel, *Fields in Vision: Television Sport and Cultural Transformation* (London: Routledge, 1992).

66   Michael Schudson, *Advertising, The Uneasy Persuasion: Its Dubious Impact on American Society* (London: Routledge, 1993), p. 107; McAllister, *Commercialization of American Culture*, pp. 24–7.

67   See, for example, Briggs, "Television in the Home and Family," pp. 116, 118; Baughman, *Republic of Mass Culture*, pp. xv, 158.

68   Quoted in Ian Buruma, "From Hirohito to Heimat," *New York Review of Books* (October 26, 1989), p. 40.

69   Roland Marchand, "Visions of Classlessness, Quests for Dominion: American Popular Culture, 1945–1960," in *Reshaping America: Society and Institutions 1945–1960*, ed. Robert H. Bremner and Gary W. Reichard (Columbus: Ohio State University Press, 1982), pp. 168–70; Lipsitz, "Consumer Spending as State Project," pp. 142–3; Barker, *Global Television*, pp. 153–81.

70   See Benjamin M. Friedman, "The Power of the Electronic Herd," *New York Review of Books* (July 15, 1999), p. 40.

71   See Joseph Turow, *Breaking Up America: Advertisers and the New Media World* (Chicago, IL: University of Chicago Press, 1997).

72   See Williams, *Television*, pp. 126–8.

9 Media, Information, and Entertainment

1   Quoted in Garth Jowett, *Film: The Democratic Art* (Boston, MA: Little, Brown, 1976), p. 349.

2   James L. Baughman, *The Republic of Mass Culture: Journalism, Filmmaking, and Broadcasting in America Since 1941* (Baltimore, MD: Johns Hopkins University Press, 1992), p. 9.

3   Jowett, *Film: The Democratic Art*, pp. 473, 475.

4   Ibid, p. 482.

5   US Bureau of the Census, *The Statistical History of the United States: From Colonial Times to the Present* (New York: Basic Books, 1976), p. 400.

6   Baughman, *Republic of Mass Culture*, pp. 141–2.

7   See Gregory D. Black, *The Catholic Crusade against the Movies, 1940–1975* (Cambridge: Cambridge University Press, 1998); Frank Walsh, *Sin and Censorship: The Catholic Church and the Motion Picture Industry* (New Haven, CT: Yale

University Press, 1996); and Leonard J. Leff and Jerold L. Simmons, *The Dame in the Kimono: Hollywood, Censorship, and the Production Code from the 1920s to the 1960s* (New York: Grove Weidendeld, 1990).

8 Thomas H. Guback, "Hollywood's International Market," in *The American Film Industry*, ed. Tino Balio (Madison: University of Wisconsin Press, 1985), p. 481.

9 See Richard Pells, *Not Like Us: How Europeans Have Loved, Hated, and Transformed American Culture Since World War II* (New York: Basic Books, 1997), pp. 219, 229.

10 Jowett, *Film: The Democratic Art*, p. 430.

11 Guback, "Hollywood's International Market," p. 479.

12 See ibid; Peter Lev, *The Euro-American Cinema* (Austin: University of Texas Press, 1993), pp. 24–5; and William H. Read, *America's Mass Media Merchants* (Baltimore, MD: Johns Hopkins University Press, 1976), pp. 56–7.

13 Quoted in the *Sydney Morning Herald*, May 12, 2001.

14 David Parkinson, *History of Film* (London: Thames and Hudson, 1995), p. 245.

15 Matthew P. McAllister, *The Commercialization of American Culture: New Advertising, Control and Democracy* (Thousand Oaks, CA: Sage, 1996), pp. 67–9, 81, 138–44, 161–8, 171–5.

16 Leo Bogart, *Press and Public: Who Reads What, When, Where, and Why in American Newspapers*, 2nd edn (Hillsdale, NJ: Lawrence Erlbaum Associates, 1989), pp. 15–24; McAllister, *Commercialization of American Culture*, p. 30; Baughman, *Republic of Mass Culture*, p. 189; Daniel C. Hallin, "Commercialism and Professionalism in the American News Media," in *Mass Media and Society*, 3rd edn., ed. James Curran and Michael Gurevitch (London: Arnold, 2000), p. 222.

17 Ibid, pp. 219–21; Daniel C. Hallin, *We Keep America on Top of the World: Television Journalism and the Public Sphere* (London: Routledge, 1994), pp. 24–6, 170–2; Baughman, *Republic of Mass Culture*, pp. 13–14, 32–3, 118–20.

18 Ibid, pp. 175–83; Robert J. Donovan and Ray Scherer, *Unsilent Revolution: Television News and American Public Life, 1948–1991* (Cambridge: Cambridge University Press, 1992), pp. 257–82; Hallin, *We Keep America on Top of the World*, pp. 25, 47–55, 170–6. The quotation is from ibid, p. 25.

19 Hallin, "Commercialism and Professionalism," pp. 221–3.

20 Quoted in Donovan and Scherer, *Unsilent Revolution*, p. 267. See also Ian Hargreaves, "Is There a Future for Foreign News?," *Historical Journal of Film, Radio, and Television*, 20, 1 (2000), pp. 55–61; and Godfrey Hodgson, "The End of the Grand Narrative and the Death of News," *Historical Journal of Film, Radio, and Television*, 20, 1 (2000), pp. 23–31.

21 McAllister, *Commercialization of American Culture*, pp. 21–2; Baughman, *Republic of Mass Culture*, pp. 192–3.

22 Kevin Williams, *Get Me a Murder a Day! A History of Mass Communication in Britain* (London: Arnold, 1998), pp. 217–19.

23 Ibid, pp. 226–7; James Curran and Jean Seaton, *Power Without Responsibility: The Press and Broadcasting in Britain*, 5th edn. (London: Routledge, 1997), pp. 77–81.

24 Curran and Seaton, *Power Without Responsibility*, pp. 72–7. The quotation is from p. 74.

25 Williams, *Get Me a Murder a Day!*, p. 224. See also Curran and Seaton, *Power Without Responsibility*, pp. 93–100, 106–7; Hargreaves, "Is There a Future for Foreign News?;" Hodgson, "End of the Grand Narrative;" Shelley McLachlan and Peter Golding, "Tabloidization in the British Press: A Quantitative Investigation into Changes in British Newspapers, 1952–1997," in *Tabloid Tales: Global Debates over Media Standards*, ed. Colin Sparks and John Tulloch (Lanham, MD: Rowman and Littlefield, 2000), pp. 75–90; and Dick Rooney, "Thirty Years of Competition in the British Tabloid Press: The *Mirror* and the *Sun* 1968–1998," in Sparks and Tulloch, *Tabloid Tales*, pp. 91–110.

26 Baughman, *Republic of Mass Culture*, p. 66.

27 Michael Emery, Edwin Emery, and Nancy L. Roberts, *The Press and America: An Interpretive History of the Mass Media*, 9th edn (Boston, MA: Allyn and Bacon, 2000), p. 372.

28 Susan J. Douglas, *Listening In: Radio and the American Imagination* (New York: Random House, 1999), p. 285.

29 Ibid, pp. 294–8, 347–54.

30 Ibid, pp. 284 327. The quotation is from p. 285.

31 Williams, *Get Me a Murder a Day!*, pp. 246–7.

10 Media, War, and International Relations

1 Phillip Knightley, *The First Casualty: The War Correspondent as Hero and Myth Maker from the Crimea to Kosovo* (London: Prion, 2000), p. 452.

2 Stephen Badsey, "The Boer War as a Media War," in *The Boer War: Army, Nation and Empire*, ed. Peter Dennis and Jeffrey Grey (Canberra: Army History Unit, Department of Defence, 2000), p. 70.

3 Knightley, *The First Casualty*.

4 Peter Young and Peter Jesser, *The Media and the Military: From the Crimea to Desert Strike* (South Melbourne: Macmillan Education, 1997), pp. 40–1; J. Fred MacDonald, *Television and the Red Menace: The Video Road to Vietnam* (New York: Praeger, 1985), pp. 31–7; see also John E. Mueller, *War, Presidents and Public Opinion* (New York: John Wiley and Sons, 1973); Knightley, *The First Casualty*.

5 Robert Elegant, "How to Lose a War," in *Major Problems in the History of the Vietnam War*, ed. Robert J. McMahon (Lexington: D. C. Heath, MA, 1990), pp. 528–36.

6   Daniel C. Hallin, *The "Uncensored War": The Media and Vietnam* (New York: Oxford University Press, 1986), p. 213. Other critics included Phillip Knightley, *The First Casualty*; Michael Mandelbaum, "Vietnam: The Television War," *Daedalus* 3 (Fall 1982), pp. 157–69; William M. Hammond, "The Press in Vietnam as Agent of Defeat: A Critical Examination," *Reviews in American History*, 17, 1 (1989), p. 318; William M. Hammond, *Public Affairs: The Military and the Media, 1962–1968, United States Army in Vietnam* (Washington, DC: Center of Military History, United States Army, 1988); William M. Hammond, *Public Affairs: The Military and the Media, 1968–1973, United States Army in Vietnam* (Washington, DC: Center of Military History, United States Army, 1996); William M. Hammond, *Reporting Vietnam: Media and Military at War*. Modern World Studies. (Lawrence: University Press of Kansas, 1998); Carlyle A. Thayer, "Vietnam: A Critical Analysis," in *Defence and the Media in Time of Limited War*, ed. Peter Young (London: Frank Cass, 1992), pp. 89–115.

7   Based on Mueller, *War, Presidents and Public Opinion*; see also Hammond, "The Press in Vietnam," p. 318; Thayer, "Vietnam," p. 107.

8   Hallin, *The "Uncensored War,"* p. 168.

9   Knightley, *The First Casualty*, p. 437; Hallin, *The "Uncensored War,"* pp. 175, 190, 214.

10   Valeria Adams, *The Media and the Falklands Campaign* (Basingstoke: Macmillan, 1986).

11   Young and Jesser, *The Media and the Military*, p. 98.

12   Robert E. Denton, Jr., *The Media and the Persian Gulf War* (Westport, CT: Praeger, 1993), pp. 8–10.

13   Warren P. Strobel, *Late-Breaking Foreign Policy: The News Media's Influence on Peace Operations* (Washington, DC: United States Institute of Peace Press, 1997), p. 41. See also Young and Jesser, *The Media and the Military*; Philip M. Taylor, *War and the Media: Propaganda and Persuasion in the Gulf War* (Manchester: Manchester University Press, 1992).

14   Ibid; Hedrick Smith (ed.), *The Media and the Gulf War* (Washington, DC: Seven Locks Press, 1992); W. Lance Bennett and David L. Paletz (eds.), *Taken by Storm: The Media, Public Opinion, and US Foreign Policy in the Gulf War* (Chicago, IL: University of Chicago Press, 1994).

15   John J. Fialka, *Hotel Warriors: Covering the Gulf War* (Washington, DC: Woodrow Wilson Center Press, 1991); see also Denton, *The Media and the Persian Gulf War*.

16   For example, Taylor, *War and the Media*.

17   Jonathan Mermin, *Debating War and Peace: Media Coverage of US Intervention in the Post-Vietnam Era* (Princeton, NJ: Princeton University Press, 1999); William V. Kennedy, *The Military and the Media: Why the Press Cannot Be Trusted to Cover a War* (Westport, CT: Praeger, 1993); Young and Jesser, *The Media and the Military*.

18   Martin Shaw, "Global Voices: Civil Society and the Media in Global Crises,"

in *Human Rights in Global Politics*, ed. Tim Dunne and Nicholas J. Wheeler (Cambridge: Cambridge University Press, 1999), ch. 8, pp. 214–32; Strobel, *Late-Breaking Foreign Policy*.

19   Philip M. Taylor, *Global Communications, International Affairs and the Media since 1945* (London: Routledge, 1997), pp. 145–92.

20   Phillip McCarthy, "US Networks Turn into Censors," *The Age* (October 31, 2001); David Shaw, "A Patriotic America Turns on Its News Media," *The Age* (November 11, 2001).

21   Duncan Campbell, "Foiling the Terrorist Net Work," *Sydney Morning Herald* (November 17–18, 2001); Bobbie Johnson, "The Net Tightens," *Sydney Morning Herald* (October 27–8, 2001); Tony Judt, "America and the War," *New York Review* (November 15, 2001); Hussein Ibish and Ali Anunimah [column], *The Age* (October 27, 2001).

22   Jacinta Thomler and Daniel Fallon, "Ripple Effect," *Sydney Morning Herald* (September 22–3, 2001).

23   Ibid, pp. 6, 8.

11 New Media

1   Peter Forman and Robert W. Saint John, "Creating Convergence," *Scientific American* (November 2000), pp. 34–5.

2   Gillian Appleton, "Converging and Emerging Industries: Video, Pay TV and Multimedia," in *The Media in Australia*, 2nd edn., ed. Stuart Cunningham and Graeme Turner (St. Leonards: Allen and Unwin, 1997), p. 180; Trevor Barr, *newmedia.com.au: The Changing Face of Australia's Media and Communications* (St. Leonards: Allen and Unwin, 2000), pp. 23–4.

3   Wilson Dizard, Jr., *Old Media/New Media: Mass Communications in the Information Age* (London: Longman, 1994), pp. xv, 2; Ray Eldon Hiebert and Sheila Jean Gibbons, *Exploring Mass Media for a Changing World* (London: Lawrence Erlbaum, 2000), p. 304.

4   Appleton, "Converging and Emerging Industries," p. 170.

5   Dizard, *Old Media/New Media*, p. 129; Appleton, "Converging and Emerging Industries," pp. 164–5.

6   Ibid, p. 168.

7   http://web.ukonline.co.uk/jeremy.thompson/rediffusion.htm; Dizard, *Old Media/New Media*, p. 107.

8   Chris Barker, *Global Television: An Introduction* (Oxford: Blackwell, 1997), pp. 52–3.

9   Dizard, *Old Media/New Media*, pp. 117, 82.

10   Ibid, p. 42.

11   Appleton, "Converging and Emerging Industries," pp. 180–1.

12   Brian Winston, *Media Technology and Society: A History; From the Telegraph to the Internet* (London: Routledge, 1998), pp. 322–4.

13   Hiebert and Gibbons, *Exploring Mass Media for a Changing World*, ch. 15. Other histories of the Internet are available in published print versions and online. There is a useful account in Barr, *newmedia.com.au*, pp. 120–3; see also Stuart Cunningham and Terry Flew, "Media Studies towards 2000," in Cunningham and Turner, *The Media in Australia*, pp. 425–40. The following site provides links to a number of online histories: http://www.isoc.org/Internet-history

14   Winston, *Media Technology and Society*, p. 333; Hiebert and Gibbons, *Exploring Mass Media for a Changing World*, pp. 308–9; Barr, *newmedia.com. au*, p. 122. Websites that provide historical and current data on Internet growth and use include: http://www.mit.edu/people/mkgray/net/printable/Internet–growth–summary.html and http://www.netsizer.com

15   Bruce M. Owen, *The Internet Challenge to Television* (Cambridge, MA: Harvard University Press, 1999), p. 231.

16   Hiebert and Gibbons, *Exploring Mass Media for a Changing World*, p. 311; Korinna Patelis, "The Political Economy of the Internet," in *Media Organisations in Society*, ed. James Curran (London: Arnold, 2000), pp. 95–8.

17   Ibid, pp. 93–5; Jenny Sinclair, "Why the Internet Is Out of Africa," *The Age* [Melbourne] *IT1* (April 10, 2001); Rajiv Chandrasekaran, "Isolated Cambodians Join the Global Village," *Guardian Weekly* (June 14–20, 2001), p. 22.

18   Anthony Faiola and Stephen Buckley, "Poor Embrace the Internet's Promise," *Washington Post*, reprinted in *Guardian Weekly* (July 20–6, 2000), p. 29.

19   Patelis, "The Political Economy of the Internet," p. 91.

20   Brendan King, "Global Village – or Global Market?" *Times Literary Supplement* (January 26, 2001), p. 29.

21   Darren Yates, "The PC Blues – Where to Now?" *The Age IT2* (May 8, 2001).

22   Jane Schulze, "Marketers Set to Harness the New 'Media' of Mobiles," *The Age* (November 30, 1999), p. 5.

23   Andrew Ross Sorkin, "European Consumers Still Await WAP," *The Age Business* (April 11, 2000); Cecilia Leung, citing British technology consultant company Logica estimates, in "Getting the Message," *The Age IT1* (May 1, 2001).

24   Andrea Petersen, "Wireless Web Ads New Can of Worms," *The Age Business* (July 25, 2000).

25   David Salter, "Netting Is All About Eyeballs," *Sydney Morning Herald* (June 19, 2000).

26   Alex Berenson, "Web Stops News from Being Caught on the Wires," *The Age Business* (October 10, 2000).

27   Pew Research Centre survey cited by Steve Geimann, "Audiences Tune out TV, Turn on the PC," *The Age Business* (June 13, 2000).

28   Jane Martinson, "News, Net Tie-ups Prove Marriages of Convenience," reprinted from the *Guardian* in *The Age* (January 5, 2000).

29   Hiebert and Gibbons, *Exploring Mass Media for a Changing World*, p. 305.

30   Owen, *The Internet Challenge to Television*.

31   Christina Ho, "The Triumphant Trio of TV, Radio and the Web," *The Age News* (September 26, 2000).

32   Dizard, *Old Media/New Media*, pp. 129, 131.

33   James Fallows, "Internet Illusions" [review article], *New York Review* (November 16, 2000), pp. 29–30.

12   Globalization and Media

1   Jeremy Hardie, "Why the Market Is Flawed" [review article], *Times Literary Supplement* (April 20, 2001), p. 12; on global financial markets see Trevor Barr, *newmedia.com.au: The Changing Face of Australia's Media and Communications* (St. Leonards: Allen and Unwin, 2000), pp. 32–3.

2   Frank J. Lechner and John Boli, *The Globalization Reader* (Oxford: Blackwell, 2000), p. 1.

3   Jean Seaton, "Global Futures, the Information Society, and Broadcasting," in James Curran and Jean Seaton, *Power Without Responsibility: The Press and Broadcasting in Britain*, 5th edn. (London: Routledge, 1997), pp. 261–2.

4   John B. Thompson, "The Globalization of Communication," in *Global Transformations Reader: An Introduction to the Globalization Debate*, ed. David Held and Anthony McGrew (Cambridge: Polity Press, 2000), pp. 203–8.

5   Ibid, p. 210; and Barr, *newmedia.com.au*, p. 161.

6   Donna A. Demac and Liching Sung, "New Communication Technologies and Deregulation," in *Questioning the Media: A Critical Introduction*, ed. John Downing, Ali Mohammadi, and Annabelle Sreberny-Mohammadi, 2nd edn. (London: Sage, 1995), p. 281; Chris Barker, *Television, Globalization and Cultural Identities* (Buckingham: Open University Press, 1999), p. 50.

7   Edward Herman and Robert McChesney, "The Global Media," in Held and McGrew, *Global Transformations Reader*, p. 220.

8   Ibid, pp. 220–1; Barr, *newmedia.com.au*, p. 160.

9   Herman and McChesney, "The Global Media," pp. 221, 222.

10   Rory Carroll, "Il Cavaliere Closes in on Power with a Little Help from His Media," *Guardian Weekly* (May 10–16, 2001): 3; Antonio Tabucchi in *Le Monde*, cited by Simon Mann, "All Hail Silvio," *The Age News Extra* (May 19, 2001), p. 5.

11   On News Corporation see, for example, Denis McQuail in Downing, Mohammadi, and Sreberny-Mohammadi, *Questioning the Media*, pp. 153–4; Gill Branston and Roy Stafford, *The Media Student's Book*, 2nd edn. (London: Routledge, 1999), pp. 299–307.

12   Peter Chernin quoted by Brian Hale, "Analysts Buy into News's Digital Spin," *The Age Business* (February 12, 2000).

13   Jim Rutenberg and Geraldine Fabrikant, "Satellite Dream Closer for Murdoch," *The Age Business* (May 8, 2001); Kim Chapman, "Murdoch's Sky Is Not the

Limit," *The Age Business* (May 10, 2001); James Harding, "News Corporation: The Internet Retreat; how Rupert Murdoch Ended the Dotcom Joyride," *Financial Times* (January 16, 2001), 24; Edward Helmore, "DirecTV Will Not Be a Bundle of Joy," *Guardian Weekly* (May 17–23, 2001), p. 14.

14 Jane Martinson, "Merger 'Launches Internet Revolution'," *Guardian Weekly* (January 13–19, 2000); Jane Schulze, "Warner Deal Puts Local Media in the Spotlight," *The Age Business* (January 12, 2000); Paul Kalina, "A Nose for News," *The Age Green Guide* (May 17, 2001).

15 Sean MacBride and Colleen Roach, "The New International Information Order," in Lechner and Boli, *The Globalization Reader*, pp. 286–92.

16 John Sinclair, Elizabeth Jacka, and Stuart Cunningham (eds.), *New Patterns in Global Television: Peripheral Vision* (Oxford: Oxford University Press, 1996).

17 Stuart Cunningham and Elizabeth Jacka, *Australian Television and International Mediascapes* (Cambridge: Cambridge University Press, 1996); Lechner and Boli, *The Globalization Reader*, pp. 2–3; Thompson, "The Globalization of Communication," p. 210; Barr, *newmedia.com.au*, pp. 164–5.

18 Sinclair, Jacka, and Cunningham, *New Patterns in Global Television*.

19 Paula Uimonen, "The Answer Is Flowing in the Wire," *The Age IT1* (November 19, 1999); Barr, citing Manuel Castells, *newmedia.com.au*, p. 132.

20 Lewis A. Friedland, "Covering the World," in Lechner and Boli, *The Globalization Reader*, p. 296.

21 Murdoch's statement quoted in Mark Wheeler, *Politics and the Mass Media* (Oxford: Blackwell, 1997), p. 176; Barr, *newmedia.com.au*, p. 163.

22 Matt Pottinger, "China Slaps Strict Curbs on Internet Content," *The Age IT1* (February 1, 2000); John Gittings, "China Bans Use of 'State Secrets' on Internet," *Guardian Weekly* (February 3–9, 2000); John Schauble, "China Tries to Weave Tighter Web," *Sydney Morning Herald* (April 24, 2000); John Gittings, "Internet Boom in China Poses a Dilemma," *The Age Business* (May 18, 2000); John Schauble, "Foreign Media Sites Barred as Beijing Tries to Stop Information," *Sydney Morning Herald* (October 28, 2000); Jennifer Lee, "US Sets Out to Foil China Web Censors," *Sydney Morning Herald* (September 1, 2001).

23 John Vidal, "The world@war," *Guardian Weekly* (February 3–9, 2000).

24 Seaton, "Global Futures, the Information Society, and Broadcasting," p. 255.

INDEX